Grace Livingston

Grace Livingston Hill (1865–1947) re_____ore than fifty years after her death. She wrote dozens of ____ ____ carry her unique style of combining Christian faith with tasteful and exciting romance.

Isabella Alden (1841–1930), an aunt of Grace Livingston Hill, was a gifted storyteller and prolific author, as well, often using her writing to teach lessons espoused by her husband, Gustavus R. Alden, a minister. She also helped her niece Grace get started in her career as a best-selling inspirational novelist.

The Chance of a Lifetime, by Grace Livingston Hill
Alan MacFarlan encounters the chance of a lifetime when his former high school professor invites him to go to Egypt on an archaeological expedition. Alan must choose whether to go or to stay and manage his father's hardware business. He soon finds that his choice could provide a chance of a lifetime for his old football rival. Then his longtime friend, Sherrill Washburn, also encounters a decision that could mean a wonderful opportunity for her—and for others in her family. An endearing story of how God moves in mysterious ways, not by chance.

Dec. 011

Under the Window, by Grace Livingston Hill
It's the night before Christmas, and Polly Bronson is alone with her cat, Abbott. She decides to invite a few children to a little party on Christmas Day. Meanwhile, Porter Mason is in search of light and finds it under the window of Polly's apartment. There he hears about the party and, having no one with whom to spend the holiday, plans a way to be invited. A heart-warming story for reading curled up in front of a fire.

May 013

A Voice in the Wilderness, by Grace Livingston Hill
As Margaret Earle steps off the train into the darkness, the howl of coyotes and a leering old man force her to seek safety at the top of a water tower. Lance Gardley, a tough young cowboy, finds her and escorts her to the town where she's to teach at the local school. There she discovers a minister intent on winning her, a hostile young girl, and a deadly scheme that leaves her stranded in the desert. Will Gardley and his men reach her before it's too late?

April 011   March 013

The Randolphs, by Isabella Alden
Maria Randolph, the youngest in her family, feels she's too much in demand by others. But when her brother starts a business, an older sister becomes engaged, and her invalid father goes to the mountains, she finds herself at a loss. So she starts her own business—much to her family's chagrin. But a chance misstep and her whole life is changed forever. Only then does she find true rest.

Oct. '08

Grace Livingston Hill

COLLECTION NO. 8

FOUR COMPLETE NOVELS

Updated for today's reader

BARBOUR
PUBLISHING, INC.
Uhrichsville, Ohio

Edited and updated for today's reader by Deborah Cole.

© 2000 by R. L. Munce Publishing Co., Inc.

ISBN 1-57748-826-1

Published by Barbour Publishing, Inc., P.O. Box 719, Uhrichsville, Ohio 44683
http://www.barbourbooks.com

ecpa Member of the
Evangelical Christian
Publishers Association

Printed in the United States of America.

The Chance
of a Lifetime

Chapter 1

The morning Alan MacFarlan's father broke his leg, Alan received a special delivery letter from his former high school professor, inviting him to accompany him as an assistant at a small salary on an archaeological expedition to Egypt. They would sail from New York in three days.

"I would have given you more notice if it had been possible," wrote Professor Hodge, "but the vacancy just occurred through the resignation of a young man who was taken seriously ill. I've recommended you, and I hope you can accept. It will be the chance of your lifetime. The salary isn't large or the position notable, but the experience will be great. I'm sure you'll enjoy it. You're young, of course, but I have great belief in your character and ability and have told our leader I'm sure you'll do well. You must wire at once if you wish to hold the job, since there are three other eager applicants. But you have priority."

A list of items Alan must bring with him followed, with directions for where to meet the rest of the expedition.

Alan was sitting at his father's desk in the Rockland Hardware store reading this letter. He'd come from home at his father's request to open the mail and answer one or two important letters that were expected. This letter was brought to him at the store by mistake instead of being delivered at the house. So the great temptation of his young life was presented to him alone, away from the loving eyes of his mother and father.

Alan's first reaction was wonder and awe that he, just a graduate of the Rockland High School, had been chosen for such a marvelous honor, a place in the great expedition to Egypt! He couldn't think of another honor in the world he desired more. He had always been interested in archaeology, and his soul throbbed with eagerness. To go with Professor Hodge, who had given him his first interest in ancient things, seemed the height of bliss. His eyes shone as he read, and his breath came in gasps. He looked up at the last word with a dazed expression.

A chance like that! A smile broke over his face as he sat with the letter still in his hand and gazed through the iron grating that surrounded the cash desk. Across the store were shelves filled with neat boxes, green and brown and red, all labeled, and gimlets and screwdrivers and chisels in orderly rows. But he saw instead a wide desert under a hot orient sky and workers in the sand bringing forth treasures of the ancients. He saw himself with a grimy, happy face, part of the great expedition, exploring tombs and pyramids and cities of another age.

Suddenly the desert faded, and the immediate environment snapped into his consciousness—bright gleaming tools of steel and iron saws and hammers and nails and plows. They fairly clamored at him for attention like so many helpless humans.

"What are you going to do about us?" they asked. "Your father is helpless, and we are your responsibility."

Alan's smile suddenly faded even as the desert had.

"But this is a chance of my lifetime!" he cried out indignantly to himself. "Surely Father would want me to accept. Surely he would let nothing stand in my way."

"Yes, but are you willing to put it up to him?" winked an honest oatmeal boiler aghast. "You know what your father told you this very morning! You know how touched you were when he told you he could bear the pain and being laid aside, since he knew you were free to take over the store, and he could trust you to run it as well as he would himself."

"But there's Uncle Ned!" cried out Alan's eager youthfulness. "He has nothing in life to do now since he's retired, and surely he could look after things for a little while till Dad is on his feet again!"

Then conscience spoke. "You know what your father said this very morning about Uncle Ned. Your uncle let everything run down and got the books mixed up those six weeks he had charge while your father went to California last year. And you know your father said there was a crisis just now in his affairs, and if he couldn't tide things over for the next few weeks, he would lose all he'd gained in his lifetime."

Alan's head made a quick, nervous movement as he laid down the letter, and a heavy paperweight in the form of a small steam engine, a souvenir of the last dinner of the United Hardware Dealers the elder MacFarlan had attended, fell with a clatter to the floor.

Alan stooped and picked it up, and all the blood seemed to rush in one anguished flood to his face and throb in his neck and head. Was he actually going to consider whether or not it was right to accept this wonderful offer? Surely his father wouldn't permit him to make such a sacrifice!

Then conscience held up before him his father's picture as he'd seen him a few minutes before, his face white with pain, his lips set firmly, his voice weak from shock. And again he heard the trembling sentences from those strong lips that had never acknowledged failure before.

"There's a note to be met, son, the first of next week. The man needs money badly and will foreclose if it isn't paid. I thought I had it all fixed up. But I got his letter last night, and I reckon that's what I was thinking about when I crossed the street in front of that car. You see, the worst of it is he has a buyer ready to take over the store and give him cash at once on foreclosure. I suspect it's that evil-eyed Rawley who's been hanging around asking questions the last three weeks, and we'll just have to raise the money somehow. Those city lots we've been saving for Mother will have to go, unless you can get Judge Whiteley to fix up another mortgage somehow to tide us over—"

The voice had failed with a new wave of pain, and Alan's mother had signaled him in alarm.

"That's all right, Dad," Alan's strong young voice had rung out with assurance. "I'll fix that up OK. Don't worry a minute! And of course I can run the store. You don't need to think anything's going wrong because you're taking a few days' rest!"

That was how he had cheered his father one short hour before and then walked down the street with his shoulders back and a feeling of responsibility to take over the business and make it succeed. How his heart had responded to his father's appeal!

And here he was considering dropping the whole thing, shedding the whole responsibility like a garment and running off to dig up gold vases in some dead king's tomb! Calling it the chance of a lifetime and crying out for an opportunity to fulfill his dreams and ambitions, while his father lay in pain and discouragement, seeing his own life struggles and ambitions end in failure, too late to mend!

Well, he couldn't do that. He couldn't lead his own life at the expense of all Dad had done, not now as things were nearing a fulfillment of his dreams. And in a sense Dad was doing it all for his sake and Mother's. Who was he to live his own life at his parents' expense? Why should his life be any more important in the universe and in God's eyes than his father's life and fortunes were?

He was sitting up now with the paperweight in one hand and the letter in the other, staring about at the four walls of the hardware store that had always seemed so important and so friendly to him. First a bright chisel was shouting these questions at him as it caught the sunlight through the window, then a keg of gleaming wire nails behind the counter took up the theme, and finally a bundle of ax halves bunched together in the corner beside a burlap bag of grass seed all but answered for him. Even a box of seed packets left over from the spring seemed to reproach him. And then he felt he had to defend himself to them all—the son of the house now in command and expected to bring order out of chaos. What made any of them think he would desert? His upper lip stiffened, and his chin lifted a bit.

Alan laid down the paperweight and, grasping his father's pencil, began to write on the back of Professor Hodge's envelope.

Deeply grateful for your thought of me. Would like above all things to go, but impossible. Dad run over by automobile this morning. Fractured leg and other injuries. May be some time recovering. Meanwhile business responsibility on me. Great regrets and many thanks. Suggest Bob Lincoln. Here's wishing. Alan.

He counted the words carefully and then reached out his hand for the telephone, but instead of calling Western Union as he'd intended he hesitated, his fingers on the receiver, looked about thoughtfully, as though the matter were settled, stuffed the scribbled envelope in his pocket and called his home.

"How's Dad, Mother? The doctor been there? What does he say? What? Ohhh-h! He does? Did you say he thinks it's a difficult fracture? What? He said he might be a long time in bed? What's that word? Complications? Oh! Worry? Why, no, of course not! There's nothing whatever to worry about. Tell Dad I'm at the helm, and the ship is sailing fine. I'll get all this mess straightened out in great shape. Tell him so! Tell him—I'm having—the time of my life! Why—tell him—I'm having"—he caught his breath as if a pain had shot through him and ended in a bright voice—"tell him I'm having the chance of a lifetime. See? And don't you worry, Mother! Dad'll pull though beautifully. This is just his chance to rest. He's worked hard for years. It's my turn to take the helm!"

He hung up the receiver sharply and shut his lips in a fine firm line, his eyes taking on a look he wore when he had to break the enemy's line on the football field or win in a race or climb a ladder to rescue someone in a village fire.

Then glancing defiantly at the inanimate objects that had accused him, he seized the telephone again and called Western Union, giving his message word for word in a clear crisp voice, feeling he'd cut his own throat but was glad. Then he opened the morning mail in a mature, businesslike way. He had a job to do and would do it. And surely he was no worse off than before he got that letter from Professor Hodge. He should be glad the professor thought him worthy to go on such an expedition. Maybe it wasn't the only chance in the world, even if good old Hodge had called it "the chance of a lifetime." Well, if it was, this store was the chance of a lifetime, too. He might never have another opportunity to help Dad and start repaying all he had done for him. Good old Dad!

Something misty got into Alan's eyes as he opened the next envelope, and he cleared his throat and brushed his hand across his forehead. Then suddenly he forgot Egypt and Hodge, the expedition and the honor, his loss, everything. For here in this letter was a challenge greater than any buried cities could give. It was even worse than Dad had hinted. The man who held the mortgage was openly threatening him, using language that added insult to injury. What! Let that man insult his father? Not if he knew himself! If he couldn't do anything else he would thrash him. But he knew he would do something else. He would get that money somewhere and put Dad on the top, if he had to sell his own skin to do it. Alan's lips shut thin and hard, and his eyes took on a steely look. Other fellows could go to Egypt and unearth the secrets of the ages. But he was the only one who could put his dad right with the world again.

All day he worked frantically, not going home for lunch but holding long telephone conversations and writing letters. He interviewed his father's lawyer, got in touch with the president of the bank, made an appointment with a real estate agent in the city for the next day and wrote letters to two or three powerful friends of his father's whom he couldn't reach over the wires and sent telegrams.

A thrill came to him as he realized his own responsibility and the need for good judgment. But he longed for someone to consult, someone closer than bank presidents or real estate agents. Of course there was Keith Washburn—and Sherrill! Sherrill had amazing good sense for a girl. But of course he couldn't tell either of them, good friends though they were, about his father's business. He must weather it alone. If only he could ask Dad a question or two. But his mother's messages reporting the beloved invalid's condition made it plain Dad shouldn't be bothered for some time yet.

Alan went home late to dinner that night and put on a cheerful face to cover his tiredness. Now that his work was done until morning, he could think of his own disappointment. Suddenly it cut deep into his heart, and he sank wearily into a chair. Perhaps he could have gone after all if he hadn't been so hasty. Perhaps his plans would carry through smoothly, and by tomorrow everything would be straightened out and the business safe. Surely someone could be found who would take over the store for a while till Dad got well. But no! He mustn't even think of that. Mother must never suspect, and Dad must never know what he'd given up. He would have wanted him to go.

His father was under opiates and in the hands of a capable nurse from the city. Alan could only tiptoe up to the sickroom door and peer into the cool dim shadows. That sleeping form with the closed eyes, the strange, unnatural breathing, stabbed his heart. Of course he couldn't have gone off to a desert and left his father like that.

Perhaps his need of reassurance after visiting his father led him out across the lawn and down the next street to the Washburn house. His mother didn't need him. He'd tucked her into bed for a nap and told her not to worry.

Sherrill was playing the piano, the lamplight falling from the shaded lamp on her head and shoulders, bringing out the glint of gold in her hair, the delicate curve of cheek and chin, the fine molding of her slim shoulders. He stood a moment and watched her wistfully. How sweet she was and wise! What would she have advised him to do? Would she have said he must stay? But of course she would! He couldn't imagine asking her. He wouldn't want her to think he'd had any other thought but to stick by his father. And yet— she was young and sane. Perhaps he'd been oversentimental. He wanted to hear her say it. Yet he couldn't ask her. The only person he could ask was God, and he thought he knew what God would have him do.

She had stopped playing and was pulling a chair up to the light. He strolled up to the open window.

"Sherry, come out in the hammock and talk to me."

She came at once, pausing for a second in the doorway. "Only out in the hammock, Mother—I won't be long. Alan is here!"

They sat down in the roomy swinging seat under the pines. Sherrill had had letters from two of the girls. Priscilla Maybrick was in the Catskills having a wonderful time, and Willa Barrington had gone with an aunt to Atlantic City. They talked for a while about the merits of seashore and mountains, and then a pleasant silence fell between them, such as that of good friends.

"Had a letter from old Hodge today," said Alan nonchalantly. Somehow he had to tell someone, and Sherrill was safe.

"You did!" she said with interest. "What did he have to say? Is he still in that suburb of New York? Keith heard he'd resigned."

"Why, no," said Alan, "he isn't. He didn't resign. Hadn't you heard? He's leading an expedition to Egypt. Archaeological, you know. Digging up some of Tut's relatives and things like that."

"You don't mean it! Really! Isn't that wonderful? Did he say when they start?"

"Friday," said Alan grimly. And then he added casually, "He asked me to go along."

"Oh, Alan!" said Sherrill, clapping her hands.

"Yes, he gave me all the information for meeting him in New York, day after tomorrow."

"Day after tomorrow!" the girl gave him a quick look, and sympathy broke into her voice. "Oh, Alan! Then you can't go, of course. But it isn't that hard. You wouldn't want to leave your father now. Does he know about it?"

"No, and I don't mean for him to," said Alan decidedly. "Please don't say anything to Mother either, Sherry. It would worry her, and she has enough without that."

"But wouldn't they both feel you should tell them? It's so important. Perhaps they could make other arrangements and let you go."

"No chance!" said Alan briskly, thinking of his hard work that day. "Nobody else knows about Dad's business the way I do, and I wouldn't trust anybody to take things over. Besides, Dad may be hurt worse than we think. The doctor can't tell everything yet. Of course, I know it's a chance of a lifetime, as Hodge said, but it can't be helped. The way isn't open. I mentioned it because I thought you'd like to know Hodge asked me. I guess it's an honor. He must know a lot of other fellows better fitted than I am."

"Of course it's an honor," said Sherrill eagerly, "a great honor! But I'm not a bit surprised. I don't believe Professor Hodge knows anyone else your age as dependable as you. But as for being the chance of a lifetime, you can't tell. Maybe staying at home is the chance of yours. Things we want aren't always what's best for us. This may not be the chance of your lifetime at all."

"Evidently not!" said Alan, with a laugh that was edged with bitterness. "Well, it was nice of him to ask me anyway, and I have it to remember."

"Have you answered him yet?" asked Sherrill thoughtfully.

"Sure! Wired him within an hour after the letter came."

They were silent a moment, swinging back and forth under the old pine trees, Sherrill's white dress making a patch of white in the shadows.

In the silence they could hear footsteps coming quickly up the sidewalk. The steps paused at the rose vine arch over the gateway, then turned in and walked more slowly up the stone flagging to the house. About halfway up they paused again, but Alan and Sherrill couldn't tell who it was. It didn't seem to be any of the boys who often came around.

"Oh, I say, Mac, is that you?" called the visitor.

Alan rose from his seat and stepped forward. "Yes, did you want me?"

Chapter 2

The newcomer came forward then and held out his hand. Sherrill saw it was Bob Lincoln, Alan's former rival on the football field.

"Hope you'll pardon me for intruding," he said. "I won't keep you long. I just got a wire from Professor Hodge and had to come and thank you. I say, Mac—you were great to recommend me after all that's passed, and I sure appreciate it. I won't forget it."

"Oh, Bob, is that you?" said Alan. "You say he wired? Did you get the job? Congratulations!"

"Sit down, Bob," said Sherrill, rising. "I'm going in the house for a sweater. It's a little chilly out."

"Don't go," said young Lincoln. "It's nothing private. You don't mind if I tell Sherrill, do you?"

"There's nothing to tell," said Alan diffidently.

"Oh, I think there is," said Bob, turning to Sherrill. "Alan's put me in for the chance of my life. I'm going with Professor Hodge to Egypt. Starting day after tomorrow. Can you beat it? And I owe it all to old Mac here. I never even heard of the job till I got the wire, and I needed something in the worst way."

"Mac," he said, turning back to Alan, "I owe you something more than thanks. I owe you an apology. I've said some unkind things about you in the past, and the time you thrashed me I guess I deserved it even more than you knew. But I never knew you were like this. I thought you were a hypocrite. Now I'm asking your pardon. I've never known a man to do something like this for his enemy."

"Oh, Bob, cut it out," growled Alan. "What I did wasn't so great. I knew you liked such things and heard you wanted to go away. Since I couldn't go myself I didn't see any reason why you shouldn't profit by it."

"I'll have to admit that if the chances had been reversed I doubt I'd have done the same thing. I'd have said if I couldn't go you shouldn't either."

"Oh, you aren't like that, Bob. Besides, I was sore I couldn't go myself, but I'm thrilled to death you can, since I can't."

"But why can't you go, Mac? Don't you want to?"

"Sure! It's like the pot of gold at the end of a rainbow. I'd rather go than get rich. But it can't be done. My dad got run over this morning, and I've got to stay by the store and take his place. It'll be weeks and maybe months before he's around again. Lucky if it isn't years!"

"Say! That's tough luck. I hadn't heard. Been groveling in the factory all day. But, say, Mac, why couldn't I take your place? I'm a year older than you, and I could take orders. I'd put my heart into doing something like that. You go, Mac, and I'll stay!"

Alan looked at him. "Would you do that for me, Bob?" he asked, his voice husky with feeling.

"I sure would," said Bob. "You're the first person since my sister died that's cared a straw what became of me. Look at what you've done for me! I'll do it gladly!"

Alan put out his hand and grasped Bob's hand warmly.

"Guess I've got an apology coming, too, old man," he said still huskily. "You're great. I won't forget this. I can't accept, of course, because Dad needs me, but you've taken half the sting of saying no away from me. When I suggested you, I didn't think you'd even know I was connected with it. But I'm glad now it happened. I'd—like—to feel—we're friends!"

"Suits me!" said Bob, smiling. "I don't have many. You might even head the list if you don't mind. Oh, by the way, I guess I'd better find out more about the trip. Professor Hodge said you had all the directions. Do you mind letting me copy them? I know you'll want to keep the letter. It's some honor to have been asked."

"That's all right," said Alan, with a smile. "We're partners in this in a way. And when you get out there, write me a card now and then to let me know what I'm missing, all right?"

"Sure!" said Bob. "You'll be mother, home and heaven to me. I'm not very popular around here, you know. Oh, Sherrill, may I step over to the light at the door and copy this?" he asked, turning to the girl, who had listened quietly as the young men talked.

"Oh, come into the library and sit at the desk," said Sherrill. "Both of you come in. I've got a pitcher of lemonade in the refrigerator and a big chocolate cake that needs eating."

"Oh, say! Lead me to it!" exclaimed Bob. "I'm boarding at the Copper Kettle and ate half a chicken wing and a lettuce leaf for my supper."

They laughed and went in the house, where Sherrill settled the young men at the library desk. Then she stepped into the kitchen, and in a moment Alan followed.

"He insists on copying it so the paper doesn't get lost," he said, "so I'll help you get the food together."

Sherrill turned to him with shining eyes. Then she carefully closed the dining room and pantry doors.

"Alan MacFarlan, you blessed old hypocrite! Did you ask Bob Lincoln to go to Egypt in your place?"

"Oh, I just suggested his name," he said, reaching for the glasses out of the cupboard. "I thought he might as well have the chance."

"But I thought you were sworn enemies!" said Sherrill. "It hasn't been long since you gave him an awful thrashing!"

"Well, he needed it," said Alan thoughtfully, "but he almost got me too. He's smart. I think he'll do well."

"But I thought you didn't like Bob and didn't approve of him at all."

"Well, I don't!" said Alan, with an odd smile on his face. "At least I thought I didn't. But I guess I'll have to change my opinion. He certainly has shown up in great shape tonight, offering to stay in my place."

"Maybe he doesn't really want to go," suggested the girl.

"Oh, yes, he does!" protested Alan. "He told me in there it's been his dream to do something like that, and he promised he'd do well. Bob's had a rotten deal lately. His sister died last month, you know, and she was the only one who ever cared for him. His brother-in-law is as hard as nails. He gave Bob a job in the canning factory carrying out peelings at six dollars a week and his board. Told him if he didn't like that he could get out; it was all he'd ever do for him. I think he's been up against it. You know Bob. He would never stand being humiliated by that old grouch. He would get into trouble pretty soon, and nobody would care."

"But how do you know what he'll do in Egypt? Do you trust him?"

"Sure! He used to be crazy about old Hodge—it was the only thing we ever had in common. I think he'll turn out all right. He's really excited about the job."

Sherrill had been buttering thin slices of bread for sandwiches, and now she turned around with the knife in her hand.

"Alan, I think you're wonderful!" she said, her eyes shining.

"Nothing of the kind, Sherry. I've been clenching my teeth all day to keep from feeling sorry for myself because I can't go."

"Well, I think you're wonderful anyway. This may be the chance of Bob's life, but I think you've got a bigger one coming still. Here"—she handed him the plate—"these are ready. Get the pitcher out of the right-hand door, please. And put that cake plate on the tray. I'll take these in."

"Say, this is great, Sherry!" said Alan, surveying the full tray. "I'm glad you did it. I think he's real hungry."

Sherry smiled at him and carried the plate of sandwiches into the library.

Bob looked up from the letter he'd been copying, his face flushed with eagerness. His radiant smile made him seem like a new person, not the boy they'd disliked through the last three years of high school.

"Say, that looks good! You two are making me feel I'll be leaving some real friends when I go away. I didn't think I'd ever regret leaving this little burgh, but I certainly think I've missed a lot not having you for friends. No, don't say anything. You probably wouldn't care for me if I stayed, so let me go with the illusion that you would, all right? A fellow has to have someone to tie to!"

"You make us feel ashamed, Bob, that we've been so unfriendly," said Sherrill. "Won't you put it this way—that we just haven't gotten to know the real you? We didn't mean to be horrid—really we didn't."

"You make me feel more than ashamed," said Alan, draping his arm across the other's shoulder. "Let's make up for the loss, shall we? We can be real partners in this job across the sea. You're the representative on the field, and I'm the home correspondent or something."

"Okay with me," said Bob heartily. "Boy, you don't know how it feels to have you say that. I can't ever thank—"

"Here," said Alan huskily, handing him the pitcher. "Have some more lemonade!"

They ate every scrap of sandwich and every crumb of cake, drinking the lemonade to the last drop, talking and laughing all the while. Then suddenly Bob jumped up.

"I must go!" he declared, looking at his watch. "It's late, and I have a lot to do tomorrow. First off I need to hand in my resignation to the Rockland Canning Factory, which I'll sure enjoy doing. Then I have to gather up all the junk on that list and pack. A few things on the list I don't think I can manage, but I guess it won't matter. I've learned pretty much to get along without things lately." He gave the same little laugh he'd always given to cover his sore feelings.

Sherrill and Alan looked at him with sudden understanding. This was the old Bob they hadn't liked. Had he covered up his loneliness with this attitude, and they simply hadn't understood him?

Then Alan spoke quickly.

"Look here, old man," he said. "You and I need to talk tonight. Suppose you come home with me for the night. Then we can get everything figured out. You're taking my place, so it's up to me to make sure you have everything you need. How about it?"

Bob looked at Alan in awe.

"Wow! That's terrific!" he said with deep feeling in his voice. "What a fool I was! I always thought all that church-going was a fake. Once I called you a hypocrite right in the schoolyard! And I believed you were. But now—well, I can't tell you how I feel about this. I'm not going to let you do anything more for me, of course, but—it's fine of you to talk that way."

"Well, we'll settle our differences in private," said Alan, laughing. "Come on—we have no time to waste."

Alan nudged him toward the door.

"Good night, Sherrill," Bob said, pausing. "You've given me a terrific evening, and I'll always remember it. I used to think you were high-hat, but now I see you're real. I can't thank you enough for letting me in on this pleasant evening."

Sherrill walked to the door with them and called out a cheery good night, as they went down the walk, Alan's arm flung across Bob's shoulders as if they'd been comrades for years.

Suddenly Alan turned and stepped quickly back to her.

"I'm carrying off some of your property, Sherry," he said with a laugh, handing her a handkerchief. "You dropped this under the hammock when we came in the house, and I absentmindedly put it in my pocket."

Their fingers touched as Sherrill took her handkerchief, and she heard Alan's low whisper: "It was great of you to do that, Sherry. He thinks you're wonderful. Thank you!"

"Oh, I was glad to have a part in it, Alan," whispered Sherrill. "And you know what? I wouldn't be surprised if this didn't turn out, after all, to be the chance of your lifetime. I think you've gone a long way toward bringing Bob to the Lord."

He squeezed her fingers gently and then caught up with Bob. And the two young men walked down the street together, whistling an old school song.

"Who was that other boy, Sherrill?" asked her mother, glancing up and smiling pleasantly.

"That was Bob Lincoln, Mother."

"Not that Lincoln boy Alan dislikes so much? The one who made so much trouble in school and was always doing wild things? The one Alan fought with?"

"Yes, Mother, one and the same. But you'd be surprised how nice he is and how grateful he was for the sandwiches and cake. He hadn't had much supper. You know his sister died not long ago, and he has to get his meals almost anywhere he can."

"Well, but, my dear! How did he come to call on you? I'm sure he's not the kind of boy you'd want to have for a friend. I hope he isn't going to start in now and bother you by coming in here. I'm sure your brother wouldn't like it at all. Keith's very particular about you, you know."

"Oh, he didn't come to see me, at all, Mother. He stopped by to speak to Alan a minute—on business—and we asked him in."

"Well, but, my dear, it isn't wise to get too intimate with a boy like that. He'll think he can come again. I'm surprised Alan didn't take him away at once. It's all well enough to be kind, but I really couldn't have you asking a boy like that here regularly. Sherrill, you never stop to think of things like that—"

"Listen, Mother, you don't need to worry about Bob. He's going to Egypt day after tomorrow for three years on an archaeological expedition with Professor Hodge. So you see there's nothing to worry about. He came to ask Alan something, and we were just being kind to him. We found out he's been lonely, and, Mother, he was so pleased to have somebody be a little friendly! You should have heard him. I felt so ashamed that I didn't know what to do."

"Is that the red-haired Lincoln boy who used to drive by here in that old noisy Ford?" asked Sherrill's grandmother, looking up with sudden interest. "I always liked that boy's looks. He reminded me of a cousin of mine who ran away and joined the Navy. He came back a first-rate man too. I always thought his aunt who brought him up never understood him. She fussed over him a lot."

"Now, Mother!" said Sherrill's mother with a tender smile. "You always were a romantic dear. Who would ever have thought you noticed a boy going by on the street?"

"Well, I did!" said Grandma. "And I'm glad you were nice to him, Sherrill. If he's going to Egypt he can't do you any harm, and anyway, I'll bank on your good sense to take care of yourself anywhere."

"Now, Mother, you're spoiling Sherrill!" smiled the mother. "However did a boy like that get a chance to go on such an expedition? That's a great honor. Professor Hodge must have approved of him or he wouldn't have asked him."

It was on Sherrill's lips to tell about Alan, but remembering his request that she keep it to herself, she closed her mouth and turned away smiling. Someday when it didn't matter, she would tell Mother what a wonderful boy Alan MacFarlan had been. She said good night and went up to her room, singing.

"She's a good girl, Mary!" said her grandmother.

"Yes, she is, Mother. I didn't mean that about your spoiling her."

"Humph!" said Grandma, folding away the skirt she was hemming and taking off her glasses. "Yes, she's a good girl, and that Alan MacFarlan is a good boy. I'm glad they gave that other fellow a pleasant time. He hasn't looked very happy."

Over at the MacFarlan house the young men entered quietly, Bob protesting that he shouldn't go in for fear of disturbing the invalid. They took off their shoes and moved silently up the stairs, but Alan's mother heard them nevertheless. She came out to the landing in her blue evening robe, her eyes bright and a look of peace on her face. Bob watched her in wonder, as she reassured her son about his father.

"He's resting very well," she said softly. "The doctor thinks he may have a better day tomorrow."

Alan introduced Bob, and Mrs. MacFarlan smiled warmly in welcome and clasped his hand in hers.

"I thought I shouldn't come," he said, "but he made me."

"Alan's friends are always welcome," she said, "and you won't disturb anybody. Alan's room is over in the tower, and no one can hear you talk."

"I wish I had a mother," said Bob, as they entered Alan's room and the light was switched on. "It must be great. I hardly remember mine."

He stopped then and looked around the room.

"Say! If I had a room like this and a mother like yours," Bob said, looking around the room, "you couldn't drag me to Egypt. I'd stay right here in my home!"

Alan glanced about at the comfortable furnishings and conveniences evidently chosen to suit his tastes.

"Well, there's something in that!" he said, smiling. "It's pretty comfortable here. I hadn't thought of it, but it would be something to leave. Let's look at that list, though, and see what you need. Here—sit in this chair. You look all in."

Bob dropped into the chair, and the two went to work in earnest on the list.

When they finally turned in there was a good understanding and a hearty liking between them that neither would have believed possible a few hours before. It was with genuine regret they parted the next morning after eating breakfast together and walking downtown as far as the bank. Alan had insisted he be allowed to provide Bob with whatever he didn't have, but he only succeeded in getting him to accept a loan until he could repay it. They stopped at the bank where Alan cashed a check from his own private fund he'd been saving for a new car.

"This is coming back to you out of the first bit of salary I can spare from actual expenses," said Bob, slipping the bills into his inside pocket.

"If you scrimp yourself, old boy, I'll take it unkindly. Remember—you must stay in good condition, and this is the only share I can have in this affair. It really makes me feel good to have this much."

"You can't know how much I appreciate it," Bob said again, with a hearty grip of the other boy's hand. "And the odd thing is, I wouldn't have taken a red cent from you twenty-four hours ago. That's how different I feel toward you."

"Same here!" said Alan. "What fools we were! Might have had three great years to look back on. What a team we could have made out of that high school scrub if we'd hooked up forces instead of fighting! I hope I remember this lesson."

They parted at the street corner, Bob promising to report late that evening and spend the night again at Alan's house since he was leaving for New York early the next morning.

As soon as Alan was alone the burden of his father's responsibilities settled down on his shoulders. The day before him looked long and hard. He must try to get in touch with the judge again. Perhaps he'd have to run up to the city and see those real estate people on the ten o'clock train! How hot the sun seemed and how uninteresting his life! His heart was going shopping with Bob, selecting the right sweaters and shoes for the trip. But life wasn't all trips to Egypt. He had business that should engross all of his energy.

A stack of mail awaited him in the store, with another threatening letter from the enemy, which conveyed a confident undertone that left him uneasy. If he could only read this one letter to Dad and see what he thought should be done—but that was out of the question.

The day proved to be even harder than he'd feared. The judge was out of town, and no one knew when he would return. Alan decided he would have to act as if the judge wouldn't return, for time was short, and the crisis was at hand.

He took the ten o'clock train for the city and followed a member of the real estate company about for two hours from place to place, finally locating him at his office at two o'clock. There he discovered that the purchaser, so anxious to buy the MacFarlans' city lots a few weeks earlier, had gone to Europe for the summer. The only price that could be raised on them in a short time would be so inadequate to meet the family's needs that it would scarcely be worth the sacrifice.

His father had suggested two other reliable mortgage and loan companies, but they both seemed unwilling to undertake negotiations outside the city. By five o'clock all the offices were closing, so Alan, not knowing what else to do, took the train home, discouraged and hungry, since he hadn't stopped for lunch. Had he been a much younger fellow he might have laid his head on the car window sill and let a tear escape. As it was, the breeze that swept in at the window was so hot he felt as if he would suffocate and thought instead of the desert to which he wasn't going. He tried to send up a prayer, but it seemed so aimless he wondered if it reached even the car ceiling.

"Oh, God, please do something for me about this mortgage. I'm about to give up and don't know what more to do. And help me stop wishing I could have gone to Egypt."

That was his constant prayer till the train arrived in Rockland.

Chapter 3

Alan looked anxiously out of the car window as he stepped into the aisle, with a vague hope of glimpsing the tall form of Judge Whiteley among the people on the platform. But all he saw was Bob Lincoln with his arms full of bundles watching the people coming out of the car, an eager look on his face, a light in his eyes. Somehow it thrilled Alan's heart that this young man, once his enemy, was looking for him. And he felt doubly glad when he saw the smile on Bob's face at the sight of him.

"I thought you might be on this train," he said, rushing up to Alan. "The boy you left in the store told me you'd gone to town, so I took a chance and met the train. Just thought I'd like to report progress and show you the wire that came from Hodge this morning. I didn't expect to hear from him again. You certainly must have given him some line about me. Look at this," he said, handing Alan a telegram.

Glad you're going. I remember you favorably. Don't worry about qualifications. Anyone MacFarlan recommends is worth having. Will reserve you as my personal assistant. Meet you at twelve thirty at the ship. Hodge.

Something broke loose in Alan's heart that lifted his spirits. It was good to have this other fellow going and to have put him into it.

"That's great!" he said, smiling. "But I didn't do a thing—just suggested your name."

"Well, it shows how much your suggestion is worth. In a sense it's really you going on this expedition, not me. While I'm gone, I'll be thinking that I'm you, and I want to be what you would be if you had gone!"

Months later Alan thought of Bob's words, when he questioned which course of two he should follow; then he remembered Bob, and his way cleared. Why, that was how it was with a Christian. It wasn't he, Alan MacFarlan, who was deciding whether to do this or that; it was Jesus Christ living in him. Strange he'd never thought of that before. And it took Bob Lincoln, a fellow who wasn't a Christian, to show him.

Bob declined Alan's invitation to supper. He needed to see his brother-in-law, and it was the only time he could find him at home. But he promised to come back and spend the night and be there as early as he could make it after nine o'clock. He still had to pack. He showed Alan the sweater he'd bought and eagerly tore the paper from his new shoes.

"And I've saved on several things," he said, "so I can return ten dollars to you now."

"Not at all—you may need it!" said Alan, waving his hand and walking down the street to the hardware store.

"I'll make it up to you yet!" Bob called out with a smile as he headed in the opposite direction from his brother-in-law's house.

A sort of sick premonition came over Alan as he approached the store.

"Any phone calls?" he asked the clerk, who was at that moment staring at the clock. It was his night to play baseball with the Twilight League, and he wanted supper before that.

"Yep, guess so," he answered languidly. "A real estate man in the city, Spur and Holden, said they've had an offer from a man on them lots. He'll give you a thousand less than your price, and they said it's best you accept. Said it's the best you'll get this time of year. And then some man named Rawlins called and said he has a proposal to make, but you got t' come t' terms before eleven o'clock t'morrow, or it's all off."

"Thank you, Joe," said Alan, with no change in his expression, though both messages were overwhelming. "Just stop in the restaurant on your way out and ask them to send me in a cup of coffee and a ham sandwich, won't you? I have no time to go home now."

Then Alan sank down wearily in his father's desk chair and attacked that day's mail. All but two of the letters were bills, and most of them asked for immediate payment. Why did everyone seem to need money at once? The two that weren't bills occupied him the rest of the evening, telephoning and telegraphing, trying to reach men who seemed to have hidden themselves beyond recall.

Alan called his mother and found that his father was still under opiates. The doctor said he couldn't tell for several days yet how severe the injuries were, but he was still holding his own. Alan could hear the anxiety and tiredness in his mother's voice. She wanted to know how business was going, and he tried to reassure her, but his voice almost broke.

It was growing dark in the store when Alan shoved the thick restaurant cup and saucer aside and dropped his head in his hands. How hot and tired he was! What a failure he was in trying to take his father's place in the store! And out a few blocks away his substitute was preparing for the desert. Only another day and he would be stepping into a new world filled with wonderful experiences.

And only another day and the enemy would be upon him and his father's business, and the judge was still away. The judge was his only hope now. He didn't know where else to turn. Tomorrow morning he'd have to deal with that awful Rawlins, and what would he propose? If he only knew! If he only had someone to consult with! There would be some humiliating terms offered, of course. Oh, he'd like to take that Rawlins out behind the store and thrash him and set matters straight. Perhaps he would, if matters took a turn for the worse. Perhaps he wouldn't be able to control his anger and would get into a fight, and then they'd have a lawsuit along with all the other trouble—or even something worse. Then what would Dad say?

He groaned as he thought of the possibilities. Then suddenly the clock struck nine, and he remembered Bob had promised to meet him at the house. He must go back and look cheerful and hear Bob talk eagerly of his plans.

"Life is hard," he told himself again, reaching for his hat.

Just then the telephone rang out sharply in the empty store. With a wild hope that this might be Judge Whiteley, Alan grabbed the receiver. But it was only Sherrill Washburn.

"Is that you, Alan?" Her voice sounded to him like a cool, sweet breeze. "Your mother said I'd find you at the store. I've been thinking. You know that fund we have for Bibles? Why don't we give one to Bob Lincoln to take with him? Do you think he'd be offended? He's never been to any of our meetings or been with our crowd very much. But I thought, well, we haven't tried very much. Maybe you could give it to him somehow. I wouldn't like him to feel— we were—well—trying to convert him or anything! What do you think?"

"Sure!" said Alan heartily, though with a twinge of jealousy he recognized at once. If he'd been going to the desert, Sherrill would be getting this Bible for him.

"How wonderful," a voice whispered to his mind's ear, "to have a Bible like that to take out in the desert and read and feel they were praying."

"Sure!" said Alan, ignoring the voice. "Make it a good one. I think he'll be glad for it. Can we get it in time? He leaves early in the morning, you know."

"Yes," said Sherrill, "we had two, you remember, as premiums for those who passed the exams in the Bible course. Cameron left before the course ended, so we had one left over."

"Sure, I remember. That's a great idea, Sherry!"

"Then you'll give it to him?"

"Yes, but not as my gift. It'll be from the crowd, as a reminder of us all at home or something like that. We can give him that list from the Bible study we're taking together. Don't you have an extra copy?"

"Oh, yes, that's good. Tell him to join our group in reading, and then we can send him the exam slips every month. Tell him we want to consider him one of our group."

"Like a connection to home. How about getting word to everyone and have them come down to the train in the morning to send him off? Do you think they'd do it?"

"Oh, I think they would, and that's a great idea. May I tell them you suggested it? They'll—be a little surprised, you know—since they've always considered you enemies."

"I'd like them to know we aren't anymore," said Alan quietly.

"That's great!" said Sherrill, with a lilt to her voice. "And I'll send the Bible right over to your house. Keith is going past there now, and he can leave it at the door without troubling anybody, can't he? I'll start calling everyone right away. Is it the eight-thirty train? All right. And we'll have the farewell hymn ready too. How's that?"

"That would be perfect!" said Alan, trying to swallow down the lump in his throat at the thought. He wished once more that he had made the effort to know Bob, instead of letting his anger get in the way and judging him, thus rendering powerless a positive influence over him.

But now the musty old office looked almost glorified to his eyes as he hung up the receiver and glanced about him. Well, at least if he couldn't go to the desert he could have a part in preparing his substitute. And wasn't it good of Sherrill to remember the Bible!

He reached for his hat again and then caught sight of the open safe. He must lock that before he left. How careless of him. He'd better keep his mind sharp for these things.

He leaned over to shut the safe door and recalled something else. What had his father said about papers in the safe? He should have looked them over earlier in the evening. How careless of him to go to the city and leave the safe unlocked. But then Dad had always trusted Joe. Alan needed to be more careful, though.

Papers? Yes, now he remembered—the deed to the city lots. Well, he should have taken those with him, of course. If he'd had a chance of selling he would have needed them. Yes, and the Westbrook Securities and the insurance papers. Yes, and what were these? He drew forth an envelope and opened one of the crisp, crackling documents with a frown. The other papers lay beside him on the floor.

Suddenly a noise startled him, and he glanced up.

A window behind the desk furnished light in the daytime, and its shade was stretched high, for Joe had been reading a book late in the afternoon and wanted all the light he could get. Instinctively Alan looked toward the window from where the sound had come. Had he seen a face vanishing as he looked up, or were his nerves on edge? It must be nerves, for who, he reasoned, would want to look in at the back window of a hardware store at this time of night? It opened on a back alley. Nevertheless, it was careless to work at the safe so near an open window.

He reached up and pulled the shade down with a snap and then turned back to the papers that were lying on the floor in the bright light from the drop lamp, their titles standing out clearly. Anyone looking in the window could have read them. But of course no one had been looking in.

Should he take those papers home with him now and get acquainted with them? Or would they be safer here behind a time lock? Safer? Why, they were safe enough anywhere, weren't they? What were they anyway? Of course he should know what was under his care. Or would there be time enough for that tomorrow? He was late now for his meeting with Bob. He must go at once.

When he'd turned out the lights and locked the door he glanced back uneasily, as an inexperienced nurse might look anxiously at the sleeping infant placed in her care, and wondered if he'd done everything that was usually done at night in leaving the store.

Then his mind switched ahead to Bob and the Bible and Sherrill. Great girl, Sherrill. She wasn't an ordinary girl. She was as good as a fellow in some ways. A real comrade.

Bob met him at the corner.

"I thought I'd wait for you here," he said, "and not disturb the house twice."

"That was thoughtful of you, Bob. You know, it's going to be tough losing you, now that we've become friends."

"Same here!" said Bob.

They walked up the street, exchanging bits of news about their days and deepening their friendship that had so quickly formed over the ashes of a dead hatred.

As they approached the MacFarlan house, a car stopped, and someone leaned out and signaled.

"That you, Mac?" called Keith Washburn. "Here's a package Sherrill sent over. Evening, Bob."

"Thanks awfully, Keith. Won't you come in?" said Alan, taking the package.

"Wish I could, Mac, but I'm on my way over to West Grove. I just received a wire from a man I've been wanting to see for some time, and he's taking the midnight train, so I'm hurrying to get there in time to ask him a few questions before he leaves. How about going with me, both of you? I'd be glad of company."

"Sorry, Keith, but Bob is leaving in the morning, and we've got some things to do before he goes."

"Oh, yes, Sherrill told me about it. Great chance, Bob. Wouldn't mind being in your boots. Dig up a few kings and buried cities for me, won't you? Hope you have a wonderful time. We'll think about you. Let us know how you're coming on now and then. Well, sorry you can't go with me. So long!"

Bob gazed after the car in wonder. Somehow the town and its people had taken on a friendly look they'd never shown before.

"I like him," he said suddenly, as if he were thinking aloud.

"He's a terrific fellow," agreed Alan, as he took out his key.

The boys went quietly upstairs to Alan's room and sat down to talk. As they turned on the light they saw a big pitcher of milk in an ice bucket and a plate of sandwiches and cake.

"Let's eat something first," said Alan. "I guess my mother thinks I haven't had any supper."

"Is that the kind of thing mothers do?" said Bob wistfully. "And you wanted to go to the desert! Well, if I had a mother like that I might have turned the job over to some other fellow too."

"You know," said Alan, a reflective tone in his voice, "I'm starting to think I haven't appreciated what I have. You're helping me see that."

When they'd cleared the plates and finished the milk Alan reached for the package.

"This is for you, Bob. It's from everyone. They want you to take it with you. Think you've got room to carry it?"

He felt a little embarrassed now that he'd begun. He wasn't quite sure how Bob would take the gift of a Bible. Perhaps, as Sherrill had suggested, he might resent it. He was known for not caring much for religion or churches.

"For me? Say, what have you been telling them? They never cared a red cent for me."

"Well, that's all you know about it, Bob. I haven't said a word to them. Sherrill Washburn is president this year and called me awhile ago to ask if I thought you'd mind their giving it to you."

"Mind?" said Bob. "Indeed I do. I mind so much I'll carry it all the way in my hands if there isn't any other place for it. What is it?"

"Well, that's the rub. I guess maybe they thought it wasn't quite in your line. They thought you might like something else better. You see, it's—a Bible!"

Alan unwrapped the package and handed the beautifully bound Bible to Bob, who took it with a look of awe and reverence that astonished Alan. He held it in his hand, almost caressing the soft leather binding. Then he opened the book carefully, noting the suppleness and the gold edges and fine paper with its clear print, and after a moment looked down at the ground.

"I've never had a Bible," he said at last. "But I'll see to it after this that it's in my line. I sure am grateful."

"I think they've written something in the front," said Alan, to cover his own deep feeling. He reached over and turned the pages back to the flyleaf.

To Robert Fulton Lincoln, with the best wishes of his friends of the West Avenue Young People's Group.

A long string of autographs followed, most of them belonging to Bob's former schoolmates, and at the bottom, in small script, was written "2 Timothy 2:15."

"Here, I've got to get my name in that space they left there," said Alan, getting out his fountain pen. "You see, I happen to be vice president."

Bob watched him write his name, and an embarrassed silence filled the room till it was written.

"Thanks a lot," he said deeply affected, studying the names one by one. "Do you know—I wouldn't have expected—that is—well, I've never thought anyone there liked me. I've always felt alone in this town. I guess that's what made me act so rotten to you all. I thought you were a—well, a lot of hypocrites!"

A look of shame crossed Alan's face.

"I'm sorry, Bob," he began. "I hope I can forgive myself. I'm starting to think your estimate of us was true, though. But we had no idea. Why, we prayed for you the time you got hit by that automobile. We prayed in our Sunday night meeting for you."

"I know you did, and I hated it. One of the little kids told me, and I thought you did it for show. But—say, Mac, I wish you'd pray for me again. I need it. It isn't easy to live in this world alone, even if I do have the chance of a lifetime."

A wave of love and joy suddenly filled Alan's heart.

"I sure will!" he said. "Let's do it now. And I wish you'd pray for me. If ever a Christian felt mean and self-centered and foolish, I do. Come on."

They knelt beside the big leather couch at the foot of the bed, with Bob shyly, awkwardly, wondering just what he had brought upon himself by his impulsive words, and Alan in young eagerness, flinging his arm across his companion's shoulders.

"Oh, God," he prayed, "I've been a fool, but I thank You that You've shown me before it was too late. Thank You for giving me this friend, and may we be friends always. And now please bless him and show him what the Lord Jesus has done for him. We thank You together that the blood of Jesus Christ covers all our sins and mistakes, both of ours, and that even such carelessness as I've been guilty of, not letting Christ live through me, can't keep either of us from wearing the robe of righteousness. It's Christ's righteousness that we may wear and not our own. Help Bob surrender himself to You before he goes, and when he goes may he know You're with him and that he'll never be alone. We ask it in the name of Jesus."

Silence filled the room as they continued to kneel, and then Alan said softly, "You pray too, Bob. It'll be good to remember, you know, till you come back."

Bob caught his breath softly and then after a pause spoke hesitantly: "Oh, God—I'm pretty much of a sinner, I guess. I don't think I'd be—much good—to You. But I need somebody—mighty bad! If you'll take me—I'm Yours."

He caught his breath again in a gasp and added, "Thanks for sending Mac into my life—and for this great chance to go in his place."

They talked a long time after the light was out. Alan explained what it meant to be born again and what he'd meant by "the robe of righteousness," showing his new friend how Christ had taken his sins on Himself and nailed them to the cross when He died. And if he accepted the freedom from the law that had been purchased on the cross, he had a right to stand clear and clean before God, not in his own righteousness, but in the righteousness of Christ.

Bob asked a lot of questions. The whole subject was new to him. The clock struck two before they decided to get some sleep. Alan had forgotten all about his own worries in the joy of leading another soul into the light. Both young men were drifting off into unconsciousness when they became vaguely aware of a car stopping before the house. A moment later a pebble struck the window, and a low whistle followed this signal.

They were alert at once, and Alan sprang out of bed to the window.

"Who's there?" Alan called softly.

"That you, Mac?" whispered Keith Washburn. "Say, Mac, did you leave a light on down in the store?"

"Why, no!" said Alan. "I know because, as I was leaving, I stumbled over a box of things Joe had left in the way."

"Well, there's one down there now," Keith said emphatically. "I just saw it as I went by. And what's more it's moving around like a flashlight in the back of the store."

"Wait! I'll be right down!" said Alan, at once reaching for his clothes.

Chapter 4

D on't get up, Bob," said Alan, struggling into a sweater. "You've got to start your trip tomorrow. It's likely nothing. Go to sleep. I'll be right back."

"Forget it!" said Bob, fumbling with his shoes. "What do you take me for, man?"

Keith was waiting for them downstairs, the engine running softly, and he started the car before they were fairly in.

"Sure you weren't dreaming, Wash?" asked Alan, wondering why his teeth were chattering and trying to remember whether he'd brought those papers home or left them in the safe. He had a sick feeling he'd left them in the safe. Oh, if only Dad was well!

"Dreaming? Ha!" said Keith, with a little contempt in his voice. "Well, I might have been, of course. I saw the light when I first rounded the corner by the post office, and I thought it was odd. Thought you must have forgotten to turn it out or else decided to leave it burning. But when I got around in front of the store it was all dark, so I concluded I'd been mistaken. Thought it was just a reflection or something. When I reached your corner I looked back, though, and it flashed up again and moved around. Then I decided you'd gone down to the store after something. But I didn't feel easy and thought I better try to get in touch with you. Thought maybe you could explain it."

They were rounding the corner onto the main street now, and suddenly Bob laid a detaining hand on the wheel.

"Better stop here, Washburn," he suggested. "If you go nearer, the engine can be heard."

"That's right, Lincoln. I should have thought of that. I'll park here in the shadow, and we'll sneak up. Probably it's only some trick of the streetlights reflecting somewhere, and I'll feel like two cents. I probably just have a case of nerves from riding half the night. If it is I'll hate it that I woke you up, but it's better to be on the safe side."

"For sure!" Alan stepped to the ground softly and wondered for the fortieth time whether he'd taken those papers home or left them in the safe.

"There's a light all right!" whispered Bob as they stole along, walking on the grass at the edge of the pavement so their feet made no sound. "There! Look! It's moving around! Now it's gone! No, there it is again!"

"I'll slide around to the alley!" whispered Alan. "Maybe I can look in the back window. They're operating down by the safe, whoever it is. You two watch this side and the front, will you?"

"Don't do anything rash, Mac! Perhaps we better call the officer. He should be in the area about now."

"No, wait! I want to get a line on things first," said Alan.

He slid off into the darkness, rushing down the alley separating his father's store from the milliner's just beyond, and passed the window behind his father's desk.

Keith and Bob stepped up to the front of the store and tried to look through the front windows, but the window decorations prevented them from seeing more than a small light dancing here and there and sometimes disappearing entirely.

Keith stepped to the door and peered through the glass, but a stand full of brooms blocked his vision, and he couldn't be sure. Once he thought he saw a dark form move across the dim distance, and the light appeared from a new angle.

How did someone get into the store?

He slid his hand down to the door latch and tried it, taking great care. But the rusty latch gave forth a grating sound, and at that moment the light inside the store went out. There followed a dull thud, as of heavy books falling, and then a crash of metal, a lot of heavy metal articles falling against one another, a sort of scuffling sound, and then silence. Ominous silence.

Frantically Keith put his shoulder to the door and tried to push it open, but the old door was held by heavy bolts at top and bottom and made of strong oak planks. Keith could only rattle it.

"We'd better call Mac and break this door open," said Keith. "This looks odd!"

But Bob had already disappeared down the alley, and Keith tiptoed to the corner of the store, with a sharp eye out toward the front so no one could escape in that direction.

Meanwhile, Alan, as he ran down the alley, was still trying to solve the problem of what he'd done with those papers. And what were they worth anyway? If deeds and securities and insurance papers were lost or stolen, did that spell calamity, or was everything recorded so they'd lose nothing? And why would anyone want those papers? It must have something to do with the people who were trying to foreclose the mortgage—unless this was a common thief looking for money in the safe. What was that paper his father had spoken about? The "agreement," he'd called it—something about not foreclosing under certain conditions. It was odd how his father's words came back now under stress. Oh, how careless he was not to attend to this matter right away!

But there was no more time to think about it now. Arriving at the end of the alley, under the window behind the safe, he saw to his horror that the window was wide open, and the light was dancing about inside.

Cautiously he approached. If he only had a box or something to stand on so he could see inside and know what to do. There might be more than one person inside, and then he'd need help. He should perhaps have brought his little revolver along, but he hadn't thought of it when he left home, nor had he considered there might be any serious danger.

While he was watching the window, he heard the thud of the ledger falling, knew what it was, saw the light go out and then heard a hurried step and the crash of metal. He figured that last was the stack of children's hoes and shovels and rakes clattering together. He could almost visualize the intruder now and knew which way he was moving.

Almost instantly a dark form appeared at the window. He could see a white hand reaching for the window sill as the light from the next street illumined it. The man was coming out!

Alan crouched close to the wall. He had no time to signal his friends. He held his breath as the intruder climbed out on the window sill, hesitated an instant and then dropped—straight into Alan MacFarlan's arms. The two struggled together and fell, rolling over and over in the alley.

Alan held on tightly, though his prisoner kicked and struggled and even sunk his sharp teeth into Alan's left arm.

Gasping and snorting they rolled about in the alley, until Alan finally gained the upper hand. But he still hadn't caught a good look at the man's face. Suddenly the man wrenched his right arm loose and gave Alan a smashing blow to his nose, stunning him and sending him crashing to the floor of the alley, unconscious.

It was Bob Lincoln who dislodged the man's hand from Alan's throat as he was choking him. The man, sensing he was outnumbered, disappeared in the darkness, but not before Keith saw him running and followed hard on his tracks, meanwhile issuing a sharp warning whistle. The police came at once. But the burglar was gone! Keith had sped after him but, reaching the end of the alley, found no one there or any trace of him. He ran up and down the street in either direction but finally gave up and returned to the place where Alan was lying.

Bob had brought him back to consciousness and was wiping the blood from his face. One of the officers had a big flashlight turned on, and they were talking in low voices. Alan, his voice a little shaky, told what had happened.

Alan presently insisted on standing to his feet. He was all right, of course. Just a little punch in the nose—what was that? He was just sorry the man escaped.

They stepped inside the store and saw the safe, which had been blown open with noiseless powder. Papers were strewn about on the floor, and the children's garden tools were lying across them. The day book and ledger were on the floor where they'd fallen when the man fled.

Alan set his lips in a firm line. *Who would have done this?* he wondered. And what would his father say when he heard of this new disaster? How much had the man gotten away with? Was it his fault in any way? Yes, at least in part, for he never should have opened the safe with the shade up and a light inside. Besides, he now recalled he'd left the iron shutters of that window, always closed at sundown, wide open. He hadn't even remembered to fasten the window. It might have been open, too. He hadn't done anything to it except draw the shade.

They went home at last and back to bed, leaving the police in charge. They could find no trace of the intruder.

Alan felt a little shaky and found he had a black eye as well as a bloody face and several minor bruises.

"Bob, you saved my life, you know," he remarked as they went up the walk to the MacFarlan house.

"Oh, I just helped out a little. You'd have been up in a second."

"No," said Alan seriously, "I was gone. He had me by the throat. I was choking to death. I remember thinking it was all over with me. You came just in time. I won't forget it."

Bob threw his arm across Alan's shoulder.

"That's great of you, Mac," he said. "Then we both have something now. I'll never forget either."

While Alan cleaned his wounds, Bob picked up his new Bible again and turned the pages reverently, reading again the inscription and the names. Then he studied the reference at the bottom of the page.

"Say, Mac, what's this down at the bottom—'2 Timothy 2:15'?"

"Oh, that?" said Alan, coming into the room. "That's the group's text for the year, Second Timothy, two fifteen. You know the verse: 'Study to show yourself approved unto God, a workman who needs not to be ashamed, rightly dividing the word of truth.' You'll likely find the verse marked in the Bible. Trust Sherrill for that. Here, I'll show you."

Alan fluttered the pages over and handed the Bible back to Bob, open to the chapter, and with the fifteenth verse marked clearly in black lines.

Bob read the verse over slowly, thoughtfully, and then looked up with a smile.

"So it seems I have a higher boss than old Hodge, do I?" he said thoughtfully. "One that comes first. Well, if I have God's approval, I guess old Hodge should be satisfied, don't you think?"

"Yes, for sure!" said Alan, pulling his sweater off and tossing it across a chair.

"But what does this last line mean? 'Rightly dividing the word of truth'?"

"Oh, that means understanding the word of truth, the Bible, that God has given us—the old and new covenants, faith, salvation, forgiveness, grace and all that. And here's our study course. I promised Sherry I'd give it to you. Stick it in the book. We want you to keep up with us, and we'll send you the exams when they come in. Then we can all be learning the same things."

Bob accepted the study course eagerly and was sitting down to examine it. But Alan reminded him it was almost four o'clock, and he had less than four hours to sleep before his trip.

"That's all right, Mac. I'll have plenty of time on the ship. But you need your sleep, so I'll turn in now, too."

Morning came all too soon for the two young sleepers, but they were alert early.

"Say, what a sight!" announced Bob, rubbing his eyes and gazing at Alan. "You look as if you'd been in a fight for sure."

Alan laughed.

Suddenly he sprang out of bed. "Oh, no! I never looked to see if I brought those papers home last night."

He dashed over to the closet where his coat was hanging and fumbled in first one pocket and then another, finally pulling out a bundle of documents fastened together with rubber bands.

"What a relief!" he exclaimed, a look of joy spreading over his face. "Here they are! Now how about that? Brought 'em home after all and didn't remember a thing about it. Now the next thing is, is that agreement among them, or did that poor fish get away with it?"

"What are you talking about?" asked Bob, glancing at the sheaf of papers. "Was there something in that safe somebody wanted? Do you have any idea who that intruder was?"

"Well, not exactly, but a man's been trying to put something over on Dad, and I'm guessing he might be hunting for certain papers. I don't know for sure, because I can't ask Dad till he gets better. I've got to figure it out myself. But I sure wish I'd had a good look at his face before he cleared out. I don't suppose we'll ever get a line on him."

"H'm!" said Bob thoughtfully. "Wish I was staying a day or two. I'd like to help you out."

"Here's an agreement," said Alan, opening an envelope. "Might be it." He read the papers quickly and then folded and slipped them in his coat pocket again. "Guess I'll put these in the safety deposit box in the bank this morning. Come on, Bob—we need to hurry. You don't want to miss that train. We'll go downstairs and eat a bite. What do you have left to do? Anything but gather up your baggage?"

"Oh, just one or two little things," said Bob. "It won't take me long."

Alan's mother had ordered breakfast served at once when they came down —honeydew melon, chops, fried potatoes, waffles and coffee. She came in smiling as the boys sat down.

"Why, this is a banquet, Mrs. MacFarlan," said Bob, standing and stepping over to pull back her chair. "You shouldn't have done all this. And I'm sure you don't have breakfast at this hour every morning."

"You're going on a trip, Bob," said the mother, "and will need a good breakfast. Besides, we've had good news this morning. Alan, your father is better, the doctor says. It will be a long time before he's back to normal, but he's passed the worst, he hopes."

They enjoyed breakfast together, and Bob's heart warmed with feeling he belonged and might help rejoice in the happiness and relief of these new friends. It was soon time for the young men to leave, but as they were going out the door the telephone rang, and Alan was called back to answer.

"I'll start on," Bob told him. "Meet you at the post office. How's that? I need to leave my address, or my brother-in-law will examine any letters that come."

But Bob didn't go at once to the post office. Instead he sprinted down the back street and entered the alley, the scene of the fracas the night before. He looked over the ground thoroughly and then followed the path down among the weeds into the fields where the man had disappeared. Yes, he saw tracks in the grass where the tall weeds lay flat as if a heavy foot had crushed them. But they ended in a group of elderberry bushes near the railroad with no sign of footsteps beyond that. He studied the vague path a moment and then retraced his steps.

He didn't notice a girl watching him from behind the fence until he stood opposite her. It was Lancey Kennedy, the niece of Mrs. Corwin who kept the millinery store on the other side of the alley and lived in a small apartment over the store. Bob didn't know the girl very well. She was quiet and had been in town for about a year. She had come to live in Rockland with her aunt after the death of her parents. But she'd been in his class in high school and was one of the best students in the class.

He would have passed her with a brief nod, but she motioned to him to wait.

"I've been hoping to speak to you," she said in a voice that seemed almost frightened. "Weren't you here last night? I thought I heard someone say 'Bob,' and it sounded like your voice that answered."

"Sure, I was here," he answered, stepping a little closer. "Did they wake you up?"

"I wasn't asleep," she said. "I was worried. You see my room is in the third-story back, and just as I turned my light out I heard a noise out here in the alley. I looked out and was sure I saw a man's feet disappearing into the window of the store."

"You did?" said Bob, with a whistle of astonishment.

"But I wasn't sure at all," said Lancey. "It's awfully dark in the alley. But I waited, and pretty soon I saw a light in the store. Sometimes I wasn't sure and thought it must be my imagination. Then I got so excited I didn't know what to do. I thought I should tell someone, but I couldn't go downstairs without waking my aunt, and I knew she wouldn't want me to call anybody. She would have said I was imagining it. So I waited, but I guess I should have gone anyway. But before I had my courage up I saw someone else come down the alley, and a man jumped out of the window, and then it all happened. I wanted to scream out, but I was so frightened I couldn't make a sound. When I got control of myself I saw two other people running and heard Keith Washburn call out, "Get him, Bob!" You answered, and I knew there was no need.

"But I saw the man run down in those bushes, and then it was so dark beyond I couldn't see him any longer. I knew you were all onto him, and I didn't know if the police had caught him. But after they'd all gone I stayed there awhile just watching that group of elderberry bushes till it seemed to move and walk up across the grass. Pretty soon I saw it was a man moving in the darkest places across the end of our back fence. He'd come right out of the bushes or from behind the bushes. He must have hid till you all went away. And he kept so close to the fence I could only see the top of his head sometimes. He would move a few steps and then stop."

Bob was watching the girl's face as he listened. He wondered why he'd never noticed her delicate features before.

"When I saw he was turning in between our store and the bakery," went on Lancey, "I slipped out of my room and went down in the store to watch and see if he came out into the street. As soon as I was in the store he passed by the window. He was limping and had no hat on. He moved slowly, glancing up and down the street, and finally crossed and went into Mrs. Brower's boardinghouse. I could see he had a latch key. He was a long time getting the door open and kept looking each way, and once he dropped the key. I heard it fall on the door stone."

"Was there any light at Mrs. Brower's?" asked Bob.

"Not for a while," answered Lancey. "Just when I was about to give up, a light came on in the third-story back room. It has a side window that looks down on the road to their garage, and I saw a hand jerk the shade down. I could make out only a hand and an arm.

"Then I wondered what to do. I felt somebody should know but wasn't sure who. I've slipped out here every time I could get away, to see if somebody wouldn't come back, so I could tell without being noticed. I knew my aunt would be furious if her name got tangled up in it. And I wasn't at all sure I should make it known anyway, except to the people concerned about it. After the light went out I was so cold I went back to my room, but I couldn't sleep all night. Do you think it's important? Do you think I should tell the police?"

"You poor kid!" said Bob, his voice full of compassion. "Don't worry any more about it. Sure, I think it's important, but you don't need to do anything about it. I'll tell MacFarlan, and then if he wants to know more he can ask you. I'll tell him to keep your name out of it. He'll understand."

"Oh, thank you!" said Lancey with a sigh of relief. "I was afraid my aunt would have to know about it, and she isn't—well—it isn't easy to make her understand. She would think I shouldn't have been watching and was to blame somehow."

"You poor kid!" Bob said again. "Leave it to me! I'll try to talk with you about it another time without the town knowing. May I call you?"

"Oh, no," said Lancey, shrinking back against the fence. "My aunt would be sure to answer the telephone and ask questions and be unpleasant."

"All right! I'll get word to you somehow—write you a note or something. Don't worry. If anybody questions you, I'll make sure they do it discreetly. Thanks for giving me the information. You're some detective. Oh, there's Mac's car. I'd better go. I'll see you later if I can."

He strode up the alley and appeared quite casually beside the car as Alan drew up at the drug store. Then he turned briefly and saw the girl standing in the back garden among the hollyhocks, her bright hair blowing in rings around her face.

Lancey watched as the young man departed and remembered his comforting words: "Leave it to me!"

Then suddenly a voice burst forth from the doorway. "Lancey Kennedy! What on earth are you doing out there in the garden at this hour? The coffeepot has boiled over, and the toast has burned to a crisp. I declare! The Kennedy in you comes out stronger every day. Whatever do you think you're worth in life anyway?"

"You're some detective," Lancey could hear Bob Lincoln's voice saying. She turned in dismay to go into the house. "And he thought it would be important, too," she told herself, as she entered the kitchen and faced her aunt's dark frown.

Chapter 5

Lancey stood there quietly while her aunt lashed out at her with her sharp words, until she asked a pointed question.

"Who was that man walking out of the alley? Didn't I see you talking to him? If you're going to turn out to be that kind of girl you can go. I'll harbor no hussies in my home, running after every man who comes along!"

The color drained out of Lancey's cheeks, and her eyes fairly blazed as she faced her angry aunt.

"He was one of the boys from high school, Aunt Theresa. I scarcely know him at all, but there was nothing unusual in his stopping to say good morning, was there? We were in the same classes everyday last winter."

"Well, when it starts it never stops at good morning. But you're not to have anyone hanging around. I won't stand for it!"

Lancey's cheeks flushed crimson, but she kept her voice steady and her chin up. "Well, you won't be troubled with him, Aunt Theresa. I understand he's leaving today for Egypt."

"Hmph!" said the aunt. "Now eat your breakfast in a hurry. You'll have to take what you can find since you've burned the toast. You have to finish wrapping that package to be returned to New York and get it to the station in time for the train. I've told them in the letter that it starts on the same train with the letter, so be quick about it. And while you're there you might as well wait for the local train to come out and bring back those things I ordered by baggage master's stamp last night. I can't do a thing till I get that velvet, and Mrs. Treadwell wants her hat this afternoon. Now for mercy's sake don't get to mooning again. I'm sure I don't know what you'll eat. The bread hasn't come yet, and you burned the last two slices."

"I'm sorry," said Lancey cheerfully, her eyes lighting up despite her efforts not to. "I'll just take a cracker and hurry. I think this clock is a little slow."

Lancey was thrilled at the chance to go to the station and see Bob Lincoln off to Egypt. Sherrill Washburn had come in yesterday and told her about it while her aunt was out for a few minutes. But Lancey hadn't thought she could get off so early in the morning, and she'd sooner have bitten her tongue than try to explain and ask permission to go. She would have fifteen minutes between those trains, and the express would pass the other way just after the local on which her package was due. Nobody knew how much she wanted to be on the platform in the farewell party to see her classmate off and help in the farewell song. And now the way was miraculously opened.

She fairly flew up the stairs to get her hat. Then she wrapped and addressed the package carefully, with hands that trembled with their eagerness and haste, and was soon on her way to the station. The morning seemed suddenly golden.

Her old classmates were there on the platform, chattering like blackbirds when Alan and Bob arrived at the station, and Lancey Kennedy shyly among the rest. No sooner had they sighted Bob than they set up a cheer, led by Phil Mattison.

Lincoln! Lincoln! Link! Link! Lincoln!
Lincoln! Lincoln! Robert of Lincoln!
Bob O'Link! Bob O'Link!

Then Riggs Rathbone, who owned a rich tenor, sprang upon the baggage truck and, signalling for attention, broke forth into a ballad to the tune of "Old Grimes Is Dead."

Wake up, good Rockland citizens;
Wake up from your long nap!
Bob Lincoln's sailing Egypt way
To put us on the map, my friends,
To put us on the map, my friends,
Put Rockland on the map!
Bob Lincoln's sailing Egypt way
To put us on the map!

Amidst laughter and cheers he began another verse in stentorian tones, and everybody hushed to listen, smiling broadly.

Look out, King Tut, you poor old mutt!
Warn all your mummy friends!
Bob Lincoln's sailing down their way!
All secrecy now ends—

Each of the eleven verses was funnier than the last, and everyone was laughing when the song was finished. Then a quiet seemed to fall upon them as they gathered in small groups and began to talk. Several stepped up to Bob, wishing him well and congratulating him on the honor he'd won of going on such a notable expedition and in such distinguished company.

Bob's face was pale with astonishment and humble surprise. He was almost embarrassed by their friendliness. It needed only a distant glimpse of his disagreeable brother-in-law driving by as the crowd set up another cheer to be fairly overwhelming. He turned his face as the brother-in-law stared in amazement.

Lincoln! Lincoln! Rah! Rah! Rah!
Bob Lincoln! Bob Lincoln!
Egypt! Egypt! Egypt!

Glancing around again, he noticed Lancey Kennedy, standing quietly behind him, with shining eyes and a glow on her face that reminded him of the pink hollyhock she had stood next to an hour ago. He stepped quickly to her side and leaned over to speak to her.

"I told Mac," he said in a low tone. "He's sure glad to know about it. He says it makes things a lot plainer. They won't bring your name in. He seemed terribly grateful to you."

Lancey's heart warmed, and her smile gave all the answer that was needed, even without the "I'm glad" she managed to murmur.

Then suddenly the crowd stirred. The train was coming. Far down the track it showed a speck of unfolding black with a plume of gray.

Riggs Rathbone jumped on the baggage truck again and began to sing. As everyone around took up the words, Bob Lincoln, on a sudden impulse, whispered into Lancey's ear: "Would you mind if I wrote to you sometimes?"

"Oh, that would be wonderful!" answered Lancey softly.

"Thanks! It'll mean a lot to me to have a friend back home!" He caught her hand in a quick warm clasp and dropped it again before anyone could notice. And then the tide of song swept around them, and Lancey joined her voice with theirs, singing from her heart:

God be with you till we meet again—

The train was coming faster now. It had just stopped at Millville Junction for a second to take on a passenger at the signal, and now it was approaching rapidly.

When life's perils thick confound you,
Put His arms unfailing round you!

The train was upon them, and everyone said their good-byes at once, while Bob stood on the platform, a Rockland pennant in his hand that someone had given him, and Alan on the step below.

The train began to move, and Alan swung off with a quick hand grip. Bob waved his pennant, smiled at them all and then found Lancey, standing against the station, waving a bit of handkerchief and smiling through misty eyes. Her pink dress was the last thing he saw as the train swept him out of sight of the town that had suddenly become dear to him.

"That's the greatest thing you ever did, Alan," Sherrill said, as she stepped into Alan's car for the ride back to her home. "You may do some things greater in your life, but I'll always think this was the greatest."

"Great?" asked Alan. "Nothing great about it. I was having the time of my life. He's a fine person! I wonder who else I'm misunderstanding and under-rating. I'd better get out the list of the people I consider my enemies and see if I can't clean them off the slate. I shouldn't wonder if I find out I'm a pretty mean kind of cuss and didn't know enough to realize it."

"Oh, stop that! Did you see how happy and surprised he looked when they cheered? And he told me he was going to study the Bible with us and that you'd talked with him."

Meanwhile, Lancey was walking back to the millinery store with her bundle, unmindful of the sharp words she would probably receive because she was a minute late from watching the express vanish out of sight. But for once she didn't care.

Alan left Sherrill at her home and drove back to the hardware store, his heart growing heavier with each block he passed. The affairs of his father's business settled down on his shoulders. He had to check over all the papers from the safe to make sure nothing was gone. How would he know? Was there a list somewhere? He must find out.

Rawlins was coming at eleven o'clock, and he felt less prepared to meet him than ever. If he could only take him outside and let him have it as he had the intruder the night before—but perhaps he had already! If the tale Lancey Kennedy had told Bob was related to this, it might mean that. In which case, would the man come at all? And would he recognize his assailant? He should investigate that at once and put police on it. He must see Lancey. But how and keep his promise to Bob not to let her aunt see him talking to the girl? Well, he must do it somehow!

Then there was the mortgage—the major trouble. What should he do, and how soon would Judge Whiteley come home?

Lancey solved one problem by running in for a paper of tacks as soon as he arrived at the store. And though she was in a hurry, she answered all his questions clearly. By the time she left he felt fairly certain Rawlins was the intruder, for the man was boarding at Mrs. Brower's. But what could he have wanted from the safe? And did he get whatever it was? If only he could ask his father a few questions! But the doctor's orders were strict: He mustn't be disturbed for several days yet.

Alan spent an hour reviewing the papers he could find and grew more perplexed. He knew his father would want him to confide only in Judge Whiteley, who seemed to have vanished for the time. He groaned inwardly.

At half past ten a telegram was delivered from the city.

Was in bad automobile accident yesterday. Am in hospital. My representative will call this afternoon at five, fully empowered to act. This will be your last chance.

Rawlins

Alan read the telegram carefully, crossed the street to the Brower boarding-house and asked if he might see a man named Rawlins who was boarding there.

Mrs. Brower seated him in her dismal parlor and climbed the stairs to the third-story back. It was some minutes before she returned bearing an open note in her hand.

"He isn't here. He was called to the city on the early train this morning," she said, glancing down at the paper in her hand as if to verify her statement.

"When will he return?" asked Alan, trying to glimpse the handwriting on the note.

"Well, I can't say for sure," said the woman. "I guess for supper. He generally turns up for meals. He 'lowed he had business here for another week yet."

Alan thanked her and departed, feeling reasonably sure he knew his man, but clearly unsure what his next move should be.

The day wore on, and the store was filled with customers most of the time. The story of the burglary was leaking out despite Alan's efforts to keep it quiet. Many people came in just to ask questions, and the five o'clock hour was drawing on when Rawlins's representative would arrive. Perhaps he should have confided in Bill Atley; he knew how to keep his mouth shut. But Bill was chief of police and was on night duty this week. He would still be asleep. And already it was five minutes after four.

Joe had taken a customer down to the cellar to look over some different sizes of chicken wire, and no one else was around for the moment. With nowhere else to turn Alan dropped to his knees beside the desk and began to pray.

"Oh, God, I don't know what to do! I can't do this alone, and there's no one but You to ask. Won't You help me somehow? For Dad's sake—for Christ's sake—won't You help? I've reached my limit!"

The hot tears stung his eyes, and he felt a great wave welling up from within, as he used to feel when he was a child. But he was a man now and must control his emotions. What would people think if they saw him?

Suddenly the telephone on the desk rang. Startled, he found his hand trembling as he reached for the receiver. It was probably that snake Rawlins or his man, and he wasn't ready for either yet.

"Hello!" he said, almost in a whisper.

"Hello!" Judge Whiteley's voice boomed over the wire. "Is that you, Alan? This is Whiteley. They tell me at the house you've been trying to reach me. Is there something important? I called the house, and your mother told me about your father's accident. Anything I can do? I'm sorry to hear it. I'm at Socker's Point. I came up yesterday to try a case and couldn't get away last night. I thought I'd better call you."

"Oh, Judge Whiteley!" Alan exclaimed, drawing a deep sigh of relief. "When may I see you? I'm in a terrible bind and need your advice."

"I can't get back before eleven o'clock Monday. The case is holding over.

Would three o'clock Monday suit you all right? I expect I'll have a lot of business to clean up when I get back to the courthouse."

"Oh—!"

"What's the trouble, son—anything you can tell me now? Is it personal or business?"

"Business!" said Alan, choking over the word and wondering what he could tell over the phone.

"Business? What's the nature of it?"

"Somebody's trying to skin Dad out of everything, Judge!"

"You don't say!" said the judge. "We can't have that, of course. What can I do? Who is it? What is it?"

"It's—quite a story!"

"I see. Too long to tell over the phone?"

"Only a mortgage and a man who wants his money right away and wants to sell Dad out. I've tried everything Dad told me but can't make any of them work, and Dad's too sick to ask now."

"What did your dad suggest?"

"He said to sell some property in the city if I could, but the only price I can get in a rush sale is a crime and wouldn't be a drop in the bucket."

"I see. What about a new mortgage?"

"That's what Dad thought was a last resort if it could be done, but two companies I went to in town won't handle it, and I don't know where else to try."

"H'm!" he said reflectively. "Well, now that shouldn't be a hard proposition. How much time do we have?"

"Only till Monday, and some guy is coming around here at five to make some sort of proposition—I don't know what."

"Well, you just absent yourself," said the kindly voice. "Clear out and don't have a thing to say. Let me handle this. I'll phone Charlie Ambler right away and arrange things. You take Charlie the papers—do you have the papers?"

"Yes, but somebody broke into the store last night and blew open the safe. I'd taken all the papers home to check, though."

"You don't say!" the judge exclaimed, catching his breath. "Well, don't worry. Take the papers around to Charlie at the bank the first thing Monday morning, and we'll have it all fixed up. Do you know how much it is?"

"Twelve thousand."

"All right, son," said the judge. "That's only a pint of trouble. Don't worry a minute more. Just get those papers over to Charlie as soon as the bank opens, and we'll have that guy helpless before he has a chance."

"Oh, thank you," said Alan, trying to swallow the lump that was forming in his throat. "I'm really grateful. I—"

"There, son. That's nothing," said the judge in a cheery voice. "Of course I'd look after things. Your father and I have always been close. And, by the way, better put Bill Atley wise to that man who's coming. It might save trouble, and you can always trust Bill. All right, son! See you Monday. Call me here if you need me before."

Alan hung up the receiver in astonishment. God answered! The telephone rang while he was praying. "Before they call I will answer." Why, it was even true for him. And he'd always taken it as a figure of speech before. He hadn't really expected an answer when he was praying.

The screen door from the street was suddenly swung open and then fell shut on its patent hinges with businesslike precision, and Alan remembered it was nearly five o'clock. He looked up with sudden panic, and there stood Bill Atley.

Was God sending all the answers at once? Relief and gratitude filled his heart, and his eyes lit up with joy.

"I just stopped in to see if you found anything more wrong," said Bill, glancing at the safe and the desk. "Find all your papers?"

Alan walked quickly to the officer and drew him behind the desk. He told him in low tones what Lancey had seen and of his visit to Mrs. Brower, showed him the telegram and gave a brief explanation about the mortgage and what had happened.

Atley's face remained unchanged during the recital. Only his keen eyes studied the young man's face, and he nodded as the story went on.

"Judge Whiteley is fixing up the mortgage all right. I'm going to pay off the other," finished Alan, with a note of triumph in his voice. "But I thought maybe you'd like to look over this guy that's coming—if he comes!"

"I sure would!" said Bill dryly. "Suppose you just beat it out the back way and leave me in charge. Anybody else here? Joe? All right. Let him stay. He can look after the customers. Where is he? All right! I'll give him his orders. You beat it! Don't go to your house. The guy might chase you and try to annoy you. Why don't you go down and see that Washburn girl you had out riding this morning? Nothing like a lady to make a good getaway behind. I'll call you there if I need you. All right now—run along."

Something in Atley's kindly tone stung Alan. But he turned with a flash of something in his eyes.

"Say, Bill—I'm no quitter. I'll stay here and face it. I just thought you might like to look him over for future reference if he comes."

"I sure would!" Atley said fervently. "But I mean what I say. I'll handle this. What you don't say can't do any harm, see? We may need this guy's fingerprints. Remember we had a burglary last night. The fact that he didn't get away with much doesn't cut any ice. We want to catch that bird and keep an eye on him, and we can keep him less suspicious with you out o' the way. Beat it, kid. Them's orders!"

Atley slapped him on the back with a brotherly smile, and Alan made no further protest.

He went out the back door of the store and walked across the back lots and through the meadow till he reached the Washburns' back fence, vaulting it. Sherrill was out in the garden picking raspberries, and he joined her.

"Sherry, I've just had an incredible answer to prayer that's knocked me silly!" he said, plucking off the ripe berries and dropping them into a bowl.

"Was that all the faith you had, Alan?" she asked, laughing. "It 'knocked you silly'? Then why did you pray if you thought you had no faith?"

"I was desperate," he said. "I didn't know what to do, and I'd reached the end of my rope."

"I read a little book the other day that said God sometimes lets us reach the end so we'll reach out to Him."

"Well, I guess that's right. I was proud of the way I was going to handle my father's business alone. Then something came along I couldn't manage, and I didn't know at all what to do. All my schemes failed. I didn't think of praying till I got in a hole. And then the telephone rang the answer to my prayer right in my ear, and I jumped. And other answers walked right into the store afterward. I didn't know answers to prayer would come like that!"

"God would probably give us answers like that everyday," said Sherrill, shaking her bowl to get more berries into it, "if we trusted Him and listened. Why, most of the time I imagine we would hear His answers if we looked only to Him and less to ourselves. But, Alan"—her voice grew quiet—"I have a feeling God is preparing you for something."

"Sure looks like it," said Alan, almost glumly. Suddenly his expression changed. "Leaving me here in this little town in a hardware store? Some chance I have to get ready for anything! I have to stay here and keep my dad's business from going to pieces while he's laid up."

"Well, I know better than that," said Sherrill. "You're reaching beyond that already and doing a lot in this town right now. What you've done for Bob Lincoln has shown a great many people what Christ can do to change someone's hatred and hostility. The others in the group sure see that. I heard some of them talking. And don't forget that your influence will reach out to the desert in Egypt and, in fact, is traveling there now as fast as the ship can go. You might even find it stronger than if you'd gone yourself. I saw a look in Bob's eyes when he told me how you prayed with him. I feel sure he'll follow through on what he promised."

"Sherry," Alan said, looking at his friend, "I feel ashamed. Here I've been pitying myself because I couldn't do anything, and you talk like that. Say—I wish you'd pray for me. I've got some big problems to face and need all the help I can get."

"I've been praying all morning," the girl said quietly.

"Oh, that must be why that answer came so quickly," he said, smiling. " 'Where two of you shall agree—.' But we didn't agree, actually. It was wonderful, though."

"We have the same God, you know—"

Just then they could hear the telephone clamoring, and Sherrill ran in the house to answer it. Her mother was out, and her grandmother was taking a nap.

Alan plucked the berries thoughtfully, and in a moment Sherrill called him from the door.

"It's you they want, Alan!"

"It's all over, Mac," he heard Bill Atley saying, "all but the shoutin'. Very obliging guy he was—tough as they come—but he gave me some nice clean fingerprints in a convenient place—'course he didn't know he was—and his autograph on a note to you, together with a telephone number where he said you could call the Rawlins bird.

"I had Joe tell him you wouldn't deal with nobody but Rawlins, see? And then I had him give 'm a private wire number where he can call you direct. Only it's the p'lice headquarters' private wire, and if he calls, he'll talk with me, see? We've gotta sift this matter, and I guess we've got some good stuff now. I know a man in the city force and will put him wise, too. So if anything else happens we'll know how to act."

Alan stayed for supper at the Washburns' and helped eat some of the raspberries with cream and angel food cake and other good things. Afterward he and Sherrill sat in the hammock and talked more about the power of prayer and the people for whom they would pray.

"I wonder," said Alan, standing on the sidewalk now, a thoughtful look on his face, "if we were meant to live this way everyday, praying for things and expecting them—and receiving them in startling ways sometimes."

"Of course," said Sherrill, "and not receiving them sometimes when God sees it isn't best. This spring at our Bible conference I heard a man from Germany say that God has different ways of answering prayer. He said the very lowest answer was yes. A higher answer was wait, and God gave it to those who could trust Him more. And sometimes He gave the answer of no to those who could trust Him most."

Alan was silent.

"That's not why He said no to me about going to the desert," he said after a moment. "I've never trusted Him like that. But I'd like to. It would be a wonderful way of living."

"I think He's going to trust you that way, Alan. I'm sure He has a good reason for keeping you home from the desert."

Chapter 6

Sherrill Washburn turned from the door with the mail the postman had brought.

Shuffling through it quickly, she saw one for her grandmother with the return address of her weekly religious paper—probably the yearly reminder that the subscription was due. She noticed two for her mother, the square one from Cousin Euphrasia, shut in and dependent now on Mother for her personal touch with the outside world. The long one was from the church missionary society Mother served as secretary. A sheaf of receipted bills followed, with a letter from a far Western investment that had lost most of its value yet would give an occasional gasp of hope for reviving.

How well these same letters were known in the family life! But Sherrill longed for something new and exciting, just as she had for the last five years since she'd begun to grow up and be impatient for real living to begin.

She was about to put the mail on the hall table for her mother to look at later when she noticed two more letters on the bottom, both with a New York postmark. She hurried back into the living room where her mother and grandmother were sewing.

"Two real letters at last," she announced cheerfully to her mother, "one for you and one for me, and I believe mine is from Uncle West. Why in the world do you suppose he's writing to me? It isn't my birthday or Christmas, and he never writes except to send me a check to buy my present."

"Read it and see," said her grandmother eagerly.

She had already opened her meager communication and laid it in her work basket. She had another grandchild living out in the world who might have written to her. She always hoped to hear something, although she had long ago realized that modern youth has little time for grandmothers.

The room was still while mother and daughter read their letters. Only the snip-snip of the grandmother's scissors could be heard as she clipped off the thread from the napkins she was making out of an old tablecloth.

Sherrill finished first and looked up to watch her mother's face as she turned her letter over and read it again.

"Well?" she asked, as her mother folded the letter and placed it in her lap. "Did you get one too? Of course I can't go, but what on earth do you suppose made him think of it? Who wrote yours? Not Uncle Weston—I know his writing. You don't mean to tell me Aunt Eloise has broken the silence of years at last?"

The mother had been gazing out the window thoughtfully. She brought her attention back and looked at her daughter.

"Really, dear, you shouldn't speak that way about your aunt," she said. "This letter is—well—kind, I think, and after all, we may have misjudged her. You know we don't really know her at all."

"Well, what's it all about?" asked the grandmother, with an impatient tone in her voice. "Read out your letter, Sherrill. It might be interesting news."

"Yes, read your letter," said the mother with a smile. "Is it from your uncle?"

Sherrill read her letter:

My dear niece:

Your aunt and I want you to come and spend a few months in the city with us this winter. We think it's time you and your cousin get acquainted and have some good times together.

We expect to be back from the shore early in November and shall expect you as soon as you can make your arrangements to come. Your aunt is writing your mother so I won't go into details, for she'll tell you all you need to know. I'm enclosing my check to cover railroad expenses and hope we'll be able to give you a good time.

Affectionately, your uncle,
Weston Washburn

Sherrill crumpled the paper in her hand and looked up.

"Now read yours, Mother, or let me read it. For I'm certain you'll leave out something or soften it somehow, and I think I have a right to know the whole matter even if it does show my aunt in a bad light."

She reached for the other letter and began to read, while her mother, half-smiling, half-troubled, sat back in her chair and listened.

Dear Mary:

Weston thinks we ought to do something for Sherrill, so I'm writing to say she is invited to spend the winter with us and see a little of New York life. You don't need to trouble about buying her any new clothes, for Carol has plenty of things she isn't using anymore that can be altered by my maid. Besides, you wouldn't know what to buy.

We expect to be back in New York on the eighteenth of November at the latest, and you can arrange for her to come to us at once. I'm sure a winter in New York will be a great advantage to her, and if she's clever at all she may be able to make valuable acquaintances and a good marriage.

As ever,
Eloise

Sherrill's voice had a sharp, mocking tone as she finished reading the letter, folded it elaborately, and put it back into its envelope.

"Won't that be nice?" she said. "Mother, wouldn't you just love it if I made a good marriage? Lots of money, I suppose, and family and all that! Anything that would lift this family out of obscurity and place it where it wouldn't be a disgrace to her highness—"

"Sherrill, don't!" said her mother abruptly. "You mustn't make fun of your aunt. Especially if you're going to accept her hospitality!"

"Her hospitality! You don't for a minute suppose it will be her hospitality, do you? I'll wager Uncle West had to lay down the law like a tyrant before he ever got that letter out of her. But why do you suppose he did it?"

"Dear, he was your father's twin brother. He was very attached to him."

"Then why didn't he come across with something after Daddy died? When Keith was struggling to keep the business together and couldn't get security, why did he hedge out of everything?"

There was an almost bitter edge to Sherrill's tone.

"I—don't know," answered Sherrill's mother, her eyes clouding. "I've always thought—your aunt was a great expense just then. She had to have an operation and was used to everything money could buy—and—well, I suppose he wasn't as well off at that time as he is now. I think he likely wants to make up for it."

"You don't mean you want me to go!" Sherrill exclaimed.

"Well, of course you haven't had as many advantages as if your father had lived," said Mrs. Washburn. "I've always wanted you to get out in the world a little. I'd expected you to go to college, just as your brother did."

"Well," said Sherrill, "New York isn't college. I'm sure I don't see what I'd get out of a winter in New York, especially since I don't care for the clever marriage Aunt Eloise expects me to pull off."

Silence filled the room until the grandmother broke it with a laugh.

" 'As ever,' " she murmured. " 'As ever, Eloise.' She needn't have said that. We know she'll always be Eloise—wanting to dominate everything and everybody. Wanting John Washburn's child to wear Carol's old cast-offs! As if Sherrill isn't every bit as good as her Carol. As if we didn't have the finest old family anywhere around this neighborhood! And who was she to snub them? She, the daughter of a corner grocery man."

"Oh, Mother, you mustn't put such ideas into Sherrill's head. It will be hard enough for her anyway, if she goes—"

"If she goes!" snorted the grandmother. "You don't mean to say, Mary Sherrill, that you'll let her go? Let her be a target for that selfish woman and let her be a background for that precious little flapper Carol!"

"Mother, don't! I haven't said Sherrill was to go, have I? Sherrill is the one to decide. She received the invitation and is old enough to settle it herself. I'm not at all sure what Sherrill should do. I somehow feel that perhaps her father would have wanted her to go. After all, Weston is her uncle, and she needs to know her father's family."

"And you'd let her go and wear cast-off clothes and be on charity?"

"Certainly not!" said Mrs. Washburn, rising and walking over to the sewing machine. "If Sherrill goes she can somehow get the right clothes to wear. We've always been decently clothed."

"Hmph!" said the grandmother. "Eloise Washburn won't care for the clothes you make. She says as much in that letter. She doesn't want you to bring anything because you wouldn't know what was suitable."

That was the beginning of a whole week's discussion.

When Keith Washburn came home, heard the news and read the two letters, he said with a sensible, elder brother's farsightedness: "Well, I think she should go. If for nothing else than to show her aunt and cousin—yes, and uncle too—that New York isn't the last word in decency and culture and education. My sister can hold her own anywhere, if she wants to, and I'd like Uncle West to know it. As for Aunt Eloise and Carol, why bother about them? They're only people and can't do much. Sherrill doesn't need to have much to do with them if she finds them unpleasant. She'll make her own place in the household and can surely get on with anybody for six months.

"While she's in New York, she can attend concerts and lectures and meet some nice people and see the sights. It's an education, even if your relatives aren't all you wish they were. Uncle Weston seems to be asking in good faith— why not accept in the same way? If things aren't pleasant you can always come home, but it's foolish to turn it down flat. Besides, I think Dad would have liked it. He always thought a lot of his brother and wanted us to over- look Aunt Eloise's snubbing for his sake.

"Really, Sherry," he added, "I'm glad you got this invitation. I've been hoping to get on my feet soon so I could send you somewhere to glimpse another kind of life. But it doesn't look as if I can for two or three more years yet. So I hope you take this and learn what you can from it till I can do better for you."

"You don't need to do things like that for me, Keith," she said, with grati- tude in her voice. "I don't need advantages. I'd rather have home and Mother and all of you than go to a thousand New Yorks."

So day after day the discussion went on—the mother and brother urging Sherrill to accept the invitation; Sherrill hesitant and wistful, but still hold- ing back; and the little grandmother openly against it.

At last they couldn't let the invitation go unnoticed any longer.

In desperation, Sherrill rushed to her room one day and, after an hour, came down with a neatly written note she handed to her mother.

Dear Uncle Weston:

I want to thank you for your kind invitation to visit you, but after think- ing the matter over carefully I don't feel I can spare the time to be away this winter. I'm taking a position in the bank here, and my work begins next week. It was most kind of you and Aunt Eloise to want to help me to better advantages, but I feel I must make my own way in the world.

Again thanking you,
I am your affectionate niece,
Sherrill Washburn

"Oh, Sherrill," said her mother, "that won't do at all. That sounds almost rude—about wanting to make your own way. And after all he is your uncle—"

The doorbell interrupted Mrs. Washburn's sentence, followed quickly by the entrance of Mrs. Harriet Masters, an old school friend of Mary Washburn's who often spent part of her summers in Rockland. She had been traveling abroad for the past two years and hadn't seen them since before her departure.

After they greeted one another, Harriet exclaimed over how Sherrill had grown and how beautiful she was. "She's so much prettier than a good number of the girls I noticed on the continent," she added.

Suddenly she turned to her friend. "What was the discussion when I came in, Mary? You were all looking so serious I'm sure it must have been important. Do tell me about it and let me get back in touch with your family right away. I'm eager to know what's happened since I left."

Sherrill's face clouded, and she turned away with a sigh. Now they would have to go over it again, and she'd thought it was settled. But in her heart she began to wonder if, after all, she didn't really want to go to New York in spite of all the drawbacks. Was she hesitating now because of her desire for a new experience?

"Oh, Sherrill's been invited to go to New York for the winter to visit her uncle's family," began Sherrill's mother. "She's just written to decline the invitation. I think she'll regret not taking the chance someday."

"Why don't you want to go, Sherrill?" asked the visitor, searching the girl's face keenly, with the privileged eyes of a friend of long years' standing.

"Well," said Sherrill, "I don't like my aunt, and I don't like my cousin, or what I know about her. And I think she's right when she says I wouldn't know what clothes to buy. Of course I wouldn't wear her things or let them buy me anything. I could make my own if I was sure I could make them look right. Oh, I guess it's just pride."

"I see," the older woman said thoughtfully. "Well, Sherry, you're too fine to let that stand in the way of something with real advantages, even though it had some unpleasantness about it. Let's see if we can't do something about those things that stand in your way.

"You don't like your aunt, but you might like her if you knew her better. At least you could give her a chance. Your cousin is young, isn't she? You could help her, instead, and not let her bother you. In other words, be strong and fine enough so nothing unpleasant can touch you.

"I heard once of a tiny white flower growing on the edge of the coal mines. It's so white and fine like velvet that it stands out in terrible contrast to the sooty blackness all around it. You would think it would turn black from the soot, but they say it's protected by some substance that won't hold the soil. The dirt rolls off and doesn't stick. In the same way you've always seemed to be surrounded by your mother's faith and love. So what harm can any snobbishness do you if you live above it and just let it roll off?"

"Yes, I know," Sherrill said. "I've tried to think that way—but—that doesn't solve the clothes problem."

"Oh, I might be able to help you solve that part. I brought back a trunk full of clothes from Paris, and you're welcome to copy any you like and adjust them to your age. Come over tomorrow morning with your tape measure and thimble, and we'll get started. It will give me a new interest in life after my trip.

"Oh, by the way, dear, I brought you a present—an evening dress! I wasn't sure you'd have much use for it in this little town, but I thought it looked like what you'd be by now, and I had to buy it. Oh, now don't look so troubled, Mary." This she said to the mother. "It has a modest, simple style and will suit Sherrill. It has little puffs of sleeves, the latest thing in evening gowns, and the back isn't low-cut either. And not even a high-brow aunt could disapprove of it. I bought it at one of the most exclusive shops in Paris, and it has a lovely evening wrap to go with it. Now what's next?"

Sherrill's grandmother gave a satisfied sigh. Nobody had ever suspected her of caring for fine clothes, but she had for some time desired something lovely for the treasure of her heart, her granddaughter. And if she had one besetting sin it was family pride. For she had cherished a secret desire that in some way her side of the family might outshine the unpleasant aunt, daughter of a corner grocery man, who had married into the Washburn side and alienated the delightful uncle from the entire family.

"You've helped a lot, Aunt Harriet," Sherry said, with a look of awe. "It was wonderful of you to bring me a real evening dress and wrap from Paris! I can't believe they'll be mine. Thank you!"

"Well, wait till you see them. You may not like them. In which case I suppose I'll have to give them to Maria Hodgkins."

Maria Hodgkins was a stout and faithful servitor of most uncertain age, in the boardinghouse where Harriet Masters always stayed, and the vision of Maria in evening dress brought laughter from them all.

The guest didn't stay long. She had arrived back in town only a short time earlier, and her trunk hadn't been sent up yet by then.

"Well, I must run," she said, standing up suddenly. "John promised to have the trunk up inside of an hour, and I want to get settled by night. But, Sherry, I'll see you the first thing in the morning."

Chapter 7

"Yes, but what will I copy them in?" said Sherrill, in a puzzled tone as she turned away from watching the guest down the walk. "It costs money, Mother, to buy materials, and I don't intend to have you and Grandma and Keith going without while I take off for the city and play millionaire."

"Oh, don't worry about that!" said Mrs. Washburn happily. "We'll manage somehow to get what you need without scrimping anybody. We always have. Now take that cloud away from your brow, Sherrill, and sing a little. I've missed your voice for a whole week, ever since your uncle's letter came. That's no way to start a vacation. Don't you want to go, child?"

"Why, yes, I suppose I do," Sherrill admitted, "if I could go right. I'd like to see New York and how our relatives live. But I can't help feeling it won't be congenial."

"Well, even if it isn't, it will be a good experience for you. Now run upstairs and get out your old things. Let's see what you have before we plan for new things."

"Why don't you go up to the attic and look in my mother's trunk?" said Grandma. "You might find something there. When your great-grandmother was young they wore skirts with nine breadths in them. That should be plenty for the little makeshifts they wear now. Here—I'll get the key and you go look. It's the little haircloth trunk under the eaves."

"Oh, Grandma, you wouldn't want me to cut up any of Great-Grandmother's dresses!"

"Why not?" said Grandma Sherrill proudly. "She can't wear them anymore, and I'm certain I won't! I don't see making a museum of the attic. Nobody ever goes up there. If it can be of any use to you now, why, consider it your great-grandmother Sherrill's contribution. It goes with the name, don't you see?"

So Sherrill went up in the attic and came down with her arms full of quaint garments, satins and brocades and one fine rose pink taffeta, soft and lovely as the dew on a rose, with a big bertha of fine old lace yellowed with age. There were kerchiefs and under sleeves of old hand embroidery, sweet with lavender, a few lovely handmade collars and several yards of real Valenciennes on undergarments of an antique cut.

"They're wonderful!" said Sherrill, her eyes shining. "Do you really think I should use them?"

"Of course you'll use them!" said Grandma, touching the silk and giving the lace a firm little tug to see if it was rotten.

Then Sherrill went up to her room, foraged out some of her own last winter's dresses and brought them down to the sitting room. Mrs. Washburn unrolled the pieces, rejecting some and laying aside others for possible use.

By the time Keith came home the air was charged with excitement.

"Well, she's going!" Grandma told him with a twinkle in her eye.

"That's the girl! I knew she would!" said the elder brother, glancing about the room. "What's all this—you aren't packing already?"

Keith went around genially, looking at everything they showed him and listening to the generous offers Harriett Masters had made. Presently he went up to his room and came down in a few minutes with a check.

"There's a starter," he said. "I can give you more later, sis. But that'll buy a few shoes and things. You can't make over shoes."

The check was for a hundred dollars. Sherrill knew Keith would have to wait even longer now for the car he'd hoped to purchase soon for his business.

"Oh, Keith!" she cried, wrapping her arms around him. "I can't bear the thought of leaving you dear people and taking everything you've got with me! I don't need all this, really."

"Oh, that's not much! Wait till I get rich! You'll see what I'll do for you then!"

"Well, wait till I make this clever marriage Aunt Eloise is planning for me to pull off!" Sherrill said, laughing. "Then I'll be off your hands, and you can roll in wealth!"

"If I thought you'd do that, sis, I wouldn't let you go!" he said in mock seriousness. "I don't want any New York brother-in-law. I want a real one from the country."

Despite their laughter and teasing, the tears stood very near the surface, for they knew that even a temporary separation would be a trial. They were a tightly knit family, especially since the death of the beloved father, and kept closer than ever to one another.

Nobody felt like eating that night, and they lingered so long over the evening meal that Alan MacFarlan came to pick up Sherrill for the church social before she was ready.

"What's all the excitement?" he asked, looking about on the family he considered second to his own.

"Sherrill's going to New York," Grandma said, searching the young man's face for his reaction. She liked to give the news and see the effect on a listener.

"Going to New York!" echoed Alan. "Why are you going to New York, Sherry?"

"To make a clever marriage!" Sherrill said, with a twinkle in her eyes. "At least that's what my unbeloved aunt expects me to pull off."

Alan had a stricken look. "Why, you're much too young to get married!"

"I'm nineteen!" said Sherrill lightly. "It's been done even younger than that, you know," she added, trying to hide the pleasure she felt at seeing Alan look so miserable.

"That's all right, Alan," Keith said. "If we don't like her choice we'll wring his neck, won't we?"

Alan tried to smile, but the stricken look remained.

"The fact is, Sherrill's been invited to spend the winter with her uncle in New York," Keith said. "It's an opportunity we think she should take. Don't you agree, Alan?"

"I suppose so," agreed Alan, somewhat doubtfully. "But what's to become of the young people's society and all our winter plans without our new president?"

And now the stricken look appeared on Sherrill's face, for the work they'd planned was dear to her heart also.

"It's probably your opportunity to take her place," said Keith. "You're the first vice president, aren't you? Besides, the winter won't last forever."

"It certainly won't come this way again, not this one anyhow. Of course, we don't want to stand in Sherry's way if she wants to go out among 'em."

"Well, she's not so keen on it," said Keith, with a warning glance at Alan. "So it's up to you to encourage her. Okay?"

"I see," said Alan, setting his lips. "Make me the goat, eh? All right, I'll think it over. All set, Sherry!"

"He'll feel her going," said Grandma when they were gone.

"Nonsense, Mother. You're always so romantic. They're just good friends. They're only children yet, you know."

"Well, he's a nice child anyway," said Grandma, with a little sigh. "She won't find many in the city cleverer than he is, either."

"He's been a pleasant friend," said her daughter firmly. "I hope Sherrill won't think of anything deeper than that for some time to come. But of course Alan is a good boy."

"Yes, Alan's all right!" said Keith, preparing to go back to his office for the evening. "But don't worry about him, Grand. Alan won't waste away for a winter of separation. His head is set on straight. And it won't hurt him to be a little lonely."

Out in the moonlight Alan and Sherrill, as they walked, were talking about their committee and the plans for the evening.

Suddenly, a silence fell upon them.

"Say, Sherry, what's all this talk about marriage?" Alan asked at last, his voice breaking.

Sherrill laughed. "Oh, that's a joke. Didn't Keith tell you?"

"You heard all he told me," said Alan gravely.

"Oh, don't take it seriously, Alan. That aunt I don't like, Aunt Eloise, is always saying something disagreeable. She wrote that if I was clever I might make a good marriage while I was up there. Get me off the family hands and all that." Sherrill laughed again. "Imagine me!"

But Alan didn't laugh.

"Well," he said glumly, "it's what's to be expected, of course, when you go away like that for a whole winter."

"Alan MacFarlan!" said Sherrill, stopping suddenly on the sidewalk. "If you talk like that I'm going back home! I thought you were my friend and understood me, and I thought you had a sense of humor." Tears were forming in Sherrill's eyes.

Alan put out a hand and touched the tip of Sherrill's elbow protectively, as if he were years older than she, though in fact he was only seven months older.

"There's usually some kind of truth behind all jokes," he said. "I just didn't like the idea, that's all. It means—well—sort of the end."

"The end of what?" Sherrill asked sharply.

"Well, the end of this. We've been friends for a long time."

"Now, look here, Alan! You've got to stop this nonsense," she said, half-indignant, half-amused. "Why, I'm still young. You said so yourself only a few minutes ago. I haven't an idea of getting married for ages yet."

"Corinne Arliss was only sixteen when she was married."

"Well, if you want to class me with Corinne Arliss, I guess you will. But you know my mother didn't bring me up that way."

"Well, you needn't get angry with me, Sherry," said the boy disconsolately. "It just seems so strange for you to go away like this for a whole winter, when we'd planned all these things. And then to hear you talk about marrying, well, it seems as if you've suddenly grown up."

"I haven't really wanted to go, Alan. In fact, I held off for a week saying I wouldn't go, till the family made such a fuss I finally gave in. Keith was the worst. He thinks my father would have wanted me to go. My uncle is his only brother, you know, and they were very close."

"I suppose he would have," said Alan. "Well, forget it. I'm an old grouch. Of course you must go—only it's going to be tough without you."

"Oh, well," said Sherrill cheerfully, "winter won't take long to pass. Remember when you went to Canada with your father? It didn't last forever, though I'll admit it seemed long at the time."

"All right!" said Alan, taking a deep breath and assuming a bright look on his face. "But what are we going to do for president of our society?"

"Nothing—I'm not moving away. I expect to return before the year is up. A winter is over in the spring, you know. And if you ask me, it'll be an early spring this year if I have anything to say about it."

"But what do you mean? We can't get along all winter without some head, can we?"

"Well, aren't you the vice president? Isn't that what a vice president is for, to take the place of president? Come to think of it—that's one more reason why I should go, to give you your rightful place in this society. You wouldn't take the office of president, though it's been offered you three times to my knowledge. So now it's being thrust upon you."

She flung a triumphant smile at him through the darkness, and Alan smiled back.

"I only said no because I wanted you to be president."

"And I only consented because I could get you to tell me how to run things right, so your modesty wouldn't keep the society from benefitting from your wisdom."

"Ha!" said Alan in a more lighthearted tone.

"No ha about it! Those are facts."

"Well, I'll do my best. But on one condition—you've got to write to me and tell me every week what you want done, and I'll report to you—"

"Why, that goes without saying. I think I hate to go worse than you hate for me to. I'm sure I'll bore you to death with directions and watch every mail for your reports—just as I did when you went to Canada. But then I got only a half dozen little postcards inscribed 'O.K.A.M.'—or something like that."

"Oh, I was only a kid then. I was too interested in that new country."

"Ha! You're still a kid now, Alan, so don't think otherwise, please. We've always grown up together, you know, and it isn't fair for you to get ahead of me while I'm gone."

"You don't think New York and all those clever marriages your aunt wants you to pursue will age you any?"

"Certainly not," said Sherrill cheerily. "Now take off that grouch and don't let everybody know we've been having a fight."

She gave his arm a friendly pat as they walked up the steps of the house where they were to spend the evening together.

The door was flung open, and happy voices and brightness greeted them. Sherrill felt a pang. How hard it would be to drop out of this dear circle where her interests had been since childhood. She entered with her own bright smile, however, feeling that for Alan's sake she mustn't let anything seem different.

They rushed upon her eagerly.

"You're late, Sherrill! You two have been making such a fuss about everybody being on time, and here you are ten minutes late."

Alan answered with a grave smile. "It couldn't be helped this time, Willa. Keith had something important to tell me. We left as soon as possible."

Sherrill glanced at him and noticed the quiet gravity on his usually merry face. So then her going was really cutting deep into Alan. She wondered why that gave her a pleasant sense of satisfaction and somehow made it easier for her to go through the evening.

Chapter 8

The social committee had outdone itself. The Barrington home, where the social was being held, was a roomy old house that paint would have improved outside and in. Some of the furniture was rare because it was very old, but the rest was plain and cheap. Yet the young people loved to go there, for it was the home of Rockland's beloved physician, Dr. Barrington. His daughter Willa and son Fred were among the most active in the younger set. And as long as they could remember, some of their most delightful times had taken place at the Barrington home.

The doctor's office was housed in a little building on the corner of the lot, facing on both streets and separate from the house, so that the noise and laughter wouldn't disturb him or his patients. The young people had helped build a tennis court at the back of the deep lot and planted a row of cosmos across the side fence, giving the court a lovely setting in the fall. They kept the lawn around it edged and trimmed, dividing the labor with the son of the house, so the young people felt as if they all but owned part of the property. Indeed they felt the same way about several other homes where they met for their activities.

But tonight the social committee had smothered the rooms with lovely fall colors. Branches of autumn leaves framed the pictures and decorated the mantels and the stair rail, while masses of pompon chrysanthemums filled the room with their spicy fragrance.

The dining room ceiling had been curiously decorated with lines of fine, invisible wires strung across the room at intervals. From it were hung single flowers of bright chrysanthemums, on silver wires, interspersed with bright autumn leaves, singly or in tall sprays, giving an effect of a fall garden.

From the chandelier above the long dining table flowed tiny ribbons, in crimson and greens and browns and gold, from a common center to each place card, cut and painted in the shape of an autumn leaf. Beside each place card stood a tiny toy candlestick containing a small yellow candle, and beside each candle lay half a cake of paraffin.

Sherrill, coming downstairs after taking off her wraps, was met by smiles and welcoming words from her friends.

"They're all here now, Prissy!" called Willa.

Sherrill looked out across the group of faithful young people and felt tears stinging her eyes. How dear they were! How could she leave them for a whole winter? What was New York compared to this?

Then her eyes were drawn to the other side of the room where Alan stood with his earnest eyes upon her. He seemed older and more thoughtful than he had been that morning when she'd met him running about in his old

Ford, collecting cakes for the evening. She smiled brightly at him, and he smiled back at once; but somehow his smile was tinged with an unaccustomed gravity.

"I don't want to go to New York! I won't go to New York!" she longed to cry out.

Yet she knew her letter of acceptance had already been mailed to her uncle, and she was bound to go now, at least for a time.

Priscilla Maybrick was calling them to order. "When the orchestra begins to play, please proceed to the dining room where you'll find your seats by the place cards."

As Sherrill turned toward the dining room, she found Alan suddenly by her side and felt a comforting sense of strength about her. His fingers clasped hers for an instant.

"You're a good friend, Sherry," he said in a low tone.

She felt the warm color spread into her cheeks and a glow about her heart, as she walked along beside him. Alan had always seemed to know when she felt sad. And suddenly she felt as if she mustn't leave Alan. Yet of course that was absurd. She must go now. And Alan would be here when she came back. It would be good to go soon and get it over with and get back to all the dear people.

When they entered the dining room the candles had been lighted, and the cakes of paraffin lay white and mysterious before them.

Amidst exclamations and laughter they found their seats, with Alan and Sherrill placed next to one another. Willa always favored friends if she could and would put them together. Besides, these two were the group's main officers.

The mysterious paraffin was then explained. Each person was to mold out of the block of paraffin any object they pleased. But they could only work with their own hands and the warmth of the little candle before them.

Nearly everyone exclaimed in dismay as each one picked up the paraffin and felt its hardness.

"Why, we never can do that!" they said. "It's too hard. Give us knives."

The social committee had some ado convincing them they could work that cold, hard substance into malleability. Finally they started, holding the wax high over the candle flame and working at it with their hands.

Sherrill discovered first that the hard wax was yielding.

"This certainly is a good example for the lookout committee," she said. "If that wax will yield to a tiny candle like that we shouldn't be discouraged when we try to bring new members, even from down on the Flats."

"You forget one thing, Sherry," Alan said. "The warm human hand has a lot to do with molding the thing. It doesn't just bring the wax into contact with the flame either, but it molds it and works over it, keeping close to it to know how near it needs to get. It gets a lot of heat from the hand too. I guess there's a lesson in that somehow, isn't there?"

He looked up with his old smile, and they all laughed.

"Listen to Alan!" said Willa. "He's caught the preaching habit from Sherrill. Pretty soon he'll be studying to be a preacher!"

"I guess that's right," said Sherrill, following out Alan's thought. "It's no good to go down after those Flats boys and girls unless we keep a warm, human interest in them every minute and follow it up continually. But we mustn't forget that it's the candle after all that makes the wax soft. The hand alone couldn't do it. I notice this wax gets cool mighty quick if I don't keep it near that flame. I expect the prayer meeting committee might get some idea of that. Wouldn't prayer have something to do with keeping close to the Flame?"

"That's all right, Sherry," called out Priscilla Maybrick from across the table where she was working on her cake of wax. "I'll go. I hate those old Flats like everything. It smells of oilcloth in the making down there and chokes me, but I'll go. I don't like that Mary Ross you sent me after, either. She needs to wash her hair, and she's coarse and loud and hard. But I'll go, and I'll pray for her too. Only, Sherry, don't rub it in tonight. Have a heart. This is a social, and I'm molding a saint out of my paraffin! See his halo?"

The others laughed at Priscilla and glanced over to catch a look of saint-likeness in the uncertain lump she held in her hand.

Amid the chatter the various lumps of wax were taking shape—a soldier, a sailor, a dog and an elephant, a Dresden shepherdess and a bust of George Washington. There were several attempts at other noted characters, but in the end, Sherrill's head of an Indian chief took the first prize, with Fred's model of Spike, the Barrington collie, as a near second.

"But I'm sure," said Sherrill, "the lookout committee must have had a hand in this amusement. I can't help feeling we've all had a wonderful lesson as to what can be made out of the most unpromising material."

"Sherrill would!" said Rose Hawthorn. "She always does. Now, whenever I see wax and a candle, I'll think of some infant down on the Flats that needs going after and working into an angel."

Sherrill smiled understandingly at Rose. Dear Rose! Did she mean anything beneath all that banter? What a helper she would be down on the Flats if she ever got near enough to the flame of the Spirit to be warmed into working for others. Dear, pretty Rose, who nevertheless had a warm, true heart.

Two charades followed, and then refreshments of apple tarts with home-made ice cream on top. Afterward Priscilla Maybrick announced that the next month's social was under Sherrill's leadership, as president of the group.

Sherrill, catching her breath, remembered the social would probably be her last for the winter, if she went to New York.

"It's our Thanksgiving social," she told the young people, with a slight tremor in her voice. "Write on a slip of paper the special things you're most thankful for during the past year and bring the paper with you. They'll be read at the close of the evening, but without the names. Make them true, of course.

"There will be a Thanksgiving dinner at half past seven in the evening, so as not to interfere with your family's plans," Sherrill continued, now in full control of her voice. "And it will be held at the home of Howard Evans."

Everyone looked at Howard Evans, who was a newcomer among them since his father had recently bought a rundown farm on the edge of town. The old farmhouse was small and unpretentious, and the young people wondered aloud whether they'd have enough room for the whole crowd. Howard almost wished he'd never suggested having them at his place, but Sherrill's voice went quietly on, with a twinkle in her eyes.

"You don't need to know the plans, except that Howard's father is building a beautiful fireplace in his new barn, and we'll all gather there and have a wonderful time. Your part is to bring the guests."

"Guests?" they all asked at once.

"Yes, guests!" said Sherrill, smiling. "This won't be just for us. Every one of us has to bring a guest. The men have to bring men, and the girls have to bring girls. You may not like this plan, but we're asking you to try it in good faith, this once anyway. The guests are to be from the Flats!"

Silence fell at once on the room.

Then back by a hallway came Rose's soft voice as if she were thinking aloud. "Sherrill would just wish something like that on us all. And she knows none of us will wear halos but her!"

The whole room burst into laughter, though some of it seemed almost touched with tears.

"Listen—you—dears!" Sherrill said, with a tender note in her voice. "I don't want to wish something disagreeable on you, but I think we need to look after those people down there and bring a witness to them somehow. Alan"—with a sudden thought she looked toward him—"would you pray that God will help us be willing and then show us how?"

Alan had always avoided leading a meeting or praying out loud or speaking before a group. He did his work quietly but would never take the lead. Now, without hesitation, his clear, steady voice was heard.

"Dear Father in heaven, make us aware of these whom You love. Help us forget ourselves and be at Your service wholeheartedly. Show us how to work wisely and let us know You are with us. We ask it in Christ's name."

The room was hushed when he finished. They said good night quietly and began to leave. A few of the girls slipped up to Sherrill and whispered, "It was wonderful of you to think of that. I'm afraid I'm not as thoughtful as you are—"

"It wasn't my thought, really. It was God's. He's been bringing it to mind a long time. But I hated to propose it because I knew it would be unpopular and hard work. In fact I'm not that eager to do it myself, but I reached the place where I must. And the girl I feel I'm to invite made faces at me when I was in the first grade at school."

"Not Maria Morse! You don't mean you'd invite Maria Morse?"

"I'm going to try," said Sherrill. "I think God wants me to. She's lost her mother, and she's taking care of her eight little brothers and sisters and working in the mill besides, and I think we girls should give her our friendship."

"Do you believe she wants it, Sherrill?" asked Rose Hawthorn thoughtfully.

"Probably not," said Sherrill, "but I guess it's up to us to give it anyway, isn't it? After all, it depends a lot on how we go about it, and I guess the only way is to pray. I feel nervous when I think of inviting her. But then we'll all need to be nice to her afterward."

Out in the starlight, Alan and Sherrill walked along silently for a block after parting from the others.

Finally Alan spoke. "You didn't tell them you were going."

"I know," said Sherrill. "I thought of it at first and then forgot until we were leaving, and then somehow I couldn't. I thought perhaps I won't tell anybody until the Thanksgiving dinner is over. Will you help me keep my secret? I can be getting ready—but—well, who knows—maybe something will turn up that I won't have to go after all!"

Alan turned to her, his eyes bright.

"Sherry, I believe you don't really want to go after all," he said, his voice vibrant with something she didn't understand.

"No, I don't, Alan. It seems as if I couldn't go," she said, with a catch in her voice.

"That makes it a lot better," said the grave young voice, and Alan gave Sherrill's hand a light squeeze in the darkness.

Chapter 9

Sherrill put it to the family the next morning at the breakfast table just before Keith left for work.

"Say, folks, I'm going," she declared, "but I want you to do one thing for me. Please don't tell anybody yet—not a soul, until I give you permission."

Keith turned from the door, his hat in his hand. "What's this, sis? You're not trying to slide out of it, are you?" he asked, studying her face.

"No, I'd rather get used to the idea myself first," she told him, her steady gaze matching his. "And I don't want the young people's group knowing about it until we've made our plans for that Thanksgiving dinner. I'm not going till after Thanksgiving anyway! I couldn't stand that!"

"We couldn't either," said Keith crisply. "We wouldn't be very thankful without you here."

"Indeed not!" Grandma agreed, smiling.

"Of course not!" Mrs. Washburn said, with a relieved sigh. It wouldn't be easy for their family to get along without Sherrill.

"I'm afraid if the group thinks I'm going away soon they won't think it necessary to carry out the plans for the dinner," she said. "And we're inviting guests from the Flats!"

"Well, you can count on me, sis. Is there anything I can do for that dinner? Suppose I furnish the ice cream? I heard of a place in the city that makes it in the shape of different flowers or fruit—or maybe something suited for Thanksgiving. How about that? Just give me a few days' notice."

"What a brother!" Sherrill said, after he had left.

"Yes," said the mother, "he likes to help out, and he's proud of you, dear. You're doing some things he'd like to do if he had time. Come, let's get these dishes out of the way and then start ripping. We should do that first and get the old things out of the way. Then we can tell what new things we need to buy. You've got a good month now to work in, and we should be able to put together a pretty wardrobe in that time. When did you tell Harriet you were coming?"

"Half past ten," said Sherrill. "I can rip up the brown and the green before that and perhaps get them sponged off so we can see how much good material we have to work with."

"I'll help rip," said Grandma, getting out her best glasses and hunting in her table drawer for the razor blade she liked to use.

"You better rip up those lace things, and I'll wash them while you're gone," said Mary Washburn. "Some of the yellowest ones we'll dip in coffee and call them ecru lace."

"Why, of course!" Sherrill said, smiling. "I read in the fashion magazine that was the style now!"

So they hurried through the dishes and then sat down with Grandma who had already ripped up a good part of the green dress. For a while only the snipping of scissors and the tearing of threads could be heard in the room.

Suddenly Grandma broke the silence. "They'll want you to do things you may not agree with, you know."

Sherrill jerked her thoughts back from her plans about the Flats young people and gave attention to her grandmother with an amused look.

"Well, let them want. I'll just tell them I don't want."

"You'll need to be courteous in declining—to say no so pleasantly they'll be as pleased as if you'd said yes. Wasn't it Longfellow who tried to do that when he had to decline an invitation to speak at some school commencement? Or was it Bryant?"

"Oh, I don't remember, Mother. But of course I'll try to be polite."

"It won't be easy!" said Grandma grimly. She had stayed awake part of the night thinking of things that might happen to Sherrill. "You'll be in their house, you know. It'll be your first trial."

"Grandma!" said Sherrill, dropping the lace and scissors in her lap in dismay. "You don't have much faith in me, do you?"

"Well, yes, I have faith in—well, in the way you were brought up. And I know you're a sweet good girl. But you put a good sound apple among a lot of rotten ones and leave it there long enough, and you know what'll happen."

"Well, Grandma, I won't stay there long enough for that. And if I see myself getting specked I'll send for Keith to come and drag me home. Also, doesn't God keep His children?"

"I'm not so sure He'll keep you when you go there. You remember what a peck of trouble the Israelites got into when they went down into Egypt—and Lot when he went to live in Sodom."

"Mother," said Mary Washburn, "you shouldn't talk that way to Sherrill. She's on the edge of backing out now."

"Well, perhaps not," said Grandma, "but I wouldn't like to see my granddaughter spoiled."

"Grandma, there's a difference you're not taking into account. I'm not going into Sodom to live or because I want to go. And can't God help me through a place like that?"

"Yes, I suppose He can—if you let Him."

"Well, I'm letting Him," said Sherrill firmly. "Now, Mother, I've got these laces ripped. Shouldn't I wash them before I go? I think there's time."

"No, you run along. Harriet likes to do things when she plans. I'll wash the lace and have it ready for you when you get back."

But Sherrill returned in less than a half hour, two large boxes in her arms and a glow on her face. Behind her came the beloved family friend, carrying two more boxes.

"I couldn't wait, Mother," said Sherrill. "I want you and Grandma to see these wonderful things."

"For the land sakes!" exclaimed Grandma, laying her ripping blade in the drawer. "If it takes all those boxes to hold what you've bought her, I don't think there's much need of our ripping up any more old clothes."

"Oh, there isn't much," said Harriet Masters. "Remember that I don't have a daughter to spend on, so I enjoyed picking these out for Sherrill. Mary always said she might be half mine sometimes."

"Of course!" said Mary Washburn quickly.

Harriet's little daughter had lived only three short months, and the baby's father had died tragically soon after that. If it gave this dear friend pleasure to take a motherly interest in her child, they mustn't let a false idea of independence spoil that pleasure. Mrs. Washburn sent Sherrill a warning glance and then smiled eagerly. After all, any mother wanted to see her dear girl dressed in beautiful garments, even if she couldn't afford to buy them for her.

So Sherrill put on the white velvet first, whose frosty sheen and simplicity of cut made her look like a young seraph just dropped down from some heavenly sphere. Silver girdled and silver clasped, the dress had an air that marked it with distinction, while yet being so simple that even to Grandma's eyes it didn't seem out of place or overdressed for Sherrill.

"She'll need a pair of silver slippers and stockings, of course," said the family adviser, "and they'll go with other evening things too."

"I'd like to see her dressed in that with other pretty girls," said Sherrill's mother wistfully.

"You might not like what many of the other girls wear these days, Mary," her friend remarked.

"I'm sure that's true, Harriet, and I imagine my sister-in-law doesn't share my views on such things."

"Well," Harriet said thoughtfully, "Sherrill has to learn to hold her own among those who don't see as she does. I hope your sister-in-law will strike a happy medium between Rockland and the ultra-extremists."

"I'm worried Sherrill will get all her ideas changed," said Grandma, "when she gets used to seeing people doing the things she's been taught to feel are wrong."

"But, dear," Harriet said, "don't you give Sherrill credit for having something more than ideas? I think they go deeper than that. Somewhere behind it all is a principle, and it's the principle that Sherrill will be true to, no matter what, or I'm very mistaken in her."

Sherrill gave the woman a grateful glance and went on admiring the lovely folds of the velvet.

"It's wonderful, Harriet," said Mrs. Washburn. "We never can thank you enough."

"Well, don't try," said Harriet abruptly. "If Sherrill gets half as much pleasure out of it as I did in buying it for her I'll be more than paid. Now, dear, get out the other things!"

"It looks like a heavenly garment," said Grandma wistfully, as Sherrill walked across the room.

But Mary said nothing more as she watched her daughter. She was thinking of what Sherrill's father would have said at the sweet vision she made and wishing he were where she might tell him about it at least.

The wrap was made of satin and embroidery. Grandma and Mother looked at their girl in the strange soft garments. The new clothes seemed to set her apart in another world from them.

Sherrill, bright eyed and pink cheeked, arrayed herself in the other outfits and, walking back and forth for their admiration, wondered if it was altogether right to be so glad over clothes.

Then she brought out boxes of exquisite lingerie and a charming kimono, with butterflies on a sky blue ground.

"It's like being Cinderella," said Sherrill, sitting down among her treasures. "I'm sure I'll never be able to eat or sleep again."

"You precious child!" said Harriet, with a tender look in her eyes. She watched Sherrill fold her new garments into their boxes and thought how her little girl would have done the same thing if she'd only lived.

"I'll be completely spoiled!" declared Sherrill. "I can feel my head is turned already!" And she twisted her brown curls around toward her mother.

"Some things don't spoil," said the guest. "I think you're one of them."

"Well, if she must go," said Grandma, "I'm glad she's going right! I couldn't stand to see that Eloise turn up her nose at Sherrill's outfit."

"Mother, I never suspected you of caring that much about clothes," Mrs. Washburn said. She hurried away to put lunch on the table and insisted her friend should stay.

Keith came home unexpectedly for lunch and had to see the new clothes and admire everything.

"Now I have only a coat to buy," Sherrill said happily. "I can make the rest of my outfits, I'm sure. Aunt Harriet is letting me copy every pretty thing she has. Isn't she a dear?"

"What kind of coat?" asked Keith thoughtfully.

"Oh, just a coat," said Sherrill. "I can buy it and all the little things I need out of that wonderful check you gave me."

"Well, don't get it right away, sis. I may have an idea."

"Now, Keith!" said Sherrill, alarmed. "You're not to do another thing for me. If you do, I'll spend this whole check on a new suit and an overcoat for you!"

Harriet enjoyed the lunch as much as anyone, entering into the plans for Sherrill's journey as if she were her own mother. They ate fried potatoes, cold ham and apple sauce, with raised biscuits, and talked so long that Keith, looking at his watch, discovered he would be late at the office.

Then Sherrill gathered pins and newspapers and her scissors and went back with Harriet to take off patterns from the imported dresses, so as to glorify her old clothes.

Chapter 10

The days passed swiftly.

Willa Barrington took the position in the bank that Sherrill had given up, and Sherrill had her time free to get ready.

Every morning and part of the afternoons she spent sewing, when she wasn't helping her mother in the house. Harriet's trunks provided a never-ending source of treasures to finish off whatever Sherrill was making. Little by little the wardrobe grew, hanging under chintz covers in the closet of the guest room. As she hung them away, one by one, proudly, her heart ached with every new accomplishment. If only she might stay at home and wear those pretty clothes among her friends whom she loved!

Yet of course with it she felt an elation at the thought of going away and seeing and doing new things. Seeing the world, living a little while in a grand mansion and not having to lift a finger for herself. Certainly that would be fun for a time. If only she could take all the dear friends with her!

Almost every evening she saw Alan MacFarlan for a few minutes at least. But Alan was hard at work, and they had little time for playing tennis or other activities. Alan was working day and night, trying to pull his father's business back into shape. With Judge Whiteley's assistance, the store looked as if it would be on a more prosperous basis than ever before. But Alan was pale and thin and wore his lips in a determined line that made him seem suddenly older. Sometimes Sherrill felt a little hurt that he had to stay away so much and couldn't even go down to the Flats with her as he used to do to call in the early evening. She had to get Keith to take her once or twice.

But one day in the third week of November Alan came early in the evening and brought a small box with him.

Sherrill was astonished. Alan had never given her presents, except now and then a book at Christmas or a box of candy for her birthday, and this was neither. She opened the box and lifted out a necklace of pearl beads.

"Oh, Alan!" she said, her face glowing with delight. "How sweet of you to give them to me! But you shouldn't have spent so much money—"

"Oh, don't say that, Sherry," the young man said, a look of joy on his face. "I've had the time of my life earning the money for those. I wanted you to have something to take that would remind you of me. I only wish they were real pearls. Someday maybe I can buy pearls. But these are good imitations. Your Harriet Masters picked them out for me in the city. She said they were what everybody was wearing and were fine enough to go with your Paris dresses."

"Oh, Alan, they're lovely! I wouldn't want real pearls. I'd be afraid they'd be stolen. And these are beautiful! They look real to me. Why"—her voice caught—"I'll—have to give you a kiss for these!"

There, with her grandmother sitting in her rocker darning some old lace and her mother setting the table for dinner and Keith looking up from reading the evening paper, Sherrill rushed over and quickly kissed the top of Alan's head. Then she slipped back to her chair and began to put the beads around her neck.

Alan's face turned bright red, and his eyes lit up. And Grandma looked quite satisfied.

"Now you know why I couldn't come over and help you with the place cards for the Thanksgiving dinner," he said to cover his embarrassment. "Mrs. Masters was going in town the next day to get the necklace, and I had to see her about it."

"Oh, and to think I was cross with you for not helping," said Sherrill.

"Oh, that's all right!" Alan said, smiling. "I'm glad you like it if it is only beads. Just put it on when your aunt brings around that other guy she expects you to land, and perhaps you won't forget old friends entirely."

He finished with a laugh, but his voice was husky, and Sherrill's eyes were misty as she gave him a look that comforted him.

Afterward they went into the parlor to try some of the songs to be sung at the Thanksgiving dinner, and Keith left to see a man on business.

"That was a nice thing for Alan to do," Grandma said, looking at her daughter.

"Yes, wasn't it?" said Mrs. Washburn quickly. "He's a dear boy."

"In my day we wouldn't have thought we could accept anything valuable like that unless we were engaged."

"Nonsense, Mother! They're only beads, and he's only a boy! Don't, for pity's sake, put anything like that into Sherrill's head."

"Well, I'm not a fool, Mary, though you seem to think I am sometimes," replied the older woman. "But I don't see how that's any worse than talking about Sherrill's going to New York to make a clever marriage."

"Oh, Mother!" said Mrs. Washburn anxiously. "That wasn't serious. We were only joking about what Eloise had said. Sherrill doesn't take anything serious from that."

"Well, I can tell you who did," said Grandma, nodding toward the parlor door. "That boy in there did!"

"Oh, Mother, no, he didn't," said Mary. "He knew we were just joking."

"He's a nice boy, Mary, and Sherrill shouldn't hurt him."

"Mother, please don't talk that way. Sherrill isn't going to hurt anybody. They'll hear you. I wouldn't have any notions put in their heads now for anything. They're just children."

"Well, Mary, I can tell you one thing," said her mother after a moment. "They won't be children when Sherrill gets back. They'll have grown up. If you want to keep Sherrill a child a little longer you better keep her at home."

"I wish I could!" said Mary, with a sudden pang that her child was to go away. "But I guess it's right that she should go."

Sherrill was in the parlor singing Thanksgiving songs with Alan, and their voices blended sweetly, the soprano and the tenor.

"We worship Thee, we bless Thee—," they sang, and their earnest faces bent over the book together, heads almost touching.

Mrs. Washburn peered into the dusk of the room lighted only by the piano lamp, saw the good sweet wholesome look on both faces and took hope. Yes, they were still children. Her mother might be right about their growing up soon, but it hadn't come yet. She felt a panic at the thought of the untried way that lay ahead of her girl. Oh, if she only dared hold her back and guard her! Yet Sherrill had good blood, a strong foundation of character and an abiding faith in Jesus Christ. Wasn't that enough to keep her through the perils of city life for a few short months? Oh, was she right in sending her out when she didn't have to?

The day before Thanksgiving Keith came home with a shiny brown box, long and narrow and distinctive looking.

"Land's sake, Keith! What's that?" Grandma asked wonderingly.

"It's something for Sherrill," said Keith. "Where is she?"

"Here I am," she said, stepping from the kitchen into the doorway. "Did you say that's for me? Keith! You know I told you not to get me anything else. I have everything I need. Since I got that new fur collar for my coat I'm fixed fine now in every particular."

"This isn't from me," said Keith, lifting his chin and smiling. "It's from Father and Mother."

A startled look crossed his mother's face, and then her eyes lit up. It pleased her to hear him give the gift in such a beautiful way.

Sherrill turned from her brother to her mother, her eyes wide with wonder.

"I knew Father would have done it if he were here. He would have wanted his daughter to have everything she should for a visit to his brother's family. So when a check came in today for the sale of that old land we thought was worthless and which Father left in my care to do what I thought best about, I turned some of it into this for you. Mother gets the rest for something equally nice that she needs."

Keith lifted the cover and pulled back a corner of the tissue paper. "Here— see if it fits," he said, handing the box to her.

Sherrill, catching her breath, bent forward and plunged in her hand.

"Oh!" she cried. "A fur coat! Oh, Keith, a squirrel coat! And I've always wanted one!" She dropped the sleeve she'd touched and flung her arms about her mother's neck.

"Oh, Mother, I can't leave you all when you've done such wonderful things for me!"

Mary Washburn held her daughter close and kissed the top of her head.

"But, dear, it's Keith you should thank. He says the present is from your father and me, but he never told me anything about it. It came out of his own thought. He's right, dear. Father would have done it if he'd been here, but it was really Keith who did it, because Father gave that land to him."

And then Sherrill hugged her brother and clung to him.

"But I can't take it," she murmured at last, "not unless you promise to get yourself that new suit and overcoat you need."

"Oh, sure, little sister, I'll get some clothes and have them ready to meet you at the train when you get back. You won't know your old brother when you ride in from New York, expecting to be ashamed of your old country family. Now try it on."

So Sherrill was prevailed upon at last to open the papers and try on the coat. She looked like a young princess in the rich fur of dyed brown squirrel. Keith had found a coat of fine quality and styling, and Mary Washburn's heart was happy about her girl. With a coat like that she would be warm and comfortable and look right wherever she went.

"Mother, it isn't right for me to have a coat like this," Sherrill said suddenly, looking at herself in the parlor glass. "You've never had a fur coat, and you should have one first."

"Well, she'll have one now, sis. I've been planning for it ever since last winter. I knew she was cold in that old black coat every time she went to church. And when this money came in I knew it was an answer to my prayers. It seems to be of good quality, too."

Alan stopped by later to see if Sherrill wanted him to run any more errands and had to look over the coat, inside and out, to notice the pretty scalloped cuffs in the sleeves, the trick of a pocket, the beauty of the skins, the shimmer of the lining, and above all how Sherrill looked as she walked across the room with it buttoned up about her chin, covering her ears and most of her hair.

"And this is the way I'll wear it when I go out in the evening to a symphony concert," said Sherrill suddenly, unfastening the coat, flinging the great scalloped cape-collar back over her shoulders and gathering the garment close about her waist. She held her head high and strolled across the room. "That's the way they wear them for evening. I've seen them in the catalogues and fashion magazines."

"Yes," said Alan gravely, "I see now how you'll go about making that clever marriage you talked about. But won't you remember to wear my pearls around your neck when you walk like that?"

Sherrill laughed, putting her hand to her throat where the pearls were, and the color flushed into her cheeks.

"Why, of course," she said, "pearls and fur like this always go together, don't they?"

Suddenly she sat down, with a grave look on her face.

"Don't you like it, sis?" Keith asked. "Tell me the truth. I'd much rather know if there's something else you'd rather have. It isn't too late to change."

"Oh, Keith, there's nothing in this world I'd rather have than this beautiful coat. But I was thinking how dreadful it is for me to have a grand thing like this. I don't deserve it. And so many people don't even have warm things. I don't believe it's right for me to have all this."

"Nonsense, Sherrill," said her mother. "That's not for you to consider. It was a gift. You have nothing to do with that. Besides, it's a sensible warm thing that will last for years, perhaps a lifetime."

"Oh, it might not last a lifetime," said her brother. "But by the time it gets shabby I hope I can buy her another one—"

"Or someone else will," added Alan in a low tone, so that only Grandma heard him.

"Grandma has been afraid I'd come back spoiled," said Sherrill, "but she miscalculated the time. I'm going away spoiled. I couldn't be worse spoiled than I am—pearls and furs and velvets! My cousin Carol won't be up with me at all. Really, Mother, I'm ashamed. A quiet Christian girl like me looking like a fashion plate! What would those girls from the Flats say to me if they knew I could dress like this? What would Mary Morse say? You know I've had a terrible time getting her to promise to come tomorrow night. I finally told her I would wear this old blue dress before she would say yes, because she said she didn't have a new dress to wear."

"Well, dear," said her mother tenderly, "you're wearing the old blue dress for Mary Morse's sake tomorrow, and next week you'll wear the blue taffeta for your cousin Carol's sake. Life, after all, is a comparative thing, and clothes suit certain places."

The little group who loved Sherrill could scarcely bear to break up that night, for how hard it would be to have her gone, even for a short time. But at last Alan stood up with a sigh and declared he must go home.

And the next day was Thanksgiving.

Chapter 11

Sherrill spent the early morning putting the last things in her trunk. Her mother insisted that she was to have no part in preparing the dinner, for she would have enough else to do.

So the turkey had been stuffed the day before and put in the oven in ample time to be ready to eat at one o'clock. Grandma would watch over it, for she was too lame to go to the Thanksgiving service. Further, she said, no one else knew how to baste a turkey to the right brown, and she enjoyed being left with the responsibility.

Keith took his mother and sister in his car to the church, and they sat in the old pew together, thinking how long it would be before they sat there together again and praying for one another.

At her brother's request Sherrill wore her new coat for the first time, with one of her new hats. He said he wanted to see how his sister looked in her "glad rags." She felt self-conscious at first, because her friends kept sending admiring glances her way.

Across the aisle Alan watched her from time to time and was glad to see she was also wearing his string of pearls. He wished he could be up in New York this winter and take Sherrill to some of those concerts and to church and museums and other interesting places. How proud he would be to take her somewhere in that coat. Perhaps he would in the spring, if spring ever came. He knew she wouldn't wear it that evening, if only for Mary Morse's sake.

He watched Keith drive his mother and sister away and let his eyes follow wistfully after them. Then he went home to his own Thanksgiving dinner, for his family was as eager to have him to themselves as Sherrill's family was to have her. But he consoled himself with the thought that he would drive Sherrill up to the Evans barn late that afternoon to set the tables, and later, when it grew dark, he would drive her down to the Flats to pick up Mary Morse. Then they would sit together at the barn dinner, with Mary on her other side. Later he would drive them all home and perhaps linger a few minutes with Sherrill to say good-bye, for she was leaving early in the morning. Oh, it would be a big evening, and Sherrill wasn't gone yet!

Though the turkey and stuffing, which Grandma had made by an old family recipe, were wonderful, Sherrill somehow couldn't eat. Tears seemed to have formed in her throat, keeping her from swallowing. She wanted to laugh and cry at the same time. But then Mother and Keith and Grandmother all felt the same way, of course, and everyone tried to be lighthearted and make the time go pleasantly. By the time the pumpkin pie was ready to be eaten, Sherrill was laughing with them and telling funny things she meant to say to her New York relatives when she arrived, although she knew she wouldn't.

Suddenly they looked up, and Alan stood among them.

With a pang Sherrill jumped up and helped her mother carry out dishes in spite of protest. They all pitched in, and soon the dishes were washed and dried and put away, amidst much laughter and talking. It was as if they were hanging on to their last minutes of being together. Her dear family—and Alan! How precious they seemed to her as she glanced up from the pantry drawer where she'd been looking for clean dish towels. Her eyes blurred with sudden tears.

And then Harriet Masters stopped by. She had declined to eat dinner with them because an elderly woman at the boardinghouse was taken suddenly ill and had begged her to stay with her. But now the woman was improved and sleeping, and Hannah Maria, the second girl, was sitting in the hall to listen if she called, so Harriet had slipped away for a few minutes.

They served her a piece of Grandma's pumpkin pie, and while she ate they finished tidying up the kitchen.

With the dishes in shining rows on the shelf, Alan and Sherrill started out on their rounds.

"And haven't you even told Willa and Rose you're going away?" asked Alan, on the way to the Evans barn.

"No, I haven't," said Sherrill, suddenly appalled at the task before her. "Somehow I couldn't before the dinner."

"Well, you'd better not tell them till the end, then. It would spoil the evening, and we want it to succeed, you know."

"Of course, and it will, I'm sure. I prayed during the church service this morning for it."

"So did I," said Alan quietly.

Two other cars were standing before the Evans barn door when they arrived, and a group of young people stepped out to greet them, all talking at once.

"The ice cream hasn't come yet, Sherrill," called out Willa Barrington. "What time did your brother say it would be here? Shouldn't I send my brother down to ask him about it? You know you can't always depend on things on holidays, and it wouldn't do to have to run after it at the last minute."

"It doesn't come till the five o'clock train, Willa. It's a special, and Holly Beach is bringing it up as soon as the train comes in. You don't need to worry a minute about it. Keith approved it last night."

And many more questions followed, from place cards and candles, to chrysanthemums and cooking, to lighting the fire and moving the piano, and Sherrill had everything in order in no time.

"The place cards are in that white box over the first stall. Alan has a whole gross of candles in the car; he'll get them. Can Dick run down to Mrs. Foster's and cut the chrysanthemums? He knows how, and she said she'd be away and couldn't. Here, I'll set that regulator. Yes, the girls on the right. No, Sam, don't light the fire yet. Yes, Rose, Keith is sending up a man from the company. He'll be here in half an hour to fix the lights. The celery is wrapped in a wet towel over there in the corner on a beam. Candles in the pumpkins, of course. It wouldn't seem real without them. No, the piano must go over there by the speaker's table so everybody can see the singers. I've brought the forks and the other cake. Of course, we'll use the same forks."

Alan stood back and watched her in admiration for an instant, then he set to work helping her. How would he ever fill her place while she was gone?

They had thought everything was ready for the dinner the day before, except to set the tables and cook the food. But now it seemed as if everything was left until the last minute, and it took every second of hard work before they felt that all was as it should be and the various members could take time to rush after their invited guests.

Alan and Sherrill were the last to leave the barn. Only the two women hired to do the cooking were at the far end busy over the two gas ranges that had been temporarily installed. They were discussing in loud cheerful tones the various ways of making turkey gravy.

Alan stood in front of the fireplace watching Sherrill as she flitted from table to table putting last touches to the flowers, scattering a few late roses on the tablecloth in front of the invited guests and a rose at each plate, changing the position of the butter plates and sugar bowls, setting out the dishes of celery, and making sure the guests were placed according to the chart drawn up by the committee.

Then she stood back and looked, her head on one side, and then with a smile walked over to where Alan stood.

"It's lovely, isn't it, Alan?" she said with satisfaction.

"Why, I guess so," said Alan, glancing about. "Yes, it is. I hadn't noticed."

"You—hadn't noticed! Why, Alan, aren't you interested? Don't you think it's wonderful?"

"Sure I do," he said, smiling, "but I was looking at you. Say, that dress you have on is just the color of your eyes. Is that one of your new dresses?"

"Oh, you're hopeless!" she said with a laugh. "This is the old blue dress I've worn two winters. I'm wearing it tonight because I promised Mary Morse I would. She felt uncomfortable about coming where she thought everybody would wear evening clothes, so I told her I would wear what I had on."

"That's like you," said Alan, studying her. "But it's not the clothes you wear. It's you. You look dressed up in anything."

"Oh, I think you've been kissing the Blarney Stone. I never knew you to be so flattering," said Sherrill, with a look of wonder on her face. "Come on—it's time to go after our guests. But I hate to leave here—it looks so pretty."

"It certainly does," said Alan, with delayed enthusiasm. "It looks nice enough to live in, doesn't it?"

"It does, doesn't it? Wouldn't it be fun to make over a barn into a perfectly beautiful house?"

"Would you like to live in it?"

"Of course I would. You could do wonderful things with some of those old barns. Take that one on the field next to our house now. Just think what wonderful porches and nooks and crannies and rooms on different levels could be made, with a wide staircase in the center and a skylight in the top story to let the sunshine in."

"I hadn't thought about it, but maybe it would. Perhaps you'd like to study architecture."

"Yes, I would, but come on—we need to go. We're supposed to be back here in half an hour, and we don't want to be late twice in one afternoon. The others have gone after their guests, and we mustn't let them arrive ahead of the officers."

Alan was still thoughtful as he stepped into the car beside her and started on their way. Sherrill turned her head and looked back.

"It's going to be lovely. See, Dick Hazelton has come on his bicycle, and he's going to light all the lanterns and touch off the fire when he sees the cars coming up the hill. It'll be so cheerful when we get back."

"It will," said Alan, looking down at her, "and you did it all. I'm afraid it's bad policy, however, beginning the season with such a success. Just look at what failures the rest will be with you gone."

"Indeed they won't. You'll make each one better than the last. Aunt Harriet has promised to help you with the next one, and she's a wonder. She knows more new things to do to get people talking and acquainted. Wait till you see what she has to suggest. She's been telling me, and you're to go over there tomorrow night and get the whole thing planned out so you can get your committees to work at once."

"Oh? Well, if you say so, I suppose I am," he said, with a dismal tone. "But it looks mighty dumb to me without you around to stir us up."

"Say! I thought you believed in being cheerful. Now don't spoil my last night!" she said, a note of appeal in her voice.

"All right, I'll try not to, if it will help you," he said, setting his mouth in a smile. "Is this the street that Morse woman lives on? Now which house in that row do you guess it is?"

"The third from the last," said Sherrill. "I went to see her yesterday, so I'm sure."

They drew up at the curb, and Sherrill watched while Alan went to the dingy, unpainted door and knocked. He lifted his hat to the slatternly neighbor who opened the door and was expecting to care for the baby while Mary Morse was away.

Mary came out presently, looking half frightened and drawing her shabby coat on over an attempt at holiday garb. A three-year-old girl toddled after her and insisted on being kissed on her soiled face. Mary bent down and spoke sharply to her instead, and the child ran back into the house, crying, and then looked after her with distress in her eyes.

"Go comfort her, Mary," Sherrill told her. "Don't leave her feeling unhappy. We have plenty of time to wait for you."

Mary gave a grateful glance toward them, then she disappeared into the gloomy house. Presently the sobbing ceased, and Mary came back out.

"She's awful spoiled," said Mary, stepping into the car. "I've had her and the baby mostly since they was born, and they don't know what to make of me going off."

"Poor little girl," said Sherrill. "Alan, didn't we have a bag of peppermints somewhere in this car? Here it is—in this pocket. They won't need them at the supper. Perhaps you would take them back to her."

"Oh, don't trouble," said Mary. "She's gotta learn I ain't handy all the time."

Alan took the peppermints back to the door, where five children were crowded with open mouths, staring at the car, and the weeping baby in the foreground.

But when he handed her a peppermint, first one and then the whole bag, she looked up in the midst of a howl and bestowed first a wondering stare and then a ravishing smile, that showed beauty even through the dirt.

Poor child, he thought. *She thinks I'm an angel from heaven. I'll remember that and take peppermints another time.*

Sherrill welcomed Mary with a warm smile and chattered pleasantly without making it necessary for Mary to answer, while they drove around to pick up Alan's guest, Sam O'Reilly.

Sam stepped into the front seat with Alan, scarcely speaking because of his embarrassment. His red hair was slicked down and wet from recent combing, and his too-tight collar kept easing up and out. He acknowledged the greetings from Sherrill with downcast eyes and a "fresh" remark, which under other circumstances might have annoyed her. But she was intent on making a success of this party and chose to ignore such trifles. She realized that was Sam's way of getting through what was to him an ordeal.

The sun had set, leaving a deep crimson streak in the west, and above in a clear emerald field a single star shone like a jewel as they drove up to the barn.

Chapter 12

The doors of the barn were open wide, and the fire flamed up around the logs in the wide fireplace, playing over the new floor boards, the gleaming tables with their white cloths and the shining glass and silver. It flickered over the beams overhead and threw furtive shadows in the distant corners where sheaves of corn and wheat were stacked, and strange pumpkin faces gleamed out unexpectedly from every shadow.

"Oh, my land! Ain't that wonderful!" said Mary Morse, with a choking sound in her voice as if she wanted to cry. "It looks just like heaven might be, don't it?"

"Say, that's great!" said Sam O'Reilly, his volubility suddenly hushed into silence after that one exclamation.

"It does look cheery, doesn't it?" said Alan, suddenly realizing how great and far-reaching had been Sherrill's scheme to get together with the young people of the Flats. Only she, of their merry bunch, could have conceived and carried out such an occasion.

They joined the other arrivals who were moving awkwardly past the wide barn door. In the soft weird light of the open fire, with pumpkin faces grinning from dark corners, it seemed an enchanted land into which the company had arrived. The strangers shrank back and stared, then entered hesitantly, giggling over the newness of everything.

The hosts and hostesses led their guests from the Flats inside and showed them where to hang their wraps on wooden pegs. Then they introduced them to those who were standing around, as if they were all strangers, although many of them had gone to the public school together several years before, when the dividing line between social classes wasn't as strongly marked. But here tonight they were all ladies and gentlemen, and the guests from the Flats felt too strange and shy to be other than polite, though the other young men had been concerned about one or two among the Flats boys, lest they might make "fresh" remarks to the girls.

Sherrill had anticipated such a possibility by arranging the affair in a somewhat formal manner. They had issued written invitations, and when everyone arrived, a receiving line was formed, with the officers first and their guests beside them. Then the committees came, each with his or her guest, and were introduced along the line and took their places to receive the rest. They all met everyone formally and shook hands, awkwardly perhaps, but still shaking hands and treating one another with respect.

Then the orchestra members took their places in the corner by the piano, not far from the fireplace, and began to play, using some of the music they had practiced at the last social. At once a line formed.

"Where is Lola Cather?" Sherrill asked Alan. They were standing near the front of the line. "And her brother Jim? I thought they were coming."

"I don't know what happened to Jim, but Mrs. Cather told me Lola wasn't coming. She said"—he lowered his voice—"she didn't care to have Lola hob-nobbing with the Flatters."

"Why, the idea!" said Sherrill indignantly. "I thought she wanted Lola to be a missionary someday. I heard her talking about sending her somewhere for a course in religious training."

"Yes, I asked her that," said Alan, "but she said that was different. She said she didn't care to have her mixed up socially with 'that class.' "

"Why not?" she asked. "Is she afraid Lola will elope with Buddy Whitlock or someone else?"

"I don't know. It's ridiculous if she is."

"Well, it seems to me if Lola's going to be a missionary she would want to get to know lots of people from all different circumstances—and learn com-passion, too. I sure hope it doesn't get out why she didn't come, or other mothers may get alarmed, although most of them are sensible. And I hope it doesn't get to the Flats. It will spoil everything.

"Well, we'll just have to pray a lot about it," she added, thoughtfully, "and then keep the gatherings friendly and well-organized. It seems strange. We all went to school together, and nobody objected. We've had the same inter-ests while we were children, and we're supposed to be going to the same heaven, if we all get there! I think there must be some pride involved."

"You're probably right," said Alan. "But I guess we have to look at our own thoughts and feelings about it all, too."

"Alan, I'm so glad you'll be looking after things when I'm gone. I know you'll do a wonderful thing here, and God will help you."

"Yes, He will," agreed the young man, smiling. "I'm sure of that!"

At that moment the music began, and everyone filed about the tables, looking for the place cards. Then Alan asked the blessing.

"Heavenly Father, we want to thank You for the good things You've given us through the year, and we ask Your blessing tonight. May every one of us know that the best gift You've given us is Yourself and yield our lives to You so we may grow in love, because You love us. For Christ's sake we ask it, amen."

Something caught in Sherrill's throat and threatened to overwhelm her for an instant. It seemed as if Alan had touched the very springs of her life with that little prayer. He himself was growing into the beautiful ways of being a Christian. Sherrill could feel a happy glow about her heart.

Then someone started playing the piano softly, and the voices nearest the piano broke into song.

My God, I thank Thee, who hast made the earth so bright,
So full of splendor and of joy, beauty and light;

So many glorious things are here, noble and right.

I thank Thee, too, that Thou has made joy to abound;
So many gentle thoughts and deeds circle us round;
That in the darkest spot of earth some love is found.

I thank Thee more that all our joy is touched with pain,
That shadows fall on brightest hours, and thorns remain;
So that earth's bliss may be our guide, and not our chain.

For Thou, who knowest, Lord, how soon our weak heart clings,
Hast given us joys tender and true, yet all with wings
So that we see, gleaming on high, diviner things.

I thank Thee, Lord, that Thou hast kept the best in store;
We have enough, yet not too much to long for more;
A yearning for a deeper peace not known before.

I thank Thee, Lord, that here our souls, though amply blest,
Can never find, although they seek, a perfect rest;
Nor ever shall until they lean on Jesus' breast.

Something about the singing was so impressive that in the hush that followed the last verse Sherrill thought she heard a little sniff beside her. Glancing at Mary Morse she saw her rough red hand steal up and wipe away a tear from her cheek. Mary was in a new world, and her heart was stirred deeply.

Sherrill felt a throb of joy. She glanced at the faces of the guests. Even Sam O'Reilly had a solemn pleased look on his freckled face. They liked it. As they sat down, she could see that all the Flatters were smiling and settling into their places with pleased anticipation.

With instrumental music playing cheerful airs and popular melodies the talk around the tables became quite comfortable, punctuated here and there by laughter. After several minutes, while they were eating, a light from behind suddenly focused on a big sheet that had somehow appeared above the fireplace without being noticed.

On the makeshift screen everyone suddenly saw the main street of Rockland before them, with some of the people they saw everyday walking toward them, smiling and greeting one another. There were Mrs. Roland with her market basket full of vegetables and Mrs. Crothers with her baby in the little express wagon. They laughed and talked and nodded good-bye and passed on. Then the bank cashier walked by on his way to the bank, and Mr. John McCormick came out and tipped his hat to the cashier. People came in and out of the post office next to the bank. Sherrill Washburn herself came out, waved her hand to somebody across the street, got into a car and drove away.

They all cheered, and everybody was excited. How did they get moving pictures of the town? They twisted their necks and watched the machine, handled by Will Rathbone, just one of those little household affairs. But Will had been preparing this surprise for three weeks. He had caught Willa Barrington drying her hair out on the back steps and Rose Hawthorn powdering her nose behind a door. He had quite a piece of reel of Jimmy Dodds in overalls repairing his old Ford, crawling under it and over it, with a streak of grease and carbon down one cheek and a wide grin on his face. He had caught almost every one of the young people's group in some funny attitude, doing something quite ordinary.

And then the scene shifted to the Flats and the streets where some of the guests had come from—not the sordid streets, but the neat ones, with little children making mud pies. Even Mary Morse's little sister, the one who had wept, was there, with a smudge on her nose, a smile on her face and a little ragged kitten upside down in her arms. Then came a cute altercation between two youngsters and after that a procession of boys from the mill, with here and there one turning and smiling straight into the camera.

Sherrill worried that the people from the Flats might be offended, but they were enjoying it as much as everyone else, even laughing at themselves. Will had selected the reels carefully. There was even a picture or two of some of the girls dressed in their best, smiling and pretty, walking down the street. He had shown the Flats young people to advantage and not made fun of them any more than he had the other young people.

Then he showed a picture of their church with the people going in, and much appreciative applause greeted this. They all wondered how he'd taken the picture, and he confessed to hiding his camera in a neighboring bush and making a long connection from the manse.

The pictures rolled on to the end amid loud applause and a general feeling of camaraderie. Afterward they ate their Thanksgiving dinner of turkey and stuffing, potatoes, vegetables, and all the accompaniments with enthusiasm and good cheer.

The program included vocal and instrumental solos and a dialogue which introduced their group to the guests, explaining its purpose and activities, and stirred some genuine interest among them.

After they had finished eating the pumpkin pie and fancy ice cream, the chairman of the prayer committee stood and announced that it was time to gather around the fire.

Several young people sat on cushions or on the bare floor, with some on either side of the fire. Then a voice started singing, "Softly now the light of day. . . ." The others took it up, and even the boys from the Flats growled away on the bass notes. Here and there a flute-like soprano or tenor lilted in, till everyone was singing. Then they melted into "Abide with me—fast falls the eventide!"

Then another member of the prayer committee invited the young people to share their verses, especially ones of thanksgiving, or mention something for which they were thankful.

He started off with his verse: "O magnify the Lord with me, and let us exalt his name together! This poor man cried, and the Lord heard him and saved him out of all his trouble!" Then he followed that by saying, "I was in a lot of trouble last week. I lost my job and couldn't get another one because of my bad leg. But I made out to pray about it, and God heard me and sent me the finest kind of job. So this is a real Thanksgiving for me tonight, I'll say!"

Then a voice from the other side of the circle started to sing.

Don't stop praying; the Lord is nigh.
Don't stop praying; He'll hear your cry!
God has promised, and He is true.
Don't stop praying! He'll answer you!

The guests sat quietly, sometimes stealing a glance at the others but apparently enjoying it all.

Then Rose spoke out her verse: " 'I will bless the Lord at all times. His praise shall continually be in my mouth!' I'm thankful tonight," she added, "that I belong to this group and know the Lord!"

" 'Bless the Lord, O my soul, and forget not all His benefits!' " Dick said next. "I'm glad tonight because my mother is getting well from a serious sickness."

So the verses and the testimonies were shared around the room, with now and then a hesitating word from a guest. At the end Mary Morse spoke.

"I don't know any of your verses, but I'm thankful tonight for a smile someone give me when I come in here. It was someone I use to think was real proud. Thank you for inviting me!"

Sudden tears sprang to Sherrill's eyes as she bowed her head and prayed. It was a simple prayer that seemed to bring them all within the circle of the throne and left them with a feeling that she had introduced them to a King.

Then Tom, the program chairman, invited everyone to their upcoming meeting Sunday night and asked Sherrill, as president, if she had any other announcements.

"Just one thing," said Sherrill hurriedly, "and I don't like to tell you a bit. I've been putting it off till the last minute, because I love you all so much and can't bear to be left out of everything. But I've got to go away for a little while, only a few weeks, I hope. If I can make it shorter, I will. You've made it awfully hard tonight for me to go. We've had such a wonderful time. And I mean the guests, too. You've all been wonderful, and I hope you'll come again and join in the Sunday meetings too. Our vice president, Alan MacFarlan, will carry on while I'm gone, and you know how well he can handle things. So I know my going won't make much difference, but I'll watch eagerly for news from home and will hurry back as soon as I can. I wouldn't go a step if it wasn't duty. I hope next month's social will be even better than this one and that each one of you will be present. I wish I could, too. Now let's sing a good-night song."

And quickly they started to sing, "God be with you till we meet again," till suddenly Sherrill felt she would cry.

But Mary was there and was singing, too, and just then she turned to Sherrill. "I can't ever be thankful enough that you got me to come to this. I may never have as good a time as this again, but I've got something to remember, anyhow!"

They took their guests home and said good night, and Sherrill and Alan were looking forward to the homeward ride together for their last words. But just then Tom came running up the street as they were leaving Mary at her home.

"Take me home, will you, Al? I came down with Red, and he has to drive out to Colterville with Alice, so I took the chance of catching you."

Of course they took him in and had a pleasant chat about how well everything had gone. But they had no chance to say good-bye quietly, as they'd both hoped. Alan did walk up the path to the door with Sherrill, but it was only a step away from the car. Tom was watching them, so they couldn't linger.

"Good night, Sherry!" said Alan, his voice catching. "It was wonderful and turned out as well as you hoped, don't you think? You did a great job!"

"Oh, you've worked just as hard and been—wonderful!"

Her hand was on the door latch, her other hand in his. He squeezed her fingers softly, impulsively, and then stepped away.

"I'm not going to say good-bye, Sherry," he said almost gruffly. "I'll just say good night." And he strode off through the moonlight whistling hard as he climbed into his car and drove down the street. Sherrill watched him out of sight and then went into the house, her eyes brimming with tears.

How dear he was, and this was the end of it. She perhaps wouldn't see him again for a long time. He had to go to work early in the morning, she knew. Yet she understood his rushing away so hurriedly. He hadn't felt like saying good-bye! Still, she felt a little ache in her heart. The days would come, and the crowd would meet without her. They would get used to being without her. Alan would see some other girl home, of course. Rose Hawthorn or perhaps Willa Barrington. Willa was dear and had always liked Alan. But she wouldn't be there. She was thinking about herself, and that wouldn't do. It was all going to be hard enough in the morning without letting in new heartaches. She must rush upstairs and put the last things in her trunk, for in the morning she would have no time.

Chapter 13

It was hard saying good-bye to Grandma. The soft old hands moved over her face like warm rose leaves.

"Never forget you're a Sherrill and a Washburn both, Sherrill," she said, her fine old eyes snapping. "You're just as good as any of them. But above all, don't forget you're a child of the King. You belong to the royal family. Don't let them put anything over on you."

"I won't, Grandmother dear," said Sherrill, emerging from the fragile warm embrace with Grandma's tears on her cheek.

Her brother drove her to the station in his old Ford, along with her mother. The new leather suitcase sat at her feet, almost rubbing the toe of her new pumps. Keith kept them laughing most of the way so they wouldn't cry. And then both mother and brother gave her last-minute advice on how to get along with her aunt and her aunt's expectations for her. On the way to the station they also picked up Harriet Masters.

"Now don't be afraid to wear that velvet a lot," she said, giving her hand a squeeze, "whenever you have a chance. It will clean, and you can send it to the cleaners as often as you like. The blue won't soil as easily, you know, being taffeta. And by the way I think that pink taffeta you made out of your great-grandmother's is as pretty as the blue. You look like a rose in it."

So they chattered as they drove up to the station.

And then Sherrill was astonished to see nearly all her friends waiting to send her off. The ones who worked had taken off for an hour, and those who didn't pooled their efforts in a hurry and bought her an exquisite handbag, the finest one to be found in Rockland.

"If you'd only told us sooner we might have done something really fine," said Rose Hawthorn, who wished the bag had come from the city. "But I thought you'd like to know Mary Morse suggested it last night. She whispered to me as she was going out the door that if we were going to get something for you she wanted us please to count her in for a dollar. She brought it around six o'clock this morning, before I was even up."

Sherrill was fairly overcome, and her smiles and near tears were so mingled that she could scarcely speak, while her eyes searched the crowd for Alan. Of course he had said he didn't see how he could get off, because a lawyer was coming out from the city with some papers that had to be signed. A whole week ago he'd told her that. Well, they wouldn't have had much chance to talk, of course, if he had come, with all those other dear people present. Still it would have been nice to have seen him again.

She didn't have much time for even faint regrets, though, for the train was heard whistling at the crossing. Then she had so many people to hug at once and so many last words to say that if Alan had been there she probably couldn't have distinguished him from anybody else, for they were all blurred together. She smiled at everyone from the lower step of the parlor car, kissed Keith and searched out Mother's face among the crowd to throw her one more kiss.

She waved her new handkerchief until the train swept around the curve and Bennett's Garage hid them from view. Then she turned to follow the porter into the car.

He seated her in her chair, placed her suitcase in the rack overhead and fixed a cushion at her feet. Then she slipped a quarter in his hand and swung her chair around toward the window to look out. She didn't even glance at her fellow travelers. She was too aware of the swimming tears in her eyes. She watched the coal yard and the lumberyard slip by, and there was Silas Lummis's new bungalow with the baby out in the yard in a little red hood, playing with the dog. How dear even old Mrs. Miller's clapboard cottage looked as they whirled past! And back on the horizon, miles away it seemed, was the familiar church steeple among the tree branches.

She dabbed at her eyes and tried to swallow the lump that would rise in her throat.

"Hello!" said a voice at her side from the next chair. "Aren't you ever going to notice me?"

She swung around, and there sat Alan MacFarlan, smiling broadly!

And then, in her surprise, two tears rolled down her cheeks, though her smile was lighting up her face.

"Oh, Alan, I'm so glad you've come. I thought you said you couldn't!" She struggled in vain to gain control of herself and seem quite casual.

"Oh, I found I could just as well go up to the city and meet the lawyer, and it suited us both a lot better," he said, with a twinkle in his eyes. "I wish I could go all the way up to New York with you, but I couldn't quite manage it today. If Dad had been on his feet I would have—that is, if you didn't mind. By the way, I got a letter from Bob this morning. He's doing great! He says he reads his Bible every day and thinks it's terrific—says he never knew the Bible was like that."

Of course Alan had to get off in three quarters of an hour, but it seemed to make all the difference in the world in the day, to have him to herself for that little while. How they talked, chattering about the dinner and rejoicing together over the news from Bob Lincoln.

As they neared the city Alan grew serious. "I say, Sherrill—don't grow up too much while you're gone. You won't, will you? It wouldn't be good if you grew up while you were gone and I was still only a kid when you came back."

She laughed and promised she wouldn't think of it.

But after that they sat quietly and watched the city approach and the station where he must leave her, and they couldn't think of anything else to say because the last words they wanted to say were stuck in their throats.

Finally Alan stood up as the train drew to a stop. Bending over her he said in a low tone, "I'm going to pray for you every night and morning, and you're going to do the same for me, see?"

Sherrill's face lighted with joy. "Oh, yes!" she agreed, looking steadily into his eyes.

Then he stooped and kissed her lips reverently, as if he were sealing a compact, and went quickly out of the car and swung himself down the steps to the platform.

Their eyes met as the train moved past him on the platform. He lifted his hat, and then the train swung into motion, and she couldn't see him anymore. But her heart was happy as she sat there for a long time with her eyes closed, remembering all he'd said and his good-bye kiss. It seemed sacred to her, binding them to God and prayer and a life of the Spirit. It made her feel happy and warm in her heart, and it seemed to make possible the long days that must pass before she might return to her home once more.

It was a long time before she noticed the new landscape sliding by. And then she saw that she had flung her new fur coat carelessly over the back of her chair, as if she were used to wearing such grandeur every day. She had been lost in remembering the dear faces she'd left behind.

Late that afternoon the train reached New York, and Sherrill roused herself to gather her belongings and be equal to the new demands upon her. She felt excited now, as she approached New York, a strange city that had always held an attraction for her. And here she was entering the outskirts of the metropolis.

She sat on the edge of her chair and stared into the blankness of the tube as they were being whirled under the river, with its deep waters flowing over her head. She watched the people about her as they prepared to leave the train and tried to look as if this wasn't her first trip to New York. Keith had told her what to do at every stage of the trip. So now she gathered her coat about her, noted that the richly attired woman across the aisle looked at her with respect and felt the prestige her coat gave. *Was that wrong?* she wondered. No, it wasn't pride. It was just a pleasant sense of being dressed appropriately and that no critic could find anything noticeably odd about her. Well, anyhow, the dear ones who had given her the coat wanted her to enjoy it. She would rest in that and be happy and satisfied about her clothes. She needed them right now to support her in her approaching ordeal. She found she was inwardly quaking at the thought of meeting her relatives.

She had been told to go immediately on arrival to the telephone desk in the ladies' waiting room and stand there until someone came for her.

The red-capped porter took her luggage and led her up the iron stair from the train into Pennsylvania Station. Although she'd heard it described many times she was filled with awe over its vastness and the great spaces framed in white marble that stretched away in every direction from it.

The porter left her in the appointed place, and Sherrill stood staring around her anxiously, wondering what the aunt or the cousin would be like. She glanced eagerly at every well-dressed woman or young girl who came that way.

Back and forth, up and down, sometimes not two feet from where she stood, a man in livery paced, watching everyone who approached. Once he stopped a plain-looking girl in a blue serge suit and asked her something, but she shook her head and walked on.

Sherrill watched the clock and everyone who came, and her heart began to have strange misgivings. Perhaps they'd forgotten her! It was a quarter to five, and no one had come yet. What should she do? Would her uncle discover it soon and come after her?

Had she made a mistake about the place she was to meet them? She asked the telephone operator if there was more than one telephone desk in the ladies' waiting room and was coldly told no. Finally she decided to telephone her uncle's house and find out what to do. Of course she could take a taxi, but they might come for her just after she'd left. And perhaps they wouldn't like that. She mustn't make a mistake right at the start. She would telephone. Surely that could do no harm. She would say she wasn't sure she'd found the spot where they'd told her to meet them. "Someone will meet you," the letter had said.

So she looked up the telephone number and finally approached the operator and asked for it.

Just then at her elbow a voice spoke respectfully: "I beg your pardon, miss, but I couldn't help hearing the number. Are you waiting for Mrs. Washburn's car?"

"Oh, yes!" said Sherrill, turning around with a relieved smile. "Do you know where they are? I must have missed them."

"Right this way, miss," said the man, stooping to pick up her baggage. "I wasn't sure whether it was you or not," he added, glancing at Sherrill's squirrel coat. He didn't say his instructions had been to look for a shabby-looking country girl.

So Sherrill was stowed away in a handsome car, her checks were taken by another red-capped official, and she rolled in state out a stone corridor into the great new city.

But she felt a strange new heaviness in her heart. This wasn't the way they welcomed guests in Rockland, sending a chauffeur after them. But perhaps everybody was sick, or something had happened. She took a long breath, settled back on the downy cushions and tried to prepare for whatever might be before her.

Chapter 14

It was a handsome house on Riverside Drive where they finally arrived, but there was no welcoming door flung open, no eager relatives waiting to greet her. Not even a costly curtain drawn back to indicate any watcher at the window.

Instead the door was opened in answer to the chauffeur's ring by a white-capped maid who stared at her with a brief questioning glance and said, "Is this Miss Washburn?" as if she were surprised, and with another appraising glance said, "Come this way, please."

Sherrill was led up a wide staircase, glimpsing stately rooms below as she passed, and down a narrow hall toward the back of the house. She had a sense of being isolated in a large boardinghouse, but the room they came to proved to be large and light and overlooked a row of backyards.

A bathroom was connected with the room, as well as a large closet, and Sherrill looked about on her new quarters with a degree of relief. It would be quite possible to feel at home in a room like that, everything else being equal.

"Mrs. Washburn said she would be busy until seven, and Miss Washburn is at a tea. But you'd better lie down and refresh yourself, for there's a dinner and party this evening you're to attend. She said she would see you at seven and arrange about your dress. The dinner is half past eight."

"Oh!" said Sherrill, bewildered. "Oh, well, I don't think I'd better go anywhere tonight. I'd rather stay right here quietly and get rested."

She was beginning to feel in a panic. No one to meet her or greet her. A party flung at her right at the start and no chance to get her bearings. This was even worse than she'd expected. But the person in cap and apron was speaking firmly, as if she had the right to order affairs.

"Oh, but I'm thinking you'll have to, miss. Mrs. Washburn has already accepted for you. Madam would never hear of your declining. She always says a dinner engagement is a thing you simply have to keep. If you'll let me fix a nice hot bath for you, miss, I'm sure you'll feel quite refreshed. I'll put some of Madam's bath salts in it. They're very helpful. And then you can lie down till it's time to go in to Madam about the dress. I believe she has had some things sent up that she wants you to see."

"Oh, certainly, I guess I don't want to upset any plans," said Sherrill, yet with some doubt. "I'll go, of course, if it's that way. They promised to send my trunk up at once. I suppose it will be here soon."

"Yes, miss, likely," said the maid. "And would you like it sent immediately to the trunk room for the night out of your way, or is there something you must have out of it first? I can unpack it for you this evening after you've gone, if you wish."

"Oh, no," said Sherrill in a new panic, "please have it brought right here. I'd rather unpack it myself if you don't mind. I know just how things are, you know," and she smiled pleasantly. "But thank you just the same."

The maid looked at her, opened her lips as if to speak, then glanced at the lovely fur coat Sherrill was taking off and closed her lips again. Finally she said, "Well, Madam thought you would want your trunk to go directly to the storeroom. But if you prefer, of course."

"Yes, I do, please," said Sherrill firmly.

When she was alone, instead of taking off her hat and following the directions for rest, Sherrill stood looking out her window blankly, trying to think what all this meant. How strange for her aunt not to greet her! She mustn't let her mother or Keith know how she'd been received. Especially she mustn't let Grandma know. She would feel it keenly.

Then suddenly she went and knelt down by a chair.

"Oh, my dear heavenly Father, help me not to misjudge. Help me to be strong and sweet and go through this trial You've given me, for Christ's sake."

Then she came back to the window and tried to interest herself in the small vision of the new city she could get from these back upper windows. Were those great masts over there far beyond the buildings, or were they steeples?

A tap on the door put an end to her investigations, and she opened it to find the maid with a tray containing tea and tiny sandwiches and cakes.

"Oh, you needn't have troubled to do that!" said Sherrill and then realized that was the wrong thing to say. Probably tea was a regular meal in this house. She must take things as they came. That was what Harriet Masters had said, and she knew.

It was six o'clock before Sherrill's trunk was delivered to the room, but she had lain down for a few minutes and felt quite rested. She had thought out the matter of clothes, comparing as much as she knew of the occasion with Aunt Harriet's guidelines, and decided the blue taffeta was the right thing to wear tonight.

She laid out the things she would need for the evening, hung her dresses in the closet and put some of her other things away in the bureau drawers and her hats on the closet shelf. It didn't take her long. Somehow she didn't linger as she'd expected to do when she laid those pretty garments away in the trunk. She had, in spite of her prejudices, pictured an eager cousin hovering near and admiring, and she was chagrined to find how much difference it made to her that no one was near to see what pretty things she had. Real Paris clothes and copies of them, and no one to know it. It served her right for caring so much about them. Well, she would just enjoy them and forget they were different from what she always wore.

She was about to slip into her dress when the maid tapped at the door.

"Madam says she is ready for you now," she announced, "and you will please not put on a dress. Just wear a kimono. She wants you to try on something."

Sherrill's face flushed, and she was about to rebel at the order, when she remembered her prayer to be kept sweet and do the right thing, so she closed her lips and tried to be pleasant. Well, at least she had a pretty kimono and lovely lingerie. She swept the bright folds of silk about her and rejoiced in the embroidered butterflies. They looked pretty with the silver shoes and stockings she had put on.

She walked down the long hall to the front of the house and waited while the maid tapped at the door of her mistress. It seemed strange to be greeting her relative in a kimono first. At least it was pretty, she told herself.

Mrs. Washburn lay on her bed, draped in a negligee of lace and orchid silk, with her face swathed in hot cloths which the attendant from time to time changed. There was no opportunity for Sherrill to give the sacrificial kiss she had earnestly resolved upon after many soul struggles.

"So this is Sherrill, is it?" said a sharp thin voice from the steaming towels. "Well, I'm glad you arrived on time. I had to substitute you as a dinner guest for a friend who was visiting me and was suddenly called home by a death in the family. So annoying. But there isn't much time, so we'll have to set to work. I have a dress here which I think should fit you. If it doesn't, the maid knows how to take it up. Suppose you put it on right away. Where did you find that kimono? Is that something Carol has been buying again on my charge account? If it is, it will simply have to go back. I can't have her doing that when she has an account of her own. Come over nearer so I can see it. What are those? Butterflies? It really is stunning! I can't say I blame her much. Perhaps I'll keep it for myself. Did she tell you you could borrow it?"

"What? This?" asked Sherrill, following the direction of the glance that came from between the hot towels. "Oh, no, this is mine. It is pretty, isn't it?"

"But it looks elegant," said the aunt in her superior tone. "Where on earth could you get it?"

"Yes," said Sherrill, "it came from Paris. A friend of Mother's brought it to me a few days ago."

"You don't say!" said the aunt thoughtfully. "A friend of your mother's. I didn't suppose she had friends who traveled abroad."

Sherrill's color rose, and she drew a deep breath. This was the kind of thing to expect from Aunt Eloise, of course, but it was irritating. She must be careful.

She gathered the lovely silken folds about her and said nothing.

"Well, there isn't much time, especially if the dress has to be altered. Take off your kimono and anything you have on underneath. This dress has garments that go especially with it. You can go over behind that screen. Maida will dress you."

Sherrill stood hesitantly, eyeing the maid over whose arm were slung billows of bright green silk and malines, and then looked toward the swathed face on the pillow.

"I don't think that will be necessary, Aunt Eloise," she said, with a smile as sweet as if she were really grateful. "It's very kind of you, of course, but I have plenty of clothes with me."

The woman on the bed waved an impatient hand.

"Don't argue!" she said sharply. "I haven't time to discuss the matter. I want that dress tried on you at once. Afterward we'll discuss it if there's time. Don't annoy me right at the start. It's so irritating when young people always object to things. Marie, this pack is getting cold. You'd better change it."

Sherrill was vexed, and her eyes had a flash of Grandmother Sherrill in them, perhaps even of Great-Grandmother Sherrill. But she remembered her resolve and after a moment said gravely, "Oh, very well," and followed the maid behind the screen.

She saw at once when she threw back her kimono that her pretty lingerie commanded the woman's respect. Nevertheless, she handed forth a minute garment she insisted should be substituted for the things Sherrill wore.

"Can't I try on the dress over these?" asked Sherrill.

"You heard Madam say the under things went with the dress," said the maid coldly.

So, much against her will, Sherrill put on the flimsy substitute. And when the maid flung the green dress over her head and she saw herself in the long glass she realized why her own lingerie wouldn't do. Her own white back gleamed at her from the looking glass, without any covering.

Sherrill surveyed herself in dismay, saying nothing at first, marveling that any girl would go out into company so nearly naked as she looked to herself. Then her sense of humor rose to the occasion, and she almost laughed aloud at herself in such array. She couldn't help picturing the faces of her mother and her grandmother if they could see her now. A bare back to the waist, with a long green tail of fluffy malines and silk, and a front that was all too revealing for her sense of fineness. And what would her friends in Rockland say if she appeared in a garment like this?

But while she was studying herself and trying to think what to say and how to decline the use of the dress, the maid moved a leaf of the screen back, and she stood revealed before her aunt.

"It couldn't fit better if it was made for her, Madam." said the maid, "and it's just her size. There won't need to be a thing done to it."

"Well, that's a relief," said the aunt, suddenly emerging from the towels and showing a steamed complexion almost like a baby's. "Put on the wrap and let her see how it's to be worn, and then she'll be set."

Before Sherrill could object Maida threw about her shoulders a long black velvet wrap with a high fur collar.

"Stunning!" said the aunt, submitting to vigorous applications of ice wrapped in cheesecloth bags over her cheeks and chin and forehead and nose. "That's that! Sherrill, you better go right downstairs and sit in the library to wait for us. Your uncle hates to be kept waiting, and it's a relief to know you're ready early enough. I won't be long now. Thank fortune you have naturally good hair, and you seem to have arranged it becomingly. Slightly ingénue, but I guess it'll have to do tonight because I simply can't spare Marie now, and Maida will have to dress Carol. Just go right down now. Those silver slippers look fine with the green. Are they the ones that came with the dress, Maida? Oh, her own? Well, they're not so bad. Maida, show her how to find the library. I'll tell you on the way about how to behave at the dinner, Sherrill. That's all now. I haven't another minute."

"But, Aunt Eloise," began Sherrill in dismay, "I'm sorry to disappoint you, but I really would prefer to wear my own dress. I'm sure Mother wouldn't like—"

"It makes no difference what your mother would like," the aunt interrupted. "She isn't here, and she wouldn't know what was proper if she were. You're under my care and advisement now, and you're in my house. I expect you to be properly dressed when you go out with me or any of my family. Understand? Now go!"

Mrs. Washburn arose haughtily from her elegant couch and stepped into the silken garment that the maid held out for her, and Sherrill realized she was dismissed.

In growing dismay she followed the maid down the hall.

At the head of the stairs the maid paused and said coldly, "You'll find the library to the left of the stairs. You can't miss it. I'll put Mademoiselle's garments in her room."

Sherrill hesitated at the head of the stairs, looking after the woman as she disappeared into a door farther down the hall, then slowly walked down the stairs trying to think what to do.

She heard the woman come out of the room a moment later, close the door and go down the back stairs. Instantly she turned and fled back to her room, the green taffeta making an alarming rustle as she went.

Once in her room she locked the door and went to the mirror. The girl who looked back at her over the fur collar seemed an alien somehow. The wrap was pretty, but far too rich and ornate for her tastes. The long green freakish tails hanging below filled her with dislike. With a quick motion she flung off the wrap and laid it on the chair beside her and took another quick survey of herself, not omitting her bare back. Then she disrobed, casting aside the borrowed garments and stepping into her own which Maida had left neatly folded on a chair.

Her own blue taffeta was lying on the bed where she'd left it, and she put it on, thankful it took only a moment to adjust. She unfastened the gaudy costume jewelry that had been put on her neck and slid out of the bracelets, clasping on her own string of pearls Alan had given her. Then she was ready, and her eyes told her she looked much better than in the borrowed clothes.

But then, of course, her aunt might be angry. Still, she couldn't help that. She wouldn't go anywhere dressed like that. Her family would have upheld her in her course, and she simply didn't feel comfortable in that dress. Probably no one else would even realize why she disliked it, but not even for peace and courtesy would she dress as her aunt had commanded.

She paused hesitantly and looked at the rich wrap lying on the bed. Should she put that on instead of her own coat so they wouldn't discover what she had done until it was too late to make a fuss about it? Perhaps they would insist on waiting for her to go back and change into the green after all.

Well, let them. Then she could remain at home. But even if it did make a coldness between her and her aunt, she felt she should take a stand at once about wearing her own clothes.

So she left the velvet wrap lying on the bed where she'd flung it and got her own fur coat from the closet. If her beautiful squirrel coat wasn't good enough to go to anything, then she would stay at home. Harriet Masters had assured her it was appropriate, and if she didn't know then no one did.

So Sherrill put on her fur coat, took out her lovely blue chiffon head scarf from Paris and was ready. Changing had taken scarcely ten minutes; yet she felt sure none of the family had gone downstairs yet.

With her hand on the doorknob she paused, dropping to her knees with a prayer: "Dear Father, help me through this hard place, and keep me and guide me every moment this evening, for Jesus' sake."

Then she hurried downstairs to the library and sat down in a shadowed corner where she wouldn't be noticed if anyone came into the room, for only a single heavily shaded lamp was burning. She was glad to sit back and close her eyes and rest. She was more tired than she'd realized, and she dreaded the evening. At that moment if anyone had offered her a quick transport back to Rockland she would have accepted it eagerly.

She had a full half hour to sit in the leather chair and wait, and time to calm her heart and think over what she'd done. It looked to her as if her stay in New York would be a stormy one unless she took a stand now. Yet she found herself trembling in anticipation. Oh, why had she come?

At last she heard doors opening upstairs. A man's voice which she thought she recognized as her uncle's, her aunt's cold thin one answering, and then another door hastily flung back and a girl's high petulant tones. That must be her cousin.

Simultaneously, Maida appeared in the doorway and peered into the elegant gloom of the room.

"Madam says you're to go right out to the car and get in, Miss Washburn," she announced. "They're late already." Turning, she disappeared.

Chapter 15

Sherrill went into the hall and found her uncle coming down the stairs. "Uncle West!" she called joyously and hurried to meet him. Here at least she might be natural. Uncle West had always been kind—whenever he'd had time.

He stopped suddenly, his eyes lighting.

"Ho, ho! Little girl, so you've come! They didn't tell me! Well, I'm glad to see you! I hope we'll have a beautiful winter together. It's going to be nice to have two little girls instead of one." He took her in his arms and kissed her.

"Now come on right out to the car," he added. "Your aunt will be down in a minute. She found a button off her slipper or something that had to be remedied, I believe, but she said we were to get in. Carol? Where are you, child? Carol is always the last one. Well, come on—you and I will go out and get settled."

He led her out to the car and seated her comfortably, and Sherrill suddenly felt warm around her heart again. It wouldn't be so bad perhaps, after all, if she had one friend in the family.

Mrs. Washburn came almost at once, stopping at the door to give directions to the butler and making a great fuss about getting settled in the car. Carol came trailing behind, fretting at having to go to the dinner.

"You know I can't abide Amelia Van's dinners, Eloise," she drawled, without even glancing toward her newly arrived cousin. "Why did you have to bring me in on this? If your Mrs. Pearly and her stupid daughter had to go to an old funeral I don't see why that should affect me. Amelia's a pest anyway, and her dinners are never worth eating."

"Carol, that's no way to speak of your hostess," chided her father mildly. "Mrs. Van Gorton is one of your mother's friends, and that should be enough for you."

"Well, it's not enough!" retorted the girl. "I don't see being a slave to anybody merely because Eloise is fool enough to accept her invitations. Here I have to go and be made a martyr when I might have been resting up a little for the dance this evening. I'll be bored to extinction. She always seats me beside that doddering old Max Pyle, just because he likes to appear young. I can't abide him, the old cradle snatcher."

"Carol, you haven't spoken to your cousin yet," reproved her mother coldly, as if to close the subject of the dinner.

"Oh!" said Carol, staring suddenly at Sherrill and then pausing to appraise her.

"Oh, hello," she said indifferently. "But, say, Eloise, you've certainly done her up in a stunning coat. I like that! You wouldn't get me a new fur coat this winter. What's the idea, anyway? I'm certainly not going to stand for that!"

"Fur coat?" said Mrs. Washburn, turning questioning eyes toward Sherrill's corner, where the light from the top of the car shone full upon her. "What do you mean?"

Then she stared.

"Where on earth did you get that coat, Sherrill?" she demanded. "That's not the wrap I gave you to wear."

"No," said Sherrill, smiling and trying to speak naturally, "I thought it would be better to wear my own things. They seemed more suited to me. You see, in the others I felt a little like David in Saul's armor."

"David?" asked Mrs. Washburn, with raised eyebrows and a tone that implied something questionable in Sherrill's acquaintances. "Who is David? And Saul? You seem to have a great many gentlemen friends. I hope they don't live in New York."

Sherrill, with difficulty, controlled a wild burst of laughter rising to the surface. She tried to answer pleasantly with a casual smile.

"Oh, I meant David of the Bible, you know."

"The Bible!" exclaimed her aunt. "I've always considered it irreverent to bring the Bible into daily conversation in such a trivial way. I'm surprised. I always heard your family was very religious. But who was this other man you mentioned, this Saul? You must excuse me, but I feel I should understand about all your acquaintances. I really couldn't have ordinary persons coming to see you at the house, you know, on Carol's account. And what could this person have to do with your wearing my evening wrap?"

Sherrill's eyes danced, and she longed to make a sharp reply. "Oh, Saul was a king who offered to lend David his armor to fight the giant," she said instead. "David declined because he felt he wasn't used to the armor and could do better without it."

"Well, I'm sure I think this David person was very rude," said Aunt Eloise haughtily. "I wonder why they persist in putting such ridiculous stories in the Bible and then expect people to read them. But I'd rather not hear any more about it. Suppose you tell me how you happen to be wearing that elegant coat. I hope you didn't borrow it for the trip."

Sherrill was suddenly so angry that she had to take a deep breath and hold her tongue between her teeth till the impulse to speak harshly had passed. Finally she managed to say steadily, although a bit coldly, "The coat is my own, Aunt Eloise."

"Then I suppose you got a job and spent an entire year's wages on it!" snapped the aunt. "It's a pity someone couldn't go around teaching poor working girls a sense of value and the fitness of things. What's your job? Something in a bank, I think your mother wrote. It certainly can't pay much. I suppose you bought it on the installment plan."

Here Uncle Weston interfered.

"Really, Eloise—don't put the child through such a catechism on the first night she's here. Let's talk of something pleasant. I'd like to know how the family's doing. We've scarcely had a chance to speak a word together yet. Perhaps she doesn't care to tell all her family affairs."

"Well, Weston, since she's here I feel it my duty to know all about her," said the aunt.

Sherrill's eyes were bright as she turned to her uncle and tried to speak pleasantly. "I have no objection to telling anything, Uncle Weston," she said. "I didn't suppose it would be of interest."

Turning back to her aunt she said, "No, I have no job as yet. I'm just out of school, you know, but I was to have gone into the bank this month if I'd stayed at home. And, no, I didn't borrow the coat from a neighbor, and I didn't buy it myself. My brother bought it for me and gave it to me as a present just before I left."

"Your brother bought it for you? And where did he get the money?" This came from the aunt in a low tone as if she thought she'd been deceived.

"Why, I don't *think* he stole it," Sherrill said, with a mischievous twinkle in her eyes. She could usually see the funny side of everything and often took refuge in a laugh when she felt more like crying.

"Oh, does he steal?" asked Carol, lifting her chin with sudden interest. "I never heard he was dishonest."

"Carol! Really—you—"

"There now, Daddy, don't get tiresome! I'm sure she said she didn't *think* he stole it. What else could I think but that he was in the habit of stealing?"

"Carol, you're out of bounds!" said her father angrily.

But Sherrill suddenly broke into laughter, clearing the atmosphere in her own heart at least.

"Don't scold her, Uncle Weston," she laughed. "She's only kidding. Of course she didn't mean it. I'm not as touchy as that!"

But the aunt didn't join in the laughter, and the cousin only stared.

"I'm sure I've always been given to understand your brother was very poor," said the aunt rather indignantly. "Didn't he at one time try to borrow something from you, Weston, to pay a bill or something?"

"No," said Mr. Washburn, looking down at his gloves uncomfortably, "not a bill. He suggested I might like to loan him some money for a year's time at a good rate of interest to help him buy a small business he had an opportunity to acquire. I would have been glad to do it if it had been possible, but that was when you went to the hospital for an operation, Eloise. Then you were ordered abroad for a year afterward, and I couldn't see my way clear to do it. I took up the matter with him two years later, but he said he no longer needed it. By the way, Sherrill, who is he working for now? Is he getting along all right?"

"Very nicely," said Sherrill quietly. "But he isn't working for anybody. He has his own business. He bought it at the time when he wrote you. The bank gladly loaned him the money, and he's paid off the entire loan now and is independent."

"You don't say!" said Uncle Weston, with a light of satisfaction in his eyes. "He must be very enterprising."

"Well, but I don't understand," began Aunt Eloise, fixing her husband with a glassy stare that implied she'd been deceived in something. "I was led to believe the family was in straitened circumstances. When you wanted me to invite—"

"Eloise!" said Uncle Weston, with a sternness in his voice. "We'll talk of something else if you please. Remember that Sherrill is our guest."

"Oh, very well," said Mrs. Washburn and relapsed into haughty silence.

"Well, that's a peach of a coat!" said Carol grudgingly. "I'll borrow it sometimes. It'll just go with my new brown velvet."

"You'll do nothing of the kind, Carol," said her father still sternly. "You have plenty of coats of your own, and if you haven't I'll get you what you need. But you're not to impose on your cousin. Understand? That's a command! If I find you disobeying it I'll take back my promise about getting you a new car in the spring."

"I don't see that you need to take it out on Carol," said the mother disagreeably. "The fact is, you don't understand the whole thing anyway. I told Sherrill to wear certain articles I gave her, which I felt were suitable for her to wear as our guest, and she has ignored my request."

"I'm sorry, Aunt Eloise," said Sherrill, in a pleasant voice that nevertheless had a note of firmness in it, "but I'd much rather wear my own things. Think how you would feel if you came to Rockland and had to wear Mother's dresses. You wouldn't like it a bit."

"I should say not!" said the aunt, curling her lip. "That's hardly a parallel case."

"I want it thoroughly understood," declared Uncle Weston, "that Sherrill is to wear what she likes while she is with us. She's not to be badgered."

"Don't be silly," said his wife. "Do you want me to let her be laughed at among our friends?"

"It seems to me," said the uncle, "that Sherrill can be trusted not to do that. She seems to have turned herself out very well as far as I can see!"

"A lot you know about clothes, Westy!" exclaimed his daughter. "If I were you I'd keep out of this. You won't get a rise out of Eloise, no matter what you say!"

"You are impertinent, Carol!" said her father.

"I meant to be, Weston!" said his daughter.

And then the car stopped, and the chauffeur opened the door.

"There," said Mrs. Washburn, "you've taken up all the time, and I meant to tell Sherrill what she would have to do and how to act!"

"I should think she would do very well without instructions," said her husband.

"You would!" said Carol, pushing past Sherrill and running up the steps of the house.

Sherrill got out and walked beside her uncle up to the door.

"You mustn't mind your aunt, Sherrill," said her uncle in a low tone, helping her up the steps. "She doesn't mean to sound unpleasant. She's just anxious to have everything go well and is plain spoken."

"Of course!" said Sherrill, trying to look cheerful. She felt comforted for the ordeal before her by this little word.

Once inside the house, the women went upstairs to take off their wraps. Sherrill slipped out of her coat and scarf, patted her hair in front of the mirror and, forgetting about her dress, stepped aside for her aunt to take her place before the dressing table. She felt the subject of clothes was finished for the present.

But Eloise Washburn, seating herself for a last touch of lipstick, got a full glimpse of her niece in her blue French dress with its sweetheart roses, and her smile changed into an icy glare.

"So you discarded the dress I bought for you also!" she said, as if Sherrill had broken all the laws in the Decalogue. "Well, I certainly think you have been the rudest girl it was ever my misfortune to meet. I spent two days hunting for that dress, and you refused to wear it!"

"Oh," said Sherrill, feeling suddenly very tired and wishing she could run away and never come back, "I'm sorry to seem rude and disappoint you, but I couldn't wear that dress. I'm not used to such things, and I would have felt— embarrassed. I'm sure my mother would have been horrified at my dressing that way."

"I've told you before that your mother has nothing whatever to say about what you wear or do while you're with us. I'm the one to judge. And you are scarcely respectable nowadays in the evening without a low-cut back. I have no desire for my hostess to think I have imported a little country child to force into society. Where did you get that dress anyway? It surely wasn't bought in Rockland."

Sherrill was growing quite indignant and was about to make some very unkind statements, but just as she opened her mouth to give a sharp retort she remembered her mother's last injunction.

"Remember, dear, 'the tongue is a little member . . . Behold how great a matter a little fire kindles.'" She closed her eyes and, opening them again, spoke quietly.

"No, Aunt Eloise, it came from Paquin in Paris. Harriet Masters, a friend of Mother's, brought it to me last week. She's just returned from two years abroad and brought me some lovely things. You won't really need to worry about me—"

Just then two friends of Mrs. Washburn's arrived in the dressing room, ending the conversation. Sherrill turned to gaze out the curtained window on the city lights to steady her shaken nerves and say a quick prayer for help and strength.

She was interrupted by her cousin's voice behind her in a low tone.

"Did you say that came from Paquin? I don't believe it. Paquin wouldn't put on a back that wasn't cut low. Show me the label."

"It's in the back of the neck," said Sherrill wearily, "if you care to look. I'm sure I don't see what difference it makes."

"Well, it makes this difference," said Carol disagreeably, "that I don't like it if you try to dress better than I do. If that's a Paquin I've got to have one. But I don't see how you managed to get yourself in style when you're only a hick."

"Come, girls—we're going down now. Don't keep us waiting," came Mrs. Washburn's command, and Sherrill closed her lips on the hot words that were forming on the tip of her tongue and went down to her first formal dinner in New York.

Chapter 16

Sherrill walked quietly downstairs behind the others, keeping herself as much in the background as possible. She realized almost at once that her French dress was a great asset. She felt inconspicuous and well dressed and that the other members of the party had accepted her as properly attired. Her fingers touched the soft blue silk, thankful it had helped her through the first hard minutes. She found no pleasure in attending her first dinner party with the disapproval of an aunt who had compelled her to be there.

But she made it through the introductions more comfortably than she had hoped and went to dinner with a gracious elderly gentleman who paid her several compliments with his first sentences, told her she looked as if she'd just stepped out of an old-time valentine and called her his sweetheart in a pleasant, impersonal way that made her feel young and at ease.

She was seated at the table between him and a young man with a tiny mustache on his upper lip that resembled a smudge of soot. In conversing with Sherrill he almost neglected the woman he had brought with him; so between the two she scarcely had opportunity to eat.

But most of the conversation was froth, and Sherrill, usually quick at repartee, scarcely knew how to take some of the things that were said to her. The young man talked of plays or pictures, and Sherrill had seen neither of them, nor did she enjoy the questionable jokes and stories he told. Then, to direct the conversation along other lines, she mentioned certain treasured books he had neither heard of nor read.

On the other side, the elderly man paid open court to her in polite flattery that was almost embarrassing. In the few intervals she had to herself she studied the people gathered around the table and realized from the scraps of conversation she heard that they were nearly all conversing in the same manner.

She studied the priceless lace cloth that covered the banqueting board and the heavy silver, the glittering crystal and the monogrammed china, and compared it to the Thanksgiving dinner she had attended the night before in a barn with the guests from the Flats. She wished she were back there again. She compared the guests at this table with those in the barn, and a startling thought came to her: They were of the same blood, made by the same Creator, living on the same earth, bound for the same ending as far as this earth was concerned. She knew she preferred the talk of the young people from the Flats to what was going on about her. Doubtless the Flats could win out in rough, uncultured talk against these people when they were off guard, but so far as last night's dinner was concerned they had been interested and courteous and well behaved. What was it about these people that made her feel as if she were in an alien land? Not just that they were strangers. No, they were almost talking a strange language, alluding to things with which she had nothing in common.

She tried to imagine any of these men and women and young people as having been present at that supper last evening. How would they have fitted in? Well, she could select several of them that might have been good sports and entered into the fun, enjoyed the singing and the color and the pleasantry, but would they have fitted in around the fire at the close any better than the people from the Flats? Would they have bowed their heads in prayer and entered into that hush that made heaven seem so near?

"Do you know," said the young man beside her, "it's criminal to look as serious as you are now?"

Sherrill's face lighted with a smile. "Oh, I didn't mean to look serious. I was just thinking."

"But you shouldn't," he said. "It isn't being done. People as young as you often die of thinking. And why aren't you drinking your champagne? That isn't at all wise, you know."

"I don't care for it," said Sherrill.

"Oh, but you should," said the young man, whose name was Elbert Girard. "It's old and costly. Are you really serious that you don't want it? Well, then, would you mind, since it's sitting so close to me?" And he lifted her glass and drained it as if it were his own. Presently a servant filled it again, and again he drained it.

At last the dinner was ended, and they all moved to the reception room. It seemed to Sherrill that she had been in this alien world for ages, and she was feeling terribly weary. She slipped into a seat in a corner behind a table and pretended to examine a book lying there. Her aunt presently discovered her.

"Sherrill, you're to go with Carol now. I've made your excuses to your hostess, and all you need to do is stop beside her and say how sorry you are that it's impossible for you to remain for the evening. She understands you have a previous engagement and only came here to fill in."

"Engagement?" echoed Sherrill blankly, the momentary relief changing to dismay. "Is Carol going somewhere else? I thought she was going home."

"Home! At this hour of the evening? Certainly not. You're going to one of the brightest dances of the season, and you're quite lucky to be here in time to go. Not everyone is invited."

"Oh, I'm sorry to seem unappreciative, Aunt Eloise, but I'm very tired, and I'd be so glad to get to bed after traveling."

"Nonsense!" said the older woman. "You're young. You mustn't mind being a little tired. You can sleep till noon tomorrow. You mustn't humor yourself that way."

"Well, then, would you mind if I stay here, please? I think I would only be a burden on my cousin."

"No, certainly you must go! I've accepted this invitation for you, and it's very rude to stay away. Do hurry. Carol is waiting for you in the dressing room."

Sherrill arose abruptly and hurried to the dressing room, wondering if she could persuade Carol to leave her at the house. But when she reached the dressing room she saw no sign of Carol, and the maid told her the young ladies had gone down to the car. Sherrill dashed after them but found to her dismay that Carol had gone off with the first car and left her to go with strangers, most of whom she'd barely met. She saw no use in asking them to take her back to her uncle's house, even if she could have made herself heard. They were all talking at once, and the young man who had sat next to her at the dinner table seemed impatient to be off. So Sherrill took the place they assigned her and tried to think of some other way out. She felt as if she couldn't go through another thing tonight. Every nerve was sore and tired. She would get hold of Carol somehow and tell her she was almost sick from being so tired, and perhaps Carol would find a way to send her home or go home early too.

But Carol was not to be interviewed. The party was already in full swing with her in the midst of it. When the raucous music broke and changed she seemed to disappear utterly.

Sherrill drifted into another room finally. She was becoming almost hysterical in her weariness. She felt out of place and disgusted by the behavior around her and the jokes she'd overheard. Liquor was flowing freely, and some of the young people were already silly from its effects. Carol was conspicuous for her loud voice and laughter. Sherrill's cheeks burned with shame for her. It seemed dreadful to think she belonged to her. Did her father know she acted this way when she was out of his sight? Why didn't her mother guard her?

From her seat in the library Sherrill could see her cousin circling unsteadily about the room, and each time she came within view Sherrill grew more troubled and fearful. It almost seemed as if she, the guest, were responsible for what her cousin was doing. Finally, when she saw Carol sit down across the large room alone, she made her way to her side and suggested pleasantly that they might both go home now, pleading her own weariness.

But Carol only stared at her vacantly and then broke into a loud mirthless laugh of contempt, finishing with a ribald improvisation whose chorus changed into the old drunken song, "We won't go home till morning."

With burning cheeks, Sherrill retreated to the library and ensconced herself in a big chair near a light with a book. She didn't even notice what the book was.

She sat thus for some time, wondering if the night would ever end, when she heard a voice at her elbow.

"My! Why the seclusion? Am I intruding? Say, you don't look as if you belonged here with this mob!"

"Oh, I don't," she said, standing to her feet in a panic. She laid the book down on the table and looked up to see a tall handsome youth with mocking laughter in his eyes. He was perhaps three or four years older than she was and sophisticated in appearance; yet he seemed sober and respectful, and her fear disappeared.

"You—don't seem to belong, either!" she added, with relief in her voice.

"Oh, but I do!" said the young man. "I very much belong. I'm Barney Fennimore, and this party happens to be in my honor. Not that I care much for this sort of thing, but my aunt does so she gives it. But if you mean I'm not drunk like the rest you're entirely correct. I don't go in for it. Don't care for the bad taste the next day. Besides, I'm in training."

"In training?" asked Sherrill, studying the young man's face.

"In training for flying. Record breaking and that sort of thing, you know. I want to keep what brains I've got steady. Say, you're something like a flower in the desert. So unexpected."

"Well, then perhaps you're a palm tree yourself," Sherrill said, laughing. "You see, I was looking around for an oasis and had started to think there wasn't such a thing."

"Here, let's sit down and talk," said the young man, drawing up a chair. "I'd like to know more about you. I didn't know there were girls like you anymore."

"I'm not so unusual in the town where I live," said Sherrill lightly. "It's a small town, and many of my friends are Christians—that's all."

"Really?" said young Fennimore. "What does that mean exactly? I don't think I've ever seen a real one."

"Why, most of us believe God loves us and forgives us for the things we do wrong. And when we believe in Him, we find peace and purpose in our lives—and happiness too. And because He loves us, we love Him, too."

The young man was looking at her perplexedly.

"Peace? Do you really have peace? And happiness? I didn't think anyone could have either one, not really anyway."

"Oh, yes," she answered quickly, "peace and happiness both! They come from knowing we belong to the Lord Jesus. You see, God loves us so much that He sent His Son Jesus to die for us and take away our sins. Believing that makes a big difference inside me—that's where the peace and happiness come in. And that doesn't depend on earthly things, either."

She looked up at him with a smile so bright on her weary face that he was puzzled.

"Please tell me more," he said wistfully. "This is news. You're sure you're not a spirit? Yet you look healthy like any other girl, flesh and blood, blue taffeta and silver slippers."

Before Sherrill knew it she was telling Barney Fennimore about salvation and faith. Perhaps he was only making fun of her quietly; yet for some reason God had sent her to this party. She hadn't wanted to come. And surely if it was in God's plan for her to be here tonight, then she was glad to share her faith with someone. It seemed a bit odd to her, though, that she was doing so a few feet from the maudlin hilarity in the next room.

"Say, you said something about purpose. I'd guess, from hearing them talk, that most of the people in that room," he said, "feel they have no purpose. I'm glad I have my flying, but maybe if I didn't have that and a few other interests, I might feel the same way. But you said it doesn't depend on 'earthly things.' What does it depend on then? Is it as easy as you make it sound?"

Then she told him that because Jesus died for him he no longer had to carry his own sins or guilt. Jesus had paid the price when He sacrificed His life. And now he, Barney Fennimore, by faith could enjoy a new life in Christ and know that God loved him and was living in him. He had only to believe and receive that gift of resurrection life.

The young man listened in wonder. He had never heard anything like it before—especially not at a party! He watched her face with admiration and respect.

"You're speaking almost in a foreign language to me," he said at last. "I think I'd like to learn the alphabet, though, and find out what it's all about! But say! I'm making you talk and not doing a thing to give you a good time. Can't I get something for you to eat—or drink?" he asked, smiling.

"Not anything, please," she said, a sudden weary look passing over her face. "There's only one thing I want, and I don't suppose that's possible. I'd like to go home, to my uncle's house. Could I get a taxi or something and just slip out and go? I've been on a long trip today and am really tired."

"Sure! I have my own car in the garage, and I'd like nothing better than to get away from this crowd and take you."

"Oh, but this is your party! You mustn't leave! I wouldn't want to do anything rude—"

"Rude? To them?" he said, looking into the other room at the noisy bunch. "You couldn't possibly. Besides, they won't even know I'm gone. I'm not important in their young lives now, except a good excuse for a party! Get your wraps, and I'll be at the door with the car. I'll speak to my aunt and tell her you have to go, and she'll be looking for you when you come down. Don't worry! Everybody else does exactly as he likes, so why shouldn't you? I'm sorry for you to go, of course, but I don't blame you at all, and I'll be glad to miss as much of this rotten stuff as possible."

So Sherrill got away at last and took in the cool, crisp air with relief, as she stepped into Barney Fennimore's expensive car and was whirled away to her uncle's home.

Barney thought of parking his car in some secluded nook overlooking the Hudson and the moonlit palisades and holding Sherrill's hand in his. Almost any other girl he knew would have expected that sort of thing. He would have enjoyed taking her in his arms and kissing her sweet lips. He felt more stirred by her than by any girl he'd met, and many girls would have given a great deal to ride with him and sit in the moonlight, leaning on his shoulder and listening to his tender words.

But something about this girl kept him at his distance. He didn't want to mar his thought of her by any cheap intimacies. She was of another world and seemed to have a shining wall about her.

"I can't tell you how grateful I am for this," Sherrill told him when she reached her uncle's home at last.

"When may I come and see you again?" he asked. "You'll be here for some time?"

"I'm not sure," said Sherrill, suddenly guarded.

"Meaning you hope not if tonight is a sample of what you'll have to endure?"

She laughed. "It's been very pleasant meeting you."

"Then may I come again?"

"Why, I don't know why not."

And so they said good night.

Sherrill was surprised to find that her uncle and aunt hadn't returned, although it was long past midnight. But she felt relieved she didn't have to explain why she had come home before Carol, though that might happen, too, in the morning.

Sleep didn't come immediately. She had a great deal to think over and was too excited to sleep. She began to see that New York life wouldn't be a pink dream of joy. This "chance of a lifetime," as her family had considered the visit, was going to turn out to be more of a testing, she thought, than anything else. Grandma was right. It wouldn't be easy. As far as her limited experience of one evening extended, it would be almost impossible, and she decided then and there that if she ever had a daughter she wouldn't put her in such a position. And yet she believed she had been led to come. *Why?* she wondered. Why had God let everybody insist on her coming? Was she supposed to gain something here? Did He have something for her to do here? If so she didn't want to miss the leading when the time came.

And so at last with a prayer on her lips she fell asleep.

The reckoning came the next morning at about half past eleven, the earliest hour the feminine portion of the family stirred. Sherrill was summoned to court in her aunt's room.

Chapter 17

A unt Eloise was sitting on a chaise lounge in her room, attired in a pink chiffon negligee and surrounded by lace pillows.

Carol sat on the upholstered window seat, leaning against more pillows, sulking. She didn't even look up as her cousin entered. The altercation had begun with Carol's demand for a real Paquin model.

"Before you sit down," said her aunt coldly, "you may go to your room and bring that dress you wore last night. You said it was a Paquin model. I'd like to see that label."

The color mounted in Sherrill's cheeks, and for an instant her eyes flashed, and she was about to refuse. But she finally turned and went for the dress without a word.

"Dear Lord, keep me!" she prayed as she brought back the pretty silk garment. "Keep me from feeling triumphant."

Eloise Washburn looked at the label, and Carol sauntered over and looked too, all the while frowning.

"Well, I'm glad to see you tell the truth at last," she said, tossing the dress aside and letting it fall to the floor in a heap. "But what is this Carol tells me about your behavior last night? I suppose I shouldn't have expected it, but I thought you would know the first principles of decency without being told."

Sherrill picked up the dress, laid it over her arm and stood waiting, but she said nothing.

"Carol said she was nearly embarrassed to death over you. She says you sat out all the dances and were rude to everyone who asked you, then refused to accept the refreshment offered and finally left without a word to anyone."

"Yes, and you forget the worst!" Carol burst forth. "She hogged the host! A stranger just come, and she flung herself at Barney Fennimore so he couldn't get away and talk to the rest of us. I was mortified, and the rest of the girls were furious. And they found out it was *my* cousin who was doing it!"

Sherrill, her face pale, her lips set, gazed from her aunt to her cousin in amazement.

"Well, don't you have anything to say?"

"I don't know what one could say," answered Sherrill quietly, "except that not a word of it is true. If you feel that way about me I think I'd better go home at once." Something in her voice made the Weston Washburns think suddenly of their husband and father, on the rare occasions when he was roused to white anger.

"Oh, now don't get mad!" Aunt Eloise hastened to say. "You must remember I'm answerable to your mother for your behavior, and I'll be obliged to write her what has happened if this isn't understood and made right. Just explain if you can. Of course if there's any reasonable explanation—"

Mrs. Washburn realized her husband would look thoroughly into any sudden flight of the guest, and she had no desire to bring him into the matter.

"I really don't see that I have anything to explain," said Sherrill, in a steady voice. "I sat out most of the dances in a room alone, partly because I was uncomfortable among the people who were there. I was introduced to almost no one present and felt embarrassed by the whole affair. I've never attended a gathering where the young people were intoxicated and found it very distasteful. Their actions were so wild and the conversations I overheard so silly and unfitting that I simply didn't want to be in that room. You may be angry to hear this, but I was mortified to be in a place like that. My mother would be very disappointed to know I was taken there."

Sherrill's eyes were flashing now, and her cheeks were red.

"I certainly did decline liquor," she went on, her head up, her voice firm. "I've never been in a group where it was offered to me. But my cousin is mistaken if she thinks I was rude about it or anything else. I simply said, 'No, thank you.'"

"And you didn't know that was very rude?" said her aunt with uplifted eyebrows. "You didn't know that isn't being done? Well, of course! What can one expect of a girl brought up in the country and by a fanatical mother!"

Sherrill's indignation was growing, especially when her mother was mentioned in this way.

"If you had been there last night, Aunt Eloise, and seen the condition of my cousin, Carol, you would have wished you were a fanatical mother, too. I heard one of the young men say she was 'silly drunk.'"

At once she realized she was saying the very things she had resolved and prayed not to say.

"Indeed!" said her aunt icily. "Of course it's to be expected you'll try to get something on Carol. Fortunately I have sense enough to realize you're exaggerating and speaking out of your ignorance. In this age of the world, my dear, a true lady knows how to carry her liquor without losing her poise as well as a man does. But that's a small matter. What about your rudeness in monopolizing the host of the evening and then in running away without a word?"

"Aunt Eloise, I didn't even know the name of the young man who came into the library where I was sitting quietly alone, until he introduced himself to me. I did nothing to make him come or stay. He asked if he could get anything for me, and I asked him if I could get a taxi to take me home without disturbing the rest. I told him I was very tired and had a bad headache, which was quite true. Then he offered to take me in his car; he called his aunt and made my apologies, and she was very kind about it. I'm sorry if you feel I mortified you, but I'm sure if you knew the facts you would see I did nothing out of the way."

"Oh, of course, if you're going to take that saintly attitude, there's very little I can do for you," said Aunt Eloise. "It's bad enough to be rude and ignorant, but to add egotism and self-satisfaction to the list makes you impossible."

Sherrill set her lips firmly and remained silent.

"I have no more time to argue with you, though. I can see it's useless. You're determined to have your own way as I feared you would be," the aunt said, frowning. "Well, I called you in this morning to advise you of our program for the rest of the day. I'm giving a tea at four-thirty for a friend of mine and her daughter who are going abroad next week, and I'll expect you to be in the receiving line. You can wear the Paquin. None of the same people you saw last night will be there, so it's all right. Carol will explain to you what to do in the receiving line. I don't suppose you've ever been in one before. And then in the evening we have tickets for the symphony orchestra. Carol and I have another engagement, but your uncle thought you might like to go with him. We may be there later, but he always goes so frightfully early, and it bores me to sit through that long program. So you'll have to be ready at eight. The same dress will do, of course, though I would prefer you wear the green I bought for you. Then on Sunday—well, we can see about that later perhaps."

"That will be pleasant, Aunt Eloise," she said simply.

"Now go!" said the aunt, with a sneer. "I'm sick of the whole subject."

Sherrill went at once to her room, struggling to keep back the angry tears and resolving to pack at once and leave before anything else happened.

Locking the door, she knelt beside her bed, the tears streaming down her face. She felt defeated. There could be no peace in this household. Oh, why had she come? Were Mother and Keith and Harriet Masters wrong in thinking she must make this trip? Was she mistaken in thinking God had led her here? And if so, must she go back like a whipped kitten and admit she couldn't stay sweet and happy through the trials?

An hour later she went down to lunch with a serenity she wouldn't have believed possible. Somehow, on her knees, she came to understand she mustn't run away, not yet anyway. She was going to give New York a chance to show her why she had come.

During the luncheon hour a florist's box arrived for Sherrill. Carol looked at her cousin in angry amazement as the maid carried the box around to Sherrill's seat and asked if she could open it.

"There!" exclaimed Carol. "Now I hope you see, Eloise. She certainly must have done some funny business to get flowers from Barney the first day."

But Sherrill had been examining the card the maid brought and looked up with a pleasant smile.

"Don't worry," she said, with a twinkle in her eyes. "They're only from one of the boys at home." She laid the card down on the table where her cousin could read it.

"Alan MacFarlan," Carol read insolently. "Who is he?"

"Oh, just someone I've known all my life. We've been schoolmates."

The maid had opened the box now, and the flowers showed their lovely faces—masses of forget-me-nots and baby's breath.

"Say! He must have plenty of money. They're out of season. I didn't know you could get them anywhere."

"You can get anything, child, for money," said her mother, studying the name on the box.

"Forget-me-nots!" Carol observed. "Love stuff! You would be that way. Mid-Victorian!"

"You might put them on my tea table this afternoon," suggested Aunt Eloise. "Since they're out of season it's a pity to waste them upstairs."

"Why, yes," agreed Sherrill, "I'd like to. I'll take a few upstairs for that pretty vase on my dressing table, and you can use the rest any way you like."

"Is he rich?" asked Carol.

"Oh, not especially," said Sherrill amusedly.

"Is he good-looking?"

"That depends on what your standard is," said Sherrill. "I always felt he was all right."

"Are you engaged to him?" Carol always went to the point.

"Oh, no," said Sherrill, still smiling. That would be one thing she wouldn't tell Alan in the letter she meant to write him that afternoon. But she could tell Mother—or no—perhaps not. Mother might read it to Harriet Masters, and she in turn might think it would be fun to tell Alan—no, she mustn't. Meanwhile her thoughts helped to keep her smiling and not ruffled at the cross-questioning she was enduring.

"You certainly are odd!" her cousin said at last, smothering her cocoa with whipped cream.

Sherrill refrained from giving her opinion of her cousin. As soon as lunch was over she took a handful of the blue-eyed flowers and went upstairs to her room, leaving the expensive out-of-season masses to the general public. But when she saw them again in a crystal bowl on the tea table she smiled tenderly at them as if she felt they understood. They were perhaps doing more for her on the tea table than they could have done on a corsage or in her room, and the blessed thing about it was that Alan would understand. He always understood.

The tea wasn't so bad, Sherrill thought. Some very nice people were there. She had a lovely talk with a sweet white-haired old lady who wore one or two magnificent diamonds and exquisite old lace in the folds of her plain black velvet gown.

Sherrill wore her great-grandmother's rose taffeta and looked charming.

"That's not a Paquin, is it?" asked Carol coldly, before the tea.

"Oh, no, it's a Washburn," answered Sherrill brightly.

"A Washburn? I never heard of him. Is he somebody new?"

Sherrill laughed.

"Very new," she said. "I made it myself, Carol, out of Great-Grandmother's nine-breadth gown from long ago. But I copied it after a model made by Lanvin."

Carol stared. "I don't believe it!"

"If you don't believe it get me some silk, and I'll make one like it for you."

"Are you a dressmaker then? Where did you ever learn?"

"Making doll clothes when I was young," said Sherrill. "I'm not a dressmaker, of course, but I often make my own clothes."

A number of guests entered the room at that moment, interrupting the conversation, but Sherrill caught her cousin studying her gown several times that afternoon. She even heard her telling another girl, "It's a Lanvin—my cousin gets all her clothes abroad."

What an extraordinary world this was! She had a feeling she would be in it a very brief time, however. She longed for home and her dear ones.

By her choice she wore the white velvet to the symphony concert. It seemed to belong with beautiful harmonies, and besides she was going out with her uncle and wanted to look her best. Her uncle was the only one of the family she felt she had anything in common with. Also she still had her doubts about staying very long in New York and wanted to wear it at least once.

Carol and her mother were not in sight when she came down to go with her uncle, so she felt no critical eye upon her. But later in the evening, during the last beautiful number on the program, they rustled in and made quite a disturbance getting settled. Almost at once Sherrill felt their glances turned toward her, and was she imagining it, or did her aunt seem more pleased with her after studying the lines of the white velvet?

Sunday started out very well. Sherrill came down dressed for church, but finding that no one in the family usually rose before noon she went off by herself to find a service and happened, or was guided, to a place where a well-known speaker gave a burning message of truth. She came back refreshed, with her heart throbbing with eagerness, and resolved to bear any unpleasantness, if she might be used somehow.

But the rest of the day was anything but satisfactory. Carol turned on the radio and filled the rooms with loud music whose lyrics were anything but pleasant and uplifting. Many of her friends stopped by, laughing and calling out to one another, telling more of their jokes and making "fresh" remarks, while some stared at Sherrill, before leaving to ride about the city.

The remaining company, an equally rowdy bunch, presently resolved itself into various amusements. At this point Sherrill was planning to steal away to her room, but to her dismay Barney Fennimore arrived to call upon her, and she was forced to remain.

He was there when Carol and her friends returned, and Sherrill felt embarrassed and unhappy, knowing Carol's icy stare and set lips boded no pleasant tomorrow. But Barney was oblivious to it all and pursued the even tenor of his way, chasing his new admiration.

The evening was no better. More people came, with more loud music and games. A young man with long hair and a languid air arrived with a violin under his arm and played some of his new compositions. To Sherrill's trained ear they sounded coarse and jarring, like evil spirits creeping stealthily out into the open. She had never thought music could express anything but the highest and best emotions.

All sense of the Sabbath was lost for her, and she was glad when she could slip away to the quiet of her room. She hoped she might get away before another such day came around.

And then Barney sent her a great box of orchids the next day which didn't improve relations between Carol and her, for Carol resented the attention paid her cousin.

Sherrill wrote a long letter home the next morning describing in detail her uncle's beautiful home, how her aunt and cousin looked, the furnishings of her room, the city of New York in general. But she didn't tell her family what they really wanted to know.

"She's not having a good time," Grandma declared, after the letter was read. "Don't be surprised if we see her back pretty soon. She's all right—that girl is."

"Oh, I hope she doesn't come back yet," said Keith, with a disturbed look. "I'd like her to get all the benefit of this visit. She'll scarcely get another opportunity at such luxury and culture. Why, it *is* quite some chance in a way."

"Well, I'm glad she has the right dresses," sighed Mrs. Washburn. "I suppose that's a mother's pride, but I couldn't stand to see Sherrill patronized."

"Well, there's one thing, Mary," said Harriet Masters, who was listening to the letter. "Only someone who was miserable would attempt to patronize that girl."

Harriet Masters had a letter from Sherrill, too, telling her how her clothes had been received and thanking her again for making it possible for her to appear at ease among these people who seemed to judge others only by their clothes.

While they were talking, Alan came in to see Keith about some tools he had ordered for the store, and the letter had to be read again. Alan had a letter of his own, but he was hesitant to mention it. He might tell Keith later, but right now he wanted to keep the joy of it to himself.

Alan had been hard at work. With Judge Whiteley's help the business was improving. The judge had fixed up the note and helped pay off the mortgage. He had also offered to be a consultant during Mr. MacFarlan's illness and suggested that Alan stop by every evening for a few minutes and discuss any questions or problems from that day.

Alan had eagerly followed this suggestion, and it resulted in a warm friendship between the two, as well as the avoidance of some serious mistakes the inexperienced young man might have made.

He was also busy following up Sherrill's work with the Flats people and had finally won enough friends to organize a weekly Bible study there with a teacher from the city. Some of the young people from the church went over, too, and served lemonade and cake afterward. So the work grew, and Alan reported the progress for Sherrill's approval and suggestions.

Further, Alan was maintaining a correspondence with Bob Lincoln in Egypt. He'd received three letters from Bob, filled with wonder about his new life and with shy questions about the Bible, which, along with the study suggested by the class, he had started to read through from the beginning.

So three weeks passed, and Rockland was beginning to feel Sherrill Washburn's absence—and Alan MacFarlan's influence. Even the other business leaders in the community called him MacFarlan, instead of Mac, or Al, as it had been. And Mrs. MacFarlan looked up one day from the coffee she was pouring and was suddenly struck with the idea that her son was growing up and looked and acted like a man, and she sighed even while she was rejoicing over him.

Alan's father was decidedly better. He was even well enough now to confer with his son for a few minutes each day and approve of the various measures that had been taken.

"I guess I had to get sick so you would put things on their feet for me," he said in his slow pleasant way one day. "I guess I had to find out what a fine son I have. It was the chance of a lifetime for me, son!"

Alan looked up startled and then smiled to think how often that phrase had come to mind lately. He had thought that about the desert trip, and Bob had said it was his chance, and Sherry's family thought her going to New York was the chance of her lifetime. He sighed at that thought. What if it proved to be a chance that would take her away from him forever? Who was that poor fish that had brought her home from that villainous party anyway? Couldn't he do something besides send forget-me-nots?

"Say It With Flowers," an advertisement declared from the pages of the local weekly newspaper. So he went out and said it with Parma violets.

Then, strolling home, he passed her house and saw the old stone barn set way back in the lot next door, with a big elm etched against the evening sky at one end and a group of spruce trees down in one corner near the street. That was an idea! Why hadn't he thought of that before? Sherrill wanted to rebuild that into a house. Well, why not someday? He would see if Henderson would give him an option on it. He could pay a sizeable deposit on it if he used his old car for another year instead of turning it in, and that would give him something to think about and plan for while Sherrill was gone. So Alan went to see Henderson.

And the busy days whirled by.

Chapter 18

Sherrill talked openly, but kindly, with her uncle on the way to the symphony concert that evening. Afterward he must have said something very decided to the rest of the family, for no more was said about parties or such. When an invitation came that Sherrill felt would be out of her sphere she was allowed to stay home.

Of course, Carol was quite jealous of her cousin and was pleased for her to stay at home, rather than having to compete with her winsome personality and attractive clothes.

That Sherrill had landed the catch of the season right off was also a sore trial to young Carol, for Barney Fennimore continued to stop by every day or two and ask for Sherrill. Carol always acted as if he were calling on her and did her best to claim his attention, but she knew in her heart he had come to see her cousin.

A climax was reached one Friday afternoon when Carol and her mother had been out that day shopping and attending social functions. They arrived home in time to see Barney Fennimore leaving, with a serious look on his face. Uncle Weston had been gone that week on a business trip, making it a difficult time for Sherrill.

"I think something must be done about this!" Carol burst forth suddenly. "Eloise, are you going to sit and see my cousin take away my men friends right from under my nose?"

"Really, Sherrill," said Aunt Eloise, giving her niece a withering glance, "for a saint and a novice, you're doing very well. I scarcely anticipated when I invited you here that you would pursue the most inaccessible man in town. I think you scarcely realize his position and his wealth and family. He wouldn't *marry* you, you know. He's just playing. Young men like that play around with a girl without any thought of settling down. He doubtless thinks you have money because you have some clever clothes, but when he finds out, he'll have some excuse—"

Sherrill's cheeks turned crimson, and her eyes flashed. Without stopping to think she turned to her aunt, her hands clenched by her side, her voice trembling.

"Stop! You have no right to talk to me like that! I have never asked that young man to come and see me or encouraged him in any way. I have no desire to marry him or anyone else at present. And if I had I wouldn't have left home to find somebody. I will not let you speak to me that way! I think you are—*disgusting!* Oh!"

Horrified at what she had said, she pressed her hands to her cheeks and dashed out of the room.

"Oh, so the little saint has become a spitfire!" she could hear her aunt saying as she hurried down the hall.

Locking the door Sherrill knelt beside her bed and wept. She had failed. She had lost control of her tongue, humiliated herself and hurt what little opportunity she may have to speak of her faith to any of them. She could never undo what she had said. No one, especially Aunt Eloise, would forgive being called disgusting! Oh, why had she cared so much after all? Their nasty comments were the enemy's way of testing her, and she had failed miserably.

She recalled the words concerning Jesus in His hour of trial: "And He answered not a word." Oh, if she only could have done that! If she had but remembered she wasn't striving against flesh and blood, but against the rulers of the darkness of this world. If she had only thought of the resurrection power inside her, to claim in any trial or temptation, for overcoming the weakness of the flesh.

She knew she must go to her aunt and apologize. She said a quick prayer for strength, stood up, washed her face and walked quietly back to her aunt's door, tapping on it gently.

Sherrill received permission to enter, though she could hear the irritation in her aunt's voice. Opening the door, she stepped softly into the room.

"Aunt Eloise," she said, going straight to the point, "I'm sorry I lost my temper and spoke to you as I did. I suppose you didn't realize how angry it would make me to hear you say what you did, but I was very wrong to let my tongue—"

Her aunt stopped her. "Is this supposed to be an apology? Because if it is you may spare your breath and my time. I never listen to apologies. People never make apologies except to show how much better they think they are than anyone else. Actions speak louder than words. Just let the matter rest. I have my opinion, and you have yours!"

Sherrill stared at her aunt blankly for a moment and then with a quiver of her lip turned and went back to her room. This was the end surely. One couldn't live with a woman who wouldn't even allow an acknowledgment of wrong done. She was impossible!

Sherrill knelt down again and prayed quietly, "Please, Father, let me go home now. I can't stand this any longer."

Then she arose and began to pack. It gave her pleasure to be folding her pretty garments and putting them into her trunk. She had prevailed upon the maid to leave her trunk in the closet and not send it to the trunk room, so now she didn't have to make public what she was doing. She felt that she must get ready before she told anybody she was going, even send her trunk off if possible.

She worked rapidly, carefully, and soon the closet was empty and the trunk almost ready to close. Then she went downstairs.

Maida came from the dining room to gather the mail from the post box, and Sherrill asked her if she knew whether the chauffeur was going down-town that afternoon again. She wanted him to do an errand for her.

"He's just taken the Madam to that tea, but he'll be back soon. He has to take Miss Carol's suitcase to her at the dressmaker's, and perhaps he can do your errand then. I'll leave word with the cook to tell him, and he'll let you know when he comes. I have to pack now for Madam and Miss Carol. They're going to that weekend house party on Long Island. They go for din-ner. You're not going, Madam said?"

The words were a statement, but the tone was a question.

"No," said Sherrill brightly, "I've changed my plans, and—I'm going home. I find I have to."

She passed on into her room, her head up.

The house party! She had forgotten it. The question had been raised, and she had wanted to get out of it, but the hostess was the sweet old white-haired woman in black velvet and old lace whom she had met at her first tea in New York. The invitation had been especially pressing so that her aunt had been insistent. But now it seemed she was going without her. She drew a breath of relief. Just so easily had the way been made plain for her to go home. They would all be out of the way, and she might write a farewell note and take the midnight train. But she must work quickly.

Taking advantage of everyone's temporary absence, Sherrill went to the telephone booth and called up the Pennsylvania Station to inquire out about trains. Then she sent a telegram to her brother: "Taking midnight train from New York. Homesick for you all. Sherrill."

They would wonder and be a little worried, but not much, and they wouldn't have long to worry. Anyway, they would get used to the idea of her return before she had to explain it. It was humiliating to be a failure, of course, but she shouldn't have come at all. That was very plain. She had prayed to be shown the way and why she was here, and nothing had come but more trouble. Now it was good to be going home.

Swiftly she put the last things in her trunk, made sure everything she needed for her trip was left out, packed her overnight bag and was ready when the chauffeur tapped at her door.

"I'm having to leave tonight, Morton," she said pleasantly, slipping a bill into his hand. "I'm wondering if you could find it convenient to look after checking my trunk. Here's my ticket, and it's the midnight train South. Can you reserve a place on the sleeper too?"

Sherrill knew the tip was generous, even for New York, but she wanted ser-vice and had done it intentionally. The man melted and was gracious accord-ingly. In another hour Sherrill received her tickets and checks and saw her trunk depart to the station. She drew a long breath of relief and began to feel thrilled at the thought of being at home in the morning. Home! Dear home! She would never leave it again. It was all the chance in life she wanted.

She had one more errand to run before she left New York, and that was to return a couple of books she had borrowed from the public library on her uncle's card which he had put at her disposal. No one else in the family read books, and she didn't wish to trouble anyone to return them.

The bus at the corner would take her downtown near the library. It was good not to have someone there to question her actions. Her aunt would probably not return from the tea before half past five, and she could be back in her room by that time. Then if her aunt wished to speak with her she would send for her. She didn't wish to go away like a coward, but on the other hand there was no use trying to explain anything to Aunt Eloise. She was impossible!

So Sherrill climbed happily into the bus with a sense of freedom she hadn't had since she'd come to New York. Suddenly she remembered Christmas was almost at hand, and she must get something for the dear ones at home. Christmas at home! A wave of joy swept over her.

She knew what she meant to give each one. She had saved enough from the money Keith had given her for clothes for that purpose. She reviewed the items and decided to stop at the library first and leave the books so she wouldn't have to carry them about the stores. It was late, and she must hurry. She glanced at her watch. Four o'clock! Perhaps she'd better shop first.

During the past three weeks she had looked at the gifts and priced them, and now she went straight to the store and purchased them quickly, then made her way outside into the late afternoon traffic.

Suddenly, there in the Fifth Avenue crowd, appeared the tall attractive form of Barney Fennimore. Sherrill lowered her eyes in hopes of not being seen, but he had noticed her and greeted her with a broad smile and a light in his eyes.

"Do you know—I was just going back to see you? I felt I'd left too soon."

"Oh," said Sherrill, an anxious tone in her voice, "I was on my way to the library. You see—I find—I have to go home!"

"Go home!" echoed the young man. "Oh, no—I don't want you to go home." Sherrill laughed. There was something so genuine and friendly in his tone. "You haven't received bad news, have you?"

"Oh, no, it's all good."

"When do you plan to go?" he asked, frowning.

"Tonight!"

"Tonight?" he said, truly dismayed. "And just when I was getting to know someone like you exists! Well, then, you and I must get busy. May I go with you? And why all these bundles? Where's your car?"

"Oh, I'm walking, and these are gifts for the folks. I'm on my way to return some books to the library."

"Good! That's a much better place than the house with your ever present relatives getting in the way. You haven't answered my question of whether I may go with you, but I'm going anyway so it's all right. I need to talk with you."

Sherrill could only give him a welcoming smile, although she had momentary visions of the Washburn car driving by, with Carol and Aunt Eloise looking out at her.

But she was presently within the sheltering walls of the stately library, and what did it matter anyway? She was going home. No words of malice Aunt Eloise could write would ever turn the dear hearts of home folks against her, and she wouldn't have to bear contempt anymore. Why not be happy?

When she had returned the books, Barney led her to one of the small reading rooms, deserted for the moment, and put her in a chair, sitting down close enough to talk in low tones and yet study her face.

"Now when may I come to see you?"

Sherrill's face flushed pink, but she tried to keep her voice steady and light as she replied. "Oh, are you coming to see me? Why, that will be nice. I'm sure my family and all my friends would enjoy knowing you, but it's a long trip to make a visit."

"Not when the girl is you. I'll be very plain with you. I've fallen for you mighty hard and think we could hit it off well. I don't see why we should waste any time, if you're agreeable. I know we haven't been acquainted long, but what difference does it make if we know what we want? I was just coming back to hunt you up and ask you if you'd marry me. I like to settle matters once I decide."

Sherrill had turned pale, and one hand flew up to her throat and caught the string of pearls she was wearing as if they were a lifeline.

"Oh, don't, please! You mustn't!" she cried.

The joy in his face faded at once. "But why not? Why shouldn't I ask you? I love you with all my heart, and I'm sure there's nothing wrong in telling you so. I hoped you would care for me, too."

"I'm sorry," said Sherrill, alarmed. "I never thought of such a thing. You were only—a pleasant—stranger. I like you, of course, and you've been awfully kind—but you mustn't—you really mustn't!" Nevertheless she wouldn't have been human not to feel a bit of triumph when she remembered her aunt's words.

"But why?" demanded Barney again. "Are you engaged to someone else?"

"Oh, no! Not engaged!" said Sherrill, drawing a long breath and trying to be natural, but still clinging to the pearls.

Barney eyed her intently. "Not engaged, but—there is *someone?*"

Sherrill's eyes said yes, but her lips only trembled into a wan little smile. She pressed her fingers along the pearls, and Barney's eyes followed them.

"Then there is somebody—," he said again slowly, watching her, "and *he* gave you *those pearls!* Am I right?"

Sherrill started, and the pink color flooded her face with a glow.

"Who is he?" asked Barney sadly. "Is he rich? Is he good looking? Would

I stand any chance of cutting him out if I tried?"

"You wouldn't try," said Sherrill. "You're too fine for that!"

"I'm not so sure about that," said the youth under his breath.

"And you couldn't if you did," she finished softly.

"Really?" he said, studying her face. "Is it that far?"

"It isn't far at all," said Sherrill. "We've never talked about such things. We've just been friends since we were little. And, no, he isn't rich, and he doesn't resemble a movie star, but he's wonderful! At least I think so. Of course you're wonderful, too, in quite another way—but—we seem to agree on lots of things—"

"And we don't, you think," finished the young man. "But say—I've decided to go into this thing and try to please you. Wouldn't you like to take me and reform me and make something real out of me?"

"Oh, I couldn't do that," said Sherrill. "Only the Lord Jesus could do that, and if you really wanted to take Him into your life you wouldn't let it depend on whether I was around or not. You would take Him anyway above everything else. And it wouldn't be genuine if you did it to please me."

"So!" said Barney Fennimore, suddenly realizing that here was something he couldn't have and money couldn't buy. Then he drew out of his pocket a small white box and took from it a blue velvet case.

"I want to show you what I bought for you today," he said. "At least I can show it to you."

He opened the case, and gleaming forth was the most beautiful diamond Sherrill had ever seen, set in a hoop of emeralds.

"Oh!" she said tenderly, sadly, as if she had looked upon the death of something sweet and tender.

He watched her a moment, his eager look appearing again, and then a sternness seemed to settle about his features.

"And you won't wear it?"

"I couldn't."

He snapped the case shut and stuffed it in his pocket out of sight.

"You're real!" he said. "You're the dearest thing that ever happened." He took hold of her small hand with his firm, well-kept one and grasped it briefly. "If I had a girl like you I might amount to something."

"You will," said Sherrill. "I hope you'll trust in Christ and His love for you. And then let Him bring the right girl to you—if He will someday. Keep the ring till then and tell her I'm glad for her when she gets it."

He looked at her tenderly and then pulled his hand away from hers with a gesture of finality.

"I will," he promised, "and I won't forget all you've tried to teach me. Perhaps I'll search it out and discover what it all means. I wouldn't expect to get into quite the same heaven with you, of course, but I'd like to be where I could see you sometimes. Say, would you mind if I run down later to see if you're still wearing those pearls?"

"Oh!" said Sherrill, with tears in her voice. "Oh, I'll be glad to see you—and to introduce you—to my friends—but I think—I'm sure, I'll still be—wearing them."

"You sweet child!" said the young man with a sigh and, rising, helped her on with her coat.

It was quite dark when they reached the street, and Sherrill feared she wouldn't get home before her aunt arrived and would have to encounter her in the hall. She didn't want to see her unless she sent for her.

Barney called a taxi, took her to the door and bid her good-bye gravely. They didn't talk much on the way. But his handclasp at the parting was heartening and reassuring.

Once inside the home she was relieved to find that her aunt hadn't returned, but she had scarcely reached her room before she heard the querulous voices of her aunt and cousin hurrying up the stairs. She waited quietly in her room expecting a summons, but presently she heard the sound of their going away again—Morton carrying out bags and suitcases, and Maida hurrying along with wraps. They were leaving without saying a word to her! Had Maida told her mistress that her trunk had gone to the station? Well, whatever they knew she was being punished. She was being left behind like a naughty child with no apology.

But it didn't matter now. It made it easier for her. Of course if her uncle had been at home, matters would not have happened like this. She would write him a nice note and leave it where he would see it, perhaps in his dressing room. She would say she felt she must go, thanking him for his kindness, and never let him suspect how she had been treated in his house.

She sat down at the desk and began to write. But suddenly she thought she heard slow, hesitant steps coming up the stairs a little way and then stopping as if to rest. Her aunt couldn't have returned. It couldn't be the butler, for she had heard him go back to the kitchen. She tiptoed over to the door and opened it a crack to look down the hall, and then she saw her uncle with such a strange look on his face that it frightened her. His face was pale and drawn, and his eyes were like two burning coals. He stared as though dazed, clutching the hand rail, then stumbling on the stairs. Could he be drunk? No, he looked more like one stricken with some terrible illness.

As she stood there he shuffled his way slowly to his dressing room door and opened it. He almost fell as he went in, leaving the door open behind him.

"Uncle Weston!" she cried, staring after him in alarm. "Has something happened? Are you sick? What's wrong?"

Chapter 19

She hurried to his door and saw him lying across his big leather couch as if he had fallen. He must have hit his head against the wall.

"Uncle Weston! You're sick!"

"Yes, sick," he mumbled. "I couldn't think what it was."

"Oh, shall I get someone? Do you want me to send for Aunt Eloise?"

"No, she would be of no use—she hates illness. Call a doctor, child, at once—." He fell back on the couch, as though unconscious.

Sherrill left the room and hastened down the hall to call one of the servants, but to her amazement no one answered the bells. Even the butler had disappeared. With the master and mistress out, they had apparently gone out also or simply didn't care to respond. She rushed to the telephone. She had no knowledge of the family physician, either his name or number. But it was evident there was great immediate need.

She called the operator.

"Call a doctor at once, please—the nearest one to this number. This is an emergency—a very sick man—and I'm a stranger in the city."

She gave the address, hung up and rushed back to her uncle, who was moaning now as if in pain and moving his head from side to side. She laid her hand on his forehead and found it hot to the touch, but he only moaned again and shrank away from her. Then she heard the telephone ring and ran to answer it, praying that help might come quickly.

"This is Dr. Grant, from around the corner. Did you give an emergency call?"

"Yes," said Sherrill, her voice trembling. "My uncle, Mr. Washburn, has come home very sick, and I'm the only one in the house. The servants have all gone out, and I'm a stranger here. Will you come at once? I think he's terribly ill, and I don't know what to do."

The doctor asked one or two questions and then said he would come.

"He's a very sick man," the doctor told Sherrill a short time later. "He's evidently been sick for several days and has a bad case of smallpox. Where's the family?"

"They've gone to a house party on Long Island."

"That's good," said the doctor. "They wouldn't be much help. How long have you been near him? Well, I'm afraid you may be in for quarantine, but we'll try to keep you from taking the disease. Wash your hands with this antiseptic soap, and put those clothes you're wearing out in the sun tomorrow. You'd better stay in another part of the house for a while until the danger is past."

"But I can't leave my uncle alone," said Sherrill, an anxious look on her face.

"Well, if you don't go now you won't be allowed to go, you know. I would send him to the hospital, but I'm afraid it might be fatal. The weather has changed in the last two hours, and it's bitter cold out and sleeting. I wouldn't dare risk moving him now. Besides, it would take time to make arrangements to admit him. Unfortunately, not all hospitals will take a case like this. I can't imagine where he picked it up. No cases have been reported around New York that I know of for some time, at least nothing as bad as this. You say he's been away? Well, call your aunt and find out what she wants done. She'll probably want to come right home and nurse him, but that wouldn't be wise. She has the right to say, though. Of course I'll phone the hospital and try to secure an experienced nurse at once."

Sherrill searched through her aunt's desk and after some difficulty found the invitation with the address and telephone number.

"This is Sherrill—," she began.

"Well, what do you want? You've made enough trouble for one day without interrupting me at a dinner. Don't you know—"

It was Sherrill's turn to interrupt.

"Uncle Weston has come home and is very sick!"

She heard silence at the other end, and then her aunt said impatiently: "Well, I can't do anything about it now. What's the matter with him? What do you suppose I can do at this distance? Tell him to call the doctor."

"I called a doctor, the one around the corner. Uncle Weston is delirious. I couldn't ask him who to call."

"How tiresome! Well, what does the doctor say is the matter?" the aunt asked sharply.

"It's a bad case of the smallpox!"

"What nonsense! I don't believe it. There's no smallpox around. But have him sent to the hospital anyway. Any hospital the doctor suggests will be all right."

"The doctor says he's too sick to be moved. It might be fatal."

"For pity's sake! I never heard of such a thing! They take people to the hospital for everything. Well, I'm sure I don't know what to do. I'm not there. You'll have to do what you can. I suppose they can call a nurse. Of course Carol and I can't come back now if it's really that. But probably they'll find out it's a mistake by morning. Weston always gets sick and thinks he's going to die if he just scratches his fingers. Call Dr. Grayson—he's our doctor. He'll know what to do. I'll call up in the morning and find out what you've done. Meanwhile, do not under any circumstance let the contagion spread through the house. Tell the servants to close the rooms downstairs and keep everyone out. This certainly is tiresome! I can't think how it happened. Smallpox! How horrid! It seems so plebeian. Weston should be ashamed to come home with such an illness."

Sherrill hung up the receiver and turned away, feeling nothing but disgust for her aunt and fear for her uncle. Her own plans must be laid aside now. She couldn't go to her dear home, and her trunk was on its way already. She was glad at least that her beautiful clothes had escaped the germs and wouldn't have to go through fumigation. Oh, why hadn't she left a few hours earlier?

Her conscience stirred. Who would have cared for her uncle? Who would have sent for a doctor and notified the family?

All at once Sherrill knew why she had been sent to New York. This then was the opportunity, the "chance of a lifetime," they had talked about. Well, if it was the chance God had planned for her, then He had something for her to do here for Him, and she mustn't complain.

With new resignation she walked upstairs and talked with the doctor. Then she went to her room and took off her dress, hanging it in the open window. She took off her shoes and put on Pullman slippers, donned the Pullman cap Grandmother had made to wear in the sleeper and, pausing briefly, pulled out the china silk kimono from her overnight bag and slipped it on. It was light and would wash easily and was better than a heavy dress.

Then she went down to the kitchen and hunted out a maid's apron. Back upstairs she presented herself at the door of the sick room.

"Now what shall I do? I can obey orders," she said firmly.

The doctor was a quiet man who possessed a genius for healing and worked hard to make a living. He had done his best to reach Dr. Grayson, the great favorite of the wealthy, but was told Grayson was up in Canada "shooting things for his health" and would not return for a month. Whereupon he turned his attention to securing a nurse, two if possible; but it appeared there was a sudden shortage of nurses for contagious diseases. No one would be free until sometime the next day, possibly not until evening.

"You're just a child!" said the doctor, turning in despair from the telephone. "I can't leave you here, even to go out and look for someone."

"Tell me what to do," Sherrill told him, smiling, "and don't waste time worrying about me."

So at last the doctor decided to go out and try to find a nurse. He thought the servants would return sometime that night and told her to warn them to come up the back stairs and observe certain precautions used in quarantine.

"You're a brave girl," he said, unbending from his brusque manner. "Aren't you afraid?"

"No," said Sherrill, "I'll be all right. It must be what I was sent here for."

He went away wondering what she meant and determined to relieve her duty as soon as possible.

The servants didn't return that night. They had evidently gone away for the weekend also. So Sherrill sat alone in the great house, with the many strange noises that step abroad in the silence of midnight. She listened to her uncle's moans and his muttered words, and it filled her with a deep longing for him to know the Lord and have peace and rest in his heart. While she waited, administering the medicine as the doctor had directed, she prayed.

Once in the night she realized she hadn't eaten anything in a long time, so after washing her hands very carefully in antiseptics, she went downstairs and found some bread and sliced turkey for a sandwich. She was pouring a glass of milk when she remembered her telegram to Keith. She knew they would be alarmed if she didn't arrive in the morning, so she called Western Union.

Unavoidably delayed. Don't worry. Will wire later. Please get trunk, check no 1021365; started on midnight train.

The doctor called up a short time later to ask how things were going and report that he hadn't found a nurse yet but thought he would soon. The night wore on, the longest night of Sherrill Washburn's life, and morning dawned at last, creeping in at the windows, throwing long gray shadows on the sick man's face.

The doctor came presently and took her place beside the patient, ordering her to lie down, and blessed sleep enveloped the girl for a time. But she was too young and too anxious to sleep long and returned after only an hour. And thus began another day.

Sherrill knew her family would have been alarmed by her nonappearance and more so by her telegram, and after talking with the doctor she decided to give them a more complete account of her uncle's sickness and the situation.

Uncle Weston has the smallpox. He's very sick. Am under quarantine. Cannot get away at present. Doctor is watching out for me and says you needn't be alarmed. Don't worry. I'm all right, only disappointed, but I guess this is why I had to come. Can't write at present but will telegraph any change. Pray for Uncle Weston.

> *Lovingly,*
> *Sherrill*

Two hours later the telephone rang. Keith called long distance from the store, to find out the whole story and not worry the others. Sherrill laughed for sheer relief to hear his dear voice. Grandmother called up while her daughter was out shopping for groceries and told Sherrill she might tell her everything and she would keep it to herself. Sherrill laughed again and told Grandmother all the funny things she could think of but gave no hint she was still the head nurse.

Mother called up shortly after she arrived home so Grandmother wouldn't hear her and said precious things as mothers can and gave encouragement she didn't feel herself. She made Sherrill promise she would take care of herself, run no risks and wire at once or phone if she felt the least bit sick—and all the other things mothers make you promise at times of great distress.

Then Alan called up, made her laugh and cry, and found out the truth, the whole truth and nothing but the truth about the case.

"Well, I knew you would. It's like you. Sure I'll pray—I have been already. And I won't let on. But if you don't have a real nurse before tomorrow night, I'm coming, see? I may be inexperienced, but I can take orders, and I don't want you sick. I can get someone to take my place in the store if you need me."

Somehow the day went easier after that, and by night the nurse had arrived, a capable experienced elderly woman who had had the smallpox and bore its marks on her face. But she was motherly and knew her business and sent Sherrill to bed at once.

Sherrill called Alan first, however, and told him the news.

Monday morning the servants returned, stealthily, as if they'd never left. But when they saw the sign on the door and heard the news Sherrill called out to them down the back stairs, they slipped into their rooms, claimed their worldly goods and threw them out a window. Then, gathering them up below, they left, without a word of concern or offer to help the weary girl who stood at the top of the stairs and watched them depart.

Then Sherrill set to work in earnest and planned out a daily routine, for now she had a house to manage and meals to prepare.

She prayed much in those days, as the sick man lay between life and death, hour after hour, and besought God to save him and restore him to health. Then after long days of waiting he began to improve, and at last the doctor told her he would recover.

Telegrams were common in those days, flying back and forth between New York and home. Alan used long distance almost every night. It was a great comfort to Sherrill in her exile to talk with him a few minutes before she slept. Christmas came, and the telephone was her only celebration—except the flowers Alan sent, a box of delicious food from Mother and a check from Keith. But at last the day came when Uncle Weston was so much better he wanted Sherrill to read to him.

She sat behind an antiseptic curtain the nurse had hung and read snatches from books or short articles from the newspaper. Finally she ventured to read a story from the Bible and then a psalm every night, and he seemed to like it. At such times she began to see the chance that had been given her to reach this dear member of her father's family with the Word of God.

Then one day her uncle asked about the Scriptures she had been reading, and she had an opportunity to make plain the way of salvation to him.

He lay a long time thinking after she had stopped talking. At last he said, "Little girl, you've been wonderful to your old uncle. You've stuck by me and saved my life. I can never repay you—"

"I don't want pay, dear Uncle Weston," she said eagerly.

"No, I know you don't," said the uncle. "That's the best of all. Little girl, you've made me see what Jesus Christ is. I never believed much before in the Bible or religion, but now I've seen Him in a human life. And if it means anything to you, I want you to know you've brought me to a place where I know I need Jesus, your Jesus, and I want to serve Him the rest of my days."

Wasn't that reason enough for Sherrill to rejoice? Hadn't she seen at last why she had to go to New York and experience the hard things? Oh, God was great!

Uncle Weston was well enough to walk about his room now and read to himself and take part in planning again. And finally the doctor signed her release, gave her a clean bill of health, took the quarantine sign off the door and sent Sherrill home.

With a heart full of joy she gathered up her few belongings. Scarcely anything was left but her letters, several plain garments they'd sent her through the mail and a few dried rosebuds from the multitudes Alan had sent her almost daily.

Aunt Eloise and Carol were wintering in Florida, and her aunt called by long distance, sweetly, almost every day to know how things were going. She was negotiating plans to sell the Riverside house and live abroad for a time, as soon as the husband and father was well enough to leave. Aunt Eloise said she could never enter "that pestilential house" again. Smallpox was so devastating to a complexion. Besides, Carol was growing up and needed foreign advantages.

"You will pray for your old uncle, little girl?" said Weston Washburn, with a tired look on his face. "You know it won't be easy for me to keep steady under fire. Pray that I won't fail. Pray for my wife. I know she's been hard on you, child, but pray for her. She needs it. And don't forget your old uncle needs you. Good-bye, little nurse—my precious missionary!"

And with these words ringing in her ears Sherrill went home. Back to the dear hometown and the dear home folks. Back to new opportunities and new understandings—back from the chance of her lifetime.

The first evening Sherrill spent at home Alan came to dinner. After they had listened to stories of her visit, often softened to hide some of the hardest places, the family soon slipped out of the room on one excuse or another and left Alan and Sherrill alone.

"There's no such thing as the chance of a lifetime, Alan," Sherrill said, lifting her eyes to his. "Every opportunity is the great chance, and the only thing is to find out where God is leading."

"You're right," said the young man, looking into her eyes. "I've been learning that all winter. If through nothing else, Bob's letters would have been enough. You should see how he's changed and grown. He loves the Bible. He seems to devour it every chance he has. And now that he's in Egypt he's hunting up things that prove the Bible stories. I've never seen anything like it. You must read his letters."

"I heard a little about it this afternoon from Lancey Kennedy. Did you know he's been writing to her? I didn't know they were friends, did you? But she came over this afternoon for a few minutes and told me about it. She said he told her how he found Christ and that he wished she would give herself to Him too. So she came to me to find out what to do. She was so eager—ready to kneel down right there and pray. Why, it choked me all up so I could hardly pray with her. It was so wonderful! And do you know, Alan, if you had gone to Egypt, maybe none of these things would have happened. Maybe Bob would have taken a worse turn in life, and Lancey would never have wanted to find the Lord Jesus. So you really were offered the chance of a lifetime in that telegram, don't you see?"

"I sure do!" answered Alan heartily. "The biggest chance I could have asked for. And there are other things, too, not as important, but still worthwhile, connected with Dad's business. I'll tell you later, though. But there's something else, Sherrill—"

Alan stood up and came and sat beside her on the couch.

"Sherry—," he began and then reached out and clasped her small hand in his. "Sherry, I want to tell you something. I love you, you know—I've always loved you—for that matter, but this is different—"

Sherrill looked up, half frightened, but he hurried on.

"Sherry, you didn't pull off any of those grand marriages or engagements your aunt suggested, did you—not yet?"

He waited breathlessly for an answer, and Sherrill's eyes had a hint of mischief in them.

"Not yet!" she said, laughing.

"Well, then, Sherry, may we—do you—that is, can I—?" He plunged his free hand into his pocket and brought out something bright and thrust it forward. It was a ring with a large pearl in a quaint setting.

"Will you wear this for me? I told your mother and Keith about it, and they thought it was wonderful. I wouldn't have dared ask you so soon, but I saw you still wore my pearls, and I hoped. Will you? I love you, Sherry, and I've missed you so much."

Sherrill held out her hand quietly and let him place the ring on her finger. He drew her close and set his lips reverently upon hers.

"Oh, Sherry, my darling!"

"You know we're only kids yet!" Sherrill reminded him, laughing, with her head resting against his shoulder. "You said so yourself only three months ago."

"Yes, that's the wonderful part of it! If God wills, there'll be more time ahead for us together. But, Sherry, dear, it's not half so bad as it sounds. Dad has sold a lot of land he thought was worthless and insists on my having the whole proceeds. He says it's my bonus for staying home from Egypt and pulling the business out of a hole while he was sick. Yes, he found out about it. Judge Whiteley told him. Well, it's a good sum, and Sherry, I—we can start as soon as you say. Dad's made me a partner. Isn't that great! That is, we'll wait till your mother feels we've had a long enough engagement, of course—"

"Oh, Alan, I didn't know anything could be so sweet. And God had this waiting for me all the while I thought I was having a hard time. That and what He let me do in reading to my uncle. Oh, I must tell you about that, too. There's so much to tell."

"Yes, but I have something else, too. I bought the old barn, and if you still think you'd like to rebuild it into a house, why, you can begin on your plans tomorrow. Dad says we can fix a way to finance it, and he's willing. Then I wouldn't have to take you far away from your family, and it wouldn't be so hard for them all. I had a chance to buy the lot cheap, and I thought it was a wonderful chance—that is, if you like it, darling."

Sherrill's eyes were shining.

"How good God's way is when we trust everything to Him. Oh, I'm so happy! All my dearest dreams are coming true!"

Mary Washburn stepped to the door to offer some late refreshment in the way of cake and lemonade, but she changed her mind and concluded she would leave her tray on the dining room table. The two seemed to need no other refreshment than one another's presence. It was a moment that would never quite come to them again, this first time of understanding between them.

So she smiled and slipped away, murmuring, "And we thought going to New York was the chance of a lifetime for her, and here God had her joy planned close by, for her and for us all. The chance of a lifetime! There is no such thing as chance."

Under
the Window

The little bronze clock on the shelf over the fireplace chimed out seven and then took up its next hour's work of counting out the seconds to the sleeping cat on the hearth.

The room was all alone and very still having a quiet time by itself. The fire winked and blinked at the lamp, and the lamp beamed brightly back from under its homemade shade of rose-colored tissue paper and cardboard. The carpet, a neat ingrain, looked as if it knew its place and what was expected of it—to look prettier than it was, to wear long and not show dirt—and it would not presume upon its privileges, even when the mistress was out. The sofa was deep and comfortable, made of a dry-goods box, with a wide board nailed on for a back, and the whole deftly padded and covered with an old crimson shawl, with fringes too shabby to be used any longer as an outside wrap.

There were curtains too, but you wouldn't have had them in your room. They were nothing but cheesecloth with rows of threads pulled back and tied. But they were cheap and gave a pretty air of grace and homeliness to the room. Broad yellow satin ribbons held them back from the windows. To be sure, the ribbons were only old pink ones, washed and dyed with diamond dye. But they were yellow and added a dainty touch to the plainness of other things.

A small table with a red cover held the lamp. Beside it stood two wooden chairs, with a little rocker covered with cretonne and a stool near the hearth. Above the table was a little shelf with a Bible and a few other books.

The only elegant things in the room were the bronze clock and two delicate vases of Parian marble. But these were presents from former pupils of the mistress and, as such, occupied the place of honor—the broad shelf over the wide, old-fashioned fireplace. But they seemed to have made friends with the ingrain carpet, the homemade sofa and the cheesecloth curtains and to feel as much at home with the yellow ribbons as though the latter had been real and new, not old and dyed. A few pictures and bright cards smiled down from the walls—and the room kept still and waited, all alone.

Now and again the white cat stirred in his sleep and opened one eye up at the clock, as though he had just heard it strike those seven clear strokes. Pushing his forepaws slowly, tremblingly forward, in the luxury of a stretch, he opened his mouth to the utmost extent, then turned over to cuddle down again, one paw over his nose and a contented smile on his pink cat mouth.

The room had two windows, one looking out on the little strip of ground between the house and the street, the other opening to a sort of lane or alley. The lane window was down several inches from the top, for the mistress had ideas on ventilation. The wind came in and stirred the curtains, even waving the least mite of white fur on the end of the cat's tail. But the cat was used to drafts and didn't mind. He only gave his ear a little nervous jerk, as if he imagined it to be summer and a fly were biting him.

He knew better, of course, if he had only stopped to think, for here blazed the fire, and outside the snow was blowing, and the breath of air that had touched his tail was decidedly cold. There were other reasons too. His mistress hadn't taken that pile of books and started off to school for three whole days. By that he knew it was the winter vacation. Then hadn't old Mr. and Mrs. Updike, from whom he and his mistress rented their rooms, left that very morning to spend the holidays with their daughter Hester? The cat and his mistress were alone in the house, except for Peter Kelly, who was probably at that moment sitting in his room over the kitchen, his chair tilted back against the wall, and looking straight at the sputtering flame of his candle.

And why didn't his mistress go away to spend the holidays and not stay during the happy Christmastide shut up in her little room with her cat? Well, in the first place, she couldn't afford to go away. She was just a poor schoolteacher, with a small salary, barely enough to support herself and her cat—for a cat she would have, she said, if she had to go without something herself. Second, she couldn't leave her cat. Who would take care of it? Not Mrs. Updike, for she hated cats. Besides, she wasn't at home. Third, she had nowhere to go and so stayed at home. She had told the white cat only a few days ago that she was all alone in the world and had dropped a bright tear on his pink ear, and he had twitched his head in surprise. She was no worse off in that respect than he was, and he was contented. He saw no further need for anyone in the world besides himself and her, except, perhaps, the milkman.

But at that moment the front door opened and closed with a bang. He heard the sound of stamping and brushing in the hall. Then the mistress entered, and the room seemed to smile and brighten to receive her. Bright brown eyes, golden brown hair, straight nose, cheeks glowing with the cold and exercise, straight eyebrows and small brown hands—that was Polly Bronson. She wore a dark-blue flannel dress, a black jersey coat, black mittens and a little black crocheted cap with balls on the top. The snowflakes glistened over all. She shook them lightly off, laid her parcels on the table and went to hang up her things in the small bedroom adjoining. Coming back, she seated herself on the little stool and proceeded to poke the fire, making it blaze up brightly.

"Come here, Abbott," she said merrily, "while I tell you the news."

The cat arose slowly, humped his back up high, curled his tail into an impossible position, stuck out each particular hair of his white coat, until he looked like a porcupine, and yawned. Then he closed one eye and went and rubbed his head sideways against Polly's foot.

"Oh, you lazy Abbott, wake up!" cried Polly, as she caught him in her arms and shook him gently.

"Listen, Abbott! I've something nice to tell you. Tomorrow is Christmas, you know."

Abbott winked gravely. Polly was in the habit of telling her plans to him, and he was a good listener, always agreeing with her.

"Well, now, if you and I were rich, Abbott, we would give each other presents, beautiful presents. People do that at Christmas—did you know?"

The cat looked inquiringly at her with his bright green eyes. Polly's face was a picture of mock gravity as she said, "I wish I had a present to give you, my poor little cat, but I'm so sorry I have none." The cat looked disappointed. "But you shall have an extra saucer of milk tomorrow for breakfast." The cat brightened. "And, Abbott, we'll have a party, you and I, and we'll invite Susie and Mamie Bryce and Joey Wilkes and little Sam. They're poor children, Abbott, without any Christmas at all. And you must be a good cat and play with them and not go to sleep on the hearth for the whole evening."

Abbott uttered a feeble "Meow!" as protest.

But Polly went on: "We can't have turkey; it costs too much. Abbott, did you know they always have turkey on Christmas? Yes, and cranberries, but you wouldn't like those; they're sour. We'll have baked beans—they're cheap, you know, and you like them—and an Indian pudding, baked nice and brown, with plenty of big, fat raisins in it. And, Abbott, some oysters! Yes, really, just once. They won't cost much, and you shall have two all to yourself, perhaps three!"

Abbott purred contentedly and settled himself in her lap for another nap. But a gust of air from the window sent Polly in haste to close the forgotten shutters, and the cat concluded it was best to go back to the hearth.

Just as those seven strokes had sounded from Polly's bronze clock, a young man stood on the snowy pavement not many blocks away, hands in his pockets, wondering how he could spend Christmas Eve. He was all alone in the city, too, without even a cat to cheer him. He had acquaintances, of course—a few—but what were they on Christmas Eve? Some were out of town, and some were in their homes at their own merrymakings, to which they hadn't even thought to invite him. He told himself he wouldn't have gone if they had, and he ground his heels into the hard snow and thought of his mother's cheerful kitchen, with its wide old fireplace and pleasant Christmas odors, the dear father and mother and brother and little sister, even the cat who blinkingly thought over her vanished youth, gazing into the glowing fire. How their faces would brighten if he could walk in upon them now! Indeed, he must stop such thoughts as these. He told himself he wasn't a child, to expect always to be at home for Christmas and to hang up his stocking.

But it was cold, and he couldn't stand there much longer. Should he go back to his office? No. He had endured that as long as he could for that evening. John Brewer and his smiling wife, who rented the room just behind his, were having a little tea-drinking, and the peals of merry laughter which issued from there every few minutes didn't make the young man feel less lonely. He dismissed as quickly the idea that he should go to his dingy little room in the grim boardinghouse on High Street.

He decided he would call on the gentleman who had left his card that day at the office, with the message that he had some important business matters to talk over with him at his earliest convenience. This would be as good a time as any to call, and the gentleman would likely be in his room, as he was a stranger in town. He turned and walked down the little alley, the nearest road to Park Avenue, the Grand Hotel and the stranger.

Halfway down the alley he discovered he couldn't recall the man's name, for he had only glanced at the card hastily as it lay on his table. He fumbled in his pocket for it, so he might consult it at the next lamppost. But a nearer opportunity offered itself in the shape of Polly Bronson's bright little side window, and he stepped up to it as Polly entered with her bundles. He had just found the right card when he heard the cheery voice calling: "Abbott, come here!"

Of course he looked up, and of course, having seen and heard so much, it wasn't in the nature of a lonely man to tramp off hastily to make a business call on a stranger. He saw in that fireplace a little of the home cheer of his mother's hearth. He saw in the white cat's face something of the thoughtfulness of the home cat. He saw in the young girl—well, I'm not sure what he saw in her; you'll have to ask him. She was just Polly, you know—something new and bright and beautiful.

Yes, he stood and watched the pretty tableau enacted before him. He let his eyes rove around the little room, and he called it pretty! He didn't know the curtains were cheesecloth and the ribbons dyed. He heard every word Polly said, too—for you remember the window was down from the top— from the presents down to the Indian pudding and the oysters, and wished with all his heart that he was poor little Sam or somebody who could be invited to that party. Listening? He never thought of such a thing. Indeed, he didn't think of anything but the interesting picture and the story that had unfolded before his eyes.

He did recover his sense sufficiently to remember he wasn't invisible when Polly came toward the window, and he stepped back into the shadow. There was a sort of blank when the shutters were closed and the cheery room was shut from his view. He didn't feel in the least like making that call now. It was scarcely five minutes, and yet he felt he had some new friends in the city. He had a feeling of pity for the lonely girl and so, in thinking of others, lost sight of his own loneliness.

He soon discovered he was standing in a snow bank. Stamping himself out of it, he made his way mechanically to the Grand Hotel, thinking, meanwhile, of what he had seen, reading between the lines of the bit of a story he had been allowed to hear. He was relieved to find that the gentleman he was searching for wasn't in, and he went home with a pleasant little plan taking shape in his brain. It was too bad the girl shouldn't have any Christmas present, he thought. What if he should send her one himself? It didn't seem exactly the right thing, to send an anonymous present to a young lady who had never seen him. But there certainly could be no harm in sending one to the cat. No one ever heard of any harm in that.

Early on Christmas morning, when few in the city were stirring, with only the milk wagon or the baker's cart rattling over frosty stones of the street, and now and then a sleepy clerk taking down shutters and opening doors, he was walking with a brisk step toward a flower store kept by a little old woman from whom he had once or twice bought flowers to send to his mother. He bought a wealth of roses this morning—great yellow Maréchal Niels, delicate Safranas only halfway open and buds of Bon Silines with their wonderful perfume. Then he selected a satin ribbon of faint green tinge for the old woman to fasten them together with, and the whole was put in the prettiest white basket, well wrapped in cotton and white tissue paper, and a card fastened to the handle: "For my friend Abbott, a very Merry Christmas."

Then the young man walked with a smiling face and calmly deposited the basket on Mr. Samuel Updike's front doorstep and retreated, wishing much that he dared remain and watch the outcome. Polly, who was allowing herself nice long holiday sleeps, slept on with one brown hand under a rosy cheek and never dreamed something was on her doorstep that would fill her with delight and wonder all day and for many days after. But Abbott must have heard a noise; for he shivered a little, opened one eye at the dying fire, wondered why his mistress didn't get up, then rolled to the edge of the rug nearest the fire and went to sleep again.

Polly did wake up by and by, made up the fire and got breakfast. After breakfast Abbott sat on the hearth licking his whiskers and washing his paws, thinking how very nice it was to have an extra saucer of milk, while Polly brushed up the room, opened the windows and stood the hall door and the front door wide open. There was the basket! Polly's exclamation brought Abbott to the door. He thought it must be another milkman, and he always went to meet the milkman, unless it rained. He sniffed around the basket and looked as curious as his mistress while she read the card aloud.

"Why, Abbott! It's a Christmas present for you! But who sent it? And what is it? Where did you get a friend I don't know about? It certainly isn't Mr. and Mrs. Updike or Peter Kelly or the milkman, and I'm sure I don't know who else knows you. Oh, Abbott, I wish you could talk!"

Abbott tried to let her know by eyes and ears, as well as a cat can, that if he could talk he could give her no information on the subject.

"Let's open it, Abbott."

Thereupon the cat and the basket were transferred to the sofa. Amid many exclamations the roses came to light, filling the little room with their elegant fragrance. Polly caught the cat up and kissed the tip of his pink ear. It was dreadful, I know. But then Polly was very happy, and she had no one else to kiss.

"You dear cat! You shall invite your friend to the party, so you shall, if you will give the invitation."

Perhaps Abbott understood, for he went to the door and sat looking out. Presently he walked down the steps and over the snowy path, putting each paw down carefully, lest it might get too much mixed with the snow. When he reached the gate he gave one spring to the top of the gatepost and paused a moment, looking up and down the street, and then, seeming to decide which way to go, sprang down and trotted off as though he had business that would require haste.

Polly talked to everything that morning while she worked. She called to Abbott at the door that he should wear the green ribbon to the party, and he looked back and winked assent as he put the first velvet paw into the snow. She told the vases they were dear, beautiful things, and she was glad at last they had something to hold, and she hoped they would keep them very carefully a long time. Polly worked fast and was soon ready to go out to do her marketing and give her invitations. She decided to have her party at night, because Mamie Bryce had to go down on Sycamore Street and take care of Mrs. Dobell's baby, while Mrs. Dobell went to a dinner party, and she couldn't get back until four o'clock. So Polly told them all to come at five, and their eyes shone brightly as they promised.

It was beginning to grow dark. Little flurries of snow filled the air. The young man—Porter Mason was his name—hurried along the street, hands in his pockets, collar turned up and hat drawn over his eyes. He had been off to the other end of the city on some good errand or other. He was cold and tired and hungry, and it was still a long walk home. He was wondering if he dared venture around to that alley again when it grew quite dark, if the window blinds would be open, if he would see the roses anywhere and if the party would be over. In a lull between the chime of sleigh bells came a faint "Meow!" and he looked sharply around. The "Meow-ow-ow-ow!" came more distinctly now, and soon just ahead of him he spied a weary white form moving dejectedly through the fast-falling snow. He stooped and picked it up, brushing the snow off and holding it up to the light of a nearby street lamp.

"I believe you are the very cat!" he said, speaking aloud. "But how in the world did you get here? Is your name Abbott?"

"Meow!" said the cat.

"All right, then, you're my friend. Jump right in here and make yourself comfortable." He opened his big overcoat and tucked the cat snugly in. "I shouldn't wonder if I had my invitation, after all," he told himself as he went on briskly.

Within Polly Bronson's cheery room all was not as serene as it might have been. The little party had assembled. They were sitting on the edges of their chairs, undergoing the first embarrassment of arrival, but a shadow besides embarrassment hung over them. Two of them were missing. The one was the guest little Sam, and the other was the host himself, Abbott. Sam couldn't come, because his father was too drunk to carry him, and the streets were too slippery to trust him with his little crutch. His mother would have brought him, for it was his first bit of pleasure for many days. But she, poor soul, was on her back, scarcely able to wait upon herself. Nobody knew what had become of Abbott.

That was the way matters stood when Porter Mason rang the bell of the Updike house, which so startled Susie and Mamie Bryce and Joey Wilkes that they all huddled together on one chair, like so many frightened peas in a pan when the pan is suddenly tipped up. Mr. Mason had gone straight to the lane side window and found the shutters closed. Now what should he do? Would it be safe to risk a peep in at the front window? Suppose the real Abbott were inside, snug and warm by the fire? How foolish he would feel appearing at the door of a strange young lady, in the dark of a snowy night, and saying, "Have you lost a cat, madam?" without giving a reason for supposing she had a cat.

He stood in the snowbank again and thought, while kitty purred under his warm coat. He might say he had once, when passing, seen a cat there. It wasn't in the least likely that the young lady would question him as to the circumstances under which he had seen the cat, and she would in all probability suppose him to have seen it on the doorstep. He concluded to risk this statement and so boldly rang the bell.

Polly hurried to the door. She wasn't in the habit of having evening callers. The door, being opened, let in such a whirlwind of snowflakes that Polly could distinguish nothing in the gathering darkness except the tall form of a man powdered with snow from head to foot.

He was taking off his hat and saying in a pleasant voice, "Have you lost a cat?" As he said it he cast an anxious glance through the half-open door to the glowing fireplace and was relieved to see no cat there.

"Oh, yes!" Her senses had come back to her. "Won't you come in? Do you know where he is?"

"I found one on the street, and, remembering seeing one at this house, I brought it here."

He was unbuttoning his coat now and handed Abbott, warm and somewhat damp, to his mistress.

"Oh, thank you!" she said, taking him eagerly in her arms. "I'm so glad to get him back! I was troubled about him when it began to snow so hard. I was afraid he was lost."

She paused and looked up. Abbott's rescuer looked very cold and blue as he stood there in the chilly hall. Perhaps he had come out of his way to bring the cat, she thought.

He had a chilly feeling in his heart, too. He began to think it was time he should say, "You're quite welcome. Good evening," and bow himself out and go to his cold, dingy room. He seemed to see the supper to which he would presently be called, remnants of the departed dinner.

He glanced again into the cheery room and was about to bow his good evening, when Polly's voice interrupted—"Won't you come in to the fire and get warm? You must be very cold."

Polly never thought of being afraid to ask a stranger in. She was never afraid of anything. She was twenty-two and had taken care of herself for nearly five years, and she felt as if nothing in the world could harm her. Then the children were there, and she had a secure sense of Peter Kelly in his back chamber over the kitchen. Besides, hadn't this stranger done her a kindness, and didn't she owe him something? And he had kind eyes and a gentle hand with the cat. There are reasons enough when a bright girl does anything.

But she was surprised when, instead of saying, "No, thank you," he hesitated and said, "May I?"

Polly, with glowing cheeks, ushered her caller into the bright room and seated him in the rocking chair, hardly knowing what to make of him or what to do with him when she got him there. But the children helped her with their gleeful exclamations over the lost and found cat. Abbott, however, slipped from their caressing hands and retired to the hearth to bathe. He was a neat cat and didn't like to appear before company with his white coat stiff and rough.

"Where did you say you found him?" questioned Polly.

Mr. Mason didn't say but launched into a full description of Abbott's pitiful cries and forlorn appearance, until the question was forgotten in a merry round of laughter, in which Polly joined, in spite of herself, although she had determined to be very dignified.

"Oh!" cried Susie, when the laughter had somewhat subsided. "Wouldn't we be having a lovely time if Sam were only here."

"Yes," said Mamie, the laughter all sobered out of her face. "He stood at the top of the stairs and cried and cried when we came down."

And even stout little Joey Wilkes said it was "just too awful mean for anything."

"And who is Sam?" asked the strange visitor, as soon as he had any chance to speak.

The children burst into a full explanation of the case, all at once of course, and it was some time before he could understand. Even then he was left in doubt as to whether more sorrow had been felt for Abbott or for Sam with his drunken father.

He arose at last and turned to Polly, "Having brought back one of the missing guests, I think I should complete my good work and bring the other. It would be a pity to have this perfect party spoiled by the shadow of an absent guest. Can you direct me to where I can find this boy?"

He buttoned up his coat, and the children danced for joy and clapped their hands, crying, "Goody, goody!"

Polly's face was beaming with pleased surprise. But she tried to draw up her slipping cloak of dignity and say, "Oh, no! You really mustn't go to that trouble for us tonight. It's so stormy out."

Mr. Mason, however, would listen to no such talk and obtained the desired information. He turned to go, then stopped, fumbling in his pockets. But since he couldn't find a card, he produced a bit of folded pasteboard, saying, "I have no card with me, but will this do as well? My name is the fourth one on the list of leaders, and when I come back we'll get Sam to introduce us."

The well-known letters "Y.P.S.C.E." met her eyes from the cover of the card and below, "Hartford Square Church." A little smile played over her face. She needn't be quite so careful now that she knew so much about him. Turning to the next page, she ran over the list of leaders and their subjects, especially the fourth one. She laid the card on the shelf and went back to her oil stove. The pudding was taking on the last delicate shades of brown and needed watching. She set her table, putting one more plate on. She supposed, she told herself, that the young man must be invited to supper, after he'd taken so much trouble for them. Then she thought of Peter Kelly.

Now Peter was of that nondescript age when one doesn't know what to call him. It seemed strange to designate him as a young man, and yet he wasn't a boy or an old man or even a middle-aged man. Yes, he certainly must be a young man, but it seemed so odd to call him that. He had colorless hair and expressionless eyes. The world hadn't used him badly. Indeed, it hadn't used him much at all either way, and he hadn't used it. Therefore he had no identity with it. Peter was connected with the Hartford Square Church—that is, he swept the floors and looked after the rooms and was, in short, the janitor. Remembering this, she filled a plate with some baked beans and one slice of the delicate toast that stood ready for the hot oysters, and pouring a cup of steaming coffee she walked swiftly to the back chamber and knocked.

The front legs of Peter's chair came to the floor with a bang, and he sat with his mouth wide open, staring at the door, after giving his gruff, "Come in."

Polly entered, setting down her burden and saying rapidly, "I've brought you some of my baked beans. They're hot, and I thought you might like them, Peter."

She never knew what sort of thanks he stammered out. She was busy thinking how she should put her question.

"Peter, do you know anyone at the Hartford Square Church by the name of Mason?"

This was as near the name as she would come. She wouldn't have dared so much if he had been like some people. But talking to Peter was much like talking to Abbott. He would never put two and two together or wonder why she had asked the question.

"Wal, yas," said Peter, diverted from his astonishment. "Thar's two of 'em. Thar's John—he's a carpenter. And thar's Porter—he's a law'er. I reckon you mean him. Is he tall an' han'some? Great big eyes an' black hair, an' allus a good word said jes' so's to help most?"

"I think he must be the gentleman I've met," said Polly demurely.

"Wal, he's a mighty nice feller. Give me a ticket to a church supper th' other evenin'. He's awful smart, too, an' good. They do say he wouldn't have nothin' to do with a case Judge Granger give him, 'cause he thought it wa'n't right. An' he ain't rich, neither. But you'd just ought to hear him pray! Thar's allus a big meetin' up to the C.E. when he leads."

Polly had all the information she wanted now and made haste to get away, amid a shower of rough thanks from Peter. She went gleefully to her room and found the children so busy with a picture book that they had scarcely noticed her absence. So she knelt by the fireplace and stroked Abbott. Now that he was dry and smooth, Polly tied the rich green ribbon around his neck, much to the delight of the children. She stuck a Safrana bud in the bow and set him upon a stool. There he sat, the long ends of shining satin reaching to his toes, holding his chin very high, either from the choking sensation of the broad ribbon or pride in his rich apparel—probably pride, for he seemed quite contented and sat purring at the children with his eyes half-closed.

Porter Mason, with happy Sam mounted on his shoulder, came to a sudden halt before a large fruit store.

"Sam, would you like to take Miss Bronson a Christmas present?" he asked.

They had been talking of her all the way along, and Sam had said he loved her next best to his mother in all the world. They were pretty well acquainted by then, so Sam answered, "You bet! Wouldn't I, though?"

"All right. We'll go in here, and you shall choose what it will be."

It almost took Sam's breath away to see so many good things together. But after grave consideration he pointed to a box of great white California grapes. You might have thought Mr. Mason extravagant for a man who "ain't rich" if you had heard his order to the clerk, but Sam was very happy, and his companion looked no less so.

"Well, Miss Bronson," said Porter Mason, after they were fairly in, and Sam had presented his gift, "is the courier to be allowed to stay to the party, or must I go outside and paw the pavement until my services are needed again? Or might I go off and come back at a certain hour?"

What could Polly do but give him a gracious invitation?

So he took his coat and hat to the hall and made himself quite at home, telling the children stories and giving them such a wonderful time, while Polly cooked the oysters, that they forgot how hungry they were. They had a great time getting seated at the table. Polly actually ventured to borrow four of Mrs. Updike's best splint-bottomed kitchen chairs, and they all went after them except Sam and Abbott, who sat and smiled at one another while they were gone.

They were seated at last, and then came a moment Polly wasn't altogether prepared for. She had meant to ask a blessing. She always did when she was by herself, and she didn't want to leave God out before these children and on Christmas night. But here was this stranger. Could she ask him?

Polly's daring spirit rose. She looked up and said quietly, "Will you ask a blessing?"

Then what a light of pleasure and surprise rushed into the eyes that met hers. He bowed his head, and his few earnest, clear-spoken words to God astonished the children more than his stories had done. They were evidently not used to this.

While Polly poured coffee, Porter Mason questioned the children and found they knew almost nothing at all about Christmas. So he promised to tell them the true story of it after tea, and they gave themselves up to the delights of their plates.

"Miss Bronson promised to sing some too," said Susie Bryce, with her mouth full of beans.

Now Polly didn't intend to keep that promise, with the stranger there to listen. So she passed him the sugar and asked Sam if he would have some more oysters. The Indian pudding was hailed with joy and pronounced by Mr. Mason to be "just as good as my mother's." Then they finished off some of those luscious grapes. They were such a treat to Polly and to the children something wonderful. Abbott had his three oysters and enjoyed them as much as anybody.

After supper, while Polly was clearing off the table, the children had their story. Polly, going about her work softly, so she might lose none of it, told herself she didn't wonder that they liked to come to the meeting when he led, if he talked like that. When she had finished she sat down very quietly, but the story was just closing, and Mr. Mason turned to her and said, "Now may we have the song, Miss Bronson?"

Polly somehow had to sing then. And though her voice trembled some, it was sweet and clear as she sang:

Little stars that twinkle in the heavens blue,
I have often wondered if you ever knew
How there rose one like you, leading wise old men
From the east, through Judah, down to Bethlehem?

Did you watch the Savior all those years of strife?
Did you know for sinners, how He gave His life?
Little stars that twinkle in the heavens blue,
All you saw of Jesus, how I wish I knew.

Then Polly stopped, and she wouldn't sing again for all their coaxing, for she had been too conscious of those eyes that had watched her so closely during the singing to try again. So she started some games, and they had a frolic until the clock on the mantel warned them it was getting late, and Mr.

Mason told Sam it was time for his carriage to take him home. The children sighed that the happy time was over. Sam was given some of the grapes and a rosebud or two for his sick mother. Polly bundled him up and gave each of the children a rose, and then they were ready to go.

Porter Mason walked gravely up to the fire, where weary Abbott, in spite of his elegance, had succumbed to the warmth and the remembrance of a delicious supper and had gone to sleep. But he was a polite cat and, as Mr. Mason came up, let him shake hands, or paws, with him.

Sam was mounted once more on his shoulder. Polly's hand was taken for just a second, and a few words were spoken: "I've enjoyed it all so much. May I come again soon and call?"

Of course she had to say yes. Then, with Susie and Mamie just behind and Joey Wilkes scudding on ahead, they started out into the snow, and the party was ended.

Yes, he came very soon to make the call. And then he wanted to come again and again, until it grew to be a settled thing for him to run in once or twice a week with a bit of a poem for her to read or a book to talk over. In those days roses were sent to her, instead of to her cat, and she was taken out to Sunday evening meetings quite often and now and then to a concert or a lecture. Abbott was left at home, which he didn't like after being alone all day. As spring came on, there were violets and anemones and once a lovely ride to the woods on a Sunday afternoon.

Then a note came from the mother of a former pupil, saying her little daughter was very sick, couldn't live long and wanted to have her dear Miss Bronson with her, which the doctor said would help. Would she come to them as soon as possible?

Polly sighed, packed away her bronze clock and marble vases, packed up the things she must take with her, waited a whole day hoping somebody would call—then gave Abbott into the keeping of a quaint new neighbor. She gave special directions to Mrs. Updike to tell whomever called that she had been summoned to a sick friend and would probably be back soon, and then she went.

It was a long journey, fifty miles or so, and the little pupil was very glad to see her. She grew no better as the days went by. It soon became evident that Polly couldn't be spared, for Bessie wasn't happy a moment unless her teacher was by her side. The mother was an invalid herself, who made her little girl worse by her melancholy speeches. So, although Polly was longing to be at home, she didn't feel as if she should go. She stayed, and Bessie grew day by day weaker but lingered on until the summer was nearing its close, and the winter school term was about to begin. Then she slipped into heaven, leaving Polly, who had made the way bright for her, almost worn out with loss of sleep and confinement to the sick room.

She hurried home to begin school life again. She unpacked the clock and vases and reestablished Abbott, who walked round and round her, purring and rubbing his head against her, trying as best he could to say he didn't like boarding and was glad to be at home again. When Polly received the key to her room and asked if anyone had called, she gained only a sentence about a tall man who "kep' a comin'." That was all the news of home she had.

Porter Mason had been very lonely after Polly left. He had called many times to see her, but Mrs. Updike never knew her address. And now, just as Polly had come home, he had been called away on business. When he finally reached home he found such a quantity of matters awaiting his attention that he had no time to think of doing anything for pleasure. So it happened that Polly had been at home for three weeks without once seeing him.

One evening she took Abbott in her arms and went to the front door. The air was chilly and hazy, as late September is apt to be. The stars weren't nearly as bright as usual. They had no sparkle. They looked as if they'd all gone away to spend the evening and left only a dim light in the window. It was lonesome and cold. She shivered and dropped a few tears on Abbott's thick coat.

She didn't hear the brisk steps coming down the street as she went in and shut the door, but they came on, right to Polly's bright little window, which had been so dark for many days when those same steps had sounded down the street. And when Porter Mason came in he took Polly's two hands in his own and held them—Abbott had his back turned, looking into the fire—and when he made her quite comfortable on the sofa, he sat down beside her and told her something. But we mustn't hear it. If you have heard such words yourself, you understand; if you haven't, wait until your turn comes to know.

What did Polly say? Why, she said it to Porter Mason, and no one heard, not even Abbott, for he was asleep, and Mr. Mason never told.

They both went to the cheerful home among the hills to spend their next holidays and delight the hearts of the dear father and mother and brother and little sister and the other cat. Abbott, much to his disgust, was obliged to spend his holidays with the quaint little neighbor.

When his mistress came back she took him to another part of the town to live, where the familiar objects were all about him. There was a rug he always lay on, crocheted out of strips of silk, and the yellow stripes were the yellow ribbons that used to hold back the cheesecloth curtains. He thought it rather odd that Polly never went to school anymore and that the tall stranger stayed all the time now. But he liked him, and so it was all right. He had all the beefsteak and milk and oysters he wanted and could wear a green ribbon and rosebuds any day if he chose—so he told the cats of the neighborhood.

And so the old room has seen the story—has helped it along, as it helped many before—and stands again waiting, all alone, except for the big black spider who is hanging her delicate draperies in all the corners. It waits for someone to enter and bring life and beauty to it again.

A Voice
in the Wilderness

Chapter 1

With a lurch the train came to a dead stop, and Margaret Earle, gathering her belongings, hurried down the aisle and out into the night.

She swung her heavy suitcase down the long step to the ground and then herself after it. She thought it strange that neither conductor, brakeman nor porter had come to help her off the train, when all three had taken the trouble to tell her the next station was hers. But she could hear voices ahead. Perhaps a problem with the engine detained them, and they'd forgotten her for the moment.

The ground was rough where she stood, with no sign of a platform. Didn't they have platforms in this wild Western land, or was the train so long that her car stopped before reaching it?

She tried to distinguish the two or three specks of light dancing in the distance. She could see dim figures moving up near the engine; each one evidently carried a lantern.

Suddenly the girl felt isolated. Perhaps she shouldn't have stepped out until someone helped her. Perhaps the train hadn't pulled into the station yet, and she should get back on and wait. Yet if the train started before she found the conductor she might be carried on somewhere and he would blame her for being foolish.

No building was visible on that side of the track. She tried to move back from the cars to look on the other side, but the ground sloped unexpectedly. She slipped and fell in the cinders, bruising her knee and cutting her wrist.

In sudden panic she stood up. No matter what, she must get back on that train. They had no right to put her out here, away from the station at night in a strange country. If the train started before she could find the conductor she would tell him he must back up again and let her off. He certainly couldn't expect her to get out like this.

Lifting the suitcase up the high step, she reached to the step rail and tried to pull herself up. Just then the engine gave a long snort, and the whole train, as if it were in league against her, lurched forward, loosening her grip. She slipped to her knees again, and the suitcase toppled from the lower step on top of her. Together they slid and rolled down the short bank, while the train ran off into the night.

The terror of being deserted helped the girl rise in spite of bruises and shock. She waved her hands at the cars as they hurried by—each bright window revealing a passenger, comfortable and safe inside, unconscious of her need.

A moment of useless screaming, running and trying to attract someone's attention, and Margaret stood dazed as the last car slatted past. She gazed after the train, the light on its last car swinging and blinking, as it vanished from sight into the night.

She gasped and looked about her for the station that only a short moment before had been so real in her mind, and, lo, she saw none!

The night was wide like a great floor shut in by a low, vast dome of curving blue set with the largest stars she'd ever seen. No building broke the inky outlines of the plain; no friendly light streamed out to cheer her heart. Not even a tree was in sight, except on the far horizon, where a heavy line of deeper darkness might mean a forest. Nothing, except one sharp shaft ahead like a black mast throwing out a dark arm across the track. She picked up her suitcase and made her way toward it.

A soft dripping greeted her—something splashing down among the cinders by the track. Then she saw the tall column with its arm outstretched and, looming darker among the sagebrush, the outline of a water tank. She recognized the engine's refilling tank and knew she had mistaken a pause to water the engine for a regular stop at a station.

Margaret approached the dripping water, laying her hand on the dark upright, as if it could help her. She dropped her baggage and stood trembling, gazing about in horror. Then, like a mirage against the distance, a vision appeared to her of her father and mother sitting around the library lamp at home, as they did every evening. They were probably reading and talking at this minute, trying not to miss her on her first venture away from home to teach. They had sheltered their beloved daughter all these years and let her go reluctantly, despite her youthful confidence, almost absurdly making her promise to be careful and not run any risks. What would they say if they could see her now?

Yet here she was, standing alone beside a water tank in the midst of an Arizona plain, not knowing where she was, around nine or ten o'clock at night! Perhaps she was dreaming! A few moments earlier she had been seated in the lighted car, surrounded by drowsy fellow travelers, almost at her journey's end, as she supposed. Now, having done as she thought right, she was stranded here!

She rubbed her eyes and looked again up the track, half expecting to see the train come back for her. Surely the conductor or the kind porter would discover she was gone and do something. They wouldn't leave her here alone on the prairie!

That vision of her father and mother in the distance unsettled her. The lamp looked bright and cheerful, and she could see her father's head with its heavy white hair. He turned to look at her mother to tell her something he read in the paper. They were sitting there, almost happy about her. And she—her dignity as a schoolteacher dropped from her like a garment now—she was standing in this space alone, with only an engine's water tank to keep her from dying and only the barren track to connect her with the world.

She dropped her head and let the tears fall. Then off in the distance the low howl of some angry beast reached her ears. She paused, clinging to the tank.

How confidently she had accepted this position, hoping it would lead to her desired career! Reading about coyotes and Indians and wild cowboys hadn't daunted her courage. Besides, she told her mother, a teacher going to a town was different from a missionary going to the wilds. She was to teach an important school where her Latin, German and mathematical achievements had won her a place above other applicants and where her tactfulness was expected to work wonders. But what were Latin and German and mathematics now? Could they show her how to climb a water tank? Would tact divert a hungry wolf?

The howl in the distance sounded closer. The water tank loomed high and dark above her—she must get up there. It wasn't safe to stand here. And from that height she might be able to see farther. Perhaps she could see a light somewhere and cry for help.

Margaret discovered a set of rude spikes the trainmen used to climb up. Setting her suitcase down at the foot, she untied the silk belt from her traveling suit, knotted one end to the handle of her suitcase and secured the other end to her wrist. Then she began to climb.

It seemed miles up, though in reality it measured only a short distance. The howling beasts grew louder and more constant, and her heart beat wildly. She felt stiff and bruised from her falls and weak with fright. The spikes, set far apart, made each step painful and difficult. At last she was high enough to see over the water tank and feel safer. She swung her suitcase to the top of the tank and stepped up after it.

The tank, partly roofed over, gave her enough room to sit on the edge without danger of falling in and drowning. For a few minutes she sat still in thankfulness and tried to catch her breath.

All at once the beauty of the night enveloped her. Against the deep blue sky the stars stood out brighter than any stars she had ever seen. The place reminded her of Taylor's pictures of the Bible lands. She half expected to see a shepherd with his crook and sheep approaching her out of the dim shadows or a turbaned, white-robed David with his hands lifted in prayer standing off among the depths of purple darkness. Perhaps it was on such a night and in such a scene as this that the wise men followed the star.

But she couldn't sit on the edge of a water tank and contemplate art and history. The night was cold, with no light or sign of a house anywhere and no freight train clattering down the track. Only the voices of the wild broke the silence.

The cold swept down and gripped her. She felt stiff and cramped on the high, narrow seat; yet she dared not move much. Would no help come? Must she sit there all night?

Then in the quiet between the calls of the night creatures she heard a sound—slow and plodding, far away. She thought she saw a shape move out of the sagebrush on the other side of the track. It might be only her imagination from staring so long at the huddled bushes on the dark plain.

Yet something prompted her to cry, "Help!" When she heard her own voice she cried again and louder, wondering why she hadn't done so before.

The dark shape paused and turned toward her. What if it were a beast instead of a human?

"Who's thar?" a nasal voice sounded out.

Her cry for help rang out again.

"Whar be you?" twanged the voice.

Now she could see a horse and rider like a shadow moving toward her down the track.

Chapter 2

The horse came to a standstill a little way from the track, and his rider let forth a stream of strange profanity. The girl shuddered.

"How'd yeh git up thar?" he growled. "D'j'yeh drap er climb?"

The man was short and wiry, with a bristly, protruding chin. She could see that, even in the starlight. Something about the point of that stubby chin she shrank from. She wondered if the night with its loneliness and unknown perils was safer than this man's company.

"I got off the train by mistake, thinking it was my station, and before I discovered it the train had left me," Margaret explained.

"Yeh didn't 'xpect it t' sit reound on th' plain while you was gallivantin' up water tanks, did yeh?"

"I'm on my way to Ashland station," she said icily. "Can you tell me how far it is from here and how I can get there?"

"It's a little matter o' twenty miles, more 'r less," said the man. "The walkin's good. I don't know no other way from this p'int at this time o' night. Yeh might set still till th' mornin' freight goes by an' drap atop o' one of the kyars."

"Sir!" said Margaret.

The man wheeled his horse around and looked up at her impudently.

"Say, you must be some young highbrow, ain't yeh? Is thet all yeh want o' me? 'Cause ef 'tis I got t' git on t' camp. It's a good five mile yet, an' I ain't hed no grub sence noon."

The tears suddenly rushed to the girl's eyes at the thought of being alone in the night again. This dreadful man frightened her, but the loneliness now seemed worse.

"Oh!" she cried. "You're not going to leave me up here alone, are you? Isn't there some place nearby where I could stay overnight?"

"Thur ain't no palace hotel round these diggin's, ef that's what you mean," the man leered at her. "You c'n come along t' camp 'ith me ef you ain't too stuck up."

"To camp!" exclaimed Margaret. "Are any ladies there?"

A loud guffaw greeted her question. "Wal, my woman's thar, sech es she is. But she ain't no high-flier like you. We mostly don't hev ladies to camp. But I got t' git on. Ef you want to go, you better light down pretty speedy. I can't wait."

Margaret descended her rude ladder step by step, while the coarse man stayed on his horse, making no attempt to assist her.

"This ain't no baggage car," he grumbled, as he saw the suitcase in her hand. "Well, h'ist yerself up thar. I reckon we c'n pull through somehow. Gimme the luggage."

Margaret stood appalled beside the bony horse and his rider. Did he actually expect her to ride with him?

"Couldn't I walk?" she asked.

" 'T's up t' you," the man replied indifferently. "Try 't an' see!"

He spoke to the horse, and it started forward eagerly, while the girl struggled on behind. Over rough, uneven ground, between greasewood, sagebrush and cactus, back onto the trail. The man, apparently oblivious to her presence, rode on, a silent shadow on a dark horse wending a silent way between the other shadows until the girl almost lost sight of them. Her breath came short, her ankle turned, and she fell with both hands into a stinging cactus bed. She cried out then and begged him to stop.

"L'arned yer lesson, hev yeh, sweety?" he jeered. "Well, get in yer box, then."

She grabbed hold of the back of the saddle and struggled up to the seat behind him.

From time to time the man pulled a bottle from his pocket and swallowed some of its contents, becoming even more fluent in his language. Margaret remained silent, growing more frightened each time the bottle came out. At last he offered it to her. She declined coldly.

"Oh, yer too fine to take a drap fer good comp'ny, are yeh? Wal, I'll show yeh a thing er two, my pretty lady. You'll give me a kiss with yer two cherry lips before we go another step. D'yeh hear, my sweetie?" He turned with a silly leer to enforce his command.

With a cry Margaret slid to the ground and ran back down the trail as fast as she could, till she stumbled and fell in the shelter of a great sagebrush and lay sobbing on the sand.

The man turned bleared eyes toward her and watched until she disappeared. Then jutting out his chin he flung her suitcase after her.

"All right, my pretty lady—go yer own gait an' l'arn yer own lesson." He started on again, singing a rowdy song.

Under the starry dome Margaret sat alone again, with no water tank for a defense, and took counsel with herself. The howling coyotes seemed silent for now. That man was her greatest menace now, and she must escape from him and get back to that tank and the railroad track. She stole softly to the place where she'd heard the suitcase fall and picked it up. Could she ever find the way? The trail seemed so intangible and her sense of direction confused. Yet she could do nothing else. She shuddered when she thought of the man.

When the man reached camp he set his horse loose and stumbled into the door of the log bunkhouse, calling to his woman to bring food.

Eight men sat around the room on crude benches and dusty bunks, smoking their pipes or staring into the dying fire. Two kerosene lanterns, hanging from spikes high in the logs, cast eerie shadows over the men, rough and hardened by life and weather. They boasted unkempt beards, uncombed hair and coarse cotton shirts open at the neck, and their faces were etched with the struggles of sorrow and hard living.

One other stood out, younger than the rest. His pale, smooth face was flushed like a boy's, and he wore a stern look like a mask. But behind it his fine features and spirit couldn't be hidden. They called him the Kid and thought his youth made him different from them; he was twenty-four, and the others were over forty. They were doing their best to help him overcome the fineness he'd inherited naturally. And though he stopped at nothing and lived as one wise in the ways of the world, he kept a quiet reserve about him, a kind of charm they hadn't penetrated.

He was playing cards with three other men at the table when the man came in, but he didn't even glance his way.

An old woman appeared at the door. She carried his supper to the table in silence, her face pale and wrinkled, her eyes dull.

"Brung a gal 'longside o' me part way," said the man, flinging himself into a seat by the table. "Thought you fellers might like t' see 'er, but she got too high an' mighty fer me. Wouldn't take a pull at th' bottle 'ith me 'n' shrieked like a catamount when I tried t' kiss 'er. Found 'er hangin' on th' water tank. Got off 't th' wrong place. One o' yer highbrows out o' th' parlor car! Good lesson fer 'er!"

The young one raised his head and looked sharply at the old man. "Where is she now?" he asked quietly.

The other men glanced up uneasily.

"Dropped 'er on th' trail an' threw her fine-lady b'longin's after 'er. Ain't got no use fer thet kind. Wonder what they was created fer? Ain't no good to nobody, not even 'emselves." He laughed harshly.

The Kid threw down his cards and walked out of the door. In a few minutes the men heard two horses pass the end of the bunkhouse toward the trail, but no one seemed to notice.

Margaret was resting on the ground in the shadow of a sagebrush on the trail's edge, with her suitcase beside her. She had made little progress since the man had left her. Her breath came in short gasps. The coldness of the ground and the night air penetrated her thin traveling dress. Suddenly she heard a whistle in the distance. It sounded like a bit from the tune "From the Desert I Come to Thee" that dated back some years and was discarded now as hackneyed even by the street pianos at home. But, oh, how cheerful it sounded to Margaret's ears!

The whistling grew louder. She tried to see through the shadows. Dared she call out, or should she keep still, hoping he would pass by without noticing her? Before she could decide, two horses stopped, and a rider dismounted. He stood in front of her as if it were daylight and he could see her plainly.

"You don't need to be afraid," he said. "I thought I'd better look you up after the old man got home and gave his report. He was pretty well tanked up and not a fit escort for ladies. What's the trouble?"

Even in the darkness she could see his broad shoulders, close-cropped curls and handsome profile. An air of quiet strength about him gave her confidence.

"Oh, thank you for coming!" she gasped. "I was—just a little—frightened, I think." She tried to stand, but her foot caught in her skirt and pulled her back down onto the sand.

He bent over and lifted her to her feet. "You certainly are some plucky girl! 'A little frightened,' were you? Well, I'd say you had a right to be."

"Well, not exactly frightened," said Margaret, taking a deep breath and trying to steady her voice. "I guess I was more mortified than frightened—to think I got off the train before I reached my station. I'd made up my mind not to be frightened, but when I heard that awful howl of some animal—and then that terrible man!"

"More than one kind of animal! Well, you needn't worry about him. He's eating his supper, and he'll be sound asleep by the time we get back."

"Oh, do we have to go where he is? Isn't there some other place? Is Ashland far? That's where I'm going."

"No other place where you could go tonight. Ashland's a good twenty-five miles from here. But you'll be all right. Mom Wallis'll look out for you. She isn't much of a looker, but she has a kind heart. She pulled me through once when I was just about flickering out. Come on. You'll be tired. We'd better be getting back. She'll make you comfortable, and then you can get off early in the morning."

He reached over and lifted her easily to the saddle of the second horse and placed the bridle in her hands. Then he swung the suitcase up on his own horse and sprang into the saddle.

Chapter 3

He turned the horses around and took charge as if he were accustomed to managing stray ladies in the wilderness.

Margaret settled into her saddle and looked about her. Again the wonder of the night overcame her, and she breathed a soft exclamation of awe.

The young man looked at her quickly.

"Does it always seem so big here—so—limitless?" she asked. "It's so far to everywhere, and yet the stars hang close, like a protection. I feel as if I'm alone in the universe with God. Does it always seem like that out here?"

He looked at her, as she studied the luminous blue above.

"No, it isn't always," he said quietly after a moment. "I've seen it when it was more like being alone in the universe with the devil."

She turned to look at his face. In the starlight she couldn't make out the hard lines being carved about his sensitive mouth. But his voice sounded so sad and earnest that she pitied him.

"Oh," she said gently, "it would be awful that way. Yes, I can understand. I felt that way a little, while that man was with me." She shuddered at the thought.

Again he gave her that curious look. "There are worse things than Pop Wallis out here," he said gravely. "But I'll grant you there's some class to the skies. It's a case of 'Where every prospect pleases and only man is vile.'" And with the words his tone grew almost flippant.

Without realizing it she drew farther away from him and murmured, "Oh!" as if he'd classed himself with the "man" he was describing.

Instantly he felt her withdrawal and grew serious again.

"Wait till you see this sky at dawn," he said. "It will burn red fire off there to the east like a hearth in a palace, and all this dome will glow like a great pink jewel set in gold. If you want a classy sky, there you have it! Nothing like it in the East!"

Margaret noticed a strange mingling of culture and roughness in his speech.

"Are you a—poet?" she asked. "Or an artist?"

He laughed abruptly and seemed embarrassed. "No, I'm just a—bum! A sort of roughneck out of a job."

"Have you been here long?" she asked at last.

"Three years," he said almost curtly, turning his head away.

Unconsciously her tone took on a sympathetic sound. "And do you get homesick and want to go back?"

"No!" His tone was almost savage now.

An oppressive silence followed before he finally turned and in a kinder tone asked her how she ended up being stranded in the desert.

She told him briefly about herself and why she'd chosen to come to Arizona.

"My father is a minister in a small town in New York. When I finished college I had to do something, and I was offered this Ashland school through a friend of ours who had a brother out here. Father and Mother wanted me nearer home, of course, but everybody says the best opportunities are in the West. This was a good opening, so they finally consented. They would send for me at once if they knew what a mess I've made of things already."

"But you're not discouraged?" he asked. "Some nerve you have. I guess you'll manage to hit if off in Ashland. It's the limit as far as discipline is concerned, I understand. But I guess you'll put one over on them. I'll bank on you after tonight!"

She laughed. "Thank you! But I don't see how you know all that. I'm sure I didn't do anything particularly nervy. There wasn't anything else to do but what I did, even if I'd tried."

"Most girls would have fainted and screamed and fainted again when they were rescued," he said, out of a vast experience.

"I never fainted in my life," Margaret said with disdain. "And I don't think I'd care to faint in a place like this."

She suddenly realized she was growing very friendly with this stranger in the dark and questioned him instead.

"What was your college?"

That he hadn't been to college never occurred to her. Something in his speech and manner led her to think he had.

A sharp, sudden silence followed. At last he answered gruffly, "Yale," and plunged into an elaborate account of Arizona in its early days. He described in detail the cliff dwellers and their homes, which could still be seen high in the rocks of the canyons not many miles to the west of where they were riding.

Margaret was eager to hear it all and asked many questions, declaring her intention of visiting those caves at her earliest opportunity. She was thrilled to be out where these odd things were that she had read and wondered about. It didn't occur to her until later that he had intentionally led her away from talking about himself.

He told her about the petrified forest over some low hills to the left: acres and acres of agatized chips and trunks of great trees turned to eternal stone, called by the Indians "Yeitso's bones," after the giant of that name whom an ancient Indian hero killed. He described the color of Arizona days, where one can stand on the edge of a flat-topped mesa and look off through the clear air to mountains that seem nearby but are in reality more than two hundreds miles away. He pictured the strange colors and lights of the place—ledges of rock, yellow, white and green, drab and maroon, and tumbled piles of red boulders, shadowy buttes in the distance, serrated cliffs against the horizon, not blue but rosy pink in the heated haze—and perhaps a lonely eagle poised above the silent, brilliant waste.

He told it not in book language, with turned phrase and smoothly flowing sentences, but in simple, frank words. He wasn't used to talking about the beauty of the place and found a strange delight in doing so.

She forgot her weariness as she listened to him describe the new mysterious country to which she had come. She forgot she was riding through the darkness with a stranger, to an unfamiliar place and doubtful experiences. Her fears had fled, and she responded to his story with awe.

From time to time in the distance she heard the same howls of wild beasts she'd heard when she sat alone by the water tank. Each time a shudder passed through her, and instinctively she edged a little toward her companion, then straightened up again as if she didn't notice. But the Kid saw her attempts at self-control and respected her more.

Suddenly a dark form crossed in front of them. Two eyes glared at them like green lamps, then disappeared among the mesquite bushes.

The creature was gone so quickly she wondered if she'd really seen it. Then one hand flew to her mouth, stifling a scream, and she shrank toward her companion.

"There's nothing to fear," he said, laying his hand on her horse's neck. "That cat didn't want our company any more than we wanted hers!" He raised his gun and shot into the air. "She won't come near us now."

"I'm not afraid!" said Margaret. "At least, I don't think I am—very! But everything is so new and unexpected, you know. Do people around here always shoot in that—well—unpremeditated fashion?"

They both laughed at that, and she leaned back in her saddle again.

"I'm sorry," he said. "I didn't realize the shot might startle you more than the wildcat. I don't seem fit to take care of a lady. I told you I was a roughneck."

"You're taking care of me wonderfully," said Margaret, "and I'm glad to get used to shots if they happen often."

Just then they reached the top of the low, rolling hill. Ahead in the darkness a light gleamed. Under the white stars it seemed a sickly red and out of harmony with the night.

"There we are!" said the Kid, pointing toward it. "That's the bunkhouse. You needn't be afraid. Pop Wallis'll be snoring by this time, and we'll come away before he's up in the morning. He always sleeps late after he's been off on a bout. He's been gone three days selling some cattle, and he'll have a pretty good top on."

The girl caught her breath, gave one wistful look up at the starry sky and a furtive glance at the young man's face, and let him lift her down to the ground.

Before her loomed the log bunkhouse, with only one window through which the lanterns flickered and unknown trials and possible perils beyond.

Chapter 4

When Margaret Earle entered the room the men sat up at once, bringing their heavy boots down on the rough wood floor, running their red hands through their hair and smoothing their beards, all in one motion. Their pipes hung there clenched between their teeth, and they all stared at her, unaccustomed to such beauty in their midst. Even in the dim light of the smoky lanterns and with the dust of travel on her, Margaret was beautiful.

"That's the problem, Father," said her mother, when the subject of Margaret's going West was first mentioned. "She's too beautiful. Far too beautiful to go among savages! If she were homely and old, she might be safe. That would be different."

But Margaret had prevailed. Now, standing on the threshold of the log cabin, she read in the unveiled admiration of these men the meaning of her mother's fears. It was a kind admiration not unmixed with awe, however. For in her beauty was a touch of the spiritual, setting her apart from other women and evoking adoration, not boldness, from men.

The Kid was right. Pop Wallis was asleep and out of the way. From a little shed room at one end his snoring marked time in the silence brought by the girl's advent.

In the kitchen doorway Mom Wallis stood and stared at the girl too. A wistful contortion crossed her face, as if she saw suddenly in this beautiful girl the life she had lost. A light almost flickered in her eyes, and then she shuffled away silently to prepare a meal for the stranger.

Margaret glanced uneasily about the long, low room at the rough company. The Kid introduced her as "the new teacher for the Ridge School beyond the junction." The men's names seemed to fit: Long Bill, Big Jim, the Fiddling Boss, Jasper Kemp, Fade-Away Forbes, Stocky, Croaker, and Fudge.

Despite her fears she acknowledged the introduction with a radiant smile and extended her small gloved hand. Each man accepted the offered hand with mingled pleasure and embarrassment. She followed quickly with a few cheerful words. These men were different from any she'd met before, but they didn't frighten or repel her as Pop Wallis had. And with her rescuer nearby, her nerve had returned.

The young man brought forth a crude, homemade chair, the only one the bunkhouse afforded, and helped her off with her coat and hat in his easy, friendly way, as if he had known her all his life.

The men sat awkwardly by and watched, unused to such manners. Moreover, they were astonished the Kid could talk so naturally with this delicate, beautiful woman. She was another of his kind and quite unlike them.

To hear her call him Mr. Gardley—Lance Gardley was the name he had told them the day he came among them—amused them. They hadn't heard it since. The Kid—Mr. Gardley!

They looked at the girl almost jealously, yet proudly at the Kid. He was theirs—in a way. Hadn't they found him in the wilderness, sick and close to death, and nursed him back to life? But he could become part of her world, too, and not be ashamed. For that they were glad, though they knew he would one day leave them.

She ate the coarse corn bread and pork Mom Wallis brought her, as if it were a banquet. She tasted it first and then smiled. She didn't devour it greedily, as each man knew he would after not eating for a long time. And she handled the two-tined fork and the old steel knife with grace. They watched, then dropped their eyes and scuffed their feet under the table.

Such strange talk too! But the Kid seemed to understand. About the sky—their old, common sky, with stars they saw every night—making such a fuss about that, with words like "wide," "infinite," "azure," and "gems." Much later, each man went out and surveyed the sky anew.

The Kid knew the girl was afraid. He kept the talk going, drawing in one or two of the men now and again. Long Bill forgot himself and laughed out loud, then stopped as if he'd been choked. Stocky told a funny story at the Kid's request and then turned red over his blunders. And the Fiddling Boss, after being asked, reached for his fiddle from the smoky corner beside the fireplace and played an old tune or two. Finally the men started singing, with hoarse, quavering voices that finished in a roar of wild sweetness. And Margaret and the Kid joined in a duet, and then Margaret sang alone, with a few bashful chords from the fiddle as accompaniment.

Mom Wallis had already stopped her work and was sitting huddled in the doorway on a nail keg with folded hands and a wistful look on her face. Silence had settled over the group as the girl sang on. Now and then the Kid, when he knew the words, would join in with his rich tenor.

It was a strange night. When she finally lay down to rest on a hard cot with a doubtful-looking blanket for covering and Mom Wallis as her roommate, Margaret couldn't help wondering what her mother and father would think if they could see her. Wouldn't they almost prefer the water tank and the lonely desert to her present surroundings?

Nevertheless, she slept soundly after the excitement and woke with a start in the morning, to hear the men outside splashing water and humming or whistling bits of the tunes they'd sung the night before.

And there was Mom Wallis standing over her, looking down at her hair and sleep-flushed cheeks. "You got dretful purty hair."

Margaret smiled at the woman.

"You wouldn't b'lieve it, but I was young an' purty oncet. Beats all how much it counts to be young 'n' purty! But land! It don't last long. Make the most of it while you got it."

Browning's immortal words came to Margaret's lips—

Grow old along with me,
The best is yet to be,
The last of life for which the first was made—

but she checked them just in time and could only smile mutely. How could she speak such thoughts amid these intolerable surroundings? Then with sudden impulse she reached up to the woman and kissed her sallow cheek.

"Oh!" said Mom Wallis, starting back and laying her bony hand on her cheek, as if it hurt her, while a dull red stole up from her neck to her hay-colored hair. All at once she turned her back on her visitor, and the tears streamed down her face.

"Don't mind me," she said after a minute. "It was real nice; only it kind of give me a turn." Then she added, "It's time t' eat. You c'n wash outside after the men is done."

Margaret wondered if that had been the order of this woman's life—"after the men is done."

So the morning dawned after the night passed in safety. The blue of the day, so different from the blue of the night sky, was as unfathomable with its clear light. Mountains rose in the distance on all sides, and a slender, dark line of mesquite set off the more delicate colorings of the plain.

After breakfast Margaret and the Kid rode out, before Pop Wallis was awake. The other men stood about, watching eagerly, jealously, for a hand-shake and a parting smile. They told her they hoped she'd come again and sing for them, and each one had an awkward parting word. Whatever Margaret Earle might do with her school, she had won seven loyal friends in the camp and rode away amid their admiring glances.

"Wal, that's the end o' him, I 'spose," Long Bill said with a deep sigh, as the riders passed into the valley out of sight.

"H'm!" said Jasper Kemp. "I reck'n *he* thinks it's jes' th' beginnin'!"

"Maybe so!" said Big Jim.

For Margaret, the view from the top of the mesa, the cool, dim entrance of a canyon where great ferns fringed and feathered its walls, and strange caves hollowed out in rocks far above brought to life the stories she had read of cave dwellers. It was a new world.

She decided she couldn't have picked out among her city acquaintances a better man for doing the honors of the desert. His fresh color no wind or weather could subdue; his gray-blue eyes with that mixture of thoughtful-ness, reverence and daring; his crisp, brown curls glinting with gold in the sunlight—all made him pleasant to look upon. And something about the firm set of his lips and chin made her feel he possessed a hidden strength.

When they stopped for lunch he went about making sure she was comfortable, spreading a blanket under the shade of a large Western tree and unpacking carefully the simple lunch Mom Wallis had provided.

"I don't understand," she said, "how in the world you ended up among such rough men! Of course, in their way, they aren't so bad. But you aren't like them."

They were riding out on the plain now in the afternoon light and in a short time would arrive at her destination.

He gazed ahead for a moment, and she saw the hard lines forming about his mouth.

"It's an old story I suppose you've heard before," he said, with almost a flippancy in his voice. "I didn't make good back there"—he waved his hand toward the East—"so I came out here to start over. But I guess I haven't made good here either—not as I meant to when I came."

"You can't, you know," said Margaret. "Not here."

"Why?" He looked at her earnestly.

"Because you have to go back to where you didn't do well and pick up the lost opportunities."

"But suppose it's too late?"

"It's never too late if we're sincere and not too proud."

A long silence followed, while the Kid gazed at the mountains. When he spoke again it was to point out the beauty of a silver cloud floating on the horizon. But Margaret had noticed the look in his eyes.

A few minutes later they crossed another mesa and descended to the enterprising town where she was to begin her winter's work. The houses and streets seemed to hasten to meet them those last few minutes of their ride.

Margaret dreaded saying good-bye to her rescuer and now friend, to face an unknown world. He turned and looked into her eyes, and she returned the look, knowing she would not soon forget him—nor did she want to.

Chapter 5

He was different from any man Margaret had encountered before—wild and wise in worldly ways and unrestrained by many of the principles vital to her—yet she felt strangely drawn to him and at home in his company. She couldn't understand herself or him. It was as if his soul had looked out of his eyes and spoken, untrammeled by circumstances of birth or breeding or habit, and she knew him for a kindred spirit. And yet she would never have expected to find him as a friend. Why did she dread leaving him to meet a world of strangers, when yesterday she would have welcomed it?

Now, when his face grew thoughtful and sad, she saw again the hard lines about his mouth, and her heart ached over what he had said about not making good. She wondered if she could say anything else to help him, but no words came, and the set look warned her that perhaps she'd said enough.

They rode quietly to the station to have Margaret's trunks delivered to the house where she'd arranged to board. Then she sent a telegram to her parents that she arrived safely, and they rode up the street to the boardinghouse.

The landlady left them alone for a moment while she dashed to the kitchen to take a boiling pot off the stove. Margaret glanced about the dingy parlor with its red and green ingrain carpet of ancient pattern, obscure chromos on the walls and thickly varnished furniture, scarcely taking it all in. She was filled with a homesickness she hadn't felt even when she bid good-bye to her loved ones at home. The people she would live with here were of another world from hers, and the only friend she had was leaving her.

She reached out to shake his hand and thank him for rescuing her. But the tears crowded into her throat and eyes, leaving no room for words. She chided herself for her foolishness. She had known him twenty-four hours, and, after all, what did she know? Yet he was her friend and rescuer.

At last she voiced her thanks and found him looking at her with an earnest, troubled expression.

"Don't thank *me*," he said huskily. "Guess it's the best thing I ever did, finding you. I won't forget, even if we never see each other again—and—I hope—you'll let me visit you sometime."

"Of course," she said. "Why not?"

"I don't feel worthy, but—thank you. I'll try." Then he walked out of the door and, mounting his horse, rode into the afternoon's lengthening shadows.

She stood in the forlorn room staring out of the window after him with a sense of desolation. For the moment her hopes of the future had fled. If she could slip unobserved out the front door, down to the station, and board some waiting express to her home, she would gladly do it.

She tried to summon her reasons for coming to this wild country but couldn't think of one, and her eyes were starting to tear. But Margaret Earle wasn't given to tears, nor could she afford to cry now. Mrs. Tanner would be returning, and she mustn't find the "new schoolma'am" weeping.

She turned from the window, suddenly aware of a presence in the room with her. In the doorway stood a man and a dog.

The man, of medium height and slight build, was staring at her with pale-blue eyes set in a putty complexion. His hair, the color of straw, was neatly combed, and his city business suit was cut in the latest style. But he looked as much out of place in that plain house as Margaret did in her simple but stylish dress of dark-blue crêpe.

His eyes smiled in a way the girl instinctively resented, though she wasn't sure why, while the dog, a collie, regarded her with his large brown eyes. She felt both pairs of eyes were appraising her. Of the two the girl preferred the dog's. Perhaps the dog understood, for he stepped closer and wagged his plumy tail. She felt friendliness at once for the dog; but for the man she suddenly conceived one of her violent and unexpected dislikes.

Into this scene bustled Mrs. Tanner. "Well, now, I didn't mean to leave you by yourself all this time," she said, wiping her hands on her apron. "But them beans boiled clean over, and I hed to put 'em in a bigger kettle. I put in more beans 'count o' you bein' here, an' I ain't uset t' calc'latin' on two extry." She looked happily from the man to the girl and back again.

"Mr. West, I 'spose, o' course, you interjuced yerself? Bein' a preacher, you don't hev to stan' on ceremony like the rest o' mankind. You 'ain't? Well, let me hev the pleasure of interjucin' our new schoolteacher, Miss Margaret Earle. I 'spect you two'll be awful chummy right at the start, both bein' from the East that way an' both hevin' ben to college."

Margaret nodded abruptly. She wondered why she didn't dislike the landlady because she prattled on in such a presumptuous way. But something innocent in the woman's manner caused her to disapprove, instead, of the smiling man who stepped forward just then, bowing low.

"Indeed, Miss Earle, I'm happily surprised. I'm sure Mrs. Tanner's prophecy will come true, and we'll be the best of friends. When they told me the new teacher was to board here I hesitated. I've seen something of these Western teachers in my time and scarcely thought I'd find you congenial. But I can see at a glance that you're an exception to the rule."

He offered his soft, white hand, and she accepted it rather than seem rude to her hostess. But her manner was cool, and she was thankful she hadn't removed her gloves.

If the man thought he would enjoy a lingering handclasp he was mistaken; the gloved fingertips brushed his hand and were withdrawn, and the girl turned from him to her hostess as if to dismiss him. He took no notice, however, until the dog stepped between them with his tail wagging. He pushed close to her and looked up into her face, his pink tongue hanging out.

Margaret looked down at him and then stooped and put her arms about his neck. Something in his kind dog expression made her feel as if she had a real friend.

The man, however, didn't seem to like the situation. He kicked gingerly at the dog's hind legs. "Get away! You're annoying the lady!"

The dog uttered a low growl and bared his teeth at the man, turning his body slightly so he stood across the girl's way, as if to keep the man from her.

Margaret smiled at the dog, laying her hand on his head, and he wagged his plumy tail again and walked beside her from the room. Neither one looked at the man again.

"Confound that dog!" said the Rev. Frederick West, in a most unpreacher-like tone, as he walked to the window and looked out. Then to himself he mused, "A *very pretty girl!* It will be worth my while to stay longer, after all."

Up in her room the "very pretty girl" was unpacking her suitcase and struggling with the tears. Not since her childhood when she started school had she felt so alone, and the bedroom brought the tears in the end.

The room was enclosed by unfinished walls and rough woodwork. An old wooden bed stood against one wall, the bureau with its warped looking-glass against another, and a braided rug lay on the floor near the bed. A wooden rocking chair occupied one corner, and a straight-back wooden chair sat near the bureau. Purple roses decorated a wall pocket, while the bookshelf of three thin boards strung together with maroon picture cord hung from the ceiling. A brightly colored picture card, "Moses in the Bulrushes," peered out from its frame of straws and red worsted, and bright blue paper shaded the windows.

How different from her room at home, simply and sweetly finished for her homecoming from college! It appeared before her homesick vision now: soft gray walls and rose-colored ceiling, blended by a wreath of exquisite wild roses, whose pattern was repeated in the border of the simple curtains and chair cushions; white enamel furniture; a pretty brass bed, spotless and soft as down in its luxurious mattress. She glanced at the lumpy bed with its fringed gray spread and lumpy-looking pillows in dismay. She hadn't thought of discomforts like that; yet now they loomed before her.

The tiny wooden stand with its thick, white crockery seemed an ill substitute for the dainty white bathroom at home. She knew she wouldn't have her home luxuries, of course; but she hadn't realized what a difference they would make.

Crossing to the window, she noticed for the first time the room's one luxury—a view! It stretched out far, in colors unmatched by a painter's brush, a purple mountain topped by rosy clouds in the distance. For the second time since she had come to Arizona her soul was lifted out of itself and its dismay by seeing what God had made and the greatness of it all.

Chapter 6

For some time she stood and gazed, marveling at the beauty and recalling some of the things she had learned that afternoon about the region. Suddenly a dark spot loomed in the foreground of her meditation. Looking down, she discovered the minister like a gnat between her eye and a grand spectacle, his face turned up to her window, his hand lifted in familiar greeting.

She pulled the shade down at once and, sitting on her bed, let the tears spill over. Here she was, Margaret Earle, newly elected teacher to the Ashland Ridge School, crying, when she should be getting settled and planning her new life. Along with the new surroundings and being homesick, she realized she was letting a foolish personal dislike get to her.

It was one thing to dislike a minister, but how could she find herself drawn to a young man whose life thus far had been anything but satisfactory, even to him? Had her perverse nature caused her to remember the look in the Kid's eyes and feel he had more manliness than the minister? After all, this man's profession would lead one to think he was more worthy of her respect and interest. Well, she was tired. Perhaps she would see things differently in the morning.

After a few minutes, she bathed her face in the heavy, ironstone washbowl, combed her hair and freshened her collar and the ruffles in her sleeves. Then she searched through her suitcase for every available article to brighten that forlorn room before going down for the evening meal.

The dainty dressing case of Dresden silk her girlfriends at home had given as a parting gift covered the pine bureau. She spread it out and arranged its silver-mounted brushes, combs, hand glass and sachet. Next she hung a lace cap with rose-colored ribbons over the bleary mirror, threw her kimono of flowered challis over the back of the rocker, and arranged her soap and toothbrush and her own washcloth and towel on the washstand. Somehow she felt better and more as if she belonged. Last she displayed her precious photographs of her father and mother and the dear vine-covered church and manse in front of the mirror. Her trunks would bring other things, and then she could bear it, perhaps, when she had buried the room in her home belongings. But this would have to do for tonight, for the trunk might not come till morning, and she was too weary to unpack.

She peered carefully out her window to make sure the minister wasn't still standing on the grass below. A pang of remorse shot through her. What would her father think of her feeling this way toward a minister, and before she knew the first thing about him? She must shake it off. Of course he was a good man or he wouldn't be in the ministry, and she had doubtless mistaken mere friendliness for forwardness. She would forget it and try to treat him the way her father would want her to treat another minister.

Cautiously she raised the shade again and looked out. The mountain was bathed in a ruby light fading into amethyst, and the path between was colored like a pavement of jewels set in filigree. While she watched, the picture changed, glowed, softened and changed again, reminding her of the chapter about the Holy City in Revelation.

She turned from the window at last, to go downstairs, and heard a soft tapping on her door. Opening the door, she discovered a dark figure standing in the hall. For a minute she feared it was the minister. But a shyness in the stocky figure and the stirring of a large furry creature behind him assured her it wasn't.

"Ma says you're to come to supper," said a gruff but youthful voice.

"Oh!" said Margaret, with relief in her voice. "Thank you for coming to tell me. I meant to come down and not give that trouble, but I was watching the sunset. Have you seen it?" She pointed across the room to the window. "Look! Isn't that a great color there on the tip of the mountain? I never saw anything like it at home. I suppose you're used to it though."

The boy took a step nearer the door and stared blankly across at the window, as if he expected to see some phenomenon. "Oh, *that!*" he exclaimed. "Sure! We have them all the time."

"But that wonderful silver light pouring down just in that one tiny spot!" exclaimed Margaret. "It makes the mountain seem alive and smiling!"

The boy turned and looked at her curiously. "Oh! I c'n show you plenty like that!" But he turned and looked at it a long, lingering minute again.

"We mustn't keep your mother waiting," said Margaret then, stepping toward the door and starting down the stairs. "Is this your dog? Isn't he a beauty? He seemed almost glad to see me." She stopped and laid her hand on the dog's head.

The boy's face lit with a smile. "Cap's a good old scout," he admitted, giving an appreciative look at Margaret.

"So his name is Cap. Is that short for anything?"

"Cap'n."

"Captain. What a good name for him. He looks as if he were a captain, and he waves that tail grandly. But who are you? You haven't told me your name yet. Are you Mrs. Tanner's son?"

"I'm just Bud Tanner."

"Then you're one of my pupils, aren't you? We must shake hands on that."

She extended her hand but had to go after Bud's reluctant fist, take it in a strange grasp and do all the shaking. By this time they'd arrived at the dining room door, where the minister was waiting and watching the exchange.

Bud frowned and walked away, ostensibly to put Cap out of the dining room, though he always sat behind his chair at meals. This practice was much to the preacher's discomfiture, for he was slightly in awe of the dog and hadn't been granted friendship as the lady had.

Mr. West stood behind his chair, awaiting the new boarder's arrival with an expectant smile.

In spite of her resolve to like the man, Margaret was again struck with aversion as she saw him standing there. She was relieved to find the seat assigned to her on the opposite side of the table from him and beside Bud.

West, however, stepped around the table and asked Mrs. Tanner: "Did you mean me to sit over here?" He placed his hand on the back of the chair meant for Bud.

"No, Mister West, you jest set where you ben settin'," responded Mrs. Tanner.

She'd thought the matter out and decided the minister could converse with the teacher to the whole table's advantage if he sat across from her. Mrs. Tanner was a matchmaker and felt this was an opportunity not to be despised, even if it robbed the Ridge School of a desirable teacher.

But West didn't return to his place then. To Margaret's annoyance he drew out her chair and waited for her to sit down.

But just then Cap darted away from his frowning master and stepped up to the minister's side with a low growl, as if to say, "Hands off that chair! That doesn't belong to you!"

West suddenly released his hold on the chair without pushing it up to the table and retired to his own place. "That dog's a nuisance!" he said and was answered with a glare from Bud's dark eyes.

Bud kept his eyes on the minister as he sat down, and Cap settled himself behind Margaret's chair.

Mrs. Tanner hurried in with the coffeepot, and Mr. Tanner came last, after combing his hair at the kitchen glass with the kitchen comb, in full view of the boarders. He was a thin, wiry, weathered man, with skin like leather and sparse hair. Some of his teeth were missing, leaving deep hollows in his cheeks, and scraggly gray whiskers, sticking out like a cowcatcher on a train, covered his kindly protruding chin. His shirt, though collarless, looked neat and clean. He greeted the new guest heartily, sat down and nodded to the minister.

"Naow, Brother West, I reckon we're ready fer your part o' the performance. You'll please to say grace."

Mr. West bowed his sleek, yellow head and muttered a formal blessing with an offhand manner, as if it were a mere ceremony.

Bud glared at him, and Cap growled low. Margaret felt a sudden desire to laugh but didn't, wondering instead what her father would think about it all.

The genial clatter of knives and forks broke the stiffness after the blessing. Mrs. Tanner bustled back and forth from the stove to the table, talking all the while. Mr. Tanner joined in with his flat, nasal twang, and the minister, with an air of contempt for them both, endeavored to set up a private conversation with Margaret across the narrow table. But Margaret had begun a conversation with Bud about the school and had to be addressed by name each time before Mr. West could get her attention. Bud, with a boy's keenness, noticed her aversion and put aside his own backwardness, entering the contest with voluble replies. The minister, if he would be in the talk at all, was forced to join theirs and found himself worsted and contradicted by the boy at every turn.

But this only made the man more eager to talk with Margaret. She was coy, and the acquaintance would have the zest of being no lightly won friendship. All the better. He watched her as she talked, noting every charm of lash and lid and curving lip, and stared so continually that she stopped looking his way at all, even when answering his questions.

At last, the first meal in the new home was concluded, and Margaret, pleading weariness, went to her room. She felt as if she couldn't endure another moment of contact with her present world. If that had meant just Bud and the dog, and even Mr. and Mrs. Tanner, she would have stayed. But the interfering minister vexed her.

She put out her light and drew up the shade. Before her spread the heavens again, with the soft purple of the mountain under the stars, reminding her of the previous night and her companion. Why couldn't she be as interested in the minister downstairs as in the wild young man? Too tired to analyze it tonight, she knelt beside her window to pray. And as she did, her thoughts returned to Lance Gardley, and she felt her heart reach out to him, that he might find a way to "make good," whatever his trouble had been.

She stood up then and, glancing down, saw the minister pacing back and forth in the yard, his hands clasped behind him, his head thrown back raptly. He couldn't see her in her dark room, but she pulled the shade down quietly and crossed to her bed. Would that man obstruct her vision everywhere, and must she try to like him because he was a minister?

At last she fell asleep.

Chapter 7

The next day was filled with unpacking and writing letters home. Margaret stayed too busy to think about the minister, despite his attempts to obtrude himself at every possible turn.

Two steamer trunks and a large box arrived, stirring up the household. Not since they'd moved into the new house had they seen so many things coming in. Bud helped carry them upstairs, while Cap ran back and forth barking, and the minister stood by the front door and gave impractical advice to the man who brought them. Margaret heard the man and Bud murmuring about Mr. West in the hall as they entered her door, and she couldn't help feeling she agreed with their opinions though she mightn't have expressed her own in the same terms.

The minister tapped at her door later and offered his services in opening the box and unstrapping the trunks. But Bud had already performed that service for her, she said, thanking him with a finality that forbade him to linger. She half hoped he heard the click as she locked the door after him and then wondered again what possessed her to feel that way. But such remorse was soon forgotten in making over her room.

The trunks, unpacked and then repacked with things she wouldn't need right away, were placed in front of the two windows. She covered them with Baghdad rugs, relics of her college days, and piled several college pillows on each, which instantly gave the room a homelike air. Then out of the box came framed pictures of home scenes, college friends and places; pennants and flags from football, baseball and basketball games she attended; photographs; a few prints of rare paintings simply framed; a roll of rose-bordered white scrim like her curtains at home. With this last she transformed the blue-shaded windows and the stiff wooden rocker and even made a valance and a bed-cover over pink cambric for her bed. The bureau and washstand were given pink and white covers, and the ugly walls disappeared beneath pictures, pennants and symbols.

When Bud came up to call her to dinner she opened the door eagerly. He stopped in wide-eyed amazement over the transformation. His eyes lit up at a pair of golf sticks, a hockey stick, a tennis racket and a big basketball in the corner. He stepped back into the hall to catch his breath, glancing around to make sure he was still in his father's house.

"I want you to come in and see my pictures and get acquainted with my friends when you have time," she said. "I wonder if you could make some more shelves for my books and help me unpack and set them up."

"Sure!" exclaimed Bud.

She hadn't asked the minister; she had asked *him*—*Bud!* He gazed around the room. What fun he would have seeing those things from the East!

Then Cap stepped into the middle of the room, mouth open, tongue lolling, panting, while he looked about as a person might have.

Bud had a proprietary air during dinner that was pleasant to Margaret and annoying to West. He plainly looked on the boy as an upstart whom Miss Earle was using to block his approach, and he was growing impatient over the delay. He suggested that she might like him to escort her about to see her new surroundings that afternoon. But with a smile she told him she would be busy all afternoon getting settled. When he offered again to help her she smiled at Bud and said she didn't think she'd need any more help; Bud was going to do a few things for her, and that was all she needed.

Bud grew two inches taller in that moment. He passed the bread, suggested two pieces of pie and filled her water glass. Mr. Tanner beamed to see his son in high favor, but Mrs. Tanner looked troubled for the minister. She thought things weren't progressing as fast as they should between him and the teacher.

That afternoon Bud built a bookcase out of the box sawed in half, with the pieces set side by side. She covered them with green burlap left over from college days, like her other supplies. Then they arranged the books, with Bud holding each book as a treasure and looking through the pages carefully. She'd brought her favorites, like old friends, to keep her from being lonely, and stirred Bud's interest in some she thought he would like to read.

At last the work was done, and they stood back to survey it. They'd kept out the schoolbooks, but the others filled the shelves. Margaret set a tiny vase on one part of the box and a small brass bowl on the other, and Bud, with a glance from his new teacher, scurried away and brought back a handful of gorgeous cactus blossoms to add the final touch.

"Say!" he said, looking around the room. "You wouldn't know it fer the same place!"

That evening after supper Margaret sat down to write a long letter home, including the details she left out of her note the previous night.

Dear Mother and Father,

I'm unpacked and settled at last in my room, and now I can't stand it another minute till I talk to you.

Last night, of course, I was pretty homesick. Things looked so strange and new and different. I knew they would, but I didn't realize how different they'd be. But I'm not a bit sorry I came, or at least I won't be when I start school.

One of the scholars is Mrs. Tanner's son, and I like him. He's been helping me this afternoon. We made a bookcase for my books, and it looks fine. I wish you could see it. I covered it with the green burlap, and the books look happy in rows over on the other side of the room. Bud picked some wonderful cactus blossoms for my brass bowl. I wish I could send you some. They're beautiful!

But you'll want me to tell about my arrival. To begin with, I was late getting here [She had decided to leave out the incident of the desert altogether, for she knew her mother would suffer during her absence once she heard of it], *which accounts for the lateness of the telegram I sent you. I hope the delay didn't worry you any.*

A nice young man named Mr. Gardley piloted me to Mrs. Tanner's house and looked after my trunks for me. He's from the East. It was fortunate for me he happened along, for he was kind and gentlemanly and helpful. Tell Jane not to worry that I'll fall in love with him; he doesn't live here. He belongs to a ranch or camp or something miles away. She was so afraid I would fall in love with an Arizona man and not come back home.

Mrs. Tanner is kind and motherly according to her lights. She's given me the best room in the house, and she talks a blue streak. She has thin, brown hair that's graying, and she wears it in a funny little knob on the top of her head to correspond with the funny little tuft of hair on her husband's chin. She wears her sleeves rolled up and bustles around noisily and apologizes for everything in the jolliest sort of way. I'd like her, I guess, if it wasn't for the other boarder. But she's decided I'll like him, and I don't, so she's a bit disappointed in me so far.

Mr. Tanner is kind and funny and looks something like a jackknife with the blades half-open. He never disagrees with Mrs. Tanner, and I believe he's in love with her yet, though they must have been married a good while. He calls her Ma and seems restless unless she's in the room. When she goes out to the kitchen to get some more soup or hash or bring in the pie, he shouts remarks at her all the time she's gone, and she answers, regardless of the conversation the rest of us are carrying on. It's like a phonograph wound up for the day.

Bud Tanner is about fourteen and is strong and almost handsome; at least he would be if he were fixed up a little. He has fine, dark eyes and a great shock of dark hair. He and I are friends already. And so is the dog.

The dog is a peach! His name is Captain, and he looks the part. He's appointed himself my bodyguard, and it's going to be nice having him. He's a big, fluffy fellow, a collie, with intelligent eyes, sensitive ears and a tail like a spreading plume. You'd love him. He has a smile like the morning sunshine.

And now I come to the only other household member, the boarder. I hesitate to approach the topic because I've taken one of my violent dislikes to him, and—awful thought—he's a minister! Yes, and a Presbyterian at that! I know it will make you feel awful, and I thought about not telling you but decided I must. I just can't bear him! Of course, I may get over it, but I don't see how, for I can't think of anything that's more like him than soft soap!

Oh, yes, there's another word. Grandmother used to use it about men she hadn't any use for, and that was "squash." Mother, I can't help it, but he does seem like squash. One of that crook-necked, yellow kind with warts and a big, splurgy vine behind it to account for its being there at all. Insipid and thready when it's cooked and has to have a lot of salt and pepper and butter to make it go down at all.

Now I've told you the worst, and I'll try to describe him and see what you think I'd better do about it. Oh, he isn't the regular minister here, or missionary—I guess they call him. He's located quite a distance off and comes only once a month to preach here. Anyhow, he's gone east now to take his wife to a hospital for an operation and won't be back for a couple of months, and this man isn't even taking his place. He's just here for his health or a vacation or something, I guess. He says he had a large suburban church near New York and had a nervous breakdown. But I've wondered if he didn't make a mistake, and the church had the nervous breakdown instead.

His hair is like wet straw, and his eyes like a fish's. His hand feels like a dead toad when you have to shake it, which I'm thankful has happened only once. He looks at you with a flat grin. He's acquired a double chin to make himself look pompous, dresses stylishly and speaks of the inhabitants of this country with contempt. He tries to be affable and offers to take me places, but so far I've avoided him. I can't think how they ever came to let him be a minister!

Yet I suppose it's my horrid old prejudice, and Father will be grieved, and you'll think I'm perverse. But I'm sure he's not one bit like Father when he was young. I never saw a minister like him. Perhaps I'll get over it. I'll try hard. I suppose he'll preach Sunday, and then, perhaps, his sermon will be grand, and I'll forget how soft-soapy he looks and think only of his great thoughts.

But I know it will comfort you to know there's a Presbyterian minister in the house with me, and I'll try to like him if I can.

There's nothing to complain of in the board. It isn't luxurious, of course, but I didn't expect that. Everything's plain, but Mrs. Tanner makes it taste good. She makes fine corn bread, almost as good as yours—not quite.

My room is lovely, now that I've covered its bareness with my own things. But it has one great thing that can't compare with anything at home, and that is its view. It's wonderful! I wish you could see it. There's a mountain at the end of it that has as many different garments as a queen. Tonight, when sunset came, it grew filmy as if a gauze of many colors had dropped on it and glowed and melted until it turned to slate blue under the night sky, and the dark about was velvet. Last night my mountain was pink and silver, and I've seen it purple and rose. But you can't imagine the wideness of the sky, and I couldn't paint it for you with words. You must see it to understand. A dark sapphire floor just simply ravished with stars like big jewels!

But I must stop and go to bed. The country air makes me sleepy, and my kerosene lamp is smoking. I guess you'd better send my student lamp after all, for I'm surely going to need it.

Now I must turn out the light and say good night to my mountain, and then I'll go to sleep thinking of you. Don't worry about the minister. I'm polite to him, but I'll never fall in love with him—tell Jane.

Your loving girl,
Margaret

Chapter 8

Margaret had arranged with Bud to take her to the schoolhouse the next morning, and he promised to have a horse hitched up and ready at ten o'clock. The school was apparently a distance from her boarding place. In fact, everything seemed to be located as far from everywhere else as possible. Even the town was scattered and sparse.

When she came down to breakfast she was disappointed not to find Bud there and was obliged to suffer a tête-à-tête with West. By asking him questions instead of letting him take the initiative, she managed to hurry through breakfast, acquiring superficial but sufficient knowledge of him.

She knew where he spent his college days and at what theological seminary he prepared for the ministry. He served three years in a prosperous New York suburban church and was taking a winter off from his strenuous pastoral labors to recover his strength, get a new stock of sermons ready and possibly write a book on his experiences. He flattened his weak, pink chin as he said this.

He said he would probably take a large city church as his next pastorate when he returned. He came out to study the West and enjoy its freedom; he understood it was a good place to rest and do as you please unhampered by what people thought. He wanted to get as far away from churches and clerical things as possible. He felt it was due him and his work that he should. He spoke of the people he'd met in Arizona as something like tamed savages, and Mrs. Tanner, sitting behind her coffeepot for a moment, heard his comments and looked at him with awe. What a great man he must be, and how fortunate for the new teacher he was there!

Margaret sighed with relief as she went to her room. She was anticipating her ride to the school with Bud. But when she came downstairs with her hat and sweater on, she found West standing out in front, holding the horse.

"Bud had to go in another direction, Miss Earle," he said, touching his hat gracefully, "and he has delegated to me the pleasant task of driving you to the school."

Dismay filled Margaret—and anger toward Bud. He had deserted her! And she thought he understood! Well, she had to go with this man, much as she disliked it. Her father's daughter couldn't be rude to a minister.

She climbed into the buckboard quickly, to avoid any contact with the man, puzzling again over her dislike of him.

West assumed all girls liked flattery. But Margaret ignored him when he told her how delighted he was to find that instead of the "old maid" he'd expected, she turned out to be "beautiful, young, and congenial."

She turned the conversation to her own advantage and asked about the countryside. What plants were growing by the trail? He knew greasewood from sagebrush, and that was about all. To some of her questions he hazarded answers that were absurd in light of Gardley's explanations. But she reflected that he'd been in the country a short time and was by nature not interested in such topics. She tried religious matters, thinking that here at least they must have common interests. She asked him what he thought of Christianity in the West as compared with the East. Did he find these Western people more alive and awake to the things of the kingdom?

West gave a startled look at the young woman beside him, thought she was testing him on his clerical side, flattened his chin in his most learned, self-conscious manner, cleared his throat and affected wisdom.

"Well, now, Miss Earle," he began, "I really haven't thought much about the matter. Ah—you know I've been resting and haven't had much opportunity to study the situation out here in detail. But, on the whole, I'd say everything is decidedly primitive—yes, ah, I might say, ah, well, *crude!*

"Why, consider this mission district. The missionary in charge seems to be teaching the most absurd old dogmas our forefathers used to teach. He's in the East with his wife for a time. I'm told she had to undergo an operation. I've never met him and really don't care to. But to judge from all I hear, he's unfit for such a position. For example, he's teaching such doctrines as the old view of the atonement, the infallibility of the Scriptures, the deity of Christ and belief in miracles. Of course, in one sense it matters little what the poor Indians believe or what people like the Tanners are taught. They have little minds and would scarcely know the difference. But you can readily see that with such a primitive, unenlightened man at the head of religious affairs, there could scarcely be much broadening and religious growth. Ignorance, of course, holds sway out here. I imagine you'll find that out soon enough.

"Whatever led you to come to a field like this? Surely many more congenial places must have been open to you." He leaned forward and cast a sentimental glance at her.

"I came out here because I wanted to get acquainted with this great country and thought there might be an opportunity to do good," said Margaret coldly. She didn't care to discuss her affairs with this man. "But, Mr. West, I don't understand you. Didn't you tell me you were a Presbyterian minister?"

"I certainly did," he answered, as though he were honoring the whole body of Presbyterians by making the statement.

"Well, then, what did you mean? All Presbyterians, of course, believe in the infallibility of the Scriptures and the deity of Jesus—and the atonement!"

"Not necessarily," answered the young man. "You'll find, my dear young lady, that a growing feeling in our church favors a broader view. The younger men and the great student body of our church have thrown out their former beliefs and are ready to accept new light with open minds. Scientific findings have opened up a vast store of knowledge, and all thinking men must acknowledge that the old dogmas are vanishing. Your father doubtless still holds to the old faith, and we must be lenient with the older men who've done the best they could with the light they had. But all younger, broad-minded men are looking at things in the new way. We've had enough of the days of preaching hell-fire and damnation. We need a religion of love to man and of good works.

"You should read some of the books on this subject if you care to understand. It would be worth your while. You look to me like a young woman with a mind. I have a few of the latest with me. I'll be glad to read and discuss them with you if you're interested."

"Thank you, Mr. West," Margaret said. "I've probably read most of those books and discussed them with my father. He may be old, but he isn't without 'light,' as you said, and he's always believed in knowing what the other side says. He brought me up to look into these things for myself. And, anyhow, I shouldn't care to read and discuss any of these subjects with a man who denies the deity of my Savior and doesn't believe in the infallibility of the Bible. It seems to me you have nothing left—"

"Ah! Well—now—my dear young lady—you mustn't misjudge me! I'd be sorry to shake your faith, for an innocent faith is beautiful, even though it may be unfounded."

"Indeed, Mr. West, that would be impossible. You couldn't shake my faith in my Christ, because *I know Him.* If I'd never felt His presence or been guided by His leading, such words might possibly trouble me, but having seen 'Him that is invisible,' I *know.*" Margaret's voice was steady and gentle.

"Well, let's not quarrel about it," he said indulgently. "I'm sure you have a charming way of stating it, and it's a relief to find a woman of the old-fashioned type now and then. It really is man's place to look into these deeper questions anyway. It's woman's sphere to live and love and make a happy home—"

His voice took on a sentimental purr, and Margaret tried to calm herself. She felt she mustn't let her temper give way, especially when talking on the sacred theme of the Christ. She found one relief. Her father would no longer expect her to respect or honor a minister who denied the very life and foundation of his faith.

"The schoolhouse can't be so far from town," she said suddenly, looking around at the widening desert in front of them. "Haven't you made some mistake?"

"Why, I thought we'd enjoy a little drive first," said West, smiling. "I was sure you'd like to see the country before you start working, and I wasn't averse to a drive in such delightful company."

"I'd like to go back to the schoolhouse at once, please," said Margaret.

Something in her voice caused the man to turn the horse around and head toward town.

"Why, yes, of course, if you prefer to see the schoolhouse first, we can go back and look it over, and then perhaps you'll like to ride a little farther," he said. "We have plenty of time. In fact, Mrs. Tanner told me she wouldn't expect us home for dinner. She packed a lunch basket under the seat for us in case we got hungry."

"Thank you," said Margaret icily now. "I don't care to drive this morning. I'd like to see the schoolhouse, and then I must return to the house at once. I have other work to tend to this morning."

Her abrupt manner finally reached him, for he stopped asking and rode straight to the schoolhouse. She remained silent during the rest of the ride, answering him with only a yes or no when necessary. He babbled away about college life and incidents of his late pastorate, at some of which he laughed immoderately; but he couldn't bring even a smile to her lips.

He hoped she would change her mind when they got to the school and praised it in a kind of contemptuous way as they drew up in front of the large adobe building.

"I suppose you'll want to go through the building," he said, producing the key from his pocket and smiling.

Margaret shook her head. "It isn't necessary. I'd like to go home now, please."

He reluctantly turned the horse toward the Tanner house, wondering why the girl was so hard to win. He flattered himself that he could always interest any girl he chose. It was bewildering. But he would win her yet.

He let her out silently at the Tanner door and drove off, lunch basket and all, into the wilderness, vexed at her unfriendliness and pondering how he might break down her dignity. He would find a way. He set his weak chin, and his pale-blue eyes took on a hardness.

Chapter 9

She watched him from her bedroom window, after escaping Mrs. Tanner's exclamations. With his derby tilted down over his left eye, he looked like a small, mean creature driving out onto the plain. Margaret couldn't help comparing him with the young man who rode away from the house two days before.

"And he's set up to be a minister of the gospel and talking like that about the Bible and Christ!" Oh, what was the church of Christ coming to, to have ministers like that? How did he get into the ministry? She knew young men with honest doubts sometimes slid through nowadays, but a man like that? What ridiculous things he said! He was like those who "darken counsel with words." And what harm he could do in an unlearned community! Mrs. Tanner hung on his words, as if they were law and gospel. How *could* she?

Margaret was still trembling over his words about Christ, the atonement and the faith. She did not believe because those were empty traditions she'd been taught; she had lived her faith and proved it and felt it a personal insult for him to speak that way of her Savior. She picked up her Bible and leafed through the pages for something—she couldn't tell what—until her eye caught some verses her father had marked for her before she left home for college. He was troubled then for her going out into an unbelieving world.

As ye have therefore received Christ Jesus the Lord, so walk ye in him: rooted and built up in him, and established in the faith, as ye have been taught, abounding therein with thanksgiving. Beware lest any man spoil you through philosophy and vain deceit, after the tradition of men, after the rudiments of the world, and not after Christ. For in him dwelleth all fullness of the Godhead bodily.

How the verses crowded upon one another, standing out clearly from the pages as she turned them, underlined with her father's own hand in clear ink. It almost seemed as if God had looked ahead to these times and set these words down just to encourage His troubled servants who couldn't understand why faith was growing dim. God knew about all this doubt and had put words here to comfort troubled hearts.

For I know whom I have believed [how her heart echoed to that statement!] and am persuaded that he is able to keep that which I have committed unto him against that day.

And on a little further:

Nevertheless the foundation of God standeth sure, having this seal.
The Lord knoweth them that are his.

The words seemed to convey a triumphant sound as she read them. Then
over in Ephesians her eye caught a verse that seemed to fit the minister:

Having the understanding darkened, being alienated from the life of
God through the ignorance that is in them, because of the blindness of
their heart.

Yet he was set to guide the blind into the way of life! And he had looked on
her as one of the ignorant. Poor fellow! He couldn't know the Christ who was
her Savior, or he never would have spoken in that way about Him. What could
such a man preach? What was there left to preach but empty words when one
rejected all these doctrines? Must she listen to a man like that Sunday after
Sunday? Did the scholars in her school and their parents, the young man out
at the camp and his rough, simple-hearted companions, have to listen to
preaching from that man, when they listened to any? She knelt beside her bed
for a word with the Christ who since childhood had been a real presence in
her life.

When she arose from her knees she heard the kitchen door slam downstairs and Bud's voice calling his mother. She went to her door and opened
it, listening a moment.

"Bud!" she called

There was dead silence for an instant, and then Bud appeared at the foot
of the stairs, frowning.

"What d'ye want?" he asked abruptly.

"Bud," she said coolly, leaning over the rail, "please, next time you can't
keep an appointment with me, don't ask anybody else to take your place. It
was all right if you had to go somewhere else, but I could easily have gone
alone or waited until another time. I'd rather not have you ask Mr. West to
go anywhere with me again."

Bud's mouth flew open. His eyes suddenly danced with understanding,
and then his brows pulled together in a frown.

"I never ast him," he declared. "He told me you wanted him to go and fer
me to get out of the way 'cause you didn't want to hurt my feelings. Didn't
you say nothing to him about it this morning?"

"No, indeed!" said Margaret, her eyes flashing.

"Well, I thought he was that kind of guy. I told Ma he was lying. But she
said I didn't understand young ladies, and, of course, you didn't want me when
a man, especially a preacher, was around. Some preacher he is! This's the
second time I've caught him lying. I think he's the limit. I wish you'd see our
missionary. If he was here he'd beat the dust out o' that poor stew. *He's* some

man, he is. He's a regular man, *our missionary!* Just wait till *he* gets back."

Margaret sighed with relief. Then the missionary was a real man. Oh, for his return!

"Well, I'm certainly glad it wasn't your fault, Bud. I didn't feel happy to be put off that way," she said, smiling down on the boy's rough head.

"You bet it wasn't my fault!" said the boy. "I was sore's a pup at you, after you'd made a plan and all, to do like that. But I thought if you wanted to go with that guy it was up to you."

"Well, I didn't and I don't. I'll always prefer your company to his. How about going down to the schoolhouse today? Do you have time?"

"Didn't you go yet?" The boy's face lit up.

"We drove down there, but I didn't care to go in without you, so we came back."

"Wanta go now?"

"I'd love to. I'll be ready in three minutes. Could we carry some books down?"

"Sure! Oh! That guy's got the buckboard. We'll have to walk. Blast him!"

"I'll enjoy walking. I want to find out just how far it is, for I'll have to walk every day."

"No, you won't neither, 'nless you wanta. I c'n always hitch up."

"That'll be very nice sometimes, but I'd get spoiled if you did that every day. I'll be right down."

They walked out into the morning sunshine, and it seemed a new day had been created since she returned from her ride with the minister. She looked at the sturdy, honest-eyed boy beside her and was glad to have him for a companion.

In front of the schoolhouse Margaret paused. "Oh, I forgot! The key! Mr. West has the key in his pocket! We can't get in, can we?"

"Aw, we don't need a key. Just wait!" Bud whisked around to the back of the building, and in about three minutes his head appeared at the window. He threw the sash open and dropped out a wooden box. "There! You c'n climb up on that, can'tcha? Here, I'll hold ya steady. Take holta my hand."

And so it was through the front window that the new Ridge School teacher first appeared and surveyed her future workplace.

Bud threw open the shutters, letting the view of the plains and the sunshine into the big, dusty room, and showed her the new chalkboard with great pride.

"There's a whole box o' chalk up on the desk, too—ain't never been opened yet. Dad said that was your property. Want I should open it?"

"Why, yes, you might, and then we'll try the chalkboard, shall we?"

Bud opened the chalk box as if it were a small treasure chest and finally produced a long, smooth stick of chalk and handed it to her with shining eyes.

"You try it first, Bud," said Margaret, seeing his eagerness.

The boy stepped forward gingerly. Shyly, awkwardly, with infinite care, he wrote in a cramped hand, "William Budlong Tanner," and then, growing bolder, "Ashland, Arizona," with a big flourish underneath.

"Some class!" he said, standing back and regarding his handiwork. "Say, I like the sound the chalk makes, don't you?"

"Yes, I do," said Margaret. "It's smooth and businesslike, isn't it? You'll enjoy doing examples in algebra on it, won't you?"

"Good night! Algebra! Me? No chance. I can't never get through the arithmetic. The last teacher said if he'd come back twenty years from now he'd still find me working compound interest."

"Well, we'll prove that man wasn't much of a judge of boys. If you're not in algebra before two months are over I'll miss my guess. We'll get it right away and show him."

Bud looked at her in wonder, half believing what she said might come true.

"Now, Bud, suppose we get to work. I'd like to get acquainted with my class a little before Monday. Doesn't school open Monday? I thought so. Well, suppose you give me the students' names, and I'll write them down, and that will help me remember them. Here, suppose you sit down in the front seat and tell me who sits there and a little bit about him, and I'll write the name down. Then you move to the next seat and tell me about the next one, and so on. Will you?"

"Sure!" said Bud, entering into the new game. "But it ain't a 'he' sits there. It's Susie Johnson. She's Bill Johnson's smallest girl. She has to sit up front 'cause she giggles so much. She has yellow curls, and she ducks her head down and snickers right out this way when anything funny happens in school." And Bud proceeded to duck and wriggle in imitation of Susie.

Margaret laughed heartily at his actions. Then she turned and wrote "Susie Johnson" on the board in beautiful script.

Bud watched with admiration, saying softly under his breath, "Say! That chalkboard's great, ain't it?"

Amelia Schwartz came next. She was long and lank, with the buttons off the back of her dress, and hands and feet too large for her garments. Margaret couldn't help but see her in the boy's clever pantomime. Next was Rosa Rogers, daughter of a wealthy cattleman, the school's pink-cheeked, blue-eyed beauty, with all the boys at her feet and knowledge of her power over them. Bud didn't, of course, state it that way, but Margaret gathered as much from his simpering smile and the coy way he looked out of the corner of his eyes as he described her.

Down the long list of students he went, row after row. When he came to the seats where the boys sat, his tone changed. She could tell by the shading of his voice which boys to look out for.

Jed Brower could ride any horse that ever stood on four legs, he could outshoot most of the neighborhood boys, and he never allowed any teacher to tell him what to do. He was Tex Brower's only boy and always had his own way. His father served on the school board. Some of the younger boys held Jed in awe, even while despising his methods. He was big and powerful, and nobody dared fool with him.

Bud didn't exactly warn Margaret to keep on Jed's good side, but she understood. She knew also that Tad Brooks, Larry Parker, Jim Long, and Dake Foster were merely henchmen of the worthy Jed, not negligible quantities by themselves.

But over the name of Timothy Forbes—"Delicate Forbes," Bud explained, was his nickname—the boy lingered with that loving admiration a younger boy will sometimes have for a husky, courageous older lad. The second time Bud spoke of him he called him "Forbeszy," and Margaret perceived that here was Bud's model of manhood. Delicate Forbes could outshoot and outride even Jed Brower when he chose, and he possessed the courage of a man when it came to cattle. Moreover, he would pitch a baseball with the younger boys when he had nothing better to do. From the description Delicate Forbes evidently didn't lack for any inches to his stature. He had whipped every man teacher in the school and deceived every woman teacher in six years. Bud's loyalty was evident; yet he plainly felt Margaret's greatest hindrance in the school would be Delicate Forbes.

Margaret mentally underlined the names belonging to the back seats in the first and second rows. Then she went home praying for wisdom and patience to deal with Jed Brower and Timothy Forbes and through them to manage the rest of her school.

She surprised Bud at the dinner table by handing him a neat diagram of the schoolroom desks with the correct names of all but three or four of the scholars written on them.

"Say, that's going some! Guess you won't forget nothing, no matter how much they try to make you."

Chapter 10

The minister didn't appear until late in the evening, after Margaret had gone to her room, for which she was thankful. She could hear his voice, fretful and complaining, as he called loudly for Bud to take the horse. It appeared he'd lost his way and wandered many miles off the trail. He blamed the country for poor trails and the horse for not finding the way better.

"Now that's too bad!" said Mrs. Tanner, by way of comfort. "Dearie me! Bud oughta hev gone with you. *Oh*, Bud, you ain't gonta sleep yet, hev you? Wake up and come down and take this horse to the barn."

But Bud only shouted some sleepy directions from his loft and said the minister could look after his own horse; he "wasn'ta gonta!" There was "plentya corn in the bin."

The minister grumbled his way to the barn and back, disturbing the calm of Margaret's evening view of the mountain. He wasn't accustomed to handling horses and thought Bud might have stayed up and attended to it himself. Bud chuckled in his loft and stole down the back kitchen roof while the minister ate his late supper. And Margaret, from her seat by the window, saw the boy slide off the kitchen roof and run to the barn, and she smiled.

The Sabbath dawned brilliantly and, at the same time, flooded the girl with a sense of desolation. She heard no church bells and had no sense of the Sabbath in the air. The mountain greeted her with what seemed a holy light, but mountains don't depend upon humankind for Sabbath worship, for they are "continually praising Him."

Margaret wondered how she woudld get through this dreary first Sabbath away from home and her Sabbath school class and her church with Father preaching. She'd been away, of course, many times before, but never to a churchless community. That's how Ashland seemed to her. On the walk to school and the ride through town, she hadn't noticed anything that resembled a church, and all the talk had been of the missionary. They must have services of some sort, and probably that so-called minister was to preach. But her face grew pale at the thought of listening to a man who had confessed to such unbeliefs. Of course, he would surely keep such doubts to himself; but nothing he could say now would change her opinion of him.

She sighed and looked at her watch. It was late. At home the early Sabbath school bells would be ringing, and little girls would be holding hands with their little brothers as they hurried down the street. Father was in his study, going over his morning sermon, and Mother was getting ready to go to her Bible class.

Margaret got up and dressed quickly, putting on a white dress she wore to church at home. She hastened downstairs to discover the family plans for the day but found, to her dismay, the atmosphere unchanged from other days. Mr. Tanner sat tilted back in his chair, reading the weekly paper. Mrs. Tanner was carrying in hot corn bread. Bud sat on the front steps teasing the dog. And the minister entered just then, his hair uncombed, his coat wrinkled and his eyes downcast, not looking at all like a man who expected to preach in a few minutes. He declined to eat his egg because, he said, it was cooked too hard. Mrs. Tanner tried two more before she produced a soft-boiled egg that suited him. Only the radiant outline of the mountain, which Margaret could see over the minister's head, looked peaceful and Sabbathlike.

"What time do you have service?" Margaret asked.

"Service?" Mr. Tanner echoed her question.

Mrs. Tanner raised her eyes from her belated breakfast with a worried look, like a mother hen stretching her neck about to make sure her chicks were safe.

It was the minister who answered. "Um! Ah! There's no church as such here, Miss Earle. The mission station is located some miles distant."

"I know," said Margaret, "but they surely have some religious service, don't they?"

"I don't know," said the minister loftily.

"Then you're not going to preach this morning?" In spite of herself her tone held relief.

"Certainly not," he replied. "I came out here to rest and selected this place largely because it was so far from a church. I wanted to be where I wouldn't be annoyed by requests to preach. Ministers from the East would be a curiosity in these Western towns, and I'd get no rest if I'd gone where my services would have been in constant demand. When I came out here I was in much the same condition as that minister you've doubtless heard of. He was starting on his vacation and said to a fellow minister, with a smile of joy and relief, 'No preaching, no praying, no Bible reading for six whole weeks!' "

"Indeed!" said Margaret. "No, I'm not familiar with ministers like that."

She turned sharply from him and looked at Mrs. Tanner. "Then you really have no Sabbath service in town?"

Mrs. Tanner's neck stretched up a little longer, but before she could say anything Bud spoke up.

"We gotta Sunday school, Ma!"

His tone held a kind of pride and a triumph over the minister, albeit Bud had adjured Sunday school since his early infancy. He was ready now, however, to be offered on the altar of Sunday school, if that would please the new teacher—and spite the minister.

"I'll take you ef you wanta go," he said, glaring at the minister.

But at last Mrs. Tanner seemed to grasp the matter. "Why, you mean preaching service!" she clucked out. "Why, yes, Mr. West, wouldn't that be fine? You could preach for us. We could post it up at the saloon and the crossings and out a ways on both trails, and you'd gather quite a crowd. They'd come from over to the camp and up the canyon way and around. They'd do you credit, they surely would, Mr. West. And you could have the schoolhouse for a meeting house. Pa's on the school board. There wouldn't be a bit of trouble—"

"Um! Ah! Mrs. Tanner, I assure you it's quite out of the question. I told you I was here for rest. I couldn't think of preaching. Besides, it's against my principles to preach without remuneration. It's a wrong idea. The workman is worthy of his hire, you know, the Good Book says."

"Oh! Ef that's all, that 'u'd be all right!" she said with relief. "You could take up a collection. The boys would be real generous. They always are when any show comes along. They'd appreciate it, and I'd like fer Miss Earle to hear you preach. It 'u'd be a real treat to her, her being a preacher's daughter and all."

She turned to Margaret for support, but that young woman was talking to Bud. She had promptly accepted his offer to take her to Sunday school, and now she hurried away to get ready, leaving Mrs. Tanner to make her clerical arrangements unaided.

The minister, meanwhile, looked after her doubtfully. Perhaps he should have preached. He might have impressed her since she pretended to be so interested in religious matters. He turned to Mrs. Tanner and asked questions about the feasibility of a church service. The word "collection" sounded good to him. He wasn't averse to replenishing his depleted treasury.

He was still trying to impress the Tanners with the importance of his late charge in the East when Margaret came downstairs. His pompous tones, raised to overcome the deafness he took for granted in Mr. Tanner, reached her ears.

"I couldn't think of doing it every Sunday, you understand. It wouldn't be fair to me or the work I've just left. But, of course, if there were sufficient inducement I might consent to preach some Sunday before I leave."

Margaret closed the front door and went out to the waiting Bud.

The Sunday school was presided over by an elderly man, who nursed his elbows and rubbed his chin meditatively between the slow questions he read from the lesson. The woman who usually taught the children was called away to nurse a sick neighbor, and the children were huddled together in a restless group. A few voices joined faintly in singing, and the exercises, including the prayer, stirred little enthusiasm. The few women present stared at the visitor as if she were intruding. Bud lingered outside the door and finally disappeared altogether, reappearing when the last hymn was sung. The new teacher felt homesick as she walked back to the Tanners' beside Bud.

"What do you do on Sunday afternoons, Bud?" she asked, as soon as they were out of hearing of the others.

The boy turned wondering eyes toward her. "Do?" he repeated, puzzled. "Why, we pass the time away, like most any day. There ain't much difference."

No church! Worse than no minister! No Sabbath! What kind of land had she come to?

She could smell tobacco smoke on the boy and knew he'd gone off somewhere while she attended the Sunday school. He smoked, of course, like most boys his age, took no interest in God and didn't think the Sabbath was different from any other day. She felt discouraged and wondered if she shouldn't give up now and go back where her ideas would be welcome. Of course, she knew things would be different from home, but this experiment had held more promise from a distance. It looked hopeless now, and she didn't think she could do any good in a place like this.

Yet the place needed somebody! That Sunday school! She almost regretted going and even dreaded her first day of school tomorrow.

Then, as she and Bud neared the Tanner house, she saw a familiar horse and rider coming down the road. Her eyes lit up on seeing Gardley, and she saw a warm smile spread over his face.

She wondered at her reaction to him—a stranger with sorrow and failure in his life—yet he had rescued her from the fearful desert night. Yes, he seemed a goodly sight to her amid these uncongenial surroundings.

Chapter 11

The sun glinted off his hair, and his blue-gray eyes looked into hers, as he dismounted. He greeted her, and Bud stepped back and watched in surprise. This was the man who had shot all the lights out the night of the big saloon riot. He'd also risked his life in other ways, so the reports said. Like most boys, Bud admired the young man, and his adoration of the teacher yielded her to a fitting rival. He stayed behind, walking beside the pony, who was following his master.

"Oh, and this is my friend, William Tanner," Margaret said, turning toward Bud.

Whatever made her call him William? Bud wondered. He blushed and grinned.

"Glad to know you, Will," said the newcomer, extending his hand in a hearty shake that warmed the boy's heart. "I'm glad Miss Earle has such a good protector. You'll have to look out for her. She's pretty plucky and is apt to stray around the wilderness by herself. It isn't safe, you know, for someone like her. Look after her, will you?"

"Right, I will," said Bud, straightening up tall and squaring his shoulders. He might have stopped to wonder how the man of the plains was acquainted with the new teacher, but he was too excited just then to do so.

The little procession walked down the road slowly. The young man had found Margaret's handkerchief at the camp after she left and brought it to her. He produced it from his inner pocket, but nothing in his manner was presumptuous or hinted of any intimacy other than their chance encounter in the wilderness. He didn't look at her as West had. She didn't resent his glance when it rested upon her, for she saw only respect and friendship.

The men had sent gifts: arrowheads and a curiously fashioned vessel from the canyon of the cave-dwellers; chips from the petrified forest; a fern with fronds, root and all, and a sheaf of blossoms carefully wrapped in wet paper and fastened to the saddle.

He showed them to her one by one and told her the history of each and a message from the man who sent it. And Mom Wallis had included an odd little cake she'd baked. The young man's face softened then, as if he knew what Margaret's visit had meant to her. Margaret recalled the morning she awakened in the bunkhouse and found the wrinkled old woman watching her with tears in her eyes. Poor Mom Wallis, tired and ill-used, with her pretty girlhood behind her and such a blank, dull future ahead!

"They all want to know," said the young man, "if sometime, when you get settled and have time, you'd come out again and sing. I explained that, of course, you'd be busy with other friends and your work, and you wouldn't want to come. But they wanted me to tell you they really enjoyed your singing. I heard Long Jim singing 'Old Folks at Home' this morning when he was saddling his horse. And the men even straightened up the bunkhouse. Jasper made a new chair yesterday—for when you come again, he said. But you needn't feel you must," Gardley added with a half laugh.

But Margaret looked up eagerly. "Of course I'll come—as soon as I can. You tell them we'll have another concert."

The young man's face lit up, and his eyes flashed their pleasure.

At the same time the Rev. West was stalking up and down in front of the Tanner house and staring down the road. He had spent the morning poring over the "show sermons" he brought with him and was about to accede to Mrs. Tanner's request and preach in Ashland before he left. And now he was eager to announce his decision to the teacher. Further, he was hungry and couldn't understand why that impudent boy and that young woman should stay at Sunday school so long.

He could smell Mrs. Tanner's fried chicken every time he turned toward the house. They shouldn't keep dinner waiting this way. He turned the other way and started thinking about his sermon. He was recalling a particularly eloquent passage when he glanced at the road again, and there they were, almost upon him! But Bud was no longer walking with the teacher. She'd acquired a new escort. Where had he seen that man before? He watched them as they approached, his pale eyes narrowing under their yellow lashes.

He noticed the look that passed between them. At the same moment he recognized the man, or at least recalled where he last saw him, and rejoiced at his advantage.

He pulled himself up, flattened his chin upward, pulled his yellow brows together in a frown and stepped forward to meet the little party as it neared the house. He looked as if he might oust the stranger, upon inspection, having assigned himself the role of protecting the lady. From the way he surveyed them, they might have been a pair of naughty children returned from a forbidden frolic. But they didn't notice him until they arrived at the house.

"Well, Miss Margaret, you're home at last!" he exclaimed, eyeing her companion.

Margaret stopped abruptly, and a look of disdain crossed her face. She didn't like his using her first name in that familiar tone.

But Gardley was already scrutinizing the minister. Something in his look made West shrink back. Then Gardley turned to Margaret.

"Is this man a friend of yours, Miss *Earle?*" he asked, with marked emphasis on the last word.

"No," said Margaret, "he's a boarder in the house." Then she added formally, "Mr. West, my *friend* Mr. Gardley."

Undaunted, the minister stood his ground, with no sense of being dismissed. He wasn't accustomed to accepting dismissal, however, as his recent church in New York might have testified. Rather than acknowledge the introduction, he stood with his hands clasped behind his back, scowling.

Gardley gazed at him a moment, a look of mingled contempt and amusement growing on his face. Then he turned away.

"You'll come in and take dinner with us?" asked Margaret. "I'd like to send a small package to Mrs. Wallis if you wouldn't mind taking it with you."

"I'm sorry I can't stay for dinner. I have an errand at some distance in another direction. But I'm returning this way and, if I may, will call and get the package toward evening."

"Oh, yes," Margaret said, smiling.

After a few more words the young man sprang on his horse, said, "So long, Will!" to Bud and rode away, not even glancing at the minister.

They watched him a moment, then Margaret started toward the house.

"Um! Ah! Miss Margaret!" began the minister, waving his hand for her to stop.

Margaret turned back to him. "Miss *Earle,* if you please!"

"Um! Ah! Why, certainly, Miss—ah—*Earle,* if you wish it. Will you kindly remain here a moment? I wish to speak with you. Bud, you may go on."

"I'll go when I like, and it's none of your business!" muttered Bud under his breath. He glanced at Margaret. He thought this might be one of the times he was to look after her.

She smiled at him. "William may remain, Mr. West," she said sweetly. "Anything you have to say to me can surely be said in his presence." She laid her hand lightly on Bud's sleeve.

Bud looked down at the hand and grew inches taller enjoying the minister's frown.

"Um! Ah!" said West, unabashed. "Well, I merely wished to warn you about the character of that person who has just left us. He's really not a proper companion for you. Indeed, I may say he's quite the contrary and that to my personal knowledge—"

"He's as good as you are and better!" growled Bud.

"Be quiet, boy! I wasn't speaking to you!" said West. "If I hear another word from you I'll report you to your father!"

"Go 's far 's you like and see how much I care!" taunted Bud.

But Margaret's gentle pressure on his arm stopped him.

"Mr. West, I thought I made you understand Mr. Gardley is my friend."

"Um! Ah! Then, Miss Earle, I must say you've formed an unwise friendship and should stop it. Why, my dear young lady, if you knew all there is to know about him you wouldn't speak to him."

"Indeed, Mr. West! I suppose that might be true of many people, mightn't it, *if we knew all there is to know about them?* No one but God could get along with some of us."

"But, my dear young lady, you don't understand. He's nothing but a common ruffian, a gambler, in fact, and frequents saloons. I've seen him myself sitting in a saloon at a late hour playing cards with a bunch of low-down creatures—"

"And why were you in a saloon at that hour, Mr. West?" Her eyes held a gleam of mischief.

The minister's face reddened. "Well, I—ah—I was called from my bed by shouts and gunshots. There was a fight in the room next to the bar, and I thought my help might be needed." (Bud snorted at this.) "But imagine my astonishment when I learned the drunken brawl I was witnessing was a nightly occurrence. I stayed a few minutes, partly out of curiosity, since I wanted to see all kinds of life in this new world for a book I may write. I noticed the people there and identified the person who just rode away as one of the chief factors in that evening's entertainment. In fact, he pocketed all the money on the gaming table, stood up, took out his pistol and shot out the lights in the room—"

"And you came within an ace of being shot, Pa says. The Kid's a dead shot, and you were right in the way. Served you right for going where you had no business!"

"I didn't stay longer, as you may imagine," West continued, ignoring Bud. "I found it was no place for a—ah—minister of the gospel. But I stayed long enough to hear from the lips of the man you were just walking with some of the most terrible language my ears have ever—ah—witnessed!"

"Mr. West, I think you've said all that's necessary. You evidently don't know some things about Mr. Gardley, but I think you'll learn them if you stay in this part of the country long. William, isn't that your mother calling us to dinner? Let's go in—I'm hungry."

Bud followed her up the walk, glancing over his shoulder at the minister and smiling cheerfully, and they disappeared into the house. But when Margaret went up to her room and took off her hat, her eyes were filled with angry tears. Yet she knew she mustn't cry, for dinner would be ready and she must go down. And never should that meddling man see that his words had pierced her.

For, angry as she was at the minister, much as she loathed his petty nature and saw through his tales, something told her his picture of Gardley's wildness was probably true. It was just what had made its shadowy way into her heart when he'd hinted at his being a "roughneck." Yet to have it put into words by an enemy both angered and frightened her.

"Margaret Earle, have you come out to the wilderness to lose your heart to the first handsome sower of wild oats you meet?" Her true eyes asked herself in the glass, and she saw a sadness reflected there. Then she dropped upon her knees beside her rocking chair and buried her face in its flowered cushions.

"Oh, Father, don't let me be weak. But I ask You to save him. Help him find You and serve You, and if he's failed—and he says he has—make it right for Jesus' sake! And if there's anything I can do, show me how and help me.

Jesus, Your power is great. Let this young man feel it and yield himself to it."

She prayed a little longer, putting her whole soul into the prayer and sensing she was called to pray for him until her prayer was answered.

She came down to dinner a few minutes later, with a calmness on her face and no hint of her recent emotion, talking eagerly at the table with Mr. Tanner about her hometown and her father and mother. By the time the conversation had turned to other matters, no one there had reason to think the new teacher was careless about her acquaintances or had cultivated anything but the highest principles from her family.

But West had retired into a sulky mood and said nothing except to ask for more chicken and coffee and a second piece of pie. He decided then that it would be best for him to preach in Ashland on the following Sunday. The young lady would be impressed with his dignity in no other way.

Chapter 12

When Lance Gardley returned to the Tanners' the sun was setting in its glory, and the mountain was robed in its rosy veil.

Margaret was waiting for him on the porch, with Cap beside her, watching her mountain. She was relieved to find that the minister occupied a room on the first floor in a kind of ell on the opposite side of the house from her room and the mountain. He hadn't been visible that afternoon, and with the dog beside her and Bud on the steps reading *The Sky Pilot* she felt safe. She'd read to Bud for an hour and a half, and he was absorbed in the story. But she was sure he'd keep the minister away at all costs. As for Cap, he and the minister were sworn enemies by now. He growled every time West came near or spoke to her.

She sat there with her hand on Cap's shaggy head, the lace of her sleeve falling back from her arm, her other hand raised to shade her face as she looked at the mountain, a slim, white figure gazing off at the sunset. The young man removed his hat and rode up softly.

The dog lifted one ear and quivered once as the rider approached. But the girl turned, alert, and met him with a smile. The hardness seemed smoothed away from his face for now. Studying him in light of the morning's revelations, she could hardly believe they were true; yet she sensed they were.

The young man dismounted and left his horse standing quietly beside the road. He wouldn't stay, he said. Yet he lingered by her side, talking for a few minutes, watching the sunset and pointing out its changes.

She gave him the package for Mom Wallis. A simple lace collar lay in a white box, with a small book bound in russet suede with gold lettering.

"Tell her to wear the collar whenever she wants to dress up."

"That won't happen," he said. "Mom Wallis never dresses up."

"Oh, then tell her I hope she'll dress up evenings for supper, and I'll make her another one to change with that and bring it when I come."

He smiled at her again in wonder.

"And the little book—I suppose it's foolish to send it," she said. "But something she said made me think of some of the lines in the poem. I've marked them for her. She reads, doesn't she?"

"A little, I think. I see her now and then reading the papers Pop brings home. I don't imagine she's read much literature, though."

"Probably not, and maybe she won't understand any of it. But tell her I sent her a message. She must see if she can find it in the poem. Perhaps you can explain it to her. It's Browning's 'Rabbi Ben Ezra.' You know it, don't you?"

"No, I don't. I was too intent on other things when I was supposed to be paying attention to Browning. But I'll do my best. What's it about? Could you give me a pointer or two?"

"It's the one beginning,

Grow old along with me!
The best is yet to be,
The last of life, for which the first was made:
Our times are in His hand
Who saith, "A whole I planned,
Youth shows but half; trust God: see all nor be afraid!"

"Grow old along with you?" he said and then smiled. "You don't look as if you would ever grow old."

"That's it!" she said. "That's the whole idea. We don't ever grow old or finish with it all. We just go on to bigger things, wiser and better and more beautiful, till we understand and become part of God's great plan!"

He regarded her for a moment with a quizzical, grave look as if he were considering the matter seriously. She waited, unable to find the right words. Then he looked away.

"That makes living different from the way most people take it," he said at last.

"Does it?" she asked, gazing with him toward the sunset.

After some minutes she realized she must speak. "I've been thinking about what you said on the ride," she began hesitantly. "You said you didn't make good. I—wish you would. I—I'm sure you could—"

She glanced up and saw a gentleness spread over his face as if his soul, long sealed, had opened and he saw a possibility for the first time through her words.

In a moment he turned to her again, smiling. "Why should you care?" he asked. The words would have sounded harsh if his tone hadn't been so gentle.

Margaret hesitated. "I don't know how to—express it," she said slowly. "There are a few lines later in that poem. Perhaps you know them—

All I never could be,
All, men ignored in me,
This, I was worth to God, whose wheel the pitcher shaped.

I want it because—well, perhaps because I feel you're worth all that to God. I'd like to see you be that."

He looked at her again and was quiet so long she wondered if he'd understood.

"I hope you'll excuse my speaking," she added. "There—are so many grand possibilities in life, and for you—I couldn't bear to have you say you hadn't made good, as if it were all over."

"I'm glad you spoke," he said quickly. "I guess I've been very foolish. You've made me feel that more."

"Oh, no!" she protested.

"You don't know what I've been," he said. Then, with sudden conviction, as if he'd read her thoughts, he added, "You *do* know! That prig of a parson told you! But it's just as well you should know."

A wave of misery crossed his face, erasing its brightness. Even the gentleness was gone. He looked haggard all at once.

"Do you think *anything* that man said would matter to me?" she asked, with sympathy in her voice.

"But all he said was true, probably, and more—"

"It doesn't matter," she said. "The other is true too. Just as the poem says—all that man ignores in you, just that you are worth to God. And you *can* be what He meant you to be. I've been praying all afternoon that He would help you."

"Have you?" he asked, his eyes glowing. "Thank you."

"You helped me when I was lost in the desert," she said shyly. "I wanted to help *you* back—if—I might."

"You'll help—you have already!" he said. "And I was far enough off the trail too. But if there's any way to get back I'll get there." He grasped her hand and held it a moment. "Keep up that praying," he said. "I'll see what can be done."

Then, suddenly, a discordant sound reached their ears.

"Um! Ah!—"

The minister stood in the doorway, barred by Bud in scowling defiance and Cap, who gave an answering growl.

Gardley and Margaret glanced at each other, smiled, then walked over to his horse. He touched her hand lightly, mounted and rode away.

"Come, William—let's sing," she said, pausing beside him.

"Sure! What'll we sing?" asked Bud, moving over to let her sit down beside him.

She sat with her back to West, while Cap lay at her feet with one eye on the minister and a growl ready to issue forth. The minister couldn't get out unless he jumped over them or went out the back door.

"Well, do you know this?" she asked and started singing quietly.

When peace like a river attendeth my way;
When sorrows like sea billows roll;
Whatever my lot Thou hast taught me to say,
"It is well, it is well with my soul."

Bud didn't know the song, but he didn't intend to be balked with the minister standing right behind him, doubtless ready to jump in and take over. So he rumbled out a bass note, turning it over and trying to make it fit, and managed to keep time and make it sound a little like singing.

Dusk was falling fast as they finished the last verse, with Margaret singing the words clearly and Bud rumbling unintelligibly and snatching at words he'd never heard before. Then she sang,

Abide with me; fast falls the eventide;
The darkness deepens; Lord, with me abide!
When other refuge fails and comforts flee,
Help of the helpless, oh, abide with me!

Out on the lonely trail, heading toward the purple mountain and the camp bunkhouse, in that clear air where sound travels, the rider heard the song and wondered.

Margaret sang on, for she didn't want to talk about commonplace things just then. Song after song was carried through the night's wideness. Mr. Tanner had long since dropped his paper and tilted his chair back against the wall, with his eyes closed, listening. His wife had settled down comfortably on the carpet sofa, with her hands folded in her lap. The minister tried to join his raspy voice to the chorus, while Cap growled now and then, as if the minister's voice put his nerves on edge. And by and by Mr. Tanner quavered in with a note or two.

Finally Margaret sang,

Sun of my soul, Thou Savior dear,
It is not night if Thou art near,
Oh, may no earth-born cloud arise
To hide Thee from Thy servant's eyes.

During this hymn the minister stole out the back door and around to the front of the house. He couldn't stand being in the background any longer. But as the last note died away Margaret stood up and, bidding Bud good night, slipped up to her room.

There beside her darkened window, with her face toward the mountain, she knelt to pray for the wanderer who was trying to find his way out of the wilderness.

Chapter 13

Early Monday morning Bud hitched up the buckboard and drove Margaret to the schoolhouse.

One by one the students trooped in, hung their hats on the hooks, put their dinner pails on the shelf, looked at her and sank into their usual seats—that is, the seats they'd occupied during the last school term. The older boys remained outside until Bud, under instructions from Margaret, rang the bell. Even then they shuffled in, scuffing their feet and loitering about the door until the last possible moment. Jed and "Delicate" came in last, scarcely glancing toward the teacher's desk.

She didn't need to be told which was Timothy and which was Jed. Bud had described them perfectly. She felt drawn instantly to Timothy. But Jed was another proposition. His heavy brows and hardened mouth seemed set for trouble.

Margaret stood by the desk, watching them all with a pleasant smile. She didn't frown at the unnecessary shuffling of feet or the boys' loud remarks as they settled into their seats. She just watched them with interest.

Jed and Timothy were carrying on a rumbling conversation, even after taking their seats. They knew their influence in that school and wanted her to know it too. If they didn't like her and couldn't manage her they didn't intend for her to stay, and she might as well understand it at once.

Margaret understood. Yet she stood quietly and watched them with almost mischief in her eyes, while Bud grew redder over the way his two idols were treating the new teacher. Gradually the other students noticed the twinkle in the teacher's eyes and grew silent to watch, and gradually they began to smile over the coming scene when Jed and Timothy discovered it and, worst of all, found out it was directed toward them. They'd expect severity or fear or a desire to placate; but a twinkle—they couldn't imagine what would happen. No one in that room would ever laugh at those two boys. But the teacher was almost laughing now, and the twinkle had taken the rest of the room into the secret.

The room grew deathly still, except for the boys' whispered growls. Still the silence deepened, until they themselves perceived it was time to look up and take stock.

Bud alone didn't grin. What a dreadful mistake the new teacher was making right at the start! She was antagonizing the two boys who held the whole school in their hands. There was no telling what they'd do to her now. But, no matter what they did, he'd have to stand up for her! Even though he lost his friends, he must be loyal to her. He didn't dare look at them but kept his eyes on Margaret. Then suddenly he saw her face break into a smile, without a hint of reproach or offended dignity in it—just a smile of comradeship, understanding and pleasure in the meeting. And it was directed to Jed and Timothy.

With wonder he turned toward the two boys and saw an answering smile on their faces—reluctant, half sheepish at first, but with lifted eyebrows of astonishment and enjoyment of the joke.

A ripple of approval passed around the room in half-breathed syllables, but Margaret gave no time for restlessness.

"I'm not going to say much now," she said eagerly. "I'll wait till we know one another. I do want to tell you, though, how glad I am to be here. I hope we'll like one another immensely and have many good times together. But we've got to get acquainted, and perhaps we'd better give most of the time to that today. First, let's sing something. What shall it be? What do you sing?"

Little Susan Johnson, bold from seeing the teacher at Sunday school, raised her hand and suggested, "Thar-thpangle Banner, pleath!"

So they tried it. But when Margaret found that only a few knew the words, she took a piece of chalk from the box on her desk and stepped to the chalkboard.

The students watched her hand move gracefully over the smooth surface, leaving behind it clear, beautiful script. They'd never seen such perfect, easy curves and twirls. Every eye in the room was fastened on her as they watched and spelled out the words one by one.

"Say!" said Bud under his breath, not knowing he'd spoken, but no one else moved.

"Now," she said, "let's sing."

When they started off again, with Margaret's strong, clear soprano leading, every voice in the room growled out the words and tried to get in step with the tune.

After two verses Jed seemed to think it was time to start something. Things were going too smoothly for an untried teacher, even if she *was* handsome and unabashed. If they went on like this the students would lose all respect for him. Though quite able to sing a clear tenor, he puckered his lips, frowned and began to whistle a somewhat erratic accompaniment to the song. He watched the teacher, expecting to see color flame in her cheeks and anger flash in her eyes; he'd tried this trick on other teachers, and it always worked. He winked at Timothy, and he too left off his bass and began to whistle.

But instead of the anger and annoyance they expected, Margaret turned appreciative eyes toward the two back seats, nodding her head and smiling with her eyes as she sang. When the verse ended she held up her hand for silence.

"Why, boys, that's beautiful! Let's try that verse again, and you two whistle the accompaniment a little stronger in the chorus. Or how about if you just come in on the chorus? I believe that would be more effective. Let's try the first verse that way. You boys sing during the verse and then whistle the chorus as you did now. We really need your voices in the verse part; they're so strong and splendid. Let's try it now."

She started off again, with the two astonished boys doing as they were told. When the whole song was finished they were surprised to hear her say, "Now everybody whistle the chorus softly," and then pucker up her own lips to join in. That finished the whistling stunt. Jed realized it would never work again, not while she was there, for she turned the joke into beauty and made them all enjoy it. It hadn't annoyed her in the least.

They watched again as she wrote another song on the chalkboard, this time a hymn—"I Need Thee Every Hour."

When they began to sing, however, Margaret found the tune went slowly, uncertainly.

"Oh, how we need a piano! I wonder if we can't get up an entertainment and raise money to buy one. How many will help?"

Every hand in the place shot up, with Jed's and Timothy's last and only a little way, but she noted with triumph that they were raised at all.

"All right, we'll do it! Now let's sing that verse correctly." And she began to sing again, while they all joined in, trying to do their best.

The instant the last verse died away, Margaret's voice caught their attention.

"Two years ago in Boston two young men, who belonged to a group of Christian workers who went from place to place holding meetings, sat talking together in their hotel room one evening."

Silence fell on the room. This wasn't like the beginning of any lesson other teachers had given them.

"They'd been talking over the day's work, and finally one of them suggested they choose a Bible verse for the whole year—"

An impatient movement was heard from a backseat, as if someone sensed a sermon, but Margaret continued speaking.

"They talked it over, and at last they settled on 2 Timothy 2:15. They made up their minds to use it on every possible occasion. It was time to go to bed, so the man whose room adjoined got up and, instead of saying good night, said, 'Well, 2 Timothy 2:15,' and went to his room. Pretty soon, when he put out his light, he knocked on the wall and shouted, '2 Timothy 2:15,' and the other man responded heartily, 'All right, 2 Timothy 2:15.'

"The next morning when they wrote letters, each one wrote '2 Timothy 2:15' on the lower left-hand corner of the envelope and sent out a great handful of letters to all parts of the world. Those letters passed through the Boston post office, and some of the clerks who sorted them saw that odd legend written down in the lower left-hand corner of the envelope. They wondered at it, and one or two wrote it down to look it up afterward. The letters reached other cities and were put into the hands of mail carriers to distribute. They saw the odd little phrase '2 Timothy 2:15' and wondered, and some of them looked it up."

By this time the students' entire attention was on the story, for they perceived that it was a story.

"The men left Boston and crossed the ocean to hold meetings in other cities, and one day at a railway station in Europe a group of people were gathered, waiting for a train, and those two men were among them. The train came, and one of the men got on the back end of the last car, while the other stayed on the platform. As the train pulled out, the man on the last car took off his hat and said in a loud, clear tone, 'Well, take care of yourself, 2 Timothy 2:15,' and the other one smiled and waved his hat and answered, 'Yes, 2 Timothy 2:15.' The man on the train, which was moving fast now, shouted back, '2 Timothy 2:15,' and the man on the platform responded still louder, waving his hat, '2 Timothy 2:15.' Back and forth the odd phrase was flung until the train was too far away for them to hear each other's voices.

"Meanwhile the people on the platform had been standing there listening and wondering what such a strange salutation could mean. Some of them recognized what it was, but many didn't know. Yet the sentence was repeated so many times they couldn't help remembering it, and some went away to recall it and ask their friends what it meant.

"A young man from America was on that platform and heard it, and he knew it stood for a Bible passage. His curiosity was so great he returned to his boardinghouse and hunted up the Bible his mother had packed in his trunk when he left home. He searched through the Bible until he found the place, '2 Timothy 2:15,' and read it. It made him think about his life and decide he wasn't doing as he should.

"I can't tell you the whole story about the odd Bible verse, how it went here and there and what a great work it did in people's hearts. But one day those Christian workers went to Australia to hold some meetings, and one night, when the great auditorium was crowded, a man who was leading the meeting got up and told the story of this verse, how it had been chosen and how it had gone over the world in strange ways, even told about the morning at the railway station when the two men said good-bye. Just as he got to that place in his story a man in the audience stood up and said: 'Brother, just let me say a word, please. I never knew anything about all this before, but I was at that railway station. I heard those two men shout that strange good-bye, and I went home and read that verse, and it's made a great difference in my life.'

"There was a great deal more to the story, how some Chicago policemen got to be good men through reading that verse and how the story of the Australia meetings was printed in an Australian paper and sent to a lady in America who sent it to a friend in England to read about the meetings. This friend in England had a son in the army in India. She was sending him a package and wrapped it around something in that package. And the young man read all about it, and it helped change his life.

"Well, I thought of that story this morning when I was trying to decide what to read for our opening chapter, and it occurred to me that perhaps you'd be interested in taking that verse for our school verse this term. If you'd like it I'll put it on the chalkboard. Would you like it?"

She paused and then heard a low, almost inaudible growl of assent. A keen listener might have said it was impatient, as if they were in a hurry to find out what the verse was that had made such a stir in the world.

"Very well," said Margaret, turning to the board. "Then I'll put it where we can see it. While I write it, will you please say over where it is, so that you'll remember it and hunt it up for yourselves in your Bibles at home?"

They snickered at that, for there were probably not half a dozen Bibles represented in that school. But they took her hint as she wrote, chanting, "2 Timothy 2:15, 2 Timothy 2:15," and then spelled out after her rapid crayon, "Study to show thyself approved unto God, a workman that needeth not to be ashamed."

They read it together then, with a half-serious look on their faces.

"Shall we pray now?" she asked.

The previous teacher hadn't opened her school with prayer. It had never even been suggested in that school. Margaret might have met with more resistance if she'd attempted it sooner. As it was, feet shuffled in the back seats at her first word. But the room grew quiet again, perhaps out of curiosity to hear a woman's voice in prayer.

"Our heavenly Father, we want to ask You to bless us in our work together and help us be such workers that we won't be ashamed to show You our work at the close of the day. For Christ's sake we ask it. Amen."

They didn't have time to resent that prayer before she had them interested in something else. In fact, she had planned out her whole first day so there wouldn't be a minute for misbehavior. She argued that if she became acquainted with them she might prevent a lot of trouble before it ever started. Her first business was to win her students. After that she could teach them easily once they were willing to learn.

She offered them a set of mental arithmetic problems next, some difficult and some easy enough for the youngest child who could think. She timed their answers and wrote on the board the names of those who raised their hands first and had the correct answers. The questions were put in a fascinating way, many of them having curious little catches in them for the scholars who weren't on the alert, and Timothy presently discovered this and set himself to get every one, winning in the end. Even Jed roused himself and was interested, and some of the girls distinguished themselves.

When a half hour of this was over she put the word "TRANSFIGURATION" on the board and started them playing a game out of it. If the school board had come in then, they might have raised their hands in horror at the new teacher's setting the whole school to playing a game. But they would have been delighted to see a quiet, orderly room with bent heads and knit brows, all intent upon papers and pencils. Never before in that school had the first day held a full period of order. It was expected to be a day of battle, of trying out the teacher and proving his or her worthiness to cope with the active minds and bodies of Ashland's young bullies. But the expected battle had been forgotten. Every mind was busy with the matter at hand.

Margaret had given them three minutes to write as many words as they could think of, of three letters or more, beginning with T and using only the letters in the word she'd written on the board. When time was called they rushed to write a last word, and then each student had to tell how many words he had, and each was called on to read his list. Some had only two or three; some had ten or eleven. They were allowed to mark their words, counting one for each person present who didn't have that word and doubling if it had two syllables, and so on. Excitement ran high when it was discovered that some had actually made a count of thirty or forty. When they started writing words beginning with R, every head was bent intently from the minute time was started.

Never had three minutes seemed so short to those unused brains, and Jed yelled out, "Aw! I only got three!" when time was called next.

By recess they'd finished every letter in that word and, adding all up, found that Timothy had won the game. Was that school? Why, a barbecue couldn't be named beside it for fun! They rushed out to the schoolyard with a shout, and the boys played leap-frog loudly for the first few minutes.

Margaret, leaning her tired head in her hands, elbows on the window seat, closing her eyes and gathering strength for the after-recess session, heard one boy say, "Wal, how d'ye like 'er?" And the answer came: "Say! I didn't think she'd be that kind of guy! I thought she'd be some stiff old Ike! Ain't she a peach though?" She lifted up her head and laughed to herself, her eyes alight, strengthened for the fray. She wasn't wholly failing then.

After recess came a spelling match with choosing sides, of course. "This is only the first day, and we must get acquainted before we can do real work," she explained.

The spelling match proved exciting also, with new features. The girls shone, but there were few good spellers, and they were presently reduced to two girls—Rosa Rogers, the school beauty, and Amanda Bounds, a stolid, homely girl with deep eyes and a broad brow.

"I'm going to give this as a prize to the one who stands up the longest," said Margaret, as she saw the boys stirring restlessly in their seats. She unpinned a tiny blue silk bow that fastened her white collar.

The girls said "Oh-h-h!" while everyone in the room straightened up. The next few minutes the two girls spelled, each keeping her eye fixed on the blue bow in Margaret's hands. Even the boys sat up and took notice, each secretly thinking Rosa would win it.

But she didn't; she missed the word "receive," putting the i before e. Amanda, catching her breath, spelled it right and received the blue prize, pinned gracefully at the throat of her old brown gingham by the teacher. The school looked on with admiration, and red rolled up the back of her neck and spread over her face and forehead. Rosa went crestfallen to her seat.

At noon, during lunch, Margaret tried to get acquainted with the girls, calling most of them by name, to their surprise, and hinting of delightful possibilities in the winter's work. Then she slipped out among the boys and watched their sports, laughing and applauding when someone made a fine play, as if she understood and appreciated.

She managed to stand near Jed and Timothy just before Bud rang the bell. "I've heard you're great sportsmen," she said to them. "I've been wondering if you'll teach me how to ride and shoot. Do you suppose I could learn?"

"Sure!" they chorused, their embarrassment forgotten. "Sure, you could learn fine! Sure, *we'll learn you!*"

And then the bell rang, and they all trooped in.

The afternoon was arranged informally with classes and a schedule for the next day. Margaret passed out slips of paper with questions for each to answer, to find out where to place them. While they wrote she stepped from one to another, talking and suggesting what they wanted to study. This was new! They weren't used to caring what they were to study. Now it almost seemed interesting.

When the day was over, the schoolhouse locked, and Bud and Margaret started for home, she realized she was weary. Yet it was a weariness of success and not of failure, and she looked forward to tomorrow.

Chapter 14

The minister had decided to preach in Ashland the following Sabbath. If he wished to be noticed by the haughty new teacher he knew he must do something to establish his superiority. He reviewed the sermons he always carried with him and selected "The Dynamics of Altruism."

Elaborate notices were posted in saloons, stores and the post office and on trees along the trails. He made them himself after completely tabooing Mr. Tanner's kind and blundering attempt, and they gave full information concerning "the Rev. Frederick West, Ph.D., of the vicinity of New York City, who had kindly consented to preach in the schoolhouse on 'The Dynamics of Altruism.'"

The coming Sabbath services were more talked about than anything else for miles around, except the new teacher and her extraordinary way of gaining the students' adoration. West might not have been so flattered at the size of his audience if he knew how many came mainly to see the new teacher.

But the community read the notices and seemed quite interested in the preacher. Under this attention he swelled and bowed whenever anybody noticed him. He even dropped his severity at the table toward the end of the week and expanded into dignified conversation, mainly addressed to Mr. Tanner about the political situation in Arizona. By this he thought to ignore the teacher and chastise her for disregarding his warning about "that young ruffian."

Out on the trail Long Bill and Jasper Kemp paused before a tree that bore West's church announcement and read it in silence.

"What d'ye make out o' them cuss words, Jap?" asked Long Bill. "D'ye figger the parson's goin' to preach on swearin' ur gunpowder?"

"Blowed ef I know," answered Jasper, eying the sign. "But by his looks he can't say much to suit me on neither one. He resembles a yaller cactus bloom out in a rainstorm as to head, an' his smile is like some of them prickles on the plant. He can't be no 'sky pilot' to me, not just yet."

"You don't allow he b'longs in any way to *her?*" asked Long Bill, after they'd been on their way for a half hour.

"B'long to *her?* Meanin' the schoolmarm?"

"Yes—he ain't sweet on her nor nothin'?"

"Wal, I guess not," said Jasper. "She's got eyes sharp's a needle. You don't size her up so small she's goin' to take to a sickly parson with yaller hair an' sleek ways when she's seen the Kid, do you?"

"Wal, no, it don't seem noways reasonable, but you never can tell. Women gets notions."

"She ain't that kind! You mark my words—*she ain't that kind.* I'd lay she'd punch the breeze like a coyote ef he'd make up to her. Just you wait till you see him. He's the most no-'count, measleyest little thing that ever called himself a man. I'd like to see him try to ride that colt o' mine. It would be some sight for sore eyes, it would."

"Mebbe he's got a intellec'," said Long Bill after another mile. "That goes a long ways with women-folks with a education."

"No chance!" said Jasper. "Ain't got room fer one under his yaller thatch. You wait till you set your lamps on him once before you go to gettin' excited. Why, he ain't one-two-three with our missionary! I wish *he'd* come back an' see to such goin's-on."

"Was you figgerin' to go to that gatherin' Sunday?"

"I sure was," said Jasper. "I want to see the show, an', besides, we might be needed ef things get too high-soundin'. It ain't good to have a creature at large that thinks he knows all there is to know. I heard him talk down to the post office the day after that little party we had when the Kid shot out the lights to save Bunchy from killin' Crapster. It's my opinion he needs a good spankin', but I'm goin' to give him a fair show. I ain't much on religion myself, but I like to see a square deal, especially in a parson. I've sized it up he needs a lesson."

"I'm with ye, Jap," said Long Bill, and the two rode on their way in silence.

Margaret was so busy and happy with her school all week that she forgot her annoyance at the minister. She saw little of him, for he was always late to breakfast, and she took hers early. She went to her room immediately after supper, and he had little opportunity for pursuing her acquaintance. Perhaps he judged it wise to let her alone after he'd made his grand impression on Sunday—and let her "make up" to him.

Sunday morning she suddenly recalled he was to preach that day. She'd seen the notices, of course, for a large one was posted in front of the schoolhouse, and some anonymous artist had produced a fine caricature of the preacher in red clay under his name. Margaret had remained after school Friday and removed as much of the portrait as possible, being unwilling to make it a matter of discipline to discover the artist. In fact, it was so true to the model she felt a growing sympathy for the perpetrator.

Margaret started to the schoolhouse early Sunday morning with Bud. Of course, he had no more intention of going to Sunday school than he had the week before, but it was pleasant to escort her. Jed and Timothy had walked home with her twice during the week, and he didn't intend to lose his place to them. Besides, he had orders to protect her.

Margaret had promised to help in Sunday school that morning; the woman who taught the little ones was still away with her sick neighbor.

"You'll be secretary for me, won't you, William?" she asked Bud on the way. "I'm going to take the left front corner of the room for the children and seat them on the recitation benches, and that will leave the back part of the room for the older people. Then I can use the chalkboard and not disturb the rest."

"Secretary?" asked Bud. He was getting used to surprises, and "secretary" sounded interesting.

"Yes, take up the collection, see who's absent and so on. I don't know all the names yet, and I don't really like to do that when I have to teach."

Margaret didn't intend to leave Bud floating around outside the schoolhouse. And though she'd prepared her lesson and chalkboard illustration for the children, she had hidden in it a truth for Bud.

The old gentleman who taught the adults was seated with his back to the platform, his spectacles resting on his long nose. He presented the questions on the lesson page as usual, but before he was half through he perceived by the long pauses between questions and answers that he didn't have his class's attention. He turned around to see what they were looking at and became so engaged in listening to the lesson the new teacher was drawing on the chalkboard that he completely forgot to go on. Before he knew it, Bud rang the desk bell for the end of Sunday school, and Margaret, looking up, saw in dismay that she had been teaching the whole school.

While they sang a closing hymn more people filed in reverently, filling up the room. Presently the minister entered, carrying his sermon in an elaborate leather cover under his arm. His chin was flattened upward, his eyes rolled importantly, and a severe clerical coat and collar set off his pink face.

Behind him in single file walked the eight men from the bunkhouse: Long Bill, Big Jim, Fiddling Boss, Jasper Kemp, Fade-Away Forbes, Stocky, Croaker, and Fudge. They had been lined up along the path outside, scowling, as the minister approached, eyeing them warily. As he neared the door the last man followed in his wake, then the next and so on. They arranged themselves across the room on the recitation bench in front of the platform, removing a few small children for that purpose. Behind the men, Mom Wallis scuttled shyly into a back seat and sank out of sight.

Margaret, sitting halfway back at the side of the schoolhouse near a window, saw through the trees a wide sombrero over a pair of broad shoulders. But she didn't see the owner enter the schoolhouse.

The minister was disturbed at first because they had no hymnbooks. He didn't seem to know how to conduct a divine service without hymnbooks, but at last he compromised on the long-meter doxology, pronounced with deliberate unction. Then, looking about for a possible pipe organ and choir, he finally started it himself. But no one would likely have recognized the tune if Margaret hadn't taken it up.

Thus they came to the prayer and Bible reading. These were performed with a formal, perfunctory style calculated to impress the audience with the preacher rather than the words he was speaking. The audience was quiet, as if reserving judgment for the sermon.

Margaret couldn't remember afterward how she missed the text. She'd averted her eyes from the minister, for it made her homesick to compare him with her father. Then her mind wandered to the sombrero outside and how its owner was coming along with his resolves and the difference they'd make in his life. Suddenly she awoke to the fact that the sermon had begun.

Chapter 15

Considered in the world of physics," began the imposing tones of the preacher, "dynamics is that branch of mechanics that considers the effects of forces in producing motion and of the laws of motion thus produced—sometimes called kinetics, opposed to statics. It is the science that considers the laws of force, whether producing equilibrium or motion—in this sense including both statics or kinetics. It is also applied to the forces producing or governing activity or movement of any kind—and the methods of such activity."

The big words rolled out over the awed gathering, while the minister tilted his chin and gazed about upon the people.

Margaret's eyes sought the row of men on the front seat, sitting with folded arms, each one from under his shaggy brows regarding the preacher as they might have an animal in a zoo. Did they understand what was said? It was impossible to tell from their serious faces.

"Philanthropy has been called the dynamics of Christianity; that is to say, it is Christianity in action," went on the preacher. "It is my purpose this morning to speak on the dynamics of altruism. Now altruism is the theory that inculcates benevolence to others in subordination to self-interest—interested benevolence as opposed to disinterested—and the practice of this theory."

He lifted his eyes to the audience again and nodded his head slightly, as if to emphasize the deep truth he'd just given them, and the battery of keen eyes before him never flinched from his face. They were searching him.

Margaret wondered if he had no sense of the ridiculous, that he could pour forth to this audience such a string of technical definitions. They sounded strangely like dictionary language. She wondered if anyone else had an inkling of what his subject was. Surely he would drop to simpler language, now that he'd laid out his plan. It never occurred to her the man was trying to impress *her* with his fluent language and store of wisdom.

On and on he droned much as he'd begun, with now and then a flowery sentence or whole paragraph of meaningless eloquence about the "brotherhood of man"—with a roll to the r's in brotherhood.

The wilderness men endured fifteen minutes of this profitless oratory with fixed attention. Then, suddenly, a sentence of unusual simplicity struck them.

"For years the church has preached a dead faith without works, my friends, and the time has come to stop preaching faith! I repeat: The time has come *to stop preaching faith* and begin doing good works!" He thumped the desk vehemently. "Men don't need a superstitious belief in a Savior to save them from their sins. They need to go to work and save themselves! As if a man dying two thousand years ago on a cross could do any good for you and me today!"

At that moment Margaret noticed a ripple pass down the front line and

Long Bill lean slightly forward and frown into the face of Jasper Kemp, and the latter, frowning back, winked solemnly.

Immediately Long Bill cleared his throat, stood up and, looking the minister in the eye, turned and walked slowly, noisily down the aisle and out the front door.

The minister, annoyed, concluded that his remarks had been too deep for the rough creature and proceeded.

"We need to work at our duty toward our fellow men. We need to down trusts and give the laboring man a chance. We need to stop insisting that men believe in the inspiration of the entire Bible and work at something practical!"

His pause was interrupted by the sharp, rasping sound of Big Jim clearing his throat and shuffling to his feet. He, too, looked the minister in the face, shook his head sadly and strode down the aisle and out the door.

The minister paused again, frowning.

Margaret sat in wonder. Could these rough men be objecting to the sermon from a theological perspective, or did they just happen to leave at those moments? Of course, the men must have only been weary of the long sentences, she decided, which they doubtless couldn't understand. She began to hope Gardley couldn't hear. Most likely few others understood enough to be harmed by the sermon, but she boiled with indignation that a man could call himself a minister of an evangelical church and talk such heresy.

Big Jim's steps died away on the clay path outside, and the preacher resumed his discourse.

"We've preached long enough of hell and torment. It's time for a gospel of love to our brothers. Hell is a superstition of the Dark Ages. *There is no hell!*"

Fiddling Boss turned sharply toward Jasper Kemp, as if waiting for a signal, and Jasper nodded slightly. Fiddling Boss cleared his throat loudly and arose, faced the minister and marched down the aisle, while Jasper Kemp remained quietly seated as if nothing had happened, a vacancy on each side of him.

By this time the color was rising in the minister's cheeks. He looked at Fiddling Boss's retreating back and then down at the remaining men. But each one of them sat with folded arms and eyes intent upon the sermon, as if their comrades hadn't left them. The minister thought he must have been mistaken and tried to take up the broken thread. But he'd lost his place in the manuscript, and the only clue was a quotation of a poem about the devil. To be sure, the connection was somewhat abrupt, but he clutched it with his eye and began reading dramatically:

Men don't believe in the devil now
As their fathers used to do—

But he got no further when he heard a chorus of throats clearing and saw

Fade-Away Forbes stumble to his feet and bolt down the aisle. He hadn't reached the door when Stocky clumped after him, followed at intervals by Croaker and Fudge, and each just as the minister began:

"Um! Ah! To resume—"

And now only Jasper Kemp remained of the front-seaters. He stared at the minister as he floundered through the remaining portion of his manuscript, until he reached the words "And finally," which opened with another poem:

I need no Christ to die for me.

The sturdy, gray-haired Scotchman suddenly lowered his folded arms, slapping a hand resoundingly on each knee, bent his shoulders to pull himself to his feet, pressed his weight on his hands till his elbows were akimbo and uttered a deep sigh with a "Yes-well-*ah!*"

With that he stood to his feet and dragged them out of the schoolhouse.

By this time the minister's face was red. Never before had he been so grossly insulted, and by such rude creatures! Yet nothing could be said or done. These men appeared to be simple creatures who had wandered in idly, perhaps for amusement and, finding the discourse above their caliber, innocently wandered out again. It appeared that way. But such actions had cruelly upset his plans. He struggled and spluttered about.

At last he spoke: "Is there—ah—any other listener who desires to withdraw before the close? If so, he may do so now, or—ah"—he paused to find a suitable ending; familiar words rushed to his lips without awareness of their meaning—"or forever hold his peace—ah!"

Silence hung over the schoolhouse. No one offered to go out, and Margaret, looking out the window, wondered what had become of the men and how much more she herself could endure.

At last the service was over. Margaret looked about for Mom Wallis, but she had disappeared. She signalled to Bud, and together they hurried out. No one from the camp was in sight.

But as soon as the minister had shaken hands with the few worshippers and walked with Mr. Tanner to the schoolhouse door, there stood the eight men in a solemn row, four on either side of the walk. Each held his right elbow in his left hand and his chin in his right hand. All eyes looked to Jasper Kemp, who was gazing up at the sky.

"H'w aire yeh, Tanner? Pleasant 'casion. Mind steppin' on a bit? We men wanta have a word with the parson."

Mr. Tanner hastened away, and the minister stood alone in the doorway.

Chapter 16

U m! Ah!" began the minister, trying to summon his best clerical manner to meet—what? He didn't know. It was best to assume they were a penitent band of inquirers for the truth. But their recent exodus from the service was etched too clearly in his mind for him to be pleasant toward these rough creatures. He should give them a lesson in behavior!

"Um! Ah!" he began again.

But the eight men before him grew more grim and menacing in their silence.

"What does all this mean?" he burst forth.

"Calm yourself, elder!" spoke up Long Bill. "There ain't any occasion to get excited."

"I'm not an elder. I'm a minister of the gospel!" exploded West. "Who are you, and what does all this mean?"

"Yes, parson, we understand who you are. We understand quite well, an' we're a goin' to tell you who we are. We're a band of al-tru-ists! That's what we are. We're *altruists!*" said Jasper Kemp of the keen eyes and sturdy countenance. "And we've come here in brotherly love to exercise a little o' that dynamic force of altruism you was talkin' about. We just thought we'd begin on you so's you could see we got some works to go 'long with our faith."

"What do you mean, sir?" said West, looking from one grim face to another. "I–I don't understand." The minister was becoming frightened; he couldn't tell why. But he wished he'd kept Brother Tanner with him. It was the first time he'd ever thought of Mr. Tanner as "brother."

"We mean just this, parson. You been talkin' a lot of lies in there about there bein' no Savior an' no hell ner no devil. We ain't much credit to God ourselves, bein' just common men. But we knows all that stuff you said ain't true about the Bible an' the devil bein' superstitions, an' we thought we better exercise a little of that altruism you was talkin' about an' teach you better. You see, it's real brotherly kindness, parson. An' now we're goin' to give you a sample of that dynamics you spoke about. Ready, boys?"

"Ready!"

Swiftly, suddenly, the minister was caught from where he stood in that doorway, hat in hand, and hurled from man to man. Across the walk and back, across and back—until it seemed to him a thousand miles in a minute. He jammed his high silk hat on his sleek head and grasped his sermon case to his breast. The sermon pages were flung to the four winds. In time each of the eight men recovered and retained a portion of that oration, and Mom Wallis, not quite understanding, pinned up as a sort of shrine the portion about doubting the devil. But as a sermon, the parts were never assembled on this earth, nor could be, for some were ground to powder under eight pairs of heels. But the minister was too engaged to notice that the child of his brain lay scattered on the ground.

Up and down he made the rounds of that merciless group, tossed like a thistledown from man to man. At last, breathless and faint, he was bound and cast into a wagon. How strange that only a few minutes earlier the place had seemed to swarm with worshipful admirers thanking him for his sermon! He called out with his raucous voice until all the states around might have heard his cry; yet no one came.

The men carried him down to a waterhole. When he threatened to evoke the law of the land upon them, they looked at him sadly, then set him on his feet and stood around him. He looked from one to another, trembling. He'd heard strange tales of this wild, free land, where every man was a law unto himself. Would they drown him there?

"Mr. Parson," Jasper Kemp said in a kind but firm voice, his eyes twinkling, "we've brought you here to do you good, an' you oughtn't to complain. This is altruism, an' we're but actin' out what you been preachin'. You're our brother, an' we're tryin' to do you good—an' now we're about to show you what a dynamic force we are.

"You see, Mr. Parson, I was brought up by a good Scottish grandmother, an' I know a lie when I hear it, an' when I hear a man preach error I know it's time to set him straight. So now we're goin' to set you straight. I don't know where you come from, who brang you up or what church set you afloat. But I know enough by all my grandmother taught me—even if I hadn't been listenin' off and on for two years back to Mr. Brownleigh, our missionary—to know you're a dangerous man to have at large. I'd as soon have a mad dog let loose. Why, what you preach ain't the gospel, an' it ain't the truth, and the time has come for you to know it an' own it and recant. Recant! That's what they call it. That's what we're here to see't you do, or we'll know the reason why. That's the *dynamics* of it. See?"

The minister saw the muddy waterhole and nothing more.

"Folks're all too ready to believe them things you was gettin' off without havin' 'em *preached,* to justify 'em in their evil ways. We gotta think of those poor ignorant brothers of ours that might listen to you. See? That's the *altruism* of it!"

"What do you want me to do?" West asked faintly.

His Prince Albert coat was torn in three places; one tail hung down over his hip, and one sleeve was ripped halfway out. The ends of his collar flew up over his cheeks. His necktie was long gone. His once-sleek hair stuck out about his eyes, and his hat had been "stove in" and jammed down until his ears stuck out like sails at half-mast. He stood ankle-deep in the mud, with his silk socks torn and black with slime.

"Well, in the first place," said Jasper Kemp, winking around the company, "that matter about hell needs adjustin'. Hell ain't no superstition. I ain't dictatin' what kind o' hell there is. You can make it fire or water or anything else you like, but *there is a hell,* an' *you believe in it.* D'ye understand? We'd just like you t' state that publicly here an' now."

"But how can I say what I don't believe?" West said in a whine.

He had come through a trial by Presbytery on these same points and posed as a man with the courage of his convictions. He couldn't easily surrender his original thought and broad-mindedness. He'd received congratulations from a number of noble martyrs who had left their chosen church for just such reasons, congratulating him on his stand. It was the first notice from important men he'd ever attracted to himself. Give that up for a few miserable cowboys! News of it might travel back East. He must think of his reputation.

"That's just where the dynamics of the thing comes in, brother," said Jasper Kemp quietly. "We're here to *make* you believe in a hell. We're the force that will bring you back into the right way of thinkin' again. Ready, boys?"

"Oh, I say, that isn't necessary. No, no, wait!" he cried, as they seized him. "I'll say it! I believe—yes, I believe in hell!"

But too late, for the Rev. Frederick West was plunged into the waterhole, from whose sheep-muddied waters he came up spluttering, "Yes, I believe in *hell!*" And perhaps he did, for indeed he thought he was in it.

The men were standing knee-deep in the water, holding their captive lightly by his arms and legs, their eyes on their leader, waiting.

Jasper Kemp stood in the water, also, looking down on his victim.

"An' now there's that little matter of the devil," said Jasper. "We'll fix that next while we're near his place of residin'. You believe in the devil, Mr. Parson, from now on? If you'd ever tried resistin' him I figger you'd have b'lieved in him long ago. But *you believe in him* from *now on,* an' you *don't preach against him anymore!* We're not goin' to have our Arizona men gettin' off their guard an' thinkin' their enemy is dead. There *is* a devil, parson, and you believe in him! Duck him, boys!"

Down went the minister into the water again and came up sputtering, "Yes, I–I—believe—in—the—devil!" Even in this strait he was loath to surrender his pet theme—no devil.

"Very well, so far's it goes," said Jasper. "But now, boys, we're comin' to the most important of all, and you better put him under about three times, for there mustn't be no mistake about this matter. You believe in the Bible, parson—*the whole Bible?*"

"Yes!" gasped West, as he went down the first time and got a mouthful of the bitter water. "I believe—." The voice was fairly anguished. Down he went again. Another mouthful of water. "*I believe in the whole Bible!*" he screamed and went down the third time.

His voice, weaker now, spewed out the words, while he was lifted out onto the mud. The men from the bunkhouse were succeeding better than the

Presbytery back East. His eyes downcast, his teeth chattering, he seemed suddenly to know he must believe in something as near his end as this.

"Just one more thing to reckon with," Jasper said. "That talk you was handin' out about a man dyin' on a cross two thousand years ago bein' nothin' to you. You said you *an' me,* but you can speak for *yourself.* We may not be much to look at, but we ain't goin' to stand for no such slander as that. Our missionary preaches all about that Man on the cross, an' if you don't need Him before you get through this little campaign of life I'll miss my guess. Mebbe we haven't been all we might 'a' been, but we ain't goin' to let you ner anybody else go back on that cross!" Jasper's tone was tender and solemn.

As the minister lay panting on his back in the mud he remembered two other times when a tone of voice had so arrested his attention and filled him with awe. When he was a boy he was caught copying off another student's paper at exam time and was sent to the principal's office. And many years later, at his mother's funeral, he sat in the dim church listening to the old minister. For a moment now he was impressed with the wonder of the cross, and it suddenly seemed as if he were being arraigned before the eyes of Him with whom we all have to do. His face paled, the smugness gone, and he saw himself a wretch in his accusers' hands. Jasper Kemp, standing over him on the bank and looking down at him, seemed like God's emissary sent to condemn him, and his soul recoiled.

"Near the end o' yer *dis*course you mentioned sin was only misplaced energy. Well, if that's so there's a heap o' your energy gone astray this mornin', an' the time has come for you to pay up. Speak up now an' say what you believe or whether you want another duckin'—an' it'll be seven this time!"

The man on the ground shut his eyes and gasped. The silence was solemn. There seemed no hint of the ridiculous. It was serious business now to those men. They watched their leader.

"Do you solemnly declare before God—I s'pose you still believe in God, as you didn't say nothin' to the contrary—that from now on you'll stand for that cross and for Him that hung on it?"

The minister opened his eyes and gazed up into the sky, half expecting to see horses and chariots of fire standing about to do battle with him.

"I do!"

In silence the men stood with half-bowed heads, as if some solemn service were being performed in which they sympathized but didn't understand.

Then Jasper Kemp said softly, "Amen!" After a pause he added, "I ain't any sort of Christian myself, but I just can't stand to see a parson floatin' round that don't even know the name of the firm he's workin' for. Now, parson, there's just one more requirement, an' then you can go home."

The minister glanced about, fear in his eyes, but no one moved.

"You say you had a church in New York. What was the name and address o' your workin'-boss there?"

"What do you mean? I had no boss."

"Why, him that hired an' paid you. The chief elder or whatever you called him.

"Oh! Um. Ezekiel Newbold, Hazelton."

"Very good. Now, parson, you'll kindly write two copies of a letter to Mr. Ezekiel Newbold statin' what you said to us concernin' yer change o' faith, sign yer name, address one to Mr. Newbold an' give t' other to me. We just want this little matter put on record so you can't change yer mind any. Get my idea?"

"Yes," said the minister dispiritedly.

"Will you do it?"

"Yes."

"Well, now I got a piece o' advice fer you. It'd be just as well fer yer health if you leave Arizona about as quick as you can pack, but you won't be allowed to leave this town, day ner night, cars ner afoot, until them letters're all okay. D'you get me?"

"Yes."

"I might add, by way o' explainin', that if you'd come to Arizona an' minded yer own business you wouldn't 'a' been interfered with. You mighta preached whatever bosh you pleased s' far as we was concerned. Only you wouldn't 'a' had no sorta audience after yer first try o' that stuff today.

"But when you come to Arizona an' put your fingers in other folks' pie, when you tried to 'squeal' on the young gentleman who was keen enough to shoot out the lights to save a man's life, why, we ain't no further use for you. In the first place, you was all wrong. You thought the Kid shot out the lights to steal the gamin' money, but he didn't. He put it all in the sheriff's hands some hours before yer 'private information' reached him through the mail. You thought you were awful sharp, you sneak! But I wasn't the only man who saw you put yer foot out an' cover a gold piece that rolled on the floor when the fight started. You thought nobody was a-lookin'. But you'll favor us, please, with that identical gold piece along with the letter before you leave. Well, boys, that'll be about all. Untie him!"

Silently the men untied him and left him, tramping solemnly away to their horses nearby.

Jasper lingered a moment, gazing down at the man. "Want us t' carry you back t' the house?"

"No!" said the minister bitterly. "No!"

Without another word Jasper Kemp left him.

Into the mesquite bushes crept the minister, groaning. He who had made the hearts of a score of old ministers sorrow for Zion, who split in two a pleasantly united congregation, disrupted a session and brought about a scandalous trial in Presbytery, was at last conquered. The Rev. Frederick West had recanted!

Chapter 17

When Margaret left the service at the schoolhouse with Bud, she had walked only a few steps when she remembered Mom Wallis and turned back to search for her. But she found no trace of her or anyone else from the camp. The curtain hadn't yet risen on West's undoing.

"I suppose she must have gone home with them," she said. "I'm sorry not to have spoken with her. She was good to me."

"You mean Mom Wallis?" Bud said. "No, she ain't gone home. She's hiking 'long to our house to see you. The Kid went along of her. See, there—down by those cottonwood trees? That's them."

Margaret turned eagerly and hurried with Bud. She knew he referred to the Kid in that tone of voice. It was the way the men had spoken of and to him. Her cheeks flushed, and her heart fluttered pleasantly.

They caught up with the two before they'd reached the Tanner house. Cap ran out to meet them but suddenly turned to chase a cottontail, and Bud took off after him. Margaret greeted Mom Wallis with a warm hug, and the old woman's eyes shone with gratitude as she trudged along shyly between Gardley and the girl.

"He was bringin' me to see where you was livin'," Mom Wallis said suddenly, nodding toward Gardley. "We wasn't hopin' to see you, except mebbe just as you come by goin' in."

"Oh, then I'm so glad I caught up with you in time. I went back to look for you. Now you're coming in to dinner with me, both of you," declared Margaret. "William, your mother will have enough dinner for us all, won't she?"

"Sure!" said Bud, with that assurance born of knowing his mother, who'd never failed him as far as things to eat were concerned.

Gardley forgot to answer for himself in wondering why the girl's face was so different from those of other girls he'd known.

But a wave of red rolled up from Mom Wallis's withered neck over her leathery face to the roots of her thin, gray hair.

"Oh, I couldn't do that! Not in these 'ere clo'es. 'Course I got that pretty collar you give me, but I couldn't never go out to dinner in this old dress an' these shoes. I know what folks should look like, an' I ain't goin' t' shame you."

"Shame me? Not at all! Your dress is fine, and who will see your shoes? And I'd like to take you up to my room and show you pictures of my father and mother and my home and church."

Mom Wallis looked at her wistfully but still shook her head. "Oh, I'd like to mighty well. It's good o' you to ast me. But I just couldn't. 'Sides, I gotta go home an' git the men's grub ready."

"Oh, can't she stay, Mr. Gardley?" asked Margaret. "The men won't mind, will they?"

Gardley looked into her eyes, then turned to the old woman. "Mom, she seems to want us to stay, and the men will manage. They can cook. We'll stay."

"That's wonderful!" exclaimed Margaret. Then her face sobered. "Mr. Wallis won't mind, will he?" She didn't want to stir up trouble for Mom Wallis when she went home.

Mom Wallis turned startled eyes toward her. "Pop's gone off. He went yist'day. But he ain't got no call t' mind. I ben waitin' on him nigh on to twenty year, an' I guess I'm goin' to a dinner party, now't I'm invited. He'd better *not* mind, I guess!"

Margaret realized how much her invitation must mean to the woman. She took the guests into the dingy parlor and slipped out to ask Mrs. Tanner. That woman was pleased to have more guests around her table, particularly since Margaret promised to compensate her with money, and sent Mr. Tanner to get more pickles and apple butter and added another pie.

Meanwhile, Gardley went outside to ask Bud to run back to the church and tell the men to leave the buckboard for them, since they wouldn't be home for dinner. When Margaret returned to the parlor, she found Mom Wallis sitting alone and took her up to her room to remove her bonnet and smooth her hair.

Mom Wallis had doubtless never seen such a room. She stopped on the threshold, caught her breath and put out her hand to steady herself against the door. Not until her eyes rested on the mountain framed in the open window did she feel anchored and sure this was a real place.

Margaret opened the door wider and drew her into the room, placing her gently in the rose-ruffled rocking chair, where she sat with tears in her eyes.

Perhaps Margaret couldn't imagine what that room meant to Mom Wallis, who had dreamed as a young girl of having such a room but laid those dreams aside for a life of hardness and self-repression. Now here she was, seated amidst her dreams, reality for the young woman beside her.

Margaret brought out the pictures of her father and mother, her home and her church, and she led her around the room, pointing out the various pictures and reminders of her college days. When she saw the woman was overwhelmed she ushered her to the window and directed her gaze to the familiar mountain again.

Mom Wallis only gasped as she looked from one object to another, unable to give voice to her feelings. But when she saw the mountain again, she looked back at the girl in wonder.

"Now ain't it strange! Even that old mounting looks diffrunt from inside a room like this. Why, it looks like its hair got combed an' its best collar's on!" She glanced down and patted the simple net ruffle about her throat. "Why, it looks like a picter painted an' hung up on this yere wall—that's what that mounting looks like! It kinda ain't no mounting anymore; it's jest a picter in your room!"

Margaret smiled. "It's a picture, isn't it? Just look at that silver light over the purple place. Isn't it wonderful? I like to think it's my mountain. And yet it's just as much yours. It will make a picture of itself framed in your bunkhouse window if you let it. Try it."

"Do you mean that ef I should wash them bunkhouse winders an' string up some posy caliker an' stuff a chair an' have a pin cushion, I could have that mounting come in an' set fer me like a picter the way it does here fer you?"

"Yes, that's what I mean," said Margaret softly, marveling at how the woman caught the thought. "God's gifts will be as much to us as we let them."

The woman gazed at the mountain for some minutes. "Wal, mebbe I'll try it!" she said, turning back to survey the room again.

The mirror caught her eye, and she saw herself, a strange self in a soft white collar. She stepped over to get a closer view, laying a finger on the lace and looking half embarrassed at seeing her own face.

"It's a real purty collar," she said. "It's too purty fer me. I told him so, but he said you wanted me t' dress up every night fer supper in it. It's 'most as strange as havin' a mounting come an' live with you, t' wear a collar like that!"

Margaret's eyes were suddenly bright with tears. Who would have suspected Mom Wallis of having poetry in her nature? Then, as if her thoughts anticipated the question in Margaret's mind, she continued.

"He brung me your little book," she said. "Thank yeh ain't 'nuf for me to say. He read me the poetry words in it. I got it wropped in a hankercher on the top o' the beam over my bed. I'm goin' t' have it buried with me when I die. Oh, I *read* it. I couldn't make much out of it, but I read the words *thorough*. An' then *he* read 'em—the Kid did. He reads just beautiful. He's got education. And he talked a lot about it. Did you mean that we ain't really growin' old at all; we're just goin' on, *gettin'* there, if we go right? Did you mean you think Him's planned it all, wanted some old woman right thar in the bunkhouse, an' it's *me?* Did you mean there was goin' to be a chanct fer me to be young an' beautiful somewheres in creation yit, 'fore I git through?"

The old woman had turned around from staring in the mirror and faced her hostess. Her eyes were bright, her cheeks had taken on an excited flush, and her hands were clutching the bureau. She looked into Margaret's eyes earnestly, as though her life depended upon the answer.

"Yes, Mrs. Wallis, that's just what I meant. Listen—these are God's own words about it: 'For I reckon that the sufferings of this present time are not worthy to be compared with the glory that shall be revealed in us.' "

"Did you say them was God's words?"

"Yes, they're in the Bible."

"But you couldn't be sure it meant *me?* They wouldn't put *me* in the Bible, o' course."

"Oh, yes, you could be sure. If God was making you and had a plan for you, as the poem says, He'd be sure to put down something in His book about it, don't you think? He'd want you to know."

"It does sound reasonable now, don't it?" said the woman wistfully. "Say them glory words again, won't you?"

Margaret repeated the verse slowly and distinctly.

"Glory!" repeated Mom Wallis, turning toward the glass and gazing in it a moment, as if she couldn't believe it.

"I useta have purty hair onct," she said, tugging at the hair pulled tightly away from her face.

"Why, you have pretty hair now!" said Margaret. "It just wants a chance to show its beauty. Here, let me fix it for dinner, will you?"

She whisked the bewildered woman into a chair and began unwinding the hard, tight knot of hair at the back of her head and shaking it out. The hair was thin and gray now, but it showed signs of having been fine and thick once.

"It's easy to keep your hair looking pretty. I'll give you a little box of my soap powder that I use to shampoo my hair. You take it home and wash your hair with it every two or three weeks, and you'll see it will make a difference in a little while. You just haven't taken time to care for it—that's all. Do you mind if I wave the front here a little? I'd like to fix your hair the way my mother wears hers."

Now nothing could have been more different from this weathered woman than Margaret's gentle, dove-like mother, with her abundant soft gray hair, her cameo features and her pretty dresses. But Margaret had a vision of what glory might bring to Mom Wallis and wanted to help it along. Glancing out the window, she saw with relief that Gardley was occupied talking with Mr. Tanner.

Mom Wallis sat gazing at the mountain while Margaret was at work. And, Sunday though it was, Margaret lighted her alcohol lamp and heated a tiny curling iron she kept for emergencies. In a few minutes the woman's astonished gray locks lay soft and fluffy about her face, pinned in a smooth coil behind, instead of the tight knot, making a wonderful difference in her old, tired face.

"Now look!" said Margaret and turned her about to face the mirror. "If you don't like anything about it I can change it, you know. You don't have to wear it this way if you don't like it."

The old woman looked in the mirror, back at Margaret and then back to the vision in the mirror again.

"My soul! It's come a'ready! Glory! I didn't think I could look like that! I wonder what Pop'd say! My land! Would you mind ef I kep' it on a while an' wore it back to camp this way? Pop might uv come home, an' I'd like to see ef he'd take notice t' it. I used to be purty onct, but I never expected no sech thing like this again on earth. Glory! Mebbe I *could* get some glory too."

" 'The glory that shall be revealed' is a great deal more wonderful than this," said Margaret gently. "This was here all the time, but you didn't let it out. Do wear it home this way and all the time. It's very little trouble, and before you go home I'll show you how to fix it. Let's go downstairs now. We don't want to leave Mr. Gardley alone too long, and besides I smell dinner. They'll be waiting for us soon."

Margaret gathered up some photographs quickly to show the others, and the two walked downstairs then and out into the yard, where Gardley was looking at the mountain. Margaret suddenly realized the minister would be returning to the house soon. He would disturb the pleasant company with his disagreeable talk and might hurt Mom Wallis's feelings. She glanced around as she came out the door, but no minister was in sight.

Gardley stopped short in his walk across the yard and stared at Mom Wallis. When he was convinced she was the same person, he looked at Margaret with wonder.

Then suddenly he noticed the old woman's embarrassment and stepped toward her, his hands outstretched.

"Mom Wallis, you're beautiful. Did you know it?" he asked gently, taking her hand and leading her to a rocking chair by the front door. Then he stood off and surveyed her, while her cheeks flushed. "What did Miss Earle do to glorify you?"

There was that word again, she thought. *Glory!* She had some glory then, and it was brought out by such a simple thing as arranging her hair. Tears filled her tired old eyes.

It was well for Mom Wallis's equilibrium that Mr. Tanner came out just then with the paper, for her lifetime stolidity was almost breaking up. But, as he turned, Gardley gave her a smile of sympathy and understanding rare for a young man to give an old woman, and Margaret, watching, admired him for it.

They had discussed the article in the paper and looked at the photographs Margaret brought down. And Mrs. Tanner had walked to the door countless times, gazed down the road, hurried back, glanced in the oven, peeped in the kettle, sighed and hurried back to the door again. At last she stood there, arms akimbo, looking down the road.

"Pa, I don't see how I can keep the dinner waitin' a minute longer. The potatoes'll be sp'iled. I don't see what's keepin' that preacher-man. He musta been invited out, though I don't know why he didn't send word."

"That's it, likely, Ma," said Mr. Tanner, who was growing hungry. "I saw Mis' Bacon talkin' to him. She's likely invited him there. She's always tryin' to get ahead o' you, Ma, 'cause you got the prize fer your marble cake."

Mrs. Tanner blushed and looked down apologetically at her guests. "Well, then, ef you'll just come in and set down, I'll dish up. My land! Ain't that Bud comin' down the road, Pa? He's likely sent word by Bud. I'll hurry in an' dish up."

Bud slid into his seat after a brief ablution in the kitchen, and his mother questioned him sharply.

"Bud, wher you be'n? Did the minister get invited out?"

The boy grinned and slowly winked at Gardley. "Yes, he's invited out, all right," he said. "You don't need to wait fer him. He won't be home fer some time, I don't reckon."

Gardley watched the boy's twinkling eyes and resolved to gain a fuller understanding later.

It was the first time in twenty years Mom Wallis had eaten anything she hadn't prepared, and now, with fried chicken and company preserves before her, she could scarcely swallow. To be seated beside Gardley and waited on like a queen; smiled at by the beautiful girl across the table; deferred to by Mr. and Mrs. Tanner as "Mrs. Wallis" and offered more pickles and another helping of jelly—and did she take cream and sugar in her coffee? It was too much, and Mom Wallis was struggling with the tears. Even Bud's round, blue eyes regarded her with approval and interest. She couldn't help thinking, if her own baby boy had lived, would he have been like Bud? And once she smiled at him, and Bud smiled back, a frank, hearty grin. To her it was like taking dinner in the kingdom of heaven and getting glory before.

The afternoon passed swiftly. Gardley walked back to the schoolhouse, where the horses waited, and Bud accompanied him to explain that wink at the table. Mom Wallis retired to the rose-garlanded room, learned how to wash her hair and received a roll of flowered scrim for making curtains for the bunkhouse. Margaret had intended it for the schoolhouse windows in case it was needed, but that could wait.

And there in the rose room, with the new curtains in her trembling hands and the mountain in view, Mom Wallis knelt beside the rocking chair. And Margaret knelt beside her and prayed that the heavenly Father would show Mom Wallis how to let the glory show through her now on earth.

Then Mom Wallis wiped the tears with her faded calico sleeve, tied on her old bonnet and rode away with Gardley to the camp, with a smile warming her face.

Late that evening the minister returned.

He came in slowly, grimacing with every step, shunning the light. His coat was torn and splattered with mud. He mumbled something about a "slight accident" to Mrs. Tanner, who met him in the hallway with a candle in her hand. He devoured the slice of pie she offered, with cheese and cold chicken.

"Very pleasant!" he replied to her query about dinner. "The name? Um—ah—I disremember! I really didn't ask—that is—"

The minister stayed in bed for several days, professing to be suffering from rheumatism. He was watched over by the anxious Mrs. Tanner, who was quite disconcerted and couldn't understand why the schoolteacher wasn't more interested in the invalid.

On the fourth day, however, the Rev. Frederick West crept forth, pale and shaken, with his sleek hair combed elaborately to cover a long scratch on his forehead, and announced he was leaving Arizona that evening.

He stole cautiously to the station as evening drew on but found Long Bill there and Jasper Kemp not far away. The two letters were stuffed in his pocket, with the gold piece, although he'd hoped to escape without forfeiting them. But he was obliged to wait until Jasper Kemp had read both letters twice, and the train about to depart, before he could board.

"Watch your steps spry, parson," Jasper said. "I'm goin' to see you're shadowed wherever you go. You needn't think you can get shy on the Bible again. It won't pay."

West bowed his head low, boarded the train and vanished from sight. But not without one regret—he had failed to capture the schoolteacher's heart.

"And she was such a pretty girl!" he said with a sigh as the Arizona landscape sped by. "Still, there are plenty more! What was it I heard before I left home? 'Never run after a streetcar or a woman. There'll be another one along in a minute.' Um—ah—yes."

Chapter 18

School had settled down to real work by the opening of the new week. Margaret knew her students and had gained a personal influence over most of them already. Her teaching had enough novelty to keep the school in a pleasant state of excitement and wonder about what she would do next, and word had spread throughout the nearby country that the new teacher had taken the school by storm. Not infrequently men would turn off the trail to glimpse the school, just to make sure the reports were true. Rumor stated the teacher was very pretty; that she'd take no nonsense, not even from the big boys; that she never threatened or punished, but that every boy was her devoted slave. There had been no uprising, and it almost seemed as if that popular excitement was to be omitted this season and school was to sail along in an orderly and proper manner.

In fact, the entire school and the surrounding population were eagerly talking about the new piano, which seemed to be a coming fact. Not that anything had been done toward it yet, but the teacher had promised that as soon as everyone was studying hard and doing his best, she would start preparing them for an entertainment to raise money for the piano. They couldn't begin until everybody was in good working order, because they didn't want to take the interest away from the real business of school. But it would be a Shakespeare play, whatever that was, and therefore of grave import. Some people talked learnedly about Shakespeare and hinted of poetry. But the main part of the community spoke the name joyously and familiarly and without awe, as if it were milk and honey in their mouths. Why should they reverence Shakespeare more than anyone else?

Margaret's way wasn't all smooth. There were hitches and unpleasant days when nothing went right, when some of the girls got silly and rebellious and the boys followed their lead. She had her trials like any teacher, skillful as she was, and not the least of them because Rosa Rogers, the petted beauty, manifested a childish jealousy of her in her influence over the boys. Noting this, Margaret went out of her way to win Rosa but found it difficult.

Rosa was proud, selfish and unprincipled. She forgave no one who frustrated her plans. She resented being made to study like the rest. She'd always compelled the teacher to let her do as she pleased and still give her a good report. She found she couldn't do this with Margaret and for the first time had to work or fall behind. It became a question not of how the new teacher was to manage the bad boys of the Ashland Ridge School, but of how she was to prevent Rosa and a few girls who followed her from upsetting her plans. Rosa was pretty and knew her power over the boys. If she chose she could put them in a state of insubordination, and this she chose often during those first few weeks.

Meanwhile, Margaret had grown used to seeing a head appear suddenly at one of the school windows and gaze at her, frowning, then at the school and then back to her again. Whoever the visitor was, he would stand quietly, watching the hour's proceedings as if he were at a play. Margaret would turn and smile pleasantly, then continue with her work. The visitor would often take off a wide hat, wave it and smile back a curious, softened smile. Soon he would mount his horse and pass on down the trail, wishing he could be a boy again and go back to shcool.

But one visitor didn't confine himself to looking in at the window.

One morning a black horse galloped up to the schoolhouse at recess, and a young man in a wide sombrero and leather trappings jumped off and entered the building. His spurs caught the sunlight, and he walked with the air of one who regarded himself of more importance than those who may have been watching him. The boys in the yard stopped their ball game, while the girls whispered in groups and huddled near the door.

He was from a ranch near the fort some thirty miles away and was inviting the new schoolteacher to come for dinner Friday evening and stay until the following Monday morning. The invitation came from his sister, the wife of a wealthy cattleman whose home and hospitality were well known there. She'd heard of the young teacher's arrival and wanted her to join her social circle.

The young man, Archie Forsythe, openly admired Margaret as she talked, and he spoke graciously to her. Then, while she was answering the note, he smiled at Rosa Rogers, who had slipped into her seat and was preparing her algebra with the book upside down.

Glancing up, Margaret caught Rosa's smile and the end of a look from the young man's eyes and wondered if he'd met the girl before. Something in his bold look made her feel he had. Yet he continued smiling and openly admiring Margaret and was pleased she would accept the invitation. All this was pleasant to her, since she felt isolated being tied down to only the Tanner household and the school and welcomed any bit of social life.

The young man had neatly combed light hair and light-blue eyes that were more attractive than the minister's. But Margaret sensed they were the same cold color. She wondered at the comparison, for she liked him and in spite of herself was flattered by his compliments. When she remembered him later, though, it was always with that uncomfortable feeling that if he hadn't been so handsome and polished he would have seemed a little like the minister, and she couldn't tell why.

After he left she glanced back at Rosa. The girl's eyes narrowed, and her brows pulled together in a frown. Margaret sighed and returned to the problem of what to do with Rosa as a student.

But Rosa slipped out just then and walked arm in arm with Amanda Bounds down the road.

From the door where she'd gone to watch the girls, Margaret saw the rider turn around and hurry back. He'd forgotten to tell her someone would come to escort her as early Friday afternoon as possible and intimated he hoped he might be detailed for that pleasant duty.

Margaret warmed to his smile. How could she have thought he was like West? He touched his hat and rode away, and a moment later she saw him draw rein beside Rosa and Amanda and then dismount.

Bud rang the bell just then, and Margaret crossed to her desk with a lingering look at the three figures in the distance. Half an hour later Rosa strolled in, with Amanda slipping in timidly behind her. Margaret noted the sly look in the girl's eyes. After school she called her to her desk.

"You were late coming in after recess, Rosa," said Margaret gently. "Do you have an excuse?"

"I was talking to a friend," said Rosa, tossing her head, as if to say, "and I don't intend to give an excuse."

"Were you talking to the gentleman who was here?"

"Well, if I was, what's that to you, Miss Earle? Did you think you could have all the boys to yourself?"

"Rosa," said Margaret, trying to speak calmly, though her voice trembled with suppressed anger, "I would prefer you not talk that way to me. Have you met Mr. Forsythe before?"

"It's none of your business!" Rosa exclaimed, turning on her heel and marching out of the schoolhouse.

Margaret, shaking from the encounter, stood at the window and watched the girl walk haughtily down the road. At that moment she felt she'd rather give up her school and go back home than face the situation. She knew this girl, once an enemy, would be a bitter one, and this last move had been unfortunate, coming out, as it did, with Rosa in the lead. She could, of course, complain to Rosa's family or the school board, but she hadn't chosen that policy; she wanted to settle her own difficulties. She was puzzled because she couldn't reach the girl.

That evening Margaret reviewed the different plays in her library and finally, with a look of apology toward a small photographed head of Shakespeare, decided on *A Midsummer Night's Dream*. Even if it was beyond most of the students, wouldn't a few get something from it? And wasn't it better to take a great work and help her students and a few in the community understand it than to take a silly play that wouldn't amount to anything in the end? She could meanwhile teach them about Shakespeare and perhaps help some love his plays and study them.

She had played Puck's part and knew it by heart and felt certain some of the more adept students could interpret their parts. It would at least be a good study in literature for them. As for the audience, many might not understand the play's meaning, but they would come and listen.

She reviewed the parts carefully, trying to find one she thought would fit Rosa and please her as well. It would give her an opportunity to display her beauty and charm. Margaret wondered if she were right in attempting to win the girl through her vanity—yet how else could she?

At noon Margaret drew Rosa to a seat beside her.

"Rosa," she said gently, "you seem to feel we're enemies, and I had hoped we would be friends. You see, there's no other way for us to work well together. When I spoke to you yesterday, it was because I feel responsible for the girls and boys in my care—"

Margaret paused. She could see by the hardness of the girl's eyes that she was accomplishing nothing. Rosa evidently didn't believe her.

"Well, Rosa," she said, suddenly touching the girl's arm softly, "suppose we put it away and learn to understand each other if we can. Meanwhile I want to talk to you after school about the play."

And then Rosa seemed to soften, and she looked up with interest, though still with some suspicion. She wanted to be in that play with all her heart and meant to have the showiest part too, though she suspected the teacher would want to keep that for herself.

So after school Margaret took the time to explain the play to her and let her choose her own part, for she thought Rosa would do better in the part she was most interested in.

At one point Rosa was about to choose Puck, because she caught that character's importance. But when she learned the costume must be a quiet hood and skirt of green and brown she scorned it and chose to be Titania, queen of the fairies.

Margaret taught her some of the fairy steps and found her eager to learn. The girl even seemed to forget her animosity and became almost as congenial as the other pupils.

By Friday afternoon all the parts had been assigned, and plans for the entertainment were well under way.

Jed and Timothy had been as good as their word about giving the teacher riding lessons, each vying with the other to bring a horse for her to ride at noon. She had already had several lessons and a long ride or two with her instructors. So now she looked forward to the thirty-mile ride to the fort for the weekend.

Chapter 19

Before school closed Friday afternoon, Archie Forsythe, with his sister and a young army officer from the fort, arrived to escort Margaret to the ranch.

As they were riding away from the schoolhouse Margaret glanced back and saw Rosa posing in the schoolyard in one of her sprite dances and kissing her hand laughingly toward their group. Then she saw a handkerchief flicker in Forsythe's hand. It was quite general and elusive, a passing bit of fun, but it left an uncomfortable impression on her mind. She looked at the young man as he rode up smiling beside her and again experienced that strange, sudden change of feeling about him.

By careful questioning during the ride she tried to find out if he'd known Rosa before. But he told her he'd just come West to visit his sister, was bored to death because he didn't know anyone there and hadn't laid eyes on anyone he cared to know until he saw her. Margaret enjoyed the banter, but she felt uneasy.

One shadow was cast over the weekend. Margaret thought someone from the camp might come down on Saturday or Sunday while she was away. Nothing had been said about it, and she had no way of sending word of her absence. She'd meant to send Mom Wallis a letter by the next messenger. It was written and lying on her bureau, but no one had been down all week.

Just then she noticed a rider approaching. To her surprise it was Gardley, and with a smile she drew rein and greeted him and gave him a message for Mom Wallis.

Gardley smiled warmly at Margaret and lifted his hat to the others in the party. Forsythe, meanwhile, surveyed Gardley in a surly manner and plainly resented him. Gardley returned the cold look as he rode away.

Margaret sensed he was somehow disappointed and turned once in the saddle to look after him. But he was already racing across the desert. She and the others in the group watched the distant speck clear a steep descent from the mesa at a bound and disappear from sight in the mesquite beyond.

"Your friend is a reckless rider," Forsythe noted, with contempt in his voice.

"What a handsome man! Where did you find him, Miss Earle?" Mrs. Temple asked. "I wish I'd asked him to join us. He left so suddenly I didn't realize he was going."

Margaret felt a pleasant sense of possession and pride in Gardley as she watched him. But she simply said he was from the East and was engaged in some kind of cattle business some distance from Ashland. She said nothing about how her acquaintance with Gardley began. She could imagine Mrs. Temple saying, "How romantic!" for she'd noticed her bestowing covert glances upon the young officer riding beside her. Margaret wondered what kind of husband she had and what her own mother would think of a woman like this.

The luxury at the ranch provided a happy relief from the simplicity of life at the Tanners'. She enjoyed iced drinks, cushions and easy chairs, with abundant food, music, and laughter. She was offered books and magazines too, along with other trappings of a cultured life. But these people were not of her world. Sitting alone in her room late Saturday night, Margaret remembered with joy the Sabbath spent with Mom Wallis and realized she dreaded the Sabbath she would spend here.

Breakfast was served late amidst much hilarity. No church service was mentioned, and it was too late to suggest when breakfast was over.

For Margaret the Sabbath was generally a day to spend in quiet reflection. She wanted to withdraw to her room, but she didn't wish to be rude to these people who were trying to be kind to her. At last she gathered them around the piano and, after singing a few numbers at their request, coaxed them into singing hymns. With only one hymnbook among them, they joined in heartily nevertheless, with Margaret's sweet voice and skillful playing leading them in "My Jesus, As Thou Wilt" and "Jesus, Savior, Pilot Me."

"You would be the delight of Mr. Brownleigh's heart," remarked the hostess, after the last tones of "Abide With Me" faded away.

"And who is Mr. Brownleigh?" asked Margaret. "Why should I delight his heart?"

"Why, he's our missionary—that is, the missionary for this region—and you would delight his heart because you're so religious and sing so well," she said. "Mr. Brownleigh is really a very cultured man. Of course, he's narrow. All clergymen are narrow, don't you think? They have to be to a certain extent. Why, he believes in the Bible *literally*, the whale and Jonah, the flood, making bread out of stones—that sort of thing. Imagine! He's sincere too. I suppose he has to be. But sometimes one feels it a pity he can't relax a little, just among us here, you know. We'd never tell. Why, he won't even play a little game of poker! And he doesn't smoke! Imagine—*not even when he's by himself and no one would know!* Isn't that odd? But he can preach. He's really very interesting—only a little too Utopian in his ideas. He thinks everybody should be good and lives that way himself. But he's a wonderful person.

"I feel for his wife, though," she added, with sympathy in her voice. "She's quite cultured. Was wealthy—a New York society girl. Imagine—out in these wilds taking gruel to the Indians! How she's ever done it! Of course she adores him, but I can't believe she's happy. No woman could be blind enough to give up everything in the world for one man, no matter how good he was. It wasn't as if she didn't have other chances. She gave them all up to come out and marry him. She's a good sport too. She never lets you know she isn't perfectly happy."

"She *is* happy, Mother. She's happier than *anybody* I ever saw," declared the Temples' fourteen-year-old daughter, home from boarding school during a measles epidemic.

"Oh, yes, she makes people think she's happy," said her mother. "But I can't believe she's satisfied to give up her house on Fifth Avenue and live in a two-room log cabin in the desert with no company."

"Mother, you don't know! Why, *any* woman would be satisfied if her husband adored her the way Mr. Brownleigh does."

"Well, Ada, you're a romantic girl, and Mr. Brownleigh is a handsome man. You've got a few things to learn yet. Mark my words—you won't see Mrs. Brownleigh returning next month with her husband. This operation was all well enough to talk about, but I won't be surprised to hear he's come back alone or else has accepted a call to some big city church. And he's equal to the city church too—that's the wonder of it! He comes from a fine family himself, I've heard. Oh, people can't pose as saints forever, even though they do adore each other. But Mr. Brownleigh *certainly* is a good man!"

The woman sat musing by the window. Yes, Mr. Brownleigh was a good man. He was the one man of culture and education she had met in many years who had patiently refused her mild flirtations. Yet he remained her friend and respected hero.

Margaret wondered if a Sabbath in Arizona was hard to find. But after dinner she drew the children into a corner and began a Bible story in the guise of a fairy tale, while the hostess slipped away to take a nap. Several other guests lingered about, however, and Mr. Temple strayed in. They sat with newspapers in front of them but listened closely all the while. So Margaret concluded that she'd had a blessed Sabbath after all.

She went to bed at last, eager to return the next morning to her work.

Mr. Temple himself traveled part of the way with Margaret, his daughter, Forsythe and the young officer who had come over with them. Margaret rode beside Mr. Temple and talked with him about Arizona, until he took another trail. He was a kind old man who adored his frivolous wife and let her go her own gait, seeming not to mind how much she flirted.

The sky dawned pink and silver, gold and azure, and Margaret felt as if the sun had risen in its glory just for her. They lingered a moment to show her a fern-plumed canyon.

Since school was about to begin, Margaret rode straight to the schoolhouse instead of stopping at Tanners'. On the way they passed a group of girls, of whom Rosa Rogers was the center. Something in Rosa's face as she greeted her caused Margaret to look back. She saw the girl smile at Forsythe, who touched his hat and gave her a peculiar smile.

In a moment Margaret stood at the schoolhouse door, the children clustered about her and welcoming her back as if she had been gone a month.

Margaret failed to notice Rosa's absence until she called the roll. The girl finally appeared after recess, with a toss of her head, as if to say she would come in late anytime she chose. When questioned about her tardiness she said she'd torn her dress and gone home to change it. Margaret knew by the look in her eyes that she wasn't telling the truth. It troubled her all morning and followed her to a sleepless pillow that night. She could see that life as a schoolteacher in the West wasn't all she'd imagined. Her father was right. There would likely be more thorns than roses on her way.

Chapter 20

The first time Lance Gardley met Rosa Rogers riding with Archie Forsythe he thought little of it. He knew the girl by sight, because he knew her father through business. That she was very young and one of Margaret's pupils was all he knew about her. For the young man he'd conceived a strong dislike. But since he had no reason for it he put it out of his mind.

The second time he met them it was toward evening, and they were so absorbed in each other that they didn't see him until he was near. Forsythe glanced up with a frown and put his hand on his holster.

He scarcely returned Gardley's slight salute, and the two hurried up their horses and were soon out of sight in the mesquite. But something in the girl's frightened look caused Gardley to turn and watch them.

Where could they be going at that hour? The trail was seldom chosen for rides, being lonely and out of the way for travelers. Gardley had run a distant errand for Jasper Kemp and taken this short trail back because it cut off several miles. He was also anxious to stop in Ashland and leave Mom Wallis's request for Margaret to spend the next Sabbath at the camp and see the new curtains. This interruption to his thoughts was unwelcome.

But he couldn't dismiss what seemed like fear in the girl's eyes. Perhaps the fellow, new to the region, had lost his way. He may not know the road led into a region of outlaws and that its only habitation was a cabin belonging to a woman of questionable reputation.

Twice Gardley turned in his saddle and scanned the desert. The sky was darkening, with a few pale stars twinkling faintly. Now he could see the couple again, riding more slowly in the valley below, their horses close together.

Suddenly Gardley turned from the trail and set his horse at a gallop through a grove of trees. In minutes he reached the trail again some distance ahead of Forsythe and Rosa and stopped to wait for them.

By this time the full moon had risen and was at Gardley's back, silhouetting man and horse as the two riders approached.

Rosa screamed, pulling closer to her companion, and her horse swerved and reared. But Gardley's horse stood still across their path, despite Forsythe's unguarded exclamation, as he reached for his pistol.

"Mr. Forsythe," Gardley said quietly, "I thought since you're new to the area, you might not know that the trail you're on leads to a place where ladies don't like to go."

"Really! You don't say!" Forsythe retorted. "You might have saved yourself the trouble. I know where I'm going, and so does the lady, and we chose this trail. Move out of the way. You're detaining us."

"I'm sure the lady doesn't know where she's going or how the place is known," Gardley said. "At least, if she knows, *her father* doesn't know, and I'm well acquainted with him."

"Get out of the way, sir," Forsythe demanded. "It certainly is none of your business anyway, whoever knows what. Get out of the way, or I'll shoot. This lady and I intend to ride where we please."

"No, you *cannot*," said Gardley, still calm.

"Just how do you propose to stop us?" said Forsythe, pulling out his pistol.

"This way," said Gardley, putting a tiny silver whistle to his lips and issuing a peculiar, shrilling blast. "And this way," he added, lifting both hands with a gun in each.

Rosa screamed, covering her face with her hands, and shrank back in her saddle.

Forsythe lifted his own pistol but glanced around nervously. "Dead men tell no tales."

"It depends upon the man," said Gardley, "especially if he's found on this road. I imagine a few tales could be told if you happened to be the man. Turn your horses around at once and take this lady back to her home. My men aren't far off, and if you don't wish the whole story to be known among your friends and hers you'd better hurry."

Forsythe lowered his weapon. He didn't want his friends to find out about his escapade and especially not his brother-in-law, the latter for financial reasons.

Silently in the moonlight they proceeded down the trail, the girl and the man side by side, their escort close behind. Once the girl glanced back and saw three more men following like grim shadows further back. They'd fallen onto the trail so quietly she hadn't heard them. Jasper Kemp, Long Bill and Big Jim had been out for other reasons but without question answered the signal.

The ride back to the Rogers ranch seemed unending, and Forsythe glanced nervously behind him from time to time. The company seemed to grow each time he turned. He hurried his horse, but the followers kept pace on theirs.

Once he tried to placate Gardley with a few jovial words. "Look here, old fellow. Aren't you the man I met on the trail the day Miss Earle visited the fort? I guess you're mistaken in your calculations. I was merely out on a pleasure ride with Miss Rogers. We weren't going anywhere in particular. She chose this way, and I wanted to please her. No man likes to have his pleasure interfered with, you know. I guess you didn't recognize me?"

"I recognized you," said Gardley. "You should take care where you ride with ladies, especially at night. The matter, however, is one you'd better settle with Mr. Rogers. My duty will be over when I put it into his hands."

"Now, my good fellow," said Forsythe, "you surely don't intend to make a great fuss about this and tell tales to Mr. Rogers about a trifling matter—"

"I intend to do my duty, Mr. Forsythe," he replied, still holding his weapons. "I was set this night to guard Mr. Rogers's property. That I didn't expect his daughter to be part of the evening's guarding doesn't matter. I'll certainly put it in his hands."

Rosa began to cry softly.

"Well, if you want to be a fool, of course—but you'll soon see Mr. Rogers will accept my explanation."

"That's for him to decide," he replied and fell silent.

Forsythe's reflections during the rest of the ride weren't pleasant, and Rosa's intermittent crying didn't comfort him.

The procession at last turned in at the gate and rode up to the house. Just as they stopped and the front door swung open, letting out a flood of light, Rosa leaned toward Gardley.

"Please, Mr. Gardley, don't tell Papa. I'll do *anything* in the world for you if you won't tell Papa."

He looked at the young girl. "I'm sorry, Miss Rosa. I must do my duty."

"Then I shall hate you—forever!" she hissed. "And you don't know what that means. I'll take my *revenge* on you and on *everybody you like!*"

He looked at her half pityingly as he swung off his horse and walked up the steps. Mr. Rogers stood on the top step in the square of light that flickered from a great fire on the hearth inside. He looked from one to another of the group until his eyes rested on his daughter.

"Why, Rosa, what does this mean? You told me you were going to bed with a headache!"

Gardley drew the man aside and told what had happened in a few low sentences. Then he withdrew into the shadow, his horse by his side, the men from the camp behind him.

The father, his face stern, crossed to his daughter's side. "Rosa, you may get down and go into the house to your room. I'll talk with you later." To Forsythe he said, "You, sir, will step into my office. I wish to have a plain talk with you."

A short time later Forsythe left the house and mounted his horse, while Rogers watched him. The young man's lip curled and his eyes narrowed as he passed the men waiting in the shadow.

"That will be all tonight, Gardley," Rogers said, his voice clear but tired. "Thank you."

The men mounted their horses and followed Forsythe a short distance.

That young man, meanwhile, was wondering what Gardley had told Rosa's father. The interview was chastening in character, baffled him concerning the father's knowledge of details, and discouraged any further romantic rides with Rosa. Whether or not the man would inform the Temples about the episode depended upon the young people's future conduct. Forsythe hadn't removed suspicion from the father's mind or established his own innocence as he'd hoped. And some of the man's remarks made Forsythe think he knew how unpleasant it might become for him if his brother-in-law found out.

Thus Archie Forsythe feared Lance Gardley, though Gardley himself took no pride in what he'd accomplished that night. And Rosa Rogers hated Gardley and consequently her teacher, Margaret Earle.

An hour later Lance Gardley stood in the dim Tanner parlor, talking to Margaret.

"You look tired," she said.

"I went out to catch cattle thieves," he said, "but stumbled on another kind of thief. I'm not tired now, though."

He smiled at her warmly, and she noticed that the lines in his face had softened.

"So you'll really come out to see us, and it isn't asking too much?" he asked again. "You can't imagine what it will mean to the men—to *everyone!* Mom Wallis is so excited in hoping you'll come that she can hardly get her work done. If you had said no I'd be almost afraid to go back." He laughed, but his tone was earnest.

"Of course I'll come. I'm looking forward to it. I'll bring Mom Wallis a new bonnet like one I made for Mother, and I'll show her how to make corn gems and steamed apple dumplings. I can bring some songs and some music for the violin. And I've got something for you to help me do, if you will."

Her eagerness to visit the rough men and old woman living in a shack touched him. He smiled and pressed her hand quickly as he left, mounted his horse and rode back to the camp.

Margaret hastened up to her "mountain window" and watched him far out on the trail, her heart swelling with an unnamed gladness over his smile and the touch of his hand.

"Oh, God, keep him safe and help him do well!" she prayed.

Chapter 21

The inhabitants of the bunkhouse and even Margaret remembered her visit at the camp for a long time. Late Thursday evening, while she was braiding a gray bonnet out of folds of malines and styling it for Mom Wallis, she realized she was more excited about this trip than the one the week before to the Temples. She had enjoyed being among cultured people then, of course. But she would have such fun surprising Mom Wallis with that bonnet and seeing her face light up when she saw herself in the small folding mirror Margaret was taking her.

She had also selected gifts for the men—books, pictures, a piece of music, a brightly colored cushion and some picture magazines. The bundle weighed more than she'd hoped, but Bud assured her it "wasn't a flea bite for the Kid—he could carry *any*thing on a horse."

Bud, a little jealous for his teacher to be away so much, was delighted when Gardley suggested Friday afternoon that he join them. He hurried home, secured a hasty permission and clothes, and joined them on his father's old horse when they were half a mile down the trail.

Margaret had decided to stay from Friday afternoon after school until Monday morning. Her one fear about going was set at rest on the way when Gardley told her Pop Wallis had been off on one of his long trips, selling cattle, and probably wouldn't return for a week. Margaret, much as she trusted Gardley and the men, dreaded meeting the old man again.

The bunkhouse looked almost like new, with the grass cut, some vines twining about the door and the windows sparkling from Mom Wallis's washing.

Mom Wallis herself stood in the doorway to greet her guest, in her best white apron, stiff with starch, her lace collar, and her hair in her best imitation of how Margaret had styled it. But more than anything else Margaret noticed Mom Wallis was smiling. She was letting the glory shine through the hardness of her life and brighten things around her.

The interior of the bunkhouse looked much improved, also. The men had built three chairs—one out of a barrel—and upholstered them roughly. The cots around the walls blazed with their red blankets folded neatly over them, and on the floor in front of the scrubbed hearth Gardley had spread a Navajo blanket he had bought from an Indian.

The fireplace, piled with logs, stood ready for lighting at night, and from somewhere a lamp had been rigged up and polished till it shone in the setting sun.

The men, washed and combed, had hovered around the back of the bunkhouse, watching the road, and now they shuffled forward, taking her small, delicate hand in their rough, newly scrubbed hands. Shyness had taken possession of them, but their eyes glowed when Margaret greeted each one by name as if he were an old friend.

Bud held back and watched, his eyes twinkling. He was glad Margaret had come here, instead of to the fort. The men's "Howdy, sonny!" and Gardley's "Make yourself at home, Will" made him feel welcome.

Mom Wallis had done her best to make supper appetizing, with lamb stew, potatoes, fresh corn bread, and coffee. A white cloth, which looked like an old sheet turned and sewed together, covered the table. But, sitting there, Margaret made the tablecloth seem like the finest damask and the two-tined forks the purest silver.

After the supper was cleared away and the lamp lit, Margaret brought out her gifts. She gave Jasper Kemp a book of Scottish poetry, bound in tartan covers of the Campbell clan, and Big Jim an illustrated pamphlet of Niagara Falls—he'd always wanted to see the place and couldn't manage it. She'd brought a picture folder of Washington City for Long Bill, a book of old ballad music for Fiddling Boss, a book of jokes for Fade-Away Forbes and a framed picture of a beautiful shepherd dog for Stocky. She presented Croaker with a big, red denim pillow—he'd complained about the seats being hard when she was there the first time—and Fudge with a blazing crimson pennant bearing the name HARVARD in big letters, because he was from Boston.

For Mom Wallis she framed a text, bearing the words "Come unto Me, all ye that labor and are heavy laden, and I will give you rest" in rustic letters twined with forget-me-nots and painted in watercolors.

The men looked at all the gifts, laughing and talking at once. They hung their pictures and Mom Wallis's text on the walls and the pennant over the fireplace and put the pillow on a bunk. And while they were thus occupied, Margaret held out a small box to Gardley.

"I wondered if you'd let me give you this," she said. "It isn't much. It isn't even new, and it has some marks in it. But I thought it might help somehow."

With a puzzled expression on his face Gardley reached for the box and opened it carefully. Inside was a soft, leather-bound testament, showing the marks of usage, yet not worn. It was so thin it could fit neatly in a vest pocket and not be a burden to carry. He took the little book in his hand, removed the silken band that bound it and turned the pages reverently, noting the pencil marks scattered throughout.

"Thank you," he said in a low tone, glancing across the room. "I'll prize it greatly. It will help, and I'll carry it with me and read it often."

His voice was tender, and a flush had spread over his face. With another glance about the room—even Bud was busy studying Jasper Kemp's oldest gun—he snapped the band on the book again and tucked it in his inner pocket. He reached for her hand and pressed her fingers gently with a quiet "Thank you!"

Then Mom Wallis's bonnet was brought out and tied on her. She blushed like a schoolgirl as she looked shyly around at the others for their approval. But, when Margaret pulled out the threefold mirror and she saw herself in the new hat, she simply stared. She walked away at last, the bonnet in one hand, the box in the other and a look of wonder on her face, murmuring as she put it away, "Glory! *Me!* Glory!"

Margaret read one or two of the poems for Jasper Kemp, while they all sat and listened to her Scottish dialect and marveled that such a woman would visit them. And she gave a lesson in note-reading to Fiddling Boss, pointing one by one to the notes until he could pick out "Suwanee River" and "Old Folks at Home" to the delight of the audience.

Margaret never knew just how she came to be telling a story, one she had read recently in a magazine, that stirred national interest and searched people's hearts. But they listened to every word and then sang until the wee hours of the morning.

Just before going to sleep, Margaret, weary from the excitement, knelt with Mom Wallis in her room and prayed.

The next day Margaret rode with Gardley and Bud to the canyon of the cave dwellers. During the ride they discussed the play she was organizing at school. Gardley offered suggestions about costumes and tree boughs for scenery and promised to help if she needed him. Then, after eating supper and the apple dumplings she had taught Mom Wallis to make that morning, they told jokes, sang around the big fire and popped some corn Stocky had ridden far that day to get. Everyone asked for another story, and Margaret was happy to oblige.

But Sunday morning after breakfast Margaret stood for a moment gazing out of the small window, with the shadow of a sigh on her lips. As she turned back to the room she met Gardley's questioning glance.

"Are you homesick?" he asked. "This must be very different from what you're used to."

"Oh, no, it isn't that," she said, smiling brightly. "I'm not lonesome for home, but I do get a bit homesick about church time. Sunday is such a strange day to me without a service."

"Why not have one then?" he suggested. "We can sing and—you could— do the rest!"

Her eyes lit up, and then she glanced at the men.

"Say, boys—do you want to have church? Miss Earle here is homesick for a service, and I suggested we have one, and she can conduct it."

"Sure!" said Jasper Kemp with a grin. "I reckon she'll do better than the parson last Sunday. Get to your seats, boys—we're goin' to church."

At once the men moved the chairs around to set up the room for "church." And she started thinking about what she could read or say to help this strange congregation thrust suddenly upon her. Because of the influence of her father, whose life business was to preach the gospel, she didn't think once of declining but was eager to do what she could.

The men stirred about, donned their coats and brushed their hair, while Long Bill insisted that Mom Wallis put on her new bonnet. She sat down carefully in the barrel chair, her hands folded in her lap, her face glowing. That bonnet was doing its work in Mom Wallis.

Gardley arranged a comfortable seat for Margaret at the table and handed her one of the hymnbooks she had brought. Then he took the chair beside her and brought out the little testament from his vest pocket, laying it on the hymnbook.

Long Bill noticed Gardley's gentle manner with the girl and, turning his head, looked out the window and sneezed to excuse the sudden mist in his eyes.

Margaret chose "My Faith Looks Up to Thee" first because Fiddling Boss could play it. While he was tuning up his fiddle she hastily wrote out two copies of the words. So the odd service started with a quaver of the old fiddle and the clear voices of Margaret and Gardley, while the men growled behind, and Mom Wallis sat with shining eyes and hair fluffed softly under the new gray bonnet.

They were so absorbed in the song that they failed to hear a horse riding into the clearing. But as the last words of the final verse died away the bunkhouse door swung open, and there in the doorway stood Pop Wallis!

The men sprang to their feet, while Mom Wallis sat there, with the smile frozen on her face and a look of fear in her eyes.

Now Pop Wallis, through unusual circumstances, had gone for some hours without liquor and was relatively sober. He stared first at the men, then the beautiful stranger and finally across to the oddly unfamiliar face of his wife. A frightened look came over him. He passed his hand over his eyes, then looked again from one to another and back to his wife.

Margaret had half risen, and Gardley stood beside her. But Pop Wallis had eyes only for his wife. He blinked and stepped into the room, wonder on his face.

"Why, Mom—that ain't really—*you* now, *is* it?" he asked.

The old woman clasped her hands together, and a look of joy replaced the fear in her eyes.

"Yes, it's really *me*, Pop!" she said.

"But—but—you're right *here*, ain't you? You ain't *dead* an'—an'—gone to gl—oo—ry, be you? You're right *here*?"

"Yes, I'm right *here*, Pop. I ain't dead! Pop—glory's *come to me!*"

"Glory?" repeated the man. "Glory?" He gazed around the room at the new curtains, the pictures on the wall, the cushions and chairs, the sparkling windows. "You don't mean it's *heav'n*, do you, Mom? 'Cause I better go back—I don't belong in heav'n. Why, Mom, it can't be glory, 'cause it's the same old bunkhouse outside anyhow."

"Yes, it's the same old bunkhouse, and it ain't heaven, but it's *goin'* to be. The glory's come all right. You sit down, Pop. We're goin' to have church, and this is my new bonnet. *She* brang it. This is the new schoolteacher, Miss Earle, and she's goin' to have church. She done it *all!* You sit down and listen."

Pop Wallis took a few hesitant steps into the room and dropped into the nearest chair. He gazed at Margaret and wondered, and then he looked back at his wife.

Jasper Kemp shut the door, and they all let out a sigh of relief and dropped back into their places. Margaret, her voice quavering, announced another hymn.

After that, Margaret gave a simple prayer and read the story of the blind man from John's Gospel, chapter 6. The men listened attentively while Margaret read. But Pop Wallis stared at his wife, an awed light on his face, the wickedness and cunning faded, and only fear and wonder written there.

In the early dawning of the pink and silver morning Margaret returned to her work, Gardley by her side and Bud riding behind, now and then running off after a stray cottontail.

The horse Margaret rode, a sturdy Western pony, was to remain with her in Ashland, a gift from the men of the bunkhouse.

During the following week Archie Forsythe rode over with a beautiful saddle horse for her to use during her stay in the West. But when he returned to the ranch the saddle horse returned with him, riderless. Neither did she accept the Temples' invitation to visit the next weekend. She had other plans for the Sabbath.

That week there appeared on trees and posts about the town and on the trails a notice of a Bible class and vesper service to be held in the schoolhouse the following Sabbath afternoon. So Margaret, daughter of a minister-father, took up her mission in Ashland for Sabbaths to follow, for the school board had quickly agreed to such use of the schoolhouse.

Chapter 22

Soon the news spread that the teacher wanted to purchase a piano. To raise money she was organizing a Shakespeare play in which the students would act on a stage set with branches from live trees. The whole community was astir.

Mrs. Tanner talked about it. Wasn't Bud to be a prominent character? Mr. Tanner talked about it. The mothers and fathers and sisters talked about it, and play preparations proceeded.

Margaret discovered that one of the men at the bunkhouse played a flute, so she taught him, Fiddling Boss and Croaker to accompany the actors in the elfin dance. Sewing costumes and training the actors also occupied her time. Gardley took on the older boys and helped them learn their parts and was soon working almost as hard as Margaret. All the boys, including Jed and Timothy, admired this high-born, college-bred Easterner who could ride and shoot as well as anyone they knew in the West.

News of the play also spread to the fort and the ranches and brought offers of assistance and costumes and orders for tickets. Margaret purchased a small duplicator and set the students to printing and selling tickets. Before the play was nearly ready to open, enough tickets were sold for two performances, and people were planning to come from fifty miles around. Margaret grew uneasy at the thought of the big audience and her amateur players. Yet for children they were doing quite well and even becoming Shakespearian in their conversations.

"What say you, sweet Amanda?" one boy would ask that stolid maiden Amanda Bounds. "My good Timothy," Jed would say to "Delicate" Forbes, "I swear to thee by Cupid's strongest bow and by his best arrow with the golden head." Soon the schoolyard rang with classic phrases, and the nearby community was being addressed in phrases from another century by the younger household members.

Then one day Rosa Rogers's father stopped at the Tanners' and gave Margaret fifty dollars toward the new piano. After that, she announced they could order the piano in time for the play. Then smaller contributions came in, and before the opening date was set they'd received enough money for a first payment on the piano.

For their English exercise that day, Margaret decided to teach the whole school how to write a letter to the Eastern piano firm, ordering it to be sent at once. Sometime earlier she had requested several illustrated piano catalogues, showing by cuts how the whole instruments were made, with pictures of the factories where they were manufactured. She'd discussed the selection with the students, showing them what points they needed to consider. Finally they sent the order, even though Margaret had a musical friend in New York who would make the final decision. The students waited in suspense to hear it was on its way.

Three days in a row the students and Margaret walked down to the station to watch for the incoming Eastern train. At last the piano arrived two weeks before the play. They watched in awed silence as it was lifted from the freight car and set on the station platform.

The largest wagon in town carted it to the schoolhouse door with the students and other townspeople walking beside it. They held their breath while the box was peeled off and the instrument taken out and carried inside. Then they filed in and took their usual seats without being told, touching the shining case shyly as they passed. By common consent they waited to hear its voice for the first time. Margaret took the key from the envelope tied to the frame, unlocked the cover and, sitting down, began to play. Even the men who delivered it stood in awe around the platform, and the silence that spread over the room would have brought honor to Paderewski or Josef Hoffman.

Margaret kept playing, and they couldn't hear enough. It sounded so wonderful that they would have stayed all night listening. She let the students touch a few chords, just to say they'd played on it. Then she locked the instrument and sent them home. That was the only afternoon during the term that the play was forgotten for a while.

After the piano arrived, the students thought they were ready for the play, but Margaret and Gardley kept rehearsing each part, daily nearing their ideal. They hoped to give both audience and performers the true idea of what Shakespeare meant when he wrote it. And now Margaret accompanied some of the parts with music, along with the flute and violin, helping the students in the elfin dance with better effect.

About this time Archie Forsythe discovered the rehearsals and rode over from the fort to offer his assistance. Margaret told him no, but he still appeared at rehearsal time, finding ways to make himself useful in spite of Margaret's polite refusals. His presence particularly annoyed her because Rosa Rogers lost interest in the play and flirted openly with him while Gardley withdrew and spoke only when spoken to.

Forsythe spoke in courteous but cool tones to Gardley, like a scornful master to a slave. Margaret could only watch at such times, but a grave look settled upon her face whenever he was near. At such times Rosa would stare at her with narrowed eyes, then toss her head and flutter a smile in Forsythe's direction.

He even told Margaret he played the violin and offered to join in the orchestral parts. Margaret could think of no reason to refuse him, but it troubled her nonetheless. He was too bold with her, and she felt uneasy, with Rosa's jealous eyes upon her and Gardley's eyes strangely averted.

She planned special evening rehearsals, when Forsythe couldn't get there, and thus avoided him. But she was vexed and even shed some angry tears alone one night after Forsythe hurt Fiddling Boss's feelings with his insolent directions about playing. She restrained herself from saying anything because the Temples had helped purchase the piano, and Mr. Temple seemed to think he was doing her a great kindness in letting Forsythe off duty so much to help with the play. The Sabbath became her only relief and source of real joy.

The first Sunday after the piano arrived the entire neighborhood turned out for the afternoon class and vesper service, crowding the room. Even the men from the bunkhouse attended regularly now, often with Pop Wallis along. He hadn't yet recovered from his wife's new bonnet and fluffy hairstyle, treating her with more esteem at home and out, and often gazed at the rose-wreathed curtains with pride and awe.

Margaret had printed several hymns on the chalkboard and played over the hymns before the singing began. Everyone listened and then sang with loud, eager voices. Sometimes Margaret and Gardley, who also attended regularly, would sing duets.

She would then teach a short Bible lesson, beginning with the general outline of the Bible, its books, their form, substance, authors and the like—all brief and simple. She inserted music between this and the vesper service, into which she wove songs, bits of poems, and Scripture passages. Then she would often tell a story to illustrate the Scripture reading.

But the Sunday before the play, a group from the fort, including the Temples, arrived at the schoolhouse during the Bible lesson. The daintily dressed ladies settled their frills and smiled at one another as they watched the teacher moving about in her chair and shuffling her papers nervously. Margaret sensed they had come for amusement, not worship, and was irritated by it. They ignored the other people present, and not until Rosa Rogers entered with her father did they bow in recognition and then with an attitude that seemed to say, "Oh, you've come to be amused, too."

Gardley was sitting in front, listening to her, and she thought he hadn't noticed the strangers. With a prayer for help not to be distracted, she sat down at the piano, touched the keys with a chord or two and invited everyone to sing along. She'd sent home for some old hymnbooks from the Christian Endeavor Society in her father's church; so everyone had the notes and words now and joined in eagerly, including the people from the fort.

But Gardley, alert to the changes on Margaret's face, sensed her irritation and could guess the cause without turning around. Presently he stood to sing a duet with Margaret and didn't seem to notice the visitors in the back of the room. He sang, as Margaret did, to the children and men sitting in front, in a voice full of emotion and sympathy.

"Really," whispered Mrs. Temple loudly to an officer's wife, "that young man has a fine voice and isn't bad-looking, either. He'd be worth cultivating. We must have him up and try him out."

But this remark repeated in another loud whisper to Forsythe brought forth only a frown.

Margaret glimpsed Forsythe only once during the service, and that when he happened to smile at Rosa. But she quickly dismissed it from her mind and went on with her story.

The hunger in Jasper Kemp's eyes finally anchored Margaret's thoughts and helped her forget the visitors. She told her story with power, interpreting it now and then for the men who sat in the center of the room drinking in every word. The service concluded with another song, and Gardley's voice rang with peculiar tenderness and strength. Afterward the men filed out silently, looking thoughtful. But the visitors from the fort crowded around Margaret.

"Oh, my dear!" said Mrs. Temple. "How beautifully you do it! And such attention they give you! No wonder you're willing to forego other amusements to stay here and preach! But it was perfectly sweet the way you made them listen and the way you told that story. I don't see how you do it. I'd be scared to death!"

They babbled about her awhile, much to her vexation, for she'd wanted to speak to several other people, who, indeed, withdrew and disappeared when the visitors surrounded her. At last, however, they mounted and rode away. Forsythe had tried to persuade her to accompany them; tried to escort her to the Tanners'; tried to stay with her in the schoolhouse when she said she had something to do there. But she refused all, and he rode away with a look of injured pride on his face.

Margaret walked to the door finally and stood there alone, looking down the road. A shadow crossed her face. Everyone was gone, even Gardley. She'd wanted to tell him—

And then she turned back, and there he was, near the door, walking toward her. A light shone in her eyes, and he smiled in answer.

"Oh, I'm so glad you're still here!" she exclaimed, a flush spreading over her cheeks. "I wanted to tell you—"

He took her hands in his. He stood thus only a moment, looking into her eyes. Neither probably knew till afterward that they were holding hands. It was over in a second, but that look and handclasp meant a great deal to them later.

"I wanted to tell *you*," he said tenderly, "how much that story did for me. It was wonderful, and it helped me decide something I've been confused about—"

"Oh, I'm glad!" she said.

So, talking in low, broken sentences, they walked back to the piano and tried several songs for next Sunday, happy to be together and scarcely understanding the significance of it all. As the shadows on the schoolroom wall lengthened, they left and walked slowly to the Tanner house and then said good night.

The young man stood a moment looking upon the girl in parting, his strength made tender and beautiful by love. In his face glowed a high purpose and devotion.

And Margaret felt her heart reach out with that love, half maiden, half divine, that comes to some even here on earth. She watched him ride down the road toward the mountain and marveled how her trust had grown since she first met him. She reflected that she hadn't told her mother and father much about him yet. Perhaps it was time to do so! She hastened to her room.

That was the last time she saw him before the play.

Chapter 23

The play was set for Tuesday. Monday afternoon and evening were the final rehearsals, but Gardley didn't come. Fiddling Boss came late and said the men had been off all day and hadn't returned. He'd found it hard to come at all. They had important work going on, but there was no word from Gardley.

Margaret was disappointed and uneasy. Of course they could rehearse without him; he didn't have to be there. He knew every part by heart and could take any boy's place if necessary. He had nothing further to do until the performance. She reasoned that his work, whatever it was—he'd never explained it thoroughly to her, perhaps because she'd never asked—must have kept him.

Forsythe came presently and was more trying than usual. She had to be firm about one or two things, or some of her actors would have gone home sulking, and Fiddling Boss, whose part in the program meant much to him, would have given up entirely.

She hurried through everything, longing to get to her room and rest. Gardley would explain tomorrow, likely in the morning on his way somewhere.

But morning came, and then afternoon, and still no word. Some things he'd promised to do about setting the stage would have to remain undone; it was too late now to do it herself, and she had no one else to ask.

Just then Timothy Forbes ran breathless into the schoolhouse. "Miss Earle! Wouldn't you know—Jed's jes' broke his leg! That new horse o' his threw him, the cayuse! Nearly home, too! He'll be okay, but now what'll we do? Who'll take his part? We can't go on less'n somebody plays Nick Bottom!" The boy sat down to catch his breath.

Before she could speak, Forsythe entered the room.

"Oh, it's you, Mr. Forsythe," she said. "Have you seen Mr. Gardley today? We need him just now."

"I have indeed," Forsythe said, a satisfied glimmer in his eyes, "not two hours ago, drunk as a fish, out at a place called Old Ouida's Cabin, as I was passing. He's helpless and out of the question now. But I'm here. What can I do?"

Margaret placed her hand on her desk to steady herself, straightening some loose papers. She didn't want Forsythe to see how his words had shaken her. After a moment she found her voice.

"Oh, really, nothing at present—thank you. No, wait, there is something. Would you mind helping Timothy hang those curtains? It's a big job for him to do by himself. Now I think I'll go home and rest a few minutes before tonight."

Fussing over those curtains wasn't the job Forsythe had wanted. But he stayed anyway to do it. He saw her face pale at his news of Gardley. Why wasn't she horrified or disgusted? He watched her leave and then turned impatiently to the waiting Timothy.

Once outside, Margaret searched for Bud, who had been sent to gather sagebrush for the background. But Bud was flying down the trail to the camp on Forsythe's horse. Moments earlier he'd stood at the schoolhouse door with his arms full of sagebrush, in time to hear Forsythe's remarks about Gardley and see Margaret's pale face.

Margaret didn't go home to rest as she'd said. Forsythe's words had shocked her. "I *don't* believe it! It *isn't* true!" she told herself. She needed time to think.

A short distance from the schoolhouse she saw someone approaching. She calmed herself quickly and then saw it was Rosa, her arms full of bundles and more piled in front of her on her pony. She knew at once that Rosa must have seen Forsythe pass by her house and returned to the schoolhouse on some pretext. She couldn't let her be alone with him. Nor could she send Rosa home with orders to rest. She was certain the girl would take another way around and return to the school. She could only go back and stay as long as Rosa did.

Margaret plucked some sagebrush growing near the path and went back to the school, determined to put her thoughts aside until she was alone and could think clearly.

On seeing her, Forsythe's face lit up, and he suddenly put forth effort to help Timothy. Soon Rosa came, along with others, and they laughed and chattered around her. Margaret went about directing some and helping others, while adding little touches to the stage, as if she had nothing else to concern her. Yet all the while a peace stole over her, for as she worked she prayed, "Please, God, don't let it be true! Save him and help him be true! I *know* he's true! Please, God, bring him safely *soon!*"

She could do no more—and no less. She couldn't send Forsythe after him. She couldn't speak about it to anyone. And Bud—she couldn't leave the schoolhouse to look for him. She could only work on and pray.

Soon one of the smaller boys came, and she sent him to the Tanners' to find Bud. But he hadn't been home since morning, the boy reported. Where was faithful Bud? Had he deserted her too?

Margaret didn't stop for supper or eat a chicken sandwich Mrs. Tanner had sent. At last, the audience began to gather.

So great was her anxiety for Gardley that she forgot to supply Jed's place. If only Gardley would come! What would she do if he didn't? What if he were the kind of man Forsythe had suggested? How terrible life would seem! But it wasn't true. No, it *was not* true! She trusted him. He would come as soon as he could and explain everything. Before her flashed a picture of his last look at her on Sunday. She knew he would come!

Margaret slipped into the dressing room and put on the white dress she had sent for, with its delicate blue ribbons and soft lace ruffles. She glanced at herself in the mirror and hoped no one would notice the shadows under her eyes or the tightness about her mouth. Back outside she smiled and talked with her usual cheerfulness as members of the audience spoke to her. She could hear murmurs of "Oh, isn't it grand we attracted such a prize of a teacher!" "See how excited she is for her students to perform!" and "See how much she cares about them!"

The seats filled; the noise and clatter went on. But still no sign of Gardley or anyone from the camp, and still no sign of Bud! What could it mean?

It was past time for the curtain to go up. The girls were in a flutter in the dressing room at the right of the stage, and the boys were in the other dressing room wanting all sorts of help. Meanwhile, some of the older boys got scared when they peered through a hole in the curtain and saw some friend or relative arrive. Oh, *why* had she ever thought of putting on a play?

Forsythe, from behind the piano, whispered to her that it was time to start. The house was full; no seats were left.

"But the Fiddling Boss isn't here yet," she told him.

"Well, we can't wait all night!" he answered, looking away from her. "He should've come early if he wanted to be in it."

At that moment she turned and saw Pop and Mom Wallis standing in the doorway and the grim, towering figure of the Boss, his fiddle held high, making his way to the front amid the crowd.

Margaret longed to ask the Boss if he knew anything about Gardley. But, with Forsythe beside her and the play about to begin, she forced herself to sit down at the piano and strike the opening chords of the overture. Somehow she managed to get through it. Of course, no music critics were present, and the audience was so enraptured it wouldn't have noticed many mistakes. For instead of just a prelude to a fairy revel her fingers played the story of a soul struggling and reached hearts as the music rolled and swelled on to the end. It may be, too, that Fiddling Boss was more in sympathy that night with his accompanist than was the other violinist and thus brought forth haunting, tender tones from his old fiddle.

Near the end, she looked up and saw before her through a hole in the curtain a familiar, freckled nose. Then a bright eye appeared and solemnly winked at her twice, as if to say, "Don't you worry—it's all right!"

Somehow she kept from falling off the stool and even finished the last chords. As they died away she heard Bud whisper, "Whoop her up, Miss Earle. We're all ready. Raise the curtain there, you guy. Let her rip. Everything's okay."

With a new light in her eyes Margaret turned the pages of the music and continued playing as if nothing had been the matter. Bud was there, so everything must be all right. Perhaps Gardley had come too, or Bud had heard some news of him—and yet Bud had been gone too and didn't know he was missing.

At least the character Nick Bottom wasn't in this first scene, she thought. She could make it to the end and then see her way clear as to what to do next.

Once she turned sideways to the audience and glanced about, glimpsing Fudge's round, near-sighted face. Perhaps the others were there too. If only she could whisper to someone from the camp and ask when they'd last seen Gardley!

The curtain went up, and the first scene opened. Much to Margaret's satisfaction, the actors played their parts with ease and dexterity. The audience, silent and charmed, watched the strangers that were their own children, marching about in odd costumes and speaking in that peculiar language.

And Margaret's heart seemed to pound in time with the music.

At last, the first scene of the first act ended, the students having given forth a flawless performance, and Margaret struck the final chords on the piano. She watched the curtain drop with a calm expression on her face. But suddenly she knew she couldn't stay there another second. She must get out to the air. Before anyone had time to notice, she had slipped from the piano stool, under the curtain to the stage, and was gone.

Chapter 24

For some time Gardley had been employed by Mr. Rogers, looking after important matters of his ranch. Before that he had lived a carefree life, working a little when it suited him and having no set interest in life, only trying to erase from his mind the life he'd left behind. Now, however, everything was different. He brought to his work the keen mind and ready ability that had put him ahead of everyone else in all he undertook. Within a few days Rogers saw what he was made of and as the weeks passed depended more and more on his advice.

Rogers was losing his best herds to cattle thieves, and so far every attempt to cut the loss or catch the thieves had failed. Rogers finally put the matter into Gardley's hands to carry out his own ideas, with the men of the camp at his disposal. The camp itself was part of the rancher's outlying possessions, one of several such centers from which he worked his growing interests.

Gardley had formulated a scheme by which he hoped to catch the thieves, and he felt certain he was on the right track. But his plan required cautious work so they wouldn't suspect and take cover. For several weeks he'd suspected them of headquartering near Old Ouida's Cabin and making their raids from there. So day and night he and his men had been secretly patrolling the woods and trails near Ouida's and noting every passerby. Gardley usually knew who frequented the area and what their business was. The men from the Wallis camp and two other camps relieved one another, with Gardley in charge.

Gardley's frequent presence at the Rogers ranch caused no small problem for the petted daughter of the household. As often as he was there he never lifted an eye to admire her. She hadn't forgotten his humiliation of her in front of Forsythe and longed to humble him, and through him to humiliate Margaret, who presumed to interfere with her flirtations. It was a constant source of bitterness to Rosa that Forsythe had no eyes for her when Margaret was about.

That Sunday after the service in the schoolhouse, when the party from the fort left for home, Forsythe lingered to talk to Margaret and then rode around by the Rogers place, where he and Rosa had long ago set up a trysting place.

Rosa was waiting for him there and during their conversation casually disclosed to Forsythe some of the plans she'd overheard Gardley laying before her father. Rosa had little idea of the importance of Gardley's work to her father, or she might not have prattled of his affairs. She thought only of humiliating him and hoped he could be prevented from appearing at the play Tuesday evening. She thought it would be easy to do so. Forsythe questioned Rosa keenly. Did she know whom they suspected? Did she know exactly how they planned to catch them, and when?

Forsythe wasn't averse to getting rid of Gardley either and saw more possibilities in Rosa's suggestion than she had. When at last he bade Rosa good night and rode back to the trail he was already formulating a plan.

And as it happened, a few miles farther along the trail, he encountered a dark-browed rider whose identity he'd learned only a few days before.

Now Forsythe might not have entered into a contract against Gardley with men of such ill-repute had it been a matter of money and bribery. But, armed as he was with information valuable to the criminals, he suggested to them that detaining Gardley would be to their advantage. This would appear to be just friendly advice from a disinterested party deserving a good turn sometime in the future and not get Forsythe into any trouble. As such, the man clutched at the information with a wicked gleam in his eyes and rode on into the dark night.

Forsythe made his way to the Temple ranch, with no thought of the forces he had set in motion. He had always aimed to please himself, even at others' expense, with whatever amusement the hour afforded.

Indeed, back in the East, where he had spent his early life, a young woman awaited his letters, patiently enduring the months of separation until he established a home and a living and was ready for her to come to him. And in the South, where he'd idled six months before going West, another girl treasured mementoes of his tarrying and wrote him loving letters in reply to his occasional notes. And out on the California shore a girl with whom he'd traveled West, along with a party of friends and relatives in her uncle's private car, cherished hopes of a visit he'd promised to make during the winter. And other countless young women of the world, wise in what crushes hearts, remembered him with a sigh now and then but held no illusions.

But young Rosa Rogers wept every time he cast a languishing look at her teacher, while those worldly wise ladies of the fort only sighed at his glance or gentle pressure of his hand. Girls like Margaret Earle, perhaps at first attracted, soon distrusted him. And the blithe Lothario went his way without a scratch on his heart, till one wondered if he even had a heart.

When Gardley left camp the Monday morning after the Sabbath service, he'd intended to be back at the schoolhouse by the time the rehearsal began later that afternoon. He'd planned for relays from other camps to guard the suspected area for the next three days so he could be free. Forsythe had told the stranger that Gardley would likely pass a certain lonely crossing of the trail at about three o'clock that afternoon. If that arrangement had been carried out, the men who lay in wait for him would doubtless have been pleased for their plans to mature so easily. But they wouldn't have been pleased long, for Gardley's men were nearby, watching that spot with eyes and ears and long-distance glasses, and their chief would soon have been rescued and the would-be captors themselves be captured.

But the men from the farther camp, called Lone Fox men, didn't arrive on time, perhaps through some misunderstanding, and Gardley and Kemp and their men had to pull double shifts. At last, late in the afternoon, Gardley volunteered to go to Lone Fox and bring back the men.

As he rode he thought about Margaret and felt again the thrill of her hands in his, the trust of her smile. It was incredible to him that God had sent someone like her into the wilderness to help him. Now he wondered if he could ever be good enough to ask her to marry him. He was earning good wages now. In two more weeks he would have enough to repay the sum that had caused him to flee his old home and come out West. He would go back, of course, and make amends. Then what? Should he stay in the East and return to his old business or come back to this untamed land again and start over?

His mother was dead. Perhaps if she had lived and cared he would have succeeded at first. His sisters were married to wealthy men and not deeply interested in him. He had disappointed and mortified them; but they were busy with social duties and had probably never missed him. His father had been dead many years. As for his uncle, his mother's brother, whose heir he was to have been before he disgraced himself, Gardley had decided to avoid him. He would make restitution, visit his sisters and then come back. Then he would let Margaret decide what she wanted to do—that is, if she would consent to link her life with someone who had once failed. If she thought he should return and be a lawyer, he would—even if he had to enter his uncle's office in a subordinate position to do so. He loathed the idea, but he would do it if Margaret thought it best. And so his thoughts went.

When he reached the Lone Fox camp and dispatched the men on their belated task, Gardley decided not to accompany them to meet Kemp and the other men. Instead he sent word to Kemp that he had taken the shortcut to Ashland, hoping to make part of the evening rehearsal.

Now that shortcut led him to the lonely trail crossing sooner than Kemp and the others could reach it from the rendezvous. There in cramped positions four masked men had concealed themselves for four long hours.

Gardley rode through the still twilight. His long day's work was done, and though he couldn't return when he had planned, he was free now until the day after tomorrow. He would go at once to see if Margaret needed him for anything.

Then he began to sing, his voice reaching the ears of the men in ambush.

Oh, the time is long, mavourneen,
Till I come again, O mavourneen—

"And the toime'll be longer thun iver, oim thinkin', ma purty little voorneen!" replied a voice through the gathering dusk.

Gardley's horse stopped, and his hand reached for his revolver, while his other hand lifted the silver whistle to his lips. But four guns bristled at him. Someone knocked the whistle from his lips before his breath had reached it, caught his arms from behind and wrenched his revolver from his hand, causing it to go off. Someone else flung a heavy blanket over his head and drew it tightly about his neck, stifling his cry and almost strangling him. Struggling only made it worse. So he lay like one dead and tried to listen. Muffled and gagged and now bound hand and foot, he could hear little and was scarcely able to breathe.

He could tell they were leading him off the trail and up over rough ground, for the horse stumbled and strained to carry him. He tried to think where they might be taking him, but the darkness and suffocation numbed him. Then he remembered with a pang that his men would think him safely in Ashland, helping Margaret. They wouldn't be alarmed if he didn't return that night; they would think he stopped at the Rogers ranch on the way and perhaps stayed all night, as he had before. *Margaret!* When would he see her? What would she think? And then he knew no more.

Sometime later, when he started to come to, he found himself in a close, stifling room where candlelight threw weird shadows over the adobe walls. He could hear a woman and a girl laughing harshly, half suppressed, and could make out the profile of someone, whose face was covered, holding a glass to his lips. The smell sickened him. He hated the thought of liquor. He'd never cared for it and had resolved never to taste it again. But whether he chose to or not, it was poured down his throat while strong hands held him. He was still bound and too weak to resist.

The liquid burned its way down his throat, searing his brain, and darkness, mingled with men's angry, coarse voices, swirled about him. Deeper darkness engulfed him and with it relief from pain.

Hours passed. He heard occasional sounds and dreamed dreams he couldn't distinguish from reality. He saw terror etched on the faces of his friends, while he lay there immobile. He saw tears on Margaret's face. And once he was sure he heard Forsythe speaking with contempt: "Well, he seems to be well occupied! No danger of his waking up for a while!" The voices grew dim and distant again, and only the old woman and the girl whispered harshly over him. Then his early sins seemed to melt away and flood him with their horror. Then tears came and an awareness that he should be doing something for Margaret now and couldn't. Then more darkness.

Chapter 25

Margaret darted behind the curtain, rushing past the excited young people and through the dressing room. She felt her breath leaving her and everything about her spinning into blackness. The cool air struck her face, reviving her, and the starry Arizona night calmed her.

And there before her, in Nick Bottom's somber costume, eating one of Mrs. Tanner's chicken sandwiches, stood Gardley, pale and weak-looking— but there! She could scarcely believe it! He turned and saw her at the same moment. Forgetting everything else, he crossed the schoolyard and pulled her gently into his arms.

At last he had come, and Margaret's heart had found its home. There behind the schoolhouse, under the starry dome, while audience and actors clamored for them, these two pledged their love, his lips upon hers, with no word spoken.

Just then voices from inside roused them. "Where's Mr. Gardley? Isn't he here yet? We need him. It's time for the curtain, and everybody's ready. And where on earth has Miss Earle vanished to? Miss Earle! Oh, Miss Earle!" They could hear feet scrambling about in the dressing room.

But Bud stood in the doorway with his back to the outside and called loudly: "They're comin'. Go on! Get to your places. Miss Earle says get to your places."

He pressed her hand softly as they stepped apart and hurried in.

With cheeks glowing and eyes shining, Margaret dashed across the stage and took her place at the piano as the curtain opened.

Forsythe, uneasy because of the look on her face as she left earlier, wondered at the change and leaned forward to tell her how well she looked. But she was watching the curtain rise and didn't notice. He suddenly remembered this was the scene in which Jed was to appear. What had Margaret done? The part couldn't be left out. Why hadn't he thought of it sooner and offered to take it? He could have bluffed his way through; he'd heard it so much. And why hadn't Rosa suggested it?

The curtain was open now, and Bud's voice as Peter Quince, a bit high and cracked with excitement, broke the stillness, while the audience gazed in awe upon the strange world before them.

"Is all our company here?" lilted out Bud's voice.

And Nick Bottom replied, in Gardley's clear voice: "You were best to call them generally, man by man, according to the scrip."

Forsythe's face paled. He glanced about, as if to steal away, then, seeing Jasper Kemp's eyes upon him, sat back with a strained look on his face. Once he looked at Margaret and caught her face glowing and felt rebuked somehow by the sight.

She had no eyes for him. And if she had, he knew it would be with contempt. A woman now and then may pierce the soul of a man who plays with love and trust and womanhood for selfish gain. Such a woman seldom knows her power. Indeed, Margaret Earle, herself unaware, by her indifference and disdain, had revealed this man to himself.

He slipped away at last, when he thought no one was looking, to the open door of the girls' dressing room. Rosa, in her character Titania, would be there between acts. He questioned her angrily, as if she had foiled their plans. Was her father home all day? Did anything happen? Had Gardley come? Had that short, thickset Scotsman with the ugly grin been there? She suggested the scheme in the first place, and it was her business to keep watch. There was no telling now what might happen.

Forsythe turned, and there stood Jasper Kemp at his elbow, his short stature drawn up to its full height, his shoulders squared, a menacing grin on his face.

Forsythe let forth a stream of words usually absent from a gentleman's code and stepped away from the frightened girl.

"Was you addressing me?" he asked. "Because I could tell you a few things a sight more appropriate for you than what you just handed me."

Forsythe hurried to the front of the schoolhouse, but Jasper kept pace with him.

"Nice evening to be *free*," Jasper Kemp continued, gazing up at the stars. "Rather unpleasant for some folks that have to be shut up in jail."

Forsythe wheeled around, his face pale. "What do you mean?"

"Oh, nothing much," drawled Jasper. "I was just thinking how much pleasanter it was to be a free man than shut up in prison on a night like this. Much healthier, you know."

Forsythe stared at him a moment, a light flickering across his face. Then he turned and walked over to his horse.

"Where're you going?" demanded Jasper. "It's 'most time you went back to your fiddling, ain't it?"

But Forsythe only mounted his horse, which, unknown to him, had traveled many miles since he last rode him.

"You think you have to go then?" said Jasper. "Well, now, that's a pity, seeing you was fiddlin' so nice an' all. Shall I tell them you've gone for your health?"

"Tell her—tell her—I'm suddenly ill." And he set his horse at a gallop toward the fort.

"I'll tell her you've gone for your health!" called Jasper, with his hands to his mouth like a megaphone. "I reckon he won't return again soon either," he chuckled. "This country's better off without such pests as him an' that measley parson."

Then, turning, he saw Rosa, pale and staring after the departed rider. "Poor little fool!" he muttered under his breath.

"Don't you go for to care, lassie," he said tenderly, stepping to her side. "He ain't worth a tear from your pretty eye. He ain't fit to wipe your feet on—your pretty wee feet!"

"Go away, you bad old man!" she shrieked, stamping her foot, then fleeing into the schoolhouse.

Jasper stood looking after her, shaking his head. "The little de'il!" he said aloud. "She'll get her dues aplenty afore she's done."

Meanwhile, inside the schoolhouse, the play went gloriously on to the finish, and Gardley as Nick Bottom took the house by storm. Jed's father, sent by the sufferer to report it all, stood at the back of the house with mixed emotions of pride and disappointment—pride that Jed had been so well represented and disappointment that his son couldn't have been up there.

The hour was late when the play ended, and Margaret stood at last in front of the stage to receive the congratulations of the entire community. The young actors posed and laughed and chattered excitedly, then left by twos and threes, their tired, happy voices echoing along the road.

The Temples and their friends from the fort were the first to crowd around Margaret. "So sweet, my dear! So perfectly wonderful! You really have some fine actors! Why don't you try something lighter—a little simpler? Something really popular that these poor people could understand and appreciate? A farce, perhaps! I could help you pick one out!"

And while they gushed, Jasper Kemp and his men stood like a cordon to protect her, with Gardley just behind her. At last the schoolhouse was empty, except for Margaret, Gardley and the men. Outside the door Bud was talking to Pop and Mom Wallis.

With this bodyguard Gardley took Margaret home. She wondered a little that they all went along, but she attributed it to their pride in the play and wanting to talk it over. And she never dreamed that she and Gardley rode in the buckboard because he wasn't fit to walk.

Jasper and his men had burst into his prison and freed him, rushing him to the schoolhouse, with Bud racing wildly ahead. Gardley hadn't had time to realize all that had transpired in those terrifying hours before, and now he could only think how glad he was to be sitting beside Margaret. Her hand lay beside him on the seat, and without intending it his own brushed it. Then he laid his gently, reverently, upon hers with a quiet pressure, and her small fingers thrilled and nestled in his grasp.

In the shadow of a large tree beside the house he bade her good-bye, while Fudge and Croaker noisily turned the buckboard about and Bud scuffed his way to the back door to get Long Bill a drink of water.

"What happened?" Margaret asked anxiously, noticing the cuts on Gardley's wrists. "You've suffered somehow—"

"I'll tell you tomorrow," he said. "We've got to get back to camp now. I'll have a great deal to tell you tomorrow—if you'll let me. Good night, *Margaret!*"

Their hands lingered in a clasp, and then, with Big Jim's help, he climbed up into the buckboard and rode to the camp with the men.

But Margaret didn't have to wait until the next day to hear the story, for Bud was fairly bursting to tell it.

Mrs. Tanner had prepared supper—more cold chicken, pie, doughnuts, coffee, marble cake and preserves. She insisted on Margaret's coming into the dining room and eating it, though the girl would rather have gone with her happy heart up to her room.

Bud didn't wait. He began at once when Margaret was seated.

"Well, we had *some ride!* The Kid's a great old scout."

"Why, what became of you, William?" Margaret asked. "I hunted everywhere for you. I really needed your help."

"Well, I know," Bud said. "I'd oughta let you know before I went, but there wasn't time. You see, I had to pinch that guy's horse to go, and I knew it was just a chance if we could get back anyway. But I had to take it. You see, if I could a gone right to the cabin it woulda been a dead cinch. But I had to ride to camp for the men, and then, takin' the short trail across, it was some ride to Old Ouida's Cabin!"

"Now, Buddie—Mother's boy!" Mrs. Tanner cried, her mouth open, her eyes round with fright. "You don't mean to tell me *you* went to *Ouida's cabin?* Why, sonnie, that's an *awful place!* Don't you know your pa told you he'd whip you if you ever went on that trail?"

"I should worry, Ma! I *had* to go. They had Mr. Gardley tied up there, and we had to go and rescue him."

"*You* had to go, Buddie—now what could *you* do in that awful place?" Mrs. Tanner was almost in tears. She saw her offspring at the edge of perdition.

But Bud ignored his mother. "You jest oughta seen Jap Kemp's face when I told him what that guy said to you! Some face, b'lieve me! He saw right through the whole thing too. I could see that! He ner the men hadn't had a bite o' supper yet. They'd just got back from somewheres. They thought the Kid was over here all day helping you. He said yesterday when he left 'em that here's where he's a-comin'.

"When I told 'em, he blew his little whistle—like what they all carry—three times, and those men jest stopped right where they was, whatever they was doin'. Long Bill had the comb in the air gettin' ready to comb his hair, an' he left it there and come away, and Big Jim never stopped to wipe his face on the roller towel—he jest let the wind dry it. And they all hustled on their horses fast as they could and beat it after Jap Kemp.

"Jap, he rode alongside o' me and asked me questions. He made me tell what the guy from the fort said over again, three or four times, and then he ast what time he got to the schoolhouse and whether the Kid had been there at all yest'iday ur t'day and a lot of other questions. Then he rode alongside each man and told him in just a few words where we was goin' and what the guy from the fort had said. Say! But you'd oughta heard what the men said when he told 'em! My, but they was some mad!

"By 'n' by we came to the woods round the cabin, and Jap Kemp made me stick alongside Long Bill. He sent the men off in different directions in a big circle and waited till each man was in his place. Then we rode hard as we could and came softly up round that cabin just as the sun was goin' down.

"My! But you'd oughta seen the scairt look on them women's faces. There was two of 'em—an old un an' a skinny-looking long-drink-'o-pump-water. I guess she was a girl. I don't know. Her eyes looked real old. There was only three men in the cabin. The rest was off somewheres. They wasn't looking for anybody to come that time o' day, I guess.

"One of the men was sick on a bunk in the corner. He had his head tied up, and his arm, like he'd been shot. The other two men came jumping up to the door with their guns, but when they saw how many men *we* had they looked awful scairt. *We* all had *our* guns out, too!—Jap Kemp gave me one to carry—," Bud tried not to swagger as he told this, but it was almost too much for him.

"Two of our men held the horses, and the rest of us got down and went into the cabin. Jap sounded his whistle, and all our men done the same just as they went in the door—some kind of signals they have for the Lone Fox camp! The two men in the doorway aimed straight at Jap and fired, but Jap was onto 'em and jumped to one side, and our men fired too. We soon had 'em tied up and went in—that is, Jap and me and Long Bill went in. The rest stayed by the door—and it wasn't long 'fore their other men came riding back in hot haste. They heard the shots—and some more of *our* men came—why, most twenty or thirty there was, I guess, altogether. Some from Lone Fox camp watching off in the woods came, and when we got outside again there they all were, like a big army. Most of the men belonging to the cabin was tied and harmless by that time, for our men took 'em one at a time as they came riding in. Two of 'em got away, but Jap said they couldn't go far without being caught, 'cause there was a watch out for 'em—they'd been stealing cattle long back something terrible.

"Well, so Jap Kemp and Long Bill and I went into the cabin after the two men that shot was tied with ropes and handcuffs, and we went hunting for the Kid. At first we couldn't find him. Say! It was something fierce! And the old woman kep' a-crying and saying we'd kill her sick son, and she didn't know nothing about the man we was hunting for. But pretty soon I spied the Kid's foot stickin' out from under the cot where the sick man was. When I told Jap, that sick man pulled out a gun he had under the blanket and aimed it right at me!"

"Oh, Mother's little Buddie!" cried Mrs. Tanner, with her apron to her eyes.

"*Aw, Ma,* cut it out! *He* didn't *hurt* me! The gun just went off crooked and grazed Jap Kemp's hand a little. Jap knocked it out of the sick man's hand just as he was pullin' the trigger. Say, Ma, ain't you got any more of those cucumber pickles? It makes a man mighty hungry to do all that riding and shooting. Well, it certainly was something fierce—say, Miss Earle, you take that last piece o' pie. Oh, g'wan! *Take* it! You worked hard. No, I don't want it, really! Well, if you won't take it *anyway,* I might eat it just to save it. Got any more coffee, Ma?"

But Margaret wasn't eating. Her face was pale, her eyes filled with unshed tears.

"Yes, it certainly was something fierce, that cabin," went on the narrator. "Why, Ma, it looked as if they'd never swept under that cot when we hauled the Kid out. He was tied up in knots, and great heavy ropes wound tight from his shoulders down to his ankles. They were bound so tight they made great heavy welts in his wrists and shoulders and round his ankles when we took 'em off. And they had a great big rag stuffed into his mouth so he couldn't yell. My! It was something fierce! He was 'most dippy too. But Jap brought him round pretty quick and got him outside in the air. That was the worst place I ever was in myself. You couldn't breathe, and the dirt was something fierce. It was like a pigpen. I sure was glad to get outdoors again.

"And then—well, the Kid came around all right, and they got him on a horse and gave him something out of a bottle Jap had, and pretty soon he could ride again. You'd oughta seen his nerve. He just sat up there straight, his lips all white yet and his eyes strange. But he looked those rascals in the eye and told 'em a few things, and he gave orders to the other men from Lone Fox camp for what to do with 'em. He had the two women disarmed—they had guns, too—and carried away and the cabin nailed up and a notice put on the door. And every one of those men was handcuffed—the sick one and all—and he told 'em to bring a wagon and put the sick one's cot in and take 'em over to Ashland to the jail, and he sent word to Mr. Rogers.

"Then we rode home and got to the schoolhouse just when you was playing the last chords of the ov'rtcher. Say! It was some fierce ride and some *close shave!* The Kid hadn't had a thing to eat since Monday noon, and he was some hungry! I found a sandwich on the window of the dressing room, and he ate it while he got togged up—'course I told him 'bout Jed soon's we left the cabin, and Jap Kemp said he'd oughta go right home to camp after all he'd been through. But he wouldn't. He said he was goin' to *act.* So 'course he had his way! But, my! You could see it wasn't any cinch game for him! He 'most fell over every time after the curtain dropped. You see, they gave him some kind of drugged whisky up there at the cabin that made his head feel odd. Say, he thinks that guy from the fort came in and looked at him once while he was asleep. He says it was only a dream, but I bet he did. Say, Ma, ain't you gonta give me another doughnut?"

Quiet in her room at last, Margaret knelt before her window toward the shadowy mountain and gave thanks for Gardley's deliverance. And Bud, in his comfortable loft, lay down to his well-earned rest and dreamed of pirates and angels and a hero who looked like the Kid.

Chapter 26

The Sunday before Lance Gardley started East on his journey of reparation, two strangers slipped quietly into the back of the schoolhouse during the first hymn. They sat down in the shadow by the door.

Margaret was playing the piano when they came in and didn't see them, and when she started the Scripture lesson she only caught a glimpse. She supposed they must be visitors from the fort, since they were speaking to Mrs. Temple, who occasionally attended the Sunday service—perhaps because she could ride with one of the young officers. Visitors who came for amusement and curiosity had ceased to trouble Margaret. Her real work was with the men, women and children who loved the services for their own sake, and she tried to forget the outsiders.

So that day everything proceeded as usual, with Margaret putting her heart into the prayer, the dramatic reading of the Scripture and the story-sermon that followed. And then she and Gardley sang a bit from an oratorio they had practiced.

At the close Margaret gave an opportunity, as she often did, for others to take part in sentence prayers. One of the strangers from the back of the room stood up and began to pray—and such a prayer! Heaven seemed to bend low and earth to kneel and beseech. The man, with the face of a saint and the sturdy frame of an athlete in brown-flannel shirt and khakis, besought the Lord to bless the gathering and the leader who had helped them see the Christ and their need of salvation.

Margaret didn't need Bud's whispered "The missionary!" to know who he was. His face and prayer told her that here, in truth, stood a man of God.

"Oh," she said, as soon as the prayer had ended, "if I'd known the missionary was here I wouldn't have tried to lead this meeting today. Won't you please come up and talk to us now, Mr. Brownleigh?"

At once he stepped to the front. "Why, yes, I'm so glad to see you all and experience the wonderful teacher you found after I left. But I wouldn't have missed this meeting today for all the sermons I ever wrote or preached. You don't need any more sermon than the remarkable story you've heard, and I have only one word to add," he said.

"I've found since I left that Jesus Christ, the only begotten Son of God, is the same Jesus to me today that He was the last time I spoke to you. He's ready to forgive your sin, comfort you in sorrow, help you in temptation, raise you in the resurrection and take you home to a mansion in His Father's house—just as He was the day He hung on the cross to save you from death. I can rest as securely upon the Bible as the word of God as when I first tested its promises. Heaven and earth may pass away, but His word shall *never* pass away."

"*Go to it!*" said Jasper Kemp under his breath in the tone some men say

"Amen!" Margaret wondered if he were thinking of the Rev. Frederick West just then.

Afterward John Brownleigh brought his wife, Hazel, forward to meet Margaret, and the two young women loved each other at once. Hazel was lovely, with a delicacy of feature that marked the high-born and high-bred, but dressed in a dainty khaki riding costume, if that uncompromising fabric could ever be called dainty. Margaret wondered later what had given it that distinctiveness and decided it was a combination of cut, finish and accessories. Creamy lace on the collar, golden-brown velvet in a gold clasp, a shimmering jewel on her finger, a small, brown cap with its two eagle quills—all set her apart and made her fit for any well-dressed company of riders in a city park or on a fashionable drive. Yet here in the wilderness she wasn't overdressed.

The men from the camp stood quietly, waiting to be recognized, and behind them, grinning with embarrassment, Pop and Mom Wallis. Mom wore her new gray bonnet, and Hazel had to look twice to be sure who she was.

"Hazel, we must have these dear people come over and help us with the singing sometimes. Can't we try something right now?" he asked, looking first at his wife and then at Margaret and Gardley. "This man has come since I left, but I'm sure he's the right kind, and I'm glad to welcome him—or perhaps I'd better ask if he'll welcome me!"

The missionary extended his hand to Gardley, who grasped it eagerly.

It would be rare to find four voices like those even in a cultured music center, and they blended in beautiful harmony. The men from the bunkhouse and others from the community slipped back into their seats to listen. The missionary took the bass, his wife the alto, while Margaret added her clear soprano and Gardley his rich tenor. And they sang to souls, so their music, classical though it was and of the highest order, appealed to the hearts of those rough men and made them feel that heaven had opened for them, as once long ago for shepherds in the field.

"I'll feel better about leaving you here while I'm gone, since they've come," said Gardley that night. "I couldn't bear to think you had no one about you. The others are devoted and would do for you with their lives if need be, as far as they know. But I'm glad you have some real Christian friends. This man may be the first minister I've met who seems to believe what he preaches and lives it. I suppose there are others, but I haven't known many. That man West was a mistake!"

"He didn't even preach anything worthwhile," Margaret said, "so how could he live it? This man is real. And there are others. I've known a lot who lead lives of sacrifice and loving service and are as strong and happy as if they were millionaires. But they haven't thrown away their Bibles and their Christ. They believe all of God's promises and rest on them daily, testing and proving them over and over. I wish you knew my father!"

"I'm going to," said Gardley, smiling. "I'm going to him as soon as I finish my business and straighten out my affairs. And I'm going to tell him everything—with your permission, Margaret!"

"Oh, how wonderful!" cried Margaret, with tears in her eyes. "To think you're going to see Father and Mother. I've wanted them to know the real you. I couldn't half *tell* you, the real you, in a letter!"

"Perhaps they won't look on me with your sweet blindness, dear," he said, smiling tenderly at her. "Perhaps they'll see only my dark, past life—for I mean to tell your father everything. I'm not going to have any skeletons in the closet to cause pain later. Perhaps your father and mother won't feel like giving their daughter to me after they know. Remember—I realize what a rare prize she is."

"No, Father isn't like that, Lance," said Margaret, her smile lighting up her eyes. "Father and Mother will understand."

"But if they don't?" A shadow of sadness flickered in Gardley's eyes as he asked the question.

"I belong to you, dear, anyway," she said softly. "I trust you even if the whole world turns against you!"

For answer Gardley took her in his arms, a look of awe on his face, and, stooping, laid his lips on hers in reverence.

"Margaret—you wonderful Margaret!" he said. "God has blessed me more than I could imagine in sending you to me! With His help I'll be worthy of you!"

Three days later Margaret was alone with her school work, her two missionary friends thirty miles away, and her faithful attendant Bud nearby. Eagerly she waited for the mail to come, and for comfort she would watch the purple mountain with its changing glory in the distance.

A few days before Gardley left for the East he was offered a position by Rogers as general manager of his estate at a fine salary. After consulting with Margaret he decided to accept it. But they left the question of their marriage unsettled until Gardley returned. Then he hoped to offer his future wife a record made as fair and clean as human effort could after human mistakes had unmade it.

Meanwhile Margaret worked and waited, wrote letters to father, mother and beloved, and enjoyed her happy thoughts with only the mountain for confidant. She dreamed hazily of the future, waiting to plan with Gardley when he returned. Probably they couldn't marry until they'd both earned some money. She must keep the Ashland School for another year. She had agreed, when she came out, to remain at least two years, if possible. It was hard not to think of going home for the summer, but the trip cost too much. A summer session of the school had been suggested; if that passed she would stay in Ashland, of course. Not seeing her father and mother for another long year was hard to think about too. But perhaps Gardley would return before the summer ended, and then it wouldn't be so hard. She tried to put these thoughts out of her mind, however, while she worked. But, for some reason, Arizona had suddenly become dull and empty.

Margaret had written to her father and mother sometime ago about that first night in the desert when Gardley found her. She had lived in Arizona long enough by then and felt they would no longer be alarmed or picture her sitting on stray water tanks. She wanted them to know Gardley as he was to her, and the letters traveling back and forth between New York and Arizona were filled with bits about him. But Margaret hadn't told her parents how it was between them. Gardley had asked that he might do that. Yet it would have been a blind father and mother not to have read long ago between the lines of those letters and understood. Margaret thought she detected a certain relief in her mother's letters when she knew Gardley had gone East. Were they worrying about him, she wondered, or was it just the natural dread of a mother to lose her child?

So Margaret settled down to routine and confided more in Bud concerning little matters of the school. If it hadn't been for Bud, Margaret would have been lonely indeed.

After Gardley left, the Brownleighs rode over to Sunday services and stopped once briefly during the week on their way to see someone in a distant community. These occasions delighted Margaret, for Hazel Brownleigh was a kindred spirit. She was looking forward to visiting them at the mission station as soon as school closed. She'd gone once with Gardley before he left, but the ride was too long to go often, and the only escort available was Bud.

Meanwhile spring commencement was approaching. Margaret hoped to institute a real commencement with class day and as much form and ceremony as she could to create good school spirit. But such things aren't done with the turn of a hand, and she missed Gardley's help in carrying out her plans.

Another challenge, however, was brewing in the background. Since the night Forsythe had quit the play and ridden away, Rosa Rogers had regarded her teacher with an ominous look in her eyes. She hated Gardley too and was waiting with smoldering wrath until she could take revenge. She felt that, had it not been for those two, Forsythe would still be with her.

Margaret had learned over time that the girl's passionate, undisciplined nature had developed in part from losing her mother at an early age and having only a father too occupied with business and too blind to her faults to guide her. So she tried repeatedly to befriend the girl. But every attempt was repulsed with scorn.

Rosa had been too long her father's petted darling, and her own way ruled her. In turn she had ruled every nurse and servant about the place and coaxed her father into letting her have her way. Twice her father, through friends' advice, had sent her away to school, to an Eastern finishing school and to a convent on the Pacific coast. But she returned shortly at the school's request, more willful than ever. And now she ruled supreme in her father's home, disliked by most of the servants except those she chose to favor because she could persuade them to serve her purposes. Her father, engrossed in his business, was also away much of the time. But when, on rare occasions, he noticed a fault in her, he dealt with it severely and grieved over it in private, for the girl was much like the mother whose loss had emptied the world of its joy for him. But Rosa knew how to manage her father and so hid most of her actions from him.

And in school Rosa knew how to use her dimples and coquettish looks to bring the pupils to her feet, ready to obey her slightest wish. She wielded her power to its fullest as summer drew near, torturing Margaret daily.

Some days an air of insurrection fairly bristled in the room, and Margaret couldn't understand how some of her most devoted followers seemed to be in the forefront of battle. But one day she looked up and caught Rosa's glance as she turned from smiling at the boys in the backseat and knew Rosa had cast her spell over the boys. It was the age-old battle of sex, of woman against woman to win the man to do her will: Margaret, using her strength of character and personality to uphold standards of right thinking and pure living among the students, and Rosa, striving with her impish beauty to lure them into mischief and foil the other's purposes.

One day Margaret detained the girl after school.

"Rosa, why do you always act as if I'm your enemy?" She searched the girl's face with her own steady gaze.

"Because you are!" Rosa retorted, with a toss of her head.

"Indeed I'm not," she said, reaching out to touch the girl's shoulder gently. "I want to be your friend."

Rosa jerked her shoulder away. "You can *never* be my friend. I *hate* you!"

"Rosa!" said Margaret firmly, following the girl to the door, with the color rising in her cheeks. "I cannot have you say such things. Tell me why you hate me. I'm sure if we talked it over we might come to some better understanding."

Rosa stood defiant in the doorway. "We could never come to any better understanding, Miss Earle," she declared in a cold, hard tone, "because I understand you now, and I hate you. You tried your best to get my friend away from me, but you couldn't do it. And you'd like to keep me from having any boyfriends at all, but you can't do that either. You think you're popular, but you'll find out I always do what I like, and you needn't try to stop me. I don't have to come to school unless I choose, and as long as I don't break your rules you can't complain. But you needn't think you can pull the wool over my eyes the way you do the others by pretending to be friends. I won't be friends!" And Rosa turned and marched out of the schoolhouse.

Margaret stared after her in stunned silence. How had she failed with this girl? Was there something else she could have done? Had she let her personal dislike of the girl influence her conduct? She sat for some time at her desk, her chin in her hands, her eyes fixed on the distance. Suddenly she sensed another presence in the room. Glancing around, she saw Bud sitting motionless at his desk, his forehead wrinkled, his jaw set and a look of such pity and devotion in his eyes that her heart warmed to him at once and a smile of comradeship broke over her face.

"Oh, William! Were you here? Did you hear all that? What do you suppose is the matter? Where have I failed?"

"You ain't failed anywhere! You should worry 'bout her! She's a nut! If she was a boy I'd punch her head for her! But seeing she's only a girl, *you should worry!* She always was the limit!"

Bud was the only boy who had never yielded to Rosa's charms. He always sat in glowering silence when she created havoc for the teacher in the classroom. Bud's loyalty was a source of strength to her, and his words expressed a touch of manliness and gentleness unwonted for him.

"Thank you, William!" she said smiling. "If everyone were as splendid as you, we'd have a model school. But I wish I could help Rosa. I can't see why she hates me so! I must have made some big mistake with her in the first place to antagonize her."

"Naw!" said Bud. "No chance! She's just a *nut*, that's all. She's got a case on that Forsythe guy, the worst kind, and she's afraid somebody'll get him away from her, the poor stew, as if anybody would get a case on a tough guy like that! Say! You should worry! Come on—let's ride over t' camp!"

With a sigh and a smile Margaret accepted Bud's consolations. She continued in her way, while trying to find some means of reaching Rosa, and Rosa continued in her way, stubborn and hateful. She regarded her teacher with haughty indifference except when she was called upon to recite. And then, depending upon her mood, she would recite with condescension, perfection or sarcasm, which would in turn send the other students into gales of laughter.

Margaret's patience was at an end. She had considered asking that the girl be withdrawn from the school, but commencement was only a few weeks away and Rosa hadn't openly defied any rules. Then, too, if she were taken out of school she had no other good influence at present. Margaret prayed daily about it, hoping something would make her way plain.

She decided finally to let Rosa take part in the commencement program and the class-day activities as if nothing were wrong. Certainly nothing in public school rules banned a scholar who didn't love her teacher. Why should that disqualify the pupil from participating in her class as long as she performed her duties? And Rosa did hers promptly and deftly, with a certain piquant originality that Margaret couldn't help but admire.

Sometimes, as she glanced at the girl working at her desk, she wondered what was hidden behind the lovely mask. And then Rosa would look up, and a sly gleam would enter her eyes.

Rosa's hatred had indeed taken root. Whatever heart she hadn't frittered away in willfulness had been caught and won by Forsythe, the first man who had ever dared to be intimate with her. Her jealousy knew no bounds. To think of him with Margaret, talking, smiling, walking, riding, sent her writhing upon her bed during many wakeful nights. The nails of her small hands dug deep into her pink flesh and brought the blood. And her sharp white teeth would pierce the pillow as she muttered, "I hate her! I could *kill* her!"

The day Rosa received her first letter from Forsythe, she fluttered about the school as if she were a princess and Margaret the dust under her feet. She felt the crackle of his letter inside her blouse. She gazed at the distant mountain and thought of his tender words: "Little wild Rose of my heart," "No rose in all the world until you came" and others like them. A love letter all her own! No sharing him with anyone! He hinted that she was the only person in that region he cared to write to and he would come back someday to get her. Her young, wild heart exulted.

When he came she would be sure he stayed close by her. No conceited teacher from the East would lure him from her side. She would smile her sweetest. She would wear her finest garments from abroad and show him she could outshine that quiet, common Miss Earle. Yet to the end she studied hard. She didn't intend to be left behind at graduation. She would please her father by taking a prominent part in the activities and outdoing the others. Then he would give her what she liked—jewels, silk dresses and everything due a girl who had won a lover like hers.

The last days before commencement wore upon Margaret's nerves. The children seemed possessed with the spirit of mischief, and she couldn't help but see that Rosa, sitting demurely in her desk, provoked it all. Only Bud's frowns at his unruly classmates' antics kept Margaret from giving up. Indeed, all but Rosa loved her and would have stood by her in a pinch. But what was the harm in having a little fun these last days of school, especially when the school beauty, who usually condescended to only a few of the older boys, was daring them to do it? Rosa's smiles flattered them so much that they failed to see their teacher's weariness.

Late one afternoon Bud walked into the schoolhouse searching for Margaret after the other students had gone. He found her with her head down on the desk and her shoulders shaking with soundless sobs. He paused in the doorway, staring helplessly at her grief. Then he slipped back outside the door and stood in the shadow, grinding his teeth.

"Say!" he said under his breath. "Oh, my! I'd like to punch her fool head. I don't care if she is a girl! She needs it. If she was a boy wouldn't I settle her, the mean little sneak!"

Something was bound to happen if this strain kept up. Margaret knew it and felt inadequate to meet it. Rosa knew it and was awaiting her opportunity. Bud knew it and could only stand and watch for where the blow would strike first and hope to ward it off. He fervently wished for Gardley's return. He didn't know just what Gardley could do about "that little fool," as he called Rosa, but it would be a relief to share the burden with somebody. If only he dared leave he would ride out to camp and tell Jasper Kemp. But as it was he must stick to the job. So the days hastened by to the last Sunday before commencement, which was to fall on Monday.

Chapter 27

After spending all day Saturday in rehearsals, Margaret slept late on Sunday morning, awaking unrested from a troubled dream. She considered asking someone to read a sermon at the afternoon service and let her sleep but suddenly thought of Mom Wallis and the men from the camp. She must get up and prepare something for them.

Margaret walked into the schoolhouse at the hour, looking worn, with dark circles under her eyes.

Mom Wallis in her front seat watched her keenly. "It's time for *him* to come back," she said quietly. "She's gettin' peeked! I wisht he'd come!"

Rosa Rogers didn't always attend the service, but lately she had been quite regular. She would arrive late with her father after the story had begun, giggling and whispering and creating a diversion from the speaker.

But today she came in early and sat directly in front of Margaret, staring at her with such intensity that Margaret shrank as if from some unknown danger. At that moment she wanted only to lay her head down from exhaustion and cry. She drew some comfort from knowing a battalion of friends from the camp would surround her at once and shield her with their lives if necessary.

She wondered how she would talk, with Rosa staring at her that way. But she turned to the piano and started a song, breathing a quick prayer in her heart. Then, to her immense relief, she saw the Brownleighs entering the room.

While everyone was singing the first verse, Margaret slipped from the piano stool and down the aisle to John Brownleigh's side.

"Would you please talk to them a little while today?" she asked. "I feel as if I just couldn't today."

Instantly Brownleigh followed her back to the desk and took her place, pulling out his Bible and opening it to a favorite passage.

"Come unto me, all ye that labor and are heavy laden, and I will give you rest."

The words fell on Margaret's heart like balm. She leaned her head against the wall and closed her eyes to listen, forgetting her burdens and resting on her Savior. Every word he spoke seemed meant just for her and refreshed her as nothing else could. When she finally stepped up to the piano again for the closing hymn she felt new strength for the week ahead. She turned, smiling, to speak to those who crowded around her.

Hazel Brownleigh hugged her as soon as she could reach the front. "You poor, tired child! You're worn out. You need a big change, and I'm going to plan it for you as soon as I can. How would you like to go with us on our trip among the Indians? Wouldn't that be great? It'll be several days, depending on how far we go, but John wants to visit the Hopi reservation. They're such an interesting people. We'll have a delightful trip, sleeping out under the stars. Don't you just love it? I do. I wouldn't miss it for the world.

"I can't be sure for a few days yet when we can go. John has to travel in the other direction first and doesn't know when he'll be back. But it might be this week. How soon can you come to us? How I wish we could take you home with us tonight. You need to get away and rest. But your commencement is tomorrow, isn't it? I'm so sorry we can't be here, but this other matter is important, and John has to leave early in the morning. Someone very sick wants to see him before he dies—an old Indian who didn't know a thing about Jesus till John found him one day.

"Do you have anyone who could bring you over tomorrow night or Tuesday? No? Well, we'll see if we can't find someone. There's an old Indian who often comes this way, but he's away buying cattle. Maybe John can think of a way we could send for you early in the week. Then you'd be ready to go with us on the trip. You'd like to go, wouldn't you?"

"Oh, yes!" said Margaret. "I can't think of anything more pleasant!"

Just then she turned, and there, just behind her, almost touching her, stood Rosa, with that gleam in her eyes, like a serpent waiting to strike.

Instantly Margaret drew back but rallied, smiling faintly at the girl.

Hazel was watching her. "You poor child! You *are* worn out! I'm afraid you're going to be sick."

"Oh, no," said Margaret. "I'm just a bit tired. I'll be all right when tomorrow night is over."

"Well, we'll send for you very soon, so be ready!" Hazel said, following her husband out and waving as she left.

Rosa was still standing behind her when Margaret turned back to her desk. The younger girl gave her one last look, a glitter in her eyes so vindictive that Margaret felt a shudder run through her whole body. She was glad when Rosa's father called her to go home.

Only one more day of Rosa, and she would be finished with her, perhaps forever. The girl had completed the school course and was graduating. She probably wouldn't return another year. Her opportunity was over to help her, and she had failed. Why, she couldn't tell.

"Sick nerves, Margaret!" she said to herself. "Go home and go to bed. You'll be all right tomorrow!" And she locked the schoolhouse door and walked quietly home with Bud.

Meanwhile, Rosa, young, wild and motherless, was finding life exciting now—with no one to restrain her or warn her she was playing with forces she didn't understand. She had easily subjugated the boys in school, keeping them exactly where she wanted them and using methods that would have done credit to a woman of the world. But her infatuation with Forsythe consumed her.

The letters had traveled back and forth many times since Forsythe wrote that first love letter. He found a whimsical pleasure in her deep devotion and naive readiness to follow as far as he led her. He realized that, young as she was, she was no innocent, which made the acquaintance more interesting. In the meantime, he idled away a few months on the Pacific coast, affecting mild love for a rich California girl and toying with the idea of settling down.

Then his correspondence with Rosa took on such a nature that his volatile, impulsive nature was stirred with a desire to see her again. Once out of sight of a victim he seldom looked back, but Rosa had shown a daring spirit in her letters and challenged his senses. Moreover, the California heiress was going on a journey, and an old enemy of his who knew altogether too much of his past had appeared on the scene. Since Gardley was removed from the Ashland vicinity for now, Forsythe felt it might be safe to venture back again. There was always that pretty, spirited teacher if Rosa failed to charm. But why shouldn't Rosa charm? And why shouldn't he yield? Rosa's father was a good sort and had all kinds of property. Rosa was her father's only heir. On the whole, Forsythe decided his best move would be to return to Arizona. If things turned out well he might even think of marrying the girl.

With this in mind Forsythe wrote to Rosa that he was coming, throwing her into a panic of joy and alarm. Rosa's father had been explicit about her ever spending time with Forsythe again. It was the most relentless command he'd ever given her, spoken in a tone she rarely disobeyed. But Rosa was fearfully jealous of Margaret. If Forsythe came and hung around the teacher, the girl felt that she would go wild. She set her sharp teeth into her red under lip and vowed that he would never see Margaret again if she could prevent it.

The letter from Forsythe reached her on Saturday evening. It would be hard enough to evade her father's vigilance once he found out the young man had returned. But she *must* get rid of Margaret! Hoping to find a way, she came to the Sunday service. Standing close to the teacher at the end she overheard Hazel Brownleigh's words and flashed a look of triumph at Margaret as she left the schoolhouse—she had found a way at last, and just in time!

Forsythe was to arrive on Tuesday and wanted Rosa to meet him at one of their old trysting places, out some distance from her father's house. He knew school would be over and she would be free, for she'd written him about commencement. But he didn't know the place he'd selected was situated on one of Margaret's favorite trails. She and Bud often rode there in the late afternoons. Further, he didn't know Rosa wished to avoid, at all costs, any possibility of her teacher's seeing them. She feared not only that Forsythe's attention would be drawn away from her, but also that Margaret might report the clandestine meeting to her father.

Rosa's heart was pounding loudly as she rode home from the Sunday Service with her father, answering his questions with smiles and dimples and a coaxing word, just as he loved her to do. But behind the mask she was forming a plan. If only Mrs. Brownleigh would do as she'd hinted and send someone Tuesday morning to escort Margaret, Rosa's way would be clear. But she dared not trust such a possibility. Not many escorts traveled their way from Ganado, and Rosa knew the old Indian who frequently escorted parties had gone in another direction.

Arriving home she went at once to her room and sat beside her window, gazing off at the purple mountains. Then she lit a candle and searched for a certain testament, long since neglected and covered with dust. She found it at last on top of a pile of books in a dark closet and dragged it forth, eagerly turning the pages. Yes, there it was and in it a small envelope directed to "Miss Rosa Rogers" in a fine angular handwriting. The letter was from the missionary's wife to the little girl who had recited her texts so beautifully that she earned the testament.

Rosa carried it to her desk, secured a good light and sat down to read it over.

No thought of her innocent childish exultation over that letter came to her now. She was intent on one thing—the handwriting. Could she seize the secret of it and reproduce it? She had done so before with great success. She could imitate Miss Earle's writing so perfectly that she often changed words in the questions on the chalkboard and made them read absurdly for the school's benefit. It was such fun to see the amazement on Margaret's face when the laughing class would call her attention to it and to watch her troubled brow when she read what she thought she had written.

When Rosa was a child she used to boast that she could imitate her father's signature perfectly; she often signed some trifling receipt for him for amusement. A dangerous gift in the hands of a girl without conscience! Yes, this was the first time Rosa planned to use her art in any serious way. Perhaps it never occurred to her that she was doing wrong. At present her heart was too full of hate and fear and jealous love to care for right or wrong. It's doubtful she'd have hesitated a second, even if her plan suddenly appeared to her as a great crime. She seemed almost like a creature without moral sense, so swayed was she by her own desires and feelings. She was blind now to everything but getting Margaret out of the way and having Forsythe to herself.

Long after her father and the servants were asleep Rosa's light burned as she bent over her desk, writing. Page after page she covered with careful copies of Mrs. Brownleigh's letter written to her almost three years before. Finally she wrote out the alphabet, bit by bit as she picked it from the words, learning just how each letter was formed, with the peculiarities of connecting and ending. At last, when she lay down to rest, she felt capable of writing a letter in Mrs. Brownleigh's handwriting. The next thing was to devise a plan and compose her letter. She lay staring into the darkness, thinking.

First, she settled it that Margaret must be gotten to Walpi at least. It wouldn't do to send her to Ganado, where the mission station was, for that was a short journey, and she could easily go in a day. When the fraud was discovered, as of course it would be when Mrs. Brownleigh heard, Margaret might return to find out who had done it. No, she must be sent all the way to Walpi if possible. It would take at least two nights to get there. Forsythe had said his stay was to be short. By the time Margaret got back from Walpi, he would be gone.

But how to get her to Walpi without her suspicions being aroused? She might word the note so Margaret would be told to come halfway, expecting to meet the missionaries at Keams. A trail ran straight up from Ashland to Keams, cutting off quite a distance and leaving Ganado at the right. Keams was nearly forty miles west of Ganado. That would do. Then if she could have another note left at Keams, saying they couldn't wait and went on, Margaret would suspect nothing and go all the way to Walpi. That would be fine and would give the schoolteacher an interesting experience that wouldn't hurt her in the least. Rosa thought it might be rather interesting than otherwise. She had no compunctions about how Margaret might feel when she arrived in that strange Indian town and found no friends awaiting her.

Her only worry was where to find a suitable escort, for she felt certain Margaret wouldn't start out alone with one man servant on an expedition that would keep her out overnight. And where in all that region could she find a woman she could trust to send on the errand? It almost looked impossible. She lay tossing and puzzling over it till gray dawn stole into the room. She mentally reviewed every servant on the place on whom she could rely to do her bidding and keep her secret, but for some reason each one wouldn't do. She scanned the country, even considering old Ouida, who had been living in a shack beyond the fort ever since her cabin was raided. But old Ouida was too notorious. Mrs. Tanner would keep Margaret from going with her, even if Margaret herself didn't know the old woman's reputation. Rosa considered wheedling Mom Wallis into the affair but gave that up, remembering Jasper Kemp's suspicious eyes.

At last she fell asleep, with her plan still unformed but her determination to carry it through as strong as ever. If worst came to worst she would send the half-breed cook from the ranch kitchen and put something in the note about his expecting to meet his sister an hour's ride out on the trail. The half-breed would do anything in the world for money, and Rosa had no trouble getting all she wanted of that commodity. But the half-breed was evil-looking, and she feared Margaret wouldn't like to go with him. She would not be balked in her purpose, however.

Chapter 28

Rosa awoke early, for her sleep had been light and troubled. She dressed hastily and sat down to compose a note which could be altered in case she found someone better than the half-breed. Before she was through she heard a disturbance below her window and a muttering in guttural tones. Glancing out, she saw some Indians below, talking with one of the men, who was shaking his head and motioning to them to go on, that this was no place for them to stop. The Indian pointed to his squaw, sitting on a dilapidated burro with a papoose in her arms and looking dirty and miserable. He muttered as though pleading for something.

We believe God's angels follow the feet of His children to protect them. Does the devil also send his angels to lead unwary ones astray and protect the plans of the erring ones? If so, then he must have sent those Indians that morning to further Rosa's plans. Instantly she recognized her opportunity.

Leaning out of her window, she spoke in a clear, reproving voice: "James, what does he want? Breakfast? You know Father wouldn't want any hungry person to be turned away. Let them sit down on the bench and tell Dorset I said to give them a hot breakfast and some milk for the baby. Be quick about it too!"

James started and frowned at the clear, commanding voice. The squaw turned grateful eyes up to the beauty in the window, muttering some inarticulate thanks, while the stolid Indian's eyes glittered hopefully, though the muscles of his masklike countenance didn't change.

Rosa smiled and ran down to see that her orders were obeyed. She tried to talk a little with the squaw but found she understood little English. The Indian spoke better and gave her their brief story. They were on their way to the Navajo reservation to the far north. They'd lost their last scanty provisions by prowling coyotes during the night and needed food. Rosa gave them a place to sit down and a plentiful breakfast and ordered a small store of provisions for their journey after they'd rested. Then she hurried up to her room to finish her letter. She had her plan fixed now. These strangers should be willing messengers. Now and then, as she wrote she lifted her head and gazed out of the window, where she could see the squaw busy with her little one. Her eyes flashed with satisfaction. Nothing could have been better planned than this.

She wrote her note carefully:

Dear Margaret,
I've found just the opportunity I wanted for you to come to us. These Indians are thoroughly trustworthy and are coming in just the direction to bring you to a point where we'll meet you. We've decided to go on to Walpi at once and

will probably meet you near Keams or a little farther on. The Indian knows the way, and you needn't be afraid. I trust him perfectly. Start at once, please, so you'll meet us in time. John has to go on as fast as possible. I know you'll enjoy the trip and am so glad you're coming.

Lovingly,
Hazel Radcliffe Brownleigh

Rosa read it over, comparing it carefully with the little yellow note from her testament and decided it was a very good imitation. She could almost hear Mrs. Brownleigh saying what she had written.

She hastily sealed and addressed her letter and then hurried down to talk with the Indians again.

The place she had ordered for them to rest was some distance from the kitchen door, a shed for certain implements used about the ranch. A long bench ran in front of it, and a large tree gave shade. The Indians found their temporary camp inviting.

Rosa made a detour of the shed, satisfied herself that no one could hear and then sat down on the bench, ostensibly playing with the papoose, dangling a red ball on a ribbon before his dazzled, bead-like eyes and eliciting a delighted gurgle from the dusky little mummy. While she played she talked idly with the Indians. Had they money enough for their journey? Would they like to earn some? Would they act as guide to a lady who wanted to go to Walpi? At least she wanted to go as far as Keams, where she might meet friends, missionaries, who were going on with her to Walpi to visit the Indians. If they didn't meet her she wanted to be guided all the way to Walpi. Would they undertake it? It would pay them well. They would get money enough for their journey and have some left when they got to the reservation. Rosa displayed two gold pieces temptingly.

The Indian uttered a gasp at sight of so much money and sat upright. He indicated by a solemn nod that he was agreeable to the task before him.

The girl continued her instructions. "You'll have to take some things along to make the lady comfortable. I'll see those are ready. Then you can have the things for your own when you leave the lady at Walpi. You'll have to take a letter to the lady and tell her you're going this afternoon, and she must be ready to start at once or she won't meet the missionary. Tell her you can only wait until three o'clock to start. You'll find the lady at the schoolhouse at noon. You mustn't come till noon—." Rosa pointed to the sun and then straight overhead. The Indian watched her keenly and nodded.

"You must ask for Miss Earle, the schoolteacher, and give her this letter."

The Indian grunted and looked at the white missive in Rosa's hand, noting once more the gleam of the gold pieces.

"You must wait till the teacher goes to her boardinghouse and packs her things and eats her dinner. If anybody asks where you came from you must say the missionary's wife from Ganado sent you. Don't tell anybody anything else. Do you understand? More money if you don't say anything?" Rosa clinked the gold pieces softly.

The strange, sphinx-like gaze of the Indian narrowed comprehensively. He understood. His native cunning was being bought for this girl's purposes. He looked greedily at the money. Rosa had put her hand in her pocket and brought out yet another gold piece.

"See! I give you this one now"—she laid one gold piece in the Indian's hand—"and these two I put in an envelope and pack with some provisions and blankets on another horse. I'll leave the horse tied to a tree where the big trail crosses this trail out that way. You know?"

Rosa pointed in the direction she meant, and the Indian looked and grunted, his eyes returning to the two gold pieces in her hand. It was a great deal of money for the little lady to give. Was she trying to cheat him? He looked down at the gold he already held. It was good money. He was sure of that. He looked at her keenly.

"I'll be watching and will know whether you have the lady or not," went on the girl sharply. "If you don't bring the lady with you there'll be no money and no provisions waiting for you. But if you bring the lady you can untie the horse and take him with you. You'll need the horse to carry the things. When you get to Walpi you can set him free. He's branded and will likely come back. We'll find him. See, I'll put the gold pieces in this tin can."

She picked up a sardine tin lying at her feet, slipped the gold pieces in an envelope from her pocket, stuffed it in the tin, bent down the cover and held it up.

"This can will be packed on the top of the other provisions, and you can open it and take the money out when you untie the horse. Then hurry on as fast as you can and get as far along the trail as possible tonight before you camp. Do you understand?"

The Indian nodded again, and Rosa felt she had a confederate worthy of her need.

She stayed a few minutes more, going carefully over her directions, telling the Indian to be sure his squaw was kind to the lady; on no account was he to let the lady get uneasy or have cause to complain of her treatment, or trouble would come to him. At last she felt sure he understood and hurried away to slip into her pretty white dress and rose-colored ribbons and ride to school. Before she left her room she glanced out the window at the Indians and saw them sitting motionless. Once the Indian stirred and, putting his hand in his bosom, drew forth the white letter she'd given him, gazed at it and hid it in his breast again. She nodded her satisfaction as she turned from the window. The next thing was to get to school and play her part in the commencement exercises.

The morning was bright and the schoolhouse filled when Rosa arrived. She fluttered into the schoolhouse and up the aisle with the air of a princess who knew she had been waited for and was condescending to come at all.

Rosa was in everything—the drills, the march, the choruses, the crowning oration. She went through it all with the perfection of a bright mind and an adaptable nature. One would never have dreamed, to look at her pretty dimpling face and sparkling eyes, what diabolical things were moving in her mind nor how those eyes, lynx-soft with sweetness and treachery, were watching for the Indian's appearance.

At last she saw him, standing in a group outside the window near the platform, his tall form and stern countenance marking him among the crowd of familiar faces. She was receiving her diploma from Margaret's hand when she caught his eye, and her hand quivered once as she took the dainty roll tied with blue and white ribbons. That he recognized her she was sure; that he knew she didn't wish him to reveal his connection with her she felt equally certain. She didn't look directly at him again. But she missed no turn of his head nor glance from that stern eye and knew the moment he stood at the front door of the schoolhouse with the letter in his hand, stolid and indifferent.

Someone looked at the letter, pointed to Margaret and called her, and she came. Rosa wasn't far away all the time, talking with Jed—her eyes downcast, her cheeks dimpling, missing nothing that could be heard or seen.

Margaret read the letter. Rosa held her breath and watched Margaret's expression. Did she suspect? No. A look of relief and pleasure had come into her eyes. She was glad for a way to go. She turned to Mrs. Tanner.

"What do you think of this, Mrs. Tanner? I'm to go with Mrs. Brownleigh on a trip to Walpi. Isn't that wonderful? I'm to start at once. Do you suppose I could have a bite to eat? I won't need much. I'm too tired to eat now and too anxious to be off. If you give me a cup of tea and a sandwich I'll be all right. I've got things about ready to go, for Mrs. Brownleigh told me she would send someone for me."

"H'm!" said Mrs. Tanner disapprovingly. "Who you goin' with? Just *him?* I don't much like *his* looks!"

She spoke in a low tone so the Indian wouldn't hear, and it was almost in Rosa's ear, who stood just behind. Rosa took a quick breath and frowned at the toe of her slipper. Would this common Tanner woman balk her plans?

Margaret raised her head now for her first good look at the Indian, and a chill entered her heart. Then, as if he comprehended what was at stake, the Indian turned slightly and pointed down the path toward the road. By common consent the few who were standing about the door stepped back and made a vista for Margaret to see the squaw sitting statue-like on her scraggy little pony, gazing off at the mountain in the distance, as if she were sitting for her picture, her papoose strapped to her back.

Margaret's troubled eyes cleared. The family aspect made things all right. "You see, he has his wife and child," she said. "It's all right. Mrs. Brownleigh says she trusts him perfectly, and I'm to meet them on the way. Read the letter."

She thrust the letter into Mrs. Tanner's hand, and Rosa trembled for her scheme again. Surely Mrs. Tanner couldn't detect the forgery!

"H'm! Well, I s'pose it's all right if she says so. But I'm sure I don't relish them pesky Injuns, and I don't think that squaw wife of his looks any great shakes either. They look to me like they need a good scrub with Bristol brick. But then, if you're set on going, you'll go, 'course. I jest wish Bud hadn't a' gone home with that Jasper Kemp. He might a' gone along, an' then you'd a' had somebody to speak English to."

"Yes, it would have been nice to have William along," said Margaret. "But I'll be all right. Mrs. Brownleigh wouldn't send anybody who wasn't nice."

"H'm! I dun'no'! She's an awful crank. She just loves them Injuns, they say. But I, fer one, draw the line at holdin' 'em in my lap. I don't b'lieve in mixin' folks up that way. Preach to 'em if you like, but let 'em keep their distance, I say."

Margaret laughed and went off to pick up her things. Rosa stood smiling and talking to Jed until she saw Margaret and Mrs. Tanner go off together, the Indians riding slowly along behind.

Rosa waited until the Indians had turned off the road toward the Tanners', and then she mounted her own pony and rode swiftly home.

She rushed up to her room and took off her fine apparel, arraying herself quickly in a plain little dress, and went down to prepare the provisions. She must work rapidly. It was well for her that she could send the servants about at will to get them out of her way. She invented a duty for each that would take them for a few minutes out of sight and sound. Then she gathered the provisions in a basket, making two trips to get them to the shelter where she'd told the Indian he would find the horse tied. She had to make a third trip to bring the blankets and a few other things she knew would be indispensable, but the whole outfit was carelessly gotten together, and it was by chance some things got in at all.

It wasn't difficult to find the old cayuse she intended using for a packhorse. He was browsing in the corral, and she soon had a halter over his head, for she'd been used to horses from her babyhood.

She packed the canned things, tinned meats, vegetables and fruit into a couple of large sacks, adding fodder for the horses, a box of matches, corn bread, salt pork and a few tin dishes.

These she slung over the old horse, fastened the sardine tin containing the gold pieces where it would be easily found, tied the horse to a tree and retired behind a shelter of sagebrush to watch.

Soon the caravan came, the Indians riding ahead single file, like two graven images, not moving a muscle of their faces, and Margaret behind on her pony, her face as happy as that of a child let out of a hard task to play.

The Indian stopped beside the horse, a glitter of satisfaction in his eyes as he saw that the little lady had fulfilled her part of the bargain. He indicated to the squaw and the lady that they might move on down the trail, and he would catch up with them. Then he dismounted, pouncing warily upon the sardine tin. He glanced about, then took out the money and tested it with his teeth to make sure it was genuine.

He grunted his further satisfaction, looked over the packhorse, secured the fastenings of the load and, taking the halter, mounted and rode toward the north.

Rosa waited in her covert until they were far out of sight, then hurried back to the house and climbed to a window where she could watch the trail for several miles. There, with a field glass, she kept watch until the procession had filed across the plains, down into a valley, up over a hill and into a farther valley out of sight. She looked at the sun and drew a breath of satisfaction. She had done it at last! She got Margaret away before Forsythe came! The fraud wouldn't likely be discovered until her rival was far enough away to be safe. She laughed too harshly, and her voice had a cruel ring to it. Then she threw herself upon the bed, burst into a passionate fit of weeping, and soon fell asleep. She dreamed Margaret returned like a shining, fiery angel, a two-edged sword in her hand and all the Wallis camp at her heels, with vengeance in their wake. That hateful boy, Bud Tanner, danced around and made faces at her, while Forsythe forgot her to gaze at Margaret's face.

Chapter 29

To Margaret the day was fair and the omens auspicious. She carried with her close to her heart two precious letters received that morning and scarcely glanced at, one from Gardley and one from her mother. She had only had time to open them and be sure all was well with her dear ones and left the rest to read on the way.

She was dressed in the khaki riding habit she always wore when she rode horseback. In the bag strapped on behind she carried a couple of fresh white blouses, a thin, white dress, a soft dark silk dress that folded almost into a cobweb and a few other necessities. She'd also slipped in a new book her mother had sent her, which she hadn't had time yet to look in, and her chessmen and board, besides writing materials. She prided herself on getting so many necessities into such a small space. She would need the extra clothing if she stayed at Ganado with the missionaries for a week on her return from the trip, and the book and chessmen would amuse them all along the way. She had heard Brownleigh say he loved to play chess.

For the first hour Margaret just let herself be glad school was over and she could rest with no responsibility. The sun shimmered on the white, hot sand and gray-green of the greasewood and sagebrush. Tall spikes of cactus like lonely spires shot up to vary the scene. It was all familiar ground to Margaret here, for she'd taken many rides with Gardley and Bud, and for the first part every turn and view were fraught with pleasant memories that brought a smile to her eyes as she recalled some quotation of Gardley's or some prank of Bud's. Here was where they sighted the cottontail the day she took her first ride on her own pony. Off there was the mountain where they saw the sun drawing silver water above a frowning storm. Yonder was the group of cedars where they'd stopped to eat their lunch once, and this waterhole they were approaching was the one where Gardley had given her a drink from his hat.

She was almost glad Bud wasn't along, for she was too tired to talk and liked being alone with her thoughts for these few minutes. Poor Bud! He would be disappointed when he got back to find her gone. But then he expected her to go in a few days anyway, and she'd promised to take long rides with him when she returned. She had left a note for him, asking him to read a certain book in her bookcase while she was gone and be ready to discuss it with her when she got back, and he would be fascinated with it, she knew. Bud had been dear and faithful, and she would miss him; but for this little while she was glad to have the great outdoors to herself.

She was practically alone. The two sphinx-like figures riding ahead of her made no sign but rode on hour after hour, not even turning their heads to see if she was coming. She knew Indians were this way; still, as time passed, she began to feel an uneasy sense of being alone in the universe with two bronze statues. Even the papoose had erased itself in sleep, and when it awoke still held its peace and made no fuss. Margaret began to feel the baby was hardly human, more like a doll set up in a missionary meeting to teach children what a papoose was like.

Presently she brought out her letters and read them, dreaming and smiling over them and getting precious bits by heart. Gardley hinted he may visit her parents soon, since it looked as if he might have to make a business trip in their direction before he could go further with what he was doing in his old home. He gave no hint of when he'd return to the West. He said he was awaiting the return of one man who might soon be coming from abroad. Margaret sighed and wondered how many weary months it would be before she would see him. Perhaps, after all, she should have gone home and stayed with her mother and father. If the school board could see it would be better to have no summer session, perhaps she would still go when she returned from the Brownleighs'. But she would decide nothing until she was rested.

Suddenly she felt herself overwhelmingly weary and wished the Indians would rest for a while. But when she stirred up her sleepy pony and spurred ahead to broach the matter, her guide shook his head and pointed to the sun.

"No get Keams good time. No meet Aneshodi."

"Aneshodi," she knew, was the Indians' name for the missionary, and she smiled her acquiescence. Of course they must meet the Brownleighs and not detain them. What had Hazel said about having to hurry? She searched her pocket for the letter and then remembered she'd left it with Mrs. Tanner. What a pity she hadn't brought it! Perhaps there was some caution or advice in it she hadn't noted. But then the Indian likely knew all about it, and she could trust him. She glanced at his face and wished she could make him smile. She cast a sunny smile at him and said something about the beautiful day, but he only looked through her as if she weren't there. After one or two more attempts she fell back and tried to talk to the squaw. But the squaw only shook her head. She seemed unfriendly. Margaret drew back into her old position and feasted her eyes on the distant hills.

The road was growing unfamiliar now. They were crossing rough ridges with cliffs of red sandstone, and every step was interesting. Yet Margaret felt more that she wanted to lie down and sleep. When at last in the dusk the Indians halted not far from a little pool of rainwater and indicated they'd camp here for the night, Margaret was too weary to question the decision. It hadn't occurred to her that she'd be traveling overnight before she met her friends. Her knowledge of the way and of distances was vague. She probably wouldn't have ventured if she'd known she must spend the night in company with two strange creatures. Yet, now that she was here and it was inevitable, she wouldn't shrink but make the best of it. She tried to be friendly again and offered to look out for the baby while the squaw gathered wood and made a fire. The Indian was off looking after the horses, evidently expecting his wife to do all the work.

Margaret watched a few minutes, while pretending to play with the baby, who was both sleepy and hungry yet held his emotions as if he were an adult. Then she decided to take a hand in the supper. She was hungry and couldn't bear for those dusty hands to set forth her food, so she went to work cheerfully, giving directions as if the Indian woman understood her. She soon discovered, however, that her talk was babbling to the other and she might as well hold her peace. The woman set a kettle of water over the fire, and Margaret forestalled her next movement by cutting some pork and putting it to cook in a skillet she found among the provisions. The woman watched her, not seeming to care; so each went silently about her own preparations.

The supper was a silent affair too, and when it was over the squaw handed Margaret a blanket. Suddenly she understood that this alone was to be her bed for the night. The earth provided a mattress, the sagebrush lent a partial shelter, and the canopy of stars shone overhead.

Panic seized her. She stared at the squaw and found herself longing to cry out for help. She could scarcely bear this awful silence of the mortals who were her only company. Yet she realized she must make the best of things. So she took the blanket and, spreading it out, sat down on it and wrapped it about her shoulders and feet. She wouldn't lie down until she saw what the others did. Somehow she shrank from asking the bronze man how to fold a blanket for a bed on the ground. She tried to remember what Gardley had told her about folding the blanket bed to keep out snakes and ants. She shuddered at the thought of snakes. Would she dare call for help from her companions if a snake bothered her in the night? And would she ever sleep?

She remembered her first night in Arizona out among the stars, alone on the water tank, and her first frenzy of loneliness. Was this as bad? No, for these Indians were trustworthy and well known by her dear friends. It might be unpleasant; but this, too, would pass, and tomorrow would come soon.

The dusk dropped down, and the stars loomed. The world grew wonderful, like a blue jeweled dome of a palace with the lights turned low. The fire burned brightly as the man threw sticks upon it, and the two Indians moved about in the darkness, passing silhouetted before the fire and then at last lying down wrapped in their blankets to sleep.

It was quiet about her. The air was so still she could hear the hobbled horses munching in the distance, moving with the halting gait a hobble gives a horse. Off in the farther distance the blood-curdling howl of the coyotes rose, but Margaret was used to them and knew they wouldn't come near a fire.

She was growing very weary and at last wrapped her blanket closer and lay down, her head pillowed on one corner of it. Committing herself to her heavenly Father and breathing a prayer for father, mother and beloved, she fell asleep.

It was yet almost dark when she awoke. For a moment she thought it was still night and the sunset wasn't gone yet, for the clouds were rosy tinted.

The squaw was standing by her, touching her shoulder roughly and grunting something. She perceived, as she rubbed her eyes and tried to summon her senses, that she was expected to get up and eat breakfast. She could smell pork and coffee in the air, and scorched corn bread lay beside the fire on a pan.

Margaret got up quickly and ran down to the waterhole to get some water, dashing it in her face and over her arms and hands. The squaw meanwhile watched her curiously, as if she thought this some oblation paid to the white woman's god before she ate. Margaret pulled the hairpins out of her hair, letting it down and combing it with a side comb. Then she twisted it up again in its soft, fluffy waves straightened her collar, set on her hat and was ready for the day. The squaw looked at her with both awe and contempt, then turned and stalked back to her papoose and prepared it for the journey.

Margaret ate hurriedly and was scarcely finished before she found her guides waiting like two desert pillars and watching keenly, impatiently, her every mouthful, anxious to be off.

The sky was still tinted pink with the semblance of a sunset, and Margaret felt, as she mounted her pony and followed her companions, as if the day was upside down. She wondered if she hadn't slept through a whole twenty-four hours and it was evening again, till the sun rose clear and the cloud-tinting melted into day.

The road lay through sagebrush and barren cedar trees, with rabbits darting between the rocks. Suddenly from a hilltop they reached a spot where they could see far over the desert. Forty miles away three square, flat hills, or mesas, looked like a giant train of cars, and the clear air gave everything a strange vastness. Farther on beyond the mesas dawned the Black Mountains. One could even see the shadowed head of Round Rock almost a hundred miles away. Before them and around was a great plain of sagebrush, and here and there was a small bush the Indians called "the weed that wasn't scared." Margaret had learned all these things during her winter in Arizona and enjoyed the splendid view before her.

They passed several little mud-plastered hogans Margaret knew for Indian dwellings. A band of ponies off in the distance made an interesting spot on the landscape, and twice they passed bands of sheep. She had a feeling of great isolation from everything she'd ever known and seemed going farther from life and all she loved. Once she ventured to ask the Indian what time he expected to meet her friends, the missionaries, but he only shook his head and murmured something unintelligible about "Keams" and pointed to the sun. She dropped behind again, vaguely uneasy, though she couldn't tell why. Something in the two faces seemed so sly and wary and unfriendly that she almost wished she hadn't come. Yet the way was beautiful, and nothing unpleasant was happening to her. Once she dropped the envelope of her mother's letter and was about to dismount and recover it. Then some strange impulse made her leave it on the desert sand. What if they should be lost and that paper guided them back? The notion stayed with her, and once in a while she dropped other bits of paper along the way.

About noon the trail dropped off into a canyon, with high, yellow-rock walls on either side and stifling heat, so she felt as if she could scarcely stand it. She was glad when they emerged again and climbed to higher ground. The noon camp was hasty, for the Indian seemed hurried. He scanned the horizon far and wide and seemed searching keenly for someone or something. Once they met a lonely Indian, and he held a muttered conversation with him, pointing off ahead and gesticulating angrily. But the words were unintelligible to Margaret. Her uneasy feeling was growing, and yet she couldn't tell why and laid it to her tired nerves. She was beginning to think she was foolish to start on such a long trip before resting from her last days of school. She longed to lie down under a tree and sleep for days.

Toward night they sighted a great blue mesa about 50 miles south, and at sunset they could just see the San Francisco peaks more than 125 miles away. Margaret, as she stopped her horse and gazed, felt a choking in her heart and throat and a great desire to cry. The glory and awe of the mountains, mingled with her own weariness and nervous fear, were almost too much for her. She was glad to get down and eat a little supper and sleep again. As she fell asleep she comforted herself with a few precious words from her Bible.

The angel of the Lord encampeth round about them that fear Him and delivereth them. . .Thou wilt keep him in perfect peace whose mind is stayed on Thee because he trusteth in Thee. . .I will both lay me down in peace and sleep, for Thou, Lord, only makest me to dwell in safety. . . .

The coyotes' voice, now far, now near, boomed out on the night; great stars shot darting pathways across the heavens; the fire snapped and crackled, died down and flickered feebly. But Margaret slept and dreamed that the angels kept close vigil around her lowly couch.

She didn't know what time the stars disappeared and the rain began to fall. She was too tired to notice the drops falling on her face. Too tired to hear the coyotes coming nearer. Yet in the morning one lay there dead, not thirty feet from where she'd slept. The Indian had shot him through the heart.

Somehow things looked dismal that morning, in spite of the sun's brightness after the rain. She was stiff with lying in the dampness. Her hair was wet, her blanket was wet, and she woke without feeling rested. Almost the trip seemed more than she could bear. If she could have wished herself back that morning and stayed at the Tanners' all summer, she certainly would have rather than be where and how she was.

The Indians seemed excited—the man grim and forbidding, the woman appealing, frightened. They were near Keams Canyon. "Aneshodi" would be somewhere about. The Indian hoped to be rid of his burden then and travel on his interrupted journey. He was growing impatient. He felt he'd earned his money.

But when they tried to go down the Keams Canyon they found the road washed away by flood and had to go a long way around. This made the Indian surly. His countenance was more forbidding than ever. Margaret, as she watched him with sinking heart, altered her ideas of the Indian as a whole to suit the situation. She'd always felt pity for the poor Indians, whose land had been seized and kindred slaughtered. But this Indian was no object of pity. He was the most disagreeable, cruel-looking Indian Margaret had ever seen. She felt it the first time she saw him, but now, as the situation brought him out, she knew she was dreadfully afraid of him. She felt he might scalp her if he tired of her. She altered her opinion of Hazel Brownleigh's judgment regarding Indians. She didn't think she would ever send this Indian to anyone for a guide and say he was trustworthy. He hadn't done anything terrible yet, but she felt he was going to.

He had a number of angry discussions with his wife that morning. At least, he did the discussing, and the squaw protested. Margaret gathered after a while it was something about her. The furtive, frightened glances the squaw cast in her direction, when the man wasn't looking, made her think so. She tried to say it was all imagination and that her nerves were getting the upper hand, but in spite of her she shuddered sometimes, just as she had when Rosa looked at her. She decided she must be about to get sick and that just as soon as she reached Mrs. Tanner's again she would pack her trunk and go home to her mother. If she was going to be sick she wanted her mother.

About noon, they halted on the top of the mesa, and the Indians had another altercation, which ended in the man descending the trail a steep way, down four hundred feet to the trading post in the canyon. Margaret looked down and gasped and thanked a kind Providence that hadn't made it necessary for her to make that descent. But the squaw stood at the top with her baby and looked down in silent agony. Her face was terrible to look upon.

Margaret couldn't understand it, and she went to the woman and put her hand out, asking gently: "What's the matter, you poor thing? What is it?"

Perhaps the woman understood the tenderness in the tone, for she suddenly turned and rested her forehead against Margaret's shoulder, giving one great, gasping sob, then lifted her eyes to the girl's face as if to thank her for her kindness.

Margaret's heart was touched. She threw her arms around the poor woman and drew her, papoose and all, toward her, patting her shoulder and saying gentle, soothing words as she would to a child. Soon the woman lifted her head again, the tears coursing down her face, and tried to explain, muttering her odd gutturals and making eloquent gestures until Margaret felt she understood. She gathered that the man had gone down to the trading post to find the "Aneshodi" and that the squaw feared he would somehow procure firewater either from the trader or from some Indian he might meet and would come back angrier than he'd gone and without his money.

If Margaret also suspected the Indian wanted to leave her at that desolate trading station in the canyon until her friends called for her, she put the thought from her mind and set herself to cheer the poor Indian woman.

She took a bright, soft, rosy silk tie from her own neck and knotted it about the astonished woman's dusky throat, and then she put a silver dollar in her hand and was thrilled to see what a change came over the poor, dark face. It reminded her of Mom Wallis when she put on her new bonnet, and once again she felt the thrill of knowing the whole world kin.

The squaw cheered up after a little, got sticks and made a fire, and together they had quite a pleasant meal. Margaret exerted herself to make the poor woman laugh and finally succeeded by dangling a bright-red knight from her chessmen in front of the delighted baby's eyes till he gurgled out a real baby sound of joy.

The middle of the afternoon the Indian returned, sitting his struggling beast crazily as he climbed the trail. Margaret, watching, caught her breath and prayed. Was this the trustworthy man, this drunken, reeling creature, clubbing his horse and pouring forth a torrent of indistinguishable gutturals? His wife's worst fears were verified. He had found the firewater.

The frightened squaw put things together as fast as she could. She knew what to expect, and when the man reached the top of the mesa he found his party packed and mounted, waiting to take the trail.

Silently, timorously, they rode behind him, west across the great wide plain.

In the distance gradually appeared dim mesas like great fingers stretching out against the sky. Miles away they seemed, and nothing intervening but a stretch of varying color where sagebrush melted into sand, and sagebrush and greasewood grew again, with tall cactus startling here and there like bayonets at rest but bristling with menace.

The Indian had grown silent and sullen. His eyes were like deep fires of burning volcanoes. One shrank from looking at them. His massive, cruel profile stood out like bronze against the evening sky. It was growing night again, and still they hadn't come to anywhere or anything, and her friends seemed just as far away.

Since they'd left the top of Keams Canyon, Margaret was sure all wasn't right. Besides the fact the guide was drunk now, she was convinced something had been wrong with him all along. He didn't act like the Indians around Ashland. He didn't act like a trusted guide her friends would send for her. She wished again she'd kept Hazel Brownleigh's letter. She wondered how her friends would find her if they came after her. Then she began in earnest to leave a trail behind her. If she'd only done it thoroughly when she was first uneasy. But now she was so many miles from anywhere! Oh, if she hadn't come at all!

First she dropped her handkerchief, because she had it in her hand—a dainty thing with lace on the edge and her name written in tiny script by her mother on the narrow hem. And then, as soon as she could scrawl it without being noticed, she wrote a note which she twisted around the neck of a red chessman and left behind her. After that she dropped scraps of paper, as she could reach them out of the bag tied behind her saddle; then a stocking, a bedroom slipper, more chessmen. When they halted at dusk and prepared to strike camp, she had a good little trail blazed behind her over that wide, empty plain. She shuddered as she looked into the gathering darkness ahead, where those long, dark mesas looked like barriers.

Then, suddenly, the Indian pointed ahead to the first mesa and uttered one word—"Walpi!" So that was the Indian village to which she was bound? What was before her on the morrow? After eating a pretense of supper she lay down. The Indian had more firewater with him. He drank, uttered cruel gutturals at his squaw and even kicked the feet of the sleeping papoose as he passed by till it awoke and cried sharply, which made him more angry; so he struck the squaw.

It seemed hours before all was quiet. Margaret's nerves were strained to such a pitch that she scarcely dared to breathe. But at last, when the fire had almost died down, the man lay quiet, and she could relax and close her eyes.

Not to sleep. She mustn't go to sleep. The fire was almost gone, and the coyotes would be around. She must wake and watch!

That was the last thought she remembered—that and a prayer that the angels would keep watch again.

When she awoke it was broad daylight and far into the morning, for the sun was high overhead and the mesas in the distance were clear and distinct against the sky.

She sat up and looked about her, bewildered, not knowing at first where she was. It was so still and wide and lonely.

She turned to find the Indians, but there was no trace of them anywhere. The fire lay smoldering in its place, a thin trickle of smoke curling away from a dying stick, but that was all. A tin cup half full of coffee was beside the stick, and a piece of blackened corn bread. She turned frightened eyes to east, to west, to north, to south, but no one was in sight. Over the distant mesa a great eagle poised alone in the vast sky, keeping watch over the brilliant, silent waste.

Chapter 30

When Margaret was little her father and mother had left her alone for an hour with a stranger while they made a call in a city they were passing through on a summer trip. The stranger was kind and gave the child a large green box of bits of old black lace and purple ribbons to play with. But she turned from the array of finery, the only thing by way of amusement the woman had, and stood staring out of the window on the strange, new town, a feeling of utter loneliness upon her. Her little heart was almost choked with the awful thought that she was a human atom drifted apart from every other atom she'd ever known, that she had a personality and a responsibility of her own and must face this thought of herself and her aloneness forevermore. It was the child's first realization that she was a separate being apart from her father and mother, and she was almost consumed with the terror of it.

As she rose now from her bed on the ground and looked out across that vast waste, in which the only other living creature was that sinister, watching eagle, the same feeling returned to her and made her tremble like the child who had turned from the box of ancient finery to realize her own little self and its terrible aloneness.

For an instant even her realization of God, which had from early childhood been present with her, seemed to have departed. She could grasp only the vast empty silence that loomed about her. She was alone and about as far from anywhere or anything as she could be in Arizona. Would she ever return to human habitations? Would her friends ever find her?

Then her heart flew back to its habitual refuge, and she spoke aloud and said, "God is here!" She looked about again on the bright waste, and now it didn't seem so dreary.

"God is here!" she repeated and tried to realize this was part of His habitation. She couldn't be lost where her Father was. He knew the way out. She had only to trust. So she dropped upon her knees in the sand and prayed for trust and courage.

When she rose again she walked steadily to a height above the campfire and, shading her eyes, looked carefully in every direction. No, there was no sign of her recent companions. They must have stolen away in the night, soon after she fell asleep, and gone so fast and far that they were beyond the reach of her eyes, and nowhere was there sign of a living thing, except that eagle still sweeping in great curves and poising again above the distant mesa.

Where was her horse? Had the Indians taken that too? She searched the valley but saw no horse. With sinking heart she returned to her things and sat down by the dying fire to think, putting a few loose twigs and sticks together to keep the embers bright while she could. She had no matches, and this was probably the last fire she would have until somebody rescued her or she got somewhere by herself. What was she to do? Stay right where she was or start out on foot? And should she go backward or forward? Surely the Brownleighs would miss her soon and send out a search party for her. How could they trust an Indian who would leave a woman unprotected in the desert? And yet perhaps they didn't know his temptation to drink. Perhaps they'd thought he couldn't get any firewater. Perhaps he would return when he came to himself and realized what he'd done.

And now she noticed what she hadn't seen at first—a small bottle of water on a stone beside the blackened bread. Realizing she was hungry and this was the only food at hand, she sat down beside the fire to eat the dry bread and drink the miserable coffee. She must have strength to do whatever was before her. She tried not to think how her mother would feel if she never came back, how anxious they'd be as they waited daily for her letters that didn't come. She reflected with a sinking heart that she had, just before leaving, written a hasty note to her mother telling her not to expect anything for several days, perhaps even as much as two weeks, since she was leaving civilization for a little while. How she'd unwittingly sealed her fate by that! For now, not even by way of her alarmed home, could help come to her.

She put the last bit of hard corn bread in her pocket for a further time of need and looked about her again. Then she spied a moving object far below her in the valley and decided it was a horse, perhaps her own. He was a mile away at least, but he was there, and she cried out with sudden joy and relief.

She stepped over to her blanket and bags, which had been beside her during the night, and stood thinking what to do. Should she carry the things to the horse or risk leaving them here while she went after the horse and brought him to the things? No, that wouldn't be safe. Someone might come along and take them, or she mightn't be able to find her way back again in this strange, wild waste. Besides, she might not get the horse and would lose everything. She must carry her things to the horse.

She stooped to gather them up, and something bright beside her bag attracted her. The sun was shining on the silver dollar she'd given to the woman. Tears rushed to her eyes. The poor creature had tried to make reparation for leaving the white woman in the desert. She'd given back the money—all she had that was valuable! Beside the silver dollar rippled a chain of beads curiously wrought, an inanimate appeal for forgiveness and a grateful return for the kindness shown her.

Margaret smiled as she stooped again to pick up her things. There was a heart behind that stolid countenance and some sense of righteousness and justice. Margaret decided that Indians weren't all treacherous. Poor woman! What a life she had—to follow her grim lord wherever he would lead, even as her white sister must sometimes, sorrowing, rebelling, crying out, but following! She wondered if into the heart of this dark sister ever crept any of the rebellion that led some of her white sisters to cry aloud for "rights" and "emancipation."

But it was a passing thought to be remembered and turned over at a more propitious time. Margaret's whole thoughts now were bent on her present predicament.

The packing was short work. She stuffed everything into the two bags that were usually hung across the horse and settled them carefully across her shoulders. Then she rolled the blanket, took it in her arms and started. It was a heavy burden to carry, but she wouldn't part with her things until she'd at least tried to save them. If she was left alone in the desert for the night the blanket was indispensable, and her clothes would at least do to drop as a trail by which her friends might find her. She must carry them as far as possible. So she started.

It was already mid-morning, and the sun was intolerably hot. Her burden was not only cumbersome, but warm, and she felt her strength leaving her as she went; but her nerve was up and her courage strong. Moreover, she prayed as she walked, and she felt now the presence of her Guide and wasn't afraid. As she walked she faced several startling possibilities in the immediate future which were likewise undesirable. There were wild animals in this land—not so much in the daylight, but what of the night? She had heard that a woman was always safe in that wild Western land. But what of the prowling Indians? What of a possible exception to the Western rule of chivalry toward a decent woman? One small piece of corn bread and less than a pint of water were small provision on which to withstand a siege. How far was it to anywhere?

Then she remembered for the first time that one word—"Walpi!"—uttered by the Indian as he halted the night before and pointed far to the mesa. She lifted her eyes now and scanned the dark mesa. It loomed like a great battlement of rock against the sky. Could people be dwelling there? She'd heard, of course, about the curious Hopi villages, each village a gigantic house of many rooms, called pueblos, built upon the lofty crags, sometimes five or six hundred feet above the desert.

Could that great castle-looking outline against the sky before her, standing out on the end of the mesa like a promontory above the sea, be Walpi? And if it was, how was she to get up there? The rock rose sheer and steep from the desert floor. The narrow neck of land behind it looked like a slender thread. Her heart sank at the thought of trying to storm and enter, single-handed, such an impregnable fortress. And yet, if her friends were there, perhaps they'd see her when she drew near and come to show her the way. Strange they went on and left her with those treacherous Indians! Strange they trusted them in the first place! Her own instincts had been against trusting the man from the beginning. During her reflections now her opinion of the Brownleighs' wisdom and judgment dropped several notches. Then she berated herself for being so easily satisfied about her escort. She should have read the letter more carefully. She should have asked the Indians more questions. She should, perhaps, have asked Jasper Kemp's advice or asked him to talk to the Indian. She wished with all her heart for Bud now. He would be saying some comical boy-thing and finding a way out of the difficulty. Dear, faithful Bud!

The sun rose higher, and the morning grew hotter. As she descended to the valley her burdens grew intolerable, and several times she almost cast them aside. Once she lost sight of her pony among the sagebrush, and it was two hours before she captured him and strapped on her burdens. She was almost too exhausted to climb into the saddle when all was ready. But she mounted at last and started out toward the rugged crag ahead of her.

The pony had a long, hot climb out of the valley to a hill where she could see far again, but still that vast emptiness reigned. Even the eagle had disappeared, and she imagined he must be resting like a great emblem of freedom on a point of the castle-like battlement against the sky. It seemed as if the end of the world had come, and she was the only one left, forgotten, riding her weary horse across an endless desert searching for a home she would never see again.

Below the hill stretched a wide, white strip of sand, about two miles, shimmering in the sun and seeming to recede ahead of her as she advanced. Beyond was soft greenness—something growing—not near enough to be discerned as cornfields. The girl drooped her head on her horse's mane and wept, her courage leaving her with her tears. In that wide universe seemed no way to go, and she was so tired, hungry, hot and discouraged! That bit of bread in her pocket and that muddy-looking, warm water were a last resort; she must save them as long as possible, for there was no telling how long it would be before she had more.

She had no trail now to follow. She had started from the spot where she found the horse, and her inexperienced eyes couldn't have searched out a trail if she'd tried. She was riding toward that distant castle on the crag. But if she ever reached it, would she find anything there but crags and lonesomeness and the eagle?

Drying her tears, she started the horse down the hill. Perhaps her tears blinded her, or because of being dizzy with hunger and the long stretch of anxiety and fatigue she wasn't looking closely. For suddenly the ground fell away steeply as they emerged from a thicket of sagebrush. The horse plunged several feet down, striking some loose rocks and slipping to his knees, snorting, scrambling, making brave effort, but slipping, half rolling. At last he was brought down with his frightened rider and lay on his side with her foot under him and a sensation like a red-hot knife running through her ankle.

Margaret caught her breath in quick gasps as they fell, lifting a prayer in her heart for help. Then came the crash and the sharp pain, and with a conviction that all was over she dropped back unconscious on the sand, a blessed oblivion of darkness rushing over her.

When she came to herself the hot sun was pouring down upon her unprotected face, and she was conscious of intense pain and suffering in every part of her body. She opened her eyes and looked about. Sagebrush waved over the crag down which they'd fallen; the sky was mercilessly blue without a cloud. The great beast, heavy and quivering, lay solidly against her, half pinning her to earth, and her helpless position was like an awful nightmare from which she felt she might awaken if she could only cry out. But when at last she raised her voice its empty echo frightened her, and there, above her, with widespread wings, circling, then poised, with cruel eyes upon her, loomed that eagle— large, fearful, suggestive in its curious stare. The desert monarch had come to see who had invaded his precincts and fallen into one of his snares.

With sudden frenzy burning in her veins Margaret struggled to get free, but she could only move the slightest bit each time, and every motion was agony to her ankle.

It seemed hours before she writhed herself free from that great, motionless horse, whose labored breath only showed he was still alive. Something terrible must have happened to the horse or he would have tried to rise, for she had coaxed, patted, cajoled, tried in every way to rouse him. When at last she crawled free from the hot, horrible body and crept in front of him, she saw that both his forelegs lay limp and helpless. He must have broken them in falling. Poor fellow! He, too, was suffering, and she could do nothing for him!

Then she thought of the water bottle but, searching for it, found her good intention of dividing it with him useless, for the bottle was broken and the water already soaked into the sand. Only a damp spot on the saddlebag showed where it had departed.

Then indeed did Margaret sink down in the sand in despair and pray as never before.

Chapter 31

The morning after Margaret's departure Rosa awoke with no feelings of self-reproach, rather a great exultation at the way she got rid of her rival.

She lay for a few minutes thinking of Forsythe, trying to decide what she would wear when she met him, for she wanted to charm him as she had never charmed anyone before.

She spent some time arraying herself in different costumes, but at last she decided on her commencement dress of fine white organdie, hand-embroidered and frilled with filmy lace, the product of a famous house in the Eastern city where she'd attended school for a while and acquired expensive tastes.

Daintily slippered, beribboned with a coral-silk belt and wearing a rose from the vine over her window in her hair, she sallied forth at last to the trysting place.

Forsythe was a whole hour late, as became a languid gentleman who had traveled the day before and idled at his sister's house over a late breakfast until nearly noon. Already his fluttering fancy was apathetic about Rosa, and he wondered, as he rode along, what had become of the interesting young teacher who had charmed him for more than a passing moment. Would he dare call upon her, now that Gardley was out of the way? Was she still in Ashland, or had she gone home for vacation? He must ask Rosa about her.

Then he came in sight of Rosa sitting in the shade of an old cedar, reading poetry, a little lady in the wilderness, and he forgot everything else in his delight over the change in her. For Rosa had changed. There was no mistake about it. She bloomed into maturity in those few months of his absence. Her soft figure had rounded and developed; her bewitching curls were put up on her head, with only a stray tendril here and there to emphasize a dainty ear or call attention to a smooth, round neck. When she raised her head and lifted limpid eyes to his she possessed a demureness, a coolness and charm he imagined only city ladies could attain.

Oh, Rosa knew her charms and had practiced many days before her mirror till she had appraised the value of every curling eyelash, every hidden dimple, every curve of lip. Rosa had watched well and learned from all she'd met. She had left no woman's guile untried.

And Rosa was sweet and charming. She knew just when to lift up innocent eyes of wonder; when not to understand suggestions; when to exclaim softly with delight or shrink with shyness that didn't repulse.

Forsythe studied her with wonder and delight. No city maiden had ever charmed him more, and withal she seemed so innocent and young, so pliable in his hands. His pulses beat high, his heart was inflamed, and passion came and sat within his handsome eyes.

It was easy to persuade her, after her first seemingly shy reserve was over-come, and before an hour passed she had promised to go away with him. He had very little money, but what of that? When he spoke of it Rosa declared she could easily get some. Her father gave her free access to his safe and kept her supplied for the household use. It was nothing to her—a passing inci-dent. What should it matter whose money took them on their way?

When she went demurely back to the ranch a little before sunset she thought she was happy, poor silly sinner! She met her father with her most alluring but most furtive smile. She was charming at supper and blushed as her mother used to do when he praised her new dress. But she professed weariness from the last schooldays—to have a headache—so she went early to her room and asked that the servants keep the house quiet in the morn-ing, that she might sleep late and get rested. Her father kissed her tenderly and thought what a dear child she was and what a comfort to his ripening years. And the house settled down into quiet.

Rosa packed a bag with some of her most elaborate garments, arrayed her-self in a charming silk outfit for the journey and dropped her baggage out of the window. When the moon rose and the household slept quietly, she visited her father's safe and then stole forth, taking the trail by a winding route known well to her and secure from vigilant servants ever on the lookout for cattle thieves.

Thus she left her father's house and went forth to put her trust in a man whose promises were as ropes of sand and whose fancy was like a wave of the sea, tossed to and fro by every breath that blew. Long before the sun rose the next morning the guarded, beloved child was as far from her safe home and her father's sheltering love as if alone she had started for the mouth of the bottomless pit. Two days later, while Margaret lay unconscious beneath the sagebrush, with a hovering eagle for watch, Rosa in the streets of a great city suddenly realized she was more alone in the universe than she could have been in a wide desert, and her plight was far worse than the girl's with whose fate she had so lightly played.

Early on the morning after Rosa left, while the household was still keep-ing quiet for the supposed sleeper, Gardley rode into the enclosure about the house and asked for Rogers.

Gardley had been traveling night and day to get back. Matters had sud-denly arranged themselves so he could finish his business at his old home and see Margaret's father and mother. He'd visited there and hurried back to Arizona, hoping to reach Ashland in time for commencement. A delay because of a washout on the road had brought him back too late. He'd ridden to camp from a junction forty miles away to get there sooner and this morn-ing rode straight to the Tanners' to surprise Margaret. It was, therefore, a deep disappointment to find her gone and only Mrs. Tanner's voluble explanations for comfort. Mrs. Tanner exhausted her vocabulary in trying to describe the "Injuns," her own feeling of protest against them and Mrs. Brownleigh's foolishness in making so much of them. Then she bustled in to the pine desk in the dining room and produced the letter that had started Margaret off as soon as commencement was over.

Gardley took the letter eagerly, as if it would connect him with Margaret, and read it through carefully to make sure how matters stood. He'd looked troubled when Mrs. Tanner told how tired Margaret was and how worried she seemed about her school and glad to get away from it all; and he agreed the trip was probably a good thing.

"I wish Bud could have gone along," he said, as he turned away from the door. "I don't like her to go with just Indians, though I suppose it's all right. You say he had his wife and child along? Of course Mrs. Brownleigh wouldn't send anybody that wasn't all right. Well, I suppose the trip will be a rest for her. I'm sorry I didn't get home a few days sooner. I might have looked out for her myself."

He rode away from the Tanners', promising to return later with a gift he'd brought Bud that he wanted to present himself, and Mrs. Tanner bustled back to her work again.

"Well, I'm glad he's home," she remarked aloud to herself as she hung her dishcloth over the dishpan and took up her broom. "I ain't felt no ways easy 'bout her sence she left, though I suppose there ain't any sense to it. But I'm *glad he's back!*"

Meanwhile Gardley was riding toward the Rogers ranch, wondering whether he should follow the expedition and enjoy at least the return trip with Margaret or remain patiently until she came back and go to work at once. Nothing important demanded his attention, for Rogers had arranged to keep the present overseer of affairs until he was ready to undertake the work. He was on his way now to report on a small business matter he'd attended to in New York for Rogers. Then he would be free to do as he pleased for a few days more if he liked, and the temptation was great to go at once to Margaret.

As he stood waiting beside his horse in front of the house while the servant went to call Rogers, he looked about with delight on the beautiful day. How glad he was to be back in Arizona! Was it the charm of the place or because Margaret was there, he wondered, that he felt so happy? By all means he must follow her. Why shouldn't he?

He looked at the clambering rose vine covering one end of the house and noticed how it crept close to the window casement and caressed the white curtain as it blew. Margaret must have such a vine at her window in the house he would build for her. It might be a modest house he could give her now, but it should have a rose vine just like that. He would train it around her window where she could smell its fragrance every morning when she awoke and where it would breathe upon her as she slept.

Margaret! How impatient he was to see her again! To look upon her dear face and know she was his! That her father and mother had been satisfied about him and sent their blessing, and now he might tell her so. It was wonderful! His heart thrilled with the thought of it. Of course he would go to her at once. He would start as soon as Rogers was through with him. He would go to Ganado. No, Keams. Which was it? He drew the letter out of his pocket and read it again, then replaced it.

The fluttering curtain up at the window blew out and in, and when it blew out again it brought with it a flurry of papers like white leaves. The curtain had knocked over a vase or something that held them and set the papers free. The breeze caught them and flung them about erratically, tossing one almost at his feet. He stooped to pick it up, thinking it might be of value to someone, and caught the name "Margaret" and "Dear Margaret" written several times on the sheet, with "Walpi, Walpi, Walpi" filling the lower half of the page, as if someone had been practicing it.

And because these words were keenly in his mind he reached for the second paper a foot or two away and found more sentences and words. A third paper contained an exact reproduction of the letter Mrs. Tanner gave him purporting to come from Mrs. Brownleigh to Margaret. What could it mean?

In astonishment he pulled out the other letter and compared them. They were almost identical except for a word here and there crossed out and rewritten. He stood looking mutely at the papers and then up at the window, as though an explanation might be wafted down to him, not knowing what to think, his mind filled with vague alarm.

Just at that moment the servant appeared.

"Mr. Rogers says would you mind coming down to the corral. Miss Rosa had a headache, and we're keeping the house still for her to sleep. That's her window up there—." He indicated the rose-bowered window with the fluttering curtain.

Dazed and half suspicious of something, Gardley folded the two letters together and crushed them into his pocket, wondering what to do about it. The thought of it troubled him so that he gave only partial attention to the business at hand. But he gave his report and handed over certain documents. He was thinking he should see Miss Rosa and find out what she knew of Margaret's going and ask how she came to possess this other letter.

"Now," said Rogers, as the matter was concluded, "I owe you some money. If you'll just step up to the house with me I'll give it to you. I'd like to settle matters at once."

"Oh, let it go till I come again," said Gardley, impatient to be off. He wanted to get by himself and think out a solution of the two letters. He was more than uneasy about Margaret without being able to explain why. His main desire now was to ride to Ganado and find out if the missionaries had left home, which way they had gone and whether they'd met Margaret as planned.

"No, step right up to the house with me," insisted Rogers. "It won't take long, and I have the money in my safe."

Gardley saw the quickest way was to please Rogers, and he didn't wish to arouse any questions, because he supposed, of course, his alarm was foolish. So they walked together into the rancher's private office, where his desk and safe were the principal furniture and no servants entered without orders.

Rogers shoved a chair over for Gardley and crossed to his safe, turning the little nickel knob. In a moment the thick door swung open, and Rogers drew out a japanned cashbox and unlocked it. But when he threw the cover back he uttered an exclamation of angry surprise. The box was empty!

Chapter 32

Mr. Rogers strode to the door, forgetful of his sleeping daughter overhead, and thundered out his call for James. The servant appeared at once, but he knew nothing about the safe and hadn't been in the office that morning. Other servants were summoned and put through a rigid examination. Then Rogers turned to the woman who answered the door for Gardley and sent her up to call Rosa.

But the woman returned presently with word that Miss Rosa wasn't in her room, and there was no sign her bed had been slept in during the night. The woman's face was sullen. She didn't like Rosa but was afraid of her. This to her was only another of Miss Rosa's pranks, and likely her doting father would blame the servants.

The man's face grew stern. His eyes flashed angrily as he climbed the stairs to his daughter's room. But when he came down again he was holding a note in his trembling hand, and his face was ashen white.

"Read that, Gardley," he said, thrusting the note into Gardley's hands and motioning at the same time for the servants to leave.

Gardley took the note. Yet even as he read he noticed the paper was the same as those he carried in his pocket. A peculiar watermark made it noticeable.

The note was a flippant little thing from Rosa, telling her father she'd left to be married and would let him know where she was as soon as they were located. She added that he'd forced her to this step by being so severe with her and not allowing her lover to come to see her. If he'd been reasonable she would have stayed at home and let him give her a grand wedding. As it was she had only this way of seeking her happiness. She added that she knew he would forgive her, she hoped he would come to see her way had been best, and Forsythe was all he could desire as a son-in-law.

Gardley uttered an exclamation of dismay as he read and, looking up, found the miserable eyes of the stricken father upon him. For the moment his own alarm concerning Margaret and his perplexity about the letters was forgotten in the grief of the man who had been his friend.

"When did she go?" asked Gardley.

"She took supper with me and then went to her room, complaining of a headache," said the father, hopelessness in his voice. "She may have gone early in the evening, perhaps, for we all turned in about nine o'clock to keep the house quiet for her."

"Have you any idea which way they went, east or west?" Gardley was the keen adviser in a crisis now, his senses on the alert.

The old man shook his head. "It's too late now," he said, still in that colorless voice. "They'll have reached the railroad somewhere. They'll have been married by this time. See, it's after ten o'clock!"

"Yes, if he marries her," said Gardley fiercely. He had no faith in Forsythe.

"You think—you don't think he'd *dare!*" The man straightened up, fairly blazing in his righteous wrath.

"I think he'd dare anything if he thought he wouldn't be caught. He's a coward."

"What can we do?"

"Telegraph detectives at all points where they'd likely arrive and have them shadowed. Come, we'll ride to the station at once. But, first, could I go up in her room and look around? There might be some clue."

"Certainly," said Rogers, pointing hopelessly up the stairs, "the first door to the left. But you'll find nothing. I looked everywhere. She wouldn't have left a clue. While you're up there I'll interview the servants. Then we'll go."

As he went upstairs Gardley was wondering whether he should tell Rogers about the two letters. What possible connection could there be between Margaret's trip to Walpi with the Brownleighs and Rosa's elopement? Furthermore, what possible explanation was there for a copy of Mrs. Brownleigh's letter blowing out of the girl's bedroom window? How did it get there?

Rosa's room was in beautiful order, the roses nodding in at the window, the curtain blowing back and forth in the breeze and rippling open the leaves of a tiny testament lying on her desk, as if recently read. Nothing showed that the room's owner had taken a hasty flight. On the desk lay several sheets of notepaper with the peculiar watermark. These caught his attention, and he picked them up and compared them with the papers in his pocket. It was strange that the letter sending Margaret off into the wilderness with an unknown Indian should be written on the same kind of paper as this. Yet, perhaps, it wasn't so strange. It was probably the only notepaper in that region and must all have been purchased at the same place.

The rippling leaves of the testament fluttered open at the flyleaf and revealed Rosa's name and a date with Mrs. Brownleigh's name written below. Gardley picked it up, startled again to find Hazel Brownleigh mixed up with the Rogers family. He hadn't known they had anything to do with each other. And yet, of course, they would, being the missionaries of the region.

The almost empty wastebasket next caught his eye, and here again were several sheets of paper written over with words and phrases he recognized as part of the letter Mrs. Tanner had given him. He emptied the wastebasket on the desk, thinking something might give a clue to where the elopers had gone. But there wasn't much else in it except a little yellowed note with the signature "Hazel Brownleigh" at the bottom. He glanced through the brief note, gathered its purport and then spread it out on the desk and compared the writing with the others, a wild fear clutching at his heart. Yet he couldn't explain why he was so uneasy. Why would Rosa Rogers forge a letter to Margaret from

Hazel Brownleigh?

Suddenly Rogers stood behind him looking over his shoulder. "What is it, Gardley? What have you found? Any clue?"

"No clue," said Gardley uneasily, "but something I can't understand. I don't suppose it has anything to do with your daughter, and yet it seems almost uncanny. This morning I stopped at the Tanners' to let Miss Earle know I'd returned and was told she left yesterday with a couple of Indians as guide to meet the Brownleighs at Keams, or somewhere near there, and take a trip with them to Walpi to see the Hopi Indians. Mrs. Tanner gave me this letter from Mrs. Brownleigh, which Miss Earle left behind. But when I reached here and was waiting for you, some papers blew out of your daughter's window. When I picked them up I was startled to find that one of them was an exact copy of the letter I had in my pocket. See! Here they are! I don't suppose there's anything to it, but in spite of me I'm uneasy about Miss Earle. I just can't understand how that copy of the letter came to be here."

Rogers was leaning over, looking at the papers. "What's this?" he asked, picking up the note that came with the testament. He read each paper carefully, took in the little testament with its fluttering flyleaf and inscription, studied the pages of words and alphabet, then suddenly turned away and groaned, hiding his face in his hands.

"What is it?" asked Gardley, awed with the awful sorrow in the strong man's attitude.

"My poor baby!" groaned the father. "My poor baby girl! I've always been afraid of that fatal gift of hers. Gardley, she could copy any handwriting in the world perfectly. She could write my name so it couldn't be told from my own signature. She's evidently written that letter. Why, I don't know, unless she wanted to get Miss Earle out of the way so it would be easier for her to carry out her plans."

"It can't be!" said Gardley, shaking his head. "I can't see her object. Besides, where would she find the Indians? Mrs. Tanner saw the Indians. They came to the school after her with the letter and waited for her. Mrs. Tanner saw them ride off together."

"A couple of strange Indians were here yesterday, begging something to eat," said Rogers, settling down on a chair and resting his head against the desk as if he'd suddenly lost the strength to stand.

"This won't do!" said Gardley. "We've got to get down to the telegraph office, you and I. Now try to brace up. Are the horses ready? Then we'll go right away."

"You better question the servants about those Indians first," said Rogers.

As Gardley hurried down the stairs, he heard groan after groan from Rosa's room, where her father lingered in agony.

Gardley got all the information he could about the Indians, and then the two men galloped away to the station. As they passed the Tanner house

Gardley drew rein to call to Bud, who hurried out to greet his friend, his face lighting with pleasure.

"Will, get on your horse in double-quick time and beat it out to camp for me, will you?" said Gardley, as he reached down and gripped Bud's rough young hand. "Tell Jasper Kemp to come back with you and meet me at the station as quick as he can. Tell him to have the men where he can signal them. We may have to hustle out on a long hunt. And, Will, keep your head steady and get back yourself right away. Perhaps I'll want you to help me. I'm a little anxious about Miss Earle, but you needn't tell anybody that but Jasper. Tell him to hurry for all he's worth."

Bud, his eyes large with loyalty and trouble, nodded, returned the young man's grip with a clumsy squeeze and sprang away to get his horse and do Gardley's bidding. Gardley knew he would ride as if for his life, now that he knew Margaret's safety was at stake.

Then Gardley rode on to the station and was indefatigable for two hours hunting addresses, writing telegrams and calling up long-distance telephones.

When all possible had been done Rogers turned a haggard face to the young man. "I've been thinking, Gardley. That rash little girl of mine may have put Miss Earle into some dangerous position. You should look after her. What can we do?"

"I'm going to, sir," said Gardley, "as soon as I've done everything I can for you. I've already sent for Jasper Kemp, and we'll make a plan between us and find out if Miss Earle is all right. Can you spare Jasper, or will you need him?"

"By all means! Take all the men you need. I won't rest easy till I know Miss Earle is safe."

He sank down on a truck that stood on the station platform, his shoulders slumping, his whole attitude like one fatally stricken. Gardley thought how suddenly old he looked, and gray! What a thing for the selfish child to do to her father! Poor, silly child, whose fate with Forsythe would probably be anything but enviable!

But they had no time for sorrowful reflections. Jasper Kemp, stern, alert, anxious, came riding furiously down the street, Bud keeping pace with him.

Chapter 33

While Gardley briefly told his tale to Jasper Kemp, and the Scotsman hastily scanned the papers with his keen, bright eyes, Bud stood frowning and listening intently.

"Say!" he burst forth. "That girl's a mess! 'Course she did it! You oughta seen what all she didn't do the last six weeks of school. Miss Mar'get got so she shivered every time that girl came near her or looked at her. She sure had her goat! Some nights after school, when she thought she's all alone, she just cried. Why, Rosa had every one of those guys in the back acting like the devil, and nobody knew what was the matter. She wrote things on the chalkboard right in the questions, so's it looked like Miss Mar'get didn't know who did it. And she was jealous as a cat of Miss Mar'get. You know what a case she had on that guy from the fort; she didn't like him even to look at Miss Mar'get. Well, she didn't forget how he went away that night of the play. I caught her looking at her like she'd like to murder her. Good night! Some look! The guy had a case on Miss Mar'get too; only she was onto him and wouldn't look at him or let him spoon ner nothing. But Rosa saw it all and hated Miss Mar'get.

"Then once Miss Mar'get stopped her from going out to meet that guy too. Oh, she hated her all right! And you can bet she wrote the letter! Sure she did! She wanted to get her away when that guy came back. He was back yesterday. I saw him over by the run on that trail that crosses the trail to the old cabin. He didn't see me. I got my eye on him first and ducked behind some sagebrush, but he was here, and he didn't mean any good. I follahed him awhile till he stopped and fixed up a place to camp. I guess he must a' stayed out last night—"

A heavy hand was suddenly laid from behind on Bud's shoulder, and Rogers stood over him, his dark eyes on fire, his lips trembling.

"Boy, can you show me where that was?" he asked, with an intensity in his voice that showed Bud something serious was wrong. Boylike he dropped his eyes indifferently before this great emotion.

"Sure!"

"Best take Long Bill with you, Mr. Rogers," advised Jasper Kemp, alive to the whole situation. "I reckon we'll have to work together. My men ain't far off." He lifted his whistle to his lips and blew the signal blasts. "The Kid here'll want to ride to Keams to see if the lady is safe and has met her friends. I reckon mebbe I better go straight to Ganado and find out if them mission folks really got started and put 'em wise to what's been going on. They'll mebbe know who them Injuns was. I have my suspicions they weren't any friendlies. I didn't like that Injun the minute I set eyes on him hanging round the schoolhouse, but I wouldn't have stirred a step toward camp if I'd a' suspected he was come fur the lady. 'Spose you take Bud and Long Bill and go find that camping place and see if you find any trail showing which way they took. If you do, you fire three shots, and the men'll be with you. If you want the Kid, fire four shots. He can't be so fur away by then he can't hear. He's got to get provisioned 'fore he starts. Lead him out, Bud. We ain't got no time to lose."

Bud gave one despairing look at Gardley and turned to obey.

"That's all right, Will," said Gardley, with an understanding glance. "You tell Mr. Rogers all you know and show him the place, and then when Long Bill comes you can take the cross-cut to the long trail and go with me. I'll just stop at the house as I pass and tell your mother I need you."

Bud gave one radiant, grateful look and sprang upon his horse. Rogers had hard work to keep up with him at first, till Bud got interested in giving him a detailed account of Forsythe's looks and acts.

In less than an hour the relief expedition had started. Before night fell Jasper Kemp, riding hard, arrived at the mission, told his story, procured a fresh horse and after a couple of hours' rest started with Brownleigh and his wife for Keams Canyon.

Gardley and Bud, riding for all they were worth, said little by the way. Now and then the boy stole glances at the man's face, and the dead weight of sorrow settled like lead upon his heart. Too well he knew the dangers of the desert. He could almost read Gardley's fears in the white, drawn look about his lips, the ashen circles under his eyes, the tense, strained pose of his whole figure. Gardley's mind was urging ahead of his steed, and his body couldn't relax. He was anxious to go a little faster, yet his judgment knew it wouldn't do, for his horse would play out before he could get another. They ate their corn bread in the saddle and only turned aside from the trail once to drink at a waterhole and fill their cans. They rode late into the night, with only the stars and their wits as guides. When they stopped to rest they didn't make a fire but hobbled the horses where they might feed and, rolling quickly in their blankets, lay down upon the ground.

Bud, with the fatigue of healthy youth, would have slept till morning in spite of his fears. But Gardley woke him in a couple of hours, made him drink some water and eat a bite of food, and they went on their way again. When morning broke they were almost to the entrance of Keams Canyon, and both looked haggard and worn. Bud seemed to have aged in the night, and Gardley looked at him almost tenderly.

"Are you all in, kid?" he asked.

"Naw!" answered Bud promptly, with an assumed cheerfulness. "Feeling like a four-year-old. Get on to that sky? Guess we'll have some day! Pretty as a red wagon!"

Gardley smiled sadly. What would that day bring forth for the two who went in search of the one they loved? His great anxiety was to get to Keams

Canyon and inquire. They would surely know at the trading post whether the missionary and his party had gone that way.

The road was still almost impassable from the flood. The two dauntless riders picked their way slowly down the trail to the post.

But the trader could tell them nothing comforting. The missionary hadn't been that way in two months, and no party and no lady there that week. A single strange Indian came down the trail above the day before, stayed awhile, picked a quarrel with some men and rode back up the steep trail. He might have had a party with him on the mesa, waiting. He'd said something about his squaw. The trader admitted he might have been drunk, but he frowned as he spoke of him. He called him a "bad Indian." Something unpleasant had evidently happened.

The trader gave them a good, hot dinner, of which they stood sorely in need, and because they realized they must keep up their strength they took the time to eat it. Then, procuring fresh horses, they climbed the steep trail in the direction the trader said the Indian had taken. It was a slender clue, but all they had, and they must follow it. And now the travelers were silent, as if they felt they were drawing near to some knowledge that would settle the question for them one way or the other. As they reached the top at last, where they could see out across the plain, each drew a long breath like a gasp and looked about, half fearing what he might see.

Yes, there was the sign of a recent campfire and a few tin cans and refuse bits, nothing more. Gardley got down and searched carefully. Bud even crept about on his hands and knees, but a single tiny blue bead like a grain of sand was his only reward. Some Indian had doubtless camped here. That was all the evidence. Standing thus in hopeless uncertainty of what to do next, they suddenly heard voices. Something familiar once or twice made Gardley lift his whistle and blow a blast. Instantly a silvery answer came ringing from the mesa a mile or so away and woke the echoes in the canyon. Jasper Kemp and his party had taken the longer way around, instead of going down the canyon, and were just arriving at the spot where Margaret and the squaw had waited for their drunken guide. But Jasper Kemp's whistle rang out again, and he shot three times into the air, their signal to wait for some important news.

Breathlessly and in silence the two waited and cast themselves down on the ground, feeling the need of support. Now with a possibility of some news they felt hardly able to bear it, and the waiting for it was intolerable, so tense and strained they were.

But when the party from Ganado came in sight, their faces wore no brightness of good news. Their greetings were quiet, sad, anxious, and Jasper Kemp held out to Gardley an envelope. It was the one from Margaret's mother's letter she'd dropped on the trail.

"We found it on the way from Ganado, just as we entered Steamboat

Canyon," explained Jasper.

"And didn't you search for a trail off in any other direction?" asked Gardley, almost sharply. "They haven't been here. At least only one Indian has been down to the trader's."

"There was no other trail. We looked," said Jasper sadly.

"We saw a campfire twice and signs of a camp. We felt sure they'd come this way."

Gardley shook his head, and a look of abject despair crossed his face. "There's no sign here," he said. "They must have gone some other way. Perhaps the Indian has carried her off. Are the other men following?"

"No, Rogers sent them in the other direction after his girl. They found the camp all right. Bud tell you? We made sure we'd found our trail and wouldn't need them."

Gardley dropped his head and almost groaned.

Meanwhile the missionary had been riding around in radiating circles from the dead campfire, searching every step of the way. Bud, taking his cue from him, looked off toward the mesa a minute, then struck out in a straight line for it and rode off like mad. Suddenly a shout loud and long was heard, and Bud came riding back, waving something small and white above his head.

They gathered in a little knot, waiting for the boy, not speaking. When he halted in their midst he fluttered down the handkerchief to Gardley.

"It's hers, all right. Gotter name all written out on the edge!" he declared radiantly.

The sky grew brighter to them all now. Eagerly Gardley sprang into his saddle, no longer weary, but alert and eager for the trail.

"You folks better go down to the trader's and get some dinner. You'll need it! Bud and I'll go on. Mrs. Brownleigh looks all in."

"No," declared Hazel. "We'll just snatch a bite here and follow you at once. I couldn't enjoy a dinner till I know she's safe." And so, though both Jasper Kemp and her husband urged her otherwise, she ate a hasty meal by the way and hurried on.

But Bud and Gardley didn't wait for the others. They plunged wildly ahead.

It seemed a long way to the eager hunters, from the place where Bud had found the handkerchief to the little note twisted around the red chessman. It was perhaps nearly a mile, and both riders had searched in all directions for some time before Gardley spied it. Eagerly he seized upon the note, recognizing the little red manikin with which he'd whiled away an hour with Margaret during one of her visits at the camp.

The note was written large and clear on writing paper:

I am Margaret Earle, schoolteacher at Ashland. I'm supposed to be traveling to Walpi, by way of Keams, to meet Mr. and Mrs. Brownleigh of Ganado. I'm with an Indian, his squaw and papoose. The Indian said he was sent to guide me, but he's drunk now, and I'm frightened. He's acted strangely all the way. I don't know where I am. Please come and help me.

Bud, sitting anxiously on his horse, read Gardley's face as Gardley read the note. Then he read it aloud to Bud, and before the last word was out of his mouth both man and boy started as if they'd heard Margaret's beloved voice calling them. Soon Bud found another scrap of paper a half-mile farther on, and then another and another, scattered at great distances along the way. The only way they were sure she'd dropped them was that they seemed to be the same paper the note was written on.

How that note with its brave, frightened appeal wrung Gardley's heart as he thought of Margaret, unprotected, in terror and perhaps in peril, riding to she knew not where. What trials and fears she must have already passed through! What mightn't she be experiencing even now while he searched for her?

Perhaps two hours later he found the little white stocking dropped where the trail divided, showing which way she'd taken. Gardley folded it reverently and put it in his pocket. An hour later Bud pounced upon the bedroom slipper and carried it gleefully to Gardley. So by slow degrees, finding here and there a chessman or more paper, they came at last to the camp where the Indians had abandoned their trust and fled, leaving Margaret alone in the wilderness.

Then Gardley searched in vain for any further clue and, riding wide in every direction, stopped and called her name again and again, while the sun grew lower and shadows crept in lurking places waiting for the swift-coming night.

It was then that Bud, flying frantically from one spot to another, got down upon his knees behind a sagebrush when Gardley wasn't looking and mumbled a rough, hasty prayer for help. He felt like the old woman who, on being told that nothing but God could save the ship, exclaimed, "And has it come to that?" Bud had felt all his life that a remote time occurred in every life when one might need to believe in prayer. The time had come for Bud.

Margaret, on her knees in the desert sand praying for help, remembered the promise, "Before they call I will answer, and while they are yet speaking I will hear," and knew not her deliverers were on the way.

The sun had been beating hot down upon the white sand, and the girl had crept under a sagebrush for shelter. The pain in her ankle was sickening. She had removed her shoe and bound the ankle with a handkerchief soaked with half her bottle of witch hazel and so, lying quiet, had fallen asleep, too exhausted with pain and anxiety to stay awake any longer.

When she awoke again the softness of evening was hovering over everything, and she started up and listened. Surely she'd heard a voice calling her! She sat up sharply and listened. Ah! There it was again, a faint echo in the distance. Was it a voice, or was it only her dreams mingling with her imagination?

Travelers in deserts, she had read, took all sorts of notions, saw mirages, heard sounds that were not. But she hadn't been out long enough to catch such a desert fever. Perhaps she was going to be sick. Still that faint echo made her heart beat wildly. She dragged herself to her knees, then to her feet, standing painfully with the weight on her well foot.

The suffering horse turned his anguished eyes and whinnied. Her heart ached for him; yet she had no way to assuage his pain or put him out of his misery. But she must make sure if she'd heard a voice. Could she possibly scale that rock she and her horse had fallen down? For then she might look out farther and see if anyone was in sight.

Painfully she crawled and crept, up and up, inch by inch, until at last she gained the height and could look afar.

There was no living thing in sight. The air was clear. The eagle had found his evening rest somewhere in the quiet crag. The long corn waved on the distant plain, and all was deathly still again. There was a hint of coming sunset in the sky. Her heart sank, and she was about to give up hope entirely, when, rich and clear, it came again! A voice in the wilderness calling her name, "Margaret! Margaret!"

The tears rushed to her eyes and crowded in her throat. She couldn't answer—she was so overwhelmed—and though she tried twice to call out, she could make no sound. But the call kept coming again and again, "Margaret! Margaret!" And it was Gardley's voice. Impossible! For Gardley was far away and couldn't know her need. Yet it was his voice. Had she died, or was she in delirium that she seemed to hear him calling her name?

But the call came clearer now. "Margaret! Margaret! I'm coming!" And like a flash her mind went back to the first night in Arizona when she heard him whistling, "From the Desert I Come to Thee!"

Now she struggled to her feet again and shouted, inarticulately and gladly through her tears. She could see him. It was Gardley. He was riding fast toward her, and he shot three shots into the air above him as he rode, and three shrill blasts of his whistle rang out on the still evening air.

She tore the scarf from her neck that she had tied about it to keep the sun from blistering her and waved it wildly in the air now, shouting in happy, choking sobs.

And so he came to her across the desert!

He sprang down before the horse had reached her side and, rushing to her, took her in his arms.

"Margaret! My darling! I've found you at last!"

She swayed and would have fallen but for his arms, and then he saw her white face and knew she must be suffering.

"You're hurt!" he cried. "Oh, what have they done to you?" And he laid her gently down on the sand and dropped on his knees beside her.

"Oh, no," she gasped joyously, with white lips. "I'm all right now. Only my ankle hurts a little. We had a fall, the horse and I. Oh, go to him at once and put him out of his pain. I'm sure his legs are broken."

For answer Gardley put the whistle to his lips and blew a blast. He wouldn't leave her for an instant. He wasn't sure she wasn't more hurt than she said. He set about discovering at once, for he had brought with him supplies for all emergencies.

Bud came riding madly across the mesa in answer to the call, reaching Gardley before anyone else. Bud with his eyes shining, his cheeks blazing with excitement, his hair flying wildly in the breeze, his young, boyish face suddenly grown old with lines of anxiety. But from his greeting it seemed like only a pleasure excursion he'd been on the past two days.

"Good work, Kid! Watcha want me t' do?"

Bud arranged the camp and went back to tell the other detachments that Margaret was found. He led the packhorse up, unpacked the provisions and gathered wood to start a fire. Bud was everywhere, with a smudged face, a weary, gray look around his eyes, and his hair sticking "seven ways for Sunday." Yet once, when his labors led him near Margaret, lying weak and happy on a couch of blankets, he gave her an unwonted pat on her shoulder and said in a low tone: "Hello, gang! See you kept your nerve with you!" And then he gave her a grin all across his dirty, tired face and moved away as if he were half ashamed of his emotion.

But it was Bud again who came and talked with her to divert her so she wouldn't notice when they shot her horse. He talked loudly about a coyote they shot the night before and a cottontail they saw at Keams, and when he saw she understood what the shot meant, and tears were in her eyes, he gave her hand a rough, bear squeeze and said gruffly: "You shouldn't worry! He's better off now!" And when Gardley came back he took himself thoughtfully to a distance and busied himself opening tins of meat and soup.

In another hour the Brownleighs arrived, having heard the signals, and they had a supper around the campfire, everyone so exultant their voices still quivered. And when anyone laughed it sounded like the echo of a sob, so great had been the strain of their anxiety.

Gardley, sitting beside Margaret in the starlight afterward, her hand in his, listened to the story of her journey, and the strong, tender pressure of his fingers told her how deeply it affected him to know the peril through which she had passed. Later, when the others were telling merry stories about the fire, and Bud lying full length in their midst had fallen fast asleep, these two, a little apart from the rest, were murmuring their innermost thoughts in low tones to each other, rejoicing they were together again.

Chapter 34

They talked it over the next morning at breakfast as they sat around the fire. Jasper Kemp thought he should get right back to attend to things. Mr. Rogers was broken up and might need him to search for Rosa if they hadn't found her yet. He and Fiddling Boss, who had come along, would start back at once. They'd had a good night's rest and found their dear lady. What more did they need? Besides, there weren't provisions for an indefinite stay for such a large party, and there were none too many sources of supply in this region.

The missionary thought that, since he was here, he should go on to Walpi. It wasn't more than a two-hour ride there, and Hazel could stay with the camp while Margaret's ankle had a chance to rest and let the swelling subside under treatment.

Margaret, however, rebelled. She didn't wish to be an invalid and was sure she could ride without injuring her ankle. She wanted to see Walpi and the strange Hopi Indians, since she was so near. So they reached a compromise. They would all wait in camp a couple of days, and then if Margaret felt well enough they would go on, visit the Hopis and so go home together.

Bud pleaded to be allowed to stay with them, and Jasper Kemp promised to make it right with his parents.

So for two whole, long, lovely days the little party of five camped on the mesa and enjoyed sweet converse. And never in all Bud's life would he likely forget or get away from that day's influences in such company.

Gardley and the missionary proved to be the best of physicians, and Margaret's ankle improved hourly under their united treatment of compresses, lotions and rest. About noon on Saturday they broke camp, mounted their horses and rode away across the stretch of white sand, through tall cornfields growing right up out of the sand, closer and closer to the great mesa with the castle-like pueblos five hundred feet above them on the top. It seemed to Margaret like suddenly dropping into Egypt or the Holy Land, or some Babylonian excavations, so curious and primitive and altogether different from anything she'd ever seen.

She listened, fascinated, while Brownleigh told about this strange Hopi land, the strangest spot in America. Spanish explorers found them years before the Pilgrims landed and called the country Tuscayan. They built their homes up high for protection from their enemies. They lived on the corn, pumpkins, peaches and melons they raised in the valley, planting the seeds with their hands. They reportedly got their seeds first from the Spaniards years ago. They made pottery, cloth and baskets and were a busy people.

Seven villages were built on three mesas in the northern desert. One of the largest, Orabi, had a thousand inhabitants. Walpi numbered about 230 people, all living in one great building of many rooms. They were divided into brotherhoods, or phratries, with each brotherhood having several large families, and were ruled by a speaker chief and a war chief elected by a council of clan elders.

Margaret learned with wonder that all the water these people used had to be carried by the women in jars on their backs five hundred feet up the steep trail.

Presently, as they drew nearer, a curious man with his hair "banged" like a child's and garments like those worn by scarecrows—a shapeless kind of shirt and trousers—appeared along the steep and showed them the way up. Margaret and the missionary's wife exclaimed in horror over the children playing along the edge of the cliffs above as carelessly as birds in trees.

High up on the mesa at last, how strange it seemed! Far below the yellow sand of the valley; fifteen miles away a second mesa stretching dark; to the southwest, a hundred miles distant, the dim outlines of the San Francisco peaks. Some children on burros crossing the sand below looked as if they were part of a curious moving picture, not as if they were little living beings taking life as seriously as other children do. The great, wide desert stretching far! The bare, solid rocks beneath their feet! The curious houses behind them! It seemed unreal to Margaret, like a great picture book spread out for her to see. She turned from gazing and found Gardley's eyes upon her adoringly, a tender understanding of her mood in his glance. She thrilled with pleasure to be here with him; a soft flush spread over her cheeks, and a light came into her eyes.

They found the Indians preparing for one of their most famous ceremonies, the snake dance, which was to take place in a few days. For almost a week the snake priests had been busy hunting rattlesnakes, building altars, drawing figures in the sand and singing weird songs. On the ninth day the snakes were washed in a pool and driven near a pile of sand. The priests, arrayed in paint, feathers, and charms, came out in line and, taking the live snakes in their mouths, paraded up and down the rocks, while the people crowded the roofs and terraces of the pueblos to watch. Helpers whipped the snakes and kept them from biting, and catchers saw that none got away. Then the priests took the snakes down on the desert and set them free, sending them north, south, east and west, where it was supposed they would take the people's prayers for rain to the water serpent in the underworld, who was in some way connected with the god of the rain clouds.

That night in Walpi was a strange experience: the primitive accommodations; the picturesque, uncivilized people; the shy glances from dark eager eyes. To watch two girls grinding corn between two stones and, a little farther off, their mother rolling out her dough with an ear of corn and cooking over an open fire, her pot slung from a crude crane over the blaze—it was too unreal to be true.

But the most interesting thing about it was to watch the "Aneshodi" going about among them—his face alight with warm, human love, his hearty laugh ringing out in a joke the Hopis seemed to understand, making himself one with them. Margaret suddenly remembered the Rev. Frederick West's pompous figure and tried to imagine him moving about among these people, attempting to do them good. Before she knew what she was doing she laughed aloud at the thought! Then, of course, she had to explain to Bud and Gardley, who looked at her inquiringly.

"Aw! Say! *Him?* He wasn't a minister! He was a *mistake!* Fergit him, the poor simp!" growled Bud. Then his eyes softened as he watched Brownleigh playing with three little Indian maids, having a fine romp. "Say! He certainly is a peach, ain't he?" he murmured, his whole face kindling appreciatively. "My! I bet that kid never forgets that!"

Sunday was a wonderful day, when the missionary gathered the people together and spoke to them in simple words of God—the One Who made the sky, the stars, the mountains and the sun, Whom they called by different names, but Whom he called God. He spoke of the Book of Heaven that told about God and His great love for men, so great that He sent His Son to save them from their sin. It wasn't a long sermon but a beautiful one. The visitors were moved as they listened to the simple, wonderful words of life that fell from the missionary's earnest lips and were translated by his faithful Indian interpreter, who always went with him, and as they watched the faces of the people taking in the marvelous meaning.

Even Bud, awed beyond his wont, said shyly to Margaret, "Say! It's something fierce not to be born a Christian and know all that, ain't it?"

Margaret and Gardley walked a little way down the narrow path that led out over the neck of rock less than a rod wide, connecting the great promontory with the mesa. The sun was setting in majesty over the desert, and the scene was one of breathless beauty. One might imagine it might look so to stand on the hills of God and look out over creation when all things have been made new.

They stood for a while in silence. Then Margaret looked down at the narrow path worn more than a foot deep in the solid rock by the ten generations of feet that had been passing over it.

"Just think," she said, "of all the feet, little and big, that have walked here in all the years and of all the souls that have stood and looked out over this wonderful sight! It must be that in spite of their darkness they've reached out to the God Who made this and found a way to His heart. They couldn't look at this and not feel Him, could they? It seems to me that perhaps some of those poor creatures who have stood here and reached up blindly after the Creator of their souls have pleased Him as much as those who've known about Him from childhood."

Gardley was used to her talking this way. He hadn't sat in her Sunday meetings for nothing. He understood and sympathized, and now his hand reached softly for hers and held it tenderly.

After a moment of silence he said, "I surely think if God could reach down and find me in the desert of my life, He must have found them. I sometimes think I was a greater heathen than all these, because I knew and wouldn't see."

Margaret nestled her hand in his and looked up joyfully into his face. "I'm so glad you know Him now!" she murmured happily.

They stood for some time looking out over the changing scene, till the crimson faded into rose, the silver into gray; till the stars bloomed out one by one, and down in the valley across the desert a light twinkled here and there from the camps of the Hopi shepherds.

They started home at daybreak the next morning, the whole company of Indians standing on the rocks to send them on their way, pressing simple, homely gifts upon them and begging them to return soon again and tell the blessed story.

A wonderful ride they had back to Ganado, where Gardley left Margaret for a short visit, promising to return for her in a few days when she was rested, and hastened back to Ashland to his work. He was happy now and at ease and felt he must get to work at once. Rogers would need him. Poor Rogers! Had he found his daughter yet? Poor, silly child-prodigal!

But when Gardley reached Ashland he found in the mail awaiting him a telegram. His uncle was dead, and the fortune he was brought up to believe was his, idly tossed away in a reckless moment, had been restored to him by the uncle's last will, made since Gardley's recent visit home. The fortune was his again!

Gardley sat in his office on the Rogers ranch and stared hard at the adobe wall opposite his desk. That fortune would be great! He could do such wonderful things for Margaret now. They could work out their dreams together for the people they loved. He could see the shadows of those dreams—a beautiful home for Margaret out on the trail she loved, where wildness and beauty and the mountain she called hers were nearby. There would be horses in plenty and a luxurious car when they wanted to take a trip; journeys East as often as they wished; some of the ideal appliances for the school Margaret loved; a church for the missionary and convenient halls where he could speak at his outlying districts. And Mom Wallis could take a trip to the city, where she might see a real picture gallery, her one expressed desire this side of heaven, now that she'd taken to reading Browning and had some of it explained to her. Oh, and a lot of wonderful things! These all hung in the dream-picture before Gardley's eyes as he sat at his desk with that bit of yellow paper in his hand.

He thought of what that money had represented to him in the past. Reckless days and nights of folly as a boy and a young man at college; ruthless waste of time, money, youth; shriveling of soul, till Margaret came and found and rescued him! How wonderful that he had been rescued! That he'd come to his senses at last and was here in a man's position, doing a man's work in the world! Now, with all that money, he had no need to work and earn more. He could live idly all his days and have a good time—make others happy too. But still he wouldn't have this exhilarating feeling of supplying his own and Margaret's necessities by the labor of hand and brain. The telegram in his hand seemed to be trying to snatch from him all this material prosperity that was the symbol of that spiritual regeneration which had become so dear to him.

He put his head down on his clasped hands upon the desk then and prayed. Perhaps it was the first great prayer of his life.

"O God, let me be strong enough to stand this that has come upon me. Help me be a man in spite of money! Don't let me lose my manhood and my right to work. Help me use the money in the right way and not dwarf myself or spoil our lives with it." It was a great prayer for a man such as Gardley had been, and the answer came swiftly in his conviction.

He lifted up his head with purpose and, folding the telegram, put it safely back into his pocket. He wouldn't tell Margaret of it—not yet. He would think it out—the right way—and he didn't believe he meant to give up his position with Rogers. He had accepted it for a year in good faith, and it was his business to fulfill the contract. Meanwhile, this money might enable him to marry Margaret sooner than he'd hoped.

Five minutes later Rogers telephoned to the office.

"I've decided to take that shipment of cattle and try that new stock, provided you'll go out and look at them and see that everything's okay. I couldn't go myself now. Don't feel like going anywhere, you know. You wouldn't need to go for a couple of weeks. I've just had a letter from the man, and he says he won't be ready sooner. Say, why don't you and Miss Earle get married and make this a wedding trip? She could go to the Pacific Coast with you. It would be a nice trip. Then I could spare you for a month or six weeks when you got back if you wanted to take her East for a little visit."

Why not? Gardley stumbled out his thanks and hung up the receiver, his face full of the light of a great joy. How were the blessings pouring down upon his head these days? Was it a sign God was pleased with his making good what he could where he'd failed? And Rogers! How kind he was! Poor man, with his broken heart and his stricken home! For Rosa had come home again a sadder, wiser child, and her father seemed crushed with the disgrace of it all.

Gardley went to Margaret that very afternoon. He told her only that some money was left him by his uncle, which would make it possible for him to marry at once and keep her comfortably now. He was to be sent to California on a business trip. Would she be married and go with him?

Margaret studied the telegram in wonder. She had never asked Gardley much about his circumstances. The telegram merely stated his uncle's estate was left to him. To her simple mind an estate might be a few hundred dollars, enough to furnish a plain little home, and her face lit with joy over it. She asked no questions, and Gardley said no more about the money. He'd forgotten that question, comparatively, in the greater possibility of joy.

Would she be married in ten days and go with him?

Her eyes met his with an answering joy, and yet he could see trouble hiding somewhere. He presently saw what it was without needing to be told. Her father and mother! Of course, they would be disappointed! They would want her to be married at home!

"But Rogers said we could go and visit them for several weeks on our return," he said, and Margaret's face lit up.

"Oh, that would be wonderful," she said. "Perhaps they won't mind so much—though I always expected Father to marry me if I ever married; still, if we can go home so soon and for so long—and Mr. Brownleigh would be next best, of course."

"But, of course, your father must marry you," said Gardley. "Perhaps we could persuade him to come, and your mother, too."

"Oh, no, they couldn't possibly," said Margaret quickly, a shade of sadness in her eyes. "You know it costs a lot to come out here, and ministers are never rich."

Then Gardley's eyes lit with joy. His money could take this away, at least. But he said nothing about the money.

"Suppose we write to your father and mother and put the matter before them. See what they say. We'll send the letters tonight. You write your mother, and I'll write your father."

Margaret agreed and sat down at once to write her letter, while Gardley, on the other side of the room, wrote his, scratching away contentedly with his fountain pen and glancing now and then toward the bowed head over at the desk.

Gardley didn't read his letter to Margaret. She wondered a little at this but didn't ask, and the letters were mailed, with special-delivery stamps on them. Gardley awaited their replies with great impatience.

He filled in the days of waiting with business. He had letters to write connected with his fortune and arrangements to make for his trip. But occupying most of his time and thought was the purchase and refitting of a roomy old ranch house in a charming location, not more than three miles from Ashland, on the road to the camp.

It had been vacant for a couple of years past, the owner going abroad permanently and the place being offered for sale. Margaret had often admired it in her trips to and from the camp, and Gardley remembered it at once when he could think of purchasing a home in the West.

It had a great stone fireplace, and the beams of the ceilings and pillars of the porch and wide, hospitable rooms were of tree trunks with the bark on them. With a little work it could be made roughly but artistically habitable.

Gardley had it cleaned up, not disturbing the tangle of vines and shrubbery that had had their way since the last owner had left, making a perfect screen from the road for the house.

Behind this screen the men worked—most of them from the bunkhouse, whom Gardley took into his confidence.

The floors were carefully scrubbed under Mom Wallis's direction and the windows made shining. Then the men spent a day bringing great loads of tree boughs and filling the place with green fragrance, until the big living room looked like a woodland bower. Gardley visited some Indian friends of his and came back with several fine Navajo rugs and blankets, which he spread about the room on the floor and over the crude benches the men had constructed. They piled the fireplace with big logs, and Gardley took over some of his own personal possessions he had brought back from the East with him, giving the place a livable look.

Then he stood back satisfied. The place was fit to bring his bride and her friends to. Not that it was as it should be. That would be for Margaret to do, but it would serve as a temporary stopping place if they needed. If no need came, why, the place was there anyway, hers and his. A tenderness grew in his eyes as he surveyed it in the dying afternoon light. Then he went out and rode swiftly to the telegraph office and found these two telegrams, according to the request in his own letter to Mr. Earle.

Gardley's telegram read:

Congratulations. Will come as you desire. We await your advice. Have written.—Father.

He saddled his horse and hurried to Margaret with hers, and together they read:

Dear child! So glad for you. Of course you'll go. I'm sending you some things. Don't take a thought for us. We'll look forward to your visit. Our love to you both.—Mother.

Margaret, folded in her beloved's arms, cried out her sorrow and joy and lifted up her face with happiness. Then Gardley, with great joy, thought of the surprise he had in store for her and laid his face against hers to hide the telltale smile in his eyes.

For Gardley, in his letter to his future father-in-law, had written of his newly inherited fortune and not only enclosed a check to cover all extra expense of the journey but said a private car would be at their disposal, for them and for any of Margaret's friends and relatives they might invite. As he wrote this letter he was filled with deep thanksgiving that it was in his power to do this thing for his dear girl-bride.

The morning after the telegrams arrived Gardley spent several hours writing telegrams and receiving them from a department store in the nearest large city, and before noon a shipment of goods was on its way to Ashland. Beds, bureaus, washstands, chairs, tables, dishes, kitchen utensils, and all kinds of bedding, even to sheets and pillowcases—he ordered with a lavish hand. After all, he must furnish the house himself and let Margaret weed it out or give it away afterward, if she didn't like it. He was going to have a house party, and he must be ready. When all was done and he was about to mount his horse he turned back and sent another message, ordering a piano.

"Why, it's great!" he said to himself, as he rode back to his office. "It's simply great to be able to do things when I need them! I never knew what fun money was before. But then I never had Margaret to spend it for, and she's worth the whole of it at once!"

The next thing he ordered was a great easy carriage with plenty of room to convey Mother Earle and her friends from the train to the house.

The days went by rapidly enough, and Margaret was so busy she had little time to wonder and worry why her mother didn't write her the long, loving, motherly good-bye letter to her little girlhood she'd expected to receive. Not until three days before the wedding did she realize she'd had only three brief, scrappy letters from her mother, and they weren't a whole page apiece. What could be the matter with Mother? She was almost on the point of panic when Gardley came and bundled her on to her horse for a ride.

Strangely enough, he directed their way through Ashland and down to the station, and it was about time for the evening train's arrival.

Gardley excused himself for a moment, saying something about an errand, and went into the station. Margaret sat on her horse, watching the oncoming train, the great connecting link between East and West, and wondered if it would bring a letter from her mother.

The train rushed to a halt, and, behold, some passengers were getting off from a private car! Margaret watched them idly, thinking more about an expected letter than about the people. Then suddenly she awoke to the fact that Gardley was greeting them. Who could they be?

There were five of them, and one of them looked like Jane! Dear Jane! She'd forgotten to write her about this hurried wedding. How different it was going to be from what she and Jane had planned for each other in their schoolday dreams! And that young man whom Gardley was shaking hands with now looked like cousin Dick! She hadn't seen him for three years, but he must look like that now. And the younger girl beside him might be cousin Emily! But, oh, who were the others? *Father!* And MOTHER!

Margaret sprang from her horse with a bound and rushed into her mother's arms. Passengers craned their necks and looked with smiles of appreciation as the train went on its way again, having dropped the private car on the side track.

Dick and Emily rode the ponies to the house, while Margaret nestled in the back seat of the carriage between her father and mother, and Jane got acquainted with Gardley in the front seat. Margaret never even noticed where they were going until the carriage turned in and stopped before the door of the new house. And Mrs. Tanner, casting behind her the checked apron she'd worn, came out to shake hands with the company and tell them supper was ready, before she returned to her deserted boardinghouse. Even Bud was staying at the new house that night, in some cooked-up capacity or other, and the men from the bunkhouse were hiding out among the trees to see Margaret's father and mother and shake hands if the opportunity offered.

Margaret's wonder and delight when she saw the house inside and knew it was hers, the tears she shed and smiles that grew almost into hysterics when she saw some of the incongruous furnishings, are past describing. Margaret was too happy to think. She rushed from one room to another. She hugged her mother and linked her arm in her father's for a walk across the long porch. She talked to Jane and Emily and Dick and then rushed out to find Gardley and thank him again. And all this time she couldn't understand how Gardley had done it, for she hadn't yet comprehended his fortune.

Gardley had invited his sisters to the wedding, not much expecting them to accept; but they telegraphed at the last minute that they would be there. They arrived an hour or so before the ceremony; gushed over Margaret; told Gardley she was a "sweet thing"; said the house was "dandy for a house party if one had plenty of servants" but thought it would be "dull in winter"; gave Margaret a diamond sunburst pin, a string of pearls and an emerald bracelet set in diamond chips; then departed immediately after the ceremony. They thought they were the chief guests, but the relief on the faces of those guests who were best beloved by both bride and groom was at once visible on their departure. Jasper Kemp drew a long breath and declared to Long Bill he was glad the air was growing pure again. Then all those old friends from the bunkhouse filed in to the tables loaded with good things, the abundant gift of the neighborhood, and sat down to the wedding supper, heartily glad the "city lady and her gals"—as Mom Wallis called them in a suppressed whisper—hadn't stayed over a train.

The wedding was in the schoolhouse, embowered in foliage and all the flowers the land afforded, decorated by the loving hands of Margaret's pupils, old and young. She was attended by the entire school marching double file before her, strewing flowers in her way. The missionary's wife played the wedding march, and the missionary assisted the bride's father with the ceremony. Margaret's dress was a simple white muslin, with a little real lace and embroidery handed down from former generations, the whole created by Margaret's mother. Even Gardley's sisters had said it was "perfectly dear." The whole neighborhood was at the wedding.

And when the bountiful wedding supper was eaten, the entire company of favored guests stood about the new piano and sang "Blest Be the Tie That Binds"—with Margaret playing for them.

Then there was a little hurry at the last, with Margaret putting on the pretty traveling dress and hat her mother had brought and kissing her mother good-bye—though happily not for long this time.

Mother and father and the rest of the home party were to wait until morning, and the missionary and his wife were to stay with them that night and see them to their car the next day.

So, waving and throwing kisses back to the others, they rode away to the station, Bud proudly driving the team from the front seat.

Gardley had arranged for a private apartment on the train, and nothing could have been more luxurious in traveling than the place where he led his bride. Bud, scuttling behind with a suitcase, looked around before he said a hurried good-bye and murmured under his breath, "Say! Wisht I was goin' all the way!"

Bud hustled off as the train got under way, and Margaret and Gardley went out to the observation platform to wave a last farewell.

The few little blurring lights of Ashland died soon in the distance, and the desert took on its vast wideness beneath a starry dome. But off in the East a purple shadow loomed, mighty and majestic, and rising slowly over its crest a great silver disk appeared, brightening as it came and pouring a silver mist over the purple peak.

"My mountain!" said Margaret softly.

And Gardley, drawing her close to him, stooped to lay his lips upon hers. "My darling!" he answered.

The Randolphs

by Isabella Alden

Chapter 1

Whatsoever

Maria Randolph shut the door of her room and turned the key. She even flushed a little as the key rasped in the lock. Then, almost aloud, she said, "Why did I do that? You'd think I was afraid someone would catch me reading the Bible. It doesn't make a bit of sense—it's nothing to be ashamed of. Besides, whose business is it what I do? And yet I have this strange feeling. If Helen walked in, as she doubtless will, it would be awkward for her to find me reading it."

She left the key turned and reached for her dust-covered Bible from the shelf.

I don't know about other young women, but Maria, this friend of mine, sensible and sharp-witted as she was, knew almost nothing about the Bible. Of course, she knew hundreds of verses in it, and even whole chapters here and there. But she had never read with understanding this book that she accepted, in theory, as the one that of all others can throw light on the mysterious future. So with both curiosity and awe she had picked up the book this evening to see what it said about the word she had chosen to make the guide for her life.

"Where are the 'whatsoevers'?" she said, still talking to herself. "I wish Tom had given me more guidelines. I couldn't have skipped all those verses back in Sunday school. The only one I remember now is the Golden Rule. That wouldn't be a bad one to practice on, I suppose—though, if people would let me alone, I'd surely do the same for them."

Her soliloquy and fruitless turning of the pages were interrupted by the twisting of the doorknob and a sharp knock.

"Why in the world is the door locked, especially so early in the evening? What are you doing?" This was her sister Helen's greeting after, exclaiming impatiently and returning the Bible to its place on the shelf, Maria had let her in.

"Are you looking for anything in particular?" was Maria's only answer to these questions.

"No, I'm not. But Father wants you, and I've been calling you and looking for you all over the house. One would think you'd grown suddenly deaf. I wouldn't think you'd shut yourself up like this until after you'd attended to him, since you've taken on yourself the sole office of nurse."

"What does he want?" was the sister's only answer.

"How should I know? He wanted you, he said. You don't think I presume to inquire into his affairs and yours, I hope? I know my place better than that."

"Don't be so ridiculous, Helen, for pity's sake!" As she ran down the hall, the hollow sound of Helen's cough followed her, and the leaven of the Golden Rule touched her conscience. "I needn't have been such a bear," she muttered. "She *is* sick a little, I suppose—perhaps more sick than we give her credit for being. But it's so disagreeable to have her ape the martyr. I must talk to Tom about it."

Mr. Randolph's wants were easily attended to. He was one of those patient, really suffering invalids who want little and endure the absence of that little as long as they can. So in less than ten minutes Maria was at her own door again. On the landing she met her brother, Tom, who stopped her.

"How about that promise, Maria?" he asked with a pensive air, as if it meant a great deal to him.

"I'm just getting around to it," she said cheerfully. "The cares of this life and the deceitfulness of poverty have held me back for some time. But I've really gone at it with diligence—that is, I took my Bible down and dusted it. Whether I get any further than that before another interruption remains to be seen. But I'm sure I'll be old and grey before I find any of them."

"I can give you some of the verses you're searching for, if you like," he said, trying to speak as lightly as she had, though with an undertone of real anxiety.

"Come in then," she said, holding the door open. "I declare, if you aren't armed for the conflict," she added, as Tom pulled a chair up to the table and produced his little pocket Bible, with slips of paper peeping out here and there.

"I've been thinking a good deal about it," he said, smiling. "I have a verse here that's just the thing for a beginning." He turned the pages rapidly, as one going over familiar ground, and presently read: " 'What thing soever I command you, observe to do it. Thou shalt not add thereto, nor diminish from it.' Now, Maria, that's the verse for you. Can you apply it the same way you do other things?"

"Why, I don't know anything about it. I'm not conscious of having any commands."

"Maria!"

"Well, I'm not. What was ever given me to do from that source?"

"You need to study the 'thou shalts' of the Bible as well as the 'whatsoevers,' " he said. "Don't you remember any of them? 'Thou shalt love the Lord thy God with all thy strength, and with all thy soul, and with all thy mind'—what about that command?"

She shook her head impatiently. "Now, Tom, don't preach. I can stand anything better than that. I didn't promise to do any such thing. I said I would be a whatsoever *worker*. Loving and hating are abstract ideas. I'm not responsible for those feelings. The precious few people I love in this world I love because I can't help it and not because I will to."

"I know you can't will it," he said earnestly, "but you can ask for the help that is never denied."

"I don't want help," said this self-sufficient young lady. "I don't feel a need for that sort of help. Don't look so horrified, Tom, as if I'd committed murder or done something dreadful. I'm as glad as could be that you see your way clear to that sort of life. It's very becoming, and I don't mean to be hateful when I say I think *you* needed it. But now, honestly, I don't think I do. I'm not the same temperament. I always liked to manage my own affairs, and I suppose I always shall. At the same time, I don't want to be a selfish old thing. I'd like to do something for somebody and do it the Bible way too. So if you can find a verse that means work, I'll do it. But the loving and all must come of itself."

Now Maria Randolph actually thought she was making a sensible and religious talk. She had no idea how she had disheartened her brother; he had thought her only careless, not self-righteous. He couldn't think of anything else to say to her. Some of her words were true; the loving, or rather the knowledge of her insufficiency, and her need of help must come of itself. No mere words could teach her this. So he remained silent, which disappointed her. She expected remonstrance, and to argue always refreshed her soul.

"Then you give it up?" he said at last, saying it inquiringly and yet with a sound in his voice as though the question were settled. It annoyed her.

"Why, no, I don't do any such thing," she said irritably. "Why do you say that? Isn't there anything in the Bible about doing? Is it all sentiment? I don't know what's to become of practical people like me if that's the case."

Tom smiled sadly. "You know so little about it, Maria, that I hardly know how to talk to you. How can you separate the feeling and the doing? You work for Father and love him. There's practical self-denying work in that, but you work because you love him, and without the love the work would be irksome to you and not acceptable to him. Don't you see?"

"That's different," said Maria, turning her head from him so he wouldn't see the look on her face.

To this Tom made no answer.

"Come," she said, smoothing the frown from her face, "let's not be cross. We have precious few evenings to spend together. It's a pity to waste them. Find a good verse for me, and I'll practice on it in a way that will astonish you."

Tom only smiled. He was grave that evening. "I don't know what verse to give you," he said. "They're all objectionable from your standpoint. I'd think the Golden Rule would answer as well as any."

"So it would. I thought of taking that before you came, but I thought it would be refreshing to have something new. I have some objection to that, too. I don't understand how it can agree with Bible teaching."

"Why?" asked Tom, surprised and wondering what could be coming next.

"Why, suppose I'd like for you to do something for me that wouldn't be right to do at all. According to the Golden Rule I must do that thing for someone else or for you."

Tom laughed. "What a muddle your mind is in, Maria. I wonder how it ever got that way. I suspect it's addressed to those people who are trying to govern their lives from a Christian standpoint. In that case it would mean, 'Whatsoever you, as a Christian, conscientiously think would be good and right and for your best good, you are bound to do that for others as far as you can.'"

"Oh, well, if it means only Christians I'm excused from trying to live by it, am I not?" She looked up at him with a mean little laugh.

"Why, yes, I suppose so, by the same one who excused you from the obligation of being a Christian. Isn't it just as I told you, Maria? These things are mixed up together. One charge rests upon and follows another, and you can no more live by the Bible and reject some of its direct teaching than you can do any other inconsistent thing."

She obstinately shook her head. "I don't believe it. I can practice on that verse, and I can do it without going through any of the mysterious processes Christians are always talking about, too. I'm going to show you."

"Very well," he said, "I'm more than willing to be shown. You can't do better than that verse, certainly, if you're after work."

Chapter 2

Practicing

The Randolph kitchen was an uncomfortable place on a warm summer morning, such as this one, on which Maria was bound by her promise to commence life on the Golden Rule system. I think you could hardly have found a harder place for her to start in or, for that matter, a harder morning.

It was warm and cloudy, damp and lifeless. I don't know a meaner morning than that. "Sticky," Maria called it.

Kitchens are not, at their best, inviting places in June weather, but there's a difference between them. Maria said theirs was one that was "different."

It wasn't possible to make a direct draft through the room, so it was just plain hot.

Helen was trying to heat dishwater, cook dinner and iron a dress. Maria was washing, and the boiler and the flat irons were in a constant push at each other.

It was this wash boiler that was to furnish the first illustration of Maria's new rule of life. As she shoved the irons out of her way she opened her mouth to speak, with these words trembling on her lips: "Helen, *do* keep these irons out of my way. What's the use of pushing them so far forward? You won't want them in an age. You aren't through with the dishes yet and won't be till noon."

Nothing special had happened for her mood to be so threatening, but it doesn't need anything special on a warm June day to make a person of Maria Randolph's temperament uncomfortable. An uncongenial atmosphere and unpleasant work are enough.

Those words were on her lips, but they were stayed. Another sentence came to the surface, that old one: "Whatsoever ye would that men should do to you, do ye even so to them." It occurred to Maria that those words were worth pondering.

"If there's anything I hate," she told herself, "it's for someone to keep poking irons out of the way when I've put them in a good place to heat. It puts me out of sorts. I don't suppose Helen likes it any better than I do, but she doesn't need them yet for hours. She probably thinks she does, and, anyway, the boiler is all right where it is."

Having thought that, she carefully restored the irons to their place and pushed the boiler a little to one side, then went back to her washing in a genial mood.

"It isn't a very lofty beginning," she said, "but it is a *beginning*. That isn't a bad rule to work by—I wonder why I haven't started before."

It didn't have the marked effect on Helen that the girl at the washtub thought it should have. Maria watched her closely when she went to the stove, and it was certainly not inspiring to discover she didn't seem to bestow a thought or glance on the position of the irons.

Maria rubbed on with a doleful face and a dim idea that it wasn't worthwhile to pay any attention to the Golden Rule unless one could be appreciated.

As for Helen, her face always looked doleful these days. She was out of sympathy with the washing and ironing being done, for Maria had determined to take in washing, in spite of strong opposition.

"We aren't reduced to beggary yet," Helen had said scornfully.

"I don't know whether we are or not," Maria would reply. "At least I don't know how soon we would be if I hadn't moral courage enough to avert it, or physical courage. I guess *that* is what's needed after all."

So she washed and ironed for the streetcar drivers as she'd planned to do. Maria took great pains with them for two reasons: one, she liked to hear Tom tell of their exclamations of delight; and the other, she had a habit of doing well what she did at all.

This new way of earning money was very helpful, but it had its disagreeable features. Some of Maria's few friends chose to ignore her because of this new development.

"Such a low thing to do," they said. "We didn't suspect that tendency in her."

And though Maria pretended to care nothing at all about such people, and though she cared as little as anyone could, it left a sore spot. Sometimes it took all her resolution and a fond remembrance of how much her father enjoyed oranges and strawberries to keep her heart in the work.

A boiler full of clothes sat on the stove, and she settled herself on the steps to rest while she waited for them, fanning her heated face violently with her apron. It vexed her to feel such weariness creeping over her so early in her day's work.

"Imagine being tired because I've rubbed a boiler full of clothes out," she grumbled to herself. "That would do for some fine lady. I need more work of some kind. I must be growing lazy."

An unusual clatter among the dishes caused her to look around.

Helen had finished baking bread and cookies and had left the dishes until the oven work was done. An army of clean dishes was piled up before her, drained and waiting for the dish towel to do its duty, and she stood by the stove attempting to reheat the water.

As she pushed the large dishpan onto the stove with one hand she clasped her side with the other and sighed.

"Whatsoever ye would," said that persistent voice in Maria's ear.

"Fiddlesticks!" she answered it. "What's so great about washing up a few dishes? What if she'd been rubbing clothes for an hour?"

"Do ye even so," said the voice.

"Well, I won't do it," Maria said, but in two minutes more she sprang up.

"I'll wipe these dishes, Helen, while I'm waiting," she said. "Do you have a side ache again this morning?"

Now it's strange when such an action as this between two sisters can awaken surprise. Nevertheless, Helen was very surprised, not at the offer to do her work, for Maria didn't shirk work, but at the tone of kindly sympathy and inquiry. Maria wasn't heartless and unsympathetic; she was simply by nature blunt and outspoken and didn't know how to express what she felt. Further, Helen had a pleasant manner of repelling sympathy of all sorts.

On this occasion she looked her surprise but said, "My side always aches. You needn't wipe the dishes. You'll be saying you had to do your work and mine too, if you do—though I don't see why the dishes are any more my work than yours, except that you choose to employ yourself on other people's work."

Maria's red cheeks grew redder.

"Am I in the habit of saying I have to do your work?" she said. "I wish you'd show a little more sense, Helen. You know as well as I do that we're poor and that I don't wash and iron clothes for Tom, Dick and Harry for my own amusement, but because I didn't know what else to do. You can see that Father would have to go without even his medicine if I didn't earn it, and the least you can do certainly is help with the housework and give me a chance to do what I can."

"Of course," Helen said, "I should remember that I'm working for my living. It's hard for me to realize I'm dependent when I remember what my own home was, but I should by this time when such pains are taken to keep the fact constantly before me."

"Oh, fiddlesticks!" was all that Maria said, and she wiped the dishes—every one of them—and put them away. But she slammed them unmercifully and thumped them to the shelves as though they were made of pewter. On the whole, she returned to her washing with a feeling that the Golden Rule was a good deal of humbug, producing hard work and no pay.

After dinner that night, when Maria was taking in the clothes, it confronted her again.

By pushing her tubs out onto the porch, shutting the door to the kitchen and working very fast and hard, she had managed to forget about it for some hours. Not until she met Tom at dinner did her promise flash over her again. It was growing to be an irksome promise. She seemed to resent the surveillance of even her own thoughts over her actions. So with a frown she gave up her pie to Grace because there wasn't enough to go around—not that pie was a particular favorite of hers or that it ever made much difference to her what she ate or didn't eat, but because it was so "poky" to have to think about such a silly little matter as that.

"I'm all mixed up," she said to herself. "I don't want her to give her pie up to me—I'd as soon she'd eat it for herself. If people would only be good-natured and accommodating, they might eat all the pie there is in the world, and I would eat chips."

Then she laughed at the still greater confusion of her ideas. Here she was requiring people to be good-natured. According to that tiresome precept, she should be so herself, and she never felt in worse humor in her life. So she slipped from the table as soon as she could and went back to the wash.

The shape her mentor took on the clothesline was a shirt belonging to Dick Norton, a streetcar driver. What a shirt it was to be sure! Patched and torn again, and buttonless and frayed at the edges.

"Was it worthwhile to pay money to get such a shirt as that washed?" she said, giving it an unnecessarily hard twitch to get it down. Then she paused in dismay. Suppose she were Dick Norton and had only this shirt and one other in the world—what a blessed thing it would be if someone mended it neatly and restored the missing buttons! Well, then, "Whatsoever ye would that men should do to you, do ye even so to them."

"But, dear me!" she said irritably. "Where would this thing lead to? I can't mend shirts for all creation. I suppose they would all like some new shirts. I'm sure I would if I were in their place. According to Tom's notion, I should set about making some right away."

This, of course, was only a vent for her vexation, for she knew very well that even the Golden Rule didn't reach beyond the reasonable possibilities of a person's life. It ended, however, in her sitting down to mend the old shirt, while the irons heated and Helen stirred gingerbread for tea.

"Do you mend old clothes for a living, as well as wash them?" that lady asked, with a contemptuous glance at the shirt.

Maria laughed. The oddness of her position was helping make her good-natured.

"No," she said, "I'm doing this for the love of it, or the pity of it. Did you ever see such a forlorn shirt for a man to wear? I keep saying, 'What if it were Tom's?'"

Helen sniffed. "How good you are becoming! Which of those worthy car drivers does that garment belong to? I should be congratulated on my sister's brilliant prospects."

Her remark was too foolish and pointless to disturb Maria. She only laughed.

"This shirt is Dick Norton's, and he's a good-natured fellow who takes Tom's place whenever he can. I owe him a good turn on that account," she said, as she threaded her needle and set to work with energy. "Besides, Helen, there's no telling what may grow out of it. He has sharp, bright eyes. I shouldn't wonder if he becomes a rich man someday. Then what mightn't he give me for mending his shirt? You see I'm looking out for the future. Nothing like being prudent."

Helen Monroe stirred violently at her gingerbread for some minutes without speaking. Then she said, with one of her heavy sighs, "It's true there's no telling what strange changes may come. No one should realize it more than I.

What do you suppose poor Horace would say if he could see me now?"

Any reference to "poor Horace" always put Maria in ill-humor. "It's so dreadful to listen to her and reflect that perhaps everything might have been different if she'd done right." This the younger sister would say to Tom when he was exhorting her to patience. On this occasion she with difficulty kept silence and split one of Dick's few buttons with her needle in the effort.

The next episode was a ring at the doorbell.

"My patience!" Helen said. "Who can that be so early in the afternoon? It isn't time for the doctor. Maria, you'll have to go. I look like a fright."

"I!" said Maria, in real dismay. "Why, Helen, do you remember that I'm washing? I'm sure, if you rub the flour from your face and untie your apron, you'll look well enough. But I'm really not presentable."

"Well, then, they'll have to ring, whoever they are." This Mrs. Monroe said in a very decided tone. "If you persist in doing washing as late in the week as Thursday, when you might be dressed and ready to receive company, I think you should take the consequences. It's different with me. I have to bake when we get out of bread, whether it's the first of the week or the last. But I'm certainly not going to the door. Not if they ring all night," she added, as another violent peal showed the anxiety of somebody to enter.

The discussion ended, as they generally did, in Maria unpinning her dress and letting it down and drawing down her sleeves.

But she said as she closed the kitchen door, "You're the most unselfish and accommodating sister that ever was born." In the hall she added, "There! That was after the Golden Rule pattern, I'm sure. People like to be complimented. How tired I am of that verse. I wonder how Tom has lived up to it today. I hope he hasn't had such a horrid time as I have."

There was a good deal of bustle in the hall and banging of trunks and eager talking. It reached even the distant kitchen.

"Who can have come?" asked Helen. "Dear me! I hope no company. Think of having to cook for company." Then, as the voices were evidently nearing the kitchen, she slipped into the pantry and shut the door.

Chapter 3

Subsoiling

Where is she?" said a new voice in the kitchen.

Helen, in the pantry, was half pleased, half annoyed and wholly surprised to recognize the voice of her sister Ermina. She came out at once.

Mrs. Ermina Harper had been gone from home only a few months, but the instant Helen turned the knob of the pantry door and glimpsed her through the crack she felt a change in her.

Mrs. Harper wore her hair in a fashion new to Helen's secluded life and quite becoming to her. She wore a traveling dress of rich, soft grey, with a faint pinkish tinge to it that suited her complexion precisely. It was more simply made than Helen Monroe had ever made her dresses. But every fold was exactly on the bias, and every plait was exactly as large as the plait next to it, and over the whole garment hovered that mysterious, unmistakable something that marks the well-dressed lady. But the change didn't consist in all these things alone. Helen didn't know what it was and, as I said, *felt* rather than saw it.

"Where in the world did *you* come from?" Helen asked her sister. "I thought you were to be gone for a century or so and do no end of wonderful traveling before we had the honor of seeing you again."

Ermina laughed. "We were to," she said pleasantly, "but Mr. Harper had a telegram, or a series of them, that changed many of his plans. We had to come to New York, and since I was hungering for a sight of home, we ran up here. Maria, can't I really see Father until after tea? It seems a long time to wait."

"I don't think you should," Maria began, with a troubled expression. "You see he doesn't expect you, and a little excitement before he has his tea is apt to leave him with—"

"What nonsense!" interrupted Helen. "You make a perfect muff of Father and would like to do so of the rest of us. It's unlikely that seeing Ermina will injure him. She's his daughter as well as you. Come on, Ermina—I'll take you to him."

Ermina stood near her and put her arm around her waist. "Perhaps it'll be better to wait after all," she said pleasantly, "until I have a good look at all your faces. How delightful that gingerbread smells—I'm glad you hit upon this particular afternoon to make it. Mr. Harper is fond of it, and I remember you used to be quite good at it."

Again that sense of a peculiar change in Ermina came to her sister and kept her silent.

They had a merry tea. Tom and Grace, next to the youngest of the four sisters, came in as they were sitting down. Maria's heart glowed with pleasure and pride to see the cordial greeting the rich brother-in-law gave the car driver. It was a sore spot in Maria's heart that this young, handsome brother seemed pinned down to a life that effectually cut him off from society and companionship. It was strange how every avenue to better employment seemed to be closed. Tom laughed about it and made cheerful remarks about the improvements he would have when he rose to the position of stockholder in the company. But Maria couldn't laugh; she oftener cried because she coveted greater things for this young brother.

Mr. Harper followed Tom into the little sitting room after tea, while Helen went with Ermina to the bedroom where her father sat propped in the easy chair awaiting her, with glowing spots on either cheek that told how wise Maria's precaution had been.

"Well, sir, it isn't particularly congenial business, I suppose?" said the brother-in-law.

"Not remarkably so," Tom answered, with his usual laugh. He meant to be a cheerful martyr at least. "But, after all, I owe it a debt of gratitude. These are hard times, you know, and I'd have had to depend on charity except for this position. I've tried in various ways to better myself and finally concluded I'm very much to be envied. At least I don't have to be idle."

"That's the true view of life," Mr. Harper said. "Then what about all the other matters? Do you find leisure to do service for the other Master?"

"Not leisure," Tom said, smiling, "at least not much of it. But some of His work I find can be done, even while I'm busy about my own. Yes, I'm trying. I've been helped by this: 'Whatsoever ye do, do all to the glory of God.' It's great that even a streetcar driver can drive for the glory of God."

Mr. Harper turned and looked at his young brother-in-law, with added interest in his voice, not unmingled with respect. "I should think it would help, but how do you find you can do this thing to His glory? I understand you in a general way, but I'm always interested in details."

"They're small ways, of course, but I can better illustrate what I mean by giving you an example. Do you know we're required to stop at steam-car crossings and wait while the conductor sights the track for a coming train? Well, Dick Norton is a fellow driver of mine; he was on my car the other evening, going down to meet his own at the junction. Our conductor was off duty long enough for supper, and it fell to me to do his work.

" 'Drive on, Tom,' Dick said as we neared the crossing. 'I'm dead certain there's no train up for the next ten minutes.'

" 'It's contrary to one of my mottoes,' I said. Of course he was curious to know what motto could apply to car driving, and I quoted to him, 'Whatsoever ye do, do it heartily, as unto the Lord, and not unto men.' Now what I mean is, I take it that God permits all faithful service to be for His glory, and

He gave me a chance to let Dick Norton know it. The poor fellow has had few chances of knowing anything about these matters."

Maria was clearing the supper table. It had been the last smart rap that Golden Rule had given her, to let Helen go to the father's room with Ermina while she cleared the table. She heard the illustration and mused over it as she brushed the crumbs from the cloth.

"His idea of 'whatsoever' is higher than mine," she said gravely.

Then she wondered dimly if living by that word made Mr. Harper unlike any man she ever saw before and whether it was the same influence that was making the "change" in Ermina which she, too, had noticed.

Meanwhile the talk went on in the sitting room. "Is there a Young Men's Christian Association here?" Mr. Harper asked. "You'll think it strange after I stayed here so long that I don't know without asking. I was only a temporary visitor, though, and was so engrossed with other business responsibilities and trusts that weighed heavily on me that I had to break away from all my usual work and devote myself to business."

"Well, there is, and there isn't," said Tom. "At least that's the way it seems to me. They used to have a flourishing group here and did much good, they tell me. But it almost died some years ago. In my opinion it would have been better if it had. We might have made a fresh start and accomplished something."

"You'll have to revive the old institution."

Tom shrugged his shoulders. "That's hard to do," he said. "I've heard many men say it's easier to build a new house than repair the old one."

"Still it *can* be done," the brother-in-law said. "What do you need most to rebuild?"

"A head," Tom said promptly. "No one seems willing to take the lead in anything. The former president has moved away, and the vice-president died two years ago. The association is virtually dead but won't believe it is. Now there just doesn't seem to be anyone to organize things again."

"The best way might be to call it dead and move for a new creature instead of a resurrection," Mr. Harper said. "Still those things are sometimes hard to do. Why don't you make yourself its head?"

Tom flushed deeply and spoke with difficulty. "Do you remember the three years of horror I put my family through?"

"Yes, I remember. And do you think anyone knows more surely the temptations young men face and the need of helping them?"

This was a new phase of the subject. The young man looked thoughtful and after a moment spoke, more to himself than in answer. "There's truth in that. I *do* feel their need of help, and I feel anxious to help them. But how to do it is the question."

"I'll tell you what I would do," Mr. Harper said, after a moment of silence. Rising and taking a seat near Tom and leaning one elbow on the table, he bent over toward him, speaking earnestly. "I would have an association between myself and the Master. Elect Him president and put yourself in constant communication with Him to follow out His plans. As you have the opportunity to call in other subordinates, do so, and that will give you a chance to work faster. But don't wait for an association, for while they're preparing to organize, Satan is at work. He has that advantage over Christians—his working forces are never disorganized."

Tom's face was glowing again, this time from eager interest in the thought before him.

"You mean," he said, "that I'm to be on the alert in every direction to help others, especially young men—that I'm to act as if I'm a Christian association and carry out their plans as far as possible, taking such helpers as I can get and for my leader God Himself. Is that what you mean?"

"That's what I mean, now that you've said it," Mr. Harper said, with a quiet smile. "You've gone deeper into the thought than I had and made it a better thought. You'll be able to carry it out, I'm certain."

"I'll certainly try," this young man said with a quiet air.

Mr. Harper had a way of suddenly turning from a subject when he'd said just the words he wanted said, and now, changing his tone entirely, he asked, "How's the cause against liquor prospering in this part of the vineyard?"

A shadow fell over Tom's face. "It isn't. It's given over to the other side. Nothing is doing for it, and everything against."

"Yet the Lord still has a cause, I think."

It was uttered quietly. But it gave Tom that same start and flush and brought to him a strange new sense of partnership—the remembrance that he was supposed in all these things to be working *with* the Lord. He needed just this word of encouragement—a reminder rather than a revelation. Yet it came to him with all the freshness of the latter word. He felt sometimes sad and alone, having no sympathy, at least among the people he had to mingle with daily. What a sudden glow it brought to his heart to realize that the Lord of heaven and earth was looking on, helping and interested in the thought that oppressed him! Surely he could afford to be alone, as far as human helpers were concerned. It suggested another thought, that to work against *that* force was surely to fail in the end. And, apart from every other consideration, who wants to fail?

Thinking these thoughts he was still again, until Mr. Harper asked another question. "What's the greatest obstacle in the way of work in that direction?"

Again the answer was prompt: "Consecrated purses."

Mr. Harper was startled. He had talked this subject over with many people. He had asked this question often before. He had received various answers: prejudice—indifference—wrong methods—and many another hovering around the same idea, but never once this clear, ringing sentence, two words: "Consecrated purses."

Mr. Harper sat up straight and asked Tom what he meant.

"Why, I mean this. The great temptation, of course, is rum, and it is everywhere in this city. No matter how much you might desire it, you couldn't find a hotel to stop at where liquor isn't sold. If you had my job, you'd see and hear the women and children crying and begging their men, who are enraged by alcohol, to give it up and stay home."

"Is that so?" Mr. Harper said, in astonishment.

"It is—and not only that, but the large boardinghouses, where most of the working men who are without homes have to gather, have side tables where they retail beer and whiskey. Temptation is spread on every hand, not only for those who want it fearfully because of an already formed taste, but for those who, because of no better place to spend their leisure time, are compelled to look on until they too follow the example."

"And your remedy is?" Mr. Harper asked, with a respectful tone in his voice. He was learning something from his young brother-in-law.

"Why, if I had the resources, I would have a hotel that didn't make its money by damaging lives. And it wouldn't be one of those seventh-rate affairs you find in some of our large cities. I'd fight with Satan's own weapons—if they do really belong to him. I mean I would have the carpets and mirrors and sofas and brilliant gaslights and the glitter of silver, everything else that is used to entice and entrap. But when you talk to men who oppose liquor they sigh and say: 'But that would take an immense amount of money.' So I say, what we need most is consecrated purses."

To this eager outburst of words Mr. Harper answered nothing. He arose and started walking slowly up and down the room, intent apparently on studying the different shades in the carpet.

Tom, watching him curiously, concluded he was disturbed by some shadowed memory the talk had called forth. But the next question was so foreign to anything that had been said or could have been suggested that he was puzzled.

"By the way, how is Peter Armstrong?"

"Peter's working away as faithfully as ever and puzzling away over the mistakes and labors of his namesake in the Bible. He's the oddest and the best fellow that ever lived." And Tom in his heart said: "Whatever put him into your mind at this moment?"

Back and forth paced Mr. Harper through the little room several times more. Then he turned and said in a quiet voice, "Well, suppose we go in and see the dear father."

Chapter 4

Planning a Siege

Mr. Harper was unusually quiet and grave during the evening. Several times his wife's eyes rested on him anxiously, and she speculated whether the talk with Tom she'd caught a few words of had anything to do with his somber mood. She was greatly troubled about that brother. He had survived those dark years and now stepped upon the sure foundation. But it was a life full to the brim with temptation. Now, as she sat listening to the talk around her and watching the deepening gravity of her husband's face, she worked herself into a fever of anxiety and fear.

The door had scarcely closed upon them, in the privacy of their own room, before she said eagerly, "What is it? I've been so worried all evening."

Mr. Harper turned to her in surprise. "Worried, my dear! I thought this was a supremely happy evening to you. What has worried you?"

"It's your face," she said, with a little laugh. "It's looked sad and anxious and thoughtful and puzzled, all at once. I'm sure something's wrong with Tom. Will you tell me exactly what it is?"

He answered her with promptness, but still with gravity. "I believe in my heart that you may dismiss all fears regarding Tom, now and forever. The Lord Himself has put a shield around him that can't be moved. He's changed and grown. His Christian development makes me feel what can be attained and what I've been losing."

Mrs. Harper gave a half-amused laugh. It was such a strange idea that anyone could have developed to a degree that would startle her husband, who seemed to be walking with long strides on the upward journey.

"Then what can be the matter?" she asked, returning to the subject of his anxiety. "I know you've been troubled all evening. Is it Father's state?"

"I don't think I've been troubled exactly, except about details," he said, sitting down beside her. "But I've been busy thinking, and some of the plans need your judgment. They've matured rapidly, for most of them have sprung from your brother's words, spoken this evening. Let me tell you about our talk."

Maria was in the kitchen sprinkling and folding clothes for tomorrow's ironing, and Tom was with her. This half hour before bedtime, when the rest of the household had separated and there were little last things to do, was this brother and sister's special time. Tom was building a scientific fire that would snap and sputter and burn vividly the instant the morning match was touched to it. Nobody but Maria knew what a comfort that carefully laid building of chips and papers was to her. She deserved a scolding because never once did she say such a simple sentence as this: "Tom, that fire arranged overnight is a great help to me." It would have been a pleasant sound to Tom's ears. But being a sensible fellow he knew it must be a help to her, so he carefully did it every evening.

"Tom," said Maria, rolling Dick Norton's shirt into a tight little knot and patting it firmly, "do you like him as well as you used to?" She didn't mean Dick Norton, and Tom knew she didn't.

"Yes," he said, pausing in his work of breaking a pine stick in two and speaking slowly. "Yes, I like him very much. I think he's a fine man." This last part of the sentence came quick and firm, accompanied by a snapping of the pine stick.

"What is hiding behind that answer?" Maria asked, with a little laugh in which Tom joined.

"Nothing," he said. "Only somehow I feel he's rather abrupt. He goes suddenly from one pole to another in conversation. I tell him an answer to a question, that seems interesting to me, and he answers it by asking another question that has no more to do with the subject at hand than this stick has to do with the moon. It gives a fellow a sort of feeling that he's simply talking with you to pass the time away or because he thinks he must."

"I hate such talking," Maria said, in sympathy with her beloved brother and indignant that anyone shouldn't enjoy a talk with *him*.

"But he's splendid for all that," Tom said quickly. "Of course he and I can't be expected to have many topics in common. Our lives are very different." And Tom snapped another kindling, in time to cover a bit of a sigh.

About this time Ermina said to her husband: "Oh, what a splendid thought! What a man you are to plan and do. Did you really never think of this until you talked with Tom tonight?"

The three sisters spent a quiet day together. Grace went as usual to the store, where she worked behind the ribbon and lace counter, and Maria devoted herself to her ironing, interrupted by constant runnings back and forth to care for her father. Ermina's arrival had broken her practice of the Golden Rule—much to her relief, it must be confessed. Still, in a general way, she tried not to go directly against its teachings; and owing partly to that, and partly to Ermina's presence and subduing influence, Helen and her youngest sister had fewer encounters than usual.

As for Mr. Harper, he seemed suddenly to have become a man of business, even though he had boasted only the evening before that he came as a guest, with nothing earthly to do for two days but visit. He went out immediately after breakfast, and the noon meal was waiting when he returned. He waited for a few minutes' talk with the invalid, then rushed away again. Not until after tea did he sit down as one who had accomplished his work, whatever it was, and was ready for talk.

"Well, sir," he said, sitting beside Tom in the same attitude he'd taken the evening before and beginning the conversation as if they'd been interrupted only ten minutes, "are you ready to beard the lion in his den?"

"What shape does he assume?" Tom asked, laughing, without the remotest idea what his brother-in-law meant.

"It isn't a good simile. 'Fighting Satan with his own weapons,' I think you called it—that's better. Well, now, you gave me a new idea yesterday or started me on a new train of thought, and I've been following it out a little today. Now I want to have a business talk with you. What are your plans?'

Tom's face flushed. "To work tomorrow just as I have today—to the best of my abilities do what I can find to do," he said earnestly.

"But in the future?"

"I've given up the future. I don't mean I'm a lonely man without a thought or hope in life and am only engaged in waiting for the end." Tom spoke laughingly, then instantly sobered. "I mean simply that I tried planning. I made a road and meant to walk in it step by step, precisely as I had it marked out, and if ever a fellow's way was hedged, so that he couldn't turn to the right or the left, mine was. Not startling, solemnizing walls either, but miserable little thorn hedges, so that it was impossible to get over them, and yet I seemed bound to scratch myself by trying. Instead of understanding it I fought it and was very near an eternal shipwreck. You know the awful shadow that stretched around me just in time to save me." The young man's voice grew serious, as it always did when he alluded to the one dark chapter of his life. "So now I'm afraid of plans. I want to live for today. I'm not unmindful of tomorrow, and I'm not indifferent as to what it will bring. I'm only trying to be trustful."

"I understand," Mr. Harper said, and he felt again that he was talking to a man, not a boy. "But now, in keeping with that idea, is of course a certain reverent intention, with the constant reservation, 'if God wills.' Does that sort of plan include a thorough classical education?"

"No, sir."

"You're very positive in your plans, after all," Mr. Harper said, smiling.

"Well," said Tom with earnestness, "I think I'm right, and I'll try to make my position clear. That was one of my hedges I was determined to climb—not so much for the love of books as for a certain ambition I had that I'm convinced now wasn't wise, at least for me. My views have changed. I should never be a hard student for the love of study. If I were to choose a profession *now* it would be the ministry, and I don't feel that I'm specially called to that work. Instead, I feel an eager calling to something else. Besides, I don't have the time to get the necessary education. My father and sisters need my help. I'm not in a position now to give them help, but I'm here with them and am in a degree to be relied upon. While I'm doing the best I can for today, there's always a hope that the 'tomorrow' will come. In short, I feel now an earnest desire to work in the church, not as a professional worker, but as a layman. It seems to me we need strength in that direction."

"Amen!" said Mr. Harper. "But, my brother, let me ask you, is that what you mean, or rather is it *all* you mean when you speak of feeling an eager calling to something else?"

"No," said Tom, his face grave and his eyes glowing, "I feel a special grudge against one form of Satan. I have a special desire to fight that form whenever and wherever I can, and with whatever weapons I can get hold of."

"And Satan to you means the despair and devastation left by alcohol?"

"Yes, sir."

"Now we've reached our point," Mr. Harper said, rising and walking thoughtfully up and down the room. "The stronger weapons you have, of course, the better you can fight, and you think the special need now is a consecrated purse. I believe you're right. Now the question is, are we ready for work? Do you know the Burton House?"

"Yes, sir."

"Is the locality a good one for a first-class hotel?"

"I don't think a better one could be found, and it's elegantly fitted up."

"Do you know there's a trouble—a mortgage—a coming change of hands?'

"I didn't know that."

"It is. I heard of it the other day—quite by accident, we could say—and went to see about it today. It's a good chance, and everything is all right—or all wrong—with the owner. He needs money, and there's to be a sale—public, it was to have been. I stopped that. We'll have a hotel, I believe, that will be an influence for good."

Tom arose and came over to his brother-in-law, his face beaming with joy.

"There couldn't be a better place," he said eagerly, "and this is just the time for an enterprise like this. I think it'll be the grandest thing ever done for the cause. But where will you find the man? I wouldn't know where to look for him."

"I do," Mr. Harper said quietly.

"Do you? Have you planned that part already? How fast you work! Where is he to be found?"

He was very eager. Mr. Harper had never seen him so excited. Evidently his whole heart was enlisted in this enterprise. He watched his eager face a moment with a smile of satisfaction on his own before he answered, and his answer when it came was very quiet and matter-of-fact.

"I think it's just the thing for you to take hold of. The wonder is that with all my thinking I've never developed anything like it."

Tom hadn't been prepared for this conclusion. He was dumbfounded. He stood like a statue looking at the quiet gentleman before him. When at last he spoke it was in a bewildered voice.

"I don't think I understand. Do you think I would do for clerk in such an establishment? The business, you know, is utterly new to me, but then my heart would be in it. I think I might do it. But such a thing hadn't occurred to me."

"I mean nothing of the kind, my brother." Mr. Harper said those words tenderly, perhaps in part because he had loved and lost a brother in his youth. "Doubtless a clerk will be needed, and a name flashed across my mind last evening, someone I thought might be trained to serve in that capacity. But what I'm telling you is, that if you'll go into this thing with all your soul and see what you can work out for His glory, why, the building and the funds to back it to the extent of my ability shall be at your disposal. Now what do you say?"

Tom turned suddenly from him and walked to the window in silence. Then he came back, and his voice, instead of a tremble, held a ring of triumph.

"It's an effort to which I'll consecrate my life. I believe God will bless it. I hadn't hoped to see anything so grand for years and years, but I believe I can do it."

"I believe you can," Mr. Harper said, in as earnest a voice as the young man's had been. "At least it's an object worth trying for. We'll try with all our hearts."

At this point a thought, which generally is supposed to be uppermost in business transactions, seemed to cross Tom's brain.

"Do you suppose such an effort can be made to pay its way?" A touch of doubt and anxiety was in his voice.

"No," said Mr. Harper, "and you're not to trammel your ideas and effort with that consideration. Part of its expenses the thing will doubtless pay, and for the rest, don't you remember those purses you so unmercifully stormed last evening? I have one of them, please remember, and it hasn't been consecrated to this object as it should have been, and as I thought it was."

The ready blood mounted in waves to Tom's forehead.

"I didn't know—I mean, I didn't think of such a thing," he began in embarrassment. "Indeed I didn't think of you at all."

"Do you suppose I think you did?" he said. "The arrow was no less sharp because it found its mark without being aimed. I thank you for it. It's the truth. My dear brother, you and I are *brethren*."

And then the two men shook hands heartily, silently, and each had a new realization of the meaning of that word.

Chapter 5

Getting Ready

I t was curious to see how the various members of the family received the news of the projected enterprise. Each one astonished Tom.

Helen, who he thought would be gratified at what she would consider a rise in fortune, or at least occupation, was scornfully indifferent, made certain sharp and sarcastic remarks about its being a place of "temptation for a reformed person" and then lapsed into sarcastic silence. If you've ever learned how exquisitely sarcastic a certain sort of silence can be, you're fortunate.

Grace was jubilant with an ecstatic delight that bewildered Tom. He didn't know his sister Grace very well; she puzzled him. At first he judged it to be the delight which springs from having something new to enter into and enjoy. But her face had an exalted look as of one who reached beyond this, and the voice in which she said, "What a wonderful work you can do," led him to wonder whether there wasn't more to Grace than a good-natured girl who sold laces at McAllister's.

Maria surprised and disappointed him the most. She was unaffectedly dismayed. Where he had looked for utmost sympathy and encouragement he met only a look of amazement.

"You don't like it?" he said, feeling more disappointed than he liked to show.

"No, I don't." Maria was as outspoken as ever. "It's horrid business. I think you're above it."

"It's so much lower than streetcar driving—I don't wonder you're disturbed!" Of course Helen said this.

And Maria was quick with her answer: "Yes, it is. Streetcar driving is only a decent employment for a few days, while he's looking for his place. But hotel keeping has to be done for a lifetime if one accomplishes anything, and I think it's the smallest and meanest kind of business. I'd rather sell tape and codfish for a living."

"But, Maria," Tom said, and his lip almost quivered, so great was his surprise and pain, "this is to be a different kind of hotel from any you're acquainted with. I'm going to do what I've longed to do, the kind of work you and I have talked over together."

"Humph!" said Maria. She kicked a stick of wood impatiently out of her way and went abruptly to the kitchen, where she rattled dishes and pans and knives until the sound of the voices in the sitting room were lost to her.

You'll have to forgive the poor girl; she had expended a great heart on this brother. She thought him equal to reaching any heights of learning and position, and she had so hoped he would choose work worthy of him. She couldn't help looking upon this as a downfall.

Of all the family Tom dreaded most to tell his father. He began to have a dim idea of what that father's hopes had been in regard to him and how bitter his disappointments must have been. This seemed like another blow. He felt this even more, now that he understood how Maria, his friend and helper, looked upon it. But the father must be told. Tom's respect for him wouldn't allow him to enter upon any plans until he'd consulted, or at least informed, him.

He chose an evening when something kept both Helen and Maria in the kitchen, and Grace was doing extra duty at McAllister's. He sat for half an hour answering questions mechanically and imparting news in an abstracted manner, trying meanwhile to plan a way of telling the special news that would have the least uncomfortable effect on his father. He succeeded as well as people usually do in such efforts, and suddenly abandoning all attempt at care he plunged into the midst of the subject.

"Father, I'm about to desert the cars and try a new way of life."

His father was all attention and showed by the sudden glow of his cheek that this was a subject having special interest for him.

Tom hurried on: "I have a chance at last, and one very different from what I expected. I'm going to try my hand at keeping a hotel."

Mr. Randolph turned on his pillow, and the flush was very marked. "What do you mean?"

"I mean that Mr. Harper has given me a chance to try a work I never anticipated. He's offered to set me up in a first-class hotel, and I'm going to fight the enemy in that way with all the wisdom God will give me."

The young man drew in his breath quickly as he finished this sentence and prepared for an argument. It was natural that his father should feel disappointed; he couldn't be expected to look at this thing as Mr. Harper did and as he himself looked at it.

He wasn't prepared for the sudden husking of voice and trembling of lip with which his father murmured, evidently not speaking to him: "Mine eyes have seen thy salvation."

"Sir," said Tom, rising in fright and anxiety. His father's mind must be wandering, but the smile that met him was strong and bright.

"You can't understand how much I feel this," he said eagerly. "You're too young, and you don't know that when you were a little boy in your cradle I used to pray for you every night. I used to spend an hour with God asking my heart's desire for you. And it wasn't for you to be rich or wise or even successful, as men count success, but that you should be to your heart's core a sober, prayerful man, strong and brave, working with all your might to save souls from the sin that so besets them. I seem to see what you can do with this chance. It's greater than I hoped for; indeed it's greater than I ever thought of, which is just how the Lord delights to answer prayer. God bless you."

He raised himself on one elbow. Tom had never seen his eyes shine as they did.

"Shut the door," he said, "and I'll tell you something you never knew in your life and that I never meant to tell you. Your mother didn't wish it. But I believe the time has come. It will help you in your work, and it will fall like a benediction on you."

Awed and wondering, Tom went forward and closed the door joining the sitting room, not a little anxious meanwhile as to the effect of this unusual excitement. But his father's voice was still strong and well controlled.

"I stood on the very edge of the chasm," he said. "Indeed, I was *over* the edge. 'My steps were almost gone,' and your mother saved me. She clung to me and wouldn't let me be lost, even though I was determined to go. She held on with an iron grasp, and through God she conquered."

The knob turned suddenly in the door, and Maria stood before them.

"You're a lovely nurse," was her comment, as she glanced from Tom's astonished, earnest face to the eager invalid with the glow on his cheek and the unusual fire in his eye. "I thought I told you to be quiet and amusing. Is that the way you manage when you're left in charge?"

"Don't scold him," the father said with a smile and in his usual quiet, kind voice. "It's all right. No harm has been done. He's given me more helpful medicine than I've had for many days, and I've helped him if I'm not mistaken. Isn't it so, my boy?"

"Aye, you have," Tom said, and Maria turned and looked curiously at him because there was such a ring in his voice.

"I'll never forget it," he said again, and then he went away to think his astonished thoughts.

His father, the quiet, grave, controlled, prayerful man, as he'd always known him—he a drunkard! That must have been what he meant. Could anything be more astonishing than that? Yes, one thing surprised him even more—that his gentle little doll-mother had ever held anyone from doing anything they chose to do, much less anyone with such a strong nature as his father possessed. He couldn't conceive of her as having any will or wish outside of his; and yet this revelation explained many things that had always seemed strange. He could understand now the love that had seemed to have a touch of idolatry in it and to be mingled at the same time with a strange feeling of almost reverence. He could understand, as he had never before, the anxious, troubled sigh and the half-whispered "If your mother were only here" he had heard in times of trial or perplexity. The sweet, tender little woman who seemed made to be loved and petted and cared for had possibilities about her, it seemed, of which he'd never dreamed—had strength born of God and had used it valiantly.

How he loved his mother as he thought of all this. How wonderful of her to conceal all that dark past from her children and accord to her husband a deferential respect, mingled with her love, that her children had insensibly copied. Then his mother would be glad of this work he'd taken up? He understood what his father meant by saying, "It will fall like a benediction on you." It had—a benediction from the dear dead mother. Tom was stronger than before. He was better fitted for his work.

Meanwhile the work of fitting up the old Burton House went on briskly. Mr. Harper made a hurried journey to New York and planned his business there for a two weeks' absence. Then he gave himself up to the new work with energy—both as to time and to purse. When an energetic man enters into a project with an unlimited command of both of these, great things can be accomplished.

These were two comfortable weeks for the girls at home. Ermina, with her happy, satisfied face, was a blessing.

The comforts and luxuries that found their way into the invalid's room weren't to be forgotten either by the father or the grateful youngest daughter. Maria had "given the Golden Rule a vacation," as she expressed it to Tom, "because" she was in too "much of a hurry to think of such minor matters." Yet, from various unselfish acts and words, he imagined that the spirit still lingered about her.

Another comfort during these days was appreciated by Maria more than she would have liked the others to know. Mr. Harper, finding he was to be present in the family for several weeks, sought the young housekeeper out one evening and in a businesslike manner arranged for board during his stay.

"It isn't the usual custom," said Maria, with dignity and heightened color, "for a son-in-law to pay board for himself and his wife during a visit to the old home. At least, it's a custom I never heard of."

Mr. Harper had studied the character he was dealing with. He turned toward her with a genial smile and said frankly, "My good sister, I think you and I understand each other. We're working together for the dear father's comfort. He's as dear to my wife as he is to you. She has as much a duty to perform in regard to him as you have. But since we're hurried, business people and take a common-sense view of life and waste no time in sentimentality, the easiest way is to settle on a reasonable price for board and say no more about it."

Maria turned on him a pair of laughing eyes, out of which the flash had departed, and said brightly, "That's a soothing way of putting it and a truthful one perhaps, except the 'reasonable price.'" She had caught sight of the figure on the bill he was folding for her. "Even Ermina's old boarding mistress, Mrs. Skimp, never dreamed of such an extravagant rate. But I like your frankness, and under the circumstances my assumption of dignity was absurd. We're poor, and since you've known it all the time I don't suppose you'd think any more of us if we tried to pretend we could afford to have company as well as not."

Maria pocketed the large bill with good grace. It was so pleasant to be talked to sensibly without any shamming. That the money was given as payment for value received soothed a temperament like hers, and she felt justified in providing the best for her boarders that the market afforded.

One other episode during these weeks of preparation was curious as to the results it produced in this scheme.

"Oh, for the hand of a skillful woman here!" Tom had exclaimed as he arranged and rearranged the table of a certain room in the new house—a room he wanted to be home-like. "Things will look stiff here in spite of my efforts to the contrary. Men don't have the knack, and that's the whole of it."

Mr. Harper, quite thoughtful, presently remarked: "Your sister Helen has a happy talent among books and furniture. I used to notice that in her own home she seemed to give speechless things a sort of individuality. How would it do to get her interested here?"

"It wouldn't do at all," Tom said promptly. "Helen can't be trusted with money. Her tastes are royal, and her purse should be too. She has no more idea of economy than if she'd revelled in wealth all her life. Why, she could spend a fortune on what she could get into this room."

"I didn't mean to give her command over supplies but over arranging what we already have. With a touch or two she could take away the stiffness you deplore."

"I don't think I'd like it," the young man said decidedly. "Helen and I don't relate well—never did. It would be almost impossible for us to work together harmoniously. In fact, I doubt whether she would enjoy it all."

"But the question is, could it help her?"

"Help her?" repeated Tom. This time his manner wasn't positive at all, but hesitating and surprised. The question seemed to suggest a new idea.

"Yes—help her out of herself—give her an interest in something going on around her."

Tom looked amazed. "Do you think there's special need of exertion on her account?"

"Well, of course I can't tell. But it seems sad to me to see a person interested only in her own sorrows and trials. I'd like to rouse her to thinking of the trials of the world at large."

Tom finished arranging the table in silence; the new thought wasn't pleasant. The enterprise he'd embarked upon was glorified to him. He didn't like the idea of clouds coming in between, and he couldn't think of Helen as anything but a cloud. Besides, he had envisioned happy evenings with Maria in work like this; she would enter into it with zest. True, she hadn't shown any as yet; she hadn't gotten over the first disappointment. But after a while, when she saw what he was doing, or trying to do, she would be enthusiastic in her help. Could he bear to forestall her place? Besides, Helen would have nothing to do with it. And then he smiled at his own inconsistency; if this were really the case, then he had nothing to worry about.

"What do you suppose is your brother-in-law's last idea?" he said to Maria as they met in the evening on their way upstairs.

"I'd as soon think of trying to tell the name of the next planet to be discovered," Maria said, partly in sarcasm and partly in satisfaction over a man who had ideas and worked them out.

"Well, he more than hinted that I should try to interest Helen in this new project and try to get her out of herself."

"How does he propose for you to accomplish that interesting exploit?"

"Why, he suggested I ask her help in planning and arranging furniture and ornaments and the like."

Tom spoke hesitatingly and felt as if he were giving pain. Besides, he shrank from sarcastic words, for he'd decided to make the attempt, and in itself it was hard enough, without Maria's words to draw him back.

She leaned against the railing and spoke thoughtfully, without a touch of sarcasm. "It's a good idea, worthy of its source. If I were you I'd try it. Helen has a pretty hard time, I suspect. She isn't like the rest of us in roughing it and never was. Perhaps she'll really get interested."

"The leaven of the Golden Rule," said Tom to himself, in surprise and delight. Aloud he said, "But, Maria, I'd wanted you installed as commander over all such things."

"It isn't my forte," Maria said coolly. "I haven't the least idea whether books should be set squarely on the table or across the corners, but Helen knows the precise angle. I'll see whether your cook seasons the meats and sweetens the pies properly. I'm much more fitted to that work."

Tom seized her hand as she was about to run and said eagerly, "*Will* you help, Maria? I've so depended on you."

"There's no telling what I'll do," Maria said. "When I get time to dip into that text of yours again it may lead me into as foolish a scheme as it has you." She broke away from him and ran lightly upstairs.

Chapter 6

Beginnings

N ow what does this room need?" Tom said, and he halted in the center of the long, elegantly furnished room and looked inquiringly at Mrs. Monroe, who was silently following him. "I've studied it all day. In fact, I've been at it for two or three days and have made a dozen different twists and turns. But something's lacking—something that makes a fellow feel stiff and uncomfortable—and I don't know what it is."

One would have thought a reasonable mortal might have been satisfied with that room. It was long and narrow—a graceful shape for a large room. It was carpeted in soft, rich hues, looking like the shimmer of sunlight among buds and leaves. The curtains at the many windows were long and fine and beautifully clear. The sofas and easy chairs, of which there were many, were upholstered in the right shape to enhance the carpet's beauty. The tables were marble topped and graceful as to shade. The piano was a large, good one. And yet, as Tom surveyed the room from mirror to mirror, he turned back to his sister and shook his head, while he repeated his question, "What's the matter with it?"

"It looks as if you'd taken a square, made geometrical lines for everything to stand in and forbidden a person to touch them," Mrs. Monroe said.

As she spoke she put forth her hand and gave the books on the table before her a scientific *shove* to right and left. Entering into the spirit of the change the little movement had made, she passed up and down that room, setting a chair crooked here, wheeling a sofa there into a different angle and scattering the music piled squarely into a corner of the piano into a systematic confusion. There's such a thing as systematic confusion, and the people who don't understand its laws, or who ignore its existence, have rooms fixed by rule and square.

It would have amused you to note the difference those few simple changes made in that room. Tom looked on in silent surprise and approbation, until, as she wheeled a great handsome rocker into a corner where the gas jet threw the right angle of light and then sank into the rocker, he drew a long breath of satisfaction.

"It's a room at last! It's been nothing in the world but a great handsome furniture warehouse despite my efforts. You women are remarkable!"

It would have been pleasant, perhaps, if these two people could have realized how much had been done in that few minutes. Tom was conscious of feeling there was an atmosphere about Helen he hadn't appreciated before. She knew how to do certain things that looked simple enough in the doing but were worse than a geometrical puzzle to him. As for Helen, for almost the first time since she could remember she had succeeded in doing Tom a kindness and in gratifying him. It gave her a more kindly feeling to everybody.

"What's all this for?" she asked, gazing up and down the room with satisfied eyes. The beauty and the refinement displayed here actually rested her. She loved beautiful things, especially those that meant wealth and cultured taste and leisure to enjoy. She hadn't asked questions up to this time. "What is this room for? It used to be a ballroom, didn't it? I've been in it." Her eyes took on a dreamy cast as she went back into that past which had been in many respects pleasant to her, without her realizing much of the pleasure.

"Yes," Tom said. It *was* the ballroom, but it is something more now. "It's a secret," he added, with smiling eyes. "Even Mr. Harper doesn't know what it's for. He thinks it's a great parlor in which, for some reason, I have a special interest. Now I mean to tell you what it is—or, here, I'll show you what's to go above the window outside." He went to the largest sofa and, wheeling it out, displayed behind it a long board set quietly against the wall. When this was turned, it showed on its reverse side, in clear gold letters, "Young Men's Christian Association Rooms."

"Rooms!" quoted Helen, laughing, yet with a softened look in her eyes. It was something so new, and it was certainly pleasant to be having a confidential chat with Tom. "Where are the 'rooms'? I see only one."

"Oh, yes, there are more," he said eagerly, "but I haven't had time to show you yet. See here."

He showed her doors at the end of the old ballroom, where good-sized dressing rooms had opened out of it. These were fitted up elegantly—the one for dressing purposes, and the other dainty and evidently intended as a quiet little resort for two who might have a word to say to each other in private.

Helen laughed again, but she was becoming intensely interested.

"Where are the young men?" she asked, as they came back and she seated herself at the piano.

"They're to be found," he said. "There must be some of the right sort in this great city, and there must be more who can be made. This is a manufactory, Helen, and we have the very best tools the world affords." As he spoke he laid his hand with a sudden, impressive movement on the large Bible resting on the little table where it stood.

"And you're going to manufacture men?" She didn't say it scornfully or in sarcasm, as she so often spoke, but as if the idea were new and interesting.

"Will you help?" he asked, stepping nearer to her and speaking with an eager face and voice.

"I, help!" she said.

Tom thought he detected a wistful glance, as if it would be pleasant to be a helper anywhere.

"What could I do?"

"A great deal, if you will. I will surely find you work to do. Will you occasionally give us some good music here, in the early evening, when we need some?"

It was a simple thing to do and sounded pleasant enough. At least it would be pleasant if one had appreciative listeners. Helen didn't love music for its own sake. But she began to feel she was condescending a good deal in regard to a scheme she'd expressed nothing but disapproval for before this.

"I don't think I can promise to do anything," she said coldly. "You know I don't approve of the idea. It's pleasant, of course, and sounds philanthropic. But it's a great expenditure of money that doesn't belong to you and a great risk. For that matter it's more than a risk—it's a direct throwing away of money. Mr. Harper expects it to succeed financially, of course, or he would never have gone into it, and you're young and not expected to be gifted with wonderful wisdom. I'm afraid you'll come to grief and have endless embarrassments, and as a family we've had enough trouble."

This was so much nearer a feeling of interest in him and his work than Helen had ever shown before, that, though it may sound cold and disheartening to you, Tom was encouraged and not a little touched by it. He drew a chair near her and sat down.

"I understand your feeling," he said, "and it's the most natural one in the world—more so because I've never inspired you with confidence in me. But, Helen, you don't half know our brother-in-law; none of us does. I had a feeling very much like yours. I nearly gave up the hope of this thing after it was all planned. He saw something was amiss and questioned me.

" 'It's involving an entire fortune,' I said. 'It amounts to that, and if it's a stupendous failure, what then? I'm risking so much that belongs to you.'

" 'It isn't my money at all,' he said. 'It's money entrusted to me to invest in a sure thing, and I invest it here because I feel so sure of the dividends.'

"Well, Helen, I was startled. It was bad enough to be using his money, but to use up another's—a stranger's—who wouldn't know if I failed whether I'd tried to do my best or not, was a thing not to be thought of.

" 'I can't do that,' I said in great heat. 'I didn't understand it that way. I can't assume such a responsibility as that.'

" 'Look here,' he said. 'Let me show you the lender's name.' And he took a book from his pocket and showed me those words, 'The silver is mine, and the gold is mine, saith the Lord of hosts.'

" 'There!' he said. 'You know the sort of return He asks—can He trust you?' And, oh, Helen, it made such a difference. I understood Mr. Harper's feeling. He meant that God had called him to do this thing, and I believe He's called me, and I mean to try to be a faithful steward."

"You're an enthusiast," Helen said, smiling and rising as she spoke, "and Mr. Harper is another, and I'm not. But I'm sure I wish I were. It must be pleasant to have an intense interest in anything."

"You haven't answered my question yet," her brother said, rising also and walking down the long room with her.

"Oh, I'm not an enthusiast on the drinking question either, you know. I don't believe in extremes of any sort. At the same time, if you really want my help, it's a new thing for anyone to want anything of me; but if there's anything I can do, why, let me know and I'll try to do it."

As Tom held the door open for her to pass and thanked her again for her services that afternoon, he felt he at least had gained a victory. He was more interested in Helen, and he realized more her need of help than he ever had before.

"Whether she helps me or not," he said as he walked back alone, "she'll try to if I can get her into it, for I'm certain we can help her. I wonder if she's really and truly a Christian at heart. Oh, to know for a certainty whether some who have the name are really alive—and so be at rest within."

Later that evening Tom had another caller. Maria came in with haste and business. He didn't take her through the handsome room or show her the gold-lettered sign. He thought she would consider those things too visionary. Instead, he took her to the large, light, thoroughly furnished kitchen and showed her the conveniences.

"It's splendid!" she said. "It will really be nothing but fun for the girls to work, and that brings me to the subject that brought me over just now. I'm almost distracted on that question of girls. I've talked with a dozen today, and none of them will do. I thought we'd found a perfect treasure for you, to serve as cook. She came highly recommended—had worked at the Laurie House as cook for six months. You know that's a first-class house, and I told Helen if half she said about herself regarding the work she did there proved true she'd be a treasure. So I had her come in and wait while I posted off to the Laurie House. Not ostensibly—I was supposed to be going to consult you. Instead I whisked around to the Laurie House, and you needn't build your hopes on her in the least, for she won't do. All she said about herself as a cook was true, and more too—the half hasn't been told. The dreadful being drinks! Like a fish, the waiter told me—said they had some dreadful scenes with her. She would go on nicely enough for a while, and suddenly the breakfast would be *non est*. He actually said it, Tom, in those very words."

"What's become of the girl?"

"She's still waiting, I presume. I left Grace on guard for fear her pastime might be stealing, and since I had to pass by here I thought she might as well wait while I ran up for a minute, and here I am staying an hour. Grace will be distracted. But I came to say you'd do better to advertise in the evening papers. That would bring an army of them; it always does."

"What's her name?" Tom asked.

"What, the evening papers? *She* has a good many names. There are several of them if you recollect."

Tom laughed. "I mean the girl, Maria. I think we'll try her, if you have an idea she'll suit in other respects."

"Try her!" Maria's face expressed horror.

"Why, Tom, she *drinks*, I tell you. She's just recovered from a time now. That waiter said she was reeling along the streets night before last. That would be an extraordinary sign for this kind of hotel, to say nothing of the inconvenience it would cause!"

"Maria," said Tom, speaking half lightly, "if your imagination can take such a flight as that, suppose yourself to be a poor girl—"

"I am," promptly interpolated Maria.

"Out of employment."

"Oh, I'm not."

"And suppose you had the appetite of a drunkard upon you. Suppose you were willing and eager to reform—what would you want the Christian people to do for you by way of sympathy and help? Turn you aside because they were nondrinkers and couldn't encourage drunkenness, or employ you and give you a chance at reformation?"

"But aren't you jumping at conclusions? I may not be willing to try to reform."

"They all are."

Tom's face was grave enough now, and he spoke with energy.

"I know about it, Maria. I've been in the meshes. It's a horrible slavery, and everyone wants to be free. I mean to try that girl. Engage her for me, Maria."

"But, Tom, it's dangerous. She may set the house on fire."

"Not as likely as are dozens of the people who occupy the back rooms of first-class hotels all over the land. She'll have to go outside for her poison—most of them find it indoors. No, this is the place for her. If she's used to working at hotels she wouldn't be satisfied in a private family even if they'd try her, and she can find enough places at hotels where she'll breathe a daily atmosphere of temptation. I'll try her."

"All the same I think it's foolish," Maria said obstinately. " 'Charity begins at home.' That's in the Bible, isn't it? If it isn't, it should be. Don't endanger your own house trying to do a wild goodness to somebody who doesn't appreciate it—that's my motto."

"No, it isn't," Tom said, smiling. "Your motto and mine is an infinite reach above that—'Whatsoever ye would that men should do to you, do ye even so to them.' "

"Oh, that tiresome Golden Rule!" Maria said, drawing her shawl about her. "I've given that up. I was never so tired in my life as I was after chasing that up for a week. It won't do for me. It reaches too many ways. I must have more leisure before I live by that rule."

"Then you yield the point of argument, do you?"

"What, that I can't live after your mottoes? No, not at all. I simply haven't time to follow that out. It keeps me turning too many ways. But everyone knows that's the worst verse in the whole Bible to keep track of."

"Then I'll give you another. It's shorter. 'Whatsoever He saith unto you, do it.'"

"Doesn't that belong to the one I said I wouldn't have?"

"No," Tom said, "it's quite distinct, and I don't mean to take an unfair advantage of you. When you're in doubt about a question of any sort, stop to think what He says on it—or what, with your present knowledge of His character, you honestly believe He would say to you if you could speak face to face with Him—and follow that belief."

"Taking my own view of things and not yours or a commentator's? Very well—that's easy enough, for I know very little about it. When I'm in doubt I can say I haven't the slightest idea what the orthodox thing is, and then of course I'll do as I please. Yes, I'll try that. But if I find it as much of a nuisance as the other, will you release me?"

"Not unless you'll admit you're conquered. Maria, hurry home and secure that girl. I've decided to see what we can do to help her."

Chapter 7

Wise as a Serpent

One day the following week the new hotel held its grand opening. Grand in a newer sense than that word generally means, at least in reference to hotels.

The gold-lettered sign was up: "Young Men's Christian Association Rooms." Another sign also hung over the main entrance, simple and unpretentious. There had been several discussions about that sign.

"Are you going to announce your principles over the door, in words every man may read?" This Mr. Harper said when the main preliminaries were finished.

"No, sir," Tom had answered with emphatic promptness and added smiling, "that is, I prefer not to say a word about our purpose on the sign, if I have your permission to do so."

Mr. Harper looked his surprise. "I can't imagine why. Give me your line of argument, please."

Tom answered with eagerness. "A man who actually has the matter at heart, even to the degree that if he saw the announcement in passing he would take the trouble to step in, won't mind asking information of hack driver or porter, and I mean that they shall be so informed as to our whereabouts that they'll have no difficulty giving directions. But I don't propose to blazon the word so that a poor tempted fellow, who is yet in such danger that he can't resist the temptation wherever he can find it, will pass us by because we explain to him that we can't give him what he longs for. We want all sorts of people to come here and find our principles so in evidence in every area and in all we say and do that each one who comes will pass the word to someone else."

To this Mr. Harper made no answer, until Tom, disturbed that he might have been too decided, said, "At the same time, if you think the other way is better, I will, of course, defer to your judgment."

Then his brother-in-law turned to him, smiling brightly. "I think whatever way you suggest is the way to try. I'm more and more convinced of it. You've gone deeper into this thing than I have."

Maria was remarkable for keeping people to the point.

"What sign will you have then?" she asked.

"Would it be improper to use your name?" Tom asked, glancing somewhat anxiously toward Mr. Harper. He wasn't certain this would be in accordance with his taste.

"*Don't* let them do that, Ermina!" Helen exclaimed. "I wouldn't have my name blazoned on a hotel."

"I'd be proud of it," Mr. Harper said quickly, "on this sort of hotel. But we'll do a better thing than that. We'll call it the 'Randolph House,' and it won't be in honor of this young fellow either. It shall be Father's work. The honored name that has worked so well shall keep on working for him, long after rest from work has come to us all, I trust. And it shall grow to be the synonym for strong, earnest, helping hands, stretched out to our young men."

This talk went on in the invalid's room, and he was propped up among the pillows to listen. As Mr. Harper spoke he turned toward the bed and watched the glow on Mr. Randolph's cheek deepen and spread.

"He being dead yet speaketh," he said, repeating the words with difficulty, because of the tremor in his voice. "I hadn't thought any such pleasure would be mine. It's an honest name, and it belonged to your mother for many years. Put it up, and we'll watch it in heaven to see that it works faithfully."

Chosen under such circumstances, do you wonder that the young man, crossing the street to note its effect, stood and gazed at the familiar name in a new place, joined to a new word, "Randolph House," and presently took out his handkerchief and wiped away a tear? It wasn't his name, but his father's. It must never be disgraced by failure or carelessness. And today was to be the opening. The handsome house was in perfect order, and a housekeeper had been secured by Mr. Harper's sister in New York; so they were all at rest upon that point.

The cook was the very one over whom Maria had vainly protested. Even Mr. Harper thought that experiment a risk, but Grace was beaming and Tom resolute.

"We must begin to work according to our principles," he said. "If we shirk possible dangers at the very start, we won't be as helpful as we should."

And in undertone he said to Maria, "I'm working on your motto, and I'm sure He says to me, 'Lend a helping hand in this direction.'"

"I'm not at all convinced she wants to be helped," Maria said crossly.

"That's a question not at all to the point," Tom answered. "The question is, does she need to be?"

A good force of girls had been engaged for the subordinate positions, and on this particular day there was to be a family dinner party. The grand feature of the day was that Mr. Randolph, carefully propped up by pillows at back and feet, had been borne in an easy carriage from his own home to the Randolph House and was at this moment reposing quietly on one of its softest beds, gathering strength to sit at the head of the table. It was to be a royal dinner, requiring all the skill of the new cook and the planning abilities of the housekeeper to execute.

Just before the feast was ready to be served the family gathered, from their wanderings over the house, in the spacious public parlor to await the summons of the dinner bell. Helen was noticeably satisfied. She'd scorned the idea of hotel life. She had persisted, from the very first, in saying it was a descent in the family history instead of a rise. Yet to be dressed in her best and sitting, a lady of leisure, in an elegant parlor, having no personal interest in the kitchen or the service of the dinner table, and yet being serenely conscious that everything was progressing as it should and the glory would reflect upon her, as one connected with the family—all this was a joy to Helen Monroe. She believed she could be the most amiable of mortals if she could only live and breathe in the atmosphere suited to her tastes and abilities. And though these surrounding her now were found in hotel life instead of the aristocratic seclusion of a private house, she was rapidly concluding they weren't to be utterly scorned.

The social gathering was suddenly interrupted. A stranger, a gentleman, was shown into the room. He advanced a few steps, then paused and looked about him with a puzzled face.

"I beg your pardon," he said to Tom, who came forward to meet him, "but I must have made some unaccountable blunder. I thought I was in a hotel."

"No blunder at all," Tom said. "This *is* a hotel—a good one, we hope. How can we serve you? Will you have a room? Our dinner will be served in ten minutes."

To Helen it was insufferable to have the family party thus rudely broken. She would have done her part toward freezing him with her dignity had she not at that moment been struck with Mr. Harper's manner. How gracious and attentive he was! For all the world as if he'd kept hotel all his life, and his father before him, and yet he belonged to one of the most aristocratic families in Boston. And Mr. Harper's manner had its unconscious influence over her—as every person's manner must influence every other person's either consciously or unconsciously in this bewildering world.

For the family it was a little difficult not to be embarrassed by the newness and strangeness of their circumstances. The stranger seemed not a little bewildered and in doubt as to whether he must conduct himself like an invited guest to a dinner party or a passing traveler enduring hotel life. The dinner bell was a relief; so was the elegant dining room, with the table glittering in china and silver. At least Helen's eyes took in all these details, and her heart feasted upon the beauties.

There was an instant's pause as they were seated, and then Tom's clear voice rang down to the other end of the table, where his father sat in a great easy chair: "Father, will you ask a blessing?"

Something touching in the weak, tremulous voice made Mr. Pierson pass his hand quickly across his eyes as he looked upon this strange scene. The next moment his eyes danced with amusement. He had never heard a blessing asked at the public table of a hotel.

"They're a set of lunatics, playing at public life, I believe," he said to himself, vainly trying to conceal a smile. "But what a delightful play it is!"

It seemed almost necessary, as the meal progressed, to make some explanation to their puzzled guest, so Tom volunteered it.

"I'm just setting out to paddle this canoe," he said, turning to Mr. Pierson, "and my family has come to wish me well. Our house has its formal opening today, and it seems so promising that even our first meal is taken with a start of the legitimate work of the house."

The sentence put the young man at his ease, and being of an easy-going nature he was as merry as the rest. Toward the close of the meal the guest apparently began to feel a want that wasn't provided for. He glanced down the length of the table. He sent quiet side glances about the well-appointed room and saw no sideboard and no provision for liquor of any sort. "Some concession to the old gentleman's whim," thought this man, looking blandly upon him.

But when the dinner was concluded and they were returning to the parlors he approached Tom with a confidential air and said in an undertone: "Where shall I go to satisfy the thirst of the inner man? You've generously provided the substantials."

"I beg your pardon," Tom said. "I'm afraid we've been negligent. Weren't you served another cup of coffee? We're beginners, you must remember. Let me serve you myself."

"By no means," his guest said, staying his hand and vainly trying to hide the laugh in his eyes. "I think I've made a mistake and slipped into the Garden of Eden under false pretenses. You don't understand that I mean I want a glass of wine or something like it?"

"Oh," Tom said, and the stranger felt he didn't know his host well enough to be certain whether innocence or keenness was in his tone. "I beg your pardon. I understand. I'm sorry we can't serve you everything you want, but the fact is we haven't an ounce of liquor of any description in the house. I mean, of course, the poisonous liquors. We have plenty of coffee and water."

It was impossible not to laugh now; there was so much humor in Tom's eyes.

"Is it really a nonalcoholic house?" Mr. Pierson asked as they moved toward the parlors.

"To the very core," Tom said. "We've taken the most extreme and emphatic form of that. Absolutely nothing, neither brandy sauces nor currant wines. At the same time, we intend to let no other conceivable want of the stomach, at least, go ungratified."

"But you don't advertise that at all. May I ask why you didn't hang out your sign, as your *confreres* in that scheme usually do?"

Tom shot a keen glance under heavy eyebrows at the tall young stranger beside him. He thought he knew the character he had to deal with.

"You wouldn't have dined with me if I had," he said, with an emphasis on the word "you."

Mr. Pierson flushed a little and then laughed. "That's true. I presume I wouldn't."

In the course of conversation it transpired that Mr. Pierson was to be in the city during the coming fall and winter and was looking for a suitable boarding place.

"I was congratulating myself that I'd found the very Elysium of my hopes, but I'll have to admit that my recent discovery isn't according to my views. I'm a nondrinking man in the main—that is, I try to be. But I confess I like to be where I can indulge my notion for a glass of wine when the spirit moves without having much trouble to obtain it."

"As to that," Tom said, "I'm sorry to say we're very close to glasses of wine and glasses of everything else that can intoxicate. We have hotels within calling distance from our front door, where they're only too willing to supply customers."

At which item Mr. Pierson laughed, cheerfully protesting that he didn't even want the trouble of going to the front door and calling. He courteously resisted all attempts to have him look at permanent rooms and at the same time earnestly assured them he was a nondrinking man; rarely indulged in anything stronger than a glass of wine, and not even that as a daily thing; and was willing to give up liquors altogether whenever the country decided it was for the public good.

"And yet he can't stay for three months where there is none! What nonsense!" This Helen Monroe said after their guest had left them and gone to his room. And as she said it she became dimly conscious that she was more committed by those words to the principles of the house than she'd ever allowed herself to be.

So Mr. Pierson had unwittingly done a small thing for the cause, and no one knows to what great results small things may lead.

As for that gentleman, he was pacing up and down his elegant room that evening. "Confound hobbies! What a fine hotel this is likely to be! A charming family circle to drop into when one became disgusted with everything else. That one they call Helen has remarkable eyes. Why do they need to ride the most tiresome of all hobbies, and the most hopeless one possible—everlasting abstinence? I'd like to stay here if it weren't for that drawback."

Then he paused suddenly, and a curious look spread over his face. "See here—this is an odd idea. What difference does it make to me after all? Am I really so fond of that occasional glass of wine that I must always be in the house where it can be bought?"

Chapter 8

Tom and Peter Talk Things Over

Another scene during that first day at the Randolph House isn't common to the exercises of hotel openings. It was a few moments before the family from "The Little House," as the Randolph home was coming to be called, was to return. They had sent for the carriage to take the invalid back and were all gathered in what was to be called his room, though each one of them felt in their hearts that he wasn't likely to occupy it again.

"I'd like one thing, Father, very much," Tom said, "though I'm afraid you aren't strong enough for it."

The invalid smiled at his young son. "I'm strong enough for a good deal today. I feel that this look at the new departure for the cause has given me great breaths of strength. What is it?"

"I'd like"—and Tom's voice trembled with the earnestness of his thought—"to have this house and all its belongings consecrated to the work, and I'd like to have the first united prayer, offered under this roof, to be led by your voice."

"I'm strong enough for that," Mr. Randolph said, and his voice certainly had a sound of strength in it. And they knelt about him, while he prayed. If Mr. Pierson could have heard this prayer and noticed with what words he was remembered, it might have caused him to reconsider his decision that he couldn't do such an odd thing as patronize this kind of hotel.

In the evening, when the house was quiet, Tom sat alone in the room that of all the rooms was his favorite—the long, light, cheerful room, that bore over its windows that gold-lettered sign. No human being knew the hopes that centered around that room or the prayers that had already gone up from it. His reverie was broken by a light tap on the door, and Peter Armstrong was admitted. He came for directions concerning the disposal of some new furniture. With that settled, Tom pushed a chair toward him.

"Sit down, Peter, and let's talk things over. We've had so much to do that we haven't found time to talk."

Peter had changed considerably in a short time. His form was rounding out into manly proportions, and he was learning to take more pains with his dress. Tom had chosen him to be the confidential clerk of the establishment —that is, he called him that when they talked together, and he certainly was confidential with him.

Now, as he leaned back and surveyed the handsome room again, he said, "Peter, this room is my special pride and joy. I can't begin to tell you how much I think of it or how many plans I have in which it takes a prominent place."

"What's the first one, and how's it to be done?"

This manner of asking far-reaching questions was one of the essential differences between Peter Armstrong and many other young men. This made him such an interesting companion to Tom, and that made Tom eagerly detail his plans.

"The first one," he said, laughing a little, "I'm not sure I can tell you. It begins whenever we can get a chance and reaches out in every direction. I have in mind snares and traps and nets and all sorts of counter measures. We have to begin small, of course, for it's only you and I. But we'll grow. We can find others to help us. There's so much to be done—and I'm anxious to begin among strangers—young men who've come here recently and have no home and no comforts, nothing to read and no influence to keep them out of temptation. The city is full of them, and my heart goes out to them, as to no others."

While Tom poured out these eager sentences, Peter sat listening with his steady grey eyes growing keener, and his whole face showing rapt attention. "It's working out the old promise," he said, as Tom paused. "Fishing after men, isn't it?"

"The old promise? Oh, yes—you mean the one that was made to Simon Peter. So it is—I hadn't thought of it. 'I will make you fishers of men,' and the call: 'Follow me.' Yes, we're called—the commission is ours, and the promise. I'd forgotten there was a promise. That's encouraging, isn't it? By the way, Peter, I was interested in your following up your namesake, but so many things have pushed in between that I forgot about it. Are you still studying his character?"

"Yes, indeed!" Peter said. "It'll bear studying a good deal."

"Where are you now?"

"Well, I go slowly, and, to tell the truth, I gave him up for a while. I said I'd never have anything more to do with him, as long as I lived. I was never so disgusted with anyone in my life as I was with that Peter."

Tom leaned back in his chair and laughed heartily at this Peter's odd way of saying things. And Peter was blessed with that rare disposition that allowed people to laugh and be amused over his ways, without taking offense.

"What disgusted you?" the laugher said.

"Oh, that awful time at the trial! I never imagined he could be as bad as that! Not only denied Him, you know, but swore about it and said over and over that he knew nothing about Him. Why, the first night I read that, I shut up the Bible and was in a storm. I couldn't stand it. Talk about his cutting off that servant's ear! Why, it seemed to me that Peter's whole head should be cut off! And I felt as though, if I'd been there, I'd have been willing to undertake the job."

"Tell me why, Peter. I'm very interested."

"I'll never forget that lesson," Peter said earnestly. "I went around for more than a week, feeling more puffed up than I can tell you, and all the while I was mad at Peter. I felt as though I could never forgive him, and if ever I came across him in heaven I'd feel like twitting him about denying his Master. But I got cured of that."

Something in his voice and manner was intensely solemn.

"Do you mind telling me how you were cured?" Tom asked quietly.

Peter arose suddenly from the low seat he'd taken and crossed to the window, evidently not to look out upon the brightly lighted street below, but to master some deep feeling stirred within him. He came back presently, and his voice had a hushed, tremulous sound.

"I did it myself! I was mad at Peter for more than a week and then went and did that very thing."

"Do you mind telling me what you did?" Tom asked again, and his voice was gentle and sympathetic.

"I went to a place where they were laughing and talking and making fun of religion, and I never said a word—not a word. I just said by my actions as plain as Peter did, 'I never knew Him.' And what did I do it for? Why, just for some shamefaced feeling about being on the weak side! To think of my finding fault with Peter! They made fun of Jesus Christ's very words. And I sat there as dumb as if He'd never given me a tongue."

"What people could you have been with," Tom asked in wondering tones, "that in this day and age made their fun out of that?"

"Oh, they were respectable enough—at least they thought so. They were having a church social, and I thought I was getting a lift when I had a chance to go there. But I never came away from any place so ashamed of myself before."

Tom's curiosity deepened every minute. What strange experience could Peter have had that remembering it so clouded his face and solemnized his voice?

"Will you tell me what happened?" he said. "I can't imagine what could have so overwhelmed you."

"Why, it isn't a long story to tell. They played games and quoted the Bible at each other and made fun of it and roared over it, even the very words of Jesus Christ, until I was ashamed and afraid—and yet I didn't say a single word. If ever a fellow denied his Master, I did. I'll never forget the way I felt that night when I went home. I thought of Peter right away and the scorn I'd felt for him, and then I felt more sorry for him than I had for anyone. I remembered that he went out and wept bitterly. I could almost feel his tears in my heart. If I could only weep bitterly it would do me good, I thought, but the tears wouldn't come. I walked up and down the room, and I didn't know what to do. It seemed as if I was too wicked to pray, as if I shouldn't ask Jesus to hear me or forgive me. Then I wondered what Peter did and how his Master treated him after the resurrection. You see, I was so mad at Peter that I'd stopped reading about him. I got a Bible and turned the pages to see if there was any account of Peter meeting Jesus. And what do you think was the first thing I saw?"

"I don't know," Tom said, interest and sympathy in his voice. "What was it?"

"Just this word: 'Go tell my disciples—and Peter.' Think of that! A special message to Peter, the one who had treated Him the worst! Nothing has ever melted me like *that*, and I never heard anything like it before either. I got down on my knees right away, and before I asked His forgiveness I thanked Him for that wonderful message to poor Peter!"

Tom's vision was blurred when this story was concluded. Something about it touched him. Not the least was that the conscience of the Peter before him was very tender. His own conscience throbbed with recalling how many times he had denied his Lord in ways he and the world called little.

"Peter," he said, rising suddenly and laying his hand tenderly on the young man's shoulder, "you must help me in this work. You must put your whole soul into it and give it your best. And to that end we must pray much about it. I feel a deep interest in our first guest. Let's try to catch him. Shall we kneel together now here and ask the Master's help?"

And so for the second time that day the Randolph House was consecrated with the voice of prayer.

Chapter 9

A Perplexed Evening

It was a summer evening, but a dark and rainy one. Maria was in the sitting room, her work finished for the day. She had just locked the kitchen door, drawn down the sitting-room shades and tiptoed to her father's room to see if he was sleeping quietly. Now she sat down in the rocking chair, folded her hands and did an uncommon thing for Maria Randolph—gave a weary sigh.

She felt unusually alone. Helen had gone over to the hotel, as she often did. That hotel was a blessing to her, despite her indignant protest. It took so much of the time that used to hang heavily, but it also left Maria much alone—not that the young woman imagined she was any more comfortable in Helen's presence than in her absence, but for all that it was certainly more lonely to have her away.

There was Grace, of course, but Grace was often where she was at this moment—in the parlor entertaining young Alfred Parks. And as Maria thought of it and heard their voices through the half-open door, it suddenly occurred to her that Alfred Parks was fond of coming to chatter away the evenings with Grace. The thought troubled her; it kept coming back and wouldn't be dismissed, though she was angry with it.

"It's natural enough," she told herself impatiently. "They're in the store together all day, and the poor fellow has no home and few enough acquaintances. Why shouldn't he like a pleasant room to spend his evenings in and a nice girl to talk with? What talk!" she continued in disgust after a few moments, during which the voices in the parlor had grown louder, and the merriment over something became extreme. "That such stuff should be called conversation! I never heard such vapid nonsense in my life! How *can* Grace be so silly!"

This last she said after an extremely foolish sentence from the young man, followed by a burst of laughter from Grace, with several giggling "Oh, Alf's!" as if her amusement was so intense she hardly knew how to express it. Maria sat upright, with glowing cheeks.

"I wish Grace was out of that store," she said, speaking aloud in her earnestness. "She's growing silly, and I never thought she was that."

At this moment she heard a quick, decisive rap on the kitchen door. Maria arose at once, shaded her lamp with her hand as she walked past the open window and, setting the lamp down on the kitchen table, unbolted the door. Without invitation or permission, a tall girl, or woman, in a torn dress and faded shawl, walked in and sat down in the chair by the table.

Maria surveyed her coolly. If it had been a man she would have trembled a little, but the idea of being afraid of a woman was absurd. "Besides," she said to herself, "that young simpleton is in the parlor to appeal to, if she doesn't behave herself. *She* will think he's a man."

"Well," she said, speaking aloud, "that's a rather odd performance! What do you want?"

"I wanted to come in, and I knew by bitter experience that if I asked permission I wouldn't get it, so I walked in without it."

"So I perceive. Now that you *are* in, what do you want?"

"Bread!" The tone was sharp and stern and the voice decisive.

"Bread!" repeated Maria incredulously. "And what if, instead of giving it to you, I have you turned out of doors?"

A visible shiver ran through the strange girl's frame, but she answered in the same stern voice: "Then at least I won't have starved without making a last hard effort at something to eat."

The word struck sharply on Maria's ear.

"Do you mean you're actually starving?" she said, and her hand was on the knob of the pantry door. In a moment more the strange visitor was swallowing the dry bread with an eagerness Maria had never dreamed of.

"Where on earth have you been?" she asked at last. "What's the matter?"

"The matter is that I'm *starving!* Do you know how that feels? Where have I been? Everywhere. Wandering up and down your streets, first for work and then for bread, and I got neither—only doors slammed in my face and answers as angry as if I'd stolen instead of begged." The great mouthfuls of bread disappeared as she spoke.

Maria stood staring at her as though transfixed.

"Where are you going to spend the night?" she asked suddenly.

"At the poorhouse, if I can get there."

"It's three miles away!"

"I know, but I've walked three times that today. It's the poorhouse or the street for me. Or, maybe, I can get taken to the station house as a vagrant if I wander around long enough. Or I might steal something. I've had plenty of chances today and an awful temptation."

Was any talk ever wilder than this? What was to be done with the poor, forlorn, half-crazy creature? Maria still stood looking at her, feeling dreadfully perplexed. If she only had someone with whom to advise, and she looked wistfully toward the bedroom door. How much she missed that sick father!

"I might talk to those two simpletons in the parlor. Much they know about it!" she said to herself scornfully, still indignant over the talk she'd overheard.

But she had no one else to consult, so she went toward the parlor door, noting that the parlor door was in line with the chair where the poor creature was, and she needn't lose sight of her.

She called Grace and her companion to the door and in low tones explained. Before the sentence was concluded young Parks raised his hands in horror and uttered an exclamation of disgust.

"The wretched imposter! Why didn't you call on me to turn her out? I wouldn't have listened to her lies for a minute. Here, let me dispose of her." He made a movement as if to pass Maria in the door.

"Dispose of yourself," she said rudely. "I'll attend to the woman. I have your advice, and that's all and more than I need."

Grace looked timid and confused and said nothing, and Maria shut the parlor door with a bang she couldn't repress and went back to her guest.

"I'm going to let you stay here all night," she began promptly. "I've had such excellent advice that it's moved my heart. I'm going to make up a bed for you on the floor out here and lock you out, so you can't do any mischief if you have any desire to, and I don't believe you have."

The reply to this strange address was quite in keeping.

"You're an odd girl," the stranger said, looking steadily at her would-be benefactor without any expression of gratitude. "I heard every word your adviser said and fully expected to be marched out. I think you haven't done it because you hate to follow advice. But there may be another reason, and for curiosity's sake I'd like to know. Are you a Christian?"

Maria's cheek flushed.

"No, I'm not," she said shortly. "What is it to you?"

"Nothing—except curiosity, as I said. I've heard of Christianity, and I wanted to know if that's what prompted you to show me the first bit of humanity I've seen in three days at least."

Maria's thoughts went backward. That afternoon she had been in her brother's room at the hotel, and while she stood by his table, straightening the papers on it, she had glanced up at a "Silent Comforter" hanging on the wall. "Give to him that asketh thee," the verse read.

"Where's the particular comfort in that verse?" she had asked Tom.

"It's one of my bylaws, direct from the Master's hand," he had answered. "It needs to be coupled with your motto, and the two would serve well together."

That verse had persistently stayed by her during the evening, and she was conscious that it helped her bring out her bread promptly. But she wasn't disposed to tell this to a stranger, nor was there time.

The stranger rose to leave. "I'm not nearly so ready to die as I was when I came in. Bread is still good. Of course I'm grateful to you—what fool wouldn't be? But I won't stay here to get you into trouble. Good-bye. And if it comforts you to know it, you can think that you saved my life."

"But where will you go?" said Maria, trying to stay her guest's steps. "Wait! Let me think." Thinking of the verse had reminded her of Tom. "Will you go where I send you?" she asked authoritatively.

"It's likely," the girl answered, in the same half-fierce tone she had used during the interview. "I haven't much to choose from. Besides, you've earned the right to give orders."

Then Maria grabbed a torn envelope that lay on the table and wrote on it.

Dear Tom,

Here's a chance to experiment on your "bylaw." She needs it. I believe she's half crazy. But I wish you'd treat her as if she were a friend of mine, for I come nearer to liking her than any girl I ever saw, almost.

Maria

Then, with careful directions for finding the Randolph House, she sent her visitor out.

The bolt had just been pushed again when another knock came, this time a somewhat timid one.

"My patience!" Maria said, hesitating. "Another call! This is becoming exciting. Perhaps I'd better call that idiot from the parlor to protect me."

A peculiar snuffing sound from the person outside revealed his identity, and Maria unbolted the door and admitted Dick Norton. He, of course, had come for his clothes. She produced the neatly ironed little pile and, as she did them up for him, noticed the sad, tired look on his homely face. "Give to him that asketh," floated through her mind. There are different ways of asking for things. Dick's face certainly looked hungry for something—perhaps it was a kind word.

"Dick," she said cheerily, "you look as gloomy as an owl. What's the matter?"

"I *am* gloomier than any owl who ever hooted, I believe," Dick said forlornly. "And there ain't nothin' much the matter neither—nothin' more than common."

"Common things are rather dismal then. Is that what you mean?" she asked, still speaking in a cheery tone. "If you'll sit down and tell me about some of them I'll mend that rip in your sleeve, so you'll look more comfortable."

At this Dick looked surprised, confused and grateful, all in one. But it ended in his pulling off his coat and sitting down on the edge of a chair, while Maria brought her work box from the other room.

"Now what about the 'common things,' Dick? They're hateful enough. I've found that out all my life. What are your worst?"

Chapter 10

The Bewilderment Deepens

Dick wriggled uneasily in his chair, as if that were a difficult question to answer. Then he said, slowly and hesitantly, "I ain't at all sure that I *can* answer that question. You see, when you go to tell things they slip out of shape somehow, and they don't look a mite like they do when you sit all alone in the dark thinkin' about them."

Maria laughed. "I understand all about that too," she said, amused to think how nearly her own experience agreed with Dick's. "I've been through that very place, and I've sometimes thought that an excellent way to get rid of our troubles would be to come out of the dark and tell them all out in plain English to somebody."

"But then," Dick said reflectively, "the trouble is, some of 'em come back as soon as you get in the dark again. They won't *stay* gone while you're alone, and it stands to reason you can't be forever keepin' in the lamplight a-tellin' 'em to somebody."

She laughed again, but she almost had tears in her eyes. These words seemed pathetic to her somehow and touched the depths of her own silent experiences.

"That's all true," she said at last. "But after all I think you'd better try to tell me the troubles, some of them at least. It's nice to have things slip away even for a little time. What's the biggest one tonight?"

"You'd never guess it," he said, with a wistful air. "But, as true as I'm alive, I'd like to know a little somethin'. I kind of hanker after it, though I s'pose it's awful foolish at my age."

"To know something!" repeated Maria, much amazed. This wasn't the sort of trouble she'd expected to hear. "I don't understand—I'm sure you must know a good many things."

"Precious few," he said, shaking his head dolefully. "I don't suppose you have any kind of idea what an awful little bit I do know. You see, schoolin' of any kind didn't come in my line. I had to work from the time I was born, I believe. I didn't even go to school three months in the winter, as the poorest of 'em get a chance to do nowadays, and I don't know nothin' at all. Why, I can't even read the newspaper without spellin' out more than half the big words!"

This last bit of information was given in an almost whisper and with a mixture of pain and shame on his honest face that arrested the laugh on Maria's lips and filled her with pity. She had a rare way of expressing pity.

"Well, what's the use of groaning over it now? It wasn't your fault anyway if you had no chance. Why don't you go to work and make up for it, now that you're old enough to understand the value of an education."

"That's the trouble," he said, but his voice wasn't quite so forlorn as before. "You see, I'm too old."

"Nonsense!" And now every trace of softness was gone from her voice, and it was brisk and businesslike. "You aren't nearly as old as Methuselah yet. I don't believe you're even of age."

"Yes, I am. I voted last fall for the first time."

"Oh, well, I've known people who were older than you are, and they accomplished something in the world, too. If I were you I'd waste no more time in groaning over spilt milk. I'd work with all my might and show what I could do."

"I've as much a mind to as I ever did to eat," he said, with considerable energy, the very tones of her voice seeming to put hope in his heart. "Only the trouble is, I don't know where to begin or how to do it. I don't have any knowledge to start on, you see."

"Yes, you have. You know the alphabet, and I daresay you know the nine figures when you see them, and the greatest scholar who ever lived had to begin right there."

"That's true," he said, and this time his voice was full of admiration. "You have a new way of puttin' it, somehow. I never thought of it before. But then they had teachers, most of 'em."

She didn't stop to correct this false bit of history, with the long list of brilliant exceptions that might be made out. Curiously enough the sound of that verse hanging on the wall in Tom's room had come to her: "Give to him that asketh thee."

Was ever help more plainly or more pitifully asked? Not the less eloquently, perhaps, that the pleader was unconscious of his petition. Certainly the last thing Dick Norton expected on earth was the next sentence, spoken in Maria's most energetic tone.

"*I'll* help you. I never tried teaching in my life, but I've always thought it was easy enough to do. I may have to turn my hand to it someday and may as well practice." She didn't wait for him to express his awkward and intense gratitude but hurried through her next sentences. "We may as well begin tonight, if you like. There's no time like the present, especially when two people have little time. This is the only evening you have in the week, isn't it? Then we'll take *this* evening by all means. *Reading* is what seems to be the first thing needing our attention. What book do you have that you could use for a reader?"

"I've got a Bible," Dick said meekly. "Your brother Tom give me that, and he give me about every good thin' I have in the world. That's the only book I've got that's fit to read in."

This was a somewhat startling suggestion to Maria. She wasn't sure it was the thing to turn the Bible into a textbook. And it would be twice as awkward to be found blundering through a chapter in the Bible with Dick Norton as it would to take any other book in the list. Then came her naturally obstinate nature to the rescue: Why would it? What was the point of being so silly about the Bible and acting as if it were a book to be ashamed of? Why wouldn't it be just as sensible to help Dick Norton learn to read that well as some stupid extract from some old book neither of them cared for? Besides—and here was the fun—hadn't Tom been wanting her to study the Bible and discover what her commands were? Wouldn't it be fun to explain to him that Dick Norton and she had taken up the subject together? Above all, wouldn't the whole thing shock Mrs. Monroe's ideas? This last thought decided her at once, and in much less time than it has taken me to tell you her thoughts she was ready with her answer.

"Then let's take the Bible. We couldn't find any better book, I suppose, and you won't have to be troubled bringing yours along with you. I happen to have one lying around somewhere. I'll hunt it up. Meanwhile we can take the large one out of the sitting room for this evening and begin our lessons at once, if you like."

It was very strange and not a little bewildering, and the last thing that had entered Dick's head when he began to tell his troubles that evening. But how could he be anything other than glad and grateful and excited, even though he was at the same time so ashamed that his face was the color of the tea rose blossoming in the window?

In a short time, considering the remarkable future issues that were to cluster around that act, the young man was laboriously at work over the first chapter of Genesis. "We might as well know the whole story since we're about it," Maria had said.

By neither work nor look did she express the dismay she really felt as the poor fellow blundered through the first verse, his embarrassment causing him to do it much worse than usual, so that hardly a single word was pronounced correctly. But Maria had one of the first elements of a teacher's success about her, and that was a propensity for constant review, so that when Dick had repeated the verse four times he found to his surprise and satisfaction that he read it glibly enough. By the time he'd read the third verse without a mistake, some of the horrible embarrassment was passing, and he was starting to feel he could appreciate the story's beautiful simplicity.

"Wouldn't you like to do that?" he asked, looking up with shining eyes.

"Do what?" Maria questioned, a bit startled, her mind up to now occupied with the strangeness of the situation.

"Why, stand up in the very thick of some great muddle that nobody understood and say, 'Do it *so*,' and right off everythin' would move in the place you pointed out, and it would all be done."

For the second time on this strange evening Maria felt inclined to melt to tears. This was such a homely and simple, and yet wonderfully forceful way, of expressing the secret longing of one's heart for a place and a name among those who could do great things and for power over people. She had felt it herself to a degree that had made her sarcastic over the trifles that were left to her life.

"No one but God could do that, of course," she said evasively and perhaps a little sharply. It was certainly a strange discovery that this ignorant, uncultured car driver had aspirations that matched if not rivalled her own.

"Not such big things, of course," he said, "but little things, or what looked like little things to God but were big things to people. It must be nice to be above other people, to have 'em lookin' up to you and askin' you what they'd ought to do and how to do it and followin' your orders. That must be fine. Why"—and he grew excited and almost eloquent with his subject—"it was even nice to try it with horses. Some of the fellows couldn't manage the horses at all. They didn't know how to make 'em mind, and as that was somethin' I *did* know it always made me feel happy to be sent for to make 'em go across the track when an engine was whistlin' on the other side.

"They always go," he said eagerly, "and I can't for the life of me help bein' awful glad I can make 'em do it right straight off, and the others can't. And if it's so nice with horses, how grand it must be to make *men* mind."

"But how would you like doing the minding?" Maria asked, with a half-embarrassed laugh. This talk was so full of strange suggestions, was so like speaking out her own thoughts that she'd never chosen to speak but had kept hidden in her heart, that she felt embarrassed without understanding why. "It would be very nice to order, but would you like to be one who was ordered?" And in her secret soul Maria knew she would rebel at this. She could understand the desire for power, but how hateful to have to submit to it.

"Yes, I would," Dick said with glowing eyes. "I've always thought I'd like to be a soldier and have a splendid commander, a grand man everybody admired and talked about. And then I'd obey every word he said—obey in an instant, no matter what, whether it was a good thin' or a hateful thin' to do. That would be almost as grand as givin' the order myself."

"Well, *you* better go on reading. That will be more profitable than mooning over what you'll never have a chance to do."

Maria said this rather shortly, for while he spoke, across her mind had flashed the thought of the great Commander, wise and good, revered by all decent people on the face of the globe, whose soldier she had been called to be, whose orders it was her privilege to obey and whose word she had ignored.

Now, strangely enough, none of this came to her yet as a personal matter. Her conscience hadn't troubled her here, for she still considered herself entirely sufficient for *herself*. The trouble was that she believed in religion for those who needed it, and she believed that young fellows like Dick Norton needed such safeguards and that her duty was to remind the fellow, if he couldn't see it, that here was the very distinction he longed for right at hand.

But here was the prick of conscience she felt—the inconsistency of pointing out to someone a course she herself carefully turned from.

On the whole, the first lesson couldn't be called an absolute success. The teacher cut it short very suddenly and announced almost crossly that the coat was mended and that she had no more time to give. She ordered the reading over of the six verses four times every night and learning to spell every word in them before he presented himself to her on Tuesday evening.

"If you're anxious to try your skill at obeying," she said with a grim smile, "this will certainly provide you with an opportunity."

As she closed the door after him she said impatiently to herself, "Why must I be haunted with such ideas? I never had any of them before. I wish Tom's notions were at the bottom of the river. The last scrape they've led me into is stranger than any yet."

Then, as she turned from the door and the damp night wind blew out her lamp, she saw something that drove Dick Norton and his verses and his ambitions utterly out of her head, for a farewell was taking place in the parlor at that moment. The door was ajar, and a stream of light came from the gas jet under which they stood, and she saw Alfred Parks stoop and touch his hateful mustached lips to Grace's fair, rosy cheek.

Chapter 11

A Sheep in Wolf's Clothing

The hotel was fairly under way. The first few weeks had been full of work and excitement. Success had flowed in upon them until Tom was ready to believe many more people were willing to promote his mission than he'd imagined.

It was Saturday evening. Matters were in order for a pleasant Sabbath, and Tom and his faithful ally, Peter, had donned overcoats and mufflers and gone out into the winter night to do work dear to the hearts of both of them—fish for men.

That expression was especially dear to Peter's heart, because of that old promise and direction he considered as much his commission as it was his namesake's: "Follow me, and I will make you fishers of men."

Tom and Peter both longed for results. They decided to divide their forces and take different paths.

"Well, good night," Tom said, as they reached the crossing at Easton Street. "Let's see what this evening will bring us. I wish you success."

Then he turned and walked down the brilliantly lighted city street, the special favorite for business and festivity, while Peter went down an alley where life was on a smaller scale. A great many people were out on the same mission of fishing, and the eagerness and art they displayed in working for their Master were remarkable to contemplate.

How the gaslights glittered in the spacious saloons he passed! What time and money had been spent in fitting up the gilded traps where young men were to be caught!

Tom looked eagerly about him with an eye for details. He didn't mean for the devil to have one inch of ground he could legitimately occupy. If anything new in elegance or fascination couldn't be found in the Randolph House, he meant for it to find its way there speedily.

Moving leisurely along, looking in at the windows, he reached the largest and grandest of these places and came to a full stop.

At the further window stood a young man, also gazing in earnestly. His face and dress and position showed him to be a young man from the country. Here was a fish, young and unsuspecting, in danger too, for his eyes plainly said, "That is a most inviting-looking spot." No doubt he was trying to decide whether to enter and see for himself what the reception would be.

The door was suddenly opened from the inside, and a young man with a winning face and manner said, as he flung wide the hospitable door and let out a flood of light and warmth into the black night, "Come in, gentlemen. You'll find much more comfortable quarters inside. It's a disagreeable night."

He was dressed in the extreme of city fashions, and his air and manner were what we usually call "dashing." A ring in his voice expressed friendliness and good fellowship. Tom caught the thought instantly. It would be well to have someone on the alert at the Randolph House door.

This cordial invitation was certainly agreeable. He sprang forward, but not to accept the invitation. "Thank you," he said courteously, for he'd adopted it as a motto to be courteous to everyone until necessity demanded a different manner. "Thank you, not at present. And I want a word with this young man, if he pleases. Will you walk with me a few steps, sir?"

The country stranger thus addressed turned and fixed a pair of grey eyes for an instant on Tom's face. "I've no objection to that. Where do you want me to go?"

Now if Tom had been entirely frank he would have answered, "I don't know in the least what to say next to you or how to account for my sudden desire for your company. The most I want is to keep you from stepping into that glittering trap that's open for you, which I know all about and of which you are ignorant." But of course it wouldn't do to say this, so he simply said, "Oh, come this way, please. You're a stranger in town, aren't you? I thought you looked lonely, and it seemed to me it would be pleasant to have a little talk with you. Do you mind taking a walk with me?"

"Not a bit," the young man said, and his voice was strong and hearty, a voice Tom liked at once. "I'm a stranger in town—have been here only a week—and I came out tonight to walk and see what's to be seen."

So they walked down Benson Street, Tom talking briskly, pointing out objects of interest and beauty, trying to be as entertaining as he could and meanwhile wondering how he would conclude this interview and make it helpful in the least.

"Where do you board?' he asked suddenly.

As the young man named one of the poorer streets of the city, where the houses were dark and dingy, Tom thought of the swarm of third-rate boardinghouses found there and pitied him in his heart. No wonder he came out for a walk and to see what was to be seen. Why shouldn't he at once try to take him away to that beautiful upper room, where there were lights and beauty and comfort and everything the most cultured taste could desire?

"Not the most fascinating place in which to spend an evening," he said, trying to speak lightly, as the young man gave a brief description of the peculiar boardinghouse in which he lodged. "Now I happen to have a much pleasanter place than that. If you don't mind a long walk, I'd like to show you where I live." Thus easily was the undertaking accomplished, and the two were soon mounting the steps of the Randolph House.

"There!" Tom said, with a little pardonable pride, as he showed his new friend into the long, bright, elegantly furnished parlor. "You're entirely welcome to pass an evening here as often as you choose."

The two seated themselves, and Tom tried to catch his fish. He talked and laughed had pie served on elegant dishes and eaten with silver forks and apparently made no headway at all.

The cool, keen, grey eyes studied Tom as if he were a rare work of art set up for investigation. The young man allowed himself to be entertained and amused, but in no way compromised. Nor did he return his host's apparent frankness by any communications about himself, except the most commonplace, and neither by word nor sign pledged himself ever to come again.

Tom was puzzled and disappointed. How would he ensnare this fish so that the surroundings should seem as pleasant to him, and as *free* to him, as the paradise into which he'd found him peeping?

"Come upstairs with me," he said, suddenly springing up after the pie was eaten. "I want to show you a perfect gem of a room."

And the grey-coated young man followed him quietly and walked the length and breadth of the precious, consecrated room without his composed face lighting up or expressing any other pleasure than that "it was very beautiful," spoken in cool, wary tones.

Tom sat on the ottoman and leaned his head against the window in despair. "I don't know how to win him," he said to himself. "He'll never come here again—I see it in his eyes. What's lacking? I wonder what I can say or do to help him?"

"Do you know what sort of place that was where you and I met tonight?" he asked.

"A saloon of some sort, I imagine," he said quietly.

"It was more than that," Tom said, speaking earnestly. "It was the largest and worst gambling hole in the city, the very worst, because they carry on their miserable business in a very respectable and fashionable manner. They're always on the lookout for victims. They thought they'd found two this evening. I'm glad they were disappointed for once."

Still no gleam of surprise or interest from his visitor. "Isn't this room as pleasant as the one we were peeping into?" he asked suddenly.

"Quite as pleasant, I'd say. Are you trying to outdo them?"

"Yes, I am—that's it precisely. I may as well tell you out and out—I'm not good at concealments. This is a trap. It's fitted up the best way I can plan, and I brought you here tonight to see if you, looking at it for the first time, could suggest something else that would help me catch the young men of our city and make them want to come here, instead of going to such places as those where we were tonight."

The strange young man up to this time hadn't taken a seat; instead he had stayed near the door, his keen eyes alert and his whole face quiet and emotionless. Now he turned, and for the first time his expression changed to one of somewhat puzzled inquiry, and he looked steadily at Tom for several seconds without speaking.

"Before I answer your question," he said at last, "I want you to tell me what you want to do with us after you trap us. What is your object in running opposition to the places downtown, and what do you expect to gain by it? Those are fair questions. If you answer them satisfactorily I'll try to answer yours."

Tom had been keenly excited during this interview and keenly disappointed. This seemed to him like the trial hour of his beloved scheme, and he feared it was to prove a failure. He couldn't conceal his excitement or the tremor in his voice.

"I want to help save men. I want to be about the business I promised my Master I'd try to do for Him. My object is to foil Satan in his plots for ruining young men."

You should have seen those grey eyes then! They fairly glowed with light and feeling. The owner of them left his station by the door and came with a long stride over to the low seat where Tom had dropped himself.

"Here's my hand," he said now. "Why, man, I belong to the same Master. He's bought me and given me my orders. I belong to the ranks and am working for the very same end. God bless you! Why, in the name of common sense, didn't you let me know what you were about?"

Tom sprang up, smiling and eager, and the country youth and the handsome city gentleman shook hands long and heartily.

"Sit down," said Tom, at last. "Why wouldn't you sit down, and why wouldn't you show a bit of interest in my beloved scheme? You made me feel it was an awful blunder from beginning to end and that you'd go and ruin yourself twice as fast after my interference as you would without it. By the way, what's your name, please? Mine is Tom Randolph."

"And mine is David Parker, at your service." And then David Parker leaned back in his chair and indulged in a long, loud, hearty laugh.

"What on earth is the matter?" asked Tom, greatly surprised and a bit annoyed.

"Why, I'm so amazed," explained his guest, "and so mistaken. You asked a question or two that I promised to answer. I'm from the country, you know, and I come fresh from a father who knows something of city life and has cautioned me on every side, until I'm fairly bristling with cautions, to beware of sharpers in every shape and form. I hope you'll excuse me for telling you, but if I didn't take you to be the tallest sharper I'd ever heard or dreamed of, then my name isn't David Parker. You know the prince of sharpers is said sometimes to appear as an 'angel of light,' and I thought I'd come across him in exactly that shape."

"What do you mean?" asked poor, puzzled Tom.

"Mean! Why, think for a minute what you did! Where did I meet you, and what excuse did you give for suddenly pouncing upon me, a perfect stranger, to take a walk with you? And what did you tell me about yourself and your schemes and all your apparent frankness? And what kind of place is this into which you led me? And how did you entertain me without the shadow of an explanation? I tell you if I hadn't been wide awake and a little vain about my ability to remain so, and if I hadn't besides honestly desired to see how you did it—that I might better help keep other young men from falling into your hands—I'd have turned and fled from you twice as fast as from that gambling saloon, for I considered you twice as dangerous."

"I begin to see," said Tom, light breaking over his perplexed face. "I've gone at this work with the idea that every young man I met was either a scamp or an unsuspecting victim, and not by any chance a fellow-fisher. I thought I was the Master's only disciple, it seems. Well, you've answered my question. Thank you. I'm encouraged."

"What is this place?" asked David Parker, his face expressing enough curiosity and eagerness to satisfy his host.

"It's a place dedicated to saving young men from the despair of alcohol."

"And what is this room?"

"It's a Young Men's Christian Association room. That is, it is to be, when we find the men to make up the association. At present there are only three: Thomas the Skeptic—that's me; Peter the Bold, and if ever a fellow was well named it's my friend Peter; and King David—that's you. We constitute officers and rank and file. I'm certain there are more, though, especially after tonight's experience. Having found our king, we can surely make progress."

"No, I'm only the shepherd boy, keeping my father's sheep," the young man said quickly.

"And are coming to serve well against Goliath with your sling and stones, are you? Very well, so be it. Let me ask you this, though: What did you expect to find up in this room?"

"A secret chamber with padded walls and gambling tables, with bottles and glasses and iniquity of every sort. It's true," he added as Tom laughed. "I expected *that* at the very least."

"Well, then, how did you know I wasn't playing sharp when I answered your question about motives? The worst scamp can feign pure motives."

David shook his head. "No, he can't—not in that tone and with that sacred name on his lips. At least I don't believe he could deceive me. I love the Leader too well and know the sound of His voice so well that I don't believe the counterfeit can deceive me. I don't know—I won't say that either, because good men have often been deceived. I'll simply say I'm as sure of you as if I'd known you all my life—and half an hour ago I thought you were the smoothest villain in the city."

"Well," Tom said, drawing a long breath, "I went out tonight praying I might find someone to help, someone to speak a word to that would be the means of doing good. But it never entered my heart to pray I might find a friend and brother. I thank Him from my soul. Shall we kneel together while you tell Him so?"

Instantly the two men knelt, and young David showed he was used to holding audience with the great King—that He was to him an "elder brother." And he thanked God for permitting him in his loneliness and sadness to find such a spot as this and such a friend.

Chapter 12

A Crisis

Maria stood perfectly still, holding on to her darkened lamp, apparently listening to the retreating footsteps of Dick Norton. In reality she was taking in this new and bewildering and, to her, utterly distasteful situation. Grace having company that was distinctively hers, that came at stated evenings and assumed rights over her—and, above all, kissed her! It was horrid!

Why, Grace was nothing but a child—a schoolgirl yesterday and would be still but for the inconvenience of money, or rather the absence of it. To be sure Grace was two years older than she; but then Maria had always been old. Who had ever heard anyone cautioned, even in her childhood, to look after her?

But hadn't the little mother looked after them hundreds of times, as they trotted off to school, and called, "Take good care of Gracie, daughter"—not in sarcasm either, but in real earnestness. For Maria, with her strongly built figure and firm step and independent air, looked fully two years older than her frail sister, and so everyone, even the mother, fell into the habit of considering her the leader and, in a certain sense, the protector. None of the family, except Helen, had ever rebelled at the leadership, and there had been times when she was glad to avail herself of its convenience. And now Grace was in the parlor, at this moment, bidding a special good-bye to a young man! Presently Maria recovered sufficiently to go forward to the kitchen table and fumble for the match safe.

"It isn't possible!" she muttered. "She can't mean anything but girlish nonsense. It isn't like Grace to be so free. It might do for some girls, but she's been brought up differently. But then she's been in that abominable store long enough to get careless. She sees him all the time too, and I suppose he seems to her like a brother. That's much too brotherly, though. I always did detest that sort of sham relationship. To think of getting it up with such a goose as Alfred Parks! What can Grace have been thinking about? Faugh!"

Whether this last remark meant Alfred Parks or the match fumes wasn't clear, for Maria said no more. But she banged the bread bowl about with a frowning face and said "Scat!" to the old white cat in such a tone that it sent her flying down to the cellar in dismay. It wasn't all ill-humor. The young lady had that unfortunate manner of exhibiting perplexity. She didn't know what to do. It must be stopped, of course. It would never do to let Grace make a fool of herself. *But how to stop it?* she wondered.

She groaned over the store and the money coming from it regularly into the family purse. Grace was wonderfully careful and economical. She could dress herself up like a lady out of a new ruffle and her old necktie redyed. Maria looked on respectfully and could never understand how it was done. In case the clerkship ended, how would she get along without the revenue from it? And in case it continued, how would she put a stop to the nonsense?

You see there was room for perplexity, but with no one to advise. By the time Grace had seen her visitor depart and locked the front door and come out to her, Maria was in just the right mood to turn fiercely around from the bread sponge she was stirring.

"Grace Randolph, what in the world has become of your common sense, to say nothing of your decency? What's the meaning of the performance I've had the pleasure of attending tonight?"

She could hardly have done a more unwise thing. I never claimed an uncommon share of wisdom for my friend Maria. A bright red spot glowed on Grace's round, fair cheek, but she answered in a mild, low voice.

"I don't know what you mean, Maria. What have I done to disturb you? Is it about the woman? I didn't say a word, I know. But Alfred really did think it was dangerous for *you*. It wasn't because he's heartless."

"Fiddlesticks for his heart!" Maria said, growing every minute more vexed. "What do I care about his heart or whether he has one? What I want to know is, what business has he to come here so much, and what right have you to be so free with him? I couldn't believe my own eyes at first. Why, I actually saw that contemptible fellow kiss you, and you stood and endured it! Now what does that all mean? Were you afraid of hurting his feelings, or *what?*"

If Maria had taken the trouble to look away from her sponge during this harangue, she would have seen that the red spot deepened and spread, until Grace's whole face was a flame of scarlet. Her voice was still low but wonderfully firm for such a slight and yielding girl, as she answered her irate sister in a way she had never spoken before in her life.

"Maria, you've forgotten yourself. Remember—I'm two years older and am not to be called to account by you, as if I were responsible to you for my actions. If I were, you haven't spoken to me in a way to invite confidence. If I were your daughter I would be almost justified in trying to deceive you after such harsh and cruel words. But I'll tell you despite all that what it means. I meant to tell you, of course, though I hoped it would be in a different way." And just here her voice trembled a little. "Alfred Parks has the right to come and see me, and for that matter to kiss me good night if he chooses to do so. He has all the right I can give him at least. I've promised to be his wife. And since I have no mother to go to, and I dare not disturb Father, I can only give him his rights in a less ceremonious, but not less sincere, way than others have done before me. I don't know how you made the discovery that has made you so angry tonight, and I'm sorry for it, because it has disturbed a pleasant story I meant to tell you this very night and hoped you would receive with sisterly sympathy. As it is you'll have to forgive us and make the most of us both. Good night."

And before Maria had finished staring at the rosy face, for she had turned entirely away from the bread sponge now, Grace had taken up her lamp and disappeared through the stairway. The water cooled in the bread bowl, the flour gathered itself into sticky lumps, and the spoon stood upright in the miserable mass, while Maria stood staring at the spot where Grace had been, apparently unable to turn her eyes away.

What a revelation! The previous one hadn't prepared her for it in the least. It had been miserable enough to suppose Grace was sinking to the level of very common young ladies, who thought that cordial leave-takings from their gentlemen acquaintances were no harm and no disgrace. She had even feared there might be a silly little feeling in Grace's heart that she rather liked the insipid Alfred. But not for one moment did it occur to her that Grace, their little sister, who it still seemed to her she should watch over and care for, had actually given herself away, thrown herself away rather, on a brainless boy, who was her inferior from every point of view—so at least he looked to *her*.

The anger had died out now. This was something real and tangible. Utter dismay and bewilderment took its place. Would they have to sit tamely down and submit to this? See Grace, the flower and darling, just frittered away! It was true enough, as she said, that no one with authority was there to appeal to. The father mustn't even hear of this.

"It isn't," said Maria to herself, with a swelling heart, "as if he were someone Father could be fond and proud of or feel joyful about leaving Grace to him."

And with this thought the anger began to rise again, and she was enabled to turn to the unfinished sponge. She tucked it up neatly and presently sat down to think, or rather glower at the future and wonder what would be the end of it all. The next arrivals were Tom and Helen. There was a little glow of interest or satisfaction on Helen's face.

"Are you studying ways and means as usual?" she asked, in a kind voice. "If I were you I'd write a book on domestic economy and end this struggle by making us all independent. I know it would be a success." This she said while Tom was lighting a lamp for her, and she went off immediately.

Tom drew his chair near his favorite sister.

"Well, I'm prepared to report about the hopefulness of that new friendship of yours. I thought you would storm me with questions. What do you suppose is her story? Or do you know it? She didn't communicate to me at all."

The only answer Maria vouchsafed to this was to whirl herself around so that her eyes were in line with her brother's and say in her most abrupt tone: "Tom, what do you know of Alfred Parks?"

"Know of him?" Tom repeated, startled. "Why, not a great deal, but as much as I care to, perhaps—no, I shouldn't say that. He's one of the kind I'm after, but I hadn't thought of him. Is he to be one of your *protégés?* You remember you promised to help."

"How should you relish him for a brother-in-law?"

"Maria!" said Tom, with sufficient amazement, not to say disgust, in his voice to satisfy Maria. "What on *earth* do you mean? I didn't even know you were acquainted with him—and I hadn't the remotest idea you were thinking of such matters anyway."

This was perhaps just what Maria needed. It was so ridiculous that it took the sting a little from her heart and the gloom from her face, and she waited to laugh before she answered.

"You can't be such an idiot to suppose I'm talking about myself! Tom, I thought you had common sense."

"What *are* you talking about?" said Tom, and then he stopped suddenly, and the amazed look changed to understanding and then to dismay. "Gracie?" he asked breathlessly.

"That's just it. Now what's to be done? Such a thing can't be borne, you know, and I want to know how we're to put an end to it."

"That's a good deal easier said than done, and I suspect she'll tell us we have no business even to discuss it in that light. But how much of a beginning has it, and how did you discover it and all about it?"

So Maria began at her beginning, which only dated to the feeling of annoyance that had crept over her lately at the frequency of "that simpleton's" calls, and detailed the result of the evening's experiences. Tom had arisen before she finished her story and was twirling his chair on one leg, looking both annoyed and perplexed. He interrupted her while she was reporting her conversation with Grace, the beginning of it.

"You couldn't have done a more unwise thing than to pounce on the child in that style."

"I know it. Do you consider that a very helpful and encouraging remark?" Tom laughed.

"Well, go on," he said. "I see how it was. Surprise and annoyance got the better of you, and I'd probably have done the same."

"No, you wouldn't. You're not made of quicksilver." Then she finished her story. By the time it was concluded, Tom was walking up and down the room; he had learned that from his father.

"He's decent enough, I suppose," he said at last, speaking slowly, as if he were reluctant to admit even that.

"But he's such a ninny—he shows off the new styles in neckties and perfumes his handkerchiefs with the latest fashion. I never imagined there was more than that to him. To think of one of the Randolphs liking him! What can Grace mean?"

"But I don't see what we're to do. She won't listen to reason, and certainly we have no authority and would perhaps have no right to exercise it, if we had. Is she two or three years older than you?"

"Two. But you needn't think *I* am going to sit meekly down and submit to such a thing!"

"You haven't," Tom said, laughing a little. "You've entered your protest. How far have you advanced toward stopping it, do you think? I don't know—there seems to be nothing we can do. If he were a drunkard or anything like that, it would be different. But he's a fellow of very decent habits—better perhaps than the average."

"What a pity!" Maria said, imitating his doleful tone. And then this troubled brother and sister broke down in a hearty laugh.

"But I *won't* endure it, all the same," Maria said, rallying. "And you needn't think it. I'll do something. Grace is nothing but a child. She doesn't know her own mind any more than a kitten would. She thinks it's nice to have somebody interested in her and look after her, that she doesn't get her feet wet on rainy days and walk a mile out of his way to carry her umbrella for her—he's done that twice—and she imagines *that* is reason enough for promising to marry him!"

"And you're her grandmother's maiden aunt and know all about it," Tom said, finding it impossible not to laugh a little over this impetuous girl, two years younger than her sister.

But she turned to him with an unanswerable argument: "Tom Randolph, *was* I ever as young in my life as Grace is now?"

"I don't think you ever were," Tom said, speaking with utmost gravity and then walking the floor again. "If she were a Christian," he said slowly, "I could appeal to that difference, but as it is—"

"If she were, she would wheedle him into thinking he was one in less than ten minutes," Maria said, spitefully. "The greatest trouble with him is that he hasn't any brains at all. He has to borrow his ideas from her. Tom, if you could hear some of his jokes, you'd be sick for a week. And Grace actually laughs over them. So, you see, she means it. But I'll do something, I'm sure of that. I won't submit meekly. If the poor wretch ever becomes my brother-in-law, I'll be sorry for him—that's all."

At last the evening was ended. Tom said good night without having thought what to do, and Maria went upstairs, locked herself in and had a luxury she seldom permitted herself, a good cry, before she got out writing materials and set to work.

Chapter 13

Invitations

Tom had a new scheme on hand and much work to do to get ready for it. Part of the work was to talk Maria into the right mood for helping.

"What in the world do you want of me?" she asked. "I'm sure it's out of my line."

"No," her brother said, speaking positively, "you're mistaken about that. It is *not* out of your line—what I want of you, you can do. I need your help. It won't be like a prayer meeting at all. I don't want it to be the least bit stiff."

"And you think I'm not stiff? That might be a compliment, and it might not. But now *what* am I to do?"

"Why, in the first place, you're to come. There's a great deal of help in just being there. Then I want you to fit in at vacant places, repeat a Bible verse, ask a question simple enough to be understood by everyone and vital enough to be of importance to all—such questions as you know how to ask."

"In short, you want me to help conduct a religious meeting! That will be very much like the 'blind leading the blind.' Didn't they both fall into the ditch? I don't know any Bible verses."

"You've just quoted one. And, besides, there's enough time to learn a new one. Then I need your help very much in the matter of singing—we want to sing every few minutes."

"Who'll lead your singing? Are you going to have playing?"

"Yes, indeed! This is one of the main uses of that piano. Helen's going to play and lead the singing—at least I'm going to ask her if she will."

"Helen!" One exclamation point doesn't begin to convey the astonishment in Maria's voice. "Tom Randolph, you *know* she won't do anything of the kind! Why, it's months since she's been to her own prayer meeting! And do you think she'll approve anything so unheard of as a Sunday afternoon meeting at a hotel, especially where all the servants are to be invited, or that she'll lead music in which they're to join?"

"I think she will," Tom said. "At least I hope so. She knows all about it and hasn't objected to the plan."

"Well, now, you can hope until you're grey, but I *know* she won't do it. She may have discovered there's no use in objecting to your notions—I should be wise enough for that myself by now—but taking a prominent part in the entertainment is another thing. I know her better than that. Tom, you ask her when she comes down, and if after a full half-hour of argument she agrees to have anything to do with it I'll come and recite two verses and sing like a lark."

This sentence was hurried to its conclusion by the sound of Helen's step in the hall. Her brother turned as she entered and came directly to the point.

"Helen, will you play and sing for us tomorrow?"

"Sing *for* you! Oh, you mean lead the singing—they're all going to join, aren't they? Why, yes, I suppose so. Maria, your alto is so strong it'll make a good background. Are you going to help sing?"

"As loud as I can roar!" said Maria emphatically and with a significant look at Tom.

And he, with a beaming face and a heart well satisfied with that half-hour's work, went to his long room to finish preparations there.

The plans for that first meeting reached out in many directions and had been carefully studied. In the first place little notices were tacked not only in conspicuous places, but in out of the way, unexpected places. These were written in fine, round print, with dainty flourishes and graceful shadings: "Praise meeting at the rooms of the Young Men's Christian Association, 279 Burton Avenue, at four o'clock next Sunday afternoon. You are invited."

There had been diplomacy in getting up those cards. David Parker had projected the idea, and Tom in much delight had grasped it.

"That's great! I'll get them printed this afternoon."

"No, indeed," David had answered briskly. "We're poor, you know—we must economize our resources. Besides, it isn't to be a printed circular, to belong to the millions, but a special, personal invitation."

"Written," said Tom heartily. "Good! I'll bring my German text into requisition then and do them elegantly."

"With all deference to your skill in that line, may I get a fellow I know to write them for us? I've been trying to catch him for some time. He's quite fast. I used to know him when he was younger, and he hasn't changed for the better. But he can write beautifully, and it will serve as an excuse."

"I see," Tom had said, with that touch of respect in his voice that this grey-coated young man from the country often called forth. "It's a good thought—carry it out, by all means. In the meantime we'll pray that the invitation may write itself upon his heart. David, there are endless ways of fishing. I learn a new one from you every day."

The result of this planning was that young David left his work earlier than usual one afternoon and sought one of the clerks in McAllister's store. He had a favor to ask, and he presented his claims with such an expectant air that the fast young man was won over to help.

"How many of them do you want written?" he asked, reading the copy attentively. "Fifty! Why, that will take time. And you must have them for Sunday? Then they would have to be done this evening, and I had other plans in mind. But that can wait, and I'd rather like to accommodate you, even if it is in such an odd way. You stick to the old track, don't you, David? It agrees with you too; I never saw you look better. Well, you can depend on me. I'll have them ready for you when you call tomorrow."

Now another result grew out of this. Not ten minutes after David Parker had gone his way the clerk at McAllister's had another call. One of his "fast" companions came, proposing a ride into the country and supper at a certain hotel. The ride and supper included some questionable activities and enough danger to lay the foundation for ruin.

"Can't go," said the clerk promptly, but with a shade of disappointment in his voice. "I've promised to devote my evening to philanthropy or religion—both, I guess. Anyhow, it will take the whole evening, what little is left, after business."

They laughed and talked over this decision, but it was unalterable. For the young man, who was treading on dangerous ground and going ahead a few steps every day, still had this safe ground holding him back. His early education had taught him that his word once given, however trivial the cause might appear to him, was to be respected.

So he sat at home and wrote those words on that slip of paper fifty times—though, during the first dozen, he got up as many times and stared out of the window, voted it a glorious evening for a ride and called himself a fool for not having gone. But he *didn't* go.

David Parker knew nothing of this result of his plan, neither then nor afterward. I wonder how many of the events of our lives turn on such little invisible hinges as these.

David had aimed at another result, and he and Tom Randolph and Peter Armstrong prayed that evening for its accomplishment.

Alone, in his dingy little room, the young clerk sat and wrote for the twentieth time those words, "You are invited." He wrote them with many variations in the curves and flourishes. Once, as he drew a graceful line under the "you," he repeated the sentence aloud.

"I've given myself a good many invitations, seems to me," he said. "I wonder if it wouldn't be a good idea to accept one of them and see what it's like. Parker is the oddest fish that ever was. I'd like to see what sort of people he's fallen among. This can never be his own plan. He must have someone in with him. I wonder where this meeting is? I didn't know there was a hall in that part of the city. I mean to stroll down there on Sunday and see what this is about."

"I caught him," David had explained to Tom, "so far as writing the notices goes. It's quite an evening's work, but he's kindhearted, likes to accommodate and is a little bit vain of his writing. So now our part is to pray that the invitation will touch him."

"Does that mean *me?*" the writer asked the next evening, as he handed over the notices and pointed to the words "You are invited."

"Indeed it does," David said, the eagerness in his heart springing up into his voice. "Will you accept?"

"Why, I guess I will, if you won't be hard on a fellow. I don't know how to act in meetings—ain't used to it, you see. What are you up to, David? What are you trying to do?"

"Come and see," David answered. "Come tomorrow—you'll find something to enjoy." And as he went down the street the glow in his eyes deepened to reverence as he thought of the wonderful directness of this answer to the previous night's prayer.

Meanwhile Peter was at work getting ready for the meeting. In his pocket he had a dozen of the slips, and as he walked down the street he searched for just the people to whom he should give them.

It was Saturday evening, and he stood in the bakery at the west end of their street, waiting for his order to be filled. Leaning on the counter, at his left, was a young fellow of about his own age, rough in appearance and manner and gloomy-looking to the last degree.

Peter, watching him furtively, wondered if he should offer him a slip of paper. The fellow was looking, not at Peter, but at a plate of little tarts on the counter. What greedy eyes he had! It couldn't be hunger, for actual hunger would have turned toward the piles of buns and loaves of bread. He didn't seem to notice them, but the tarts fairly held him there.

Whatever the cause of the temptation, it proved too strong for the poor fellow. The hour was late for business, and the only clerk in attendance was engaged with Peter's order at the other end of the room.

It took a second to reach out two arms and hands and grasp in either hand a tart, then stuff them unceremoniously into either pocket. He seemed to have forgotten Peter's existence. As for Peter, he stood looking in pitiful dismay. To steal something to eat was such a sad thing to feel obliged to do! That's how it appeared to Peter.

He stood contemplating what to do until the clerk returned. The poor fellow meanwhile stood with an air of stolid indifference. Peter glanced over the list of articles, and while he reached into his pocket said, in a loud, clear voice, "You may add two tarts to this bill. How much are they?"

"Two tarts!" said the surprised clerk. "Oh, you mean you helped yourself to them? All right—they're ten cents apiece."

And Peter added twenty cents from his own pocket to the amount due. He was leaning carelessly against the door during this transaction, and at its close he turned suddenly to the fellow at his right and handed him a slip of paper.

"Here's an invitation for you," he said in a kind voice. "Will you accept it?"

Then he shouldered his parcel, opened the door and went out.

"Will you come?" he asked, as the young man immediately followed him.

For answer, he turned about and stared at Peter in the moonlight. "You didn't take no tarts."

"No, but you did, so I paid for them. The man shouldn't lose the price of them, you know. Besides, I couldn't bear to have you steal."

If Peter had expected gratitude he was mistaken.

"Your conscience is mighty tender," the fellow said gruffly. "It was nothing but two mean little pies, and he had lots of 'em. But I don't want you to do my payin' for me, and I ain't got no money to pay you."

A bright thought struck Peter. "If you'll come to that meeting tomorrow I'll consider it square."

"What do you want me to come for?"

"To have a good time. Will you come?'

"You're a strange chap," was the muttered answer. "But I ain't afraid of you or of no trap you can set. Yes, I'll come, if I don't get took to jail for something before the time."

So this was the character of the recruit Peter secured for the first meeting.

Chapter 14

Turning the Tables

Such a delightful room they gathered in for the meeting on that lovely Sunday afternoon! It looked like a room garnished for a festival scene. On either end of the piano and on the many little tables scattered up and down glowed sweet-smelling flowers. Nothing anywhere was stiff or somber.

The congregation assembled for this meeting was somewhat peculiar. Helen, in her handsome black silk and soft laces, presided at the piano and looked every inch a lady. At her right were two of the chambermaids, in pretty and neat-fitting calicoes, and very near them was Irish Kate, red-faced and good-natured, so encumbered with flesh that she waddled instead of walked and on this day was fairly blazing in a red and green plaid dress.

On the velvet sofa next to her were two elegant young ladies in elegant costumes: summer silks, fluttering ribbons, ruffles, tucks and puffs. They had come to the house the day before, and whether they had come to this meeting from interest or curiosity remained to be seen.

Their nearest neighbor was Dick Norton. And next to him was the young man who had written the invitations, gazing about him in amazement. He, certainly, was in a strange place.

Peter was there, and so, to his surprise, was *his protégé* of the evening before.

The meeting had no beginning and apparently no leader. But, like all successful meetings with this appearance, it meant to the initiated that much thought and time had been expended and that some *one* had done his best to make the effort a success.

The rule proved true here. Tom had never given himself more entirely to any work than he had to preparing for this little gathering.

After singing two or three favorite hymns from the books on each seat, Tom laid aside his hymnbook and said, "I've been interested in some verses which have been grouped together from the Bible. Perhaps we'd enjoy reading them over. Each Bible has a slip of paper in it, and if those who have the verses I call for care to read them aloud, it'll make the reading more pleasant. If anyone doesn't care to read and would like to look on, we hope you'll do so."

Thus invited, even Dick Norton opened his Bible, which Maria observed and inwardly hoped he wouldn't attempt to read aloud. You'll remember she was familiar with his skill in that line.

Bible readings are strange things anyway—so different from opening one's Bible in Genesis or Numbers, or *anywhere* at random, and reading a chapter.

Maria had done that a good many times in her life, but with about as little idea of what she'd read as someone who had been running her eye over a certain number of words. But this was a connected argument—simple, earnest, and as logical as the brains of Moses and David, and Paul, touched by the power of the Holy Spirit, could make it, and the subject was the reasonableness of God's requirements.

Mindful of her pledge to repeat a verse, this obstinate sister had given considerable attention to the subject during the previous evening and had finally succeeded in finding a verse she was satisfied with: "A feast is made for laughter, and wine maketh merry, but money answereth all things."

She had been happy over this verse while she was committing it to memory. The latter part of it, at least, was so like her own sentiments that it was a pleasant surprise to find that the wise men of all time so fully agreed with her.

But her brother's arrangement, with a set verse for each to read, brought to her the straightforward, plain and, she couldn't help thinking, remarkably reasonable verse: "He hath showed thee, O man, what is good; and what doth the Lord require of thee, but to do justly, and to love mercy, and to walk humbly with thy God?"

Despite her effort at unconcern, her voice held a slight shade of consternation as she read this sentence, which, viewed in the light of what had preceded it, seemed the most reasonable consequence in the world.

Maria had reason to remember that Bible reading—not only because it shed new light on the Bible as a book for study, but because every verse selected seemed to be full of barbed arrows, all pointing at her favorite theories of practical common sense.

It was an unusual hour to some present. The clerk who had written the invitations was surprised at his interest in the matter; he wondered what the people were about and what special advantage it could be for them to follow up this sort of thing and spend time and money in its development. His interest was so great that he lingered, even after the meeting closed, and sought to draw his old acquaintance out on the subject.

"This is a grand establishment you have to use for carrying out your schemes," he said, as David came over to him. "I don't think there's a finer put-together place in the city. Who runs it, and what do you have to pay for the use of this room?"

"Yonder is the man in authority, talking with the lady at the piano."

"What, that boy! Why, he's younger than you are. How in the world did he become the head of such an affair as this? And how does he happen to be mixed up with a religious performance like this?"

"This is a religious affair from beginning to end," David said, adopting his companion's phraseology. And then he proceeded to unfold the idea upon which the foundations of the Randolph House rested, to the young man's astonished ears.

"Upon my word!" he repeated slowly, after asking a dozen questions and being carefully answered. "This beats all the notions I ever heard of! And so that young fellow actually has control of a house like this! And he means to run it without any liquor! He'll get in debt, as sure as my name is Wilders.

I've heard of that kind of thing being tried before, and it won't work. I heard the biggest antiliquor man in the city say so only last week. Hotels *can't* be run without liquor. Not a man in the country can afford to do it. You can't make a living in such a way."

He of the keen grey eyes wasn't in a mood to argue, and if he had been, this young Wilders wasn't the sort of person to select when one thirsted for actual argument.

So he simply said, with a composed voice, "Suppose that were all true—proved, you know, beyond any mistake. And suppose, also, that I couldn't make a living at selling boots and shoes unless I first cut your throat. The question is, shall I do that or try to get my living in a less questionable way?"

An exceedingly dim idea of this odd young fellow's meaning glimmered in the mind of Wilders but wasn't sufficiently clear for him to return other than that easy and unanswerable answer, which is the unfailing refuge of puzzled people: "That isn't a parallel case, you know."

David knew just how much that meant, so he only laughed in reply and said, "Well, never mind—you keep in sight of the Randolph House until it fails, and then you'll have another argument for your side. In the meantime you might as well enjoy it. We're going to have an entertainment here tomorrow evening for some of our friends. Will you come and make yourself useful in amusing them?"

"What sort of entertainment?"

"Oh, music and talk and some refreshment. It's for some of those people who never have any good times. You might as well give some of your evenings to helping other people. Come and give us a lift."

This shrewd young man understood his "fish" perfectly. To be invited because of needing help to *himself* would be a terrible blow to his vanity and send him away never to come again. But to be invited to help a good cause, especially one with respectability, not to say grandeur, about it, was quite another thing. He gave the required promise so promptly that David was satisfied and especially thankful he'd received it before the young man had been committed to a scheme he knew to be among another class of entertainers.

Peter, meanwhile, wasn't idle. His *protégé* was striding out when Peter touched his arm and said kindly, "If you'll wait I'll introduce you to Mr. Randolph, the gentleman who runs this house, and he'll invite you to the gathering tomorrow evening."

"I ain't a-coming!" was the gruff, loud-spoken reply, and with a jerk he released himself from the kind hand and tore down the steps.

Peter looked after him with a sigh and said, exactly as you've said, my friend, a dozen times about some pet scheme of yours, "*That* did no good," when all the time the One who plans and works with you knows the end from the beginning as you and Peter *cannot.*

"Was it a success?" Tom said, bending eagerly over Maria.

"No, it was horrid, firing brickbats at people in that style. Why couldn't you have been content with the singing and the praying and not shoot Bible verses around in that promiscuous fashion? And you didn't tell me I was to read a verse *you* selected. It was gotten up under false pretenses. Next time I'll know enough to stay with Father and send Grace. What's become of Dick? I was afraid he'd practice on his recent lessons in reading and try to perpetrate a verse. He's the most amazing reader you ever heard in your life. I'll tell you what it is, you silly fellow—if you'd turn some of your Bible preachings into a little practical instruction on how to write one's name and add a column of figures, you might do some good in the world. Dick says four of those car drivers can't write their names, and I suppose their reading is equal to his."

"That's a good thought," Tom said. "I'm glad you mentioned it. Tomorrow evening will be a good time to consider it. Maria, will you come tomorrow and help us arrange for refreshments?"

"My patience! Are you having a party? You're the most absurd boy! I mean to write to Mr. Harper and tell him what a wild way you're going on! The idea of his trusting his fortune in your hands! He'd need to be a Rothschild at the very least. Oh, yes, I'll come over and attend to that. Refreshments are in my line, if Bible verses aren't. But, Tom, don't do another wild thing until next week at least."

And this indifferent sinner went to her home—while Tom sighed over her carelessness and the impossibility of ever getting her to think seriously—and gave her father such a gentle, tender account of the meeting that he more than once wiped a glad tear from his faded eyes and thought in his heart that this dear child wasn't far from the kingdom. And neither he nor Tom was entirely correct. Thoughtless she was not, with that verse ringing in her ears as it seemed to do; haunting her as she went about her work; following her to her room and persistently repeating itself in her ear as she lay on her pillow and impatiently refused to answer it.

"What doth the Lord require of thee, but to do justly, and to love mercy, and to walk humbly with thy God?"

Reasonable requirements, said her common sense. She was willing enough to be "just" to everybody; at least she thought she was. But to walk humbly, with all that her conscience, enlightened by Christian education, knew that sentence involved, her proud heart assured her she wasn't willing to do; nor did she want to be troubled about this matter.

At the same time her inconsistent soul was bubbling over with pride for Tom. She began to realize something of the greatness of his plans and efforts, and while she wouldn't encourage him by even a word, yet she shed delighted tears in secret that he was unlike other young men and had consecrated his life to something so grand as this outreach after men. She went to sleep with a strange contradiction of feelings tugging at her heart. She wanted her brother to work for young men, for their present and eternal welfare. In her own wayward way she was even willing to help this work on. At the same time she said that *she* was not a young man, and she *did* wish he could learn to let *her* alone.

Chapter 15

"To Be or Not to Be"

Between the last time Maria closed and locked the kitchen door after Tom and the time she arranged paper and ink before her, she had developed a plan for rescuing Grace from the misery that in her sister's estimation awaited her. This involved a letter, which she wrote and I now copy for your consideration.

My dear Ermina,

And your husband too, of course, except that I haven't got used to saying it yet. I don't indulge in letter-writing very often, you remember. Grace is proving a treasure in that direction. But this evening I have something to tell which she might put in a different light.

Do you remember that smooth-faced, yellow-haired, insignificant-looking creature—clerk at McAllister's—whom they call Al Parks? I don't suppose you do; there wasn't enough of him to remember. But you must collect your thoughts and try to descend sufficiently low in the social scale to recall him, for he's destined to make you wish he'd never been born—in this country, at least.

Not to linger over disagreeable things, the whole story in a nutshell is that Grace is engaged to him! Just think of it, Ermina! Our Grace! Doesn't it seem to you as if she were still a little girl in school, with Mother looking after her and being afraid she would take cold and have the croup? Perhaps you'll hint, as Tom does, that during those days I was younger than she—whatever may be said of me now—but you know the time never was when I was smaller than she, and I didn't belong to the croupy sort either. I remember Grace needed constant care, and I did it. She would never remember to wear her tippet and could never find her mittens, and she needs taking care of to this day.

But it isn't so easy to do as it used to be. When a girl imagines she's lost her heart, no matter in how insignificant a place it's lost, she seems to grow obstinate. Ermina, I'm so thankful we had one wedding in our family that was a comfort. You know we always had to go around feeling, if not saying, "Poor Horace," but your husband never seemed to be a special object of pity in any direction. I'm not much given to flattery, you know, but I can't help telling you I never pitied him for securing you for his wife.

Well, now, Ermina, what are we to do about this matter? Tom says, or seems to feel, that there's no use in attempting to stop it. He says Grace isn't under our control and has a right to marry without regard to us, if she chooses to do so. But that seems to me to be a heartless way of disposing of the matter, and impossible, as far as I'm concerned. I have to attempt it. If I *fail, it won't be my fault.*

My first attempt deserved to fail, I suppose; it was such a blunder. You see I've been taken by storm—never dreamed of anything so absurd until tonight. Then certain developments amazed and vexed me, and I did what Tom calls "pitching into her." She was as dignified as if she'd been my grand-mother. But I don't blame her, for Tom says I could hardly have done any-thing more ill-advised than talk to her as I did. Though I told him I didn't appreciate his telling me so, still it was the truth, and I knew it. The worst of it is that it has spoiled any further thing I might do, though I don't know what I could do except order the miserable fellow away from the house at the point of the broomstick. I'm willing to attempt that, if it's advisable.

Seriously, Ermina, I'm so distressed I hardly know what I'm writing. It isn't as if we had a mother, who in her quiet, tender way could talk over these things, or if Father were so that he could look after us. We're wonderfully alone and have to depend on ourselves. But do you suppose we have to sit down and submit to such a thing? I won't make wedding cake for this party, I can tell you.

I know you'll be at your wits' end trying to recall the fellow, and you want me to tell you something definite about him, and I can't—not because I don't know all about him, but because there's nothing of him to tell about. He parts his hair more to the left than anyone else does, and he smokes a good many cigars in a day and wears a gold ring with a large glass plate in it on his lit-tle finger. These, with his many bright-colored neckties, are all the distinctive marks he has. "Do you know anything really bad about him?" Tom said anx-iously, and I assured him I didn't, because I never had thought there was enough of him to be bad. He's simply negative.

Write and tell me what you think, or what you advise, and do be quick about it. I'm in a twitter. I expect to spoil the starched clothes tomorrow, just because of my state of mind. I wish I washed for that fellow. I'd see that his collars were stiff.

Father is as usual. He hasn't coughed quite so much for a night or two. I sleep on the sofa in the sitting room now, so as to be nearby to look after him. The new medicine really seems to strengthen him a little.

Tom is splendid. I don't tell him so, but really that boy does me credit. He's as full of schemes for usefulness as Alfred Parks is of indolence. The fact is, Alfred would make a capital foil to our Tom. Think of having to "brother" someone like him!

I hope Mr. Harper looks well to his purse. I told Tom I'd consider it my duty to warn him. He's so busy planning for young men who have no homes and no pleasures. He'll need a bank account that will reach around the world. Yet, after all, one needs to expend very little anxiety on him. I don't pretend to any goodness myself, but I'm thankful to the sole of my foot that I have such good relations.

Helen is really getting interested in life again. She goes to the hotel nearly *every day, and it's wonderful to see how Tom and she consult together. She thinks he's silly and is wasting a lot of money, but she helps him waste it with much interest. If the scheme gives Helen something to think about besides her troubles, I think it will have accomplished something.*

If I had time I'd give you an account of a lady visitor I had this evening, but that precious Alfred has occupied so much of my thoughts that all minor matter must be left to another time.

Having freed my mind I can go to bed now and try to dream some way out of the calamity staring us in the face. Good night.

Maria

Ermina, sitting in her handsome rooms at home, read this characteristic letter a day later and laughed and cried over it.

"I have a letter from Gracie's grandmother," she said, as her husband entered the room, "and it's impossible to read it without laughing, and yet it makes me feel very anxious. Sit down till I read it to you. You're called to a family council once more."

Writing the letter had been a great relief to Maria. Just what it would accomplish she had no idea. Her judgment told her it was absurd to expect it to accomplish anything. Yet she had come to have a certain assurance that whatever went into Mr. Harper's hands was sure to be acted upon, promptly and wisely. So, without reasoning about what he could do in this case, she let the satisfied feeling creep into her heart that she had secured a strong ally.

Another thought gratified this inconsistent girl, as she put away her pen and went to the window to look out into the night: Ermina and her husband would pray a good deal about the new development and get counsel as to what should be done. Though why a girl who never prayed, who apparently had more confidence in her own resources than in a lifetime of prayer, should be so satisfied that some people who believe in it would pray, I cannot explain to the satisfaction of any reasonable mortal. Unfortunately for Maria she didn't attempt an explanation, because, being a girl of good common sense, she might have felt the folly of her own position and so been driven from it.

Passing over the tiresome waiting Maria had to do and the Sabbath and two following days, I bring you down to a certain Wednesday afternoon when she sat alone in the little sitting room. The door was closed to the bedroom so her father might have his afternoon nap, and she with a frowning face sewed on the patches of his dressing gown and wondered what was to come of it all and whether another mail would come without her receiving a letter from the New York people.

"It" wasn't progressing well, so she thought. Grace had gone boldly to church Sunday evening, leaning on the obnoxious Alfred's arm, and on this very evening she was to accompany him to a concert. Helen was in a provokingly indifferent state and not inclined to interfere in any way, which, if Maria had thought of it, was an alarming feature for her to exhibit. But she didn't hesitate to declare that if Grace could get a little comfort out of such an insignificant bit of humanity as the said Alfred, she didn't see what right they had to interfere. Then she went over to the hotel to practice a new piece of music which Tom wanted sung at the next gathering.

So Maria sewed and frowned, and presently the doorbell rang, a quick, clear peal. It deepened Maria's frown; she was in no mood for entertaining the few callers who troubled themselves about the decayed and quiet family. But she put aside her sewing, drew her apron straight and brushed the threads from it while she went through the hall, giving in another moment a quick exclamation of surprise and pleasure.

"Mr. Harper! I would have as soon expected to see the president, and I'm a great deal more glad to see *you*. Where is Ermina?"

"At home and well. I came in haste and on business. She decided it wasn't best to come just now."

"Did you get my letter?" Maria asked eagerly, as he followed her in. "Did she, I mean, and what did she think of it? Has she sent me any answer?"

"We got it and read it carefully. Yes, she sent an answer by me. At least I came down to answer it to the best of our abilities. We'll see what we can do. How is Father?"

"Better than usual. I really think if we had a doctor who knew as much as he should, something could be done for Father. I don't believe he has consumption any more than I have."

"Would he miss Grace much, do you think, and would she object to leaving him for awhile?"

"No," Maria said, startled a little. Did he intend to recommend solitary confinement for Grace until she outgrew her folly? "No, he wouldn't miss her much, because he sees very little of her. She goes in the morning before he's awake, and often he's too tired to see her more than a moment or two at night. What are you thinking of?"

"We're thinking of carrying her off to New York with us and putting her where she should be, in a first-class school, for a couple of years, giving her a chance to cultivate her talent for music and for—"

"Common sense," interrupted Maria, as he hesitated for a word.

Maria was amazed at this brilliant planning. *Could it have been the result of the praying?* she found time to wonder. But her surprise never took the form of silence. Her powers of speech were much too active for that.

"It's a perfectly gorgeous idea," she said, with shining eyes. "Just the opportunity Grace should have had, and if I'd been the oldest daughter, as I ought to have been, she should have had. But I'm afraid she's infatuated to the degree that *she won't do it*—at least if he advises her not to she won't, and of course he will. He's just idiot enough to offer such advice as that, and Grace is developing; she's as obstinate as possible. The moment she hears a word from me she goes about the house in an aggrieved sort of way, as if she were a martyr instead of a dunce."

"I don't wonder," the brother-in-law said, laughing in spite of himself. "Maria, you don't believe in hearts, do you?"

"Hearts!" said Maria, in great indignation. "I believe in common sense."

"That you do—and it's most fortunate for this family that you've been given your share of that useful article," he said heartily and with genuine affection in his voice. "But, in the meantime, I respect Grace for standing up firmly for the man she thinks she's chosen. He may be a simpleton, but he doesn't look like one to her. Maria, is it possible you may be doing him an injustice? I don't mean he's perfect, and they're both absurdly young to think of such matters. But suppose they weren't, and they had a true affection for each other. Isn't it possible your natural anxiety underrates him?"

"You have a talk with him," said Maria. "Just spend half an hour in his interesting society, talk on any subject you choose and see what you think then. That's all I have to say."

The brother-in-law laughed.

"I mean to try it," he said quietly. "Well, now, Maria, are you willing to put this matter in my hands and let me manage it according to my own ideas?"

"Of course," Maria said, with energy. "If you can manage it at all, you can do more than I—and more than I suspect *you* can do, for I never knew how obstinate Grace *could* be. We've always thought her yielding, but I hope she'll be managed."

"And you'll promise not to open your lips to her on the subject, either for or against the young man or the plan or in any way whatever? Because, to tell you the truth, I'm rather afraid of your energy in this matter. You can plunge at a thing until you pitch it over, so that it can't be righted."

"Oh, I'll keep still," Maria said, a little piqued. "It isn't that I want to manage her. It isn't that. I don't want her to be miserable all her life or be nothing but a sickly little simpleton. If things are only done, I don't care to have any hand in them."

"You've had a hand in this," Mr. Harper said earnestly, "a most decided hand. Of course, but for your warning we'd have known nothing of it, and but for your appeal we'd hardly have liked to interfere. But, my dear sister, you've learned only half the verse. You speak the truth earnestly, forcibly, and with strong common sense on your side, but the verse says 'speaking the truth in love.' And don't you know you have a way of hiding that part in your heart, so that the truth sometimes wounds where you would have it heal?"

Maria laughed. Her good nature had returned.

"I knew you'd finish up with a Bible verse," she said. "Neither you nor Tom can help it. I'll be as mum as a block, and I wish you joy in your work. Now go in and see Father, and I'll get you some dinner. I know in my heart just how glad I am you've come, but I'll keep the knowledge to myself, for you hinted I couldn't tell if I tried."

Chapter 16

Alfred Parks on Examination

Mr. Harper entered upon his task of becoming acquainted with Mr. Alfred Parks without any distinct idea of the magnitude of the effort. The occasion was favorable. The young man came for Grace to attend the concert and was in holiday attire, with a new and glorious necktie, rivaling the rainbow in brilliance. To Grace he looked particularly charming, and it was with beaming eyes and a satisfied smile that she introduced "my brother-in-law, Mr. Harper" and left them together while she went to get ready. It was with a grim sense of having accomplished it that Maria closed the door on the two gentlemen and left them alone together.

Young Alfred didn't feel particularly at ease. He was sufficiently master of "small talk" to feel at home among young people of his own age and stamp and sufficiently vain to imagine that all *young* ladies, and a large portion of older ones, could be entertained with it. But with this dignified gentleman, known in their own set as "very religious," Alfred felt greatly at a loss as to how to proceed, especially since it was important to make as good an impression as possible. So he did the wisest thing under the circumstances—he kept silence.

"It's a pleasant evening," Mr. Harper said, plunging at once into the subject that chanced first in his mind, and he was duly answered.

"Yes, very."

"Is it a concert you're expecting to enjoy this evening?" This was the next question.

"Yes, sir."

"Good singers?"

"I guess so. They're a fine lot who've been largely advertised. I thought we might as well try them."

"You're fond of music, I judge?"

"Well, some."

"Do you sing?"

"Not a bit."

"Miss Grace has a very marked degree of musical talent for such a young girl, I think."

Alfred didn't seem to know what reply to make to this. He looked somewhat conscious, which, considering that he hadn't chosen to announce his personal interest in her to any member of the family, seemed to Mr. Harper uncalled for. He felt strangely at a loss what to say next. A novel and amusing feeling for Mr. Harper to have—but he'd been placed there for a purpose, and it wouldn't do to relinquish it so ingloriously. So with an amused query as to what Maria would say if she were there he made another attempt.

"How did your last course of lectures succeed here?"

"A good many people went to them, I guess."

"And pecuniarily, were they a success?"

"I don't know, I'm sure. I never heard any of the fellows say."

"You don't belong to the association yourself then?"

"Oh, no."

"Did they have much talent displayed in the list of speakers?"

"Well, I don't know. I guess they thought so. Anyway, the speakers themselves did." This was intended for a joke, and Alfred showed his appreciation of it by laughing heartily.

"I'm a school committee, and he's trying to pass examination," murmured Mr. Harper to himself, whereupon he laughed also.

"Who was the best speaker you had?" he continued, determined to get to the root of some thought.

"Oh, I don't know. I didn't hear many of them. The Fat Contributor gave us as good a one as any, I guess. He was real rich. He kept the fellows in a roar from the time he began until he sat down."

Mr. Harper didn't doubt it. He had Alfred Parks's ideas as to lectures at last. On the whole, he was glad Maria wasn't in the room. One other item he was anxious for.

"Was Mr. Beecher on your course this year?"

"Yes, but he was dry as a stick. I never want to hear him again. I don't know how people can rave about Beecher as they do. I never thought much of him."

Mr. Harper changed his seat and his subject.

"How's the Christian association getting along? Is it revived any?"

"I don't know much about it. I did hear Tom Randolph was trying to get up something of the kind, but I don't know how he succeeds."

"You haven't attended any of his Sunday afternoon meetings then?"

"Oh, no. If I get to church on Sunday evening it's about as much as I can do. Sunday is our only day of rest, you know."

Young Alfred pronounced the word "our" as though he belonged to a much-injured, ill-used class of humanity, who had more working days in the week than any other, while his companion had to do with a world that enjoyed a perpetual holiday.

"Are your evenings closely occupied?"

"Oh, no—we close at six o'clock."

"Yet he didn't attend many of the lectures." This was Mr. Harper's mental comment, and he added in the same way: "I wonder what he does with his evenings. He can't spend them all with Grace; at least if he does, I'll try to get the child to start for New York tomorrow."

"What about the evening?" he said aloud, and with the genial smile of one personally interested in the young man before him. "Do you young men have any system about them, or do you go wherever it happens?"

"Well, there's a good deal of happen about them. There's always something going on, you know—a concert or a party. And then there's always the opera, you know, and the theater for extra nights, and we have our club once a week."

"A reading circle?" asked innocent Mr. Harper.

"Oh, the dickens, no!" Alfred Parks laughed immoderately and voted Mr. Harper decidedly "green" and a man not to be afraid of in the least. Then he roused himself to be entertaining, and Mr. Harper fell more and more into listening, until Grace, blushing and pretty, came in ready for the concert.

"Well," Maria said, as her brother-in-law came out to where she was sitting and looked at her while she sewed, "how did you enjoy the society?"

"Maria," he said, "we must make every effort to get Gracie to New York."

A clear, good-natured, relieved smile blossomed all over Maria's face.

"I'm glad you had a pleasant evening," she said grimly.

Mr. Harper sat down on the arm of the sofa and folded his arms.

"The next thing is to accomplish this without doing more harm than good by it."

"I know a way," Maria said, "and I don't see any other way out of it. Tell Father her associations in the stores aren't what they should be and get him to advise her to go home with you. She won't go contrary to *his* advice. None of us ever did that."

Mr. Harper shook his head.

"That mustn't be done for several reasons. In the first place, it would be necessary to take Grace into our confidence and thus rouse an opposition that would take a lifetime perhaps to conquer. She *expects* opposition and will be even more indignant over it because of that. Also, that wouldn't subdue the danger; it would simply retard it. Maria, he isn't a young man *ever* to be received into this family. There will never be enough of him to make it a pleasant acquisition, but there must be a great deal less of him before he can be tolerated at all."

Maria laid down her sewing and turned herself around to get a full view of the speaker before she answered.

"I'd like to know what you mean. I never did understand you very well, and I'm sure I don't now. You see through the fellow as plainly as that, and yet you say my plan won't do, because we'd have to take Grace into our confidence? I'd like to know how you intend to break up this affair without letting her know anything about it. I think she'd discover it."

Mr. Harper laughed.

"It's to be done by the natural laws of causes and effects," he said. "I think, my dear, faithful sister, that I see my way clearly through the trouble and that you may go to sleep with a serene hope that the young gentleman will never have the opportunity of lecturing you. Now, in the meantime, I have a letter to write to Ermina, and if your sisterly care can suggest anything in the feminine line that Grace needs before she goes away, I hope you'll start planning it at once, for I intend to make great haste in this matter."

Following out these plans, at the breakfast table Mr. Harper, after bringing a pretty glow to Grace's cheek by telling of a remarkable music teacher then in the city, turned suddenly to her.

"By the way, Grace, I suppose you haven't an idea what brought me up here. But the truth is, I came for you. I'm going to carry you away captive."

"For me!" Grace said, holding her spoon suspended on its way to her mouth and looking the picture of astonishment. Then she laughed lightly. "Messrs. McAllister & Co. would have a word to say. They wouldn't even give me a holiday of one half day, though I coaxed."

"But they'll *have* to, if we put it in the light I mean to. You see, I'm going to assert my rights as a brother. I've never done much in that direction, and you don't begin to know my power. I propose to release you from the McAllisters—tell them we can't spare you to them any longer. The fact is, Ermina needs you this coming winter. I have to be confined to business very closely, and, besides, Ermina wants you to continue your music. She thinks, with me, that it's a pity to allow your talent in that direction to go uncultivated. Our plans are all formed, and I've been sent up to carry you off 'willy nilly,' as my Scotch nurse used to say."

Grace's face was a pretty study. It flushed and paled by turns, until Maria began to grow alarmed. Neither Maria nor anyone else knew how precious to her the study of music had been, or what a sacrifice it had been to the family good when she sweetly and quietly relinquished even her practice hour. Ermina suspected much, but even *she* didn't know the passion this thing had been to her sister; and Maria never even dreamed of it.

Mr. Harper saw his advantage and hastened on.

"We're very pleasantly situated in the city, except that, as I say, it would be lonely for Ermina. But with you there to keep her company everything will be perfect. Father, I'm glad to tell you, is decidedly on our side. He thinks you need change and rest and will be so happy to have you go on with your music that he says he'll dream of it all winter. So, you see, you have a chance to give him another pleasure."

Still no answer from Grace, unless a strange choking in her throat and a rush of tears to her soft eyes could have been called answers.

How astonished they would have been if they could have read her heart. There wasn't one at that table who didn't think they understood her perfectly, and each had a different view. The truth was, each had a little piece of her character, and another bit was hidden away in her heart that none of them saw or imagined.

Maria said within herself: "She likes the fun of it after all. She has a little sense left. I'm glad of that."

Helen pictured to herself the grandeur and beauty that enveloped the family in New York and said to *herself*, with a little sigh: "No wonder she wants to go. Why shouldn't she?"

Mr. Harper, watching her closely, said: "The child is ready to do anything to please her father."

And all this was true. What girl wouldn't look forward to the prospect of plenty of leisure to pursue her favorite study? What one, with an innate love for the refinement and beauties of wealth, wouldn't enjoy the thought of luxuriating in them? Also, Grace loved to think of her father as pleased and happy that she was having the advantages he had so craved for her.

But beyond and above all of these things, there was another motive. She had given her heart into the keeping of Alfred Parks—so she imagined. But in truth it wasn't Alfred Parks at all. In her heart was an ideal being, vested with all the grace and goodness of a saint, and she had chosen to give him mortal resemblance to Alfred Parks. How she did it, why there came such a glamor over her eyes and her senses that he seemed to her an embodiment of human excellence, passes me to explain. But haven't you seen the same thing done again and again by fresh, foolish, sweet young girls?

Grace had been very little into what we call society. The family fortunes had fallen before she came on the stage of young ladyhood. And what to Maria, with her keen-visioned brain, would have been impossible, was to Grace, with her ideal nature, not only possible but probable. Alfred was but the synonym for manhood, and he had condescended from his grand height to notice her! The simple heart was full of gratitude and humility. She wanted to go to New York, to enjoy the advantages of society and of study, so she might become *worthy of Alfred Parks!* With what horror Maria would have viewed her if she could have known how the silly young heart glowed at the thought of being able to play so that Alfred might be proud of her! It was well for Grace that she had such a wise and kind friend to help her just now as her brother-in-law. Many a bright young girl makes shipwreck of her life and her happiness just here.

Maria hadn't sense enough to be fully satisfied with the turn affairs were taking.

"You haven't said a single word to her about that fellow," she grumbled, when Grace had fluttered into the little bedroom to kiss her father good morning. "I don't see that you'll accomplish much by taking her to New York, even if she goes—which she won't. She'll go down to the store and stay all day and talk with that idiot between every yard of lace she measures, and he'll persuade her into staying at home. And if she goes she'll be writing letters to him all the time, and that will be as bad as talking with him. If I were you I'd get Father to forbid a correspondence."

Mr. Harper serenely sipped the remainder of his coffee.

"Neither of these things is going to take place, my good sister. You promised to leave the matter entirely in my hands, you remember. By virtue of that promise you're not even to whisper the young man's name, either to Grace or to Father, until I give you permission. If you feel anxious to talk about him, there is one safe place. You have my full permission to pray for him and Grace just as much as your heart prompts."

And rising from the table as Grace returned, ready for her walk, he said, "Will you take me to the store with you, Grace? I want to push my plans."

Chapter 17

"Good-bye"

On the way downtown, Mr. Harper was the most delightful of companions. Maria, watching them from the window, fondly supposed he was taking that opportunity to enlighten Grace as to her folly and give her good advice for the future. That wasn't his intention. He talked much about the proposed visit in such a hearty, matter-of-fact way that at last Grace found voice.

"I'd like it of all things, of course. But I really don't see how it's to be brought about."

"Then it will be all the more enjoyable when it's 'brought about' for you, won't it? Isn't that the way these things work? And the beauty of it is, *I* see the way very clearly, unless, indeed, you propose some objections I don't know anything about. What's the most formidable one in your mind at this present time?"

"My own importance," Grace said, laughing a little, but with an anxious side glance at him to see if he understood.

"As one of the providers of the family purse," he said quickly. "I understand all about that, and Ermina will tell you we've planned admirably concerning it. The memory of it does you credit. This part of the plan belongs essentially to Ermina, and you must allow her to do the work."

"It's all new to me," Grace said. "Ermina has never mentioned anything of the sort, either when she was at home or in her letters. I'm surprised."

"Ermina doesn't divulge her plans before they're ready for operation," Mr. Harper answered quickly, grateful he didn't need to tell Grace when this plan he was pushing with such energy was first conceived.

By the time they reached the store, Grace began to have a dim sense that this delightful scheme might some way, and sometime in the future, be carried into execution, but as yet it was too unreal a thing for her to build any strong hopes upon. In the first place, the store required a month's notice before any clerk was released. So arbitrary was this rule that Grace almost felt that if she were to be sick it would be improper not to have given ample time to fill her place. Her astonishment was therefore greater when, after introducing her brother to the principal and leaving him at the office, she was called there in an hour and abruptly asked by Mr. Harper if she could get ready to go home with him in two days if she stayed at the store during the remainder of that day.

Dumbfounded, Grace flushed and paled and looked in a frightened sort of way up at her chief and didn't know what to say. But Mr. McAllister in conference with the well-known capitalist, Mr. Harper, was a different man from the one who generally dealt in short and somewhat crusty fashion with his clerks. Grace had realized this in a measure when she entered the store earlier and was greeted by him with short dignity.

"Fifteen minutes late, Miss Randolph. It's fortunate this is a rare occurrence, or I'd have to say more about it."

To this Grace had simply bowed and replied: "My brother-in-law, Mr. Harper, Mr. McAllister." And Mr. McAllister, recognizing the name and the face, had no more to say.

After the conference he smiled down on her now in a way that was utterly new to her and said benignly: "It's against our rules, of course, Miss Randolph. But all rules fail on unprecedented occasions, and this brother of yours is very peremptory. I congratulate you on the brilliant prospect that's opening before you, and of course we're glad to do your brother a favor. At the same time, if you *could* remain during this day, it would save us from embarrassment, as two of the clerks reported illness this morning."

And having received her wages in full and a cordial dismissal at the close of that day's service, coupled with a flattering testimonial of her ability as a saleswoman and the loss it would be to them, unsophisticated Grace went back to her desk with a dim sense of the power of wealth and position dawning upon her.

"Only think, Alfred," she said to that individual in the first moment of confidence the rush of business gave to these two, "I'm going to New York for the winter!"

Alfred did think, and a blank fell upon him. He realized the store would be darker and gloomier with that face gone.

"I know it," he said rather shortly, almost crossly. "That precious brother-in-law of yours has been to inform me of it. At least he condescended to stop at my counter and hint as much. Seems to me he assumes the management of things in a little too lordly a fashion."

This was unwise in Alfred. A sense of the family's dignity was strong in Grace, and *he* was hardly of the family yet—not near enough to be allowed to criticize, at least not in that cross tone.

"We're only too glad to have him assume what authority he chooses," she answered. "He's been a true friend to us in every way. I thought you'd be pleased at my prospect of a chance to improve."

"Pleased with the prospect of not seeing you for a year!"

"Not at all that long," she said, appalled. "Just for a few months—three at the longest. And when I come home I can play some of those pieces for you that you liked so much last night. I know I can. I know the talent is in me, if I can only get a little chance to bring it out. And then, Alfred, you know you've disliked to have me in the store."

"I know it," he said, heroically. "I suppose it's the best thing. At least we may as well think so, for it seems it's decided. Only I think you might have told me about it and asked my advice."

Grace laughed a little silvery laugh.

"*My* advice wasn't asked," she said. "I was just taken by storm. I never heard a word about it until this morning, and then I supposed it was something that was to be in the future sometime, if I could get away from the store and if fifty things didn't happen to prevent it. But, Alfred, if you don't like it at all, I might reconsider it in some way. But my position here is given up, and they've sent out for help in my place, and it would make things rather awkward."

"Oh, no," Alfred said quickly, mollified by the indication that, after all, *his* judgment was the ruling one and mindful of the advantages of such a relationship as the wealthy brother-in-law. "You'll have to go now, of course. It's too late to change plans, and I daresay it's the best thing to do. We must keep on the right side of the rich brother. We may want his help in the future."

Now this was one of the rare, *very* rare occasions in which Alfred made remarks that jarred on the refined sensibilities of Grace Randolph. On such occasions it wasn't that *Alfred* was rude, not to say coarse, in his utterances, but that mankind in general was so much more outspoken on these subjects than women could ever be. This was the way Grace put it. She wished he wouldn't speak that way of Mr. Harper. She was glad Mr. Harper wasn't there to hear.

Meanwhile, the Randolph household was in a whirl of preparation.

"Helen will be horrid," Maria complained to Tom when he came over that morning to see how the new ideas were working. "If Grace decides to go— which I have no hope of—all the time we're at work getting her ready I pity *myself*. I know just how much of a martyr all this will make of Helen. No amount of explaining will make it plain there's special need to get Grace away just now. After I've exhausted my breath and my temper trying to do so, she'll remark, as if I hadn't said a word, that 'it would have been natural to suppose Ermina would have chosen her, the widowed sister, who was nearest her age, to spend the winter with her, instead of *that child*, who was well enough off at home.' I can hear her, as plainly as though she was saying it. And that thing, with variations, is what I'll be destined to listen to while I'm cutting and contriving for Grace—and how that last is to be done is more than *I* can see. There are definite inconveniences in this plan, even if it works."

Tom only laughed.

"You're borrowing trouble," he said. "Perhaps everything will come out all right. Anyway, trust Mr. Harper for getting his own way, whatever it is—and it's sure to be a good way. I'll try, meanwhile, to keep Helen so busy she won't have time to make a martyr of you."

But Helen did no such thing. She acquiesced in the arrangements with marvelous good humor, rather, like one who continued to be preoccupied and absent-minded, and helped Maria rip and turn in good-natured silence, until that bewildered girl grew seriously alarmed that Helen was really sick.

Into the midst of the whirl of preparations and the dismay as to proper wardrobe for city life came a letter from Ermina, not from the post office, but from her husband's pocket, at an opportune moment.

"Oh, by the way," he said, rising from the table and turning to Grace, "I have a note here for you from Ermina. I was to give it to you as soon as you started preparing for your journey, and I hope you've already started."

This was the note:

Gracie dear,

Now you're not to be troubled or let Maria puzzle her poor tired brains over the old, vexing question, 'Wherewithal shall I be clothed?' Tell that blessed sister it is my turn now. I'm your good old grandmother, and you're to come to me just as you are, except that you may exercise your own pretty taste about a traveling dress. For the rest, I'll accept nothing, not even an apron that isn't bought and made under my own eye. We'll have remarkably nice times arranging it all. Won't I be glad to get hold of you! You see, I take it for granted you're to come, because I know everyone in our family is gifted with common sense and because my husband has gone for you and said he would bring you back with him. The idea of his coming home without you after that is preposterous to me, who know him so well. Buy the traveling dress ready made—you can get very good ones that way—and don't scrimp, please. Let me see what your taste is when you really indulge it. You may consider the dress a birthday present. I remember that last week was the birthday.

In great haste to see you, I wait.
Ermina

Out of this fell a fifty-dollar note. Grace, with the red glowing in her cheeks, handed both without a word of comment to the sister nearest her, who happened to be Maria. Mr. Harper had considerately taken himself to the bedroom. Maria read, and the dress she was ripping, a piece of which she'd held on to as she took the letter, dropped from her hand.

"Well!" she said. "Ermina Randolph does credit to her bringing up. Grace, I think the whole story of Cinderella has been remodeled for your use. I shall rip no more on that old thing!" And she pushed the dress away, with a gesture of contempt.

While this new and important view of the subject was being discussed somewhat warmly by Grace, Mr. Harper reappeared. He judged it time for another diversion.

"Maria," he said, taking a seat beside her, "can you get her ready for the day after tomorrow?"

"My patience!" said Maria.

Then they all said such haste wasn't possible; and it ended, as Mr. Harper's plans usually did, in an energetic rush of everybody in the house to accomplish the desired end—and it was accomplished! Still Maria failed to be satisfied.

"*I* don't understand how you're improving things," she grumbled to Mr. Harper during that last evening of Grace's stay at home. Grace at that moment was alone in the parlor with the obnoxious Alfred. "There they are, as cooing as possible, I daresay. I don't see why you didn't forbid that performance or have Father do it."

"See here," Mr. Harper said gravely. "Why didn't you tell Father about this matter yourself, instead of keeping it perfectly quiet and writing to us? Didn't you fear the effect of the excitement on him?"

Maria was obliged to admit she did.

"Then won't you give me credit for sense enough to follow a good example after it's been set for me? As to avoiding this evening call, I think I could have done it, but a difficulty was in the way. I didn't think it the best thing to do. I shall do the *best* I can, Maria." And Maria was silenced if not convinced.

And Mr. Harper endured, with the utmost amiability and composure, the attendance of the said Alfred at the depot the next morning. He even allowed him to assist Grace from the carriage and check her trunk and hover around her like a moth. He was kind and gracious in his manner and entirely won Grace's confidence and gratitude, for could there be a greater contrast between Maria's frowning face and haughty voice, whenever she looked at the poor fellow, and Mr. Harper's cordial frankness and courteous "Good-bye" when they were fairly moving off?

She looked out of the window, her eyes swimming in tears. It was her first departure from the old home, her first peep into the outside world. She had no idea of the strange events that would occur before she saw that home again. In one room of the dear old house was a father who at this moment was praying for the safekeeping of his darling—praying that if he never saw her again on earth she might be sure to come up to him in heaven. Looking after the retreating train were a brother and sister who had thought and planned—and one of them, at least, prayed much for her—and who looked after her with grave faces and tender longings in their hearts. And yet this girl gave her last look, her last smile, her last tear, to the light-haired young man who paced the walk, looking after the train, indeed, but already sending a puff of cigar smoke to help it on!

Chapter 18

A Confidential Ride

Not until Mr. Harper had spent an entire day with his young sister-in-law—a day filled with all the delicate attentions and courtesies a man of wealth and refinement can bestow upon a young lady who is taking a long journey in his care—did he venture upon anything like a confidential talk with her.

The train had just left Albany, where they'd been delayed for several hours. Grace had been established at the Delevan in one of the elegant rooms and waited on with that obsequiousness wealth buys. She had dined at the most elegant hotel table and had, in short, begun to realize her brother-in-law was a person of consequence in that portion of the world estimated by money, and she had a sort of reflected consequence about her, not an unpleasant discovery to a young lady taking her first journey. A sense of deep gratitude began to rise in her heart and be added to the feeling of respect and love with which she'd always regarded him.

He disposed of satchels and wraps in that businesslike way the traveled man so well understands; arranged sash and blind and ventilator with careful regard to his young sister-in-law's comfort; arrested a passing boy and bought a dozen Havana oranges and laid them beside her with the direction to amuse herself with those; and stopped the "book boy" and bought the last new book that had created a stir in the world and that he had one day heard her express a desire to read. Then he sat down beside her and began without ceremony or preparation a very confidential talk.

"This young man, Gracie, to whom you introduced me the other evening and who was at the cars this morning—is he a friend of yours?"

Grace's cheeks glowed, but she answered steadily: "Yes, sir."

"A very special friend?"

This question was harder to answer than the last, but it was *answered* in the same way. He had evidently no intention of sparing her.

"Do you mind telling me just how much that means with young ladies your age?" he asked, not in sarcasm, but with an inflection calculated to remind her she was *young*. "Does it mean you've engaged yourself to him?"

It was very disagreeable. If there had been anything to resent, Grace would have resented it. She felt sure that Alfred Parks would have considered Mr. Harper impertinent. But yet he surely had a right in view of their relationship—and the valuable way in which he was acting upon that relationship—to a certain degree of confidence. When she answered, her voice was a little lower than before and her cheeks still glowing, as she wondered whether he would express annoyance or anything disagreeable about Alfred. She resolved in her loyal heart that she wouldn't submit to anything of that kind—no, not if he were twenty times her brother-in-law and were taking her to the royal palace to be presented to the queen!

But she noticed no change of voice, no expression of astonishment or annoyance in the next sentence, and it was certainly simple enough, hardly a question at all, rather an intimation that as a matter of course such and such was the case.

"With Father's approval, of course?"

There is an art in asking questions, a chance to display talent or to show oneself a bungler. Something either in the words themselves, in Mr. Harper's way of saying them or in the keen, clear, quiet eyes bent fully on her while they were spoken, made Grace remember that this man questioning her had a right to claim her father as his and therefore had a right to question the daughter who was under his care.

Also it overwhelmed her with a sudden sense of the impropriety of being engaged to be married to a young man of whom her father hadn't even heard! Such a strange thing to do! How could she ever explain it to this clear-eyed man who was looking so steadily at her and waiting for an answer? It had never seemed strange to her before.

She had said to herself that she was doing just what the rest of the household was doing, shielding her father from excitement or anxiety of any sort. But somehow that refuge seemed to fail her or to shrink into insignificance before those steady, inquiring eyes. She was painfully embarrassed, the blood flowed in rich dark waves up to her very temples, and she looked at her brother-in-law with a beseeching air that plainly said, "Ask me some other question, or ask me this some other way," and he quietly waited.

"No," she said at last, low-voiced and tremulous, and he said nothing. Then she went on hurriedly: "It was because Father is so feeble and so easily made nervous and wakeful. We shield him from everything that might excite or trouble him. We all do so, and therefore I've thought it best to say nothing to him, and I've told Alfred so."

Mr. Harper didn't turn his eyes away. He didn't look less grave and troubled. He didn't speak at all for as much as a minute; to Grace it seemed half an hour.

"Would you *marry* the gentleman without your father's knowledge?" he said then.

Grace started and shivered as she answered quickly: "Oh, no, no, of course not! Why, Mr. Harper, you know I wouldn't. Why do you say such things to me? I've done nothing wrong—at least I meant right. I thought—." And there she stopped. What *was* she doing or undoing? And what would Alfred think of all this?

Still the manner of the serious man before her didn't change a particle, and his tone was, if anything, more solemn than before.

"Then you're waiting for Father to die before this matter can be known?"

What a dreadful thing to say! The great tears gathered in Grace's eyes and rolled down her cheeks; she dropped the veil on her traveling hat quickly to shut in the tears and shut out that dreadful gaze.

"You are cruel," she said at last, struggling to regain her composure and speaking earnestly. "You know I had no such thought. I'm waiting and hoping that he'll get sufficiently better for me to trouble him with my affairs at all, and I didn't mean to do anything wrong."

He had certainly probed very deeply; it seemed to be time to drop in some oil if he had any. He spoke very quietly, not at all as one who had anything for which to ask forgiveness.

"I can only know you by what you *do* and not by what you think, you remember. And I'm sure your good sense sees the propriety of my understanding this matter thoroughly. I can't tell you I think you've done rightly, because some risks must be run even when a person is feeble. We didn't think for a moment of carrying out this plan of a winter in New York without your father's full consent and approval, and surely it's of much less importance than the other matter.

"But at the same time, I can see it's been an error of judgment and not of intention. What remains to be decided is—in view of what has already been done—what is to be done in the future. I needn't remind you that Father gave me many directions and cautions regarding you and that he felt he was entrusting a very precious treasure to my care. I assure you I feel the responsibility; so you'll expect me to speak plainly to you, as I could hardly be justified in doing otherwise.

"I haven't up to this time credited the statement that you were positively, seriously, engaged to this young man without condition or understanding as to your father's wishes." He spoke this sentence slowly, pausing long enough at the end for Grace to take it in. And you'll do her justice to understand it was the first time she'd realized what a strange and improper thing she had allowed herself to do.

Then he continued: "I've hoped and believed that those who were anxious for you were overanxious because they were mistaken. Now, as I say, though astonished, I can understand it was an error of judgment and one that would not have occurred doubtless had there been a mother to advise. It's right for me to tell you the responsibility is too great for me to assume."

Another pause, during which it seemed to Grace that her heart stopped beating. What *was* he going to do? Was she to be sent back to her home tomorrow morning—perhaps this very evening, as soon as the train stopped? And what would she say? Must *she* tell her father, and must she go back to McAllister's store and tell them and ask for her old position again? And what would Alfred say to all this? A dim sense that he would feel disgraced and bitterly displeased with her contributed a little to her pain. The low, clear voice went on.

"Would you be willing to write to Father and lay this entire matter before him with frankness in detail and desire, or would it be less painful to you for me to write for you and get his directions for the future?"

His voice had assumed a gentle, respectful tone, which somewhat quieted the poor child beside him, and after a moment of silence she spoke.

"Wouldn't you be afraid of the excitement resulting from such a letter? Don't you think Father is too weak for me to run such a risk, or *don't* you think there's any risk about it?"

"Yes," he said firmly, "there's a risk, undoubtedly. Father is very feeble, and I don't know what degree of strain he can endure. Of course this would be an excitement to him. If you were older he'd be expecting it and be in a sense prepared. If he knew and had known the young man as a valued family friend, it wouldn't be so exciting, but all the circumstances were against it, and I don't wonder you're bewildered. But, as I understand you, the time is past for such considerations to be weighed. The need for plain speaking is upon us and can't be avoided."

"I don't see why," she said, speaking hurriedly now. "You're cruel to me. I can't risk my father's life—and I won't. Why can't I wait until spring—until he's better, as we so hope he will be? What's the need of troubling and exhausting him just now?"

For a few minutes he didn't speak at all. Then he said, and Grace never forgot the tone in which the sentence was spoken: "Grace, you heard your father's last prayer. You heard his last words of direction to me—could I receive you into my family, knowing you were engaged to be married to a young man, knowing you were in constant and special correspondence with a young man whose very existence your father is ignorant of and be faithful to my trust? Granting that he should live to know all about it, could he hold me free from blame?"

Then Grace cried with all her might, and it was well that the twilight and the rushing train shielded her from observation or hearing. As for Mr. Harper, he waited quietly, his face sad indeed, but not really troubled.

"What *can* I do?" murmured the poor little crushed mouse at his side at last. It was the question he had been waiting for.

"Of course there's an honorable way to arrange it all. If you feel unequal to the responsibility of a frank talk with your father, you can write to this young man the whole story of your thoughts and views and explain to him the nature of the difficulty. You can say to him that you realize you shouldn't have given your word unconditionally, that you shouldn't be in correspondence with him of that nature and that you must be allowed to hold the promise back until such time as it can be honorably given. You'll understand better what should be written than I can possibly tell you."

"But," pleaded Grace, catching her breath and feeling she was going over a precipice that was to whirl her forever away from Alfred Parks, whom she was leaving standing dismally on the shore, "I *have* given my promise. It *was* unconditional. And however silly it may have been it is done, and I don't see how I have a right to undo it."

He was very prompt with his answer.

"Of course you consider this gentleman an honorable man and a man of average intelligence. Then don't you suppose he knows that a girl your age, who has a good father, has no moral right to give herself away without that father's knowledge?"

Then after a pause, during which he felt the muffled-up bundle beside him shrink and wince, he added with that quiet firmness which was characteristic of him: "At least I see no other way out of this matter. I'm not dictating, of course, what you'll do. I'm simply answering your question. But it's my duty to be very frank with you. Much as Ermina and I have looked forward to this winter together and to all the pleasant details of this plan, and sharp as the disappointment would be to us both, I cannot assume the responsibility of a correspondence like this with any living man without your father's knowledge and consent. I have no right to do it, and therefore you must be frank with him, or else I must be, or this other plan may come in to relieve us both. It's for you to decide."

Then an utter silence fell between them, broken only by one question from Grace: "Do you mean I shouldn't write to him at all?"

"No, not necessarily that, though I'd prefer it. But I think Father trusts your sister and you enough not to object to a friendly correspondence which is known in detail to *her*. But, of course, you see that such a correspondence would be very different from the one you've proposed."

Poor Grace! She saw it plainly. What long letters she was to have written him and for no eye but his. Then the silence again, until at last, more than an hour since she'd turned that last answer over again bitterly in her mind, seeing all that it involved, she spoke in that clear, decisive tone she could assume.

"Mr. Harper, you needn't be afraid. I've been wrong. I can see it plainly now, and so will Alfred when he thinks of it. I'll agree to that last. I *will* not take any risk regarding my father's health, but your responsibility won't be greater than I can help. But I want you to understand this: It is simply because of Father's health, and it won't change the actual feeling an atom.

"Maria doesn't like Alfred, and she's prejudiced you against him. All that won't be of the least consequence. I belong to him in heart and always shall. But while I have a father to ask I won't belong to him in any other way without Father's consent. And while I'm at your house I'll do nothing you disapprove of, but the actual feeling will never change. I'm not responsible to anyone for that."

"Of course I have nothing to do with that," Mr. Harper answered quietly, "and I'm entirely satisfied and trust you fully." But, for the first time since the embarrassing conversation had started, he couldn't restrain a quiet smile.

Chapter 19

Work Maria Can Do

Maria Randolph stood in her kitchen surveying the work spread out there with the air of a general preparing for battle. It was Saturday morning. Washing and ironing were disposed of for the week, and this was the grand day for sweeping, dusting and mopping, to say nothing of the bread and cookies that must bake with the same fire that cooked the dinner and heated the water for mopping. Economy of forces was rapidly reducing itself to a system in this young lady's mind. She knew almost to a splinter how many sticks of wood it took to bake four loaves of bread and two tins of cookies. Five minutes ago she had work planned to fill the day. Now, with a perplexed look on her face, she twisted a slip of paper over her finger and wondered what she should do. Finally she opened the bit of paper and read the brief note again:

> Maria, won't you come over here as quick as you can? Come prepared to stay for awhile at least and help us think what to do. We're in great trouble.
>
> Haste,
> Tom

"What in the world does the boy want, I wonder? Why can't he tell me? It would have taken less words, I daresay, than he used in *not* telling me. That's just like a man! How does he think I can come to stay and leave Father? I wonder why Helen wouldn't do?"

At this point Helen came down the back stairs with a broom and dustpan in hand and an old veil tied over her hair. Maria turned to her.

"See here, Helen—what can be the matter?"

"I don't know, I'm sure," Helen said, reading the note. "You're going to see, aren't you? It must be something serious—he says to hurry. Where are your things, Maria?"

"How *can* I go?" said Maria impatiently, who had no intention of *not* going but wanted to be talked into it. "Just look at the things to do, and Father must be taken care of and his room put in order!"

"I'll do the best I can, and perhaps you won't have to stay long. Anyway, I'd go, for poor Tom must be in trouble."

Maria turned and bestowed a searching look on her sister. In the midst of her perplexities intruded this question: "What in the world has happened to Helen? I wonder if she's going to be sick?" Then she said aloud: "Well, I suppose I must run over and see what's wanted. But I don't see how I can—anyway, I can't stay."

So into the midst of the disorder and consternation in the kitchen at the Randolph House came Maria. What a sight it was! In the great stove the fire had died down, the hearth was strewn with ashes, and the top of the stove was covered with unwashed cooking utensils, while on every table and shelf appeared the debris of the morning meal. Standing around these scenes of confusion, in various stages of bewilderment, were three or four girls, looking as though their wits had deserted them, and they didn't know which way to turn.

"What in creation is the matter?" asked Maria of Tom, who had evidently just come in and whose face expressed sorrow and disgust and dismay.

"Matter enough!" he replied briefly. "See here, Maria." He opened a door leading into a little room and motioned her to follow. "That girl—you remember," he began as soon as he'd carefully closed the door.

"What! My friend?"

"No, the other—the cook."

"Oh, *your* friend. What about her? Has she deserted? Tom, she hasn't gone to drinking again?"

"Yes, she has. She just managed to blunder through the breakfast—and such a breakfast it was! No boarder would stand a repetition of it. And it seems she's smuggled some liquor into the house and took some every little while until now she's intoxicated. Peter and I had to carry her to her room." Tom's handsome face clouded, and he shivered at the thought. "Such a sight, Maria, I hope you may never have to witness."

He paused, seeing that comforting expression, "I told you so," in every line of Maria's face, and he got it too. She wasn't one to disappoint such expectations.

"Tom, what did I tell you? I knew how it would be. You never did a sillier thing than when you tried to ignore human nature and act as if everybody who had anything to do with the Randolph House was going to be an angel."

"I know you told me," Tom said. "It can't in any sense be your fault for not warning me. But I won't pretend penitence. I'm not sorry I did it, and, given the same circumstances, I'm afraid I'd do it again. In fact, I *know* I would, for I thought I did only what was right. But for all that I'm in sore straits and don't know which way to turn. The housekeeper's gone for the day, you know, and I can get no extra help. I've been out to two employment offices without result. Those poor girls out there know no more about what should be done in this line than I do, though they're good girls. I felt I must see you for a minute, to advise with you. The house is full of boarders. Shall I call them together and send them all down to the Clinton House to dinner?"

"Nonsense!" said Maria, throwing off her shawl on one chair and her hat on another, and somehow the tone and the action inspired him with courage. "You'll do no such thing. It's a likely story that four girls can't get up a dinner of some sort. What are their names, Tom? No, never mind what their names are. You go over to the house and tell Helen to warm Father's broth at eleven o'clock and see that his feet are warm when he lies down. And give me the keys and let me know in ten minutes how many to expect to dinner. I'll look out for all the rest."

Tom was amazed and dismayed and relieved all in one. He'd expected no such whirlwind of help as this. He hardly knew what he'd expected, except that it seemed natural to think of Maria when he was in trouble. But he utterly distrusted her ability to manage a hotel dinner from the foundation.

"But, Maria, I'm afraid you can never—," he began in protest.

But she turned abruptly away from him. "I'll talk with you after dinner, Tom, if I happen to be alive at that time. It isn't talk we want just now but work, and we must fly around." Saying that, she opened the little door and went like a fresh young breeze into that dismayed kitchen, leaving Tom standing alone, in doubt whether to be relieved or more perplexed than before. He listened to her brisk voice.

"Come, girls—I hear that you and I have to get the dinner today. We'll have to be brisk, for it's getting late, and our reputation's at stake. We must have a better dinner today than was ever eaten in this house before. Who's the dishwasher? Here, let's all be dishwashers. We can't do anything in such a wild-looking room. What's your name? Kate? Well, Kate, you get the dishpans ready and the hot water, and the rest of you get the dishes in shape. I'll make up the fire and my menu at the same time. Then we'll all set to work at it—and trust we'll get it done."

Tom waited five minutes, ten minutes, and by that time the kitchen had assumed the look of a campground, with trained soldiers on drill before a masterly general. Everyone was busy and alert, the fire was roaring, and Maria was looking for fresh napkins for the dinner table. Tom turned on his heel with a relieved smile. Some kind of dinner they would certainly have, and it would appear at the proper time too—of that he now felt assured.

At the appointed hour the noisy gong sounded its summons through the halls, and the guests of the Randolph House rushed in from the balconies and down the stairs, eager to obey its voice. Tom had been there before them and drew a long breath of relief and intense satisfaction as he surveyed the scene. The most faultless cleanliness and order prevailed. Not a dish was lacking, not a spoon out of place; the silver glittered with new luster, and the glasses sparkled and glowed, while the odor of delicious coffee floated faintly through the air.

That dinner was a triumph. Certain little irregularities that had been frowned upon in the morning were forgotten in the satisfaction with which the fastidious guests disposed of their more than usually dainty desserts. They told each other that "there certainly was unusual cooking done in that house."

It hadn't been such a formidable thing after all. The startled girls were ready and willing to do, but they'd been used to a head to guide them, and when they found Maria capable and determined to *be* such a head, they fell promptly into line.

Also, they had received a special blessing in the way of desserts. The girl Maria had persistently styled her friend, and whom perhaps you remember as paying her a mysterious visit one evening, had been engaged ever since as a chambermaid at the Randolph House. Maria hadn't as yet had time to "cultivate her acquaintance," but persisted in the belief that she was worth cultivating. This girl, in one of her passages through the kitchen, saw the new leader, instantly recognized her and as instantly came to her rescue. With a half dozen skillfully put questions she gathered the story and then turned to Maria.

"I know how to cook all sorts of fancy desserts. If you want my help, my morning's work is nearly done."

"Of course we want your help," Maria had answered quickly, looking relieved; she hated desserts. "Come down as soon as you can and fix us the most distracting dish ever set on a table."

She came back in an hour and rendered such good service that more than one guest at the dinner table wondered where they found such a pastry cook this side of Paris.

Now the day was nearly done. Maria, at home in the sitting room, leaning back in the armchair, rocking and resting after the day's unusual exertions, gave a detailed account of some of the anxieties and mishaps in preparing the meal for forty fastidious people. Triumph gleamed in her face and voice, and intense satisfaction glowed through her. If this girl was guilty of any one sin it was jealousy. In her own estimation she hadn't a touch of it, and certainly her life had proved she was remarkably unselfish—a thing which very few people are.

Still, in her heart had lurked a sore, disappointed feeling about this brother Tom. Hadn't she been the favorite sister all her life? Hadn't he told her his plans and hopes and intentions, ever since she was old enough to remember anything? She'd been the one to do for him, think for him, save for him, help him in every way she could imagine, until this last scheme; and this had seemed to come between them.

In the first place, it had been her own fault—she had opposed it. But lately she had fallen in with the young man's plans with remarkable patience and helped him wherever he'd asked for it. The sore point was that he rarely asked, and he asked and received much from Helen. The younger sister understood perfectly the reason for this. She even remembered he had drawn Helen in, at her own suggestion, and that they'd often planned together to interest her for her good. Yet *Helen* was receiving little notes from Tom, asking her to come over and arrange the parlors for special occasions; to arrange flowers for the rooms of special guests; to play for a rare singer who was stopping with them; to sing with the Glee Club in the reading room! None of these things could Maria do, and a score of other trifles were shut out from her for the same reason, which made it harder.

It was well enough when she and Tom together planned ways by which Helen could be brought in and made to forget her unhappy self for a little. But gradually Maria knew Helen had become a necessity. She was often sent for, not for *her* sake, but for Tom's—sent for to fill places that she, Maria, couldn't fill. And it had hurt. She had called herself a simpleton; she had boasted of her inability to tell what flowers looked well together or whether the reception chairs should stand at the right or the left of the mirror. Yet in her heart it felt hard to have Helen slipping in where she'd been needed so long and realize she was almost never needed at the Randolph House.

So on this particular morning she had lifted her eyebrows and spoken sharply to the boy who brought the twisted note. "From Mr. Randolph. He must have told you to give it to Mrs. Monroe. He can't possibly want anything of *me*," unconsciously quoting words she'd been long used to from Mrs. Monroe's lips.

Wasn't it a bit of a triumph then to discover that at last something was more important than music and flowers? Something Helen was as unable to do as a child in the street; something that if left undone would bring dismay and disaster to the Randolph House—and then to know that *she* could make it all right, restore order where chaos was and, in short, make the wheels of domestic life roll along as smoothly as though the road hadn't thought of being rough. She wasn't glad the poor tempted cook had fallen again, but it was a real delight to find herself a necessity to her brother; to find him leaning on her again and know she was strong enough for the strain. It was largely to this feeling—if the well-satisfied guests had known it—that they were indebted for the remarkably good dinner she put forth her wits and her skill to secure for them. So now tonight she rested in her chair and was jubilant. Tom had been ignoring her lately, but he had suddenly found there *were* places where she fitted in nicely. At the particular moment when she was giving this thought expression, in tone rather than in words, Tom opened the door and walked in.

"Well," Maria said, "I didn't expect to see you again tonight. I thought you'd seen quite enough of me for one day. What's the matter now? You look as if some new trouble had overtaken you. Didn't the housekeeper come?"

"Yes, she came—"

"Oh, well, then, you'll do nicely. That friend of mine is a perfect host in herself. You'll do well to promote her. I believe I'd give her that miserable cook's place right away."

"It isn't that," Tom said, sitting down. "Maria, we seem to need your help a good deal. You're wanted at the Randolph House again—and tonight."

Chapter 20

Unequal to the Emergency

Your friend," Tom continued in answer to his sister's startled and inquiring look, "insists on seeing you tonight and at once. No one else will do.
"What does she want? Is she sick?"

"I don't think so. At least she's been at her work as usual. I think she's sick at heart—in trouble, mental trouble, I'm afraid. She came to me a few minutes ago, with such a worn, sad expression that it hurt me to look at her, and begged me to let her send a boy for you, as she must see you at once. I tried to discover the trouble, but she seemed unable to tell me. I was afraid you might not understand the message so I came myself. Will you go over and see what you can do for her?"

Maria arose composedly and with her intense satisfaction in herself not a bit lessened. "I'll go, of course," she said, "though I *did* suppose I was tired. I expect to find nothing more formidable than a broken pitcher or platter to confess. You try to make those girls of yours mortally afraid of you, while they seem very anxious to please you, but I do wish she'd left her confession until morning."

"It isn't as trivial as that. If I thought so I wouldn't let you go at all. Perhaps it would be as well to send her word you'll come over in the morning or she may come to you."

Maria's only answer was to go in search of hat and shawl and in a few minutes to announce herself ready.

At the hotel she went directly to the room assigned to the girl. That neat little room! Few chambermaids at hotels or elsewhere have such spots to call their own as that was. It had been one of Ermina's blissful whims to have the servants' rooms at the Randolph House furnished with every appliance of convenience and comfort to meet the needs of respectable girls. They even had what most mistresses would call luxuries, when found in servants' rooms, though these same mistresses would recognize such articles as common necessities when found elsewhere.

"It's safe to conclude," Maria thought, glancing around as she entered, "that *she* never had such comfortable quarters before." Maria enjoyed her having them. She believed in it with all her heart, but she wanted people to be aware of, and loyal to, the superiority of the Randolph House over the rest of the world.

"What can I do for you tonight, Maggie?" she said, trying to speak calmly.

The girl was walking up and down the room, and her eyes looked scarcely less fierce and unreadable than they did on that first meeting with her. She couldn't be half starved *now*; what could be the matter with her?

"Sit down, please—I have something to tell you," she said in a husky voice, evidently struggling to appear composed and respectful, as became a girl talking to the sister of her employer.

Puzzled and half-awed by her manner, Maria took the low chair by the stand and waited in silence for her to speak, which she didn't seem in a hurry to do. She renewed her walk through the room, and Maria studied the flushed face and hungry-looking eyes and tried to determine what could possibly be the matter.

"Does it rain?" she asked suddenly.

"Yes," Maria said, more astonished than before.

"Hard?"

"Yes, quite hard."

"Such nights drive me wild," Maggie said, and she looked as though she might really be wild. "Because, you see, I don't know where he is. He may even be out in the storm. It was on a night like this that I lost him."

"What are you talking about?" said Maria, thoroughly aroused and alarmed. "Sit down, Maggie, and don't walk the floor like an insane woman. I think you must be sick. You'd better let me call my brother and send him for a doctor."

"I'm not sick at all," Maggie said, speaking more quietly, and bringing a chair she sat down opposite her guest. "I beg your pardon for frightening you and for sending for you at all. But, Miss Randolph, I had a new thought—a new hope, I might almost call it—and it seemed to me you were the one to help me, and I couldn't resist sending for you. But first I must tell you something about myself. You think I'm insane, and I wonder that I'm not. What would you think if I told you that somewhere in this great miserable world I have a little boy, a baby, only three years old, wandering up and down in the storm maybe or lying sick in the gutter or, oh, I don't know where—dead, perhaps. If I *could only* know he was, how happy I could be! What do you think of a trouble like that?"

"Do you really mean it?" Maria said, horror and pain in her voice. "Maggie, what *can* you mean? And how could such a thing be?"

Maggie laughed a laugh that had no sweetness in it. "You may well ask," she said, "and you're dying to ask me a hundred questions. Why didn't I take care of my boy, if I had one, and not let him get lost? Oh, only God knows how I tried! My darling, I did everything and bore everything for you, and what did it amount to? It isn't a long story, Miss Randolph, to those who are familiar with such things. I could tell it in one word. Rum stole my baby and lost him, and I've been without him for two dreadful years. Now you know it all."

"But how, *how?*" repeated Maria, her face pale with sympathy and dismay. "Tell me about it. How could it be, and what have you done?"

"Done! I've done everything—no, I thought of one thing I have *not* done, and I've sent for you tonight to help me do that. His father took him, took him from his warm little crib out into the night and storm. Think of that! And he was sick too. I had run to the doctor's next door for some medicine for him, and when I came back he was gone, and I've never seen or heard of him since. And don't you wonder that my reason hasn't gone? But it won't—I'll keep that, and I'll find him yet. I'll never give it up, never."

Maria sat as one stunned. What a strange, terrible story to whirl right into the midst of her quiet, uneventful life! Could such sorrow as that be possible? She began after a little to pour out questions, and Maggie, who seemed to have grown calmer in telling her bitterness, answered each one briefly and promptly.

Her husband had been a post-office clerk in a neighboring city. They'd been very happy once. He only took a little medicated wine to strengthen him after night work, when he had to sit up late making up the books. The doctor ordered it—said, indeed, he would break down without it.

"I hate doctors," Maggie said, flashing into sudden fire, then quieting at once and going on with her story.

Little by little the habit grew, until he was very often "exhausted," and the wine was soon used without any medication, and it ceased to strengthen him, and something stronger was obtained, and, oh, me!

Maria had heard the whole story dozens of times. There wasn't a new feature about it. It's being worked out with each day's history, but it had never come to someone she could sit and talk with till she could not only know, but *feel* the sorrow. There's a great difference between the two. Helen's tragedy had been cut off in its early days by death. It might have been as terrible as this.

It took an hour to tell the story in all its pitifulness. How the drunken father had come just as she ran out. She saw him come and felt no fear, for in his wildest moments he had only been loving to the boy. She saw him go out again with a bundle in his arms, wondered what had been sacrificed now and hastened home to see, and she found an empty crib.[1]

What had been the father's object, where he went, what he did or why he did it, the poor half-wild mother didn't know and could never conjecture. She knew only too well that from that day forth she had seen neither husband nor baby; nor had any trace of them ever come to her, though she'd used all ways and means that keen brains and determined wills could devise. Before the story was concluded the poor mother had talked herself into calmness.

"I was on the very verge of insanity that evening when I came to you," she said quietly. "I can never tell anyone the story of my wanderings or of the cruel things that were said to me. I used to look at happy mothers with their darlings in their arms and think, 'If you knew, I wonder what you would say?' "

"Why didn't you tell them and see?"

"Once I did," she answered, with a flash in her eyes that told of smothered fire, "and the woman said, 'The miserable creature is not only intoxicated, but crazy. She should be taken to the mad house.' But don't let me talk of it—I can't.

"One thing I've never done. I didn't even think of it until this morning, when your brother was praying at family prayers. I've never prayed for him.

---

[1]Founded on fact—the incident came within my knowledge—Isabella Alden.

I don't mean I haven't got down on my knees and cried out wildly to God to give him back to me. But that isn't the kind of prayer I mean. My prayers aren't acceptable to God. I'm not a Christian woman. I never have been, but I *mean* to be. I want to know *now* how to be a Christian, so that I can go to God and pray for my baby and feel sure He hears and trust Him, just as your brother does. I must learn to pray.

"I didn't know who to ask. I can't talk to a man and tell him my bitter story. But today, when I worked with you and saw how efficient you were and how prompt to do the right thing at the right time, it flashed upon me how much I'd give to hear you pray to God for my darling. Then I thought you were just the one to help me learn to pray for him myself, and I thought about it and kept going back to it until I felt tonight I had to see you. Now will you help me?"

Imagine, if you can, how Maria Randolph felt! She had come over there with an assured feeling that, whatever was asked of her, she was equal to the occasion. A sense of superiority, a sense of power, had possessed her all day and grown upon her with each added call. Yet here she was, asked to pray! Not only that, but asked to show another how to pray! She who had never prayed in her life! What could she do or say? Here was this miserable mother devouring her with hungry eyes and with a hope so eager and strong springing up in her poor heart that it seemed a solemn thing to crush it.

Why hadn't she asked Tom? How gladly he'd have prayed and pointed out the way to her. Still, Maggie waited for the answer. Something must be said. Must she make the humiliating confession?

"You've come to the wrong person," she said at last, speaking desperately. "I don't know how to pray for myself; I never prayed in my life." What a monstrous admission for a sane woman to make! Maria felt it as she spoke the words. "Yes, I used to pray at my mother's knee, but I don't know how now. Why didn't you ask my brother? If anyone in the world knows how to pray he does, and he would sympathize with you in your trouble, as few people can."

Maggie had left her chair and was walking the floor again. "I felt as if I needed a woman to speak to," she said. "I felt sure you could help me. I thought you were the one, and you had been so kind to me—kind when everyone else was cruel. I'm sorry I troubled you. I shouldn't have sent for you, I suppose, but I felt so sure. I'm awfully disappointed."

"Let me call my brother," Maria said, moving toward the door, speaking in a low, subdued voice. She felt utterly humiliated.

"No," Maggie said, "not now, please. I couldn't explain. I can't talk about it anymore; it would do no good either. What good can praying do? *You* don't believe in it, do you?"

"Yes, I do, with all my heart. I had a mother who prayed, and I know God hears and answers my father. Yes, if there's anything in the world I have unshaken faith in, it's prayer."

"Then why don't you pray?"

Now what was a sensible person to answer to such a question, in the face of such a declaration as she had just made and upon which she'd prided herself? Maria felt the force of her own folly and was puzzled and embarrassed. There really seemed to be nothing to say. Being one unaccustomed to answer with silence, she said the only thing left to say under the circumstances: "I don't know, I'm sure."

Maggie regarded her fixedly, and something very like a smile hovered about the corners of her drawn mouth. Could it be a derisive smile? "I think I was mistaken in you," she said simply. "I imagined you were like your brother, but with a certain natural force that drew me and made me feel like resting on you. I thought, perhaps, you were very high in favor with God."

What a strange sentence! It sent a thrill like an electric shot through Maria's sensitive nerves. She was fond of power; she delighted in being leaned upon; she enjoyed reflected greatness; she liked being Tom Randolph's sister and Mr. Harper's sister-in-law. What a thing it would be to be high in favor with God! To be so familiar at court that she could present a friend there, as she'd been asked to do this evening, without a fear or doubt as to the result! Yet what a broken reed she'd been. She felt a bitter, utterly new sense of humiliation.

A low, quick knock was heard at the door and Tom's voice outside: "Maria, will you stay with us all night? If so, I'll go over to tell Father. I'm afraid they'll be anxious."

"No," Maria said, rising suddenly. "I can't stay. I'm coming now. Maggie, let me ask my brother to come in. He can help you."

"It wouldn't be suitable," Maggie said quietly, and that strange smile was on her face. "Don't you know the world would be shocked at such an indecorous proceeding? You see I'm shut up to your help tonight or none."

How true it was! Tom couldn't come in there at that hour, even to pray with a young and beautiful woman.

"Then go to God," Maria said, suddenly and with intense energy. "I'm sorry I can't help you, but because I've shown myself a fool you don't need to be one. Go right to Him—I know my father's God will hear you and help you."

"What a long conference!" Tom said, when his sister came out to him. "It couldn't have been about a pitcher. What did she want, if I may be told?"

"She wanted me to pray with her." Maria's voice was abrupt and hard.

Tom was very much startled.

"And did you?" he asked after a few minutes of silence, during which it appeared she had no more to tell him.

"What a foolish question!" she said bitterly. "Whatever else I may be, I'm not a hypocrite."

He was still until they were crossing the road. Then he said, "What do you think of your ability to follow out the orders of your motto now? You can't think that when a waiting soul asks you to pray, Christ doesn't say to you, 'Do it'?"

She answered nothing, It was a new sting. She had forgotten her motto, "Whatsoever He saith unto you, do it." She'd boasted of her ability to follow it. Had she? She went into the house and up to her room in utter humiliation.

Chapter 21

Waiting for Something to Happen

Life now began to take a very humdrum aspect to Maria Randolph, and if any one aspect of life above another was hateful to her it was humdrumness. Real tangible trouble was almost more endurable. She dreaded the winter; it stretched before her in interminable stupidity. One morning she grumbled to Tom over the prospect.

"I know what will happen tomorrow, as well as I do what's going on today, and the day after tomorrow will be the same. Helen is gloomy or sharp all the time, and Father sick in his room, and you at that tiresome house that swallows all your strength and all your heart, and Grace gone! The prospect is rather dismal now, *isn't* it? I don't fret very often, do I? But it does seem to me as if life is very forlorn. I like to have things happen, even if they're troublesome to manage. My washing is really the only excitement I have, and there isn't enough of that to keep me busy—though Dick Norton *does* get his clothes horribly dirty, and he manages to tear them every week just for the pleasure of seeing me mend them, I believe."

"How is his education progressing?" Tom asked. "I thought you were getting him ready for college."

"Now, Tom Randolph, you're not to make fun of him. He's doing real well, poor fellow. If he were ten or twenty years younger and had a chance, he'd make a scholar yet. He can read chapters in the Bible now without stumbling at all, and he's as interested as possible."

"I'm glad of it," Tom said, laughing, "though it seems to me some important 'ifs' are in the way of his becoming a scholar. But, Maria, don't you think Helen is better? She's less gloomy than she used to be, isn't she?"

"Why, she is different," Maria said thoughtfully. "Yes, there *is* a difference. She's preoccupied, seems to have very little time to devote to me or to finding fault, either. Now that I think of it, I've been struck with her silence several times when I expected an outburst. But she always impresses me with the idea that she's forgotten to say anything, rather than that she didn't intend to. What interests her so much over at the Randolph House? She spends a great deal of her time there."

"She's interested in everything that pertains to it," Tom said, "and she's a real help to us. I think she's very different. I wouldn't worry about the winter, Maria. Enough things may happen—things you don't want perhaps."

"Don't croak!" said Maria impatiently. "What *could* happen? Father's better—everyone thinks so. I can see he's improving every day. If we had a doctor who knew anything, I believe he'd get well. Mr. Harper thinks he's gaining ground."

"I think so myself," Tom said, with heartiness enough to comfort Maria, whose irritation arose from an excessive desire to make everyone confess that her father was at least not growing worse. "But you certainly have a care in looking to his comfort, and I know it must be a pleasure."

"Of course," she said, in her practical way. "But the thing is, what to do with myself when I've done everything for him I can, and more too. When the work is all done—there's only a little handful of work now—and when I'm alone, it's easy for you to preach contentment. But I'm *not* content—I wasn't made to be, unless my hands were so full I didn't know what to do first. I tell you I'm restless, and I can't help it."

Tom looked at her wistfully.

"It seems strange," he said, "to hear you complaining of not enough to do, when there's so much work waiting to be done. 'Whatsoever He saith unto you, do it.' Think what a broad command that is."

"Don't preach!" said Maria, and she turned away from him impatiently again. But his words seemed to have suggested to her a new train of thought. She turned back presently with a question.

"Tom, what did you do with that girl? I left her in a forlorn state, and when I met her yesterday, she smiled and bowed and looked as sunshiny as though she'd found her baby. Isn't that horrible anyway? I *would* find him. If I were she I would travel through the whole world night and day until I got him again."

"You'd do much better to earn your living, and something over, to help carry out the search intelligently and with system, as she's doing." Tom spoke so quietly that Maria's blaze of enthusiasm died down.

"What did you do for her?" she asked more calmly.

"Sent Kate up to her—she spent the night, and in the morning she told me Maggie had gone to the only One who could possibly help her much and given her cause into His hands. She feels surer of success now than she ever did."

Now Kate was the Scotch-Irish waitress at the Randolph House, a red-cheeked, broad-shouldered maid-of-all-work, with a certain native refinement of speech and manner that seemed to belong to her heart more than her education, and so in truth it did. She was being educated into the delicacy and tenderness of Christian fellowship. Maria had heard her brother speak of her before as an earnest Christian girl, whose influence was very strong for good. But what a humiliating discovery that where she utterly failed, Kate, with her disregard for the king's English—who said "ain't" and "his'n" and "your'n," with perfect indifference—had been able to give timely help! This fact irritated Maria. It was *so* hard to be recognized as a failure!

"I'm glad you have such a perfect treasure as Kate in your family," she said, speaking contemptuously, answering what she'd heard him say before rather than anything he had said then. "I'd think you had set her to reforming your precious cook, who'll burn the house down over your head one of these nights. If she's such a powerful agent for good, you should see what she can do in that direction."

"I have," Tom said, still speaking with the utmost quiet and patience. "She's doing better than you propose. She's trying to help her look to the only One Who can give her strength to reform, and we're all praying she may be helped to 'look.' You should have heard Maggie pray for her last evening in the girls' meeting. Kate said it made them all cry."

"What a melting time!" Maria said, with a scoffing voice and a sore heart.

Maggie had learned to pray, and she hadn't helped her in that or in anything, and she had felt such an interest in her, such a burning desire to help her in her great sorrow! Tom looked at his young sister with a pitying sigh.

"You need a place to rest, Maria," he said tenderly. "Why *won't* you come to it?"

Maria rallied her pride and turned to him with a laugh.

"I need a scolding," she said cheerily, "for being so cross. You know I'm not often such a dragon as I've seemed this morning. I hope you'll all get as good over there as you can, and then come here and take me over. I need it. I'm sure—Tom, who in the world is standing at the door with Helen?"

They were near the side window, and the piazza door was plainly discernible from where they stood. Tom looked.

"Don't you know him?" he said. "I thought you'd met him. He's a good man. Why, he's a home missionary—been two or three years in Southern Michigan and is going back in two months or so. He's been sent on here to collect funds toward helping forward their church building. Didn't you hear him in our church one Sunday? Oh, I remember—you stayed with Father that morning. Well, he gave us a good sermon. I know you didn't hear him now, for I remember wishing you'd let Helen stay with Father and had come to church. I thought it was a sermon which would have helped you."

"About home missions?" said Maria. "Do you think I'd make a good missionary, Tom?" She laughed gleefully.

"It wasn't on that subject," said Tom, "at least, only incidentally. It was on the need of personal consecration."

"Well, in the meantime, what's he doing on the piazza talking with Helen?"

"Why, I suppose he met her on the street and walked down with her. He told me he'd like to call on Father sometime, if he was able to see him. He met some men in Michigan whom Father once helped and who are very grateful. He said it might be pleasant to Father to hear the story from him. Perhaps that's his present errand."

"He won't see Father this morning," Maria said, "unless his business is much more urgent than that. I've been giving his room a tremendous clearing up, and he's tired out. Tom, come over to tea tonight. We're having flapjacks, and you know you're too fashionable to have them at the Randolph House—so come where you can enjoy them. He's coming in, I declare!" And

Maria suddenly vanished up the back stairs.

Now I want to take you back perhaps two months and explain to you certain items of which Maria was in ignorance.

It was Sunday morning, one of Helen Monroe's miserable days. I hardly know why Sunday seemed to be her worst day, but you'll often find it so among people to whom that day should be a blessing. She'd spent the morning in doubt about whether to drag herself to church or stay at home. If she could have stayed in her own room and spent her time on the bed, half sleeping, half crying and wholly miserable, she wouldn't have hesitated a moment. But knowing she'd either have to go to church or spend the time in or near her father's room made her undecided. He was very particular that the family should be represented at church; and the effort to invent an excuse for not going, and at the same time for not giving Maria a chance to go, would have involved more energy than she possessed. So, after delaying until it was almost too late for anyone to go, she decided that a morning church would be preferable to a morning under her father's possible questions. So she went.

A stranger preached—a common, uninteresting-looking stranger. So she called him the moment her eyes rested on him. As for him, something perhaps in the wan pale face, shrouded behind the widow's weeds, looking at him presently with earnest, haunting eyes, may have attracted him to turn often during his more pointed sentences to the Randolph pew. There were many pointed sentences in his sermon. The text was "Unpaid Vows." Nothing was particularly new in that sermon, nor was the man specially eloquent. In fact, Helen Monroe listened, or sat in the seat and pretended to listen, every Sunday of her life to sermons that had five times the rhetoric and talent shown in them than this one possessed. I don't know what it was, except the man was in earnest, and I suppose the Spirit of God had a message that day for just that woman sitting in the Randolph pew, and He chose the stranger-preacher to deliver it. Perhaps that might have been because the stranger had that very morning spent an hour on his knees, making the bold petition that God would honor his work to some *special* soul and do it *that very day*.

At least all these things occurred, and who shall say they weren't connected, each with the other? Helen Monroe had never heard such solemn truth as came home to her conscience that morning. Yes, *she* had vowed. She remembered the summer morning long ago in which she'd stood in that very church and taken the solemn vows of its covenant upon her. The gentle little mother down in that pew where she sat now brushed sweet and grateful tears from her flushed cheeks, and her father looked his gladness and his love from eyes clouded with feeling. The scene was vivid. It had made a strong impression on her at the time, and she could recall some of the language of the covenant. Now as to payment—had she deferred?

For a long time, in fact for years, Helen Monroe had had a dim, uncomfortable sense in her heart that her religion was weak and worthless. She'd felt a contempt for her own profession, even when she strenuously clung to it, as though something in it made life a little safer for her. But until that morning I don't think she'd ever stood face to face with her heart and felt it stripped of all hiding places and subterfuges.

Somehow those simple, plain words of the preacher seemed to scald her. She passed through many phases of feeling during that half hour. At first she was interested, then shocked, then angry, then alarmed, then utterly and, as she felt, hopelessly miserable! It was pitiful to see how she clung to her poor little rag she'd called religion and felt as if she actually let go and said, "I'm not a Christian," it would be settled doom to her. Yet, as the searching work went on, how could she know anything experimentally about this matter to have lived the life she had?

When the service closed she was conscious of only one strong desire—to get away from everybody, to get to her room, to lock her door, to have a chance to be utterly miserable—and I don't doubt she'd have carried out that design. She had decided, before the sermon ended, that she could never have any right to take the vows of the church upon her and that having a name to live was of small comfort after all. She would give it all up. She would never come to the communion again. She would stop going to prayer meeting (she still went occasionally). She wouldn't be a hypocrite, whatever else she might be. But this resolve did little toward quieting the tumult in her heart; for, after all, it was toward no such resolve that the preacher or the text was aiming. "Pay that which thou hast vowed" were the concluding words of the text, and she wasn't allowed to lose sight of them.

Tom came over to her the instant the benediction was pronounced.

"Won't you go over to the house with me?" he said, and he looked anxious. "I have some strangers there for the Sabbath, and they talk 'all sorts' when they get in the parlors, unless there's something to entertain them. Will you go over and give us some music?"

It was the last thing Helen felt she could do, and she was ready with a decided negative. But she had been accommodating lately, and Tom seemed to expect it and didn't wait for a negative. He turned to greet the preacher. "Good morning—Mr. Leonard, let me introduce my sister. Helen, will you walk with Mr. Leonard? He's to dine with us, and I have to go to my class, you know."

Chapter 22

Home Missions

And there was Helen standing in the aisle, with the minister calmly waiting for her, while the unsuspecting brother hurried away, supposing he'd arranged matters very satisfactorily.

She could only lead the way to the Randolph House with what grace she had, and Helen walked on before, feeling that this thing was sorely against her will, for more reasons than one.

The clergyman wasn't a difficult person to entertain. Indeed, from the first, he was unlike anyone she'd ever seen. His first opening of conversation was strikingly unlike what she expected. He made no remark on the weather or the beauty of the elegant church they'd just left.

Instead, he said suddenly, as one absorbed in the thought and imagining that all others were equally interested: "That was a remarkable text I preached from this morning, wasn't it? I don't know when any verse of the Bible has come to me with such force. Unpaid vows—only think of it. Isn't it startling when we remember to Whom they're due?"

"Very," Helen said, and something in her voice caused him to turn his eyes from space and look searchingly at her. "Who *does* pay them?" she asked, bridling suddenly, as if he'd accused her of unfaithfulness, and speaking almost fiercely. "I don't know of anyone who lives up to his profession in the sense you talked about this morning."

His answer, if answer it could be called, was certainly very peculiar.

"Don't you know *one* who's trying to?" The emphasis on the word "one" was marked. There was no escaping the fact that he meant her to understand *she* was the one meant.

"No," she said, speaking as before with sharpness.

"Do you mean you've never made any vows?"

No, she couldn't say that. It wouldn't be true. She had too recently gone over that day, when the solemn public vows were taken, to ignore them now. Her answer was less sharp, but it was distinct.

"Yes, I've vowed."

"Then you can't mean you're not trying!"

His voice held genuine dismay. To this honest man it was evidently no light thing to promise and not perform, even when the one promised was the Lord Himself. It's strange, but how can we help believing that people who would be shocked at the idea of violating their word given to other people seem to ignore without much trouble the most solemn commitments made to God!

The actual enormity of this had never struck Helen's conscience so forcibly as it did at the moment when that probing question was put. Natures like hers are rarely stirred deeply without becoming, or seeming to become, very irritable. She answered in great heat and haste.

"Yes, I mean just that! I don't think I've tried at all, not for this long time. I doubt whether I ever *really* tried. I was led into a public profession, as many other persons have been, when I didn't know what I was about. And much good I've ever done the church! I'm in a false position. I never realized it as I have today. Your sermon has accomplished so much. Perhaps you can tell me how to get out of it. Does the church release people from its roll? How shall I manage? I have no desire to be where I don't belong."

"I know of only one way," he said—his voice had lost its excited, astonished tone and was quiet and firm—"I know of only one *honorable* way—'Pay that which thou hast vowed.' It's God's command. It seems to be the way He's chosen for helping people who are in trouble and sincerely desire to get out.

"I know there's such talk as 'release from the church roll,' as though the vows were all made to the church, instead of the church being only a witness. I know people think they're doing an honorable thing to stay away from the communion when they feel they haven't lived the right life. But only see how foolish that is! If you'd made your brother a promise and called on me to witness it and had broken that promise again and again, would it make matters all right for you to refuse to have anything to do with *me*, the witness?"

This was the beginning of it. The Randolph House was some distance away, and the talk continued. It continued after they went to the parlor. And though Helen broke away from it for a time, after dinner when she came down to play, after the music was over, chance led her to the seat near the clergyman, and some sentence that seemed a chance one to her led them back into the topic.

That was weeks ago; much had transpired since then. The home missionary still lingered in the city, taking trips constantly to other cities and towns, but making the Randolph House his headquarters by the host's eager invitation. Tom felt the influence of such guests in the house. Helen saw much of this guest and heard much from him, especially at first on the subject of personal and entire consecration.

Gradually, almost imperceptibly to herself, her ideas and feelings began to change. I don't know, and I'm not sure she knows herself, whether during all those past years of church membership she was a Christian or not. She vexed her soul over the weary question for long days, but she finally had to give it up as, after all, of minor importance, compared with the vital one waiting to be answered. She came to understand that the point was not, Was I a Christian last year or last week or even yesterday? But it was, Do I mean to be one today—now?

When at last she was enabled to rest her heart on that one question, she began to feel that there was a solid rock and that she must have it for a foundation. She had no sudden experience of light and brightness; instead, the way was obscured for a good while. She had had much light given her before this and had chosen to go veiled, refusing to receive it. Why should it come in floods of glory to her now?

But, after all, she found a sense of peace, security, humility and even assurance. She walked softly, as one almost in a dream, as one who feared a rude awakening.

Maria had felt the change and wondered over it and feared at times that Helen was going to be sick. That is as far as she reached in understanding the secret. Sickness may have been the only power she recognized as a subduing agency.

Among other things about her sister that she didn't know, she had never met and never heard of this man whose sermon had been the instrument used to set these new experiences in motion.

We left him, you may remember, standing with Helen on the side piazza, or rather they were just about to enter as Maria vanished upstairs. She was gone just long enough to brush over her somewhat ruffled hair and exchange a somewhat soiled kitchen apron for a fresh one of the same fashion, and then she descended.

"Maria," Helen said, turning to her the moment the door opened, with a flush on her cheek deeper than usual, "let me introduce you to the Rev. Mr. Leonard. My sister Maria, Mr. Leonard."

"How do you do?" asked the gentleman, and his voice was genial and hearty, and he shook her hand in an altogether unconventional manner. "I've heard of this sister several times in the last few weeks. How's your father today? Do you mean to let me have a little talk with him? Or don't you think it would be prudent? They tell me you watch over his comfort with wonderful care."

Then he helped himself to a seat and continued talking about her father, asking questions about his sickness and the remedies in use and their effect, with such interest and evidently thorough understanding of sickness and common sense view of its needs, that Maria felt her stiff dignity, which she had put on to greet a stranger and a minister, thawing rapidly. She surprised herself by the detail with which she entered into a description of her father's state and became deeply interested in Mr. Leonard's suggestion about certain strength-giving potions.

Helen, meanwhile, seemed suddenly to have lost the grace and ease she'd always been known for in entertaining strangers and was silent and flushed. Maria couldn't tell what to think of her.

Presently the question of a call on the father came up again, and Maria was sufficiently thawed to admit graciously that when he awoke, if he felt as well as usual, she knew of no reason why he wouldn't like to see Mr. Leonard for a few minutes.

"I'd imagine, from some things you've said, that you've seen a sick man before and have a little common sense left for what weakness can bear, which is more than can be said of the majority of people who come to call on him."

This sentence, uttered in a half-savage tone, was as nearly a compliment as any Maria had ever spoken. It ended in her going to the sick room and returning presently with the gracious permission to make a ten-minute call or, if her father didn't seem tired, fifteen minutes.

No, it didn't end that way. Mr. Leonard had risen and was moving toward the bedroom door when he suddenly turned and said, "Perhaps this is hardly the right thing after all, Helen. I think we can be wiser than this."

"What on earth does the man mean?" was Maria's mental comment.

Then he turned to her. "The truth is, my friend, I'll have to make a *confidante* of you. I'm very willing to, and it seems prudent. Do you think your father sufficiently strong this morning for an important conversation? I'm going home in another month, and I want to take your sister Helen with me. Do you think I may ask him for such a favor, or should I wait until a more favorable time?"

Now, of all the experiences of Maria's life, and some had been startling enough, nothing had ever so amazed her. She stood still, with her hand on the knob of her father's door, and looked from one to the other of the two people standing near her, with a face in which astonishment and incredulity curiously blended. Helen's face flushed crimson before the look, the flush running up to her hair. She could realize, in a measure, what this surprise was to Maria. As for Mr. Leonard, he laughed good-naturedly.

"What do you mean?" Maria asked at last. "Where is your home, if you don't mind saying? And what can you possibly want of Helen? She isn't strong enough for a teacher, and, besides, it would be a dreadful life for her. I'd hate to have her a martyr to that extent."

Her voice trembled, and she evidently desired to shield Helen, which strangely moved that older sister. Somehow, she felt then, as she never had before, what a care-taking, burden-bearing life Maria led and was willing to lead for them all. Mr. Leonard seemed to appreciate it. He spoke quickly and with feeling.

"I'll shield her in every way in my power. Her life won't be harder than I can help. As for the trials and privations, I think she's ready for them and willing to bear the burden. My home is in Southern Michigan, and she'll have only one scholar. As her husband, I think I can make the work easier for her than if she went out alone. I'm a home missionary, you know."

Still Maria stood looking at them—the surprise in no way lessening, the incredulous look deepening, if anything. It was becoming very embarrassing, at least to Helen, until suddenly Maria declared four words, so full of pent-up astonishment that they bristled with exclamation points.

"Helen Monroe a missionary!"

They reacted on Helen's excited nerves. She had been on the verge of tears. Now she laughed. Dropping into the nearest chair she covered her glowing face with her hands and shook with laughter, in which Mr. Leonard seemed moved to join with great apparent satisfaction.

In the midst of this, Mr. Randolph's voice was heard calling Maria. She escaped into his room, and when, a few minutes later, she emerged, propriety had returned to the two in the sitting room, and they were sitting quietly waiting for a chance to make that call.

"Go on, Helen," said Maria, leaving the door ajar and motioning them in.

She seemed to have determined it was Helen's place to introduce the stranger. And Helen, followed by Mr. Leonard, went softly into the quiet room, and Maria herself shut the door after them with a little nervous click and a curious sensation in her throat.

Chapter 23

Once and Again

Maria walked to that side window out of which she and Tom had looked but a few minutes before. The world seemed to have changed a good deal in that time, for such a surprise had come into her life! That odd feeling remained in her throat, as of one who was choking back tears—though why should she cry? She heard the steady murmur of voices in the bedroom. It was an earnest conference. She'd doubted the wisdom of exciting her father with such an astounding revelation. She'd even taken time to wonder what Grace would say to their consistency when her poor little affair had to be so carefully guarded from troubling him. But nothing else seemed possible to do. This was altogether different from two simpletons like Grace and Alfred Parks playing at grown-up-ness. These were man and woman, each with years and dignity enough to decide questions for themselves, having decided they sought the father's blessing now. Maria couldn't doubt they'd get it; she knew it would be a joy to her father's heart to have the family represented in such work as the home mission cause afforded. But what an odd representative! This though almost caused a reaction. It certainly had its ludicrous side, to think of Helen Monroe in such a position!

Tom came somewhat hurriedly across the street and entered the side door.

"Why, I thought Mr. Leonard was here," he said, looking about him in surprise.

"He is," said Maria briefly, and she nodded her head toward the bedroom. "A private conference, Tom."

"Ah!" he said. "I expected that."

"You might have given me a slight hint then—at least of the existence of such a person." And Maria looked dignified.

"My dear Maria, there was nothing for me to hint. I was just suspicious without having any reasonable ground for being so. I had a presentiment, perhaps some would call it. But it wouldn't have looked well for me to tell you so. I wonder when the conference will be over? I perhaps ought to intrude. A man is waiting to see Mr. Leonard, and the business is urgent."

"Tom, isn't it the oddest thing that ever happened?"

"What, this? I think it's the best thing that's happened to the Randolph family yet."

Whereupon Tom crossed to the bedroom door and without further ceremony knocked. A half-dozen words exchanged with Mr. Leonard, and that gentleman made hurried adieus and left in his company. Helen lingered a little with her father, the door still shut. When she came out traces of tears were on her face, but her eyes were smiling. Maria seemed glued to that window seat. Helen went over to her.

"Were you very much surprised?" she asked, speaking gently.

"Surprise is no word for it. I don't think I'd have been much more bewildered if he'd come after me."

Helen laughed.

"In many respects it would have been a much better thing for him to do," she said. "But, for the comfort of the entire Randolph family, we rejoice that he didn't."

"Why? It doesn't follow that I'd have rushed out there after a home missionary life at the first opportunity. I don't think I'm fitted for such a place, and, for that matter, I don't think *you* are."

Now the Helen of Maria's acquaintance would have bridled at this and strongly hinted that she, Maria, wasn't the proper person to judge one's fitness for places and that it made little difference to anyone what she thought. Maria knew this and expected something in that line. But she felt most unusually severe; in proportion to how much her heart had been touched, and trembled under the shadow of coming changes, did her resolute will resist this invasion of feeling and resort to roughness to hide its softness. Helen remained beside her, keeping silence for two or three minutes, then she spoke.

"I don't wonder at that remark, Maria. I've been at work all my life proving to you my unfitness for any place of trust. No one certainly can feel less qualified than I in many respects feel myself to be. But I ought to tell you one thing. In some degree I'm different from what I was a few weeks ago. I hardly know what to call it—I don't try to name it—but for the first time in my life I'm sure I love the Lord Jesus Christ, and I long to show my love by anything I can do. I didn't seek for this thing—I didn't hope for it—I didn't dream of it. I simply prayed to be shown the way in which to walk, to be led as a child, and God seemed to send me this answer. How much I thank Him for *such* an answer, I can't explain even to you."

And then this reserved, oftentimes haughty, woman stooped and kissed her youngest sister as she stood there. Then she went upstairs to the privacy of her own room, and Maria stood still. The excitement didn't lessen; the bewilderment deepened by this latest development.

Only this feeling was strong and clear in the midst of the conflicting and excited thought: "There is a power beyond anything that has ever touched my life, beyond anything I've ever imagined!" The power that could make Helen Monroe acknowledge *anything* that should be humbling to her pride was a power her sister Maria didn't understand and felt compelled to respect. Then she set about getting dinner as usual.

Yet it wasn't as usual. The shadow of a surprising change had fallen over the family; she felt it and couldn't rid herself of it, even as she walked back and forth in that room, looking in every respect as it had looked for so long.

The "something" she had craved "no matter what," only an hour before, had come to her with a vengeance.

She no longer needed to mourn over not enough to do. The new plans brought a great influx of work, and not only work, but responsibility. A dozen times a day during the next few weeks Maria contrasted the lives of the two persons, the Helen as she had been and the Helen she had become, and was filled with amazement over the latter.

"Helen," she said, "aren't you going to get a new silk?"

"Dear me, no! How could I? And what would I need of one if I could? I'm going to live in a log cabin for the next few years."

"But what will you be married in?"

"Oh—why, my traveling dress."

"What is that to be?"

"I don't know, I'm sure—I haven't thought. Alpaca of some sort, I guess, or empress cloth."

"Alpaca!" Maria stood aghast.

How would Helen Randolph have looked in an alpaca! It really became bewildering as a new experience. This seemed more strange since Ermina in her long, long letter of congratulation had enclosed a bank check as a wedding gift that stood for any amount of finery and hinted that such was its intended use.

Helen and Maria had changed places. Maria was intent on sustaining the Randolph honor, and Helen was engaged in saying, "What's the use? I really won't need anything like that."

The same bewilderments occurred over the wedding arrangements.

"Where will we set the table?" Maria said. "In the back parlor or leave it in the dining room?"

"When?"

"When? Why, when the day comes. Helen, what's the matter with you?"

"Well," said Helen, laughing, "I'd say, let's have breakfast in the dining room as usual."

"And what shall we have?"

"Oh, I don't know—beefsteak and griddle cakes, I guess. I must learn how to make your kind of griddle cakes. Mr. Leonard says they're better than Westerners get."

"Helen Monroe!" Maria exclaimed, and she dropped the skirt she was basting and looked the picture of despair. "Who ever heard of beefsteak and griddle cakes for a wedding breakfast!"

"Oh, a *wedding* breakfast," repeated Helen, as if that were an entirely new idea. "Why, Maria, it needn't be different from any other breakfast. Tom will be the only one besides the Harpers."

"Don't you mean to have any company at all?"

"Oh, dear, no! Whom could I have? Father is too feeble for company, you know. Besides, I can't think of anyone I want. I'll tell you, Maria—fix it exactly as you think it should be. Then I'll know they're all right. You know more about things than I ever shall, I'm afraid. I'm only particular about this one thing—that you give yourself as little work and anxiety and spend as little on me as possible, for I honestly don't think these things are worth the trouble. If I were going to Washington or Boston or one of those cities to live and had a reputation to sustain, it would be different. But I'm to be nobody but a missionary's wife, you know, and live in the back woods." Whereupon Helen would fold up her work, looking serenely happy the while and set out for a tramp into the west end with Mr. Leonard.

"Going down in the very scum to practice," Maria would say, with a turned-up nose. "I'd think they might wait until they got out West." For the west end of that little city was another name for Five Points or some of those well-known resorts. Yet Maria, looking after them both, was proud with a pride that no sight of Helen in her silken robes, and poor Horace Monroe in his lavender kid gloves, had ever awakened. Mr. Leonard had brought his Western habits with him and wore no gloves at all.

All anxiety about the effect of such unusual excitement on the invalid was quieted by his evident satisfaction in and enjoyment of his prospective son-in-law. Mr. Randolph's own very early life had been spent in the West, and the family was intimately connected with the home mission work in earlier days. Old memories, therefore, were revived, and the spot in his heart blossomed and glowed with the thought that the Randolph blood would flow again in ministry.

Despite the confusion regarding plans, preparations for the coming event went swiftly forward. The days went forward rapidly, too, and brought them presently to the breakfast Maria had worried so needlessly about. For Tom finally declared that the care of the father and the bride was as much as Maria's nerves should manage, and a strong force from the Randolph House came over to do everything to perfection. So, though there were almost no guests, Peter Armstrong only being invited as a friend of the family and Dick Norton being added, simply because it suited Maria's fancy to include him, the breakfast was as dainty and tasteful in all its details as though the guests had been numerous.

Also Maria had worried over Grace coming home so soon and mingling again with the obnoxious Alfred. That, too, was needless, for Mr. Harper came alone. Ermina wasn't quite well, and Grace thought it unwise to leave her alone, as she was very anxious he should attend.

Maria heard and wondered whether Ermina had considerately sickened at this opportune time to arrange this convenient and satisfactory program.

Mr. Harper brought their love and remembrance in a trunk full of most satisfactory things, chosen, Mr. Leonard said, with as much wisdom as though they'd been the "granddaughters of pioneer missionaries."

And Mr. Randolph answered with pride: "They are."

To Maria came a little private note from Grace, containing only these words, much underscored:

Dear Maria,
Won't you please invite Alfred to the wedding for my sake? Please do—
that's a dear sister.

Gracie

Over this note Maria gloomed and scolded and finally settled down into the serene conviction that for once everything was going nicely, for the said Alfred thoughtfully went off on a vacation tour and didn't return in time to be either invited or slighted.

So on this morning, when Maria, having no coffee to manage or other tasks to see to, suddenly remembered that she and Grace paid a last visit to Helen that other time and had a farewell talk. Though she had no Grace to go with her, she decided to go alone. Helen was dressed and standing by the window looking out.

"All ready?" asked Maria.

Helen turned toward her. There were traces of tears in her eyes. "I've been saying good-bye to Mother's grave. Graves seem hard to leave. People who are alive and I can hear from, and to whom I can write long letters, are different. But somehow one holds on to graves and wants to be near them."

At once Maria thought of Horace's grave and wondered if that was remembered by the widow, who was almost a bride. It didn't seem the thing to ask.

But Helen, as if in answer to her thoughts, suddenly added: "Some graves are very hard to think about. There has been one very bitter spot in my life that, however much joy may come to me in the future, I can never forget. If I'd been a different woman, Horace's grave might have been bright with the light of resurrection. Think of that! Oh, Maria, I hope you'll never have to look on any grave and feel that thought."

The tears were flowing freely now.

"Come," said Maria, not knowing what to say, "I wouldn't cry. You'll look like a fright. What will Mr. Leonard think?"

"He'll know that no tears were shed over him," Helen said quickly, and her eyes flashed with a sudden brightness.

Altogether it was in striking contrast with that other call. Maria felt the difference and respected it. Life was changed, and circumstances were changed, and, yes, Helen was changed by something besides time and circumstances—some great motive power had come into her life and lifted her up. It had been that way with Ermina; it had been that way with Tom.

"I'm left at the bottom," she said to herself, with that odd, choking feeling in her throat again. And yet she *would* stay at the bottom! Wasn't she a strange girl?

Chapter 24

The Next Thing

"What next, I wonder?" Maria said.

She and Tom were turning away from the depot once more. They had been watching a departing train. Mr. and Mrs. Leonard were being whirled off on their Western journey. The last flutter of Helen's handkerchief had just disappeared from view. Mr. Harper had departed in the train headed East just five minutes before this one started West. So there was nothing to do, Maria said, but go home and be humdrum.

That wedding was a very quiet, very pretty affair. Brides can look well, even in empress cloth, as Maria discovered. *Something* about Helen was wonderfully becoming. She had never looked so well. Some discussion had been held as to the proper place for the couple to stand during the ceremony, but it finally arranged itself in a manner that hadn't been thought of till the last minute. On the morning in question Mr. Randolph appeared too feeble to sit up, so the bridal party stood directly at the foot of his bed.

"Helen Monroe being married in the bedroom!" was Maria's amazed comment to Tom, when she went to tell him of the change of plans.

"What does she think of it?" Tom asked.

"She? Why, it was her own proposal. She wouldn't mind being married in the pantry. She might even think it more convenient, and trouble could be saved by taking a cold bite off the pantry shelves! Mr. Leonard, or somebody else, has transformed her. I'd have to get acquainted with her all over again if she were going to stay at home."

That walk from the depot was the opportunity for more gloomy looks ahead into the future. They had dismissed the carriage in order to have a long walk and talk together.

"There isn't any 'next,'" Maria said, answering her own question. "Everything that can happen to our family *has* happened. There's absolutely nothing but sweeping and dusting and getting dinners for the future."

Tom shivered visibly.

"Maria, how *can* you talk so recklessly, even in sport?" And his voice was almost stern. "You surely see ways great and terrible changes could come to us as a family—changes we've almost held our breaths for fear *would* come. Let's not court them by a spirit of unrest."

"If you mean Father," said Maria with utmost coolness, as if every nerve in her heart didn't quiver, "I see that he grows stronger every hour. Mr. Harper said the improvement in him during the short time since he'd seen him was marked. Why, Tom, if you weren't as blind as a bat, you'd see it too. Imagine our allowing him, three months ago, to go through such an experience as he had this morning!"

"I do see it," Tom said, "with a very thankful heart, I assure you. And yet, Maria, you and I know he's far from well. And we don't know what our Father in heaven has decided concerning him."

Maria twitched angrily.

"Don't!" she said sharply. "I don't want to hear that sort of talk. Father's going to get well again. I know it as well as if I saw him on the street this morning. Let me have some comfort in the world."

What was the use of talking to Maria? Tom felt, with a sigh, that she wasn't in the least subdued.

Meanwhile changes were coming swiftly. Maria had hardly time to settle down after the unwonted excitement before plans started up which made a great stir in the household and especially in her heart. She was in the kitchen. The rain was falling softly outside, but before it began, sun and air had dried and whitened a great basket of clothes.

Over these, Maria, in trim kitchen apron and sleeves rolled up, was now at work, sprinkling and rolling into tight little heaps ready for the next day's ironing.

The gate clicked, and she wondered whether Tom was taking pity on them and coming over to supper. It was a quick, manly step and came around to the side door—yes, and came in without knocking. Of course it was Tom.

She turned to greet him and said, in alarmed surprise, "My conscience!"

"It's only your brother-in-law," Mr. Harper said, shaking the rain from his hat and opening the door again to let out his umbrella. "I've surprised you, haven't I?"

"What's the matter? Is it Gracie or Ermina?"

Mr. Harper laughed reassuringly.

"It's neither," he said. "They're perfectly well and send their love. The fact is, I had a plan I'm trying to develop. I came up to talk to you about it. I came around to the side door because I thought it was about time for Father's afternoon nap, and I feared the bell might disturb him. How is he?"

"He's better. I think he improves every day."

"That's encouraging for my plan then. It's about him I've come." And Mr. Harper took a seat on the corner of the table and unfolded his plan. It overwhelmed Maria with astonishment and dismay. There was an earnest argument, somewhat heated on her part. Tom found them still talking when he came, almost an hour afterward.

"What in the world is the matter?" he said, as surprised as Maria had been.

"I've come all the way from New York to unfold a plan, and to my sorrow I find that our good practical sister doesn't approve at all." This Mr. Harper said while he was shaking hands with Tom.

"Of course I don't," said Maria with energy. "I wonder how I could be expected to? Tom, he wants to carry Father off to New York now."

"To New York?" echoed Tom in astonishment.

"Yes, I feel that a change of air and physicians will work great results for him. I believe the doctors are mistaken in thinking his lungs are hopelessly diseased, and I believe he can be cured."

"Of *course* he can be," chimed in Maria, "and he's *being* cured as fast as possible! See how he's improved in the last four weeks! But if you carry him off to New York you'll just upset it all. I don't like it at all."

Though there was grim determination in this, there was also an undertone of satisfaction, as one who knew she reigned there and that it would be very hard to carry out plans to which she didn't consent. Tom seemed astonished.

"But, Maria," he said, "think how often we've said if he could *only* have salt air to breathe and be under the care of Dr. Conyers."

"What do I know about Dr. Conyers? Because he lives in New York is no sign he knows more than all creation. What I say is that a sick man needs his own home and his own things about him, and he needs my care too. You'll find that *he*, at least, will object to going away from *me*."

Mr. Harper interrupted eagerly.

"My dear sister! Did you suppose for a moment we could think of having Father go without you? I took it for granted your good sense would *know* you're included in this arrangement. Of course he needs you; no one else could take your place."

"Well, I shall *never go*, you may feel sure of that. I'm not going to have the reputation of living off my brother-in-law as long as I can earn my own living." And Maria, as she jerked these words out between lips that wanted to quiver, sprinkled the clothes with an energy that sent the water over Mr. Harper's broadcloth. He wiped the shining drops off composedly.

"That's a foolish way to talk, Maria—not at all in line with your usual good sense. I *am* your brother-in-law, however much you may feel disposed to ignore the relationship, and as such have certain rights and privileges. I know you don't mean you won't do whatever shall seem in the end to be the best thing for the father, whose health and welfare we're all to put ahead of every other consideration. What we want is to talk this matter over calmly and then decide what seems best to us all."

He might as well have talked about talking calmly with a tornado. Maria's blood was on fire; she was like a lioness afraid of being robbed of her young. Her father had so long been her charge, so entirely under her sway, that to give up the right to plan and work and sacrifice for him was like giving up her life. For the time she was incapable of reasoning or talking intelligently on the subject. So Mr. Harper decided, and, breaking off suddenly, he began to talk to Tom about the Randolph House and finally went away with him to look at certain improvements in the reading room.

They both came back to tea, and Maria had gained sufficient control to say that her father would be ready to see them at that time. At the table the subject came up again, Mr. Harper apparently being no less determined and Maria being calmer, having had time to entrench herself in the firm belief that her father would put an end to all such planning.

By mutual consent the subject wasn't broached to the invalid that night. But Mr. Harper began it promptly the next morning. It was a stormy day with Maria; also it was a day in which much planning was done.

Contrary to the expectations of anyone and the hope of one, Mr. Randolph entered with eagerness into the new plans. He had long felt that a mistake was being made in his case and lately had begun to hope and believe that if he could get a change of air, above all a whiff of sea air, perhaps he might get strength again to support his family.

He was willing, nay, *anxious,* to try the proposed change. He was deeply grateful for the thoughtful love that had planned it. And more than that, he agreed with Maria that it would be better for her to remain behind to look after the old home, the cow, the hens, the garden and all those tiresome details that are looked after so thankfully when there's someone in the house for whose comfort you're planning and to whose comforts they'll add a share.

But how utterly trivial they become when you're taking care of them only because they *must* be taken care of. Maria realized this part. But she had little more to say. Indeed you would have pitied her if you'd been in the kitchen with her while she washed the dishes from her father's room. Her hands moved slowly, as if they'd lost their energy. Every now and then a great tear splashed on the table or was brushed suddenly as it was about to fall. Her father was willing to go away, to leave the little room she'd made so sweet and fair for him and eagerly filled with all the comforts her hands could furnish! He was willing to go without *her,* to be waited upon by other hands than hers! How *could* he think *she* could bear it!

Mr. Harper felt sorry for her and objected earnestly to leaving her at home, but neither the father nor Tom helped him. Mr. Randolph said she'd been confined too closely to a sick room; she needed rest and change almost as much as he did and was growing old before her time.

"It's been a loving service," he said, looking after her with eyes that glistened, "but it's been a hard one for a girl her age. She needs her freedom for a little while. She'll stay at the Randolph House and look after Tom and get rested and brightened up, and then everything will be looked after at home."

"Then wouldn't it be better to explain to her that it's for her sake you wish her to remain and not because of the house?" Mr. Harper asked the question; he couldn't bear for the sore heart to be made sorer by being apparently underrated.

Mr. Randolph shook his head with a smile.

"You don't understand my youngest daughter as well as you do Ermina," he said. "I doubt if she would do anything for her *own* sake. She understands the art of doing for others, but she doesn't understand that each one owes a duty to himself in this world that can't rightly be neglected. She needs to learn that."

Tom said nothing until his brother-in-law and he were walking downtown.

Then Mr. Harper made the anxious remark: "It seems to be a mistake leaving Maria behind. I'm sorry for her. She's lived for Father so long that she won't know how to live without him. Besides, he'll miss her more, I'm afraid, than he realizes."

"He realizes it," Tom said, with a smile. "The truth is, my father is unselfish. He sees, I think, that it's for Maria's good. I believe she needs to learn that life *can* go on without her. Not that she's conceited in the usual sense of that word, but she's managed us all so long, and especially Father, that she feels herself absolutely necessary to the affairs of this life. She hasn't a grain of trust in her nature. I doubt if she could be persuaded to go to New York and live with your family, even for Father's sake. Independence is her weakness—a good trait carried to excess. Maria has to have everything in excess; it's her nature."

"Is she progressing any, do you think? Has she discovered yet that it's hard to live by her motto while she ignores the foundation?"

Tom shook his head.

"I don't know what she's *discovered*," he said gravely. "She's *admitted* nothing. The fact is, Maria, more than any other person I ever knew, needs to be taught the lesson of dependence. She doesn't want to depend on anybody but her own self; she even rebels at the idea of a daily dependence on God! She thinks herself sufficient to herself, apparently, not only for this life, but for the life to come. Sometimes I tremble for her and wonder how it will be necessary to teach her the lesson. I hope to do something for her while she's at the Randolph House. We have good influences there now in every direction."

He needn't have built many plans on that hope. If Maria wouldn't go to New York, neither, it appeared, would she go to the Randolph House. She was somewhat crushed by discovering her will wasn't as potent as she'd imagined—but only crushed, not broken. If she couldn't control the disposal of other people, she could at least control herself. She kept her own counsel; she worked day and night to prepare her father; she planned indefatigably for his comfort. It was her hand that arranged his collar and necktie on the morning of the prospective journey. It was her hand that arranged the pillows at his back when he was seated in the carriage. It was she who arranged a couch for him in the car that had been retained for this occasion. It was she who saw the annoying sunbeam creeping in at the wrong corner and shining right in his eyes. It was she who hovered around him, anticipating every motion, every whim. She made herself an absolute necessity until the train gave its warning whistle.

And she wrung from him with the good-bye kiss this tender whisper: "My darling child, I couldn't bear this separation even for a little while if it weren't for your good."

"My good!" she said to herself with a grim smile, as she watched the train around the curve. "What possible *good* does he think can come to me! If harm doesn't come to *him* through it all, I'll be only too thankful. But I'll have him back in a little while. They'll all see their folly. I only hope it may not do any mischief I can't repair." Then she turned to Tom.

"Well, here we are again at this depot! Can't we just take rooms here and wait for astonishing things to happen? They all seem to center around departing trains. Tom, either you or I must get married or go to Europe for the next event. That's all there is left to happen *now!*"

Tom turned away in silence. He wasn't constituted like Maria. His father had looked very pale and feeble. It was a hazardous experiment after all. Who could tell whether they would ever see the dear face again in life! He couldn't put on a cheerful voice just then, even to help Maria. But he did sleep quietly and calmly that night after his earnest prayer for his father's safety—while his sister was burying her lonely head in her pillow and sobbing aloud in her loneliness and sore-heartedness. But there was the difference between the two natures.

Chapter 25

W hen will you be over to the house?" Tom asked, as the carriage rolled toward home.

"Oh, I don't know. I'll call as usual, I suppose, whenever the spirit moves me."

"Maria, what do you mean? Aren't you coming over there to live?"

"Not by any means. So long as I have a house of my own to live in, I'm not disposed to live on charity, especially since I have a trade and can support myself."

Of course this was the beginning of a long discussion. Tom dismissed the carriage and went into the deserted house and sat down, but he might as well have discussed with the wind. Maria was even less reasonable than usual. It appeared she had her plans all formed. She was going to stay in the house, of course. How else could she take care of things properly and be ready for her father when he returned next week or next month? Of course she expected him as soon as that—sooner. She had no hope at all of this wild scheme doing him any good. She wasn't so foolish. If only it didn't do him permanent harm she would be thankful. No, she wasn't afraid in the least. What on earth was there to be afraid of more than there was when her father lay sick and helpless in that bedroom? She wasn't supposed to be afraid then—why must she be now? Do? He'd find there was plenty of work even *she* could do, if she wasn't important enough to have her opinion count for anything.

In short, she had her way, of course, as she meant to from the first—and all the more determined because she hadn't yet rallied from the disappointment and humiliation of being overmatched in this last planning.

Tom went away at last, more thoroughly vexed with her than he'd ever allowed himself to be before. The utmost concession she could be prevailed upon to make was to submit, it must be confessed with an ill grace, to Tom's quiet announcement that since she would be so foolish and unkind she must take the extra work of getting a room ready for him, for he would sleep in the house of course.

When she rudely questioned what earthly use there was in putting himself and her to that extra trouble, he answered more coldly than she'd ever known him to: "That you find it necessary to ask such a question only goes to prove how young and foolish you are and how very improper it is for you to be left to yourself."

And then Tom allowed himself to bang that door just a little, and as he went downtown he felt that he had a most heavy and unwilling responsibility. His heart would have been softer if he could have seen how bitterly the stoical sister cried the moment the door banged after him. She was sore-hearted and didn't understand the feeling.

Tom found it difficult to determine whether he felt more vexed or amused when he came the next time in the daytime and discovered the improvement that had been made. The old Randolph homestead—which had sheltered a long line of Randolphs—not imposing in any way, but eminently respectable, had a new ornament, a sign, tacked in a conspicuous spot, and the letters on it were unmistakably clear and plain: "Clear starching and fine ironing done here."

Tom was democratic. He thought no one could be more so. He was most remarkably free from false pride. Hadn't he been a streetcar driver? Yet this sign made the blood flow faster in his veins. It seemed too great a departure from the beaten track—especially since now, more than at any time during the last struggling years of their fortunes, it was unnecessary. The troubled brother walked past the house and around the block before he'd settled in his mind how to treat this new departure. Acting upon a plan thus considered he was in the house ten minutes before he made any remark concerning the sign.

"You've enlarged your business, I see," he said, in as quiet and careless a voice as he could assume. "Do you propose to take in a partner?"

"Perhaps I shall, if I can find one with enough mental capacity to be of use. Do you have a *protégée* you want to get rid of?"

"Not now. What was the object of the enlargement?"

"No special object—only you seemed afraid I'd lack for occupation. And since I didn't seem to be of use to anybody or have any sphere whatever in life, I concluded to make one for myself or to make money at least. There's money in it. If you need any to carry on your schemes you'll know where to come."

"*He* doesn't care what I do or how many signs I tack to the old house, so that I don't trouble him." This Maria said with a swelling heart as she watched that same brother walk away a few minutes later without raising his eyes to the sign.

He, on his part, drew a long sigh and said, "She'll have to learn by experience. I see no other way, and I don't know how to help her in the least."

After all, they understood each other's hearts about as well as those articles get understood in this surface world.

Outwardly I'll have to admit that Maria's plan had a fair chance of succeeding better than anything the Randolphs had ever undertaken, that is, as far as their purses were concerned. Maria had said truly there was money in it, provided (she was apt to add) you have no pride to speak of and a good strong back.

While the world seems to be full of people who are willing to teach our children to strum on the piano, to draw impossible-looking trees and people, to jabber in a dozen different tongues, the lamentable fact remains that in every town and city it's really difficult to get one's collars and cuffs starched and ironed decently without paying a fabulous price for it.

As Maria had a great deal of pride of execution and an indomitable determination and a secret plan to make herself and her father independent thereby, she worked with a will and in time actually took in, not partners exactly, but hard-working girls glad to be taught what she'd worked out by her own wits and the help of her eyes when she visited certain famous laundries. For time went on, and the father didn't return to them. In fact, she became unwilling to have him return, though this she didn't admit to anybody. But she gloated in secret joy over the wonderful accounts of rapid progress and increasing strength.

The day came when her eyes were red all day with happy tears she'd shed in the privacy of her own room the night before over a half-dozen lines actually written to her by her father's hand. In his own words he communicated to her his ambition to get well enough to go back to his clerkship, so she might have leisure and money in return for all her self-sacrificing love.

"He'll never do it if I can help it," she said with energy. And she ironed eleven shirts that day; she saw a way to help it by making it unnecessary. This she would do if they'd give her enough time. So she became reconciled to the visit to New York.

So the days passed, and snarly March and tearful April and uncertain May came and went, and, except a flying visit from Mr. Harper, none of the New York family was to be seen. Mr. Harper came with plans; they wanted to take Father to the White Mountains. Grace had been studying hard and needed the change, and the doctor said nothing wiser could be done for the father, so he'd come down to see about it. Father was anxious to have Maria go. He longed for a sight of her; besides, he felt sure she needed the change.

Unlucky sentence! Maria was inexorable. Her heart throbbed at the sad thought of getting through the long summer without one peep at her father. But she was taking care of herself and wasn't to be cuddled at the White Mountains, or any other mountains, on the plea that *she* needed anything.

"I'm willing Father should go," was her magnanimous conclusion. "I have no doubt it will do him good. Your plan of taking him to New York has resulted in a way I never thought it would. But there's no use in talking about *my* going, because I can't and won't."

I hope they appreciated this admission; it cost Maria a great deal to make it, and it was splendid of her. It was more than for most people to get down on their knees and humbly beg your pardon. It was her misfortune, perhaps, rather than her fault, that she was gifted with a marvelously obstinate disposition, though, to be sure, she'd done what she could to cultivate her gifts in that direction.

But no amount of coaxing changed her determination not to be made happy herself. Other people might be as happy as they could; she was going to wash and iron clothes. That's what it looked like to Tom and Mr. Harper; they knew nothing at all about her bank account or her cherished plans.

But our washerwoman had long, lonely hours in which she could neither wash nor iron and in which she didn't know what to do with herself. Tom was so busy and eager over his hotel, his reading room, his Sabbath services and his hundred other plans, some in which she couldn't, and others *wouldn't*, be interested and allow herself to help, that he had little leisure time to bestow.

In fact it wasn't till years after that it dawned upon Maria he actually sacrificed time and convenience to occupy at night the pleasant little room she took care to make so inviting for him. She was still skeptical over the hotel—not that she didn't see and feel the good it was doing or admire the idea. But how was Tom ever to marry and support a family on fine ideas?

She felt this even more when she was present one evening and the accounts had been gone over, closing the financial year of the house. Mr. Harper and Tom had been at work all day. An hour before, she'd heard Mr. Harper say, "Now, subtracting the expenditures for furniture and for extra matters that won't naturally come in another year, how do we balance as to accounts?" Then Tom had done some very silent and rapid figuring, until presently he sat back with the crimson creeping up on his forehead and the white lines about his mouth, showing how intense and keen his interest was in this experiment.

"We net exactly seventy-two cents," he said, trying to control the tremble in his voice.

Instantly Mr. Harper stretched his hand across the table and grasped Tom's in an eager grip.

"Victory!" he said in a voice of triumph. "Then it's demonstrated beyond the shadow of a reasonable doubt that a first-class hotel *can* be sustained with even a moderate degree of patronage and not have a drop of liquor brought into it. I congratulate you, my brother. Are you ready to go on with the work?"

"If it fell seventy-two cents behind, instead of netting that, I would try to find a way to earn that sum and go ahead," said Tom, trying to cover his evident emotion with cheerfulness. "But your property at that rate is lying waste, even if we do so well in the next year, and your expenses for furnishings have been enormous."

"My property belongs to the cause and sinks or swims with it. I'm grateful to you for letting it help." Mr. Harper said this quietly, but with shining eyes, and both gentlemen arose and shook hands again, even as they had after the first compact between them.

But I regret to state that poor mercenary Maria looked scornful. "Seventy-two cents!" she said within her heart. "How does the boy ever expect to support a family with such an income as that? And it'll grow worse instead of better, for he'll have new schemes every year." And she resolved to work harder than ever at her chosen calling. *Some* of them must have some money.

That was the evening before the Fourth of July. Maria had so far laid aside her obstinacy that she came over to the Randolph House, "bag and baggage," as she phrased it, to spend the Fourth. A curious intimacy had sprung up between Maria and the girl Maggie. For the first time in her life Maria was close to having a particular friend. Maggie interested her as no girl or woman had ever done before.

To those few among her acquaintances who were intimate enough to remonstrate with her on the strangeness of making a friend out of a "hired girl," Maria delighted to answer: "She's a pastry cook, and I'm a washer-woman. What's the difference?"

So she spent the Fourth in the Randolph kitchen, helping Maggie concoct elegant desserts for the unusual rush of visitors. She and Maggie were the only ones who didn't desert the work in the kitchen for a sight at the parade. And it wasn't until everything was in order for the night that the two girls decided to take their holiday by mounting to the highest balcony that over-looked the square and getting a view of the fireworks.

"I like bonfires better than any of these new-fashioned fizzes, rockets and Roman candles and all those. I used to like the fireballs they whirled through the air. I don't care if they were dangerous. They were a dozen times more romantic than these namby-pamby affairs."

This Maria said as she watched the flames curling slowly around a great pyramid of tar barrels, gathering strength and volume every minute and beginning to light up the square with a lurid glare.

Maggie made no answer; she was watching the curling flames like one fascinated.

"I like them too," she said after a little. "I like *power*."

The way in which she spoke those words, under her breath, made Maria smile as she looked curiously at her. "She has power," she said to herself. "I wonder what she would do in an emergency! I don't believe she would faint or scream. I'd like to know."

"I'm glad I haven't power," began Maggie again. "I'd be afraid of myself. I think I might do something dreadful, just for the sake of doing it. If I had the power of God, for instance, I'd sweep out half the people in the world at one swoop, I think."

"No, you wouldn't," said Maria, amused and yet a little startled. "You'd hate to destroy machines your own power had made."

There was something in that. Maria thought about it and found she had no reply ready. Still the flames grew and made more than sunlight in the square; the faces of the people looked weird and fantastic in the growing glare. Suddenly Maggie gave a little scream—not a scream either. It wasn't loud enough for that; it was the suggestion of a scream that a strong will had instantly suppressed. She clutched Maria's arm.

"What on earth is the—?" Maria began, greatly startled.

Before the sentence was concluded, Maggie asked, "Do you see that man standing by the lamppost, the blue light, with a child in his arms?"

Yes, he was defined distinctly against the dark background; a glow of light shone full upon the child's face.

"That man," said Maggie, and again there was that sense of a powerful, controlling will about her voice, "is my husband, and he has my baby in his arms."

All this was said in an instant of time. Swift and low her voice had been, and the grasp on Maria's arm had been like a vice. Then she was off, through the room, down the hall, down the stairs, down another hall, another flight of stairs, so swift and noiseless that she seemed almost like a spirit. Though Maria followed, breathless and panting, it was hard to keep her in sight.

Chapter 26

Emergencies

By dint of eager pushing and breathless haste Maria kept the flying feet ahead of her in sight, and at last they reached the goal. Such a wonderful change as those few minutes had accomplished! Where was the light which had made a glow on all the faces but a moment before? A sudden tumbling of a few tar barrels, a sudden change in the current wind, and that part of the square was in gloom. Besides, the people tired suddenly, it would seem, of the sight they were so eagerly gazing at a moment before, had surged and swayed and were breaking in all directions—men, women and children, in crowds and throngs, but not *the* man or *the* child—at least Maggie didn't seem to find them, as she pushed her way through, peering eagerly into the face of every man or woman who held a child by the hand.

It was a hopeless search. It looked so to Maria in a few minutes after she got among that throng. Yet she dared not speak, dared not say, "It's of no use—the child is gone. You were mistaken, or if you weren't, he's lost in the crowd." That would seem too bitter to say, so near to him and yet to have lost him. Could any pain be harder than that?

"It was perfectly awful," she said, telling the experience to Tom the next day. For the search ended, and they returned to the hotel. Maria hardly knew how. "I don't know how *Maggie* could have felt. I know *I* felt like death. Was there ever anything so dreadful?"

"The police should have been notified instantly," said Tom. "Precious time was lost."

"The police!" echoed Maria, and her countenance fell. "Why, what could they do, and how should they have been notified?"

"Do! They could have stationed guards and watched the trains and boats. There were three trains and two boats left before they were notified. They could have been sure the persons weren't on any of them. It would have been easy enough to notify them. Any decent man you met would have sent a message to headquarters. You should learn what to do in emergencies, Maria."

Now wasn't that a hard sentence to hear? She who had prided herself on her talent for managing emergencies, who had puzzled her brains half the night over the question, What *could* she do to help Maggie? And had finally settled into believing there was *nothing* to do but accept the hard fate.

Then she spent hours in planning what *might* have been done. How easily God might have ruled that they would be in time to seize that child and carry him off in triumph. This was what *she* would have arranged had she ruled the world. By so much then was she wiser and more merciful than God. She didn't see that this was the inevitable conclusion her logic reached. She would have been shocked at that thought.

Most grumblers would be shocked at the mathematical results of their reasoning. But now Maria was more than shocked; she was disgusted. And of all persons to be disgusted with in this trying world, the most trying is oneself; because one doesn't like to give oneself a talking to, though nothing would be more profitable sometimes. Maria contented herself with frowning gloomily.

"I wonder *she* didn't think of that," she told Tom at last. The necessity for blaming somebody seemed to be upon her.

"I don't wonder at that at all. She was almost wild, I suppose, and wasn't to be expected to think connectedly. The wonder is you allowed such a sensible move to be neglected for so long a time."

"How should *I* think anything about the police?" grumbled Maria. "I haven't had to do with such scrapes."

"Then I advise you to impress it upon your memory that, after this, when you want to find a lost child, the most reasonable thing you can do is notify the authorities whose business it is to help you, and the sooner you do this, the better you'll exhibit your common sense."

Tom spoke quickly, vexed by Maria's apparent hardness into a departure from his quiet manner.

"Have you been over to see Maggie this morning?" he presently asked, speaking in his usual tone.

"No, I haven't, and I have no desire to go."

"Why?"

"Because I have a little feeling left, though you seem to think you're the only one so affected. I don't want to see her. I can't imagine anything more terrible. It's a wonder to me that she keeps her senses. I wonder what she thinks of all her prayers now! Great good they did. It was as bad as losing him the second time—a tantalizing glimpse and then gone. I'd go wild or be an infidel. I have nothing at all to say to comfort her. If anybody has, I advise them to say it. All I can say is, I don't understand such dealings. There's no man living who would be so inhuman as that. Can't endure the thought of meeting her again."

Tom smiled a peculiar smile.

"You go over and see her, Maria—go as soon as you can. It'll do you good."

Now, though Maria hadn't the slightest intention of following this advice, though she assured herself she wouldn't go near there for at least a week, an irresistible impulse seemed to draw her in that direction. She went that very afternoon, up the stairs with a soft tread—such as one instinctively assumes in the presence of death—and tapped softly at the door. No answer. Was Maggie buried among her pillows in bitter weeping, or was she sitting in apathy—her senses dulled by the bitterness of her grief?

Maria waited a minute, then softly opened the door. The room was vacant. Maria preserved an outward calm but in an inward anxiety sought for her friend. Who could tell but in her despair she'd wandered away, as she had before, leaving no trace of her flight? One and another of the girls she met, asking the same question: "Do you know where Maggie is?" And she received the same answer: "No, ma'am—I haven't seen her since dinner."

It began to grow very serious, but Maria bravely kept her own counsel and kept looking. When she finally reached the storeroom she found Maggie weighing out sugar for making sponge cake for tea. She was very pale, with dark rings under her eyes, as one might look who hadn't slept much the night before and had shed some hot tears. But she turned with her usual smile to greet her friend.

"I've been hoping for you all day," she said, speaking in a quiet voice. "I was afraid the wild way I led you last night might have tired you very much."

"I'm not so easily tired, but I'm very astonished. I went to your room and expected to find you in bed."

"Oh, no, I'm not sleepy. I slept some last night, and I've had to be busy all day. I suppose there's no news yet." She looked up with a sudden gleam of wild hope in her eyes.

Maria shook her head.

"Your brother's been so kind," she said. "He was up half the night, putting the police on the track, writing out descriptions of them to post in conspicuous places, and I don't know what he *has* done—everything that could be done, I'm sure. What a blessed thing it is to have friends at such a time!"

"Do you expect any results?" Maria asked skeptically.

She was so quiet and stirred that flour and egg so dexterously that it didn't seem cruel to say *anything* to her.

"Results? Indeed I do. I feel hopeful today, more so than I have for a long time. I've had a good deal to encourage me. Think what a blessed sight it was! I saw my darling as plainly as I see you at this moment, and he looked plump and well. He clung to his papa's neck, not as if he were frightened, but as if he was happy and enjoyed it all. And his papa was sober. I know that, for I've watched him so long and so well that I can tell with one swift glance. Oh, if there was ever a direct answer to prayer, my gleam last night was one. My prayer has been a mixture of petition and thanksgiving today."

Now all this might as well have been spoken in Greek as far as Maria's understanding of such a state of mind was concerned. But what we don't understand can sometimes thrill us mightily, and Maria Randolph turned away from that pantry door with a strange sense of her own littleness and uselessness and of the wonderful nature of prayer.

"I admire her pluck anyhow," she said to herself.

But she knew it wasn't pluck. She knew it was something she didn't have and that Maggie had never possessed, until that night when she learned to pray. She had taken great strides in the Christian life in a little time. A great sorrow is a wonderful educator. But all that Maria didn't understand. She went directly home and thought about it the rest of that day.

"If you'd go and hear him," said Dick Norton, speaking to her with a sort of wistful earnestness that amused, while it surprised her, "you'd know how he says these things I try to tell you. They ain't as odd as they sound when I tell them in a blundering fashion. They're worth hearing."

"What if I *should* go?" Maria said, pausing on her way to the pantry as she cleared the tea table. Tom had been over to tea, and the table had been set with ceremony once more.

"That's a new idea. I'm eager for something new; I live a stupid life nowadays. But this is the reading-room night, isn't it? My brother will be engaged. Dick, will you take care of me if I go to the meeting with you?"

"I will that—there's nothing I'd like better."

The energy with which he spoke amused her again. And, adding to the sudden impulse to have something new in her humdrum life a kindly desire to give Dick Norton pleasure, she got ready to accompany him to the Fleet Street Church to hear the minister who had been preaching there every evening for a week and in whom Dick was greatly interested.

The church was crowded when they reached there, and the service was in progress. They found seats near the rear of the church. Maria glanced around and suddenly gasped loudly enough that Dick turned—and saw her staring at a man a few feet away. He had a child in his arms—a little boy. The boy had an arm wound half around the gentleman's neck, and his hand toyed caressingly with the locks of hair.

The sermon may have been effective; indeed I know it was. Some present will remember it, not only for this world but for the next, because of the power it had in influencing their future lives.

But Maria didn't hear a word of it. From first to last she never took her fascinated eyes away from the face of the man who held the child in his arms. She shielded her gaze by peeping through her fingers, but not a movement of the stranger's escaped her.

Something, she couldn't have told what or why, either the child's caressing hand or the likeness to the shadow she'd seen defined against the glare of light in the square or the mysterious sense of insight that seems sometimes given—either, or all of these, so powerfully impressed Maria Randolph that she had just enough self-control left to wait with feverish impatience for the benediction before she executed a bold plan.

"Follow close to me, Dick, and don't let that man escape us for the world!"

This was the tragic whisper that fell on Dick's astonished ear as the "Amen" was spoken and the crowd surged toward the door.

There was to be an inquiry meeting, and many remained quietly in their seats waiting for the people to leave.

Maria moved toward the door, followed closely by Dick. She was following eagerly the man who held the little child, now sleeping quietly in his arms.

In the vestibule he halted. So did Maria.

"Won't you go to the second meeting?" a man asked, stopping before the stranger.

"I would," he answered promptly, "if it weren't for my little boy. He needs to be resting."

"We need much help tonight," the other said. "It's a blessed time."

And the man with the child answered heartily, "Indeed it is."

Every word he spoke made it less probable that Maria was right. Yet she clung to her determination. No police could be more vigilant than she would be tonight.

She turned toward him. "Dick, stand close by me," she said in a low voice.

Then she addressed the stranger: "Aren't you Mr. Henry Reeder? And isn't this child named Wallace?"

He looked down at her quickly. "Yes," he said, and if Maria hadn't been intent on carrying out her plans, she would have noted the sudden catching of his breath. "Who are you?"

"Never mind who I am. If you'll give me that child I'll take him to his mother, and the sooner you give yourself into the hands of the police as a disreputable vagrant, the less trouble you'll make us all."

Maria prided herself on the cool contempt, stinging in every word, of this sentence. So sure was she of her man that she had been preparing this message during the sermon. She hadn't planned the result that speedily followed. She had reckoned as if the man before her were a puppet to be played on as she chose. If she had leveled a pistol at his heart and taken true aim, he couldn't have dropped more suddenly and silently than he did before her.

There was much confusion now, and Maria saw how well she could act in an emergency. Her wits served her well; she talked rapidly and to the point.

"Don't surround him so closely," she said. "The man is in a dead faint. I gave him news too suddenly. Take the child, one of you. Dick, call a carriage, or, no, one of you gentlemen, please call a carriage, and then if you'll help him into it we'll be all right in a few minutes.

"Dick, see here. Get a policeman to take a ride with us." This she said in a low tone to the amazed Dick.

Then Maria raised her eyes again and met the searching gaze of one of Tom's friends. She was equal to that.

"Dr. Preston," she said coolly, "I'll have to press you into service. Is there anything more than a faint?"

"No," he said quietly, "the man is reviving. What do you want done?"

"I want him taken to the Randolph House as speedily as possible. He's the one my brother's been searching for."

In much less time than it's taken me to tell it, the strange party was on their way to the Randolph House.

Dr. Preston, who had invited himself to go with them, rested the head of the fainting man on his shoulder. Maria held the sleeping boy in her arms, with Dick close beside her, and the policeman mounted guard with the driver and wondered why he could be wanted to accompany a respectable-looking party, three of them gentlemen, home from a religious meeting!

Tom was standing on the brightly lighted piazza, looking after a carriage-load of departing guests. He waited while the next carriage drove up.

"What now?" he asked, as the policeman swung himself to the ground.

"Don't know, sir," said the policeman, touching his hat. "I'm detailed to convey this party from Fleet Street Church to this house, and I believe they're all here."

Dick Norton was the first to alight; he could give no information as to why he was there. Dr. Preston followed, steadying the steps of the man, who seemed dizzy and bewildered.

"Preston!" exclaimed Tom, his surprise increasing every moment. "What's up?"

"A sick man is down, and we're ordered here. For the reason why, ask your sister. I must get this man in safe—he's likely to faint again."

Finally, down clambered Maria, clinging closely to the sleeping boy. She issued her orders like a general. "Is he going to faint again, did you say? Take him to the hall sofa. Dick, pay the carriage and dismiss it. Tom, here is Maggie's boy. I have him safe, you see. And—no, thank you—I mean to *keep* him safe until I can put him in her arms. But I want you to see that I notified the police, as you directed me to do. As to what his duty is in the matter, you'll have to inform him, for *I* don't know." And she vanished with her precious burden from Tom's astounded gaze.

Chapter 27

What Maria Did Next

"What that girl will do next is more than I can imagine." That was what her brother Tom said as he followed Maria in, looking after her in a dazed kind of a way, before he turned to Dr. Preston and his charge.

"The next thing, she'll be responsible for a human life, I'm afraid," Dr. Preston said, as he bent with grave and troubled face over the apparently lifeless man. "This man has had a fearful shock of some sort. Where's he to be put, Randolph?"

Whereupon Tom roused himself and gave directions right and left. The doctor looked around him, his eye falling on Dick Norton, who stood waiting and watching.

"See here, my man," he said, "can you do an errand for me?"

"Yes, sir."

The promptness of the answer and something in the tone told how eager Dick was to be helpful. Dr. Preston drew him to one side and was evidently giving careful directions, watching him meanwhile with keen eyes to see whether he took the complicated windings of the different errands into intelligent consideration. Dick listened in silent attention until the sentences were concluded; then he made one solitary observation.

"Do you want me to report on the first errand before I do the others?"

"Yes," said the doctor, his eyes lighting, "I do. I'd forgotten it."

"All right, sir," Dick said, and he was off.

It was just that little incident that had to do with Dick Norton's failure.

It was an anxious night to those interested in the family trouble. The stranger who had so suddenly come among them was wild with delirium all night. He knew neither his wife, who hovered over him, nor the sleeping boy they brought to lie beside him. Both Dr. Preston and Dick Norton spent the night, and by tacit consent it seemed to be understood that Dick was the doctor's special helper. With the morning came a change and hopefulness. The fever was subdued and the patient quietly sleeping. Dr. Preston came from the room on tiptoe.

"If he's carefully watched and not unduly excited he'll get along without a fever after all, I think," he said. "His pulse seems to be growing natural. Now what's it all about? I was so suddenly whirled into the middle of a mystery and put so steadily at work that I had no time to question my way out."

"What we know of it ourselves can be told in a dozen sentences," Tom said and gave as much of the story as he knew.

"I can guess at some of the rest," Maria said. "It seems Maggie, in her wildness, never for a moment thought the man might come to his senses and hunt for her in their old home. She left as suddenly as he did, and in the night—and has never told any of the people her whereabouts."

"What an idea!" said the doctor.

"I know. But she seems to have been haunted with the idea that he wanted to avoid her and would never come near her of his own will."

Tom drew a long sigh.

"For her sake I don't know whether we should wish him to live or die," he said sadly. "I suppose there's nothing but trouble in store for her."

Maria struggled with her dislike to say a word on the topic, but at last she burst forth: "As to that, I suppose you'll think he's all right, Tom. He's a convert, it seems, of that man who's preaching every evening down at the Fleet Street Church. He says he followed him here. Dick Norton says he's taken part every evening in the prayer meetings or inquiry meetings or whatever you call them. Done as well as the minister, Dick thinks."

She was neither blind nor insensitive to the lighting up of both her brother's and the doctor's faces.

"Thank God," they both said, speaking in the same breath. And the doctor added reverently, "His ways are certainly not as our ways."

"You're not going home?" Tom said, turning to Maria and speaking in a dismayed tone.

"Yes, I am. There's nothing for me to do just now. The boy and the patient are both asleep, and the mother is crooning over them both. In time, when there's work to do, I can come over again. But for now I have some fine ironing that *must* be done."

Dr. Preston was one of the people before whom Maria liked to parade her fine ironing. She went off with a merry good morning and in a most amiable mood. The world had righted itself once more, and she had come out on top.

Once more she was a person of importance, whose rapid and common-sense action had restored the lost child to his mother and the lost husband to his family, though she hadn't planned *that* part of it. The first half of the night had been troubled. Who supposed the man had a brain to be shocked or a heart to be over-strained? She had no idea of such responsibility, but the shadow was lifting.

Dr. Preston had pronounced him almost out of danger, and she was in a fair way to be a heroine. Not that she used that high-sounding word in her thoughts—not that she realized she was in any sense working for herself.

It was natural for her to plan and perform, and it was very fortunate for a large class of people that such was the case.

Can anyone be blamed for liking to be of importance to the world? Throughout all the duties, many and important, of that entire day, Maria carried about with her a sense of satisfaction. She was needed yet, and some realized it. As for Maggie, how would it be possible for *her* ever to repay what she'd done for her? She was glad it wasn't possible; she had no desire to work for pay.

Maria certainly had a way of making herself a necessity in the world when she chose to do so. She went back to the Randolph House the moment her fine ironing was disposed of. She worked not only in the sick room, but in the kitchen, taking Maggie's place, and in fact everywhere. Her quick wits and willing hands and skillful brain were all on the alert, proving she was mistress of the occasion, or, as she phrased it, "was capable of taking care of herself and several other things at the same time."

By evening it was almost transformed from a sick room to a place of festival. The shock had been a tremendous one, but the man rallied rapidly and drank in the medicine of his wife's face as if it were a draught from the fountain of life.

Even Maria, who had supposed herself hopelessly his enemy, felt herself warming toward him as she watched his great hungry eyes following every step of his wife, every change in her countenance.

"Well, it's fortunate there's a refuge like religion for such poor weak wretches as he!" she said as she went home at nightfall. "I'm sure I'm thankful he has a strong arm to lean on."

But as for Maria Randolph, she needs no other arm than her own. She didn't *say* that; the sound of the words would have shocked her. People often think thoughts that would sound outrageous if put into words.

Maria hurried through her preparations for tomorrow's work and treated herself to a fresh white, ruffled apron, as she sat down to await the arrival of her scholar. It was Dick Norton's evening, and his progress lately had been so rapid, his improvement so marked, that it had begun to be a source of great satisfaction, not to say pride, to his young teacher. She'd exerted herself to give him lessons, not only in spelling and writing, but in etiquette, until really among his companions he was a marvel.

Tom, too, had begun to notice the decided change in his manners and had more than once heartily commended Maria for the work she was doing and told her Dick would be thankful to her all his life for the help she was giving him now. Maria was very fond of receiving praise from Tom. She was smiling yet over the pleasant thought of being a real and lasting benefit to him and planning new ways of helping him, when she heard his quick, eager step on the walk.

Only an hour later she sat where she had been when he knocked, with her cheeks and indeed her entire face aflame, her eyes unnaturally bright and her whole face struggling with strong emotions. Whether wounded pride, anger, dismay or amusement had the master, it would have been hard to say.

"To think," she burst forth, "that all my planning for him should end this way! Oh, the idiot! What could have possessed him? Is the world made up of fools and nothing else? I never heard of anything so *ridiculously* idiotic in my whole life!"

Should she laugh, or should she cry? She felt equally able to do either, but she waived both with a sudden spring and gave her energies to getting upstairs and out of hearing before Tom, who seemed to be unusually early tonight, should let himself in. She was in no mood to talk with him.

Usually Tom let himself into the house late at night and out of it early in the morning. It was no small inconvenience often to get away from the Randolph House, but this was his patient concession to his sister's obstinacy. But the next morning he lingered late in the hope of talking with Maria. He even knocked softly at her door and waited a moment but finally thought better of it and went away.

Maria, on her part, waited in breathless silence over by the window, not choosing to leave her room until she saw him safely around the corner. She still had no desire to meet him. She was still flushed with an unusual excitement and went about her work with nervous starts, as if on the edge of expected earthquakes.

"There's no telling what may *not* happen next!" she muttered, as she found herself flushing to her temples simply at the sound of the postman's knock. He brought a sealed drop letter, addressed in Tom's familiar hand.

The letter read:

I've been trying for an hour to get over but an unusual press of business has held me. I tried to see you last night but failed in making you hear.

"No, you didn't," interpolated Maria.

My dear sister,
   I know all about it. Dick came, in his excitement and dismay, directly to me, whom, next to you, he considers his best friend. I know it's absurd, and I hardly see what can have possessed the poor fellow; but he's young, you must remember. He was in great distress and feared that you felt insulted. I comforted him—for, after all, however absurd it may be, a human heart is not to be treated scornfully. He's in dead earnest, poor fellow—at least he thinks he is, and his heart is large and honest. Of course I made plain to him the utter foolishness of such an idea, and we'll arrange so that it won't be uncomfortable for you. I'll be over during the day if possible, and I beg you not to give me the trouble of looking you up. Your family—the husband and the boy—are doing well. The doctor pronounces all danger over.
                                                    In haste,
                                                    Tom

Maria tore this note into half-inch pieces and felt like fleeing from the face of the earth, or at least from Tom. But she thought better of it and presented herself with a very glowing face when he came. It was impossible not to feel horribly embarrassed. Perhaps they did the best thing possible under the circumstances—they both laughed!

"Poor fellow!" Tom said, when the laugh was over. "I feel as sorry for him as possible. But it's absurd."

"How could he be such an idiot?" Maria said, with reddening face.

"Well, he's at the age when it's more natural to be foolish than to be anything else," Tom said. "As for considering you his best friend, I don't know that I blame him."

"What's to be done next?" Maria asked, speaking with evident disgust. It set her brother off into another laugh.

"Why, we must send one of you off to that asylum for sick and wounded hearts, I suppose. Which shall it be? I don't think we should appeal to our brother-in-law again, do you?"

"Tom, don't be more absurd than is necessary under the circumstances!"

"Why, I'll try not to be. But you see the circumstances warrant a good deal. Well, to be sensible, we have plans arranged, I think, and it may be the making of the boy. You've given him a lift educationally, and having tasted it he may be on the lookout for more. Of course he must go where he won't annoy you. In fact, it's almost time for him to start."

"What an absurd performance all around! Do you mean to say the poor fellow must be caught away from the place where he earns his bread and butter and be smuggled off, because he's made a fool of himself?"

"Well, not quite that. Of course he could stay where he is. But it will be more agreeable for him *not* to do so, and he has a splendid opportunity to better himself. He deserves a better place in life than that. Now I think so. And Dr. Preston is going back to New York this evening and takes the five-fifteen express, and he's taken a liking to Dick. So you see the way is clear. He wants an office boy, and Dick wants with all his heart to be *the* boy."

"You didn't tell Dr. Preston?" Maria said, her face aflame.

"Maria, I had to. You see he burst in upon us in such an astounding way, Dick did, last evening. Preston and I were sitting together, and in *he* came, and from his incoherent way of talking and bringing in your name, he actually startled *me*. I had to take him out of the room alone and find out what was the matter. And then I was afraid Preston would think strangely of it all, so I told him. Maria, why do you care? I tell you an honest heart is not an insult, however impossible it may be to have anything to do with it."

"Of course not," Maria said. "But then, pshaw! What a perfectly idiotic performance from beginning to end!" And she jerked open the damper and poked her clothes in the boiler with a spiteful air.

"Why are you boiling clothes at this time of day? Maria, I wish you'd give up that thing. It seems as if you might do so much to gratify me."

"I'm doing so much to keep you and your wife from the poorhouse!" Maria said, with energy. "If you go on in as philanthropic a manner in the future as you have in the past, you'll certainly have to depend on me for support. Remember, I heard what your last year's income was!"

"Well," said Tom, flushing and laughing, "I can live on it. I won't run in debt. And as for my wife, I don't think you've ever heard her complain. Why are you working so late?"

"Because I didn't work early. I was worried and vexed and bewildered. I'm sick of *plans* anyway. I had a good many for that silly boy, and there he's gone and spilled them all in the most senseless manner. Tom, help me off with this boiler. I'm going to get these clothes hung out before tea. They'll dry between now and ten o'clock."

"Do you lift that great boiler alone when I'm not here? Maria, I dislike this plan of yours above *all* things. I could wish this would be the last boiler full of clothes you would ever touch."

"Well, it won't be. I expect to touch hundreds of them and make my fortune and yours too, as I said."

"Wait a minute," Tom said, with his hand on the boiler. "The doorbell rang. I'll see who it is. Perhaps you'll need to let the creatures boil away for awhile while you attend to callers." And he went to the door.

"I'll do nothing of the kind," muttered Maria. "I can lift the boiler myself. I've done it a hundred times, and you can entertain the callers."

It was one of those little, commonplace things that happen around us every day. A hundred times she had lifted that boiler in safety; but the hundred and first time she staggered under it. Her unsteady foot hit against a block of wood she'd dropped there only a moment before, and down she went. A slight fall, just on the smooth floor, and by some miraculous intervention the boiler remained right side up, with its scalding contents. It took place in a minute of time, and Tom was back in the kitchen, beholding with dumbfounded face the scene before him.

"Lift me," said Maria, "instead of the boiler. I can't stir. I've hurt my back a little. Just open Father's room and help me in there. I'll have to lie down for awhile. Then set that horrid boiler back on the stove as you planned. I believe it was the wicked spirit in you that made all this happen. Oh, I'm not killed. I'll be up in an hour and rinse those clothes out."

Chapter 28

Facing Results

She didn't come out and finish those clothes. What a strange look into the future it would have been if, as Tom carried her in his arms to their father's room, and she gave a swift look back to see if the damper was open or shut, she could have seen the hours that would intervene before she looked around that room again!

What wasn't permitted to her is given now to you, her friends: to have a look at the *present* future without living over the waste of days that lies between. It's a summer day, in all the perfection of beauty that sentence sometimes implies. Maria Randolph sits in the little sitting room in the armchair, with her hair combed smoothly back and coiled in a not ungraceful twist. Her dress is a wrapper of flowing white. A spray of lilies-of-the-valley is pinned at her throat, and her hands, lying idly in her lap, are almost as white as the dress on which they lie.

There is still an invalid in the Randolph household. The pretty house and all its neat and lovely furnishings look much the same as they did on that day when Maria left them and was carried into the invalid bedroom.

And yet there are changes in many things. A toy cart, with one wheel off, lies against the fence in the yard. A one-armed doll is sleeping on the center table, and a doll's cradle occupies the niche between the two doors. There's an air of quiet bustle about the house; the very chairs wear a look of expectancy. The only reposeful feature of the room is Maria as she leans back in the chair.

Exactly five years and seventeen days has Maria sat in that chair and quietly watched the flow of life go on about her. That step from the stove to the outer door, tugging at the boiler, was the last step she took. What if she had known! Now, looking back and knowing it, she smiles a quiet, hushed smile, a smile that rests you to see and tells you in an instant of time that what life, busy life, and work and care and responsibility failed to bring to Maria Randolph, the quiet and pain of the sick room have wrought.

This is a gala day in the household—a family reunion, actually the first they've had since the spirit of change fluttered down upon them. Helen is at home, with her husband and her child—the broken cart and armless doll belong to her. Helen is serene in a dress of not quite the right shade of grey to suit her complexion.

"Mr. Leonard bought it," she says, laughing, "and I wasn't going to tell him it would make me look peach-colored, for, after all, what difference does it make?" It isn't as perfect a fit as Helen Monroe always used to wear, but that, too, is explainable.

"It's a bit loose and cut a little too low on the shoulders," Helen says. "A young girl made it who's just beginning. The poor thing has to support herself and her mother. I wanted to give her work, if I could, and it does very well."

Maria listens and smiles and says to herself, "How different she is! And she doesn't know it—that's the oddest of all!" And in the fact that *she* only *smiles* and says nothing, keeping all her thoughts within herself, you see how Maria Randolph has changed—and *she* doesn't know it! But everyone else does.

Mr. Randolph comes and goes with a brisk business air. He isn't a clerk. The neat, tasteful, thriving store is his own and free from debt, by the last handsome Christmas gift of the rich son-in-law. Moreover, he's well. New York and the White Mountains and the rest from caretaking helplessness have lifted the wrinkles from his white face and made him young again.

A housekeeper is flitting in and out, busy and bright and serene. Is her face familiar? It's Maria's one friend—Maggie, or, rather, Mrs. Reeder. When Maria laid down the burden of the household Maggie promptly lifted it. It took only a few hours for Maria to discover there was ample chance for the kindness she'd shown her friend to be repaid.

Mr. Reeder is the superintendent at the Randolph House, and the boy is superintendent of them all. Maggie flutters here and there, with the air of expectancy on her face, as well as on the house.

A new building sits in the backyard, long and low, from whose chimney the smoke constantly issues. Can you guess that it's a washroom and that all the appliances for carrying on Maria's chosen profession in the most approved style are there? That is Maria's pet. She watches the work from her window, day after day—a dozen girls hard at work there, girls who have been forlorn wanderers in search of employment.

Under Maggie's skillful training they do good work and earn high wages. They're bright and neat and happy. And Maria, well, sitting there in her chair, not taking a step from one year's end to another—her scheme is more nearly being realized than that of many; she is actually growing rich. "There's money in it," she had said, emphatically, and with Maggie's efficient help she proves it, even now.

The door of the little sitting room pushes open, and a yellow head bobs in and says this one sentence: "Auntie Rye, they've come." The head pops out again, and the door closes. And Maria, hearing the bustle and eager voices and the laughter, sits still and waits.

There's a wonderful homecoming. Grace is getting back to the early home for the first time since that morning when she went out so tearfully, five years ago. "Just for the winter, you know," and yet it's true that five winters have come and gone since she went away. Five years since Maria had seen the sister who used to be her charge and her care! Nobody intended it to be so long; everybody would have been shocked if they'd imagined it. It was one of those plans which shape themselves, or appear to, without intention on our part.

First, there was the White Mountain scheme, where she went with her father and his health began to come back to him. She returned to New York late, just in time for the opening of the school. A little overwork and a heavy cold kept her from coming home during the winter vacation; a sudden alarming sickness on Ermina's part kept her in the spring and a rush off to the seaside for the summer, with a summer of anxious watching, when there wasn't a day for leaving Ermina and peeping in on the helpless sister at home. Then school and the whirl of coming graduation occupied time and brain during another winter. No need to take time for running home during the short winter vacation, since she was going in the spring to stay. But what did the spring do but arrange business matters with the mercantile house that suddenly, with only twenty-four hours' notice, the junior partner had to be off for Europe. Of course he took his wife; the junior partner was one of those men who always took his wife. And of course so grand an opportunity for Grace to go abroad couldn't be lost if it did defer the long-promised going home.

And once in Europe, who can tell the numberless plans that arose to keep them there? The brief history is that, instead of staying three months, as they had planned, it was more than two years before they landed in New York again. Now, at last, they'd come home.

And there Maria sat with folded hands and *waited*, hearing the sound of the voice in the hall that was familiar and yet *not* familiar. It had a certain indefinable change that reminded one of flowers and music; one couldn't tell why. Maria waited with the color deepening on her cheeks, until presently the door opened, and a vision appeared. Both sisters looked eagerly at each other. Both spoke at once.

"Gracie!"

"Oh, Maria!"

Each voice expressed intense surprise.

Of course Maria had known that five years bring changes, especially when they come in at that period of life when the girl is changing into the woman. She knew Grace must be developed in form and manner, and yet to know a fact is one thing and to *realize* it is another. Maria hadn't realized the fair-faced shrinking Grace was utterly gone from them and in her place would come a brilliant woman.

And Grace had known Maria was an invalid and helpless, and yet she'd always imagined her bustling eagerly about, accomplishing the work of two, even as she'd always known her. To see Maria quiet and thin and, now that the flush was passing, pale was a startling surprise. Seeing is *so* different from hearing.

They had all been together for some hours and broken bread together at the home tea table, before anything like a settled feeling began to come to them. Callers were expected for the evening, and presently one and another went their various ways to get ready for the evening—all but Maria, who couldn't go and was always ready, and Mr. Harper, who, being a gentleman, had nothing to get ready.

He came over to Maria's side as the door closed on the last departure.

"What do you think of our experiment?" he asked. "I saw your eyes follow Grace. Has she changed?"

"Changed!" repeated Maria. "Oh, Mr. Harper! Think of Alfred Parks in connection with her *now*! What's to be the end of it all? Do you know he boasts of his connection with her? I heard only this week of his saying that his lady was just home from Europe."

Mr. Harper shook his head, and his voice was sad.

"I don't know what the end is to be. I hoped that long before this it would die a natural death. But Grace was more of a woman than I gave her credit for being. She still clings to her ideal friend. Whether she'll give it up when she finds it's nothing but an ideal friendship is a question that gives me anxious thoughts. In any case it will be a pain and mortification to her. People can't play at hearts, Maria, without being injured."

"I know. Yes, she clings to her imagination somewhat and to her promise a great deal. But if the promise had never been made, as it shouldn't have been at her age, this trouble would be avoided. As it is, I don't know what the end will be. Perhaps he's improved. At least we'll have a chance to see. He'll be in this evening."

"Who else is coming this evening? Who came up from New York with you? Gracie spoke of your party."

"Why, Dr. Preston came up, and several other New York friends, and stopped at the Randolph House."

"Dr. Preston. I haven't seen him since the day I was hurt. Oh, that reminds me. What has become of poor Dick Norton? Did you ever hear Dr. Preston mention him?"

"Often. He's been in New York all the time. Why, he came up today."

"Did he really? How much I'd like to see the poor fellow again. Will he come to see us, do you think?"

"I should think there'd be no doubt of it," Mr. Harper said, and his eyes had a mysterious twinkle.

The talk was interrupted by a caller—no less a person than Alfred Parks. I wish I could take his photograph for you as he sat there making talk with Mr. Harper and Maria, while he waited for the coming of his early friend. The five years had wrought changes in him also. He'd grown fleshy, and his nose had reddened suspiciously; so had his eyes. His clothes, which were evidently arranged with great care, were what those given to the use of slang phrases are wont to call "flashy." His necktie was rainbow-hued, and he had about him an uncomfortable commingling of liquor and cigar smoke, hair oil and cologne, while the ring on his little finger was far too large and flashing to be other than washed gold and paste diamonds.

Mr. Harper surveyed him with a sinking heart and tried to conceal his dismay. As for Maria, something of the old indignation throbbed about her as she watched him and tried to imagine him as the lifelong companion of Grace.

He was entirely at ease and insufferably familiar. He seemed to think the time had come for being received into familiar relations, and he said "Maria" and "Harper" without the least show of embarrassment, despite the fact that Maria put unusual emphasis on the word "Mr." whenever she addressed her brother-in-law, and he became suddenly very careful, when he spoke to her, to say "Miss Randolph."

Suddenly the young man paused in the midst of a sentence and stared toward the door as one bewildered. Maria turned quickly. Grace was coming into the room. What is there about a lady's dress when it can be called neither showy nor extremely expensive, and yet marks her as the perfect lady? Thus was Grace's dress, a rare combination of texture—soft, clinging and noiseless—and color—some of those soft, quiet colors blending together, reminding one of sunset and peace.

And without knowing what was the matter with him it had a strange effect on Alfred Parks. It embarrassed him. A sense of incongruity suddenly came upon him, as if the elements in his appearance and hers didn't assimilate. It made the contrast in their manner even more striking. It was a horribly embarrassing moment. Neither of them acted as they'd planned.

A glow on Grace's cheek deepened as she came forward. All these years she had clung to the ideal she'd fashioned in her heart when she gave it the name of "Alfred Parks," nursing it with patient zeal whenever it seemed to be fading. And now that she stood again before the original, she didn't know it! Was this ill-dressed, ill-smelling, ill-mannered man the one she'd been corresponding with and thinking of during the maturing years of her girlhood? Not that she put it in that language. She simply felt a rush of dismay, a sudden heavy sinking of her heart, a sensation as if the world was sinking away into chaos again. Then she rallied, and though every vestige of color left her face, and her voice faltered over the name, she spoke it simply and sweetly— "Alfred."

But he did the only thing for which Maria ever gave him any credit. He didn't offer to take the proffered hand, and he forgot to give the familiar greeting he'd eagerly planned—a greeting that would show her proud relatives on what footing he stood with her. He managed to stammer out, "How do you do, Miss Randolph"—and that was all.

And then Grace took the chair Mr. Harper brought for her, and through a painful half-hour they tried to converse. What had they talked about during those early days in which they had spent long evenings together? I doubt if either of them knew. But it was only too apparent they hadn't a thought in common now.

Art, history, travel, music, pictures, science, religion—Alfred Parks's brain seemed equally barren of an idea about any of them. And the absurd blunders he made in his attempt to express his views weren't amusing to the little company who had to hear them. They were simply and painfully humiliating. Each of them would have tried earnestly to make the fellow at ease had he been an accidental caller. But with the spell upon them all, that he'd actually for five years been living in the belief he was almost a member of the family, they seemed powerless to help him.

The color didn't return to Grace's cheeks. She looked as if the weight of a dozen added years had suddenly fallen upon her, and Mr. Harper at least grew silent in his sympathy for her pain. It was evidently a rude awakening. His plan, after all, hadn't worked as well as he'd hoped.

"It can't be done at all," he said to himself. "Where these solemn matters of lifelong vows are played with while people are still children and don't know their own minds or their own powers, it will leave its scar. I see plainly that it can't be helped. Grace can never marry him; it would be a horrible mockery. But then there must be broken promises and humiliating explanations and the memory her whole life of loving words and titles which didn't belong to him and should never have been given. It's miserable business. I wonder when the world will learn that promises are solemn things and living is serious business, and when we're young we aren't called upon to decide questions that belong to mature judgments. I wish I saw the way plain through the rest of this."

And he looked pitifully at Grace, who was struggling to continue the conversation with Alfred—a conversation he continually marred by coarse, slang phrases that sounded to her unaccustomed ears even coarser than they really were. And yet she was this man's promised wife!

Chapter 29

The Last of the Randolphs

The embarrassment didn't lessen as the evening waned. On the contrary, when Tom and Dr. Preston came, and the three gentlemen tried to converse with Alfred, the difference in culture and refinement of thought and feeling, and above all in purity of language and high moral tone, was even more painfully marked than before.

Grace stood her ground bravely, and beyond the pallor of her face and the occasional half-nervous, half-timid appeals her eyes made to Dr. Preston, she showed nothing of her feelings. Dr. Preston seemed to appreciate the appealing look. He tried patiently to draw the attention away from Alfred and interest the party in talk that would require only silence from that young man.

But Mr. Harper chose to be merciless. He kept up a steady fire of questions, so direct as to require from Alfred at least an attempt at answering. As his embarrassment grew upon him his blunders became more frequent and glaring, until Dr. Preston darted an angry glance at Mr. Harper and seemed to feel the misery had been carried far enough.

Maria, looking on, studied the situation and began to comprehend that it was more complicated even than she had feared. There was no mistaking the anxious light in Dr. Preston's eyes and the patient, manly way in which he tried to shield Grace from pain. Besides, the grateful and pleading glances, which she seemed almost unaware she gave him, told their pitiful story.

"It's all confusion," said Maria, within her heart, leaning wearily back on the pillow which was always at her back. "How glad I am the responsibility of working it out and making the right and wise answer doesn't rest with me."

Something of this thought she expressed in low tones to Mr. Harper, when at last he gave up the effort to draw out the guest and retired to Maria's corner, while he allowed Tom and Dr. Preston to make the conversation general.

He looked down at her, smiling quietly.

"And yet you're the young lady who once courted and coveted responsibility and bore your part in life's tangle remarkably well."

Maria smiled back.

"That was before I had an idea I wasn't responsible at all, at least in the sense in which I used to put it. I thought all the plans and successes of this family, at least, hung in my hands. And I worked so hard to prove it, not only to myself but others, that you see it was necessary to take all work and influence and power away from me before I could believe the world would move on without me. How I fought over my lesson!"

"And have only half learned it yet, I'd say, if you've ignored all responsibility. Did you ever accomplish so much in the full possession of your powers as you have since you sat here? Don't you know you have responsibilities resting upon you now three times more important than those from which you were put aside?"

"No," she said quietly. "It is blessed not to have to agree with you. My feeling is utterly different. Work I've done. Results have been shown to me. But the *responsibility* I have forever laid aside. I do now what my Master gives me. 'Whatsoever He saith unto you, do it.' Don't you remember how hard I tried to adopt that motto before I understood the first letter of it? It's my motto now and for the rest of my life—unquestioning obedience, as far as the *doing* goes; but as far as the *results* are concerned I think I have no business at all with any of them. Mine is the *doing*, when He says the word, but His is the bringing to pass. And that, you see, is the end of all worrying and planning and doubt. There is no rest or comfort outside of that conclusion."

"You're right," he said, looking at her with respectful eyes. "You've learned in your quiet chair the lesson we out in the world at work find it awfully hard to realize. Therefore much of the worrying and doubting is still my portion."

Whereupon he looked toward Grace and sighed.

"Doesn't that really worry you in the least?" he asked.

"Don't you think Grace is the Lord's very own?" she asked him.

"Aye, I do indeed, with all my soul."

"Do you think when He said, 'All things work together for good, to them that love God,' that He meant it?"

"Yes," he said, after a moment's thoughtful silence. "I think I have unquestioning faith in the truth that even our *mistakes* He'll overrule for our good. But, because of that, shouldn't we be sorry for the mistakes of our lives that made our way rough?"

"I think we should and are. But are 'being sorry' and 'worrying' synonymous? Can't I be sorry for the innumerable blunders of my headstrong girlhood and yet rejoice, and even *rest*, in the thought that the Lord has forgiven and will lead?"

"Then you think that with regard to Gracie we may rest?"

"Why, if the past blunders are to 'work together for good,' shouldn't that rest us? Those aren't my words, you know."

"Your armchair has been a good teacher," he said, smiling. Then suddenly, as though the words had in some way grown out of the conversation, he added, "Tell me about your boys. Do they come to you every Monday now?"

Maria's eyes brightened.

"Yes," she said, "and I'm doing them good. I know I am. And, if it hadn't been for my blundering with poor Dick Norton, I'd never have thought of it. Mr. Harper, do you know Dick? Has his life been forlorn?"

"Yes," said Mr. Harper, "I know Dick. Tom, I thought Norton was coming over with you this evening."

"I was to call for him at half-past eight," said Tom, glancing at his watch, "and it's nearly that now. Maria, do you feel able to see him this evening?"

And then he went at once to bring him.

Maria, relieved by her invalidism from the need to talk unless she chose to do so, leaned back among her cushions and watched the feelings on the faces before her and went back over the histories of each life and took in the changes.

Ermina hadn't grown old. Her face had the bright, fresh look of one whose life had never lost its bloom. Neither care nor trouble had come to age her, and strong, healthy work for human hearts had kept her fresh and vigorous.

Helen's face had softened. All the lines were clear and tender. The worn look, the lines of impatient martyrdom, had passed away. In their place had come a vivid, glowing interest in life and work and a healthy certainty that Mr. Leonard and his views and plans and ways of work were infinitely superior to all others. He was the same strong-souled, vigorous man who had come for her five years before, and the boy was a match for them both.

In Grace the change was more striking and startling than in the others. Sitting beside Alfred, the contrast showed more vividly still that he, too, had changed—had grown coarser in feature and grosser in mind. What grand men they were, those others! And how like a pigmy he appeared beside them!

It wasn't a pleasant subject, and she was willing to turn from it to meet Tom and her old friend, Dick Norton. Time, and the many changes in her, had removed all feeling of vexation at the foolishness of his youth, and she found herself eager to meet her old scholar again. She made the mistake common to many people of forgetting that the five years had left their stamp upon him also. And, without realizing it, whenever she thought of him she called up his image exactly as it had appeared to her the last time she saw him—tall, somewhat overgrown in fact, with a shock of wiry hair that would never lie where its owner desired, and with his ungainly figure arrayed in coarse, ill-fitting, ill-chosen garments.

"What a contrast he'll present to them all!" she said, glancing at the others. "And yet he'll be an improvement on that poor attempt at gentility." Then she turned to greet her old friend.

"Maria," Tom said, "this is your old acquaintance, Dr. Norton."

And Maria neither answered nor gave her hand in greeting. She simply stared. Dr. Norton! Who on earth could *he* be? Not certainly anyone she'd ever known. This man was tall, finely formed and finely dressed—that is, his dress was of the quiet kind which can't be described but makes you instantly think of a gentleman. Moreover, his bow was easy and graceful, and his voice, as he said, "Will you shake hands with an old acquaintance, Miss Randolph?" was smooth and cultured.

"You're not Dick!" stammered forth Maria at last, the flush on her cheek deepening and her bewilderment rapidly becoming an embarrassment.

"I am indeed the veritable Dick, though I've worked hard for the title behind which your brother has hidden me. Don't you remember me at all, Miss Randolph?"

And then they shook hands, and Tom, seeing his sister's confusion, hurried his friend away to meet the other members of the circle.

Maria listened as one in a maze to the talk that followed. Changes! Why, none of them had so utterly bewildered her or seemed so impossible to understand. She watched the newcomer as he took his place in the circle with the assured air of one who was accustomed to the society of those who greeted him as their equal. She listened to the animated talk in which, since it fell on some subject he'd lately examined, he took the greater share. And as she listened, the strangeness didn't diminish, though certain touches of tone and a sort of intensity of manner began to remind her of the Dick Norton she'd known in the days that seemed suddenly to have receded into the very distant past.

Tom came over to her for a bit of confidential talk.

"Why didn't you tell me?" she said reproachfully. "I was never so amazed in my life. They give me a strange feeling, all these changes, as if I'd suddenly lost my identity and this had become a new world, where the shadows of the people I used to know were gathering around me."

"What a ghostly scene it must be!" Tom said cheerily. Then he answered her question. "Well, there are two reasons for my not talking of Dick to you. In the first place, I had no idea there'd been such a development as this. I knew he was studying medicine. In fact, I knew Dr. Preston went away with that idea in mind. But for a long time I regarded it as a freak of his and a very unwise one. I thought nothing would come of it but disappointment for them both. Afterward, when I heard Dick had become an indefatigable student and Dr. Preston believed he was destined to distinguish himself in medicine, I thought it would be such a pleasant surprise to you that I would wait and give time a chance to do its work. But, mind you, I hadn't an idea she worked so rapidly. I expected to see him improved, but nothing at all like this. He's actually graduated and started practice with Dr. Preston, and the doctor tells me he's certainly destined to a brilliant career. Looking at him now, it isn't hard to credit the prophecy. Maria, the best of all is that he says he owes it all to you. He says he would to this day have been nothing but a streetcar driver, earning his daily wages, but for your helping hand."

"That's nonsense!" Maria said, with a trace of her old vehemence of manner. "It was his forlorn reaching after a better place in the world that first suggested to me to help him."

"No," said her brother quietly, "you forget that you helped him about those shirts before he ever dreamed of such a thing as an aspiration. That shirt business was the most sublime reach your genius ever took, Maria. Not a day passes but I hear of some fruit."

Maria was laughing. It was a novel subject to call "sublime," and it had its ludicrous side. But there were tears in her eyes—the fruit was certainly beyond anything she had dreamed.

"Is he a Christian man?" she asked suddenly.

"Aye, that he is—a grand one, Preston says. He's doing a splendid work in the city, and his headquarters are at the streetcar stations among the drivers and hostlers. Preston says every man knows him and would give their lives to serve him. Think of that! Don't you see how you are working while you sit here?"

At this point the young doctor abruptly drew his chair away from Mr. Leonard, with whom he'd been talking, and came over to Maria's side.

"Will you tell me what the different stages of your sickness have been?"

"What a formidable question to put to a girl who has been sick for five years!" she said with a seriocomic look at the earnest face.

But he was evidently very much in earnest. He began a rapid fire of questions, clear, penetrating and intensely professional. Dr. Preston evidently caught the sound of familiar professional words and came over to their side of the room, stationing himself behind Tom's chair and listening intently. At last the new doctor paused and looked up at him.

"Well, sir," said Dr. Preston, "what do you think?

"I think electrical treatment will restore her."

Maria turned suddenly and looked up in Dr. Preston's face. The sudden paling of her own face revealed the keen eagerness of her desire to be in and of the world again, instead of being shut up within the two arms of her easy chair. Dr. Preston was a name well known in the medical world. His judgment was almost proof against mistakes, and if he did anything other than smile on this young enthusiast, if he even treated the sentence with a show of gravity as though there *might* be something in it, why, then, indeed, she might almost begin to hope. Tom, too, had turned and was waiting for his answer. He didn't keep them waiting. His voice was quick and firm.

"I've been thinking of the same thing. I've been listening with keen interest to your examination. I'm almost sure you're right."

It would be difficult to describe the state of eager excitement into which this simple sentence threw the circle. They had ceased their conversation and were listening. As a family they were all in eager sympathy with his answer. They gathered around Maria and were so voluble in their exclamations of delight and hopefulness that Dr. Norton, who had the air of one called as professional adviser and therefore had the care of the patient, peremptorily advised them not to excite themselves and weary her, but to wait and see.

At this opportune moment, Alfred Parks seemed to have determined he'd endured as long as he could the strain upon *his* nerves and arose to leave. It was a somewhat embarrassing moment. Tom didn't choose to act the part of host, and Mr. Randolph hadn't yet arrived. Mr. Harper half arose as one accustomed to act in his sister's stead and then sat down again as Grace resolutely turned toward the hall door as if to accompany her guest. Dr. Preston turned promptly toward them.

"By the way, Mr. Parks," he said, "did I hear you speaking of young Wheeler? Where is he now?" And as he spoke he threw open the hall door.

A sudden and marked interest in young Wheeler seemed to have come to him, for he continued his questions, following Alfred and Grace into the hall in the most natural manner possible and keeping the former engaged in answering, while he selected his hat. It was finally Dr. Preston who drew back the night latch, opened the door for him and bowed him from the steps. Utter silence filled the hall while Grace waited, and he closed the door.

Then he said, "Gracie, are broken promises worse than false vows?"

"Oh, doctor!" she answered, while her cheeks glowed and her eyes burned painfully. "It's all a bitter humiliation."

"I know," he said. "But be careful. Don't make it worse by adding false vows. Remember that. Remember that no early mistake can be righted by adding to it a later and more serious one." Then they went back to the sitting room.

I don't know if you're interested in all these people as I am. Probably you're not. It's one thing to live lives right along with people and another to tell about lives after they've been lived.

But I really would like to tell you about the weeks and months that followed. What blessed times this united family had together during the next month. The two doctors entered vigorously upon the new treatment that was to do so much for Maria. A number of times it became necessary for the young doctor to come up from New York to be sure his directions were being carried out and the longed-for effects were being produced. New plans were being developed for the Randolph House, so that they reached out far beyond the first hopes or even thoughts of the early days of the enterprise. And in these plans our old friend, Peter Armstrong, took such an eager and practical interest that the rest said of him, laughingly, that the mantle of his namesake from the Bible must surely have fallen upon him, for such was the vim and zeal he threw into the work.

"If I should lose him," Tom said, looking after him one night, as he rushed away to fresh work, after giving a brief, rapid account of the day's grand results in reaching out after tempted men, "I'm afraid I'd give up the enterprise in awful grief and dismay. He's the most indefatigable 'fisher' I ever met. Blessed be the day when his heart took in those words, 'I will make you fishers of men.' They will be the key note to his life."

Of all these things I have neither time nor space to tell you. I must take you over months of time, down to a winter evening when there was a jubilee at the Randolph house—not the newly fitted up hotel, but the family home.

They were all gathered at the homestead, Helen unexpectedly back again from her Western home, because everybody must come home to weddings. The wedding had been, and the bridal pair were about to start on their journey.

Of course you know it was Grace, and of course you know the bridegroom was *not* Alfred Parks—that folly of her girlhood had to be atoned for as best she could and, at the best, it left sore spots and a feeling of pain and shame at the thought. But the bridegroom was Dr. Preston.

It was well that he was a patient man, for it was painful to feel that he'd been defrauded of tender words and touches that should have been his own and that were wasted before the bride was old enough to feel their sacredness.

But it had righted itself at last, as well at least as mistakes ever right themselves, and now they lingered about that side piazza door, looking wistfully after the carriage that bore away the bridal couple. Mr. Randolph walked to the end of the piazza and stood in the darkness and silence for a little. When he walked back he spoke to Maria in a husky voice.

"It's hard to give up Mother's baby."

That little mother was the name still that brought the tears to the fading eyes of this grey-haired man. Yes, he said this to Maria. She stood beside him in the doorway. It's a wonderful thing to stand in a doorway when you're doing it for the first time in six years! The new doctor's positiveness had been founded on wisdom. The dear dream was realized, and she could walk!

"Not too long," an anxious voice said just behind her. "My dear Maria, I don't want you to stand long at a time—not yet. Wait a little, and you'll be able to stand as long as you want to and walk where you choose."

"This is the first time I've been in the kitchen, you know," she said, turning smiling eyes on familiar, yet unfamiliar, objects. "I don't suppose you have any idea how strange it all seems to me. Dick, I stood just there when that horrid boiler tipped over with me."

It was a strange place for sentiment, that winter kitchen, with the coffee boiler steaming on the stove and the remains of the wedding feast strewn everywhere. But they stood there for a long time despite the caution and went over many old times the familiar furnishings of that room brought back to them.

"I must go now," Dr. Dick Norton said, as he looked at his watch. "It won't do not to be in New York early in the morning. I'll have double duty now until Dr. Preston returns. Well, Maria, I'll be down by New Year's, and by that time I have strong hope that you can travel in safety."

A moment afterward he went with brisk steps down the walk. Maria stood looking after him. Before the sound of his footsteps faded away Tom came up the same walk. He had been to look after the departing train that carried away the new bride.

"Dick will be late," he said. "I hear the train whistling."

Maria made no answer. Her brother paused in the kitchen and looked at her searchingly. Then he reached forth his hand after hers.

"The last of the Randolphs?" he said inquiringly.

"Don't, Tom," she said, laughing, though there were tears in her eyes. "You don't intend to commit suicide, do you? I'm sure you're a Randolph."

"But you intend to take care of Dick's buttons for the rest of your days? Is it so? I was sure of it. Well, let me see. Didn't you once tell me Dick was the first fruit of your first attempt to follow out the teachings of your 'whatsoever'? It was the Golden Rule, too, wasn't it? How great it is that you taught him to follow its teachings also! Maria, the story of the leadings of the Randolph family would make a book, wouldn't it?"

And you see, dear friends, it has.

Grace Livingston Hill Collections

Readers of quality Christian fiction will love these new novel collections from Grace Livingston Hill, the leading lady of inspirational romance. Each collection features three titles from Grace Livingston Hill and a bonus novel from Isabella Alden, Grace Livingston Hill's aunt and a widely respected author herself.

Collection #7 includes the complete Grace Livingston Hill books *Lo, Michael, The Patch of Blue,* and *The Unknown God,* plus *Stephen Mitchell's Journey* by Isabella Alden.

paperback, 464 pages, 5 ³⁄₁₆" x 8"

❖ ♥ ❖ ♥ ❖ ♥ ❖ ♥ ❖ ♥ ❤ ♥ ❖ ♥ ❖ ♥ ❖ ♥ ❖ ♥ ❖

❖ ♥ ❖ ♥ ❖ ♥ ❖ ♥ ❤ ♥ ❖ ♥ ❖ ♥ ❖ ♥ ❖